E.L. DOCTOROW

THREE COMPLETE NOVELS

E.L. DOCTOROW

THREE COMPLETE NOVELS

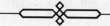

BILLY BATHGATE

WORLD'S FAIR

LOON LAKE

WINGS BOOKS
New York • Avenel, New Jersey

Continued on page 660

CONTENTS

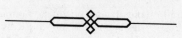

BILLY
BATHGATE

To Jason Epstein

PART ONE

ONE

He had to have planned it because when we drove onto the dock the boat was there and the engine was running and you could see the water churning up phosphorescence in the river, which was the only light there was because there was no moon, nor no electric light either in the shack where the dockmaster should have been sitting, nor on the boat itself, and certainly not from the car, yet everyone knew where everything was, and when the big Packard came down the ramp Mickey the driver braked it so that the wheels hardly rattled the boards, and when he pulled up alongside the gangway the doors were already open and they hustled Bo and the girl upside before they even made a shadow in all that darkness. And there was no resistance, I saw a movement of black bulk, that was all, and all I heard was maybe the sound someone makes who is frightened and has a hand not his own over his mouth, the doors slammed and the car was humming and gone and the boat was already opening up water between itself and the slip before a thin minute had passed. Nobody said not to so I jumped aboard and stood at the rail, frightened as you might expect, but a capable boy, he had said that himself, a capable boy capable of learning, and I see now capable of adoring worshiping that rudeness of power of which he was a greater student than anybody, oh and that menace of him where it might all be over for anyone in his sight from one instant to the next, that was what it all turned on, it was why I was there, it was why I was thrilled to be judged so by him as a capable boy, the danger he was really a maniac.

Besides, I had that self-assurance of the very young, which was in this case the simple presumption I could get away when I would, anytime I wanted, I could outrun him, outrun his rage or the range of his understanding and the reach of his domain, because I could climb fences and hustle down alleys and jump fire escapes and dance along the roof parapets of all the tenements of the world if it came to that. I was capable, I knew it before he did, although he gave me more than confirmation when he said it, he made me his. But anyway I wasn't thinking of any of this at the time, it was just something I had in me I could use if I had to, not even an idea but an instinct waiting in my brain in case I ever needed it, or else why would I have leapt lightly over the rail as the phosphorescent water widened under me, to stand and watch from the deck as the land withdrew and a wind from the black night of water blew across my eyes and the island of lights rose up before me as if it were a giant ocean liner sailing past and leaving me stranded with the big murdering gangsters of my life and times?

My instructions were simple, when I was not doing something I was specifically told to do, to pay attention, to miss nothing, and though he wouldn't have put it in so many words, to become the person who would always be watching and always be listening no matter what state I was in, love or danger or humiliation or deathly misery—to lose nothing of any fraction of a moment even if it happened to be my last.

So I knew this had to have been planned, though smeared with his characteristic rage that made you think it was just something that he had thought of the moment before he did it as for instance the time he throttled and then for good measure stove in the skull of the fire safety inspector a moment after smiling at him in appreciation for his entrepreneurial flair. I had never seen anything like that, and I suppose there are ways more deft, but however you do it, it is a difficult thing to do: his technique was to have none, he sort of jumped forward screaming with his arms raised and brought his whole weight of assault on the poor fuck, and carried him down in a kind of smothering tackle, landing on top of him with a crash that probably broke his back, who knows? and then with his knees pinning down the outstretched arms, simply grabbing the throat and pressing the balls of his thumbs down on the windpipe, and when the tongue came out and eyes rolled up walloping the head two three times on the floor like it was a coconut he wanted to crack open.

And they were all in dinner clothes too, I had to remember that, black tie and black coat with the persian lamb collar, white silk scarf and his pearl gray homburg blocked down the center of the crown just like the president's, in Mr. Schultz's case. Bo's hat and coat were still in the hatcheck in his case. There had been an anniversary dinner at the Embassy Club, five years of their association in the beer business, so it was all planned, even the menu, but the only thing was Bo had misunderstood the sentiment of the occasion and brought along his latest pretty girl, and I had felt, without even knowing what was going on when the two of them were hustled into the big Packard, that she was not part of the plan. Now she was here on the tugboat and it was entirely dark from the outside, they had curtains over the portholes and I couldn't see what was going on but I could hear the sound of Mr. Schultz's voice and although I couldn't make out the words I could tell he was not happy, and I supposed they would rather not have her witness what was going to happen to a man she might possibly have come to be fond of, and then I heard or felt the sounds of steps on a steel ladder, and I turned my back to the cabin and leaned over the railing just in time to see a lighted pucker of green angry water and then a curtain must have been drawn across a porthole because the water disappeared. A few moments later I heard one returning set of footsteps.

Under these circumstances I could not hold to the conviction that I had done the smart thing by coming aboard without his telling me to. I lived, as we all did, by his moods, I was forever trying to think of ways to elicit the good ones, the impulse to placate was something he brought out in people, and when I was engaged in doing something at his instruction I pressed hard to do my urgent best while at the same time preparing in my mind the things I would say in my defense in any unforeseen event of his displeasure. Not that I believed there was an appeals process. So I rode as a secret rider there at the cold railing through several minutes of my irresolution, and the strings of lights on the bridges behind me made me sentimental for my past. But by then we were coming downriver into the heavier swells of the open water, and the boat began to pitch and roll and I found I had to widen my stance to keep my balance. The wind was picking up too, and spray was flying up from the prow and wetting my face; I was holding the rail and pressing my back against the side of the cabin and beginning to feel the light head that comes with the realization that water is a beast of another planet, and with each passing moment it was drawing in my imagination a portrait of its mysterious powerful and endlessly vast animacy right there under the boat I was riding, and all the other boats of the world as well, which if they lashed themselves together wouldn't cover an inch of its undulant and heaving hide.

So I went in, opening the door a crack and slipping through shoulder first, on the theory that if I was going to die I had rather die indoors.

HERE IS WHAT I SAW IN THE FIRST INSTANT OF MY BLINKING IN THE HARSH LIGHT of a work lamp hooked to the deckhouse ceiling: the elegant Bo Weinberg standing beside his pointed patent-leather shoes, with the black silk socks and attached garters lying twisted like dead eels beside them, and his white feet looking very much longer and very much wider than the shoes he had just stepped from. He was staring at his feet, perhaps because feet are intimate body parts rarely seen with black tie, and following his gaze, I felt I had to commiserate with what I was sure he was thinking, that for all our civilization we go around on these things that are slit at the front end into five unequal lengths each partially covered with shell.

Kneeling in front of him was the brisk and impassive Irving methodically rolling Bo's pant legs with their black satin side-stripe to the knees. Irving had seen me but chose not to notice me, which was characteristic.

He was Mr. Schultz's utility man and did what he was told to do and gave no appearance of thought for anything else. He was rolling up pant legs. A hollow-chested man, with thinning hair, he had the pallor of an alcoholic, that dry paper skin they have, and I knew about drunks on the wagon what they paid for their sobriety, the concentration it demanded, the state of constant mourning it produced. I liked to watch Irving whatever he was doing, even when it was not as it was now something extraordinary. Each fold-up of the pant leg exactly matched the one before. He did everything meticulously and without wasted movement. He was a professional, but since he had no profession other than dealing with the contingencies of his chosen life, he carried himself as if life was a profession, just as, I suppose, in a more conventional employment, a butler would.

And partially obscured by Bo Weinberg and standing as far from him as I was but at the opposite side of the cabin, in his open coat and unevenly draped white scarf and his soft gray homburg tilted back on his head, and one hand in his jacket pocket and the other casually holding a gun at his side that was pointed with no particular emphasis at the deck, was Mr. Schultz.

This scene was so amazing to me I gave it the deference one gives to the event perceived as historical. Everything was moving up and down in unison but the three men didn't seem to notice and even the wind was a distant and chastened sound in here, and the air was close with the smell of tar and diesel oil and there were coils of thick rope stacked like rubber tires, and pulleys and chain tackle, and racks filled with tools and kerosene lamps and cleats and numerous items whose names or purposes I did not know but whose importance to the nautical life I willingly conceded. And the tug's engine vibrations were comfortingly powerful in here and I could feel them running into my hand, which I had put against the door in order to close it.

I caught Mr. Schultz's eye and he suddenly displayed a mouth of large evenly aligned white teeth, and his face of rude features creased itself into a smile of generous appreciation. "It's the Invisible Man," he said. I was as startled by his utterance as I would have been if someone in a church painting had started to talk. Then I found myself smiling back. Joy flooded my boyish breast, or perhaps gratitude to God for granting me at least this moment in which my fate wasn't in the balance. "Look at that, Irving, the kid came along for the ride. You like boats, kid?" he said.

"I don't know yet," I said truthfully and without understanding why this honest answer was so funny. For he was laughing now loudly and in his hornlike voice, which I thought was terribly careless of the solemn nature of the occasion; the mien of the other two men seemed preferable to me. And I will say something more about Mr. Schultz's voice because it was so much an aspect of his power of domination. It was not that it was always loud but that it had a substantial body to it, it came out of his throat with harmonic buzz, and it was very instrumental actually, so that you understood the throat as a sound box, and that maybe the chest cavity and the nose bones, too, were all involved in producing it, and it was a baritone voice that automatically made you pay attention in the way of wanting a horn voice like that yourself, except when he raised it in anger or laughed as he was doing now, and then it grated on your ears and made you dislike it, as I did now—or maybe it was what I'd said that I disliked because I was joining in some cleverness at a dying man's expense.

There was a narrow green slat bench or shelf hung from the cabin wall and I sat down on it. What could Bo Weinberg possibly have done? I had had little acquaintance with him, he was something of a knight errant, rarely in the office on 149th Street, never in the cars, certainly not on the trucks, but always intimated to be central to the operation, like Mr. Dixie Davis the lawyer, or Abbadabba Berman the accounting genius—at that level of executive importance. He was reputed to do Mr. Schultz's diplomatic work, negotiating with other gangs and performing necessary business murders. He was one of the giants, and perhaps, in fearsomeness, second only to Mr. Schultz himself. Now not just his feet but his legs to the knees were exposed. Irving rose from his kneeling position and offered his arm, and Bo Weinberg took it, like some princess at a ball, and delicately, gingerly, placed one foot at a time in the laundry tub in front of him that was filled with wet cement. I had of course seen from the moment I had come through the door how the tubbed cement made a slow-witted diagram of the sea outside, the slab of it shifting to and fro as the boat rose and fell on the waves.

I COULD HANDLE THE SUDDEN EVENTS, GETTING BAPTIZED AS BY A THUNDERSTORM, but this was more than I was ready for to tell the truth, I found I was not a self-confident witness here in contemplation of the journey about to be taken by the man sitting before me with his feet being cast in stone. I was working to understand this mysterious evening and the unhappy tolling of a life in its prime that was like the buoys I heard clanking their lonely warnings as we passed out to sea. I felt my witness was my own personal ordeal as Bo Weinberg was invited to sit now in a wooden kitchen chair that had been shoved into place behind him and then to present his hands for their tying. They were crisscrossed to each other at the wrist with fresh and slightly stiff clothesline still showing the loops it came in from the hardware store, and with Irving's perfect knots between the wrists like a section of vertebrae. The joined hands were placed between Bo's thighs and tied to them cat's cradle, over and under, over and under, and then everything together was roped in three or four giant turns to the chair so that he could not lift his knees, and then the chair was twice looped to the laundry tub through the handles and the final knot was pulled tight around a chair leg just as the rope ran out. Quite possibly Bo had at some time in the past seen this scoutcraft displayed on someone else for he looked upon it with a sort of distracted admiration, as if now, too, someone not himself was sitting hunched over in a chair there with his feet entubbed in hardening cement in the deckhouse of a boat running without lights past Coenties Slip across New York Harbor and into the Atlantic.

The deckhouse was shaped like an oval. A railed hatch where the girl had been put below was in the center of the deck at the rear. Toward the front was a bolted metal ladder leading straight up through a hatch to the wheelhouse where I assumed the captain or whatever he was called was duly attending to his business. I had never been on anything bigger than a rowboat so all of this, at least, was good news, that something like a boat could be so much of a construction, all according to the rules of the sea, and that there was a means of making your tenuous way across this world that clearly reflected a long history of thought. Because the swells got higher and longer, and everyone had to anchor himself, Mr. Schultz taking the side bench directly opposite where I sat and Irving gripping the ladder leading upstairs to the wheelhouse as if it were a pole on a subway train. And there was a silence for some time inside the sounds of the running engine and the waves, like the solemnity of people listening to organ music. And now Bo Weinberg was coming to life and beginning to look around him, to see what he could see, and who was here and what could be done; I received the merest glance of his dark eyes, one short segment of arc in their scan, for which I was incredibly relieved, not bearing any responsibility, nor wanting any, for these wheezing shifting seas or for the unbreathable nature of water, or its coldness, or its dark and bottomless craw.

Now there was such intimacy among all of us in this black cabin shining in the almost-green shards of one work light that when anyone moved everyone else noticed, and at this time my eyes were riveted by Mr. Schultz's small action of dropping his gun in his ample coat pocket and removing then from his inside jacket pocket the silver case that held his cigars and extracting a cigar and replacing the case and then biting off the tip of his cigar and spitting it out. Irving came over to him with a cigarette lighter, which he got going with one press of his thumb just a moment before he held it to the tip. And Mr. Schultz leaned slightly forward rotating the cigar to light it evenly, and over the sound of the sea and the grinding engine I heard the *sip sip* of his pull on the cigar and watched the flame flare up on his cheeks and brow, so that the imposition of him was all the more enlarged in the special light of one of his appetites. Then the light went out and Irving retreated and Mr. Schultz sat back on the bench, the cigar glowing in the corner of his mouth and filling the cabin with smoke, which was not really a great thing to be smelling in a boat cabin on the high seas.

"You can crack a window, kid," he said. I did this with alacrity, turning and kneeling on the bench and sticking my hand through the curtains and unlatching the porthole and pushing it open. I could feel the night on my hand and drew it in wet.

"Isn't it a black night though?" Mr. Schultz said. He rose and moved around to Bo, who was sitting facing astern, and hunkered down in front of him like a doctor in front of a patient. "Look at that, the man is shivering. Hey Irving," he said. "How long till it hardens up? Bo is cold."

"Not long," Irving said. "A little while."

"Only a little while longer," Mr. Schultz said, as if Bo needed a translation. He smiled apologetically and stood and put a companionable hand on Bo's shoulder.

At this Bo Weinberg spoke and what he said was genuinely surprising to me. It was not what any apprentice or ordinary person in his situation could have said and more than any remark of Mr. Schultz's to this moment gave me to understand the realm of high audacity these men moved in, like another dimension. Perhaps he was only admitting to his despair or perhaps this was his dangerous way of getting Mr. Schultz's sincere attention; I would not have thought of the possibility that a man in his circumstances would feel he had a measure of control over how and when his death would occur. "You're a cocksucker, Dutch" is what he said.

I held my breath but Mr. Schultz only shook his head and sighed. "First you beg me and now you go calling me names."

"I didn't beg you, I told you to let the girl go. I spoke to you as if you were still human. But all you are is a cocksucker. And when you can't find a cock to suck you pick up scumbags off the floor and suck them. That's what I think of you, Dutch."

As long as he was not looking at me I could look at Bo Weinberg. He certainly had spirit. He was a handsome man, with smooth shiny black hair combed back without a part from a widow's peak, and a swarthy Indian sort of face with high cheekbones, and a full well-shaped mouth and a strong chin, all set on the kind of long neck that a tie and collar dresses very nicely. Even hunched over in the shame of his helplessness, with his black tie askew on his wing collar and his satiny black tuxedo jacket bunched up above his shoulders, so that his posture was subservient and his gaze necessarily furtive, he suggested to me the glamour and class of a big-time racketeer.

I wished now in some momentary confusion of loyalties, or perhaps thinking only as a secret judge that the case had not yet been made to my satisfaction, that Mr. Schultz could have some of this quality of elegance of the man in the tub. The truth was that even in the finest clothes Mr. Schultz seemed badly dressed, he suffered a sartorial inadequacy, as some people had weak eyes or rickets, and he must have known this because whatever else he was up to he would also be hiking up his trousers with his forearms, or lifting his chin while he pulled at his collar, or brushing cigar ashes from his vest, or taking off his hat and blocking the crown with the side of his hand. Without even thinking about it he tried constantly to correct his relationship to his clothes, as if he had some sort of palsy of dissatisfaction, to the point where you thought everything would settle on him neatly enough if he would stop picking at it.

The trouble may have been in part his build, which was short-necked and stolid. I think now that the key to grace or elegance in any body, male or female, is the length of the neck, that when the neck is long several conclusions follow, such as a proper proportion of weight to height, a natural pride of posture, a gift for eye contact, a certain nimbleness of the spine and length of stride, all in all a kind of physical gladness in move-ment leading to athletic competence or a love for dancing. Whereas the short neck predicts a host of metaphysical afflictions, any one of which brings about the ineptitude for life that creates art, invention, great for-tunes, and the murderous rages of the disordered spirit. I am not suggest-ing this as an absolute law or even a hypothesis that can be proved or disproved; it is not a notion from the scientific world but more like an inkling of a folk truth of the kind that seemed reasonable enough before radio. Maybe it was something that Mr. Schultz himself perceived in the unconscious genius of his judgments because up to now I knew of two murders he had personally committed, both in the region of the neck, the throttling of that Fire Department inspector, and the more viciously expe-dient destruction of a West Side numbers boss who was unfortunate enough to be tilted back in a chair and having himself shaved in the barbershop of the Maxwell Hotel on West Forty-seventh Street when Mr. Schultz found him.

So I suppose the answer to his regrettable lack of elegance was that he had other ways of impressing you. And after all there was a certain fluent linkage of mind and body, both were rather powerfully blunt and tended not to recognize obstacles that required going around rather than through or over. In fact it was just this quality of Mr. Schultz's that Bo Weinberg now remarked upon. "Think of it," he said, addressing the cabin, "he makes this cheap dago move on Bo Weinberg, can you believe it? Only the guy who took out Vince Coll for him and held Jack Diamond by the ears so he could put the gun in his mouth. Only the guy who did Maranzano and bought him a million dollars of respect from the Unione. Who made the big hits for him and covered his ass for him, and found the Harlem policy he was too dumb to find for himself, who handed him his fortune, made him a goddamn millionaire, made him look like something else than the fucking lowdown gonif he is—this shmuck from the gutter. This bullethead. Listen, what did I expect, pulls me out of a restaurant in front of my fiancée? Women and children, anything, he doesn't care, he doesn't know any better did you see those waiters cringing, Irving, you weren't there you should have seen those waiters trying not to watch him shovel it in sitting there in his Delancey Street suit that he bought from the signboard."

I thought whatever was going to happen now I didn't want to witness; I had scrunched up my eyes and instinctively pressed back into the cold cabin wall. But Mr. Schultz hardly seemed to react, his face was impassive. "Don't talk to Irving," he said by way of reply. "Talk to me."

"Men talk. When there are differences men talk. If there is a misunderstanding they hear each other out. That's what men do. I don't know what you came out of. I don't know what stinking womb of pus and shit and ape scum you came out of. 'Cause you're an ape, Dutch. Hunker down and scratch your ass, Dutch. Swing from a tree. Hoo hoo, Dutch. Hoo hoo."

Mr. Schultz said very quietly: "Bo, you should understand I am past the madness part. I am past the anger. Don't waste your breath." And like a man who has lost interest he returned to his seat along the bulkhead across from me.

And from the slump of Bo Weinberg's shoulders, and the droop of his head, I thought it might be true of a man of rank that he would be naturally defiant, and it might furthermore be true that he would exhibit the brazen courage of a killer of the realm for whom death was such a common daily circumstance of business, like paying bills or making bank deposits, that his own was not that much different from anyone else's, as if they were all a kind of advanced race, these gangsters, trained by their chosen life into some supernatural warrior spirit; but what I had heard had been a song of despair; Bo would know better than anyone there were no appeals; his only hope would be for a death as quick and painless as possible; and my throat went dry from the certainty that came over me that this was exactly what he had been trying to do, effect it, invoke Mr. Schultz's hair-trigger temper to dictate the means and time of his own death.

So I understood of the uncharacteristic controlled response that it was so potent as to be merciless; Mr. Schultz had made his very nature disappear, becoming the silent author of the tugboat, a faceless professional, because he had let Bo's words erase him and had become still and thoughtful and objective in the approved classical manner of his henchman Bo Weinberg, as Bo, swearing and ranting and raving, had seemed to become him.

In my mind it was the first inkling of how a ritual death tampers with the universe, that inversions occur, everything flashes into your eyes backward or inside out, there is some kind of implosive glimpse of the other side, and you smell it too, like crossed wires.

"Men talk, if they are men," Bo Weinberg said now in an entirely different tone of voice. I could barely hear him. "They honor the past, if they are men. They pay their debts. You never paid your debts, your deepest debts, your deepest debts of honor. The more I done for you, the more like a brother I been, the less I have counted to you. I should have known you would do this, and for no more reason than you are a welsher who never paid me what I was worth, who never paid anybody what they are worth. I protected you, I saved your life a dozen times, I did your work and did it like a professional. I should have known this was the way you would make good on your debt, this is the way Dutch Schultz keeps the books, trumping up the wildest cockamamie lie just to chisel, a cheap chiseler chiseling every way he can.''

"You always had the words, Bo,'' Mr. Schultz said. He puffed on his cigar and took his hat off and reblocked it with the side of his hand. "You got more words than me, being having been to high school. On the other hand I got a good head for numbers, so I guess it all evens out.''

And then he told Irving to bring up the girl.

AND UP SHE CAME, HER MARCELLED BLOND HEAD, AND THEN HER WHITE NECK AND shoulders, as if she was rising from the ocean. I had not before in the darkness of the car gotten a really good look at her, she was very slender in her cream white evening gown hanging by two thin straps, and in this dark and oily boat, totally alarming, white with captivity, staring about her in some frightened confusion so that prophecies of an awful evil despoilage filled my chest, not just of sex but of class, and a groan like a confirmation of my feeling strangled in the throat of Bo Weinberg, who had been cursing a stream of vile oaths at Mr. Schultz and who now strained at his ropes and shook his chair from side to side until Mr. Schultz reached in his coat pocket and brought the grip of his pistol smartly down on Bo's shoulder and the girl's green eyes went wide as Bo howled and lifted his head in pain and then said from his squeezed face of pain that she shouldn't look, that she should turn away and not look at him.

Irving coming up the stairs behind her caught her as she began to fold and set her down in the corner on a cushion of piled tarpaulins and leaned her back against cylinders of coiled line, and she sat on her side with her knees drawn and her head averted, a beautiful girl, I was able to see now, with a fine profile, as in the aristocracy of my imagination, with a thin nose and under it a lovely dimpled crescent curving out downward to a mouth which from the side was full-lipped in the middle and carved back to no more than a thin line at the corner, and a firm jawline and a neck that curved like a waterbird's, and—I dared to let my eyes go down—a thin fragile chest, with her breasts unencumbered as far as I could determine by any undergarment, being slight, although apparent at the same time under the shining white satin of her décolletage. Irving had brought her fur wrap along and draped it now over her shoulders. And all of a sudden it was very close in here with all of us, and I noticed a stain on the lower part of her gown, with some matter stuck to it.

"Threw up all over the place,'' Irving said.

"Oh Miss Lola, I am so sorry,'' Mr. Schultz said. "There is never enough air on a boat. Irving, perhaps a drink.'' From his coat pocket he withdrew a flask encased in leather. "Pour Miss Lola out a bit of this."

Irving stood with his legs planted against the rock of the boat and unscrewed from the flask a metal cap and precisely poured into it a shot of neat and held it out to the woman. "Go ahead, missy," Mr. Schultz said. "It's good malt whiskey. It will settle your stomach."

I couldn't understand why they didn't see she had fainted but they knew more than I did, the head stirred, the eyes opened and all at once in their struggle to come to focus betrayed my boy's romance: She reached out for the drink and held it and studied it and raised it and tossed it back.

"Bravo, sweetheart," Mr. Schultz said. "You know what you're doing, don't you? I bet you know how to do just about everything, don't you. What? Did you say something, Bo?"

"For God's sake, Dutch," Bo whispered. "It's over, it's done."

"No, no, don't worry, Bo. No harm will come to the lady. I give you my word. Now Miss Lola," he said, "you can see the trouble Bo is in. You been together how long?"

She would not look at him or say a word. The hand in her lap went slack. The metal screw cap rolled off her knee and lodged in a crack of the decking. Immediately Irving picked it up.

"I had not the pleasure of meeting you before this evening, he never brought you around, though it was clear Bo had fallen in love, my bachelor Bo, my lady-killer, it was clear he had gone head over heels. And I see why, I do most certainly see why. But he calls you Lola and I am sure that is not your name. I know all the girls named Lola."

Irving passed forward, handing the flask to Mr. Schultz, and continuing, and it was at this moment an uphill walk, the boat riding a run of wave prow up, and he reached the forward ladder and turned to wait with all of us, watching the girl, who would not answer as the boat dropped under us, but sat now with two streams of tears silently coursing down her cheeks, and all the world was water, inside and out, while she didn't speak.

"But be that as it may," Mr. Schultz went on, "whoever you are you can see the trouble your Bo is in. Right, Bo? Show her how you can't do certain things anymore in your life, Bo. Show her how the simplest thing, crossing your legs, scratching your nose, it can't be done anymore by you. Oh yeah, he can scream, he can shout. But he can't lift his foot, he can't open his fly or unbuckle his belt, he can't do much of anything, Miss Lola. Little by little he is taking leave of his life. So answer me now, sweetheart. I'm just curious. Where did you two meet? How long you been lovebirds?"

"Don't answer him!" Bo shouted. "It's nothing to do with her! Hey Dutch, you're looking for reasons? I can give you all the reasons in the world and they all add up to you're an asshole."

"Aah that is such bad talk," Mr. Schultz said. "In front of this woman. And this boy. There are women and children here, Bo."

"You know what they call him? Shortpail. Shortpail Schultz." Bo cackled with laughter. "Everyone has a name and that's his. Shortpail. Deals in this brewed catpiss he calls beer and doesn't even pay for it. Chintzes on payoffs, has more money than he knows what to do with and still nickels-and-dimes his associates. An operation this size, beer, unions, policy, runs it like some fucking candy store. Am I right, Shortpail?"

Mr. Schultz nodded thoughtfully. "But look, Bo," he said. "I'm standing here and you're sitting there and you're all finished, and who would you rather be at this moment, Mr. class-act Bo Weinberg? Moves on the man he works for? That's class?"

"May you fuck your mother flying through the air," Bo said. "May your father lick the shit of horses off the street. May your baby be served to you boiled on a platter with an apple in its mouth."

"Oh Bo." Mr. Schultz rolled his eyes upward. He lifted his arms out and his palms up and made mute appeal to the heavens. Then he looked back at Bo and let his arms fall to his sides with a slap. "I give up," he muttered. "All bets off. Irving, is there another cabin down there that has not been occupied?"

"Cabin aft," Irving said. "The back end," he said in explanation.

"Thank you. Now Miss Lola, would you be so kind?" Mr. Schultz reached out to the seated woman as if they were at a dance. She gasped and folded herself back away from his hand, bringing her knees up in the gown and pressing back, which made Mr. Schultz look for a moment at his hand as if he was trying to see what about it was so repugnant to her. We all looked at his hand, Bo from under his lowering brow while at the same time making strange strangling noises, his ears and neck turning red with the effort to burst Irving's ropes. Mr. Schultz had stubby fingers, a plump meaty rise where the thumb and forefinger joined. His nails needed a manicure. Sparse colonies of black hair grew behind each knuckle. He yanked the woman to her feet so that she cried out and held her by the wrist while he turned to face Bo.

"You see, missy," he said, though he was not looking at her, "since he won't make it easier we'll have to do it for him. So he couldn't care less when the time comes. So he'll be only too happy."

Pushing the girl in front of him, Mr. Schultz descended to the deck below. I heard her slip on the stairs and cry out, and then Mr. Schultz telling her to shut up, and then a thin, extended wail, and then a door slamming, and then only the wind and the plash of water.

I didn't know what to do. I was still sitting on the side bench, I was bent over and gripping the bench with my hands and feeling the engine reverberate in my bones. Irving cleared his throat and climbed the ladder into the wheelhouse. I was now alone with Bo Weinberg, whose head had slumped forward in the privacy of his torment, and I didn't want to be alone with him so took Irving's place at the bottom of the ladder and started to climb it, rung by rung, but with my back to it, climbing the ladder backward by my heels and then coming to a halt halfway up between the deck and the hatch, and entwining myself there because Irving had begun to talk with the pilot of the boat. It was dark up there when I peered up, or maybe as dark as the light from a compass or some other dashboard instrument, and I could picture them staring over the prow from that height as they spoke, looking out to sea as the boat rode to its impenetrable destination.

"You know," Irving said in his dry gravelly voice, "I started out on the water. I ran speedboats for Big Bill."

"That right?"

"Oh sure. What is it, ten years now? He had good boats. Liberty motors in 'em, do thirty-five knots loaded."

"Sure," the pilot said, "I knew those boats. I remember the *Mary B.* I remember the *Bettina*."

"That's right," Irving said. "The *King Fisher*. The *Galway*."

"Irving," Bo Weinberg said from his tub.

"Come out here to the Row," Irving said, "load the cases, be back on the Brooklyn side or off Canal Street in no time at all."

"Sure," the pilot said. "We had names and numbers. We knew which boats were Bill's and which boats we could go after."

"What?" Irving said, and the word seemed conditioned by a wan smile I imagined up there in the dark.

"Sure," the pilot said. "I ran a cutter in those days, the C.G. two-eight-two."

"I'll be damned," Irving said.

"Saw you go by. Well, hell, even a lieutenant senior grade only got a hundred and change a month."

"Irving!" Bo shouted. "For God's sake!"

"He covered everything," Irving said. "That's what I liked about Bill. Nothing left to chance. After the first year we didn't even have to carry cash. Everything on credit, like gentlemen. Yes, Bo?" I heard Irving say from the top of the ladder.

"Put me out, Irving. I'm begging you, put a muzzle to my head."

"Bo, you know I can't do that," Irving said.

"He's a madman, he's a maniac. He's torturing me."

"I'm sorry," Irving said in his soft voice.

"The Mick did him worse. I took the Mick out for him. How do you think I did it, hanging him by his thumbs, like this? You think I held him for contemplation? I did it, bang, it was done. I did it mercifully," Bo Weinberg said. "I did it merci-ful-ly," he said, the word breaking out of him on a sob.

"I could give you a drink, Bo," Irving called down. "You want a drink?"

But Bo was sobbing and didn't seem to hear, and in a moment Irving was gone from the hatch.

The pilot had turned on the radio, twisting the knob through static till some voices came in. He kept it low, like music. People talked. Other people answered. They warranted their positions. They were not on this boat.

"It was clean work," Irving was saying to the pilot. "It was good work. Weather never bothered me. I liked it all. I liked making my landing just where and when I'd figured to."

"Sure," the pilot said.

"I grew up on City Island," Irving said. "I was born next to a boatyard. If I didn't catch on when I did I would have joined the navy."

Bo Weinberg was moaning the word *Mama*. Over and over again, *Mama, Mama*.

"I used to like it at the end of a night's work," Irving said. "We kept the boats there in the marine garage on a Hundred and Thirty-second Street."

"Sure," the pilot said.

"You'd come up the East River just before dawn. City fast asleep. First you'd see the sun on the gulls, they'd turn white. Then the top of the Hell Gate turned to gold."

TWO

It was juggling that had got me where I was. All the time we hung around the warehouse on Park Avenue, and I don't mean the Park Avenue of wealth and legend, but the Bronx's Park Avenue, a weird characterless street of garages and one-story machine shops and stonecutter yards and the occasional frame house covered in asphalt siding that was supposed to look like brick, a boulevard of uneven Belgian block with a wide trench dividing the uptown and downtown sides, at the bottom of which the trains of the New York Central tore past thirty feet below street level, making a screeching racket we were so used to, and sometimes a wind that shook the bent and bowed iron-spear fence along the edge, that we stopped our conversation and continued it from mid-sentence when the noise lifted—all the time that we hung out there for a glimpse of the beer trucks, the other guys pitched pennies against the wall, or played skelly on the sidewalk with bottle caps, or smoked the cigarettes they bought three for a cent at the candy store on Washington Avenue, or generally wasted their time speculating what they would do if Mr. Schultz ever noticed them, how they would prove themselves as gang members, how they would catch on and toss the crisp one-hundred-dollar bills on the kitchen tables of their mothers who had yelled at them and the fathers who had beat their ass—all this time I practiced my juggling. I juggled anything, Spaldeens, stones, oranges, empty green Coca-Cola bottles, I juggled rolls we stole hot from the bins in the Pechter Bakery wagons, and since I juggled so constantly nobody bothered me about it, except once in a while just because it was something nobody else could do, to try to interrupt my rhythm by giving me a shove, or to grab one of the oranges out of the air and run with it, because it was what I was known to do, along the lines of having a nervous tic, something that marked me but after all wasn't my fault. And when I wasn't juggling I was doing sleight of hand, trying to make coins disappear and reappear in their dirty ears, or doing card tricks of trick shuffles and folded aces, so their name for me was Mandrake, after the Hearst *New York American* comics magician, a mustached fellow in a tuxedo and top hat who was of no interest to me any more than magic was, magic was not the point, it was never the point, dexterity was to me the point, the same exercise as walking like a tightrope walker on the spear fence points while the trains made their windy rush under me, or doing backflips or handstands or cartwheels or whatever else arose to my mind of nimble compulsion. I was double-jointed, I could run like the wind, I had keen vision and could hear silence and could smell the truant officer before he even came around the corner, and what they should have called me was Phantom, after that other Hearst *New York American* comics hero, who wore a one-piece helmet mask and purple skintight rubberized body garment and had only a wolf for a companion, but they were dumb kids for the most part and didn't even think of calling me Phantom even after I had disappeared into the Realm, the only one of all of them who had dreamed about it.

The Park Avenue warehouse was one of several maintained by the Schultz gang for the storage of the green beer they trucked over from Union City New Jersey and points west. When a truck arrived it didn't even have to blow its horn the warehouse doors would fold open and receive it as if they had an intelligence of their own. The trucks were from the Great War, and still the original army khaki color, with beveled hoods and double rear wheels and chain-wheel drives that sounded like bones being ground up; the beds had stakes around the sides to which home-made slats were affixed, and tarpaulin was lashed down with peculiar and even gallant discretion over the cargo as if nobody would know then what it was. But when a truck came around the corner the whole street reeked of beer, they carried their gamy smell like the elephants in the Bronx Zoo. And the men who got down from the cab were not ordinary truck drivers in soft caps and mackinaws but men in overcoats and fedoras with a way of lighting their cigarettes in their cupped hands while the teamsters on inside duty backed the trucks into the black depths we were desperate to see into, that made me think of officers returned from a patrol across no-man's-land. It was the sense of all this purveyed lawless might and military self-sufficiency that was so thrilling to boys, we hung around there like a flock of filthy messenger pigeons, cooing and clucking and fluttering up from the ground the minute we heard the chains grinding and saw the sneering Mack hood nosing around the corner.

Of course this was just one of Mr. Schultz's beer drops, and we didn't know how many he had though we knew it was a fair number, and the truth was none of us had ever seen him though we never stopped hoping, and in the meantime we were honored to know that our neighborhood was good enough for one of his places, we were proud we enjoyed his confidence, and in our rare sentimental moments when we weren't sassing each other for our pretensions, we thought that we were part of something noble and surely had a superior standing among other kids from ordinary neighborhoods that could not boast a beer drop or the rich culture it brought with it of menacingly glancing men who needed shaves and a precinct house of cops whose honor it was never if they could help it to breathe the air out-of-doors.

Of particular interest to me was that Mr. Schultz maintained this business in all its prohibitional trappings even though Repeal had come. I thought that this meant beer like gold was by nature dangerous to handle however legal it might have become, or that people would buy better beer than his if he didn't continue to frighten them, which meant, breathtakingly, that in Mr. Schultz's mind his enterprise was an independent kingdom of his own law, not society's, and that it was all the same to him whatever was legal or illegal, he would run things the way he thought they ought to be run, and fuck woe to anybody who got in his way.

So there you see the heart and soul of what we were, in that moment in the history of the Bronx, and you would never know from these dirty skinny boys of encrusted noses and green teeth that there were such things as school and books and a whole civilization of attendant adults paling into insubstance under the bright light of the Depression. Least of all from me. And then one day, I remember it was particularly steamy, so hot in July that the weeds along the spear fence pointed to the ground and visible heat waves rose from the cobblestone, all the boys were sitting in an indolent row along the warehouse wall and I stood across the narrow street in the weeds and rocks overlooking the tracks and demonstrated my latest accomplishment, the juggling of a set of objects of unequal weight, a Galilean maneuver involving two rubber balls, a navel orange, an egg, and a black stone, wherein the art of the thing is in creating a flow nevertheless, maintaining the apogee from a kind of rhythm of compensating throws, and it is a trick of such consummate discipline that the better it is done the easier and less remarkable it looks to the uninitiated. So I knew that I was not only the juggler but the only one to appreciate what the juggler was doing, and after a while I forgot those boys and stood looking into the hot gray sky while assorted objects rose and fell through my line of vision like a system of orbiting planets. I was juggling my own self as well in a kind of matching spiritual feat, performer and performed for, and so, entranced, had no mind for the rest of the world as for instance the LaSalle coupé that came around the corner of 177th Street and Park Avenue and immediately pulled up to the curb in front of a hydrant and sat there with its motor running, nor of the Buick Roadmaster with three men that came next around the corner and drove past the warehouse doors and pulled up at the corner of 178th Street nor finally of the big Packard that came around the corner and rolled to a stop directly in front of the warehouse to block from my view, if I had been looking, all the boys slowly standing now and brushing the backs of their pants, while a man got out from the front right-hand door and then opened, from the outside, the right rear door, through which emerged in a white linen double-breasted suit somewhat wilted, with the jacket misbuttoned, and a tie

pulled down from his shirt collar and a big handkerchief in his hand
mopping his face, once a boy known to the neighborhood as Arthur
Flegenheimer, the man known to the world as Dutch Schultz.

Of course I am lying that I did not see it happening because I saw it all,
being gifted with extraordinary peripheral vision, but I pretended I was
not aware he stood there with his elbows on the car roof and watched with
a smile on his face a juggling kid with mouth slightly open and eyes rolled
skyward like a beatific boy angel in adoration of his Lord. And then I did
something brilliant, I glanced out of my orbit across the hot street and let
my face register ordinary human astonishment, to the effect of omigod it's
him standing there in the flesh and watching *me*, and at the same time
continued the pistonlike movement of my arms, while one by one my
miniature planets, the two balls, the navel orange, the egg, and the stone,
after a farewell orbit, plumed out into space, and went soaring in equidis-
tant intervals over the fence to disappear down into the New York Central
chute of railroad tracks behind me. And there I stood with my palms up
and empty and my gaze transfixed in theatrical awe, which to tell the truth
was a good part of what I felt, while the great man laughed and applauded,
and glanced at the henchman beside him to encourage his appreciation,
which duly came, and then Mr. Schultz beckoned me with his finger, and
I ran across the street with alacrity, and around the car, and there, in a
private court chamber composed of my gang of boys watching on one
quarter, and the open Packard door on another, and the darkness of the
warehouse depths on the third, I faced my king and saw his hand remove
from his pocket a wad of new bills as thick as a half a loaf of rye bread.
He stripped off a ten and slapped it in my hand. And while I stared at calm
Alexander Hamilton enshrined in his steel-pointed eighteenth-century
oval I heard for the first time the resonant rasp of the Schultz voice, but
thinking for one stunned instant it was Mr. Hamilton talking, like a comic
come to life, until my senses righted themselves and I realized I was
hearing the great gangster of my dreams. ''A capable boy,'' he said, by
way of conclusion, either to his associate or to me, or to himself, or
perhaps to all three, and then the meaty killer's hand came down, like a
scepter, and gently held for a moment my cheek and jaw and neck on its
hot pads, and then was lifted, and then the back of Dutch Schultz was
disappearing into the dark depths of the beer drop and the big doors
flattened out with a screech and locked with a loud boom behind him.

What happened now showed me all at once the consequences of a
revolutionary destiny: I was immediately surrounded by the other boys all
of them staring, as I was, at the mint ten-dollar bill lying flat in my palm.
It dawned upon me that I had half a minute at most before I became a
tribal sacrifice. Someone would make a remark, someone else would jab
the heel of his hand against my shoulder, and the rage and resentment
would flare, and a collective rationale would arise for sharing the treasure
and administering a punitive lesson—probably to the effect that I was an

asslicking brownnose whose head was going to be broken for thinking he
was better than anyone else. "Watch this," I said, holding forth the bill
but really extending my arms to hold the circle, because before the attack
comes there is a kind of crowding movement, an encroachment on the
natural territorial rights of the body; and taking the crisp bill in my fingers
I folded it once lengthwise, and once again, and then tightly twice more
to the size of a postage stamp and then I did a hocus-pocus pass of the
hands over each other, snapped my fingers, and the ten-dollar bill was
gone. Oh you miserable fucking louts, that I ever needed to attach my
orphan self to your wretched company, you thieves of the five-and-ten,
you poking predators of your own little brothers and sisters, you dumb-
bells, that you could aspire to a genius life of crime, with your dead witless
eyes, your slack chins, and the simian slouch of your spines—fuck you
forever, I consign you to tenement rooms and bawling infants, and slug-
gish wives and a slow death of incredible subjugation, I condemn you to
petty crimes and mean rewards and vistas of cell block to the end of your
days. "Look!" I cried, pointing up, and they tracked my hand, expecting
to see me pluck the bill out of the air, as I had so often their coins and
steelies and rabbits' feet, and in the instant of their credulity, as they stared
upward at nothing, I ducked under the circle and ran like hell.

Once I was running no one could catch me, though they tried, I cut
down 177th to Washington Avenue, and then turned right and ran south,
with some of them right behind me and some chasing me in parallel on
the other side of the street, and some of them fanning out down side
streets behind me in anticipation of my cutting back toward them, but I
ran a straight course, I was really getting out of there, and one by one they
pulled up panting, and I made one more change of direction for insurance
and finally I was truly alone. I was in the valley of the Third Avenue El.
I stopped in the doorway of a pawnshop, unlaced my sneaker, flattened
the bill, and slid it down as far as it would go. Then I laced up and resumed
running, I ran for the joy of it, flickering like a movie in the alternations
of sun and shadow under the elevated tracks, and feeling each warm stripe
of sun, its quick dazzle in my eyes, as Mr. Schultz's hand.

FOR DAYS AFTER I WAS MY UNCHARACTERISTIC SELF, QUIET AND COOPERATIVE WITH
the authorities. I actually went to school. One night I tried to do my
homework, and Mama looked up from her table of glass tumblers which
held not water but fire, this being the condition of mourning, that the
elements of life transform, and you pour a glass of water and hocus-pocus
it is a candle burning, and she said Billy, my name, Billy, something's
wrong, what have you done? That was an interesting moment and I
wondered if it would hold, but it was only a moment and then the candles

caught her attention again and she turned back to her enameled kitchen table of lights. She stared into the lights as if she was reading them, as if each dancing flame made up a momentary letter of her religion. Day and night winter and summer she read the lights, of which she had a tableful, you only needed one once every year but she had all the remembrance she needed, she wanted illumination.

I sat out on the fire escape to wait for the night breeze and continued with my uncharacteristic thought. I had not intended anything by juggling outside the beer drop. The quality of my longing was no more specific than anyone else's, it was a neighborhood thing, if I had lived down near Yankee Stadium I would have known where the players went in through the side door, or if I lived in Riverdale maybe the mayor would have passed by and waved from his police car on the way home from work, it was the culture of where you lived, and for any of us it was never more than that, and very often less, as, for instance, if one Saturday night years before we were born, Gene Autry came to the Fox Theatre on Tremont Avenue to sing with his Western band between showings of his picture— well that was ours and we had it, and it didn't matter what it was as long as it was ours, so that it satisfied your idea of fame, which was simple registry in the world, that you were known, or that your vistas were the same that had been seen by the great and near-great. That they knew about your street. And that's all it was, or so I had believed, and I couldn't have been planning to juggle continuously every day of my idling life until Mr. Schultz arrived, it had just happened. But now that it had I saw it as destiny. The world worked by chance but every chance had a prophetic heft to it. I sat with my ass on the windowsill and my feet on the rusted iron slats and to the flowerpots of dry stalks I unfolded my ten-dollar bill and folded it and made it disappear all over again, but it kept reappearing for me to unfold.

Right across the street was the Max and Dora Diamond Home for Children, which everyone knew as the orphanage. It was a red stone building with granite trim around the windows and along the roofline; it had a grand curving double front stoop, wider at the bottom than at the top and the two halves of it joined at the front doors one floor above the basement level. Flocks of kids were sitting and sprawling all up and down both sets of stairs and they made a birdlike chatter and moved in a constant shifting of relationships up and down the steps, and some of them on the railings too, just like birds, city birds, sparrows or grackles. They clustered on the stone steps or hung on the railings like the building was Max and Dora themselves, out with their children for some evening air. I didn't know where they put them all. The building was too small to be a school and not tall enough to be an apartment house and assumed in its design that it had the land to set it apart, which you just didn't get in the Bronx even if you were the Diamond family of benefactors; but it did have a kind of hidden volume to it and a run-down majesty all its own, and it had provided me most of the friends of my childhood as well as several formative sexual experiences. And I saw now coming down the street one of the orphan incorrigibles, my old pal Arnold Garbage. He was pushing his baby carriage in front of him and it was piled with the day's mysterious treasures. He worked long hours, Garbage. I watched him bounce the carriage heavily down the basement steps under the big curved stoop. He ignored the smaller children. His door opened on darkness, and then he disappeared.

When I was younger I'd spent a lot of time at the orphanage. I spent so much time there that I came to move around their wards like one of them, living as they lived with the orphan's patrimony of tender bruises. And I never looked out the windows to my house. It was very peculiar how I came to feel one of them, because at the time I still had a mother who went in and out of our house like other mothers, and in fact I enjoyed something like a semblance of family life complete with door poundings by the landlord and weepings unto dawn.

Now when I looked behind me into the kitchen it was illuminated with my mother's memory candles, this one room glittering like an opera house in all the falling darkness of the apartment and the darkening street, and I wondered if my big chance hadn't a longer history than I thought in the proximity of this orphans' home, with its eerie powers, as if some sort of slow-moving lava of disaster had poured its way across the street and was rising year after year to mold my house in the shape of another Max and Dora Diamond benefaction.

Of course I had long since ceased to play there, having taken to wandering away down the hill to the other side of Webster Avenue, where there were gangs of boys more my own age, because I had come to see the orphanage as a place for children, as indeed it was. But I still kept in touch with one or two of the incorrigible girls, and I still liked to visit Arnold Garbage. I don't know what his real name was but what did it matter? Every day of his life he wandered through the Bronx and lifted the lids of ashcans and found things. He poked about in the streets and down the alleys and in the front halls under the stairs and in the empty lots and in the backyards and behind the stores and in the basements. It was not easy work because in these days of our life trash was a commodity and there was competition for it. Junkmen patrolled with their two-wheeled carts, and the peddlers with their packs, and organ-grinders and hobos and drunks, but also people who weren't particularly looking for scavenge until they saw it. But Garbage was a genius, he found things that other junkers discarded, he saw value in stuff the lowest most down-and-out and desperate street bum wouldn't touch. He had some sort of innate mapping facility, different days of the month attracted him to different neighborhoods, and I think his mere presence on a street was enough to cause people to start flinging things down the stairs and out the windows. And his years of collecting had accustomed everyone to respect it, he never went to school, he never did his chores, he lived as if he were alone and it all worked beautifully for this fat intelligent almost speechless boy who had found this way to live with such mysterious single-minded and insane purpose that it seemed natural, and logical, and you wondered why you didn't live that way yourself. To love what was broken, torn, peeling. To love what didn't work. To love what was twisted and cracked and missing its parts. To love what smelled and what nobody else would scrape away the filth of to identify. To love what was indistinct in shape and indecipherable in purpose and indeterminate in function. To love it and hold on to it. I made up my mind of uncharacteristic thought and left my mother with her lights and swung myself over the fire escape railing and climbed down the ladder going past the open windows of people in their summer underwear, to swing for a minute from the last rung before dropping to the sidewalk, which I hit running. And dodging my way across the street and ducking under the grand granite steps of the Max and Dora Diamond Home for Children I went down into the basement, where Arnold Garbage maintained his office. Here the smell was of ashes, and in all seasons there was a warmth of ash and bitter dry air with suspensions of coal dust and also attars of rotting potatoes or onions that I preferred without question to the moist tang upstairs in the halls and lofts of generations of urinating children. And here Garbage was busy adding his new acquisitions to the great inventory of his life. And I told him I wanted a gun. There was no question in my mind that he could supply it.

As MR. SCHULTZ TOLD ME LATER IN A MOMENT OF REMINISCENCE THE FIRST TIME is breathtaking, you have this weight in your hand and you think in your calculating mind if they only believe me I will be able to bring this thing off, you are still your old self, you see, you are the punk with the punk's mind, you are relying on them to help you, to teach you how to do it, and that is how it begins, that badly, and maybe it's in your eyes or your trembling hand, and so the moment poses itself, like a prize to be taken by any of you, hanging up there like the bride's bouquet. Because the gun means nothing until it's really yours. And then what happens, you understand that if you don't make it yours you are dead, you have created the circumstance, but it has its own free-standing rage, available to anyone, and this is what you take into yourself, like an anger that they've done this to you, the people who are staring at your gun, that it's their intolerable crime to be the people you are waving this gun at. And at that moment you are no longer a punk, you have found the anger that was really in you all the time, and you are transformed, you are not playacting, you are angrier than you have ever been in your entire life, and this great wail of fury rises in your chest and fills your throat and in this moment you are no longer a punk, and the gun is yours and the rage is in you where it belongs and the fuckers know they are dead men if they don't give you what you want, I mean you are so crazy jerking-off mad at this point you don't even know yourself, as why should you because you are a new man, a Dutch Schultz if ever there was one. And after that everything works as it should, it is all surprisingly easy, and that is the breathtaking part, like that first moment a little shitter is born, coming out into the air and taking a moment before he can call out his name and breathe the good sweet fresh air of life on earth.

Of course I did not at the moment understand this in any detail, but the weight in my hand did give me intimations of a fellow I might become; just holding the thing bestowed a new adulthood, I had no immediate plans for it, I thought maybe Mr. Schultz could use me and I wanted to be ready with what I imagined he was looking for, but it was a kind of investiture nevertheless, it had no bullets and badly needed cleaning and oiling, but I could hold it at arm's length and remove the magazine, and shove it back in the handle grip with a satisfying snap, and I could assure myself that the serial number was filed off, which meant that it was a weapon of the brotherhood, which Garbage confirmed by telling me where he found it, in a wet marsh off Pelham Bay, in the far reaches of the North Bronx, at low tide, with its snub nose stuck in the muck like a mumbly-peg knife.

And the name of it was most thrilling of all, it was an Automatic, a very modern piece of equipment, heavy yet compact, and Garbage said he thought it would work if I could find a bullet for it, he himself having none, and quietly without dickering he accepted my suggested price of three dollars, and he took my ten into the depths of one of his piled bins where he kept hidden his El Corona cigar box with all his money, and brought me back seven very wrinkled worn neighborhood dollar bills, and the deal was done.

I was in a wonderful generous and expansive mood that night with the weight of my secret ambition in the right pocket of my knickers where I had discovered, in a confirmation of the rightness of my intuition, that the hole there allowed the gun to be slung down discreetly, the short barrel along my outer thigh, the grip transverse in the pocket, everything neat and accommodated as if by design. I went back to my apartment and gave my mother five of the singles, which was about half her week's wages from the industrial steam laundry on Webster Avenue. "Where did you get this?" she said, crumpling the bills in her fist and smiling at me her vague smile, before turning back to her latest chapter in the table of lights. And then, my gun stowed, I went back in the street, where the adults had taken possession of the sidewalks, having changed places with the children, who were now in the houses, there being some order in this teeming tenement life, some principle of the responsibility of mothers and fathers, and now there were card games on the stoops and cigar smoke drifted through the summer night, and the women in their housedresses sat like girls with their knees pointing up from the stone steps and couples strolled in and out of the streetlights and I was very moved by the sullen idyll of all this impoverishment. Sure enough when I looked up the sky was clear and a section of inexplicable firmament was winkling between the rooflines. All this romance put me in mind of my friend Rebecca.

She was a nimble little girl with black hair and dark eyes and a delicate thin black down above her pronounced upper lip. The orphans were inside now, the lights blazing in the windows of diamond-mesh translucence, and I stood outside and heard the din, louder on the boys' side, and then one of the signal bells, and I went down the alley to the small backyard and waited there in the corner of their broken-down little ball yard with my back against their chain-link fence, and in about an hour most of the upper-story lights were out, and I rose and stood under the fire escape ladder and leapt up, catching the bottom rung, and hoisted myself onto the ladder and so, hand over hand and foot over foot, rose on the black ladder of my love and at the top, swung out to a window ledge without a net below me and entered the open hallway window on the top floor, where the oldest girls slept, eleven to fourteen, and found there in her bed my witchy little friend, whose dark eyes were open when I looked into them, and absolutely unsurprised to see me. Nor did her wardmates find anything remarkable enough to speak of. I led her through the aisle of their eyes to the door that led up a half flight of stairs to the roof, a kind of games park with ruled lines of skelly and shuffleboard glowing darkly in the summer night, and in the nook made by the roof screen and the kiosk of the stair door, stood and kissed Rebecca ardently, and stuck my hand in the neck of her nightdress to brush her breastbuds with the backs of my fingers and then held in my hands her hard little ass that gave its contours to my touch under the rub of her white cotton shift, and then, before I became too far gone beside myself, when I knew her bargaining position was at its strongest, I negotiated a fair price and peeled a one-dollar bill off my depleted fold, which she took and crumpled in her fist as she first hunkered and then sat on the ground, totally without ceremony, and waited, while I stood on one leg and then the other, to remove my sneakers and everything to the waist, with some trembling awkwardness for a wizard, reflecting how odd it was that whereas men like Mr. Schultz and me folded our money neatly, no matter if our wad was thin or thick, women like my mother and little Rebecca squeezed theirs in a ball and held it, forgetting to let go, whether they sat in a distraction of candled grief with a shawl over their heads or lay on the ground and were fucked two times for a dollar.

THREE

When the boat came into the slip there were two cars waiting in the rain with their motors running. I would have liked instruction, but Mr. Schultz bundled the girl whose name wasn't Lola into the back of the first car and got in beside her and slammed the door, and not knowing what to do I followed Irving to the second car and climbed in after him. I was fortunate there was a jump seat. On the other hand I found myself riding backward facing three of the gang sitting shoulder-to-shoulder in their bulk, Irving now in an overcoat and fedora like the others, while they sat and stared forward, looking through the front window at the lead car over the shoulders of the driver and the man next to him. It was not a good feeling riding sandwiched in all of this serious armed intent. I really wanted either to be where Mr. Schultz could see me or off by myself, maybe on the Third Avenue El, alone in a railcar and reading the ads in the flicker of the bulbs while it rocked its way over the streets to the far ends of the Bronx. Mr. Schultz did impulsive and unwise things, and I worried that I was one of them. I had been more readily accepted by the executives of the organization than by the rank and file. I liked to think of myself as a kind of associate gang member, and if it was true, I was the only one, it might have been because the position had been created just for me, which should have said something to these deadheads though it didn't. I wondered if it all had to do with age. Mr. Schultz was in his thirties and Mr. Berman even older than that, but with the exception of Irving most of the men were in their twenties, and for someone with a good job and the possibility for advancement who was only twenty-one, say, a fifteen-year-old was a punk, whose presence in business situations was inappropriate to say the least, and if not unwise, certainly an affront to everyone's dignity. One of the bouncers at the Embassy Club was Jimmy Joio, who came from Weeks Avenue just around the corner from my house and whose kid brother was in fifth grade with me although it was true he was taking it for the third year when I came along; but the couple of times I'd seen Jimmy he looked right through me although he had to know who I was. With all these gunmen I could be made to feel from one moment to the next some kind of brash freak, not even a boy but a midget, or some small jester of deformity just agile enough to get out of the way of the king's big dogs. What Mr. Schultz liked lived by his protection, but I knew I needed to improve my standing with them all, although when or how that would be possible I had no idea. Sitting on a jump seat trying to keep my knees from bumping into theirs was not the circumstance I was looking for. Nobody said anything but I knew in the practical common sense of such things that I was witness to yet another of Mr. Schultz's murders, and the most intimate of them, certainly the most carefully planned, and whether it added to my credit as a trustworthy associate or put me in serious jeopardy, I was thinking now riding backward up First Avenue at two o'clock in the morning, I didn't like it and could have done without it and was a fucking dope to have exposed myself to it. I had caught on by Mr. Schultz's whim. My God. I felt weak in the legs, queasy, as if I was still on the boat. I thought of Bo perhaps even now continuing his descent with his eyes open and his arms over his head. To the extent that I could think rationally I wanted to know what was going to happen to this Miss Lola because she had been a witness too, and killers were not supposed to like outside witnesses, and I felt peculiarly of her status in this, and I needed intelligence of her. On the other hand I mustn't panic. She was still alive, wasn't she?

I didn't like the state of my mind and stared out the window to bring into myself the structure of the city, the solidity of the dark buildings, and the colors of traffic lights reflected in the black shining street. The city has always given me assurances, whenever I have asked for them. I recalled to myself my own imperial intentions. If I could not trust my own impulses to direct me, I was not in Mr. Schultz's class. He operated without sufficient thought and so must I. We were directed beings, and to the extent that I trusted myself I should trust him. What I was in was a thrilling state of three-dimensional danger, I was in danger of myself, and in danger of my mentor, and in danger of what he was in danger of, which was a business life of murdering danger; and out beyond all that were the cops. Four dimensions. I cracked a window and smelled the fresh night air and relaxed.

The cars were heading uptown. We went along Fourth Avenue, and then through the tunnel which brought us up on the ramp that curved around Grand Central Terminal and then we rolled onto Park Avenue, the real Park Avenue, going past the new Waldorf-Astoria Towers, with its famous Peacock Alley and its equally famous host the irrepressible Oscar, as I knew from my reading of the *Mirror,* an invaluable source of information; and then we turned left on Fifty-ninth Street and bumped along behind a streetcar whose bell sounded in my ears like the gong at a prizefight, and then we swerved and pulled up to the curb at the corner of Central Park in the shadow of General Tecumseh Sherman on his horse slogging up there through the rain, which fell also from the fountain of tiered basins across the plaza into the shallow pool he would have to have the horse step through if he was going to get the woman with the basket of fruit standing up there on top of everything, assuming it was a piece of fruit he wanted. I have never liked public monuments, they are ghostly foreign things in the city of New York, quite beside the point, if not actually stupid lies, and for all you can say about the Bronx you won't find generals on rearing horses or dames carrying baskets of fruit or soldiers standing in aesthetic hills of dying comrades and lifting their arms and holding their rifles up to the sky. To my astonishment the door opened and Mr. Schultz was standing there. "Okay, kid," he said and in he reached and yanked me by the arm and all at once I was standing there in Grand Army Plaza being rained on and thinking, in this world of water, that that was it for the phantom wizard juggler of the rackets, I would be found face down in a mud puddle under a bush in Central Park, and if dying depth was a measure of achievement I was worth whatever was of value to some dog snout rooting me up from an inch of water and licking the mud off my dead eyes. But he said walking me quickly to the first car: "Take the lady to her apartment. She is not to make any phone calls under no circumstances, although I don't think she will try. She will pack some things. You are to wait with her until I get back. Not long. Just stay with her and someone will call you on the house phone to bring her down. You got it?"

I nodded I did. We came up to his car, and though water was dripping off his hat brim, he only now reached in to the back seat and withdrew a black umbrella and after he opened it he bent into the car and brought her out and handed me the girl and the umbrella; it was a lovely moment, the three of us under the one umbrella, and she was looking at him with some slight and cryptic smile and he was gently stroking her cheek and smiling at her; then he dove into the car and was still pulling the door closed as it gunned away from the sidewalk with a screech of tires, the second car close behind.

We stood in a huge blowing rainstorm. It occurred to me I had no idea where Miss Lola maintained her apartment. For some reason I assumed everything was up to me, and that she would lack all volition and simply wait to be led. But she took my arm with both her hands, and huddling close to me under this great black umbrella rattling like a snare drum, she pulled me along at a half-walk half-run across Fifth Avenue so shining with rain that the rain splashed up at us after it came down. She seemed to be heading for the Savoy-Plaza Hotel. Sure enough, a doorman came out of the swinging doors with his own umbrella and rushed toward us uselessly except as he demonstrated solicitousness, and a moment later we whooshed into the carpeted, brightly lit but intimate lobby where some fellow in tails and striped pants relieved us of ours. And a flush of excitement was on Miss Lola's beautiful face, and she laughed looking down at the damp wreckage of her costume and ran her hand fetchingly through her wet hair and then shook her wrists at the carpet and received the greetings of the reception clerk as her just due—Good evening, Miss Drew, Good evening, Charles—as well as the polite salute of the police- man standing there with his hotel-staff friends as he liked to do in the warmth of the friendly lobby on inclement nights of his beat, while I, not daring to look at him, waited with a dry throat for what her explanation would be for me, a clear punk in any cop's eyes, and tried not to look back at the revolving door which was no good anyway and deciding on the curving staircase beyond the elevators which even though it led up could find me a way down. I prayed Mr. Schultz knew what he was doing, I prayed for understanding if not resourcefulness from Miss Lola, Miss Drew, whoever she was and whatever she had been through this night of the death of a man of whom she was presumably fond enough to be going to dinner and to bed with. But she made no explanations as she took her key, as if every night of the year she came in like this with strange boys in cheap scuffed imitation suede jackets and army-navy workpants and Bronx pompadour haircuts, and took my arm and walked with me into the elevator as if I was the normal companion of her nights, whereupon the doors closed, and the man took us up without having to inquire as to the floor, and I rose simultaneously in my thought to the truth that explana- tions are required of everyone but the people at the top, and to the terrible shadow of a revelation that for this Miss Drew glancing at me now with her cruel green eyes it had been one hell of an exciting ride on a tugboat.

HERE IS THE KIND OF HOTEL THIS WAS: WHEN THE ELEVATOR DOOR OPENED WE WERE already in the apartment. The floor was bare and very highly shellacked and there was a rug or tapestry hanging on the opposite wall, something going on with ranks of armored knights with lances on rearing horses, each horse standing on its hind legs at the same angle as the others, like the Rockettes, and the reason there was no furniture in this room is that it was the entrance foyer, except if you wanted to sink down into either of the two waist-high urns in the corners and put yourself in the middle of a circle of walking Greek philosophers holding wrapped sheets around themselves, or shrouds, given the mood I was in. But I preferred to follow the new Miss Drew grandly throwing open the double ceiling-high doors on our left and striding forward down a short hall hung with brownish oil paintings with fine cracks in them. And hoving up on the left was an open door from which, as she passed, a man's voice called out "Drew?"

"I have to pee, Harvey," she said in a quite matter-of-fact voice, and kept going around a corner and I heard another door open and close. And I was left standing in this doorway looking into a room that was a private library with glass-enclosed bookcases and a tall leaning ladder that rolled on rails and an immense globe in its own polished wood framework, and light that came from two brass table lamps with green shades at either end of a soft sofa, on which were sitting two men side by side, one somewhat older than the other. What I found remarkable, the older was holding the younger's erect cock in his hand.

I'm afraid I stared at them. "I thought you were out for the evening!" the older man called out, looking at me but listening somewhere else. He released his hold, rose from the sofa, and straightened his bow tie. He was a tall handsome man, this Harvey, very well groomed in a tweed suit with a vest into the pocket of which he inserted his hand as if he had some sort of pain under the cloth, except that as he came toward me he didn't appear to be in pain, and in fact looked quite healthy and like a man who took care of himself. Not only that but he commanded respect, because without thinking I stepped out of his way. As he went by me he said, "Are you all right?" loudly in my ear, and I noticed the tracks of the comb in his hair as it came back from his temples, this Harvey.

It made things so much easier, living on an explanationless planet. The air was somewhat rarefied, a bit thinner than I was used to, but then there didn't seem to be any need for exertion. With thumb and forefinger the fellow on the couch removed an antimacassar from the sofa and dropped it over himself. He looked up and laughed in a way that suggested we were complicitors, and I realized he was working-class, like me. I had not at first glance understood this. He appeared to be wearing mascara on his eyes, they were certainly bold and black eyes, and his black hair was slicked down flat without a part, and his bony wide shoulders were draped with the tied sleeves of a collegiate sweater with an argyle pattern of light maroon and gray.

Mr. Schultz was responsible for all this stunning experience so I thought I'd better attend to his business. I wandered down the hall and around some corners and found Harvey in a big padded gray-and-white bedroom, bigger than three Bronx bedrooms put together, and a mirrored bathroom door was open on a field of white tile, and Drew was in there with bathwater running and this caused him to speak loudly over the sound of it while he sat on a corner of an enormous double bed with his legs crossed and held a cigarette in his hand.

"Darling?" he shouted. "Tell me what you've gone and done. You didn't ditch him."

"I didn't, my dearest. But he's no longer a presence in my life."

"And what did he do! I mean you were so gaga about him," Harvey said with a wry and rueful smile to himself.

"Well if you must know, he died."

Harvey's back straightened and he lifted his head as if wondering if he'd heard correctly. But he said nothing. And then he turned and looked at me sitting in the far corner on a side chair that had gray napped upholstery, a boy as out-of-place here as in the library, but now visible, in this new intelligence, and I sort of straightened my own back for his benefit and stared just as rudely at him.

He immediately rose and went into the bathroom and closed the door. I picked up the phone at the bedside table and listened for a moment until the hotel operator came on the line and said Yes, please, and then I hung up. It was a white phone. I had never seen a white phone before. Even the cord was wound in white fabric. The big bed had a white upholstered headboard and big fluffy pillows, about a half dozen of them, with little lace skirts, and all the furniture was gray and the thick carpet was gray and the lights were hidden and shone out of a cornice onto the walls and ceiling. Two people used this room because there were books and magazines on both end tables, and two immense cabinets with white doors and curving white legs that were closets inside, his and hers, and two matching dressers with his shirts and her underwear, and until now I only knew about wealth what I read in the tabloids, and I had thought I could imagine, but the detailed wealth in this room was amazing, to think what people really needed when they were wealthy, like long sticks with shoehorns at the end of them, and sweaters of every color of the rainbow, and dozens of shoes of every style and purpose, and sets of combs and brushes, and carved boxes with handfuls of rings and bracelets, and gold table clocks with pendulum balls that spun one way, paused, and then spun the other way.

The bathroom door opened and Harvey came out holding Miss Drew's dress and underwear and hose and shoes all in a bundle in his two hands out in front of him, and he dropped the whole shebang into a wastebasket and then brushed his hands off, you could see he was not happy. He went to some far corner of the room and opened another door and disappeared there and a light went on, it was a walk-in closet and he came out with a piece of luggage which he threw on the bed. And then he sat down beside it and crossed his legs again and then crossed his arms over his knee and waited. And I waited back in my chair. And then the lady came out of the bathroom with a big towel around her and tucked in under the clavicle, and another towel wrapped around her head like a turban.

The argument was about her behavior. He said it was becoming erratic and disruptive. She herself had insisted they accept that dinner invitation for tomorrow evening. To say nothing of the regatta weekend. Did she want to lose every friend they had? He was entirely reasonable but he was losing me, because Miss Lola Miss Drew conducted her side of the argument while getting dressed. She stood at the armoire and let the big towel fall, and she was altogether taller and longer-waisted and maybe her ass was a little softer and flatter, but there was the prominent spinal column of tender girl bones of my dirty little Rebecca, and all the parts were as Rebecca's parts and the sum was the familiar body of a woman, I don't know what I'd been expecting but she was a mortal being with flesh pinkened by the hot bathwater, she hooked on her garter belt and stood on each thin white leg while she gently but efficiently raised the other to receive its sheer stocking, which she pulled and smoothed upward taking care to keep the seam straight till she could lower her toe-wiggling foot and sling her hip and attach the stocking to the metal clips hanging from the garter belt, and then she raised one foot and stepped in her white satin step-ins and then the other, and yanked them up and snapped the waist-band, and it was the practiced efficiency of the race of women dressing, from that assumption they had always made that a G-string was their armor in the world, and that it would do against wars, riots, famines, floods, droughts, and the flames of the arctic night. As I watched, more and more of her was covered, a skirt was dropped over the hips and zipped along the side, two high-heeled shoes were wiggled into, and then, dressed only from the waist down and with the towel still on her head, she commenced to pack, going from drawers and armoire to valise and back, making her decisions quickly and acting on them energetically, all the while saying that she didn't give a hoot in hell what her friends thought, what had that to do with anything, she was going to see whomever she damned pleased surely he knew that and so what was the point of making a fuss, all this whining of his was beginning to bore her. And then she brought the lid down on her leather valise and snapped shut the two brass locks. I had I thought heard just about everything that went on between Miss Lola and Mr. Schultz in the hold of that tugboat but clearly I hadn't, there was some pact between them she was determined to honor.

"I speak of order, of the need for some order," the fellow Harvey said, although clearly without hope of prevailing. "You're going to destroy us all," he muttered. "I mean a bit of scandal is not the point, is it? You're a very clever, very naughty little hellion, but there are limits, my darling, there really are. You're going to get in over your head and then what will you do? Wait for me to come to the rescue?"

"That is a laugh and a half."

And then she sat nude to the waist at her dressing-table mirror and unwrapped the towel on her head and ran a comb a few times through her short helmet of hair, and painted on some lipstick, then found a camisole and shrugged it over her torso and pulled a blouse on over that, and tucked it in, and then a jacket over the blouse, and a bracelet or two, a necklace, and she stood and looked at me for the first time, a new woman, Miss Lola Miss Drew, a formidable intention in her eyes, and when had I seen a woman dress herself so, all in cream and aqua, to run away with the killer of her dreams?

* * *

So THERE WE ARE, THREE O'CLOCK IN THE MORNING AND TEARING UP ROUTE 22 OUT
of the city, miles into the mountains where I have never been before, I am
sitting up front next to Mickey the driver, and Mr. Schultz and the lady are
in the back with glasses of champagne in their hands. He is telling her the
story of his life. A steady hundred yards behind is a car with Irving and
Lulu Rosenkrantz, and Mr. Abbadabba Berman. It has been a long night
in my education, but there is more to come, I am going into mountains,
Mr. Schultz is showing me the world, he is like a subscription to the
National Geographic Magazine except the only tits I've seen are white, I've
seen the contours of the ocean bed and the contours of the white Miss
Drew and now I see the contours of the black mountains. I understand for
the first time the place of the city in the world, it should have been obvious
but I had never realized it, I had never been out of it before, never had the
distance, it is a station on the amphibian journey, it is where we come out
sliming, it is where we bask and feed and make our tracks and do our
dances and leave our coprolitic spires, before moving on into the black
mountains of high winds and no rain. And what I hear as my eyes begin
to droop is the soft whistle of the wind in the half window I've left open
a crack with a turn of the knob, not a whistle entirely but the kind of
almost-whistle a person makes who is whistling to himself; and the
soundplow of the eight-cylinder car in its bassoing, and the resonant rasp
of Mr. Schultz telling how he robbed crap games as a lad, and the tires'
humslick on the damp highway, all of it really the protesting circuitry of
my brain as I wrap my arms around myself and let my chin drop to my
chest, I hear one last laugh but I can't help it, it is three o'clock in the
morning of the awesome morning of my life and I haven't even been to
sleep yet.

FOUR

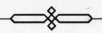

knew from Walter Winchell's column Mr. Schultz was a lammister: the federal government was looking for him because he had not paid taxes on all the money he had earned. The police one day had raided his headquarters on East 149th Street with axes and found there incriminating records from his beer business. Yet I had seen him with my own eyes and felt his hand on my face. It is spectacular enough to see someone in the flesh whom you've only known in the newspapers, but to see someone the newspapers have said is on the lam definitely has a touch of magic to it. If the papers said Mr. Schultz was on the lam then it was true; but "the lam" suggested to most people someone running by night and hiding by day when really what it is is the state of being invisible; if you don't run and you don't hide and you are on the lam then you are there all the time, you are simply controlling people's ability to see you and that is a very potent magic. Of course you do it by waving dollars over the air, you wave a dollar and you are invisible. But it is still a difficult and dangerous trick that may not always work when you want it to. It would not work in Manhattan, I decided, because that's where the federal attorneys were who were planning to try Mr. Schultz for tax evasion. It would work better in the Bronx, as for instance in the Bronx neighborhood of a beer drop. It might work best of all, I decided, in the very gang headquarters that had been raided and cleaned out by the police at the insistence of the federal attorneys.

And that is how it happened one summer day the boy Billy came to be clinging to the back of a Webster Avenue trolley as it hummed its way south toward 149th Street. It was not easy traveling this way, your fingers had only the narrowest purchase on the outer sill of the rear window, which was of course the front window when the trolley was going in the other direction, which meant it was a big window and that therefore you had to crouch while you clung so that your head didn't appear in it: when the motorman spotted you in his rearview mirror he could make the car buck, throw it into some sort of electrical braking stutter so that you had to drop off, whether there was traffic behind you or not, which was a real son of a bitch. Not only that, but your feet had only the narrowest fender to toe, so that really you attached yourself for passage more by whole-body adhesion than anything else. And therefore when the trolley made a stop the correct procedure was to drop off until it started up again, not only because you were really vulnerable clinging to a trolley car at rest when any cop could come along and whap you across the ass with his billy club, but so that you would have the strength to hang there till the next stop. You didn't want to fall off while the damn thing was moving along at a clip, especially on Webster which is an industrial street of warehouses and garages and machine shops and lumberyards all of which make for long blocks and a fast-moving trolley enjoying its run between distant stops, going fast enough to rock along side to side on its wheel carriages, banging the hell out of them and sending up sparks up there where the pole scrapes the power from the wire. It is a fact that more than one boy has died riding the back of a streetcar. Nevertheless this was my preferred mode of travel even when, as now, I had two dollars in my pocket and could easily afford the nickel fare.

I hugged the great machine and got there and jumped off, running, just shy of my stop. But I didn't have the address of the East 149th Street headquarters so for a couple of wearying hours I trudged up and down over the hills, going as far west as the Concourse and then doubling back east, and never knowing what I was looking for in that simmering heat, but coming into luck when I saw two cars, a LaSalle coupé and a Buick sedan, sitting side by side in the lot of a closed-down White Castle hamburger joint not far from the junction with Southern Boulevard. By themselves neither car would have caught my eye but together they looked familiar. Next to the White Castle was a narrow four-story office building of indiscriminate color and large dirt-encrusted windows. When I went in the place smelled of piss and wood rot. Had there been a business directory on the wall you couldn't have seen it. I was elated. I removed myself and crossed the street and sat down on the curb between two parked trucks and waited to see what I would see.

And it was very interesting. It was about noon I'd say, the sunlight flashing down the power lines, the smoke of truck exhausts puffing up white as flowers, heat shimmering over the asphalt, and the street surface giving way to my sneaker heel and leaving an indentation like a crescent moon, so that a good detective could point out This is where he sat, right here where he banged his heel down, and from the depth of the indentation I'd say it was probably noon. And every once in a while someone would come along, some guy in shirtsleeves mostly, and he'd duck into that building. And one got off the corner bus, and one came out of a car that waited at the curb with its motor running, and one pulled up in a yellow cab, but all them were in a hurry, they were urgent, and with anxious expressions on their faces, white or black, and some of them strode and some of them scurried and one of them limped, but the thing was they all carried brown paper bags going in and when they came out they had nothing.

Now you would think it was easy to find a paper bag lying around on the sidewalk or down an alley or in a trash can, but for some reason this was not so on 149th Street, to get my hands on one I actually had to locate a grocery store and go in and spend money to buy something. And then I curled the mouth of the bag closed just like they did, folded it over a couple of times so that it looked wrinkled, and then I took a deep breath and though I was a block away, just to get into the mood of it I loped along like all those guys and got up a good sweat and pushed my way through the doors of the building into the dark urinal of a lobby and bounded up wooden stairs that you could hear a cockroach walk on, and I knew they would be at the very top, it was what made sense, and the higher I got the lighter it got, and at the top floor was a skylight covered by a rusty grating, and at the end of the landing was a plain steel door that had a number of peculiar gashes and dents in it, and the knob had been chopped off so I just nudged it with my finger and it swung open and in I went.

I don't know what I was expecting but I found a short empty corridor with splintery floor and another door, a brand-new unpainted steel door this time with a little peephole and it did not give way to the touch so I knocked and stood back a foot or so so the guy could see my bag and I waited. Could they hear my heart banging to be let in, louder than a sledgehammer, louder than an ax on steel, louder than a dozen cops rushing up four flights of wooden stairs?

And then the door unclicked and swung open an inch or two so what the hell, I found myself in a pleasant large room with several old beat-up desks and a man at each desk counting slips of paper, or stacks of bills, and they all lick their thumbs when they do this, and a phone was ringing, and I stood at a counter that came up to my chest looking in at all of this with my bag proffered and tried not to mind the guy who had opened the door standing behind me six feet tall and noisy of breath, the kind of person who snore-breathes, and I could smell the garlic, and I didn't yet know his name but it was Lulu Rosenkrantz, and he had this oversized head with unkempt black hair in need of a cutting, and little eyes practically hidden by his shaggy brows and a nose broken into blossom and blue cheeks all sunken in on their pockmarks, and each wave of garlic he exhaled I imagined as fire coming out of his throat. I didn't see Mr. Schultz anywhere, the fellow who came over to the counter was a bald man with rubber bands billowing his shirtsleeves above the elbow and he looked at me for a second curiously and took the bag and turned it over and emptied it out. I remember the look on his face when a dozen or so packages of cellophane-wrapped Dugan's cupcakes, two to a package, poured out on the counter: suddenly pale and alarmed in the eyes he was, and stupid with the effort to comprehend, all in the second before he held the bag upside down and shook it to see if anything would flutter out and then for good measure looked up inside it to see the trick hidden there. "What the fuck is this?" he shouted. "What the fuck are you bringing me!"

People stopped working and grew quiet and one or two rose and came over to look. Lulu Rosenkrantz moved up behind me. We all stood there in silence looking at these cupcakes. And it was nothing I had intended, I wouldn't have bought them if I'd found a bag in the street, I'd have blown up the bag with air, so that it looked as if I was carrying something, and then when you do that to paper bags you know you can pop them, hit them like a guy playing the cymbals, you hold the neck with one hand and punch out the bottom, and supposing I had done that, exploded the bag in front of this guy, I mean with a wild boy you can't tell what he might do, and that would have been the end of me, a dozen guys would have hit the floor and Lulu Rosenkrantz would have clubbed me on the top of my head with his fist and then when I was down on the floor he would have put his foot in my back to hold me still and executed me with one shot in the base of the skull, I know that now, you don't ever want to make sudden loud sounds when you're with these people. But because I'd had to buy something to get the bag I'd chosen cupcakes, chocolate with vanilla icing, which I happen to like, maybe I figured they would heft like packs of policy slips and stacks of bills in rubber bands, but I had just swept them off the bakery rack with my two arms and dumped them on the grocery man's counter, I didn't think about it, I had paid my money and come down the street and up the stairs and run cupcakes through a steel door and under the eyes of one of the deadliest gunmen in New York right into the heart of Mr. Schultz's policy racket. And it was unerring, like my juggling had been when with aplomb I'd tossed the navel orange, the stone, the two rubber balls, and the egg into a kind of pulsing fountain over the fence behind me to the tracks of the New York Central, at this time everything I was doing was working, I could do no wrong, it was really mysterious to me, I had known without knowing that whatever my life was going to be in this world it would have something to do with Mr. Schultz, but I was beginning to suspect it now, and with the faintest intimation that I might be empowered. That is the feeling you get, that your life is charmed, which means among other things that it is out of your hands.

At this precise moment while these heavyweight brains stood in their contemplation of the Idea of the Cupcake, Mr. Schultz came out of a back office preceded by the sound of his voice and then by a man in a gray pinstripe suit walking backward while trying to stuff some papers into his briefcase. "Goddammit counselor what do I pay you for!" Mr. Schultz shouted. "All you have to do is make the deal, it's very simple isn't it, a simple deal, all this legal bullshit you're giving me, why can't you just do what you're supposed to do and stop dicking me, I'm dying here, I could go to law school myself and pass the bar in every state of the union waiting for you to move your ass.''

Mr. Schultz was in his shirtsleeves and he wore suspenders and no tie, and he had a handkerchief crumpled up in his hand, and he was mopping his neck and ears as he advanced on the lawyer. It was my first clear look at him when the sun wasn't in my eyes: thinning black hair slicked back, a lot of forehead, heavy eyelids with pink rims, a reddened nose, as if he had a cold or suffered from some allergy, a bowl of a jaw, and a wide and disturbingly undulant mouth for a voice so much like a horn in timbre: ''Stop with the papers a minute and listen to me,'' he said and leapt forward and with a swinging backhand knocked the briefcase flying. ''You see what I got here? I got twenty desks. You see the men sitting at these desks, I got ten men. Doesn't empty desks mean anything to you? They are niching me, you stupid fuckingass lawyer, every week I'm under cover I lose bets, I lose banks, I lose my men to those motherfucking dago scungili. I've been out of it for eighteen goddamn months you Ivy League dickhead, and while you are having your afternoon teatime with the D.A. they're taking everything I got!''

The lawyer was flustered but also he was red in the face with anger about that briefcase, and pursued it now and the papers as well, hunkering down and shoveling everything back in. He was one of those fair-skinned people who flush up with their dignity. I noticed his shoes, shiny black wing-tips with rows of tiny decorative holes. ''Dutch,'' he said, ''you don't seem to appreciate you do not hold the cards in this situation. I went to our friend in the state senate and you see what he accomplished. I've gone through three of the best lawyers in Washington, I have a top man working on it now, a very important and respected litigator, knows everybody, and even he's hedging. This is a tough one, these are Feds and they are impervious, and it's unfortunate but it takes time and you're just going to have to live with it.''

''Live with it!'' Mr. Schultz shouted. ''Live with it?'' I thought if he was going to kill he would do it now. He let go a string of curses that was in his voice almost a kind of litany, he strode back and forth ranting and raving, and this was really my first experience of his temper and I was transfixed, I watched the raised veins of his neck and wondered why the lawyer was not cowering in front of him, I had nothing to compare this to, the vehemence seemed to me ultimate, I could not understand as the others did that this was not new anger, but one worn down somewhat by usage, as in a family argument, which is to say running, and therefore with a necessarily ceremonial aspect to it. So I was astonished to see Mr. Schultz drift over to the counter right in front of me, where he noticed all these cupcakes, and in the midst of his harangue grab one of the packages and break it open and peel off the browned pleated paper they bake each one in and drift back into the argument while consuming a chocolate cupcake with vanilla icing, but without quite being aware of it, as if eating was a distracted form of rage, and both were the function of a generic appetite that was nameless. And this was good enough for the guy holding the empty paper bag, the Riddle of the Sphinx was cracked, he went back to his work and the others turned away and went back to their desks, and Lulu Rosenkrantz returned to his place by the door and sat down and leaned his bent-cane chair against the wall, and shook an Old Gold out of his pack and lit himself a cigarette.

And I was still here and still alive and for all anyone knew I belonged here, at least for another moment or two. Mr. Schultz had not even seen me, but one pair of shrewd and amused eyes had seen and understood everything, including I suppose the brazen genius of my ambition, and their direct and unblinking gaze now made me aware of a man sitting at a desk near the window on the far wall, and he was talking on the phone as he looked at me, he was conducting what appeared to be an intimate and quiet conversation that did not seem at all inconvenienced by the shouting and screaming of Mr. Schultz. In a flash I knew for a certainty this was the great Abbadabba Berman, Mr. Schultz's financial brain, perhaps because his slow smile at me through all the noise and over the heads of everyone else even as he spoke on the phone was the distributed concentration of a mind superior to its surroundings. He turned slightly and raised his arm and drew a figure in the air and immediately a man on the right side of the room got up and wrote the figure 6 on a blackboard. And all at once the men at the desks in unison began to strip pieces of paper off their stacks of policy pads and rain them on the floor as if a sort of abstract Lindbergh parade was passing by. As he was to tell me later, the six was the final digit before the decimal point of the total odds of the first three races of the day according to the pari-mutuel machines at the Tropical Park in Miami Florida. And it was the first element of what would be the day's winning number. The second element of the number would come the same way from the second two races. And the last digit would most of the time come from the day's final two races. I say most of the time because if the winning number happened to have been played heavily, if for instance it had been touted by the astrological dream books the players liked to consult, Mr. Berman put in a last-minute call to an associate who was an official at the track and placed a bet, thus making a minute change in the odds on the pari-mutuel machines, thus changing the last digit of the winning number to one not so heavily played, thus protecting Mr. Schultz's overall profits for the day and bringing honor to the rackets. This legerdemain had been of Mr. Berman's devising and was the sort of thing that caused him to be known as Abbadabba.

I immediately granted him all the powers of his reputation because of the way he wrote a number in the air and it passed through all the noise and shouting to become visible on a blackboard. When he finished his call and arose from his desk, he rose only a short distance; he wore a summer yellow double-breasted suit and a panama hat, which was pushed back on his head, and the suit jacket was open and hanging down at an angle which suggested to me that he had something of a humpback. He walked with a rocking lurch from side to side. His shirt was a darker yellow silk, and a pale blue silk tie was clipped to it with a silver tiepin. It surprised me that someone that physically unfortunate would want to dress sharply. His trousers were pulled up so high by his suspenders that he seemed not to have any chest. When he came up to the counter not much more of him was showing from his side than was showing of me from mine. His brown eyes were encircled by steel-rim spectacles. I did not feel menaced by their gaze, which seemed to have originated in a realm of pure abstraction. Each brown pupil had a milky blue rim. His nose was sharp with little tufts of hair curling out of each nostril and his chin was pointed, and he had a sly V-shaped mouth in the corner of which the stub of a cigarette moved up and down as he spoke. He rested a clawlike hand over a package of cupcakes. "So kid, where's the coffee?" he said squinting at me through smoke.

FIVE

A minute later I was tearing down the stairs saying over in my mind how many black, how many black with sugar, how many with cream, how many with cream and sugar, I ran down 149th Street in the direction of the Boulevard Diner, I ran faster than the cars were moving, and the horns of the buses and trucks, and the grinding gears, and the clop and rattle of horse-drawn wagons, the sound of all the traffic driving its way fiercely into the high hours of the business day, sounded like choir music in my breast. I did a cartwheel, I did two in-the-air somersaults, I did not know in that moment how otherwise to praise God for giving me my first assignment for the Dutch Schultz gang.

Of course and as usual I was in advance of the actual facts. For several days I lived on the edge of everyone's patience and was consigned for the most part to the same curbstone of my observation across the street where I had begun. Mr. Schultz had not even noticed me, and when he finally did, as I swept up policy slips from the floor, he didn't remember the juggler, he asked Abbadabba Berman who the fuck I was and what I was doing there. "He's just some kid," Mr. Berman said. "He's our good-luck kid." For some reason that answer satisfied Mr. Schultz. "We could use some," he muttered and disappeared into his office. And so I rode the Webster Avenue streetcar every morning like a fellow going to work, and if I was given a job to do, if I brought coffee, or swept up the floor, I counted the day a success. Most of the time Mr. Schultz was not present, it was Mr. Berman who seemed to run things. I had plenty of time to begin to appreciate that it was he who had made a decision. Mr. Schultz had made a judgment, but Abbadabba Berman had engaged me. And then, the day when he chose to describe the details of the numbers game to me, the concept of apprenticeship rose in my mind, and I found a dignity in myself here as a kid operator sitting on a curb that quieted me down and gave me patience.

When Mr. Schultz was not present the life was tiresome, the runners came by in the mornings with their paper bags and by noon they had all

delivered, and the first race of the day's card went off at one P.M. and the
numbers went up on the blackboard every hour and a half or so, and the
magical numeric construction was completed by five o'clock, and by six
the shop was closed and everyone had gone home. When crime was
working as it was supposed to it was very dull. Very lucrative and very
dull. Mr. Berman was usually the last to leave and he carried a leather
briefcase that I assumed held the day's take, and just as he came scuttling
out of the office building a sedan pulled up and he got in and was gone,
usually glancing at me sitting there across the street and giving me a
knowing nod through the window, and I wouldn't count my day over until
he had, I tried to learn something from every small sign and infinitesimal
clue, and that face in the small triangle of rear window, sometimes obscured further by a cloud of cigarette smoke, was my cryptic instruction for
the night. Mr. Berman was like the other side of Mr. Schultz, the two poles
of my world, and the one's rage of power was the other's calm administration of numbers, they couldn't be more unlike as men, for instance Mr.
Berman never raised his voice but spoke out of the corner of his mouth that
was not employed with his perpetual cigarette, and the smoke smoked up
his voice and made it hoarse, so that it came fragmented, as a line broken
into dots, and I found I had to listen closely to hear what he said, because
not only did he not shout, he never repeated himself. And he had the aura
of mild deformity about him, his hunch, his stiff-kneed walk, that suggested a frailness, a physical grayness that he painted over with his neat
and color-matching clothing style, whereas Mr. Schultz was all brute
health, moving about in a disorder of moods and excessive feelings that
nothing like clothing could really fit on or augment.

One day I found some slips on the floor near Mr. Berman's desk that
looked different and when I was sure no one was looking I picked them
up and shoved them in my pocket. In the evening back on my block I
looked at them, there were three scraps of paper and each was drawn with
a square divided into sixteen boxes, and all the sixteen boxes of each
square were filled with different numbers, and I looked at them for a while
and began to see something, the numbers added up to the same sum no
matter which line you added, the horizontal line or the vertical or the
diagonal. And each square was totally different, he had figured out sets of
numbers in each case that worked that way and he hadn't repeated himself. The next day when I had the chance I observed him and saw that
what I had assumed was his work was a kind of doodling idleness, he sat
there all day and did calculations at his desk, and I had assumed they had
to do with the business, but really the business didn't demand that much
of him, there was nothing to it, the numbers that interested him were the
puzzling kind. Mr. Schultz was never idle that I was able to tell, he did not
have that quality of thinking about anything but business, but I saw that
Abbadabba Berman lived and dreamed numbers, and that he couldn't help
himself, he was as helpless with his numbers and everything they could

do for him as Mr. Schultz was in the grip of his ambitions.

Not once in that first week of my hanging around did Mr. Berman ask my name or where I lived or how old I was, or anything like that. I was prepared to lie in any case but it never came up. If he spoke to me he called me kid. He said one afternoon, ''Hey, kid, how many months in the year?'' I answered twelve. ''Okay, now suppose you give each month its number, like January is the first month and so on, you got it?'' I said I did. ''Okay, now you don't tell me your birthday but take the number of the month, and then add the number of the month following, you got it?'' I had it, I was thrilled he was talking to me. ''Okay, now product that sum by five, you got it?'' I thought a moment and then said I had it. ''Okay, now you product by ten and add the number of your birthday to the result, you got it?'' All right, yes, I had it. ''Now give me the number you come up with.'' I did—nine hundred and fifty-nine. ''Okay,'' he said, ''thanks for telling me, your birthday is September nine.''

This was of course correct and I grinned with appreciation. But he pressed on. ''I'm gonna tell you how much change you got in your pocket. If I do that and I'm right, I win it, okay? If I'm wrong, I'll match the sum and you will have double what you had before, okay? Turn around and count it, but don't let me see.'' I told him I didn't have to count it, I knew how much I had. ''Okay, double the sum in your mind, you got it?'' I had: the amount was twenty-seven cents and I doubled it, fifty-four. ''Okay, add three, you got it?'' Fifty-seven. ''Okay, now product it by five, you got it?'' Two eighty-five. ''Okay, subtract the number six, you got it? Now tell me the result.'' I told him, two hundred seventy-nine. ''Okay, you've just lost twenty-seven cents, am I right?'' He was right.

I shook my head in admiration and smiled though I was smarting, and the smile felt false on my face. I handed over my twenty-seven cents. Maybe I had the sneaking hope he would give it back, but he pocketed it and turned back to his desk and left me to my broom. It occurred to me then that with his sort of mind if he needed to know my birthday, or the amount of money I had, this is the way he would go about it. What if he wanted my street address. Or the number of my public school. Everything could be translated into numbers, even names if you assigned a number to each letter as in code. What I thought was idleness was a system of understanding, and it made me uneasy. They both knew how to get what they wanted. Even a stranger who knew nothing about him, neither his name nor his reputation, would perceive in a flash Mr. Schultz's willingness to maim or kill anyone who stood in his way. But Abbadabba Berman calculated everything, he figured the odds, he couldn't walk that well but he was lightning quick, so that all events and outcomes, all desires and means of satisfying them, were translated as numerical values in his mind, which meant he never did anything unless he knew how it was going to turn out. I wondered which of them was more of a dangerous study to a simple boy just trying to get ahead and make something of himself. There was an implacable adult will in both of them. "And see if you can work out one a those number squares for yourself, it ain't so hard once you get the ruling idea," Mr. Berman said giving a dry little hack through the cigarette smoke.

A WEEK OR TWO LATER THERE WAS SOME SORT OF EMERGENCY, MR. BERMAN WAS dispatching people in the office and over the phone, and then he must have run out of people, he beckoned to me and wrote something on a piece of paper and it was an address on 125th Street, and also a name, George. I understood immediately this was a break for me. I asked no questions, not even how to get there, although I had never been to Harlem. I decided to go in a yellow taxi and let the driver find the way, I had built up a stake of four dollars from my tips from sweeping and running errands and I figured a cab ride was a good investment also because it would allow me to show how fast and reliable I was. But I had never flagged a taxicab before and I was half surprised when one stopped. I read out the address as if I'd been riding in cabs all my life and hopped in and slammed the door, I knew the proper deportment of dealing with cabs from the movies, I showed nothing on my face of the excitement I felt, but we hadn't gone a block with me sitting in the middle of the back seat with all the room in the world on the cracked red leather before I decided this was my new preferred mode of travel.

We proceeded down the Grand Concourse and across the 138th Street Bridge. The address I had was a candy store near the corner of 125th Street and Lenox Avenue. I told the driver to wait, like people in the movies did, but he said he would wait only if I paid him as much of the fare as was on the meter. This I did. When I walked in the store I knew it was George standing there behind the counter with a big puffy eye and a red bruise on the side of his face, he was holding a piece of ice under his eye and the melting ice was running through his fingers like tears, he was a light-complected Negro man with gray hair and a trim gray mustache, and he was shaken, ashen actually, two or three other men who looked not so much like customers as friends of his were there sitting at the counter, and they were black too and wore their wool working caps though it was the hot summer, they were not joyful to see me. I stayed calm and tried to act like a true business representative. I looked through the window at the black passersby on the street looking in at me as they passed, and I saw then the plate-glass window was cracked diagonally in half, and there were shards of glass on the worn linoleum floor near the newspapers, and the taxi at the curb looked as if it wasn't joined properly in the middle, nothing was joined, nothing went together, this dark little candy store had broken off from Mr. Schultz like a piece of the continent into the sea,

George reached down into one of the ice-cream containers under the fountain and came up with a brown paper bag rolled tight at the top the way they did it and he dropped it on the Belgian marble counter. "Ain't nothing I can do, I work for them now," he said holding the ice cake up to his face. "You tell him that, hear? You see what happen I try to do right. You tell him. All go to hell far as I concern, you tell him that too. All the white mens together."

And back to the Bronx I went, the paper bag clutched in my two hands, and I didn't even look inside, I knew there were hundreds of dollars there but I wouldn't look, I was happy enough to have this official standing as a runner, I wondered what had happened to George's man but didn't really care that much, I felt too good about handling the thing without a hitch, and without feeling afraid, and that this George did not question my credentials or make a personal remark about me, as angry as he was, but simply treated me as another of Mr. Schultz's men, a professional, one whose face showed no emotion in the presence of pain or misfortune but who had come for the money and gone with it, period, and who was now bumping over the bridge over the Harlem River, his heart pumping with happy gratitude for the beauty and excitement of his existence, and the river flowing with industrial muck, and the welding torches of riverside machine shops like sparklers in the July morning.

SIX

Of course as happy as I was to be catching on with them, things were not going well at that time for the Dutch Schultz gang and they wouldn't until Dixie Davis, that was the name of the lawyer Mr. Schultz shouted at all the time, was able to work out a plan for Mr. Schultz's surrender to the U.S. District Attorney's Office. If you did not know the arcane nature of these matters it would not make sense that Mr. Schultz was hoping to turn himself in for arraignment but he paced up and down dreaming of nothing but that, once actually trying to tear the hair from his head in a fury of frustration that he couldn't yet do that, for the truth of the matter was until he was booked and out on bail he wasn't free to attend to business. But he couldn't turn himself in until he had some legal guarantees that would improve his chances in a trial, as for instance that it should be held out of New York City, where, because of certain unfortunate publicity having to do with his activities, the public from which any jury would be composed tended not to see him in a good light. And that was at the core of the endless negotiations between his lawyer and the D.A.'s office, he wanted some guarantees before he turned himself in and until he had them he could not be arrested and therefore free.

He told me the crime business like any other needs the constant attention of the owner to keep it going, because nobody cares about the business like the owner and it's his burden to keep the profits flowing, to keep everyone on their toes, and most of all to keep the business growing, because as he explained it to me an enterprise can't maintain itself today just by repeating what it did yesterday, if it doesn't grow it dries up, it is like something living, when it stops growing it starts dying, to say nothing of the special nature of his particular enterprise, a very complex enterprise not only of supply and demand but of subtle executive details and diplomatic skills, the payoffs alone deserved a special department of controllers, the people you needed to rely on were vampires, they needed their blood money, and if you weren't there to give it to them they folded up on you, went numb, faded into the mist, you had to be a public presence in

criminal enterprise or it would get away from you, and whatever you built
up could be taken away from you, in fact the better you were, the more
successful you were, the surer the fuckers would try to take it away from
you, and by that he didn't only mean the law he meant the competition,
this was a highly competitive field that did not attract gentlemen, and if
they found a weakness in the armor, they went after it, and even if you had
one pissant sentry sleeping on his post say, or some gonfalong foot soldier
who could be lured off guard duty, not to speak of your own absence from
the command post not even to speak of that, why then you were finished
because they drove their tanks in through that opening whatever it was
and that was the end of you, they had no fear of you, and without their fear
of you, you were a dead man in no-man's-land, and there would not be
enough recognizably left of you to put in a coffin.

I took these concerns for my own, as how could I not, sitting on the
screened back porch of the two-story red brick house on City Island with
the great man confiding his thoughts his worries to orphan Billy, the
good-luck kid, the amazed beneficiary of this sudden and unpredictable
intimacy. He had gone from not recognizing me to remembering the first
moment he saw me across the street capably juggling, how could I not take
on the dark troubles of his heart and feel them inside myself as a matter
that would not go away, the nagging fear of loss, the dry inner sob of
unjust circumstance, and the heroic satisfaction of enduring, of seeing
things through? So this was the secret place where he stayed when he was
not temporarily present in his protected precincts, this red brick private
house just like the flat-roofed private houses you saw all over the borough
except way out here it was the only one on a short street of bungalows, on
this island that was still in the Bronx, and now I was one of the few people
who knew, Irving knew of course because it was his mother's house, and
his elderly mother knew because she cooked and kept things going normally—a woman who walked around with her hands always wet—on
this quiet side street with a few hardy ailanthus trees like the ones planted
in all the city parks, and Mr. Berman knew it because it was he who one
day allowed me to come for the ride that he took each afternoon to bring
Mr. Schultz the receipts and go over the figures. And as I sat out in the
fenced backyard while they were doing this I reasoned that all the neighbors on the street and perhaps for a few blocks around must know it too
because how can you not know when a famous visitor is on your street,
and a dark car with two men in it sits outside at the curb night and day,
this was a small place, a waterfront town really, if of a New York style, but
having not really that much in common with the endless paved hills and
valleys of Bronx tenements and stores and elevated trains and trolleys and
peddlers' carts, it was an island that got sun, and the people on it must feel
special, apart from everything, as I did now, relishing my connection with
the good life of space, of this view of the Sound, which looked to me like
an ocean, a deep horizon of gray sea sliding and shifting about in a

leisurely way, the way slate and stone would shift if not fixed to the land, with the stateliness of a monumental body too big to have enemies. Right next door on the other side of the chain-link fence was a boatyard, with sailboats and motorboats of all kinds propped up on blocks or tilting over in the sand, and there were a few sailboats moored in the water off the boatyard wharves. But the boat I had my eye on was tied up at the wharf looking sleek and ready to go, a varnished mahogany speedboat with grooved tan leather seats built in and bright brass trim on the windshield and a steering wheel like a car's and a little American flag flying from the stern. And I saw a gap in the chain-link fence between the house and the boatyard just at the waterline, and then a path to the wharf where that boat waited, and I knew this had to be the craft of Mr. Schultz's getaway, if it ever came to that. How I admired the life of taking pains, of living in defiance of a government that did not like you and did not want you and wanted to destroy you so that you had to build out protections for yourself with money and men, deploying armament, buying alliances, patrolling borders, as in a state of secession, by your will and wit and warrior spirit living smack in the eye of the monster, his very eye.

But beyond that, contriving a life from its property of danger, putting it together in the constant contemplation of death, that was what thrilled me, that was why the people on this island street would never rat, his presence honored them and allowed them to live in their consciousness of him as in a kind of light of life and death, with the moments of superior awareness or illumination the best of them might get in church or in the first moments of romantic love.

"Christ, I had to earn everything I got, nobody gave me a thing, I came out of nowhere and everything I done I done by myself," Mr. Schultz said. He sat in reflection upon this truth and pulled on his cigar. "Sure I made mistakes, that's the way you learn, the only time I ever served was when I was seventeen, I got sent to Blackwell's Island for heisting, I didn't have a lawyer and they gave me an indeterminate, meaning when I got out depended on how I acted, and that was fair enough. I tell you if I had some of these hotshot lawyers I have now probably I'd have gotten life. Hey Otto?" he said laughing, but Mr. Berman had fallen asleep in his chair with his panama over his face, I suppose he had heard Mr. Schultz complain once or twice before about how hard his life was.

"Anyways I was damned if I'd kiss ass just to be let out of there, I raised hell instead, and I was such a tough son of a bitch they couldn't take me and sent me upstate to reform school, a work farm with cows and all that shit. You ever been in reform school?"

"No sir."

"Well it wasn't no picnic. I wasn't a big guy, I was about your size, a skinny little punk, and there was a lot of bad boys there. I knew you gotta make your reputation early, where it matters, where the word can get around. So I was mean enough for ten. I didn't take any shit. I looked for fights. I took on the biggest guys I could find. God help the fucker who messed with me, as one or two did to their regret. I even escaped from the goddamn place, it wasn't hard, I went over the wire, and I was out in the bushes a day and a night before they caught me, and they added a couple of months for that, and I got poison ivy all the hell over me for good measure, and I was walking around all that time in calamine lotion like a mad zombie. When I finally got out they were glad to see me go, let me tell you. You in a gang?''

"No sir."

"Well how you expect to get anywhere, how you expect to learn anything? I hire from gangs. That's the training ground. You ever hear of the Frog Hollow gang?''

"No sir."

"Jesus. That was the most famous of all the old Bronx gangs. What's the matter with this generation? That was the gang of the first Dutch Schultz, don't you know that? The toughest street fighter who ever lived. He'd bite your nose off. He'd pull your balls out by the root. My gang named me after him I got back from the reform. It was a honorary thing. It showed I'd done my time and gone through it, and come out of my training a son of a bitch in spades. So ever since that's why I'm called the Dutchman.''

I cleared my throat and looked out through the screen over the privet hedges to the water, where a small boat with a triangular white sail seemed to be sailing the shimmering mesh. "There are some gangs now," I said, "but they are dumb fucking kids, mostly. I don't want to pay for no one's mistakes but my own. I think these days for the real training you got to go right to the top."

I held my breath. I didn't dare look at him, I looked at my feet. I could feel his gaze on me. I could smell his cigar.

"Hey Otto," he said, "wake the hell up, you're really missing something."

"Oh? That's what you think," Mr. Berman said from under his hat.

IT DIDN'T ALL HAPPEN AT ONCE BUT IT HAPPENED NIGHT AND DAY, THERE SEEMED to be no rule of time, no plan except the possible moment and whatever it was we drove to it in a car, and when you look out the window at the life you're going through to get to this moment it takes on an odd cast, so that if the sun is shining it's shining too brightly, or if it is night it is too black, all the organization of the world seems part of the conspiracy of your attention, and whatever is naturally around you becomes unnatural by the peculiarly absolute moral demand of what you are doing. This was my wish, I was training at the top. I remember for instance being dropped

off at the corner of Broadway and Forty-ninth Street and told to hang
around and keep my eyes open. That was all that was said, but it was
momentous. One of the cars sped off and I didn't see it again, the other,
the one with Mr. Berman, kept coming around the block every few minutes, a single black squarish Chevrolet sedan inconspicuous in the traffic
of black cars and the yellow checker cabs cruising for fares and the double-
decker buses and streetcars, relatively empty, and neither Mickey the
driver nor Mr. Berman looked at me as they passed, and I derived from
that not to look particularly at them. I stood in the doorway of Jack
Dempsey's restaurant that had not yet opened for the day, it must have
been nine or nine-thirty in the morning, and Broadway was fairly fresh,
the newsstands and coconut-drink and hotdog stands were open and a
couple of the stores that sold little lead Statues of Liberty but not much
else. There was a second-floor dance studio across Forty-ninth Street and
the big window was tilted open and someone was playing ''Bye, Bye,
Blackbird'' on the piano. There is a local Broadway, a community of
Broadway that you see in the morning before the penny arcades and bars
open for the day, the people who live upstairs in the tenements above the
movie marquees, who come out with their dogs on the leash to get the
Racing Form and the *Mirror* and buy a bottle of milk. And the bakery
delivery men who pull up and carry the racks of breads and big bags of
rolls into the groceries, or the butcher trucks with the guys loading big raw
sides of beef on their shoulders and dumping them on the roller chutes
leading down to the basements underneath the restaurants. I kept watching and saw the street sweeper with his big broom and his summer white
with the khaki-and-orange trim on his hat load up the horse manure and
paper and crap and trash of a Broadway night on his wide-blade shovel
and dump it all into the big ashcan on his two-wheel cart as if he was a
housewife tidying up her kitchen. A while later the tanked water wagon
came along spraying the street so that it looked shining and fresh and
almost simultaneously I saw the string of electric lights go on around the
Loew's State Theatre a few blocks below where Broadway ran into Seventh
Avenue. In the sun it was not entirely possible to read the headlines riding
in lights around the Times Building on Times Square. The black Chevrolet
came around again and this time Mr. Berman glanced at me and I began
to feel anxious, I wanted to see whatever it was I was supposed to see but
the traffic was ordinary, not particularly heavy, and the people on the
sidewalk were going about their business with no great urgency, a man in
a suit and tie came along with a crate of apples on his shoulder and set it
up on the corner with his APPLES 5¢ sign, the morning was warming up and
I wondered if what I needed was in the window behind me where Jack
Dempsey was shown in a big blowup photo of the ring in Manila with
thousands watching, and there were other photos of the great man shaking hands with famous people, show people like Jimmy Durante and
Fanny Brice and Rudy Vallee, but then in the reflection of the restaurant

glass I saw the office building across the street, and I turned around to look, up on the fifth or sixth floor a man climbed out on a ledge with a pail and sponge and affixed his safety belt to the hooks imbedded in the brick and leaned back against the belt and began to make wide arcs with his soapy sponge on the window, and then I saw another man on another window ledge on the floor above him coming out to do the same thing. I watched these men washing the windows and then for some reason I knew this was what I was supposed to see, these window washers doing the morning's work high above the street. And on the sidewalk below them was a sign, the kind that supports itself like an A, advising passersby that work was going on overhead and to take care, and it was the sign the window washers had set up in the name of their union. I had by now crossed Broadway and stood on the southwest corner of Forty-ninth Street and Seventh Avenue and I watched these guys working up there, two of them were on a scaffold hanging from the roof parapet maybe fifteen stories above the street and I saw this was the expedient for the extra large windows at the top that were too wide for a safety belt to span. And it was this scaffold with the two men and their sponges and pails and rags which suddenly lurched, the rope on one side snapping up into the air like a whip, and the two men flinging their arms back and spilling down the scaffold. One of them came down the side of the building wheeling. I don't know if I shouted, or who else saw it happen or heard it, but while he was still several stories up, some seconds above his death, the whole street knew. The traffic was stopped as if every vehicle had been pulled up taut on the same string. There was a collective screech, a total apprehension of disaster on the part of every pedestrian for blocks around, as if we had all been aware all along of what was going on above our heads in the sky, so that the moment the composition was disturbed everyone knew instantly. Then the body at a point of flat and horizontal extension hit the roof of a car parked in front of the building and the sound it made was as a cannon going off, a terrible explosion of the force of bone and flesh, and what made me gasp was that he moved, the guy moved in that concavity of metal he had made, a sinuosity of bone-smashed inching, as if it was a worm there curling for a moment on the hot metal before even that degree of incredible life trembled out through the fingers.

A cop on a horse was now galloping past me on Forty-ninth Street. The other window washer was still up there hanging from the unhinged end of the vertical scaffold and kicking his legs to find purchase where there was none, screaming up there as the platform swayed from side to side in the way least calculated to ensure his survival. What does a man have in his arms eight ten stories above the ground, what does he have in his fingers, in the muscles of his fingertips, what do we hold to in this world of unholy depth which presents for us its bottomless possibilities in air in water in the paved soil that opens up under us, cracking like a thunderstorm of the most specific density? Green-and-white police cars were converging from all directions. Up at Fifty-seventh Street a hook-and-ladder fire engine was turning into Broadway. I was breathless with the fascination of disaster.

"Hey kid!"

Behind me on Broadway was Mr. Berman's Chevrolet, which was pulled up to the curb. The door opened. I ran back the short block and got in and slammed the door behind me and Mickey the driver took off. "Don't gawk, kid, you leave that to hicks," Mr. Berman said. He was put out with me. "You are not in the sightseeing business. You're told to stay somewhere you stay there."

At this I forbore to look back out the window, which I would otherwise have done even knowing that the progress of the car down Broadway would have blocked the scene from my sight. But I felt the will in myself in not moving but sitting back silently and staring ahead.

Mickey the driver had both hands on the wheel when he didn't reach down to shift. If the wheel was a clock he held it at ten and two. He drove moderately but not slowly, he did not contend with the traffic but used it to his advantage without ever seeming to speed or cut anyone off. He did not try to make a changing light, or upon a light's turning green to speed off with it. Mickey was the driver and that's all he was, but that was everything; you knew watching him and feeling the movement of the car under you that there was a difference between driving a car and running it with the authority of a professional. I myself did not know how to drive, how could I, but I knew that Mickey would drive a car as calmly and safely at a hundred miles an hour as at thirty, that whatever he called upon a car to do it would do, and now with the vision in my mind of the helpless window washer falling to his death, Mickey's competence stood in my mind as a silent rebuke in confirmation of Mr. Berman's remark.

I don't think in all the time I knew him while he was alive I ever exchanged a word with Mickey. I think he was ashamed of his speech. His intelligence was all in his meaty hands and in his eyes, which you sometimes saw flick back for a professional second in the rearview mirror. They were light blue. He was totally hairless, with fat ridges at the back of his neck which I got to know well. His ears bulbed out in back. He had been a prizefighter who never got further than the preliminaries in club fights. His greatest distinction was having been TKO'd by Kid Chocolate in one of his earliest fights when the Kid was coming up, one night in the Jerome Arena just across the street from Yankee Stadium. Or so I had heard. I don't know why but I wanted to cry for us all. Mickey drove us over to the West Side into some truck garage, and while Mr. Berman and I went across the street to a diner for coffee, the Chevrolet was exchanged for another car, which appeared with Mickey at the wheel maybe twenty minutes later. It was a Nash with totally different black-and-orange license plates. "Nobody dies who doesn't sin," Mr. Berman had said to me in the diner. "And since that covers everybody, it's something we can all look forward to.'' Then he tossed one of those little number-square games on the table for me to amuse myself with: the one with sixteen squares and fifteen little numbered tiles which you have to put in order by shoving them around until they're in sequence. The point is you have only that one space to use to get everything around where it belongs; one space usually in the wrong place to put everything in the order in which it belongs.

BUT AS I SAY IT WAS A KIND OF ENLISTMENT, I HAD WALKED IN AND SIGNED UP. And the first thing you learn is there are no ordinary rules of the night and day, there are just different kinds of light, granules of degree, and so no reason to have more or less to do in one than in another. The blackest quietest hour was only a kind of light.

There was no attempt on anyone's part to provide explanations for why things were being done and no one sought to justify anything. I knew better than to ask questions. What I did understand is that a strong ethic prevailed, all the normal umbrages and hurts were in operation, all the outraged sensibilities of justice, all the convictions of right and wrong, once you accepted the first pure inverted premise. But it was the premise I had to work on. I found it was easiest when Mr. Schultz talked to me; at these times for a few moments things were clear. I decided I had so far the idea of it but not the feeling, it was the feeling that made for the genius of the idea as anyone could tell just being in Mr. Schultz's presence.

In the meantime I could figure out things were being done at a level of intensity that perhaps had been anticipated in the quiet afternoons on the back porch of the City Island house. I will tell here about Mr. Schultz's Embassy Club. It was a place he owned, one of his properties, and it was quite publicly visible with a fancy canopy with its name in scripted letters on East Fifty-sixth Street between Park and Lexington avenues. I knew all about nightclubs from the gossip columns, and the customers who went there and the fancy names some of them had, from high society, and how they all seemed to know each other, movie stars and actors and actresses coming in after work, and ball players and writers and senators, I knew there were sometimes floor shows with bands and chorus girls or black women who sang the blues, and I knew each place had bouncers for the unruly and the girls selling cigarettes on trays while they walked around in net stockings and cute little pillbox hats, I knew all that though I had never seen it.

So I was excited when they sent me to work there as a busboy. Imagine me, a kid, working downtown in a nightclub! But in the week I worked there it was nothing like I expected. There was first of all not one single famous person I saw while I was there. There were people who came and ate and drank and listened to the little orchestra and danced, but they were

unimportant. I knew that because they kept looking around for the important people they had come to see. Most nights the place was half empty
except toward eleven o'clock when the floor show went on. The whole
place was lit in blue light with banquettes around the walls and tables with
blue tablecloths around a small dance floor, and a small stage with no
curtain where the band played, not a great band, two saxophones and a
trumpet and a piano and guitar and drums, and there was a hatcheck girl
but no cigarette girls and no midnight reporters come to get dirt from the
famous, no Walter Winchell or Damon Runyon, the place was dead, and
it was dead because Mr. Schultz couldn't show up there. He was the
attraction. People liked to be where things happened or could happen.
They liked power. The bartender stood behind the bar with his arms folded
and yawned. At the worst possible table, by the door where it was drafty,
every night two assistant United States attorneys sat with lime rickeys they
did not touch and filled the ashtrays which I emptied conscientiously.
They did not look at me. Nobody looked at me in my short maroon jacket
and bow tie, I was so low-down as to be supposed legitimate. I was
making good in the nightclub world and took a sort of scintillating pride
in the fact that as a busboy I was beneath even the notice of the old-time
waiters. That made me valuable. Because I had been put there by Mr.
Berman with the usual admonition to keep my eyes open. And I did, and
I learned what idiots people could make of themselves who came to
nightclubs, and how they loved it if a bottle of champagne cost them
twenty-five dollars, and the headwaiter gave them a table when they
pressed a twenty-dollar bill in his hand though there were so many empty
tables they could have asked for the one they wanted and he would have
led them to it for nothing. It was a narrow room, an empty scene, and
between sets the band stood out in the alley and every one of them was a
viper, even the girl singer, and on the third or fourth night she turned her
hand upside down to me and handed me a roach and I sucked on it like
I had seen them doing and sipped it in, that harsh bitter tea, like a scatter
of embers going down my throat, and of course I coughed and they
laughed, but the laughter was kindly; except for the singer they were white
musicians not much older than I was and I don't know what they took me
for, maybe someone working his way through college, and I let them think
it, whatever it was, all I needed was a pair of Harold Lloyd horn-rim
glasses and the act would have been perfect. In the kitchen though that
was a different story, the chef there was a Negro who was in charge, he
smoked cigarettes, the ashes of which dropped onto the steaks he was
frying, and he had a cleaver with which he threatened waiters or underlings who offended him. He was a perpetually angry man who blew into
flares of rage like the flames that flew up in the fat drippings. The only one
who wasn't afraid of him was the dishwasher, an old gray-haired Negro
man with a limp who seemed to be able to stick his bare arms in tubs of
scalding soapy water with no feeling. We were close because I brought

him the dishes. He appreciated the way I scraped them. We were professionals together. You had to be careful in the kitchen because the floor was as greasy as a garage's. Cockroaches were in leisurely residence on the wall almost as if they were stuck there, and the flypaper that hung from the light-bulb strings was black, and sometimes on the counters themselves a mouse or two scurried from one food bin to another. This was all behind the padded swinging doors with the oval windows of the blue-lit Embassy Club.

Yet I stopped to listen to the girl singer when I could. She had a sweet thin voice and seemed to look far away when she sang. They would always get up to dance when she sang because the women liked her songs of loss and loneliness and loving men who didn't love them back. *The one I love belongs to somebody else. He means his tender songs for somebody else.* She stood in front of the microphone and sang with very little gesture, perhaps because of all the tea she smoked, and every once in a while, at really inappropriate moments of the lyrics, she hiked up her strapless satin gown as if she was afraid even her listless gestures would expose her breasts.

Then every morning at about four or four-thirty Mr. Berman arrived looking as fresh as the morning in some artful combination of pastel colors. At this point everyone would have left, the U.S. District Attorney's men, the waiters, the band, the place was only ostensibly open, with maybe the beat cop with his hat on the bar having one on the house. And it was my job to go pull all the tablecloths off the tables, and stack the chairs on them so that the two cleaning women who came in in the morning would be able to vacuum the carpet under the tables and mop and wax the dance floor. After this I was summoned to the basement, where a small paneled office was maintained just down the hall from a fire door leading to a kind of culvert that led up a flight of iron stairs to an alley. And in this office Mr. Berman would go over the night's receipts and ask me what I had seen. I would of course have seen nothing except what for me was the new life of Manhattan, a life of the night, where in one short week everything was inverted and I finished work at dawn and went to sleep in the daytime. What I had seen was the life of the big time and a certain fluency of money not as it was earned and collected, as on 149th Street, but as it was spent and as it was turned into blue light and fancy clothes and indifferently delivered love songs. I had seen that the hatcheck girl paid Mr. Berman for her job, rather than the other way around, but that this seemed to be profitable to her as she went off duty each night with a different man waiting under the canopy outside. But this was not what he meant when he asked the question. I had seen my witchy little friend Rebecca in my mind dressed in high heels and some kind of black lacy gown dancing with me there to the songs of the girl singer. I thought she would even be impressed with me in my waistcoat busboy jacket. I slept in that same office after Mr. Berman left, and there I dreamed of making love to Rebecca and not having to pay for it. In my dream I was in the rackets and this made her love me enough to enjoy what I was doing to her. But certainly this was not what Mr. Berman had in mind. Half the time I awoke in the morning all gummed up in my sleep, which created laundry problems, and I solved these too like a denizen of Broadway, finding a Chinese laundry on Lexington Avenue, but also buying myself socks and underwear and shirts and pants over on Third Avenue under the El. It was like my Third Avenue. I was not unhappy this week. I found I was really comfortable in the city, it was no different from the Bronx, it was only what the Bronx wanted to be, it was streets and they could be learned and I had a job which paid twelve dollars a week now, dispensed from Mr. Berman's pockets just for me to haul dishes around and keep my eyes open though I did not know for what. And after the third or fourth day of this I rarely saw in my mind the cartwheeling body of the window washer in the sun coming down alongside the office building on Seventh Avenue. It was almost as if the East Side was a different behavior even for the rackets. I slept below ground in that office on a fold-out cot and, along about noon, came up the iron stairs into the alley and walked around the corner and a few blocks down and found a cafeteria on Lexington Avenue where the cab drivers had their lunch while I had my breakfast. I ate big breakfasts. I bought rolls and buns for old men the cafeteria owner was trying to kick out the revolving door. I reflected on my competence for life and could find nothing to criticize except perhaps not going uptown to see my mother. I called her once to the phone at the candy store on the corner of our block and told her I would be away for a while but I didn't know if she would remember. It had taken fifteen minutes on an open line for someone to find her and bring her downstairs.

I mention all this as an interlude of peace and reflection.

THEN ONE NIGHT I WAS ABLE TO TELL MR. BERMAN THAT BO WEINBERG HAD COME in with a party and had dinner and paid the band to do a couple of numbers of his choice. Not that I had recognized him, but the waiters had all come alive. Mr. Berman did not seem surprised. ''Bo will be in again,'' he said. ''Never mind who he sits with. See who sits at the bar near the door.'' And so I did, a couple of nights later, when Bo reappeared with a pretty blond woman and another good-looking couple, a well-dressed man with a blond pompadour and a brunette. They took the best banquette, near the bandstand. And all those customers who had come there that evening looking for the peculiar excitement seemed now to believe it was their good fortune to have found it. It wasn't merely that Bo looked good, although undeniably he did, a tall, rugged, swarthy man impeccably groomed and with teeth that seemed to shine, but that he seemed to drink up the available light, so that blue light turned red and everyone else in the room seemed dim and small by comparison. He and his party were wearing formal clothes as if they had come from someplace important, like the opera or a Broadway show. He greeted this one and that one, he acted as if he owned the joint. The musicians came out earlier than they might have and the dancing started. And soon the Embassy Club was what I had imagined a nightclub should be. From one minute to the next the place was packed, as if all of New York City had come running. People kept coming up to Bo's table to introduce themselves. The man Bo was with was a famous golfer, but I didn't recognize the name. Golf was not my sport. The women laughed and smoked a puff or two of a cigarette and as soon as it was mushed out I changed the ashtray. It was odd, the more people there were and the noisier the place got with music and laughter, the bigger the Embassy Club seemed to be, until it seemed the only place that there was, I mean with nothing outside, no street, no city, no country. My ears were ringing, I was a busboy but I felt it was my personal triumph when Walter Winchell himself appeared and sat for a few minutes at Bo's table, although I hardly saw him, because I was working my ass off. Later Bo Weinberg actually addressed me, telling me to tell the waiter to refresh the drinks of the assistant U.S. attorneys who were sitting at the drafty table by the door. This caused great merriment. Well after midnight, when they decided to have something to eat, and I went up to the table to place the little hard rolls in their little plates with my silver tongs, as I by now knew how to do with aplomb, I had to restrain the urge to pick up three or four of the rolls and juggle them in time to the music, which at the moment happened to be "Limehouse Blues," which the band did in a very stately and deliberate rhythm. *Oh Limehouse kid, Oh Oh Limehouse kid, going the way that the rest of them did.*

But for all of that I never forgot my instruction from Mr. Berman. The man who had come in just before Bo Weinberg and sat at the end of the bar was not Lulu Rosenkrantz with the ridged brow, and not Mickey with the floret ears, and it wasn't anyone I had ever seen on any of the trucks or in the office on 149th Street, and in fact no one at all that I recognized from the organization. It was a small, pudgy man in a double-breasted pearl gray suit with big lapels and a green satin tie and a white-on-white shirt and he didn't stay that long, smoking just a cigarette or two and drinking a mineral water. He seemed to enjoy the music in a quiet and private way. He didn't talk to anyone and minded his own business and kept his porkpie hat on the bar beside him.

Later when the morning rose in the basement office in the culvert off the alley, Mr. Berman lifted his eyes from the stacks of cashier slips and said "So?" his brown eyes with the pale blue rims looking at me through his spectacles. I had noticed the man used his own matches and left the book in the ashtray and I picked it out of the trash behind the bar after he left. But this was not the moment to give my proof. It was necessary only to make the essential attribution. "An out-of-towner," I said. "A goom-bah from Cleveland."

THERE WAS NO SLEEP FOR ME THAT MORNING. MR. BERMAN SENT ME OUT TO A phone booth and I dialed the number he gave me, let it ring three times and hung up. I brought back coffee and rolls. The cleaning women came in and did up the club. It was now nice and peaceful in there with all the lights out except one light over the bar and whatever silt of the morning sun managed to drift in through the curtains on the front doors. Part of what I was learning was when to be on hand and visible, as opposed to being on hand and invisible. The second was the expedient I chose now, perhaps from no more evidence than Mr. Berman's disinclination at this time to talk to me. I sat upstairs at the bar all alone in the dusk of the morning tired as hell and not without pride in myself for having made what I knew was a useful identification. But then all of a sudden there was Irving, which meant Mr. Schultz was somewhere nearby. Irving stood behind the bar and put some ice in a glass, then he cut a lime in quarters and with his fingers squeezed lime juice into the glass, and then filled the glass with a spritz from the seltzer bottle. When all this was meticulously done, with not so much as a ring left on the bar surface, Irving drank off his lime soda in one draft. He then washed the glass and dried it with a bar towel and replaced it under the counter. At this moment it occurred to me that my self-satisfaction was inane. It consisted in believing I was the subject of my experience. And then when Irving went to the front door, where someone had been knocking on the glass for some minutes, and admitted the improvident city fire inspector who had picked just this time, and why, except that the words in the air of the great stone city go softly whispering in the lambent morning that this sachem is dead and that one is dying, as if we were some desert blooming in the smallest flowers with the prophecies of ancient tribes, I saw even before it happened what an error of thought could lead to, that presumption was dangerous, that the confidence of imperception was deadly, that this man had forgotten what a fire inspector was, his place in the theory of inspections, his lesser place in the system of fires. Irving was ready with money from his own pocket and would have had the guy out of there in another minute but that Mr. Schultz happened to come upstairs from the office with the morning's news. At another time Mr. Schultz might have genuinely admired the man's gall and peeled off a few dollars. Or he might have said you dumb fuck you know better than to walk in here with this shit. He might have said you got a complaint you talk to your department. He might have said I'll make one phone call and have your ass you stupid son of a bitch. But as it happened he gave this roar of rage, took him down and mashed his windpipe and used the dance floor to make an eggshell of his skull. A young man with a head of curly hair is what I saw of him alive in that light, maybe a few years older than me, a wife and kid in Queens, who knows? who like me had ambitions for his life. I had never seen anyone being killed close up like that. I can't tell even now how long it took. It seemed like a long time. And what is most unnatural is the sounds. They are the sounds of ultimate emotion, as sexual sounds can sometimes seem to be, except they are shameful and degrading to the idea of life, that it can be so humiliated so eternally humiliated. Mr. Schultz arose from the floor and brushed his pants knees. There was not a spot of blood on him although it was webbed out in strings and matter all around the head on the floor. He hitched up his pants and smoothed his hair with his hands and straightened his tie. He was drawing great gasping breaths. He looked as if he was about to cry. "Get this load of shit out of here," he said, including me in the instruction. Then he went back downstairs.

I couldn't seem to move. Irving told me to bring an empty garbage can from the kitchen. When I got back he had folded the body and tied it head to ankles with the guy's jacket. I think now he must have had to crack the guy's spine to get him doubled so tight. The jacket was over the head. That was a great relief to me. The torso still had heat. We inserted the folded body ass-down in the galvanized-iron garbage can and stuffed the space around with wooden straw of the kind that protects French bottles of wine in their cases, hammered the lid on with our fists and put the can out with the night's refuse just as the carter came along on Fifty-sixth Street. Irving had a word with the driver. They are private companies that take away commercial refuse, the city only does citizen garbage. Two guys stand on the sidewalk and heave the can up to the fellow standing in the truck on top of all the garbage. That fellow dumps out the contents and tosses the empty can back over the side to the guys in the street. All the cans came back except one, and if a crowd had been standing around, which there wasn't, for who in the fresh world of the morning wants to watch the cleanup of the night before, the truck motors grinding, the ashcans hitting the sidewalk with that tympanic carelessness of the profession, nobody would have noticed that the truck drove away with one packed garbage can imbedded in all that odorous crap of the glamorous night, or dreamed that in an hour or two it would be shoveled by tractor deep below the anguished yearnings of the flights of seagulls wheeling over the Flushing Meadow landfill.

*   *   *

WHAT DEPRESSED IRVING, WHAT DEPRESSED ABBADABBA BERMAN, WAS THAT THIS
had not been part of the plan. I saw it in their faces. It was not so much
a fear that there could be unforeseen complications, that was not a professional worry. It was that such poor slobs who on their own get high-and-
mighty ideas, which are in fact low ideas of what high-and-mighty is, are
unnecessary to kill. Essentially the guy was not in the business. After a
while even Mr. Schultz looked depressed. It was still morning and he had
a couple of Cherry Heerings served to him by Irving at the bar. He looked
glum, as if he understood he was getting to be a cross they all, himself
included, had to bear. There was this interesting separation he made now
from his own temperament. "I can't deal with it when it's all over the
street," he said. "Irving, you remember that Norma Floy, that gash who
took me for thirty-five thousand dollars? She run out on me with that
fucking horseback-riding instructor? What did I do? What did I do? I
laughed. More power to her. Of course I ever find her little blond head I'll
break every tooth in it. But maybe I won't. And that's the point. These
guys are putting it out on the street. I mean the fucking fire inspectors?
What next, I mean the mailmen?"

"We still got time," Mr. Berman said.

"Sure, sure. But anything is better than this. I can't take this no more.
I'm finished with this. I've been listening to too many lawyers. Otto, you
know the Feds are not going to let me pay the taxes I owe them."

"That is correct."

"I want one more meeting with Dixie. And I want to make things
really clear to Hines. After that we will confront what we must confront."

"We are not without resources," Mr. Berman said.

"That's right. We will do the one or two essential things it appears now
we must do. And then it's on to Shangri-la. I'll show those fuckhead sons
of bitches. All of them. I'm still the Dutchman."

MR. BERMAN TOLD ME TO COME OUTSIDE AND WE STOOD BESIDE THE EMPTY
garbage cans by the curb. He said the following: "Supposing you have
numbers to the number one hundred, how much is each number worth?
It is true that one number might be the value one, and another number the
value ninety-nine, which is ninety-nine ones, but each of them in the row
of one hundred is only worth a hundredth of the hundred, you get it?" I
said I got it. "All right," he said, "now knock off ninety of those numbers
and say all you got left is ten of them, it doesn't matter which ten, say the
first five and the last five, how much is each number worth? It doesn't
matter what it says its number is, it's its share in the total that matters, you
get it?" I said I got it. "So the fewer the numbers the more each one is

worth, am I right? And it doesn't matter what it says it is as a number, it's worth its weight in gold is what it's worth compared to what it was surrounded by all the other numbers. You unnerstan the point?'' I said I did. "Good, good, you think about these things then. How a number can look like one thing but mean another. How a number can look like one thing, but have the worth of another. After all, you'd think a number was a number and that's all it was. But here is a simple example how that is not so. Come take a walk with me. You look terrible. You look green. You need some fresh air.''

We turned east, came to Lexington, crossed, and headed for Third. We walked slowly as you had to do with Mr. Berman. He walked slightly sideways. He said, "I'll tell you my favorite number, but I want you to guess what it might be." I said, "I don't know, Mr. Berman. I can't guess. Maybe the number that you can make all the other numbers from." "That is not bad," he said, "except that you can do that with any number. No, my favorite number is ten, you know why? It has an equal number of odd and even numbers in it. It has the unit number, and the absence of the unit number which is mistakenly called zero. It has the first odd number and the first even number and the first square. And it has the first four numbers which when you add them up add up to itself. Ten is my lucky number. You have a lucky number?''

I shook my head. "You might consider ten," he said. "I want you to go home." He took out a wad of bills from his pocket. "Here's your salary for the busing job, twelve dollars, plus eight dollars severance pay, you are hereby fired.''

Before I could react he said, "And here's twenty dollars just for the hell of it because you can read the names of Italian restaurants on matchbooks. And that's your money.''

I took the money and folded it and put it in my pocket. "Thank you.''

"Now," he said, "here's fifty dollars I'm giving to you, five tens, but this is my money. You unnerstan how I can give it to you but it is still mine?''

"You want me to buy you something?''

"That is correct. My directions for it are I want you to buy me yourself a new pair of pants or two and a nice jacket, and a shirt and a tie and a pair of shoes with laces. You see those sneakers you're wearing? It was a personal embarrassment to me to come in the morning and to see that a busboy at the elegant Embassy Club was walking around all night in his Nat Holman basketball sneakers with the laces so far gone the tongue hanging out of the mouth, and a big toe showing for the final insult. You are lucky few people look at feet. I happen to notice such things. I want you to burn those sneakers. I want you to get a haircut so you don't look like Ish Kabibble on a rainy night. I want you to buy a valise and into the valise put some nice new underwear and socks and a book to read. I want you to buy a real book from a bookstore, not a magazine, not a comic book, a real book, and put that in the valise too. I want you to buy a pair of glasses to read the book if it comes to that. See? Glasses, like I wear."

"I don't use glasses," I said. "I got perfect eyesight."

"You go to the pawnshop and you'll find they have glasses with plain glass. Just do what I say, all right? And do this. Take a few days. Take it easy, try to enjoy yourself. There's time. When we need you we'll send for you."

We were by now standing at the foot of the stairs to the Third Avenue Elevated. It was going to be another hot summer day. I had mentally counted the money in my pocket, ninety dollars. At this moment Mr. Berman unpeeled another ten. "And buy something nice for your mother," he said, the one remark that rang in my head all the way home on the train.

SEVEN

The train to the Bronx was empty at that hour of the morning, I was alone in the car staring into people's windows as we went by. I caught glimpses of people's rooms as if I was taking snapshots, a white enamel bed against a wall, a round oak table with an open bottle of milk and a plate, a standing lamp with a pleated shade protected with cellophane with the bulb still on in the morning over a stuffed green chair. People leaned with their arms on their windowsill and stared at the train going by as if they didn't see them every five or ten minutes. What was it like with the sound filling those rooms and shaking the plaster off the walls? These crazy women hung their family laundry on clotheslines between the windows, and their drawers flapped as the train went by. It had never occurred to me before how everything in New York was stacked, one thing on top of another, even the railroads had to be put over the street, like apartments over other apartments, and there were train tracks under the streets too. Everything in New York was on levels, the whole city was rock and you could do anything with rock, build skyscrapers into it, scallop it out for subway tunnels, poke steel beams into it and run railroads in the air right through people's apartments.

I sat with my hands in my pants pockets. I had distributed my money half and half and held on to it with both hands. For some reason it was a long trip back to the Bronx. How long had I been away? I had no idea, I felt I was coming home on a furlough, like a doughboy who'd been in France for a year. Everything looked strange to me. I got off a stop early and walked a block west to Bathgate Avenue. This was the market street, everyone did their shopping here. I walked along on the crowded side-walks between the pushcarts on the curb and the open stalls in the tene-ments, every one of the merchants competing with the same oranges and apples and tangerines and peaches and plums for the same prices, eight cents a pound, ten cents a pound, a nickel each, three for a dime. They wrote their prices on paper bags which they hung like flags on wooden slats behind each crate of fruit or vegetables. But that wasn't enough. They

shouted out their prices. They called Missus, look, I got the best, feel this
grapefruit, fresh Georgia peaches just in. They talked they cajoled and the
women shopping talked back. I felt a little better now in all this innocent,
urgent, only slightly larcenous life. There was chatter and in the street the
horns of trucks blowing and kids darting from one side to another and
overhead from the fire escapes men who were out of work sat in their
pants and ribbed undershirts and read the papers. The aristocracy of the
business had the real stores where you walked in and bought your chickens still in their feathers, or your fresh fish, or your flank steak, or milk
and butter and cheese, or lox and smoked whitefish and pickles. In front
of the army-navy stores suits hung on hangers from the awning bars or
dresses hung from racks wheeled out the front doors, and clothes were
bargains too on Bathgate, where for five dollars or seven dollars or twelve
dollars you got two pairs of pants with the jacket. I was fifteen years old
and I had a hundred dollars in my pockets. I knew without question that
in that precise moment of the daily life of subsistence I was the richest
person on Bathgate Avenue.

There was a florist on the corner and I went in and I bought my mother
a potted geranium because it was the only flower whose name I knew. It
didn't have much of a smell, it smelled more like earth or a vegetable than
a flower, but it was the kind of plant she herself bought and then forgot
to water until it withered on the fire escape outside the kitchen window.
The leaves were full and green and there were small red blossoms that
hadn't opened. I knew that a geranium was not a proportionate gift but it
was sincerely from me and not from Abbadabba Berman speaking for the
Schultz gang. I felt somewhat shaky now walking home to my street. But
when I turned the corner by the candy store there before my eyes were the
Max and Dora Diamond kids running around in their underwear under the
sprinkler attached to the fire hydrant. The street was closed off, it was
maybe ten in the morning, and they were all running around in wet
underwear, the little ones, screeching, with their shiny little bodies so
beautifully fast and quick. Of course the few older children wore real
woolen bathing suits, dark blue trunks and connected tops with shoulder
straps for both boys and girls, the uniform orphan-blue wool, and not a
few suits had holes where the flesh peeked through. And there were
regular kids from the tenements all mixed in with their individual colors
and their mothers watching and wishing they could run under the water
too except for their dignity. The water made a rainbow umbrella over the
shining black street. I looked for my witchy friend Becky but I knew she
wouldn't be there, I knew she wouldn't be caught dead running under a
sprinkler any more than any of the other incorrigibles, it was not what
they could allow themselves to do no matter how hot it might be, it was
their dignity no less than the parents' to make distinctions, in fact so it was
with all of us, not excepting me, I the most rigid of all, passing into the
dark courtyard of my house, stepping out of the light, climbing through

the dark halls of chipped octagonal tile to the apartments where I had grown into my life.

My mother was at work as I knew she would be. I could look into all the rooms in the world, there was no house like my house. There had been a fire in the kitchen, the enamel on the table was burned in a big egg shape and around the edges the paint was blistered. Nevertheless the candles were lit and lined up in their tumblers. Sometimes in cold weather, when the wind came through the cracks around the windows and under the door and up through the dumbwaiter shaft, they leaned one way and then the other and swayed and shifted dissynchronously as in a kind of dance. Now they burned evenly although there seemed to be more than I remembered, the effect on me was of looking into a chandelier, that although I was upright I might just as well be lying on the floor and looking up into a grand imperial firmament. There was something majestic about my mother. She was a tall woman, she was taller than I was. She had been taller than my father as I reminded myself now looking at the wedding photo on the bureau in the sitting room which served also as her bedroom when she made up the couch. She had years ago run a crayon over the glass in a big X across his figure. This was after she had scraped away the face. She did things like that. When I was little I thought all rugs were in the shape of men's suits and trousers. She had nailed his suit to the floor as if it was the fur of some game animal, a bearskin, a tigerskin. The house had always smelled of burning wax, of candles gone out, of the smoke of wicks.

A water closet was off the kitchen, a dark cubicle with just a toilet, whereas the bathtub was in the kitchen, covered with a heavy wooden hinged lid. I put the geranium here so that she would see it.

In the little bedroom where I slept I found something new, a battered but once-elegant brown wicker baby carriage. It seemed to take up the whole room. The wheel rims were dented so that it wobbled as I pushed it back and forth. But the tires had been washed until they were white. And the top was up, that hinged part that can be put up against the weather and snapped into place with decorative stanchions on the sides. And a series of splintered holes ran diagonally down through it, so that the light from the bedroom window lit them up. An old rag doll lay askew in the carriage; perhaps she had found them together in the street, or bought them from Arnold Garbage separately and put them together herself, the carriage and the doll, and pulled them up the stairs and into the apartment and into my room for me to find when I came home.

* * *

She didn't ask too many questions and seemed happy enough to see me. My arrival split her attention, if the lights were a phone it would have been as if she maintained two conversations simultaneously, she half listened to me, half turned to the lights. We ate our dinner as always sitting beside the bathtub lid and my flowers made a kind of centerpiece and seemed more than anything to give her to understand that I had gotten a job. I told her I was working as a busboy with duties also as a kind of night watchman. I told her it was good work because there were lots of tips. That's what I told her and that's what she appeared to believe. "But just for the summer, of course, because you have to go back to school in September" is what she said, rising to adjust the position of one of the lights. I agreed. But I told her I had to dress properly for the job or I couldn't keep it, so on Saturday afternoon when she got home from work we rode the Webster Avenue trolley up to Fordham Road and went shopping for my suit at I. Cohen's, which was her choice, it was where, she said, my father had found good value in the old days, and she had good taste, she was suddenly an efficient and capable mother in the outside world, and I was very relieved on several grounds, just one of them being that I didn't know how to buy clothes for myself. But she looked reasonably normal too, she wore her best dress of large violet flowers on a white background and combed her hair up under her hat so that it did not show itself as long. One of the things that bothered me about my mother was that she never cut her hair. The fashion was for short hair but hers was long and in the morning, when she was preparing to leave for her job with the industrial laundry, she plaited it in one long braid which she coiled up on the top of her head and then stuck a lot of long pins in. She had a sour-cream jar of these long decorative pins on her bureau. But after she took her bath in the kitchen at night and prepared for bed, sometimes I couldn't help seeing all that straight long gray-black hair combed out on the couch pillow, some of it even falling off the side and touching the floor, some of it getting caught in the pages of her Bible. Her shoes bothered me too, she had bad feet from standing all day at her job, and her solution was to wear men's shoes, white ones which she put white polish on every night, summer or winter, claiming they were nurse's shoes if I happened to be in a bad enough mood to mention them. When we argued my criticism made her smile. It drove her further into herself. She never criticized me, however, being too distracted, only asking an occasional question whose anxiety was dispelled by her own wandering attention almost before she came to the end of the sentence. But on this Saturday afternoon when we went up to Fordham Road she looked very fine and acted almost all the time as if she was in the day together with me. She picked out a light gray single-breasted summer suit with two pairs of trousers and an Arrow shirt with little tabs sewn into the tips of the collar so that it would not curl up, and a red knit tie with a square bottom. We were a long time at I. Cohen's and the old gentleman who took care of us pretended not to see how poor we were, the condition of my sneakers, my mother's white men's shoes, taking us on faith, this little plump man with a tapemeasure hanging around his neck like a prayer shawl perhaps he had reason to know of the pride of poor people. But when my mother opened her purse and displayed the cash I had given her I thought I did detect a look of relief on his face, if not curiosity for this handsome tall woman who brought in this kid in rags and bought him an eighteen-dollar suit and accompaniments like it was nothing. Perhaps he thought she was a wealthy eccentric who had picked me out of the street as a charity case. I knew that night he would tell his wife that his job made a philosopher out of him because every day he saw that human nature was full of surprises and all you could say about life was that it was past understanding.

I. Cohen's did the alterations and put up the cuffs of the trousers while you waited, but we said we'd be back and I walked with my mother up the winding hill toward the Grand Concourse. I found an Adler shoe store and bought a new pair of black sneakers with nice thick soles and then I chose shoes, black wing-tips with secretly heightening leather heels of the style I had seen on the feet of Dixie Davis, Mr. Schultz's lawyer. All of this set us back another nine dollars. I carried the shoes in a box and wore the new sneakers and we continued our way up Fordham until we found a Schrafft's. And there we joined for their afternoon tea all the fine people of the Bronx. We ordered little chicken-salad sandwiches with the crusts cut off the bread, actual tea for my mother and a chocolate ice-cream soda for me, all of it set down on paper place mats in open lace patterns and served by waitresses in black uniforms with white lace aprons that matched the place mats. I was very happy to be doing something like this with my mother. I wanted her to be having a good time. I enjoyed the ceramic clatter of the restaurant, the fussy self-important waitresses balancing their trays, the afternoon sun coming through the front window and shining on the red carpet. I liked the big-bladed silent ceiling fans turning slowly as befitted the dignity of the diners. I had told my mother that I had money in my pocket to buy her some new clothes too, lots of them, and new shoes too that were better for her feet, and that we could go right now two minutes up the street to the Alexander's Department Store if she wanted, right at Fordham Road and the Grand Concourse, the main intersection of the Bronx. But she had become interested in the paper lace of the place mat and was tracing the design with her fingers, feeling the embossing with her fingertips and then closing her eyes as if she was blind and was reading it in Braille. And then she said something I wasn't sure I heard properly but was afraid to ask her to repeat. ''I hope he knows what he's doing'' were the words she said. It was as if someone else was at the table, the voice was not quite hers. I didn't know whether she had said it speaking for herself or had read it off the dots of the embossed place mat.

* * *

BUT ANYWAY I PUT FORTY DOLLARS IN HER POCKETBOOK THAT NIGHT, WHICH LEFT me with a little over twenty-five. I found I was getting used to these big sums, handling these bills as if I was to the manner born. It is true that you get accustomed to money very quickly, that the miraculousness of the idea of it wears away and it becomes unremarkable. Yet my mother's salary at the laundry was twelve dollars a week and that money remained miraculous in my mind, which is to say valuable in the old way, as my own earnings by their profligacy were not. It was an Abbadabba Berman idea. I hoped the dollars I put in her purse would take on the quality of the dollars in her pay envelope. Around the neighborhood it became clear that I had money. I bought whole packs of Wings cigarettes and not only smoked them continually but was generous with them. In the pawnshop on Third Avenue where I went for the glasses I found a reversible satin team jacket, black on one side, and then you could turn everything inside out and presto it was a white jacket, and I bought that and strutted in the evenings in it. The team name was The Shadows, not a name I recognized as local, and it was stitched in fancy white script on the black side and in black on the white side. So I was wearing that and with my cigarettes and new sneakers and I suppose my attitude, which I might not be able to discern in myself but which must have been quite clear to others, I represented another kind of arithmetic to everyone on my street, not just the kids but the grown-ups too, and it was peculiar because I wanted everyone to know what they figured out easily enough, that it was just not given to a punk to find easy money except one way, but at the same time I didn't want them to know, I didn't want to be changed from what I was, which was a boy alive in the suspension of judgment of childhood, that I was the wild kid of a well-known crazy woman, but there was something in me that might earn out, that might grow into the lineaments of honor, so that a discerning teacher or some other act of God, might turn up the voltage of this one brain to a power of future life that everyone in the Bronx could be proud of. I mean that to the more discerning adult, the man I didn't know and didn't know ever noticed me who might live in my building or see me in the candy store, or in the schoolyard, I would be one of the possibilities of redemption, that there was some wit in the way I moved, some lovely intelligence in an unconscious gesture of the game, that would give him this objective sense of hope for a moment, quite unattached to any loyalty of his own, that there was always a chance, that as bad as things were, America was a big juggling act and that we could all be kept up in the air somehow, and go around not from hand to hand, but from light to dark, from night to day, in the universe of God after all.

But anyway it was a palpable change, no matter what I wished, you do feel special and there are numerous discreet kinds of recognition granted to you on the street, as if you had entered a seminary or something like that, small registrations in the eyes of people, where now they see you and are sure they don't want to have anything to do with you, or they see you and give you a moment of their serious attention, depending on what their own ideas of the religious life might be, or perhaps political life, but in any event they see you and wonder how you can hurt them or be of use to them, and now and henceforth, you're another name in the system.

At the same time nobody knew anything, you understand, who I was with and where I worked, all of this was secondary to the mythological change of my station, except of course to those who were in the business, who for their part, as a matter of principle, would not show the least interest because these things come out in due course, first of all, and because I was to the professional eye so clearly still a punk, second of all. So this was a very subtle spirit event of my street that I speak of, and except in the public life of summer might hardly have found the currency it did; I mean never in my self-consciousness of my return did I have the illusion that anyone knew the magnitude of what had happened to me, how I had been living in the very pulsebeat of the tabloids, distributed in printer's ink and hidden like the fox in the tree leaves on the puzzle page except that I was right in the middle of the centrally important news of our time.

But one night I was sitting on the orphans' stoop in the white side of my Shadows jacket with my two friends Rebecca the Witch and Arnold Garbage and we had it mostly to ourselves, the younger kids having been herded inside because it was their curfew, and it was that moment of summer night when it is still light blue in the sky but lamppost dark in the street and it was noisy enough with everyone's window open and the radios playing and the arguments going, and there came around the corner the green-and-white prowl car of the local precinct house and when it reached us it stopped at the curb and the motor ran quietly there and I stared at the cop in the car and he looked up the steps at me, and the appraisal was keen and measured, and it seemed to me everything grew immediately quiet, although of course this was not so, and I felt my white jacket glowing in the last light coming down from the sky, I felt levitated by that light and the cop car too seemed to float away, from its dark green bottom to its upper half in white suspension over the tires, and then the head in the window turned away and said something to the cop I couldn't see, the driver, and they laughed and the headlights went on like gunshots in the street and they drove away.

This was the moment of my awareness, in this strange light, of that first anger Mr. Schultz had told me about, how it comes to you as a benefit, as an endowment. I felt the defining criminal rage, I recognized it, except that it had come to me as I sat in contentment with other strange half-children there on the steps of the Max and Dora Diamond Home. Clearly what I had sought and didn't want at the same time, that peculiar notoriety of a kid's dreams, was now official, I was another kind of citizen, there was no longer any question. I was angry because I still thought it was up to me to decide what I was, not fucking cops. I was angry because nothing in this world is provisional. I was angry because Mr. Berman had sent me home with money in my pocket for no other reason than to teach me what money costs and I hadn't realized it.

Now I remembered what he had said, that I should just take it easy and when they wanted me they would find me. I was standing at the foot of the stairs to the El. I hadn't really heard him, why don't we hear the things said to us? A minute later I had bounded up the stairs and dropped my nickel in the turnstile with its thick magnifying glass showing you under light how big an American buffalo is.

So THAT NIGHT I DID SOMETHING I HAD NEVER DONE BEFORE, I THREW A PARTY. IT seemed to me properly defiant. I found a bar on Third Avenue that sold beer to minors for the right price and bought a pony and rented the tapping equipment to go with it and Garbage wheeled it all covered up in one of his carriages and we bumped it down the steps to his cellar and that's where I threw the party. The big work was clearing enough of his storehouse of shit out of the way so that we had something like an old couch or two to sit on and some floor space to dance on. On the other hand it was Garbage who supplied the tall dusty glasses we drank the beer from and the old Victor Talking Machine with the sound horn curled like a seashell and the pack of steel needles and the box of race records that gave us our dance music. I told him I would pay rent for everything he supplied. I was determined that night to pay everybody for everything, even God for the air I breathed. And I threw the party for the incorrigibles of the Max and Dora Diamond Home after everyone else including the floor wardens and the custodial supervisor had gone to sleep. Eventually there were maybe ten or twelve kids altogether including my friend Rebecca, who arrived like some of the other girls in a nightgown, but she had earrings on too and some lipstick. All the girls wore lipstick, all the same color all obviously from the same tube. And there we were making a big deal over this beer that must have come from Mr. Schultz's drop because it was really piss water but because it was beer gave us the requisite taste of adult corruption. Someone had raided the house kitchen and come away with three salamis and several loaves of white bread in wax paper and Garbage poked around in one of his bins till he found a kitchen knife and a broken coffee table, and sandwiches were made and beer was poured and I had cigarettes for those who wanted them, and in the dry and ashen air of the basement, with suspensions of coal dust lit in the yellow light of an old standing lamp, we smoked Wings and drank our foamless beer and ate and danced to the old black voices of the 1920s singing their slow songs of doubled lines of love and bitter one-line resolutions, of pig's feet and jelly rolls and buggy rides and papas who did wrong and mamas who did wrong and people who were waiting for trains that had already gone, and though none of us knew how to dance except the square dancing they taught upstairs, the music taught us how. Garbage sat by the Victrola and cranked it up and took a record out of its blank paper jacket and put it on, he sat cross-legged on a table with a pillow under him and did this, neither dancing himself nor talking to anyone for that matter but giving by his assent to everything going on in his basement the best measure of impassive sociability of which he was capable, neither drinking beer nor smoking but only eating and engrossing himself with the endless supply of scratchy music, the cornets and clarinets and tubas and pianos and drums of sorrowful passion, and the girls danced with each other and then pulled the boys in to dance with them, and it was a very solemn party we were having, white Bronx kids holding on to each other in the sweet black music, full of the intent to live life as it should be lived, there in the orphans' home. But little by little it began to look different because some of the girls found collections of clothing in big cardboard boxes in the recesses of Arnold Garbage's bins, and he didn't seem to mind, so they dressed themselves in this and that over their nightclothes, trying and choosing different hats and dresses and high-heeled shoes of bygone times, till everyone was satisfied, and my little Rebecca wore a kind of Spanish black lace affair down to her ankles, and a gauzy shawl of rose with great looping tears in it, but continued to dance with me in her bare feet, and some of the boys had found suit jackets whose shoulders were like football pads on them, and pointed patent-leather shoes, and big wide ties they looped around their bare throats, and so by and by in the smoke and jazz we were all just the way we wanted to be, dancing in the dust of the Embassy Club of our futures, in the costumes of shy children's love, and learning as only the fortunate do that God is not only the instruction of the mind but of the hips in their found rolling rhythm.

MUCH LATER REBECCA AND I WERE SITTING ON ONE OF THE COUCHES AND SHE HAD HER legs crossed at the knees and one dirty foot swinging and her nightgown showing below the hem of her black lace dress. She was the last kid there. She raised her arms and she pulled her black hair back behind her head and did something deft back there the way girls do with their hair so that it stays the way they fix it without any visible reason to and despite the law of gravity. Maybe I was a little drunk by then, maybe we both were. Also the dancing had been warm and close. I was smoking a cigarette and she took it

out of my fingers and drew on it, one puff, and blew out the smoke without
inhaling and put the cigarette back in my fingers. I saw now she was wearing
mascara on her eyelashes and eyelids and had on that communal red
lipstick, paled somewhat since its application, and was glancing at me
sideways with her foot swinging, and those eyes dark as black grapes, and
her white neck draped in that torn shawl of dusty pink—I had no warning
or preparation from one moment to the next, I was swimming in a realm
of intimacy, as if I had just met her, or as if I had just lost her, but surely
as if I had never roof-fucked her. My mouth went dry she was so incredibly childishly beautiful. Until this moment I had been the party-giver and
big boss of the evening, dispensing his largesse and granting his favors.
All those dances—oh I knew everyone knew I favored her on my randy
forays up the fire escape, but it was athletics, I paid her, for christsake, I
must have been staring at her because she turned away and lowered her
eyes, her foot going madly—all those dances I had danced with her and
only her were the exacting ceremonies of possession. And this ancient
witch child understood before I did that everything was now up in the
heart, as if my rise in the world had lifted us to an immensity of consequence, which we were now allowed to see, like a distance ahead of us,
like a horizon. They must all have understood, every fucking kid there,
while I thought what I had been feeling was only a sweetly mellow good
time.

So when everyone else had gone we lay for the first time together
without any clothes on that same couch, everyone else asleep, even Garbage in some inner bin of his privacy. We lay in the dark cellar of dust and
ash, and I was passive and on my back and Rebecca lay on top of me and
cleaved herself on me letting herself down with a long intake of her breath
which I felt as a cool flute of air on my neck, and slowly awkwardly she
learned her rhythm upon me as I was patient to allow her to do. My hands
were on her back for a while and then on her buttocks, I followed the soft
down with my fingers, I knew it was as black as her hair, it went from the
bottom of her spine down into the crack between her ass, and then I put
my finger on her small ring of an asshole and as she raised her hips I
touched it, and as she lowered her hips I lost it in the clamp of her hard
buttocks. Her hair fell forward as she raised herself and it brushed my face,
and when she lowered herself it fell around my ears, and I kissed her
cheeks as she rested and I felt her lips on my neck and her hard little
nipples against my chest and her wet thighs on my thighs, and then I
didn't remember when it started she was making little discoveries which
she voiced in private almost soundless whimperings in my ear and then
she moved into some arrhythmic panic and went stiff and I felt around my
cock the grasp of her inner musculature and when I reached down with my
finger and touched the asshole it clamped around my fingertip and
released and contracted and released in the same rhythm as her interior
self was squeezing and unsqueezing my cock and I couldn't stand it

anymore I arched myself into her and pulled back, raising myself and lowering myself with her dead bodyweight as vehemently as if I were on top, pretty soon going so fast she was being bounced on my chest and thighs with little grunts until she found my rhythm and went stuttering and imperfectly and finally workingly, smoothly against it, meeting me when I was to be met, leaving me when I was leaving to be left, and that was so unendurably exquisite I shot into her and held her down against me with my hands while I came pulsing up into her milkingly lovely little being as far as I could go. And she held her arms around me to get me through that, and then there was peace between us, and we lay as we were with such great trust as to require no words or kisses, but only the gentlest slowest and most coordinate drift into sleep.

EIGHT

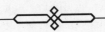

What woke me was the chill of empty air on my skin, and the degree of ashen gray light that represented morning in the basement of the Max and Dora Diamond Home for Children. A mound of black and rose lace lay on the floor beside the couch as if the witch had disembodied: My lover had gone back upstairs to her childhood. Institutional orphans know with a basic workaday cunning how not to get caught, and it occurred to me that that was not bad training for a gangster's girl. I wondered what age people had to be before they could marry. I reflected as I lay there that my life was changing more quickly and in more ways than I could keep up with. Or was it all just one thing, as if everything had the same charge to it, so that if I was remade to Mr. Schultz's touch, Becky was remade to mine, and there was only one infinitely extending flash of conformation. She had never come before, with me anyway, and I felt pretty sure with nobody else either. Her cunt barely had hair. She was growing herself up to match me.

Oh my God what I felt right then for this mysterious parentless little girl, this Mediterranean olive, this nimble nipply witchling, with her arching backbone, her downy ass, as hard-living dumb as a female could be. She liked me! I wanted to race her, I knew she could run, I would give her a head start because I was older, and I bet she could make a good race of it. I had seen her jump rope, inexhaustibly, with lots of tricks, on one foot, or with a quick two-step, or skipping through the snapping arcs, hip-hopping through a double rope, the left and right coming from opposite directions, and do it faster and longer than anyone else. She could walk on her hands too, totally careless of her falling inversion of skirt and her white panties for all the boys to see, her swarthy legs waving in the air, as she paraded the street upside down. She was an athlete, a gymnast: I would teach her to juggle, I would teach her and myself at the same time to throw-juggle till we had six bowling pins flying in the air between us.

But first I wanted to buy her something. I tried to think of what it should be. I listened. I knew the orphans' home as well as I knew my own,

I could lie there, and even hung over, and with every signal sense refracted in an atmosphere fetid with stale beer, I could tell by the degree of vibration of the building what time of day it was: they were barely beginning to get going in the kitchen. It was just dawn. I roused myself, grabbed my clothes, and sneaking up a back stairs I made it to the Boys Showers and ten minutes later was out in the new morning, the hair of my recent haircut wet and shining, my Shadows jacket turned out in satin white, and the breakfast to hand a fresh bagel lifted from the big bread bag left before light on the delivery platform by the Pechter's Bakery truck.

It was so early nobody was up yet, not even my mother. The streets were empty, the lamppost lights were still on under the white sky. I had the idea, going to Third Avenue, that I would look in the pawnshop windows for something and just wait around for the day to begin to buy it. I wanted to buy Becky a piece of jewelry, maybe even a ring.

At this hour not even the newsstand at the foot of the El station had opened. The morning papers lay baled in twine where they'd been tossed from the trucks. I knew the headline in the *Mirror* was meant for me before I looked at it, I felt the attraction of the words before I read them: GRISLY GANG MURDER. Underneath was a murky photo of a dead man in a barber chair who I thought was headless until I read the caption explaining that his head was swathed in bloodied barbers' hot towels. Some West Side numbers boss. I was so distracted, I actually put my three cents on the ground by the stack of papers before I pulled one out to get the story.

I read with a proprietary interest, I read first in the shadow of the El and then not sure I'd gotten it all I stepped into a stripe of light cast by the space between the overhead tracks, I held my arms out and I read again in the pacific glare of the morning the *Mirror* gang murder of the day, while nothing moved on any of the levels, neither train nor trolley, except the pattern of darkness striped with light up and down the cobbled avenue like a jail guard running his stick along the bars of the cells, my head beginning to hurt through the eyes, and the recognition of darkness alternating with light in the black print on the white paper as the personal message for me in this news.

For of course I knew whose work this was, there wasn't much more to the story than there was in the headline and the picture, but I read with intense concentration, not merely as one who was in the same trade, but of the same shop, I was reading of my mentor, and the proof was I didn't need any proof, I knew to the point of looking for Mr. Schultz's name in the story, and wondering why it wasn't there, numb and not thinking properly after my first night on earth of love, as if everybody in the world would know something because I did, as if I didn't know anything nobody else knew, especially the papers. I went back and pulled out a *News,* which had almost the same picture and no more information, and then I took a *Herald Tribune,* one of those hifalutin rags, and they didn't know anything more than the others, although they used more words. None of them knew. Gangsters were killed every day in the week and why and by whom was a matter of public confusion. Lines of power crossed in secret, allies became enemies, partnerships split up, any one man could be killed by just about anybody else in the business on any given day, and the press, the cops, they needed eyewitnesses, testimony, documentation, to make their tracings and figure things out. They might have their theories but it took them a while to get up an authoritative version, as with all historians going through the wreckage after the silence has set in. By contrast I immediately knew, as if I had been there. He had used whatever was to hand. He had improvised something from his rage, I mean you don't sit someone down in a barber chair to murder him, you find him there and you grab a razor. He had gone totally out of his mind the way he did with the fire inspector, I had caught on with the great Dutch Schultz in his decline of empire, he was losing control, it was a bloody maniac's portrait there on the front page, and now what the fuck was I going to do? I had this sense of being implicated in a way that wasn't fair to me, as if he had broken a trust and there was nothing after all to learn from him except self-destruction.

I broke into a clammy sweat and that most dreaded and unendurable of feelings, nausea, rose in me. At such times you just want to fling yourself on the ground and clutch it, nothing else is possible. I looked around and dropped the papers in an ashcan, as if I could be arrested for holding them, as if they were evidence of my complicity.

I sat in a doorway and put my head between my knees and waited for the awful nausea to go away. After a few minutes I felt better, the sweat turns to a chill and you're all right, you can breathe again. Perhaps this was the moment when I germinated my secret conviction that I could always get out, that they could come looking but they'd never find me, that I knew more escapes than they dreamed of. But consciously all I could think was that Mr. Schultz was a greater danger to me when I was not in his presence than when I was. He'd do another one of these things that I wouldn't know about and I'd be picked up. All of them, Mr. Berman too, the less I saw of them the more vulnerable I became. It was a most contrary proposition but as a feeling it was indisputable. If I didn't have him where I could see him, how could I get away if I didn't know when to run? Then and there I knew I had to be back with the gang, it was my empowerment, my protection. I felt, sitting there under the El, that not being with them was a luxury I couldn't afford. It wasn't safe not to be around them.

I told myself I wasn't thinking clearly. To calm down I started walking. I walked and walked, and by and by like some assurance to me that the world could take whatever happened to it, the El came along thundering overhead, cars and trucks appeared in the streets, the people who had jobs were going to them, the streetcars rang their gongs, shopkeepers opened their doors, and I found a diner and went in and sat at the counter

shoulder-to-shoulder with my fellow citizens of the world and drank
tomato juice and coffee and feeling somewhat better ordered two eggs
sunny-side up and toast and bacon and a doughnut and more coffee, and
topped everything off with a reflective cigarette, and by then the outlook
wasn't so bad. He had said to Mr. Berman in my presence: There are one
or two essential things it appears we must do. The window washers falling
twelve stories down the side of a building was one of these things and this
was another. This was a planned business murder as concise and to the
point as a Western Union telegram. The victim after all had been in the
business. He was the competition. Therefore his murder was symbolically
meaningful for the few people with whom Mr. Schultz wanted to communicate. But at the same time because it was done with a razor it would
more probably suggest to the D.A.'s office and to every crime reporter
certainly, and to the cops in the know and to the top Tammany people, and
in fact to everybody in the industry except the competition, that it must be
someone else's work because it didn't have the Dutchman's signature—
it was a Negro's type of murder, or a Sicilian's in its vindictiveness, but
in any event there was enough of everything in it to be anyone's work.

So all of this was very consoling except now I began to resent that I had
been sent away when all these important matters were being adjudicated.
I worried that my position had been changed without my knowing it, or
worse, that I had overestimated it to begin with. So I walked back up Third
Avenue beginning to feel as uneasy as I had originally and with the
identical need to be back with Mr. Schultz. I was in a very strange state.
I had looked green after the morning murder in the Embassy Club. Maybe
I shouldn't have looked so green. Maybe they thought I didn't have what
it took. Soon I was running. I was running home in shadow and light. I
ran up the stairs two at a time in case a message had come for me while
I was gone.

BUT THERE WAS NO MESSAGE. MY MOTHER STOOD TWIRLING UP HER HAIR. SHE
glanced at me curiously with her arms raised and her hands behind her
head and two of those long jeweled pins crosswise between her teeth. I
could hardly wait for her to leave for work. She had an infuriating slowness about her, as if each of her minutes was longer than anyone else's,
it was a kind of stately time she moved in of her own weird invention.
Finally the door closed behind her. I grabbed my new secondhand valise
from the back of the closet, a leather number that folded in at the top like
a very large doctor's instrument bag, and I packed my I. Cohen suit and
wing-tip shoes and shirt and tie, and my plain glass steel-rim spectacles
that looked like Mr. Berman's and some underwear and socks. I packed
my toothbrush and hairbrush. I had still not bought a book from a book-

store but I could do that downtown. I had to wheel the terrible baby carriage of my mother's affection out of the way in order to get under the bed where I had hidden my Automatic. I put that in at the bottom, underneath everything else, snapped the hasps, buckled the straps and put the valise by the front door, and I put myself on watch at the fire escape window. I was convinced they would come and get me this very morning. It was now a matter of great urgency to me that they should. It was not possible that they wouldn't. Why would Mr. Berman insist that I get new clothes if they were just going to abandon me? Besides I knew too much. And I was smart, I knew what was going on. I knew more than what was going on, I knew what was going to happen next.

The only thing I didn't know and couldn't anticipate was how they would come and get me, how they would know where I was. Then I saw the precinct prowl car come slowly up the street and stop in front my house. I thought: That's it, it's too late, it's all over, they're rounding up everyone, he's done it, he's killed us all. And when the same wiseass cop who had looked me over a few nights before got out, I experienced the meaning of the law, the power of uniform, and a desperate sense of exclusion from the future. Adept wily and swift though you may be, if the moment stuns you with its terror you are made as helpless, as transfixed by the vision of disaster, as an animal caught in headlights. I didn't know what to do. He disappeared below me into the building and came up the dark stairwell, I could hear his footsteps, but in the street when I looked the other cop was out of the car now and standing leaning against the driver's door with his arms folded right under my fire escape. They had me. I stood behind the front door and heard the footsteps. Then I heard his breathing. Oh Jesus! Then he was knocking on my door with his fist, the fucker. When I opened it he stood there filling the doorway in the darkness, a big fat cop mopping his gray hair with a handkerchief and then wiping the inside rim of his cap. "All right, punk," he said, he was all blue and bulky, the way cops are with everything they hang on themselves under their tunics—pieces and nightsticks and ticket books and bullets— "don't ask me why, but you're wanted. Get a move on."

AND HERE I WILL SUMMARIZE WHAT MR. SCHULTZ TOLD ME ABOUT THIS MURDER, because I could not even begin to render it word for word, try to understand how it was to be in his presence and his confidence when he spoke of these most intimate matters, there is horrified elation, you sometimes don't hear the details just looking at the face that speaks, you wonder at your own great recklessness to have put yourself in his line of vision, you hope he won't see that it is your deepest desire to conform your mind to his, to speak in your own mind with his voice, which means that you cannot. But listening to these confidences, dumb with pride to be receiving them, and remembering my panic of that early morning, I did feel foolish and a bit disloyal ever to have doubted him or his regard for me, because, as he said, despite the honestly improvised nature of the barbershop occasion it had that feeling about it of being right, as right as if it had been planned, except that things planned so often go wrong that it was better than planned, and he knew immediately it was a genius hit because it did so many different things at the same time, all of them dovetailing with one another, so like any good piece of business it was part luck, part inspiration, but in any event an act of mastery that was both correct as business and poetically effective, in addition of course to being solidly grounded in the only sound motive, which is simple and just retribution. He was very proud of the job. I think it eased the embarrassment of his loss of control with the fire inspector. And there was no sadness to it, he said, no lingering hurt, nothing mournful as with Bo, it was nothing that personal, it just so happened Irving fingered the guy while Mr. Schultz was availing himself of the pleasures of a cathouse not two minutes from the Maxwell Hotel. He was celebrating his return from Syracuse, where he had surrendered to the law, put up bail and walked out of the courtroom a lammister no longer, he was celebrating part one of the new plan and was having a preliminary glass of wine with the fancy girls and, I was to tell him, could anything in life be greater than that? as if I would know, to reappear and retake your old life, to be the Dutchman of old from your unshined shoes to your slightly dirty pearl gray fedora, and so, this was true luck, a good sign, he was able to get over there and work things out while the regular barber was still trimming the fucker's hair. And he was all ready by the time the chair was tilted back for the shave. The numbers boss held his piece on his lap under the striped barber sheet, as lots of guys tend to do, and two of his henchmen sat in the lobby reading the evening papers by the potted palms just outside the glass barbershop door. Those were the conditions. One henchman happening to glance over the top edge of his paper, and seeing there Lulu Rosenkrantz standing and smiling at him with his broken-toothed smile under that protuberant and bushy brow, and next to him Irving holding up his index finger to his lips, he quietly cleared his throat to capture his colleague's attention and together, with the briefest of glances between them, they folded their papers and stood, in hopes that their immediate and unanimous decision to fuck loyalty would find favor with these two well-known and formidable personages. Which it did, they were allowed to disappear through the revolving door of the hotel with no hard feelings, but only after surrendering their newspapers, which Irving and Lulu sat down to read in the vacated chairs beside the potted palms, although if the truth be known, Mr. Schultz said, Lulu couldn't read. At the same time the regular barber, who took only very special people after hours, having seen and understood the meaning of the ceremony outside his shop while applying the hot towel to his customer's face, wrapping it the way they do like a custard swirl, so that only the tip of the nose is visible, quietly excused himself forever from the profession by means of a mirrored side door leading to a supply room and to an alley leading to the street, passing with murmured apologies another barber in a white short-sleeve tunic who was just entering, Mr. Schultz himself with his thick but not muscular arms showing black hair, and a thick short neck and a blue-black shadow on his own tormentedly twice daily shaven cheeks. The Dutchman came up to the recumbent customer and applied additional hot towels in mimicry of the attentive ministrations of a barber, dripping on them especially about the nostrils a potion from a small unlabeled bottle he had had the foresight but not the detailed reasoning to borrow from the cathouse madam. And hovering about the chair and making small administrative sounds until he was satisfied that all was well, he felt under the sheet, took the piece from the slack fingers, daintily put it aside, lifted the towels where they draped over the chin, carefully folded them back from the throat, and choosing an already opened straight razor from the shelf under the mirror and satisfying himself that it was impeccably sharpened, he drew it with no hesitation across the exposed neck just below the jawline. And as the thread-thin lip of blood slowly widened into a smile and the victim made a small half-questioning movement in his chair, a slight rise of the shoulders and lift of the knees, more inquisitive than accusatory, he held him down with his elbow on his mummied mouth and wrapped layer after layer of wet hot toweling that was to hand in the chromed steamer behind the chair over his chest and throat and head, until only a seeping pinkness, the color of a slow and tentative sunset, suffused the wadding, so that he was able with unhurried insolence to wipe clean the twelve-inch razor, fold it, and drop it in his breast pocket next to the comb, and after a glance of vindication to the lobby as if there was there, watching, an audience of numbers-industry bankers, controllers, collectors, and runners, rubbed the grip of the Smith & Wesson with the striped sheet, and placed it back in the victim's hand, and placed the hand back in the lap, and smoothed the striped sheet over the body, and withdrew through the mirrored door, which closed on the scene with a click, leaving two barber chairs, two bodies, and two trickles of blood spattering the tile floor.

"There wasn't nothing grisly about it," Mr. Schultz told me, referring to the very headline that had caught my attention. "That was newspaper bullshit. You never get a break from those guys, it was as beautiful and professional as could be. Anyway, probably the knockout drops was what killed the son of a bitch. I mean he moved but so does a chicken after you cut its throat. Chickens run around after they're dead did you know that, kid? I seen that in the country."

PART TWO

NINE

We stood the first morning on the courthouse steps and looked over the town past a bridged mountain stream to the fields and pastures and hills around us, everything green and lilac on the hillsides and the field crops a darker green, the sun was shining in a deeply blue sky, and there was a lowing cow at some distance that sounded to me like a song of the great unconscious gladness of nature, and Lulu Rosenkrantz muttered, ''I don't know about this, what do you do when you wanna go for a walk?''

I had never been in the country before except if you counted Van Cortlandt Park, but I liked the smell of it and the light, I liked the peace of all that sky. Also I was instructed in the purposefulness of human settlement. Out there in the distance they grew what was needed, they farmed and kept dairy herds, and this town, Onondaga, the county seat, was their market. It was built onto the side of the hills overlooking the farmland and the stream came down from the mountains right through it. Nobody told me not to so I made an excursion to the old rattly wooden bridge and watched the water flowing fast and shallow over the rocks. It was wider when you were right on top of it, more like a river than a stream. Then a few blocks up along the river I found an abandoned lumber mill, the sheds leaning over like a good wind would flatten them, the place was long since closed but showed clearly someone's past ambition and an enterprise with natural resources that I had read about in school geographies but never fully appreciated. I mean you don't really appreciate a phrase like *natural resources,* you have to see the trees on the mountains, and the stream, and the lumberyard beside the stream to begin to get the idea, to see the sense everything made. Not that I would want such a life for myself.

A lot of people had lived and died in Onondaga and what they left behind was their houses, I could tell immediately the houses had been around for a long time, they were of wood, people in the country lived in wooden houses, one next to another, big boxy things stained dark brown or peeling gray paint and with pitched roofs and gables and porches loaded up with firewood, and there was an occasional weird house with a corner tower topped with a kind of dunce cap roof and with curved windows and shingles nailed on in different patterns and iron grillwork decorating the roof edges, as if they had a pigeon problem. Anyway this was America too I said to Lulu Rosenkrantz, though he was dubious. At least the public buildings were of stone, the courthouse was made of blocks of red stone with granite trim that reminded me of the Max and Dora Diamond Home except it was bigger and had arched windows and doors and was rounded at the corners as justice sometimes is, and the four-story Onondaga District School, the same ugly red stone as the courthouse, and also the Onondaga Public Library, a tiny one-room affair faced over in stone blocks to make it look as if people took their reading matter more seriously than they really did. Then the gray stone gothic church, modestly named the Church of the Holy Spirit, and so far the only thing in town I had found not named after this Onondaga, this Indian, who had apparently made quite an impression. There was a statue of him on the lawn in front of the courthouse shading his eyes and looking west. When Miss Lola Miss Drew came outside for the first time and saw that statue she seemed quite taken with it, she stared at it till Mr. Schultz grew irritated and pulled her away.

The grandest structure in town was the hotel, The Onondaga, of course, six stories of red brick, right in the heart of the commercial district if it could be called that, because many of the stores were closed with FOR LET signs in the windows, and the few cars parked front wheels into the curb were old black tin lizzies, Model A's and T's or farm trucks with chain drives and no doors, there was not much going on in Onondaga, in fact with our arrival we were what was going on, which came home to me when the old colored man who was the bellboy carried my bag with genuine delight to my very own private room on the top floor and didn't even wait for the tip I was figuring out to give him. This was where we were all to stay, on the sixth floor, which Mr. Schultz rented in its entirety. Each person had at least one room to himself, otherwise it wouldn't look right, Mr. Schultz said glancing at Miss Lola Miss Drew, so she had her own suite, and he had his own suite, and the rest of us had single rooms except that Mr. Berman had a second room for which he ordered a special direct phone line not using the hotel switchboard.

The morning of our arrival I bounced on my bed. I opened a door and lo! there was a bathroom with an enormous tub and several thin white towels hanging on the bar and a full-length mirror on the inside of the door. The bathroom was as big as our kitchen at home. The floor was small white octagonal tiles, just like our halls in the Bronx, except a lot cleaner. My bed was soft and wide and the headboard was like half of a big spoked wheel of maple wood. There was a reading chair with a lamp sticking out of a table right beside it, and a bureau with a mirror, and in the top drawer were little concave sections for pocket change and small items that might otherwise get lost. There were gauzy white curtains that could be drawn with a string and behind them black shades, the same as at my school, where you pulled them tight to watch slide shows or movies, with a little pulley wheel attached to the sill. Next to the bed was a table radio which crackled a bit but didn't seem to bring in any stations.

I loved this luxury. I lay back on my bed, which had two pillows and a white bedspread with a pattern of tufts, rows of little cotton nipples, each one under my fingertip making me think of Becky. I lay with my hands behind my head and poked my pelvis into the air a few times imagining she was there on top of me. Private hotel rooms were sexy places. I had noticed in the lobby downstairs a writing table with hotel stationery free for the taking and I thought in a day or two I would write her a letter. I started to think what I would say, whether to apologize or not for leaving her without saying goodbye, and so on, but was interrupted by the stillness. I sat up. Everything was very hushed, unnaturally quiet, which at first felt like part of the luxury, but then seemed to me like another presence which was making itself known. I don't mean that I felt I was being watched, nothing like that, more like there were certain expectations of the society that were trying to represent themselves to me, in the pattern of the wallpaper, for example, endless rows of little corsages of buttercups, or the pieces of maple furniture standing there so silently like elements of a mysterious rite waiting for me to perform it correctly. I sat up. I found a Bible in the drawer of the bedside table and thought someone had left it there by accident. Then I realized from the resolute neatness and orderliness of the room that it must be there as a furnishing. I looked out the window, my room was at the rear, I had a good view of the flat roofs of stores and warehouses. Nothing was moving in Onondaga. Up behind the hotel was a hillside of pine trees that managed to block out the sky.

I understood what Lulu Rosenkrantz must be feeling, the absence of life as we knew it, raucous and loud and mechanically driven, with horns and bell gongs, and grinding wheel flanges, and screeches of brakes, all that rude variousness of too many people in too small a space, where you could really be selfish and free. But he at least had Irving or Mickey, and years of loyalty to the gang to comfort him, whereas none of them had any particular fondness for me. At this moment nobody had told me what I was supposed to be doing in Onondaga. I thought I was past the point of going for coffee, but I wasn't sure. I knew things that it was deadly to know if you were not trusted. I found myself not for the first time measuring my reasons for confidence against the depth of the danger I was in. It would always be this way, every time I felt good about the way things were going and that I was living my charmed life unerringly, all I had to remember was how small a mistake was sufficient to change my fortune, maybe even without my knowing it. I was an habitual accomplice to murder. I could be arrested, tried, and sentenced to death. But that was not enough to ensure me my place. I thought of Bo Weinberg and opened the door to the dimly lit wide carpeted hall and looked up and down for a sign of life. All the doors were closed. I went back to my room and closed my own door so as not to disturb the quiet and this so oppressed me that I decided to do something so I unpacked my new I. Cohen suit with the two pairs of pants and hung it in the big dusty closet and put my shirts and things and gun away in the bureau drawer and then put the empty suitcase in the closet and then sat on the side of the bed and felt worse than ever. Part of it may have been that when you're going somewhere it is always mysterious when you arrive. Or perhaps, as I told myself, I was not used to living alone, I had only been living alone for five or ten minutes and I was not yet used to it. In any case my optimism of the early part of the day had now totally deserted me. The only thing that cheered me up was the sight of a cockroach walking up the wall between the sprays of buttercups, because then I knew The Onondaga Hotel was not all it was cracked up to be.

THE FIRST COUPLE OF DAYS I WAS MOSTLY BY MYSELF, MR. BERMAN GAVE ME FIFTY dollars in small bills and told me to spend it in as many different places as I could. This was not as easy as it sounded, Onondaga was not rich in the fruits of the earth like Bathgate Avenue. The stores were unnaturally quiet dark establishments with bare shelves and they were separated from one another by stores that were closed up and boarded. I went into the Ben Franklin five-and-ten and it was pathetic, I had stolen from some of the best five-and-ten-cent stores in New York and knew what they should be and this little place was so dismal and poor the owner kept only one light bulb on in the back and the country kids who came in barefoot got splinters from the rotted-out floor. There was hardly any stock. I bought a handful of metal toy cars and motorcycles with policemen molded to them and gave them away. I found a clothing store for women and bought a straw hat with a big brim for my mother and then I took the hatbox to the post office and had them send it the most expensive way. I found a jewelry store and bought a pocket watch for a dollar.

Through the window of the drugstore I saw Lulu and Mickey the driver sitting at the fountain drinking malted milks through straws. They would take sips and then look at the glass to see how much more had to be swallowed before their ordeal was over. I was very pleased to see they had gotten the same assignment from Mr. Berman as I had. When they left the drugstore I shadowed them for practice. They stood irresolutely in front of a window where a tractor was on display. They found a news store and went in but I could have told them there were no New York papers. They came out and lit cigars that were so stale they flared up like torches. Lulu was disgusted, Mickey had to calm him down. They bought a fifty-pound sack of onions and left it in a trash can. They went into the army-navy store and through the window I saw them choose shirts and hats and then lace-up work boots that I knew I would never see on their feet.

By the second day of this spending spree my imagination was taxed. Then it occurred to me something of the same purpose was served by making friends, so I bought ice-cream cones for some kids who were following me, and then in a little park across from the courthouse I did some juggling with three pink rubber balls. Kids were everywhere in Onondaga, they were the only human beings I saw in the afternoons, the only ones out in the sun with nothing to do in their overalls with no shirt underneath and bare feet and squinty faces of freckles, they made me think of my street and the homeful of orphans there, but there was less humor in them, they were not inclined to smile or jump around, they took their pleasures stolidly, giving my juggling feats the most serious attention, but hanging back when I offered to show them how to do it.

In the meantime of all the people not to be seen Mr. Schultz and Miss Lola Miss Drew were the most prominent, day and night there was a running route of room service to his suite. I wondered what she did to make her own suite look occupied. Then I wondered if she bothered. I tried to keep from thinking about her but it was difficult, especially at night in my room as I lay on the bed and smoked my Wings and listened to the faintest dance band music from the crackling radio. I was sorry I had seen her nude, I knew too much to be imagining her in my mind at this particular time, in fact it made me queasy to think of her. Then I became angry. She had certainly taught me how little I knew about women, I had thought first she was this fine innocent blue-blood victim of a terrible cross fire of gang life, then up in her Savoy-Plaza apartment it was clear she had flung her ass around with the best of them, I had thought only women from the wrong side of the tracks were tramps, but there were rich tramps too and she was one of them, she had some kind of marriage that was so advanced in sophisticated license as to be degenerate, she was entirely wild, she liked a kind of primordial action, I mean sitting in a Packard in the early hours of the morning and being driven you don't know the hell where while drinking champagne with the man who's just murdered your boyfriend might be considered by some to be a sordid situation with a degree of risk attached to it, but that was not the thought I saw in her eyes in the privacy of her bedroom when as you know a woman preparing to go out is her true self in shrewd preparation of her commodity, without the need to sit with her knees pressed together or stand with one foot slightly forward of the other and pointing outward.

They were in there together two whole full days without coming up for air. Late the third morning I happened to see them emerge from the hotel lobby. They were holding hands. I was worried that Mr. Schultz would notice me standing around juggling for a bunch of hick kids on the sidewalk. But he noticed nothing except her, he handed her past Mickey, who was holding open the door of the Packard, and ducked in himself. The expression on his face suggested that Mr. Schultz's two days and nights in bed with Miss Drew had somewhat elevated her in his regard. After they drove off I thought, well, if she was going to survive her deadly knowledge of that boat ride, this was indeed the way to do it, which was a laugh because she was clearly so heedless as to make mere survival the last possible thing on her mind.

But I was cheered at the end of the second day by an invitation to dinner at a big round table in the hotel dining room, and everyone was there, Mr. Schultz with Miss Lola Miss Drew on his right, and Abbadabba Berman on his left, and the rest of us, Lulu, Mickey the driver, Irving, and I fanned out facing him. Mr. Schultz was in excellent spirits and it seemed to me everyone in the gang was glad to be together, that maybe I wasn't the only one a little homesick.

There were elderly couples at two or three of the tables who kept glancing at us and then leaning toward each other to talk, the faces of passersby framed themselves in the dining-room windows and were replaced by other faces, and appearing in the doorway every other minute to smile and watch us and maybe make sure we were still there were the man from the front desk and the elderly colored bellboy. Mr. Schultz loved all this. "Sweetheart," he called to the waitress, "tell me about your cellar," which I thought was a bizarre request until she said all they carried was Taylor New York State in screw-cap bottles, which made him laugh as if he had known it all along, she was a plump young girl with blotchy skin and wore a uniform like the waitresses I had seen in the Schrafft's on Fordham Road, black with white trim, and a little starched cap on her head, but despite this she was so nervous she kept dropping things, pouring the water in our glasses to the brim, things like that, and I thought any minute she would rush out of the room crying. Mr. Schultz didn't mind, he ordered two bottles of Taylor's New York State red. I could tell Lulu and Mickey would have preferred beer if they couldn't have the hard stuff but they didn't say anything. They were not comfortable in neckties, either. "To justice," Mr. Schultz said lifting his glass, and touched the glass of Miss Lola Miss Drew, who looked at him and laughed a lovely throaty laugh, as if he was kidding, then we all clicked glasses, even I with my milk.

Our table was in the middle of the room, right under a chandelier of clear glass light bulbs that made things dim and glary at the same time so that it was hard to tell how anyone looked, I wanted to see what people looked like who had spent forty-eight hours screwing each other silly, I wanted some evidence, something tangible that I could use for my imaginative life of abstract jealousies, but it was not to be had, at least in this light, it was particularly difficult to see Miss Lola Miss Drew's face, she was so blindingly beautiful under that cut gold hair, her eyes were so green and her skin was so white, it was like trying to look into the sun, you couldn't see her through the brilliance and it hurt to try for more than an instant. She was totally attentive to Mr. Schultz and stared at him every time he opened his mouth, as if she was deaf and had to read lips.

Dinner was meat loaf with string beans and mashed potatoes and a basket of packaged white bread and a hunk of butter and a bottle of ketchup in the middle of the table. It was good hot food and I was hungry. I ate fast, we all did, we went at it with a vengeance, Mr. Schultz asked the girl to bring another platter of the meat loaf, and it wasn't till the first edge of my hunger was rounded off that I noticed Miss Lola Miss Drew hadn't touched her dinner but was leaning with her elbows on the table and intently regarding the wolfish crew of us holding our forks in our fists, chewing with our mouths open, and reaching out to spear slices of bread. She seemed quite fascinated. When I looked again she had lifted her own fork and folded her hand over it till she had made a fist around the shank. She held it one way and then another to see how it felt, and then forked the slab of meat loaf on her plate and hoisted it slowly into the air to her eye level. At this point everyone grew quite still, she had the attention of the entire table, although she no longer seemed to be aware of us. She lowered the fork and left it standing upright in the portion of meat and as if she was quite alone and thinking about something far away took her napkin from the place setting, unfolded it, and laid it across her lap. Then she looked at Mr. Schultz with a sweet distracted smile and then down at her glass, which he hurriedly refilled. Then she proceeded to dine, taking the fork in her left hand and her knife in her right, and cutting and accepting in her mouth from the fork tines, after she had laid the knife down and switched the fork to her right hand, small bites of the meat loaf and tiny dabs of mashed potato. It was an operation of pronounced gentility performed at ritual speed, just as teachers in school write words across the blackboard while enunciating them syllable by syllable. As we all watched, she took her wineglass and put it to her lips and drank without making any sound, though I listened hard, not a sip or slurp or gulp or gurgle, so that when she replaced her glass on the table I wondered if any wine had gotten into her at all. I had to conclude this was one of the most depressing displays of daintiness I had ever seen, as beautiful as she was, she momentarily forfeited her allure as far as I was concerned. Lulu Rosenkrantz frowned the frown that could terrify a hit man, and then exchanged glances with Mickey the driver, and Abbadabba stared at the tablecloth with a sad expression on his face, and even the impassive Irving lowered his eyes, but Mr. Schultz was nodding his head with his lips pouted as if a necessary point was being made. He leaned forward and, looking around the table, said in his idea of a modulated voice, "Thank you, Miss Drew, for your thoughtful comments, which I believe are offered in the best interests of watching our asses for our own good."

I knew immediately something momentous had occurred but I didn't trust myself to think what it was until later, when I was alone in my room again in bed with the lights out and the crickets in the fields of Onondaga beating away like the night's loud pulse, as if night were an enormous body, like the sea, with things living in it, making love in it, and lying dead in it. Miss Lola Miss Drew disdained memories. Technically she was a captive, her life was at risk. But she had no intention of being a captive. She had something to contribute. Of course what Mr. Schultz had said was correct in that we did have to watch our asses up here, like travelers in some dictator's foreign country. But what stunned everyone at the table was that he had sided with her, she had done this crazy pantomime, presuming to act in that way of privilege of instructing those less fortunate than she, and instead of whacking her across the face, which is probably what everyone else there would have done, he had accepted it and found value in it. It was as if they felt an announcement was being made, that she was being cut in in some way and that was how it was going to be.

Of course, I didn't know if I was right, if that was what everyone thought, but I knew from my own career with him that Mr. Schultz liked to be pursued, he was vulnerable to people who were attracted to him, followers, admirers, acolytes, and the otherwise dependent, whether show-off kids, or women whose men he killed. She was a spoil of war, after all, she had been given her delicious value by Bo Weinberg's love for her. I had to wonder if when he took her to bed Mr. Schultz enjoyed the hard-on of triumph, making love to the lady but giving it to the dead Bo.

THE NEXT MORNING BRIGHT AND EARLY, MR. BERMAN KNOCKED ON MY DOOR AND told me to get dressed in my new suit and to wear my glasses and meet Mr. Schultz down in the lobby in fifteen minutes. I did it in ten, which was enough time to run around the corner for a doughnut and a cup of coffee. I got back as everyone was coming outside. Mickey was there with the Packard, Lulu Rosenkrantz was getting in beside him, and Mr. Schultz and Miss Drew were seated in the back. I jumped in.

It was a short trip, in fact only around the corner to the Onondaga National Bank, which was a narrow limestone building with two long skinny barred windows and columns holding up the stone triangle roof over the front doors. Mickey pulled up across the street and we all sat there looking at it with the motor running.

"I once't chanced to meet that Alvin Pincus who ran with Pretty Boy Floyd," Lulu said. "A very excellent safecracker."

"Yeah, and where is he now," Mr. Schultz said.

"Well they did good for a while."

"Think about it, Lulu," Mr. Schultz said. "Going for the dough the one place it's under lock and key. You gotta be stupid. That outlaw shit ain't in the economic mainstream," he said patting the briefcase on his lap. "Okay, ladies and gents," he said, and he got out of the car and held the door for Miss Drew and me.

I didn't know what I was supposed to do. When I got out of the car Miss Drew said, "Wait a minute," and straightened my clip-on tie. I instinctively drew back.

"Just be a nice boy," Mr. Schultz said. "I know it's hard."

I could tell my black wing-tips were already raising a blister on my heel, and the wire hooks of my plain glass steel-rim glasses were pinching me behind the ears. I had of course forgotten to buy a book as Mr. Berman had told me and so as a last resort carried the Bible from my room in my left hand. My right hand was held by Miss Drew, which she squeezed as we crossed the street behind Mr. Schultz. "You look handsome," she said. I resented it that even when I wore my Elevator Shoes she was the taller of us. "That's a compliment," she said, "it doesn't call for a scowl." She was very gay.

We were shown right past the tellers' barred cages to the back office, where the president came from behind his desk and shook Mr. Schultz's hand heartily, though his eyes flicked over us all with cool appraisal. He was a portly man with a fleshy tubular underchin that looked like a hydraulic pump under his jaw when his mouth moved. Behind him was this open door and steel gate, and an inner room that was really a big safe with its thick door open and lots of drawers inside the room like mailboxes in a post office. "Well, well," he said after the introductions were made, Mr. Schultz having described me as his prodigy, and Miss Drew as my governess, "please sit down, everyone, we don't often have famous people in our little town. I hope you're finding it to your liking."

"Oh yes," Mr. Schultz said, beginning to undo the straps on his briefcase. "This is a summer in the country for us."

"Well, country is what we can offer. Swimming holes, trout streams, virgin forest," at this his eyes darted for a moment to Miss Drew's crossed legs. "Some pretty fair vistas from up the top of the hills, if you like hiking. Good fresh air, all you can breathe," he said, laughing as if he'd said something funny, and he went on with this mindless booster small talk his eyes coming back again and again to the briefcase which Mr. Schultz now leaned forward to place on his desk, the top flap folded back, so that when it was given a quick shove and then pulled back, packs of greenbacks slid out on the big green blotter. And with that, words abruptly ceased to come from the banker's mouth although the hydraulic pump didn't lift it shut for another moment or two.

It was a lot of money, more than I had ever seen, but I showed more restraint than the banker, giving no indication that I saw anything out of the ordinary. Mr. Schultz said he wanted to open a checking account for five thousand and put the balance in a safe deposit box. A moment later the banker's old secretary was summoned in and in a fluster of attentions

she and the banker went off to count the haul while Mr. Schultz sat back
and lit a cigar fresh from the humidor on the banker's desk.

"Kid," he said, "you notice how many tellers' cages are open for
business?"

"One?"

"Yeah. One teller with gray hair sitting there reading the paper. Lulu's
friends walk in they won't even find a bank dick at the door. You know
what this guy's reserves must be? Holding a lot of dirt-farm mortgages?
Spends his days foreclosing and selling off the county of Onondaga for ten
cents on the dollar. I'm telling you. He'll lay awake at night thinking of
all that cash in my safe deposit box. What it represents. Give him a week,
ten days. I will get a call."

"And you will go in on whatever it is," Miss Drew said.

"Goddamn right. You're looking at the patron sweetheart of the boondocks." He buttoned the jacket of his dark suit, and brushed imaginary
dust off the sleeves. He put the cigar in his mouth and leaned over and
pulled up his socks. "Get through here I could run for Congress."

"I would like to mention something on a different subject but not if
you're going to get all pouty and sulk," Miss Drew said.

"What. No. My words again?"

"Protégé, like proto-jay."

"What did I say?"

"You said prodigy. That's something else, like a child genius." At this
moment the banker returned all happy and hand-rubbing and put out
some forms for Mr. Schultz to sign and took the cap off his fountain pen
and slipped it on the end and handed the pen across the desk chattering
all the meanwhile. But upon the scratching of the signature he went quiet
and the documents were duly executed in a hush, as if a state treaty were
coming into effect. Then the old lady secretary came in with her receipts
and a book of blank checks and there was more fussing and heartiness,
and in a few moments we were standing for the goodbyes and thank-yous
and let-me-know-if-there's-anything-I-can-dos, it is a fact that money
exhilarates people, it puts them in hysterias of good cheer, they suddenly
care about you and want the best for you. The banker had hardly taken
notice of anyone but Mr. Schultz but now he said, "Hey, young fellow,
what's the younger generation reading these days?" as if it was really
important to him. He turned the book up in my hand so he could read the
title, I don't know what he had expected, a French novel maybe, but he
was genuinely surprised. "Well good for you, son," he said. He gripped
my shoulder and looking at my governess said, "My respects, Miss Drew,
I'm a scoutmaster myself, we don't really have to worry about the future
of the country, do we, with youngsters like this?"

He walked us to the front entrance, all our heels ringing on the marble
floor, it was like a procession, with the single teller standing up in his cage

as we passed. "Goodbye, bless you," the banker said, waving at us from the steps.

Lulu held the car door open and we settled into the back and after he took his seat up front, Mickey started the engine and put it in gear, and we drove off. Only then did Mr. Schultz say, "What the fuck was that all about?" and reach over Miss Drew to grab the Onondaga Hotel's Holy Bible out of my hands.

There was absolute silence in the car except for the flipping of pages. I stared out the window. We were going slowly downhill now along the nearly deserted main street. Here in the country they had things like feed stores. I was sitting in a new suit with long pants and my Elevator Shoes and my thigh touching the thigh of the beautiful Miss Drew right in the back seat of the luxurious personal car of the man who had existed for me only as an awesome dream a few weeks before and I couldn't have been more unhappy. I rolled the window all the way down to let out the cigar smoke. There was no question in my mind that something unimaginably terrible was about to happen.

"Hey Mickey," Mr. Schultz said.

Mickey the driver's pale blue eyes appeared in the rearview mirror.

"Stop at the church up the hill there where you see the spire," Mr. Schultz said. He began to chuckle. "The one thing we didn't think of," he said. He put his hand on Miss Drew's knee. "May I add my respects to the guy's back there?"

"Don't look at me, boss," she said, "I didn't have anything to do with it."

Mr. Schultz leaned forward so he could see me on the other side of Miss Drew. He was smiling broadly, with enormous teeth, a very big mouth of them. "Is that right? This was your brainstorm?"

I didn't have the chance to explain. "You see," he said to Miss Drew, "I know what words I'm talking about when I pick my words. The kid's my fucking prodigy."

And that was how I came to be enrolled in the Sunday Bible study class of the Church of the Holy Spirit, in Onondaga New York the interminable summer of the year 1935. To undergo orations on the subject of the desert gangs, their troubles with the law, their hustles and scams, the ways they worked each other over, and the grandiose claims they made for themselves—that was my sacred fate in the church basement with sweat dripping from the stone walls and the snivels of summer colds dripping from the noses of my fellow students in their overalls or their faded flowered dresses, always a size too big, and their feet swinging under the benches, shoed or bare, every goddamn Sunday. For all I had accomplished and as far as I had come, I might just as well have been back in the orphans' home.

* * *

BUT SUNDAY WAS ONLY THE WORST OF THE DAYS, ALL WEEK WE WENT AT IT, THERE
was nothing to do but good. We made visits to the hospital and brought
magazines and candy to the wards. Wherever there was a store open with
something to sell, as long as it wasn't tractor parts, we went in and bought
whatever it was selling. A mile out of town was a broken-down miniature
golf course, I drove out there with Mickey and Lulu on several occasions
and the three of us putted the ball through little wooden chutes and barrels
and pipes and I got pretty good at it and took a few dollars from them but
decided not to go out there anymore the day Lulu in a fit of bad sportsman-
ship broke his club over his knee. In town a small crowd of little hick kids
collected whenever I set foot out of doors, they followed me down the
street and I bought them candy and whirligigs and ice cream while Mr.
Schultz was having receptions for their fathers and mothers under the
auspices of the American Legion, or taking over the church socials, buying
up all the homemade cakes and then throwing a party for everyone to
come have cake and coffee. Of all of us, he was the one who seemed
actually to enjoy these long boring days. Miss Drew found a stable with
riding horses and she took Mr. Schultz out horseback riding every morning and I could see them from the sixth-floor corridor window trotting
down the country roads to the fallow fields where she was giving him
instruction. The post office delivered things she had ordered by phone
from a fancy store in Boston, riding outfits for both of them with tweed
coats with leather patches on the elbows and silk neck scarves and dark
green felt hats with little feathers stuck in the brim and sleek soft leather
boots and jodhpurs, those peculiar lavender pants that bloomed out at the
hips, which was fine in her case since she tended in her long-waisted way
to be a bit flat back there, but not really suited to the stolid build of Mr.
Schultz, who appeared unathletic in them, to say the least, not that any of
us, even Mr. Berman, wanted to bring this to his attention.

The only time I enjoyed was the very early morning. I was always the
first one up and I took to buying the *Onondaga Signal* from the news store
so that I could read it with my breakfast at a little tea shop kind of
luncheonette I had found down a side street. The woman there did her
own baking and made very good breakfasts but I kept this intelligence to
myself. I think I was the only one of us who read the *Signal,* it was
undeniably dull with farm news and almanac wisdom and home canning
advice and so on, but they carried *The Phantom* comic strip and *Abbie and
Slats,* and that gave me some small connection to real life. One morning
the front page had a story about Mr. Schultz buying a local farm from the
bank and giving it back to the family that had lost it. When I got back to
the hotel there were more old cars parked with their wheels against the

curb than usual, and sitting and hunkering all over the little lobby were men in overalls and women in housedresses. And from then on, there was a constant watch at the hotel, inside or outside, one or two farmers and farmers' wives or as many as a dozen, depending on the time of day. I noticed about these people that when they were skinny they were very skinny and when they were fat they were very fat. Mr. Schultz was always courteous when he came through and would take a couple of them to a corner table in the hotel dining room as if it was his office, and listen to them for a few minutes and ask a few questions. I don't know how many foreclosed mortgages he recovered, probably none, more likely he gave them the monthly payment money or a few dollars to keep the wolf from the door, as he put it. The way it worked, for the sake of their feelings, he would maintain a businesslike pretense, take their names and tell them to come back the next day, and then it would be Abbadabba Berman who issued the actual cash in a little brown envelope from his office room on the sixth floor. Mr. Schultz didn't want to be lordish about it, he showed great tact that way.

It was very mysterious to me how a countryside could be so beautiful and yet so invisibly in trouble. I wandered down to the river and across the bridge and out on the country roads every now and then, a little farther each time as I got used to it and discovered no harm would come to me from an empty sky, from hills of wildflowers, from the occasional appearance back from the road of a house and a barn and an animal or two standing around. It was clear here upstate that every city came to an end and an empty road began that required faith to travel. Encouraging were the evenly spaced telegraph poles with electricity wires dipping from pole to pole, I was happy to see also the painted white line going assiduously down the middle of the road over every little rise and fall of the land. I got used to the strawy smell of the fields and the occasional inexplicable whiff of dung coming up out of a roadside patch of heat, and what I first heard as silence turned out to be an air of natural sounds, winds and breezes, startled whirrs, slitherings through brush, pipey yelps, bugbuzz, clops, kerplunks, and croaks, none of which seemed to have any visible origin. So that it occurred to me as I made more of these excursions how you hear the life and smell it before you learn to see it, as if sight is the clumsiest of perceptions in the natural world. There was a lot to learn from the mysteriously unfolding landscape, it offered no intervening comfort between unadorned earth and a large and potent sky, so the last thing I would have expected of it was that it would suffer the same ordinary rat shames of tenements and slums. But I had by now taken to venturing off the paved roads and down this or that dirt lane and one day I was kicking along a wide rocky path when I heard an uncountrylike sound with an alarming breadth to it, and as I walked it became identifiable as a continuous rumble, like a motorized army, and I came over a rise to see a cloud of earthen dust rising from the distant fields and then saw in front of me, parked by the roadside, the black cars and trucks of the country poor, what must have been a good part of the population of Onondaga was walking out across the land in the plumes of dust made by a battery of tractors and harvest machines and trucks taking up acres and acres of potato plants, the machines pouring the potatoes down these moving belts into the truck beds, and the people following, bending down to cull the potatoes missed by the machines and putting them in burlap sacks they dragged along behind them, some even hurrying on all fours through the furrows in the urgency of destitution, men women and children, one or two of whom I recognized from Sunday school at the Church of the Holy Spirit.

And now the scope of Mr. Schultz's strategy became apparent to me. I had wondered how anyone could be fooled, because what he was doing was so obvious, but he wasn't trying to fool anybody, he didn't have to, it didn't matter that these people knew he was a big-time New York gangster, nobody here had any love for New York anyway and what he did down there was his business if up here he showed his good faith, it didn't even matter that they knew why he was doing what he was doing as long as he did it on a scale equal to his reputation. Of course he was obvious, but that's what you had to be when the fix was in with the masses, everything had to be done large, like skywriting, so that it could be seen for miles around.

He said at dinner in the hotel one night, "You know, Otto, I was paying the Chairman of the Board as much a week as all this is costing. There's no middleman up here to jack up the price on you," he said enjoying the thought. "Am I right, Otto? We're dealing direct, eggs fresh from the farm." He laughed, everything seemed to be going off in Onondaga just as he hoped it would.

But I could tell Abbadabba Berman was feeling less sanguine. "Chairman of the Board" was the code name for Mr. Hines, the Tammany man. Until the Feds had messed things up Mr. Hines got cops who were too smart for their own good assigned to Staten Island and magistrates who didn't understand their job retired from the bench and, for icing on the cake, bought the election of the gentlest and most peaceable district attorney in the history of the City of New York. It had been a wonderful way to do business. Here, the reality was that they were trying to extricate themselves from a grave situation. Also, the gang was out of its element, they lacked experience in legitimacy and could not be counted upon always to do what was right. And the other thing was Miss Drew. Mr. Berman had never been consulted about Miss Drew. There was no denying she was classing-up the act and thinking of things which her background had taught her, how to work charity, the forms it took, the dos and don'ts of it. And she seemed to be good at giving the Dutchman a little touch of style, so that it was harder for the people up here to think of him as without the shadow of a doubt a man of the rackets. But she was an X. In mathematics, Mr. Berman had told me, when you don't know what something is worth, not even if it is plus or minus, you call it *X*. Instead of a number you assign a letter. Mr. Berman had no great regard for letters. He was looking at her now as with a dead pan Miss Drew picked at her salad with her right hand and with her left out of sight under the table touched Mr. Schultz's privates which couldn't have been more apparent because Mr. Schultz started up from his seat and knocked over his wine and coughing into his napkin and turning red told her as he started to laugh that she was a crazy fucking broad.

Sitting at the far end of the dining room, in a corner by themselves, were Irving, Lulu, and Mickey the driver. They were not happy men. When Mr. Schultz cried out Lulu had not been looking in that direction and was so taken aback he rose to his feet and reached into his jacket staring around wildly before Irving put a hand on his arm. Miss Drew had split the gang, there was a hierarchy now, the four of us sat at one table each night and Lulu, Irving, and Mickey sat at another. Given the demands of life in Onondaga Mr. Schultz spent much of his time with Miss Drew and me but mostly Miss Drew, and I know I felt ill-used and muscled out so I could imagine how the men felt. Mr. Berman had to have understood all of this.

Of course once the New York press got wind of what Dutch Schultz was doing here, our situation would change rapidly, like a fever breaking, but I couldn't know that, everything seemed very weird and dizzying to me, as for instance that Miss Drew could be my mother and Mr. Schultz my father, a thought that came to me, no not even a thought worse than a thought, a feeling, when we attended a mass at the St. Barnabas Catholic Church one Sunday nice and early so I wouldn't miss Protestant Sunday school at the Church of the Holy Spirit. And he took off his hat and she pulled a white lace shawl over her head and we sat all solemn and shining in our rear pew listening to the organ, an instrument I hate and detest, the way it blurs the ears with intimidating chordblasts of righteousness, or worms inside the ear canal with little pipey slynesses of piety, and that father in silken robes swinging a smokepot up there under a poor painted plaster bleeding Christ on a golden cross, oh I tell you this was not my idea of the life of crime, but that there were things even worse than I knew, because afterward in this church at a table near the door Mr. Schultz lit a candle in a little glass for Bo Weinberg, saying what the hell, and then on the sidewalk the father came after us, I hadn't thought priests on the pulpit in their colored silks saw who was in the audience, but they do, they see everything, and his name was Father Montaine, he spoke with an accent, he said he was hoppee to see us and shook my hand vigorously, and then he and Miss Lola Miss Drew spoke French, he was a French Canadian with a limited amount of wiry black hair which he combed sideways over his head so that he wouldn't look bald, which of course he did. I felt dumb, thick-tongued, I was getting fat eating pancake breakfasts on the expense account and ham steak and applesauce dinners, I wore my fake glasses and went calling on churches and combed my hair and kept clean and neat in outfits Miss Lola Miss Drew had found for me, and that was another thing, she had taken to ordering clothes in my size from Boston, I was becoming a project of hers, as if she really was responsible for me, it was weird, when she turned her intense gaze in my direction I saw no depth of assignable character, she seemed incapable of distinguishing pretense from reality, or perhaps she was rich enough to think everything she pretended was true, but me, I didn't know what it was to flat-out run anymore, I felt I was not reliably myself, I was smiling too much and talking like a sissy and I was reduced to devious practices, doing things I would never have imagined myself doing in my Shadows jacket, like eavesdropping, listening in to conversations like some cop on a wiretap just to try to get some intelligence of what was going on.

For instance one night in my room I smelled cigar smoke and heard voices, so I went into the corridor and stood in the hall just outside the slightly open door of Mr. Berman's room that he had turned into an office and I peeked in. Mr. Schultz was in there in his bathrobe and slippers, it was very late and they were talking softly, if he'd caught me there was no telling what he would do but I didn't care, I was one of the gang now, I was running with them, I told myself what was the point of living on the same hotel floor with Dutch Schultz if I didn't take advantage of it. At least my senses were still sharp, and that was something, I stepped back out of sight and I listened.

"Arthur," Mr. Berman was saying, "you know these boys would go to the wall for you."

"They don't have to go to the wall. They don't have to do nothing but keep their eyes open tip their hats to the ladies and don't goose the chambermaid. Is that too much to ask? I'm paying them, ain't I? It's a goddamn paid vacation, so what are they complaining about."

"No one has said a word. But I'm telling you what I know. It's hard to explain. All these table-manners kinds of things are getting to their self-respect. There's a roadhouse about twenty miles north of here. Maybe you should let them blow off steam once in a while."

"Are you out of your mind? All this work, what do you think happens they get into a goddamn bar fight over some whore? That's all we need, a run-in with the state troopers."

"Irving wouldn't let that happen."

"No, I'm sorry, we're talking about my future, Otto."

"That is correct."

There was silence for a few moments. Mr. Schultz said, "You mean Drew Preston."

"Until now I had not been introduced to the lady's full name."

"I'll tell you what, call Cooney, tell him to get hold of some stag films and a projector and he can drive them up."

"Arthur, how shall I say this. These are serious grown men, they are not deep thinkers but they can think and they can worry about their futures no less than you worry about yours."

I heard Mr. Schultz pacing. Then he stopped. "Jesus Christ," he said.

"Nevertheless," Mr. Berman said.

"I'm telling you, Otto, it doesn't even take money she's got more money than I'll ever have, this one is different, I'll grant you she's a bit spoiled, those kind always are, but when the time comes I'll slap her around a little and that is all it will take, I promise you."

"They remember Bo."

"What does that mean? I remember too, I am upset too, I am more upset than anyone. Because I don't go around talking about it?"

"Just don't fall in love, Arthur," Mr. Berman said.

I went very quietly back to my room and got into bed. Drew Preston was in fact very beautiful, slender and with a clearly unconscious loveliness of movement when she was thoughtless of herself as she would be when we went out into the countryside, like the drawn young women in the children's books in the Diamond Home broken-down library of books no newer than from the previous century, kind and in communication with the little animals of the forest, I mean you'd see that on her exquisite face in moments of her reflection when she forgot where she was and who she was with, and that raised generous mouth curved back like the prow of a boat, and the clear large green eyes that could be so rude with intense curiosity or wickedly impertinent lowered under a profound modesty of lashes. All of us were subject to her even the philosophical Mr. Berman, a man older than the rest of us and with a physical impairment that he would have long since learned to live with and forgotten except in the presence of such fine-boned beauty. But all of this made her very dangerous, she was unstable, she took on the coloration of the moment, slipping into the role suggested to her by her surroundings. And as I thought about this I thought too that we were all of us very lax with our names, when the pastor had asked my name to enroll me in Sunday school I gave it as Billy Bathgate and watched him write it that way in the book, hardly realizing at the time I was baptizing myself into the gang because then I had an extra name too to use when I felt like it, like Arthur Flegenheimer could change himself into Dutch Schultz and Otto Berman was in some circles Abbadabba, so insofar as names went they could be like license plates you could switch on cars, not welded into their construction but only tagged on for the temporary purposes of identification. And then who I thought was Miss Lola on the tugboat and then Miss Drew in the hotel was now Mrs. Preston in Onondaga, so she was one up on everyone, although I had to admit I had probably gotten the wrong impression when I took her back to the Savoy-Plaza and the lobby clerk had greeted her as Miss Drew not necessarily because that was her maiden name, although for all I know in that walk of life the married women keep their maiden names, but because as an older man in professional service he might have known her since her childhood and though she was now too grown-up to be called simply by her first name, she was too fondly known for too long a time to be called by her last. Perhaps it wasn't necessary to get anything straight, not even monickers, maybe that was my trouble that I needed to know things definitely and expected them not to change. I myself was changing, look where I was, look what I was doing, every morning I put on glasses that magnified nothing and every night I took them off at bedtime like someone who couldn't do without them except to sleep. I was apprenticed to a gangster and so was being educated in Bible studies. I was a street kid from the Bronx living in the country like Little Lord Fauntleroy. None of these things made sense except as I was contingent to a situation. And when the situation changed, would I change with it? Yes, the answer was yes. And that gave me the idea that maybe all identification is temporary because you went through a life of changing situations. I found this a very satisfying idea to consider. I decided it was my license-plate theory of identification. As a theory it would apply to everyone, mad or sane, not just me. And now that I had it I found myself less worried about Lola Miss Drew Mrs. Preston than Mr. Otto Abbadabba Berman appeared to be. I had a new bathrobe, maybe I should put it on and after Mr. Arthur Flegenheimer Schultz went back to bed I would go knock on the Abbadabba's door and tell him what *X* meant. All I had to remember was what had gotten me to this point in the first place, the innermost resolve of my secret endowment. That must never change.

TEN

I slept to an unaccustomed late hour, which I realized at once when I woke and saw the room filled with light and the white curtains on the windows like movie screens with the picture about to start. The chambermaid was running a vacuum cleaner in the corridor and I heard a chain-drive truck coming around the back of the hotel to make a delivery. I got out of bed and felt very heavy in the limbs, but I did my ablutions and dressed, and inside of ten minutes I was on my way to breakfast. When I got back to the hotel Abbadabba Berman was out front with the Buick Roadmaster at the curb, he was waiting for me. "Hey kid," he said, "come on we'll go for a ride."

I got in the back and found the only available seat was in the middle, between Irving and Lulu Rosenkrantz. It was not a comfortable place to be, after Mr. Berman got in the front and Mickey started the engine, Lulu leaned forward and I could feel the tension in him as he said, "Why does this little shit have to go with us?" Mr. Berman didn't bother to answer but looked straight ahead and Lulu banged back into the seat beside me, giving me a murderous look but clearly talking to everyone else as he said, "I'm fed up with all this crap, I don't give a pig's fuck for any of this."

Mr. Berman knew that, he understood, he did not have to be told. We drove past the county courthouse and as we did an Onondaga police car backed away from the curb and swung out behind us. I glanced back to make sure and was about to say something when my instinct told me not to. Mickey's pale blue eyes appeared regularly in the rearview mirror. Mr. Berman's shoulders barely rose above the front seat, his panama hat was horizontally forward of where it should have been because of his hump-back, but to me this was the deportment of canniness and wisdom, I knew somehow the police car behind us was something else he knew and didn't have to be told.

Mickey drove across the rattly boards of the Onondaga bridge and out into the country. Everything looked baked and bleached in the high noon and it was hot in the car. After ten or fifteen minutes, he turned off the paved road into a farmyard and nudged through a protesting squawking flutter of chickens and past a gamboling goat or two and around a barn and a silo and then picked up speed down a long bumpy dirt road, with rocks making a popping against the tires and a big plume of dust billowing out behind us. He pulled up in front of a hut fenced in with chain link. A moment later I heard the brakes of the police car and a slamming door, and a policeman walked past us and unlocked the fence gate with its sign that said KEEP OUT and swung it open and we drove in.

What I'd thought was a hut was in fact a long barracks sort of structure where the Onondaga police took their pistol practice, the floor was dirt and at the far end the wall was earth, a big pile of it having been shoveled up into a sort of hill or berm, and there were overhead wires attached to pulleys at either end of the building like clotheslines. The cop pulled some paper targets out of a bin and clipped them to the lines and ran them to the berm and then he sat by the door leaning his chair back on two legs and rolling himself a cigarette, and Lulu Rosenkrantz stepped up to the railing without ceremony, unpacked his forty-five and began blasting away. I felt as if my head had burst, I looked around and saw that everyone else was wearing leather earmuffs, and only then noticed a clump of them on a table and quickly availed myself of them, clutching my hands over them for good measure while crazy Lulu shot that target into smithereens and left a smell of burning powder in the air and the echo of high-caliber concussions that seemed to press the sides of the building outward and suck them back in.

Lulu hauled the target back and didn't bother to study it but pulled it off and clipped on a new one and yanked it back down to the end and proceeded to load his pistol hurriedly, even dropping cartridges in his haste, he was so eager to go at it again, and again he shot off his rounds one after another like he was in an argument and jabbing his pointed finger for emphasis, so that a continuous roar filled the shed, it was all too much for me, I went out the door and stood in the sun leaning against the car fender and listened to my head ringing, it rang in several different notes simultaneously, like the horn of Mr. Schultz's Packard.

The firing stopped for a few minutes and when it began again I heard the discreet shots of careful aim, a shot and a pause and another shot. After this had gone on for a while Mr. Berman came outside holding up two of the white target sheets and he came over and laid them out side by side on the hood of the Buick.

The targets were printed in black ink in the shape of a man's head and torso, and one of them was peppered with holes both inside and outside the target area with the biggest a kind of jagged shell hole in the middle of the chest, so that I could see the sun reflected in the car hood underneath. The other target had small precise holes arranged almost like a design, one in the middle of the forehead, one where each eye would be, one in each shoulder, one in the middle of the chest and two in the stomach region just above the waistline. None of the shots had missed the target area.

"Who is the better shooter?" Mr. Berman asked me.

I replied without hesitation, pointing to the second target with its unerring carefully placed holes: "Irving."

"You know that's Irving?"

"He does everything this way, very neat, and with nothing wasted."

"Irving has never killed a man," Mr. Berman said.

"I wouldn't like to have to kill a man," I said, "but if I did I would want to know how like that," I said, pointing to Irving's target.

Mr. Berman leaned back against the fender and shook an Old Gold out of his pack and put it in his mouth. He shook out another one and offered it to me and I took it and he gave me his matchbook and I lit both cigarettes.

"If you were in a tight situation you would want Lulu standing up for you and emptying his barrel at everything in sight," he said. "You would know that in such a circumstance it is all decided in a matter of seconds." He flipped out his hand with one finger pointing, then flipped it again with two fingers pointing, and so on, till the whole claw was extended: *"Boom boom boom boom boom,* it's over," he said. "Like that. You couldn't dial a phone number in that time. You couldn't pick up your change from the Automat."

I felt chastened, but stubborn in my opinion too. I looked at the ground at my feet. He said, "We are not speaking of ladies' embroidery, kid. It don't have to be neat."

We stood there and he didn't say anything for a while. It was hot. I saw way up a single bird circling, way up high in the whiteness of this hot sunless day, it dipped around like a model glider, and it had a red or rust tone to it, lazing about up there drifting one way and then another. I listened to the *pop pop* of the pistol fire.

"Of course," Mr. Berman said, "the times change and looking at you I see what's in the cards, you're the upcoming generation and it's possible what is required of you will be different, you would need different skills. It is possible everything will be smooth and streamlined, people will work things out quietly, with not so much fire in the streets. We will need fewer Lulus. And if that comes to pass you may not ever have to kill no one."

I glanced at him and he gave me a little smile with his *V*-shaped mouth. "You think that's possible?" he said.

"I don't know. From what I can see it don't seem too likely."

"At a certain point everyone looks at the books. The numbers don't lie. They read the numbers, they see what only makes sense. It's like numbers are language, like all the letters in the language are turned into numbers, and so it's something that everyone understands the same way. You lose the sounds of the letters and whether they click or pop or touch the palate, or go *ooh* or *aah*, and anything that can be misread or con you with its

music or the pictures it puts in your mind, all of that is gone, along with
the accent, and you have a new understanding entirely, a language of
numbers, and everything becomes as clear to everyone as the writing on
the wall. So as I say there comes a certain time for the reading of the
numbers. Do you see what I'm getting at?''

"Cooperation," I said.

"Exactly. What happened in the railroad business is a perfect example,
you look at the railroads, they used to be a hundred railroad companies
cutting each other's throats. Now how many are there? One to each section
of the country. And on top of that they got a trade association to smooth
their way in Washington. Everything nice and quiet, everything streamlined.''

I inhaled the cigarette smoke and there was an undeniable opening-out
of excitement through my chest and into my throat like the looming of my
own power. What I was hearing was prophecy but of an inevitable event
or of a planned betrayal I wasn't sure. And why did it matter as long as
I knew that I was valued?

"But anyway, whatever is going to happen you must learn the basics,"
Mr. Berman said. "Whatever happens you have to know how to handle
yourself. I already told Irving he should show you. As soon as they're
through you'll take your turn.''

I said, "What, you mean shoot?''

He was holding out in his palm the Automatic I had bought from
Arnold Garbage. It was all cleaned and oiled, not a speck of rust, and when
I took it I saw the cartridge clip was locked into place and I knew from the
heft it was loaded.

"If you're going to carry it, carry it," Mr. Berman said. "If not, put it
somewhere else than the bureau drawer under the underwear. You're a
smart kid but like all kids you do dumb things.''

I WILL NEVER FORGET HOW IT FELT TO HOLD A LOADED GUN FOR THE FIRST TIME AND
lift it and fire it, the scare of its animate kick up the bone of your arm, you
are empowered there is no question about it, it is an investiture, like
knighthood, and even though you didn't invent it or design it or tool it the
credit is yours because it is in your hand, you don't even have to know
how it works, the credit is all yours, with the slightest squeeze of your
finger a hole appears in a piece of paper sixty feet away, and how can you
not be impressed with yourself, how can you not love this coiled and
sprung causation, I was awed, I was thrilled, the thing is guns come alive
when you fire them, they move, I hadn't realized that. I tried to remember
my instruction, I tried to breathe properly and plant myself in the sidearm
stance and sight down my arm, but it took all that day and in fact the rest

of the week of daily practice and a lot of sprays of earthclots brittle as crockery before I brought it around and turned that piece into the familiar of my own hand's warmth and got it to hit where I looked, and my natural athletic genius of coordination, the spring of my juggler's arm and the strength of my legs and my keen eyesight asserted themselves to their natural levels of achievement and I was hitting the target to kill whoever it was with every little pressure of my index finger. In a few short afternoons I could take aim and place the shot in the center of the forehead, either eye, the shoulders, the heart, or the belly, as I chose, Irving would pull the target back and take it down and put it down measuredly on the table over the previous target and the holes would match up. He never praised me but never did he seem to get bored with instructing me. Lulu didn't deign to watch. He didn't know my plan, which was to have Irving's techniques of accuracy so governed by my skills that I could lose the form, drop my arm, snap point like Lulu in the punishment of his blasting rage, and make the same holes in the same places. I also knew what he would say if I did this, that shooting at paper targets didn't mean shit, let me go out on a job with someone rising from his chair in the restaurant and people's guns coming round in my direction looking big as field eighty-eights, looking in their barrels as wide and deep as a big bertha on a railroad flatbed, let me see what I could do then.

Oddly enough, I detected this same attitude in the cop who came every day to open the gate and sit back on the two rear legs of his tilted chair and roll his cigarettes, it was only after my second day shooting I realized he was the chief, he had this braid on his cap none of the others in town had, not even the sergeants, and the arms in his short-sleeved shirt were an older man's arms of former muscle, and his abdomen slumped, I had thought a police chief would have something better to do than personally unlock the gate of the firing range for the city folks who'd paid him off and hang around to enjoy the show, but in Onondaga he had all the time in the world and it had nothing to do with the responsibilities of his office, he was watching a boy, and even as I fired my clips, I thought of the chief behind me with the slight smile on his lips, another man imbedded in his institutional job out in the country, like Father Montaine, with a very low visibility in the world but quite comfortable even so and satisfied with the rewards of his life, the smoke from his shag cigarette keeping me in mind of his presence like some farmer's on his porch sitting for his amusement to watch the passing parade.

But for the first time since coming to Onondaga County I felt I was doing proper work, those few days of squeezing off rounds, I could hardly wait to get out there, and in the evenings I came to dinner hungry, with my ears still ringing and memorial pungencies of burned gunpowder sputtering in my brain. Clearly they were bringing me along, and I could reflect how organized everything really was in the apparent chaos of Mr. Schultz's life, how patiently they were dealing with everything, from the present exigencies of the law to the anticipated needs of the future, they were managing their business interests from a distance, establishing a presence in this county seat of the north country, adjudicating their own internal problems in their own way, and also he had brought along someone pretty for the ride. It was a kind of juggling, wasn't it, keeping everything in the air. I really liked pistol-shooting, I thought I was probably the youngest expert marksman in the history of the rackets, I'm not sure I went so far as to swagger, but at night in bed I thought of neighborhood louts chasing me down Washington Avenue, how if that happened now I would stop in my tracks and turn with my gun in my hand and my arm pointed and watch them skid, brake, and tumble all over themselves even crawling under cars to get out of my sights, and the picture of that made me smile in the dark.

But nothing else I could think of doing with that gun was anything to smile about.

I SHOULD SAY HERE THAT THERE WERE THINGS GOING ON BEHIND THE LIFE I AM describing, business things that I wasn't directly involved in. Mr. Schultz was still collecting on policy, he was still selling beer and running the window washers' and the waiters' unions, once or twice he disappeared for a day or two and went down to New York but by and large he ran things long-distance, which couldn't have been a terribly comfortable way to do business if you happened to be by nature suspicious as he was and distrustful of all but your closest associates, and of them too when they were not where you could keep your eye on them. A lot of time I could hear him screaming on Mr. Berman's special phone, the walls were too thick for the words to be heard but the pitch and timbre and intonation came through clearly and like the man who woke up when the train didn't go past his window I would have been startled if one day passed not carrying his raised voice.

Mickey was gone a lot making the long drive to New York and back in a night and a day, and sometimes other men in other cars appeared whom everyone seemed to know but me, they would take their dinner with Irving and Lulu at the other table, I would say I saw two or three new faces a week. From all of this I began to appreciate the size of the operation, that the weekly payroll alone must be considerable, and from my vantage point Mr. Schultz would have to be now holding his own after the losses he had suffered as a lammister. It was difficult to judge these things because he portrayed himself so consistently as someone wronged, or double-crossed, or taken for a chump. Mr. Berman pored over the books constantly, and sometimes Mr. Schultz joined him, they really put in the time, usually late at night, and on one occasion I passed the open door of Mr. Berman's office and saw there for the first time a safe, and some deflated canvas mail bags lying on the floor beside it, and it came to me that all the money was ending up right here across the hall from me, a reality that I found unsettling. Apart from the token sums he had deposited that day for political purposes, Mr. Schultz did not keep a bank account, because bank records could be subpoenaed and assets confiscated and tax cases made against him, it was a simple precaution, the case the Feds had now was based on adding-machine slips and policy records taken in a raid on the 149th Street office, which was bad enough. So it was essential accounting practice that everything was done in cash, cash for the payouts, cash for the payoffs, cash for the payroll, it was a cash business and the profits to Mr. Schultz were in pure cash and I dreamed one night of a great tide of cash coming in and going out and what was left on the beach Mr. Schultz ran along and scooped up in packets, which he stuffed into a burlap bag like potatoes, knowing it was a dream as I dreamed it because it put the country at the seashore but realizing in the dream, which is to say reading it for the truth of the matter, that he had been doing this for some time and he had to have accumulated many many burlap bags of culled cash, or cold cash, and then it turned into a gold cache, but I didn't know in the dream where it was hidden, any more than I knew when I awakened.

AROUND THIS TIME, MR. SCHULTZ'S LAWYER, DIXIE DAVIS, WHOM I HAD SEEN THAT time in the numbers office, came up from New York and arrived at the Hotel Onondaga in a Nash sedan driven by a member of the gang I didn't know. Dixie Davis was my model for a good dresser, I had gotten my wing-tip shoes from seeing his and now I noticed his country summer shoes, which had a kind of mesh on top, they were brown with this cream-colored mesh going from the laces to the tip and I was not crazy about them although they were probably cool on the feet. He was wearing a double-breasted very light tan suit, which I liked, and a striped tie of cotton colored pale shades of blue and gray and pink, which I thought was smart, but best of all was the straw skimmer on his head, which he put on as he emerged in a crouch from the car. I happened to have been coming downstairs and so I saw Mr. Berman, himself no slouch at color combinations, greet him just outside the revolving door. Dixie Davis had his briefcase with him and it looked fat with the mysterious problems of legal life. He was somehow different from what I remembered, perhaps in anticipation of meeting Mr. Schultz he seemed to lose his self-assurance the moment he pushed into the lobby, he took off his straw hat and looked around somewhat nervously and held his briefcase in both arms, and though he was smiling and being jolly I saw that he was city pale, not handsome as I remembered under that pompadour haircomb, but somewhat toothy, and unctuous in his deportment, he had one of those smiles that went down at the corners of his mouth, what we in the Bronx called a shit-eating smile, and it was on his face as he passed with Mr. Berman into the elevator.

Mr. Schultz was going to be tied up for the afternoon so he told Drew Preston to put in the time acting like my governess. She and I had a conference standing outside the little Indian museum that they had in the red stone courthouse around the back down some basement steps. "Look," she said, "it's just a few headdresses and spears and such and there's no one there anyway to see what a good governess I am. Let's go for a picnic instead, is that all right with you?"

I said anything was all right with me as long as it didn't involve education. I took her down the side street to where my secret tea shop lady made up such good things, and we bought chicken salad sandwiches and fruit and napoleons, and then she bought a bottle of wine at the liquor store, and we set out uphill through the east side of the town into the mountains. This was a longer hike than I expected, I had done most of my exploring north and west into the farmlands, but hills always look closer than they are, and we were well beyond the end of the paved streets and still going up in wide spirals on a dirt road with the big hill behind the Onondaga Hotel looking just the way it did from my window, close enough to touch but just as far away, even when I turned around and looked down at the roofs of the city and saw what progress we had made.

She strode out ahead of me, which ordinarily would have brought out my competitive spirit, except I enjoyed watching the flex of the muscles in her long white calves. The minute we were out of the town limits, she had unwrapped and removed her governess's skirt and flung it over her shoulder, which stopped my heart beating for a moment, but she had a pair of walking shorts underneath, the hippy kind of shorts girls wear, and she was walking with a very attractive leggy stride, a smart practiced walk, head down, her free arm swinging, each buttock of her shorts rising and falling in a way that very quickly became reliably familiar to me, she was making good time uphill, her long legs her little feet pointing in their low-heeled shoes and white anklets, and then the road leveled and we were out of the sun into the shade of pines, and here the road petered out into a path and we struck off into woods, an entirely new world, very soft underfoot with a thick cushion of dried brown pine needles, and dry twigs cracking in the stillness, a brownish world with the sun breaking up high above us in the high-topped evergreens so that only speckles of it or small patches managed to reach the forest floor. I had never been in woods of such extent before, I mean there were dirt lots in the Bronx with weeds growing like trees all twisted and jungly but there wasn't enough extension of them to get lost in them, not even the wilder parts of the Bronx Zoo gave me the sense I had now, of being inside something, as in a cavern or a cave, I had not realized that about forests that you would be walking down at the bottom of them.

Drew Preston seemed to know where she was going, she found what she said were old logging trails, so I followed her trustfully, and we passed into small sun meadows that I thought might do for a picnic but still she didn't stop but kept going in a generally uphill direction, and then I knew we were really in the hills some miles from the town because I heard the sound of water, and we came to the Onondaga River, which here was shallow and not much wider than a brook so that you could walk across it on the rocks imbedded in it, which we did, and I thought then she would want to stop but she kept going away from the river steeply uphill in a dark woods and I was thinking of beginning to complain, the socks in my new sneakers rubbing up blisters and the gnats itching my bare legs, for I was in my new Little Lord Fauntleroy summer shorts of linen and my short-sleeved polo shirt of blue-and-white stripes that she had chosen for me, but we came to a large flat natural park of brown woods, and here the sound of water became louder, and she was some yards ahead of me standing still now finally and silhouetted in a corona of dazzling light, and when I came up to her I saw we were at the edge of a great sunlit gorge of falling water, falling so thick it was white and thunderous breaking on tumblings of boulders all the way down. This was where she chose to have the picnic, seated with our legs hanging over the root-tangled and mossy banks into thin air, as if she had known all along this place was here and exactly where to find it.

We unwrapped our sandwiches from the wax paper, and laid the picnic out behind us on her skirt, which she had spread on the ground, she unscrewed the cap from the bottle of New York State red wine and had the tact or carelessness to assume I would naturally take my turn drinking from the bottle as she did, and so I did, but only after removing my glasses, and we sat in silence eating and drinking and staring into this very amazingly beautiful roaring gorge of washed white boulders streaming with sun. At the very bottom there hovered a perpetually shimmering rainbow as if not water but light was pouring and shattering into its colors. This had to be the most secret of places. I had the feeling that if we just stayed here we would be free, Mr. Schultz would never find us because he couldn't imagine such a place existed. What new assumption was I making now in this romantic setting? What could I have been about to declare when I turned to her only to realize this was not a shared silence between us? She sat with her shoulders rounded in some clearly deepening meditative privacy and forgot me and forgot to eat and, holding the bottle in both hands between her knees, forgot to give me any more swigs of wine. The advantage to me in this was that I could stare at her without attracting her attention and first I looked at her thighs, you know the way thighs broaden in the sitting position especially when they are not overly muscular, and in this unsparing sun they were soft and very milk-white girl's thighs with the thinnest bluest veins of such tracing delicacy that it was with some shock I realized she was younger than I had taken her to be, I didn't know her age but the company she had kept and the fact that she was married had made me think of her as an older woman, it had never occurred to me she might be as precocious in her way as I was in mine, she was a girl, clearly older than I but still a girl, maybe twenty, maybe twenty-one, this Mrs. Preston with the gold band on her finger. You could see that just looking at her skin in the sun. Yet she lived a life so beyond mine in practiced knowledge that I was a child beside her. I don't mean just her free access as a great beauty to the most advanced realms of power and depravity, she had chosen this life for herself when, perhaps for her same reasons of staring meditation, she might have chosen life in a convent, say, or to be an actress on the stage. I mean rather how she knew this place would be here. How familiar woods were to her. She knew about horses. I remembered her invert husband, Harvey, had mumbled something about a regatta. So she probably knew about sailing and oceans too, and beaches to swim from with no crowds on them and skiing in the European mountains of the Alps and in fact all the pleasures of the planet, all the free rides of the planet that you could have if you knew where they were and had the training to take them. This was what wealth was, the practiced knowledge of these things so you could appropriate them for yourself. So looking at her now I had revelation of the great expanse of my ambitions, I felt the first acute pain of this same knowledge, which was an appreciative inkling of how much I had so far missed and my mother had missed and would forever miss and how much the little dark-eyed Becky was doomed to miss if I didn't love her and take her with me through all the chain-link fences I had to get through.

I now found myself painfully conscious of Drew Preston, I was impatient of the solitude she made for herself, it seemed to me a slight. I found myself waiting upon her, waiting for her attention, which I wanted very badly but would not abase myself to demand. I was at this point up to her profile. The heat of the hike had matted her hair off her forehead and I saw the whole line of it, a bone-white curve smooth as sculpture. The sun's rays coming up off the boulders allowed me to see through the transparency of her eye to the green oval iris with its golden lights which blurred into radiance, and the whole orb seemed to magnify and I realized she was crying. She cried silently, staring through her tears, and she licked the tears at the corner of her mouth. I turned away as you do in intimate and uninvited witness of a terrible emotion. And only then did I hear her sniff and drink it in, like a normal sniveling human being, and she asked me in a choked voice to tell her how Bo Weinberg died.

* * *

I DIDN'T WANT TO TALK ABOUT IT ANY MORE THAN I DO NOW BUT I DID AND SO I will, this was the time I told it so now I have to tell it again.

"He sang 'Bye Bye Blackbird.' "

She stared at me with the water roaring and the rainbow shimmering below us. She didn't seem to understand.

" 'Pack up all my care and woe, here I go, singing low, bye bye blackbird,' " I said. "It's a famous song." And then, as if I thought I couldn't make it more clear, I sang to her:

> " 'Make my bed and light the light,
> I'll arrive
> Late tonight
> Blackbird, bye bye.' "

ELEVEN

He begins humming it early on while Mr. Schultz is down below with her, and I stand halfway between the upper decks hooked by my heels and my elbows on the bolted ladder, which rises vertically and falls vertically as the tugboat rides the waves or drops between them. And it is as if Bo has heard it in the throbbing of the engine or a phrase of the wind, in the way that mechanical or natural rhythms around us take on the character in our minds of a popular song. He raises his head and tries to square his shoulders, he seems to have found strength from the distraction of singing, the assumption of your control in song, as when you hum while you are busy with some work of quiet concentration, and his wits were somewhat recovered, he cleared his throat and sang a bit louder now but still wordlessly, and he only stopped in order to look as much behind him as he could, and not seeing but feeling I was there he called to me, hey kid, c'mere, talk to old Bo, humming again while he waited confidently for me to appear in front of him. And I didn't want to become any closer to this situation than I already was in the same deckhouse as this dying man, his state seemed to me contaminating, I did not want any part of his experience, neither its prayers nor appeals or plaints or last requests, I did not want to be in his eyes in his last hour as if then something of my being would go down with him into the sea, and that is not a pretty thing to confess but it was the way I felt, entirely estranged, being no saint, nor priest of absolution, nor rabbi of consolation, nor nurse of ministration, and not wanting to participate in any conceivable way with anything he was going through, not even as a looker-on. And so of course I had no alternative but to come down from the ladder and stand on the rolling deck where he could see me.

He nodded his head peering up at me from under his brow, he was uncharacteristically messy, everything awry, his dinner jacket, his pant legs, his shirt half pulled out, his jacket bunched up behind him as if he had a hunchback, his thick black shining hair fallen off to the side, he nodded and smiled and said, the word's good on you kid, they have high hopes for you, you know that, anyone tell you that? You're a runty little fucker aren't you, you'll never be fat your whole life, you grow another couple inches you can fight in the featherweight class. He smiled with his even white teeth from that swarthy face, the high cheekbones elongating his Siberian eyes. Little guys make good kills in my experience, they go up on it, you see, it's an upward stick, he said lifting his head sharply for a moment to represent the knife, you use a gun it kicks up so that's to your advantage too, but if you're as smart as they say you will get to where your nails are manicured and a pretty girl sits by your chair and cleans under them every day. Me I am six one but I always killed smartly, I did not torture and I did not miss, the guy has to go? *boom*, you put his lights out, tell me who it is Dutch, *boom*, it's done, that's all. I never liked anyone who enjoyed this work apart from the pride of doing something very difficult and very dangerous very well. I never liked the creeps, I'll give you some advice from the old Bo. This man of yours ain't gonna last long. You see his behavior, he is a very emotional man, an untrustworthy maniac fuck who doesn't give a shit for other people's feelings, I mean people who matter, people who are as tough as him, and have better organizations and I'll tell you just between us better ideas for the future than this wildass. He is obsolete kid, you know what that means? He's all finished and if you're as smart as they say you are you'll listen to me and look out for yourself. This is Bo Weinberg talking. Irving upstairs knows and he's worried but he won't say anything, he's too far along he's ready for retirement he's not going to change his colors now. But he has my respect and I have his. What I've done in my life, my achievements, the quality of my word, Irving respects these things and I bear no brief against him. But he'll remember, you'll all remember, you too kid, I want you to look on Bo Weinberg for your own sake and understand the terrible usage of such a man, look him in the eye if you can so you will never forget this as long as you live because in a few minutes, in just a few minutes, he will be at peace, he will be over it the ropes won't hurt he won't be hot or cold or scared or humiliated or happy or sad or needful of anything anymore, this is the way God makes up for the terrible death, that it comes in time and the time goes on but the dying is done and our persons are at peace. But you kid are a witness and it's tough shit but that's the way it is, you'll remember and the Dutchman will know you remember and you can never be sure of anything again because you are doomed to live in remembrance of the foulness done to the man Bo Weinberg.

He looked away. And now I was startled to hear the song in a strong baritone, hoarse with defiance: Pack up all my care and woe, here I go, singing low, bye bye, blackbird. Dum de dum de dumdedum, yah dah dee, yah dah dee, bye, bye, blackbird. No one here can love or understand me, oh what hard-luck stories they all hand me. Dum de dum, light the light, I'll arrive, late tonight, blackbird, bye—and he shook his head with his eyes squeezed shut to reach the high note at the end—byeeee.

Then his head slumped and he hummed the tune to himself more softly, as if he was thinking again, almost not aware of humming through his thoughts and when he left off and began to talk again he was no longer talking to me but to some additional Bo sitting beside him perhaps in perfect elegance at the Embassy Club, drinks in front of them, while they reminisced: So I mean the guy is up there behind locked doors in the Grand Central Building, what is it, the twelfth floor? people everywhere and you know he has to have a roomful of guns and an outer office and an inner office, in this very legitimate well-cared-for building that straddles Park Avenue at Forty-sixth. So these are the conditions. But they know that and they know it is difficult, the man Maranzano has been in the business his whole life, it is not a sucker's proposition we are talking about and the Unione knows for this job they need the ace of spades. And Dutch comes to me and he says look Bo you don't have to do it this is their special Italian thing they like to clean out their generations every once in a while, but as a favor they have asked for you, and it wouldn't hurt us to be where they owe us a very big one so I say of course, I mean I was honored, of all the guns it's my gun they want, it was like I did this and I was in glory for the rest of my days, this one thing, like Sergeant York. You know I love to be reliable. I mean I like wining and dining and laying pretty women, I like the ponies I like the crap table, I like to come into a room cut an indolent swath, but under that I like best of all to be reliable, that is the purest pleasure, the pleasure of my purest being where someone will say not this one not that one, but Bo Weinberg, where someone will ask me and I will nod yes and it will be done as smoothly and quickly and easily as that nod, and they will know that and consider it done, as it will be, so when they read about it in the newspapers a day later, a week later, it's another unsolved mystery of a self-ordering world, another sweet tale of the tabloids. So I go to the meeting and I won't say his name but he's there and he says in that voice of a healed cut throat what do you need, and I say get me four police badges that's all. And his eyebrows go up but he says nothing and the next day they are in my hands, and I get my guys and take them to the haberdashery and we all dress ourselves like detectives in those raincoats and derbies and we walk right into the joint and flip open our wallets police you're under arrest, and they all go to the wall and I open the door the guy is behind his desk rising from his chair very slow on the uptake the man is seventy seventy-five he doesn't move too good I stand and brace myself on the front edge of the desk and I place the shot cleanly in the eye. But here is the funny part that building has marble halls and it sounds like no-man's-land it sounds through the open doors down the halls the stairwells the elevator shafts the shot heard round the world and everyone scrams, my guys, the hoods against the wall, everyone is running like hell and grabbing elevators and leaping down the stairs three at a time. And by the time I get out of there with this hot piece in my pocket doors are beginning to open up and down I hear those panics you know when people know something terrible has happened and they start shouting, and I lose my head I run down the stairs, I run up the stairs, and I get lost in this fucking building winding around corridors looking for exits walking into cleaning closets, I don't know I get lost, and somehow, somehow, when I get to the bottom I am not on the street I am in Grand Central Terminal and it is five six o'clock in the evening the place is like grand central, people in every direction making trains, standing waiting for the gates to open, the train announcements echoing in all that noisy mumble, and I attach myself to the crowd waiting for the five thirty-two and I slip the piece in some guy's pocket, I swear that's what I did, in his topcoat, he's holding his briefcase in his left hand he's got his *World-Telegram* folded for reading in his right hand and just as the gate opens and everyone presses forward in it goes so gently he doesn't even feel it and I saunter away as he gets through the gate and rushes down the ramp for his seat and, can't you see it, hello dear I'm home my God Alfred what's this in your pocket eek a gun!

And he is laughing now, tears of laughter in his eyes, one precious instant in the paradise of recollection, and even as I'm laughing with him I think how fast the mind can move us, the way the story is a span of light across space. I know he certainly got me off that boat that was heaving me up and down one foot at a time through an atmosphere rich in oil, I was there in Grand Central with my hand delivering the piece into Alfred's coat pocket but at the same time with my hands on the starched white tablecloth fiddling with the matchbook in the Embassy Club of the smart life, and the skinny girl singer doing ''Bye Bye Blackbird'' and outside in Manhattan the idling limousines at the curb sending their thin exhaust into the wintry night.

I became the object of his baleful stare. And what are you laughing at, he said, you think it's funny, wiseass? The story was clearly over, as in juggling when the ball you throw up finds the moment to come down, hesitates as if it might not, and then drops at the same speed of that celestial light. And life is no longer good but just what you happen to be holding.

You think it's funny, wiseass? He was a man who in his day took care of a great many people. May you last that long in your season till the last minute of your life at threescore years and ten. Then you may laugh. He was a greaser of consequence, Maranzano, not some piece of crazed slime like Coll who you couldn't ever put enough bullets in. Not like Coll that mick fuck of a child-killer for whom one death was not enough. But I killed Coll! he shouted. I turned him to spit and shit and blood in that phone booth. *Brrrrupp!* Up one window. *Brrrrup!* Down the other. I killed him! These are facts, you miserable wretch of a kid, but do you know what it is to do that, *do you know what it is to be able to do that*? You're in the Hall of Fame now! I killed Salvatore Maranzano! I killed Vincent Mad Dog Coll! I killed Jack Diamond! I killed Dopey Benny! I killed Maxie

Stierman and Big Harry Schoenhaus, I killed Johnny Cooney! I killed Lulu Rosenkrantz! I killed Mickey the driver and Irving and Abbadabba Berman, and I killed the Dutchman, Arthur. He stared at me his eyes bulging as if he was about to break the ropes that bound him. Then it was as if he could not look at me anymore. I have killed them all, he said bowing his head and closing his eyes.

LATER HE WHISPERS TO ME TAKE CARE OF MY GIRL DON'T LET HIM DO IT TO HER GET her away before he does her too, do I have your promise? I promise, I tell him in the first act of mercy in my life. For now the engine is idling and the tug rocks wildly in the wash of the ocean waves, I never knew they made a point of being out here too even bigger more ferocious with their own life in the middle of nowhere. Irving comes down the ladder and Bo and I both watch him in the economy of his movements swing open the double doors at the rear of the cabin and step outside and hook them fast. Suddenly the clean rage of air has blown out the smell of the oil and cigar, we are outdoors in here, I see the height of the heavy seas like gigantic black throats in the dim cast of our cabin light and Irving is at the stern rail, which he unhooks and lifts and stows neatly to the side. The boat is yawing in such a wallow that I have gone back to my position on the side bench, which I affix myself to by bracing my heels against a steel deck plate and clutching the bulkheads on either side of me. Irving is a true sailor mindless of the rising and falling deck and no less of the splashing he has taken about the legs of his pants. He is back inside, his thin gaunt face is splotched with sea spittle, his thin hair glistens on his shining scalp, and methodically without asking my help he jimmies up one end of the galvanized tin tub and jams a dolly under it and shoves and bangs the dolly further and further under the tub to where he can use the leverage of his whole weight to hold down the dolly with one foot and pull the tub up on it, an oddly dry scraping sound reminding me that if it were a sandpail and nobody's feet were in it, it could be turned over and tapped and leave whole a perfect cement sculpture of an overturned laundry tub perhaps even showing the embossed letters of the manufacturer. Bo's knees are now raised to a painful angle and his head is even lower, he is just about folded in half, but Irving fixes that next, after he jams wood shivs under the four rubber wheels of the dolly, he opens a steel tool kit and removes a fisherman's knife and cuts Bo's ropes, and lassoes them off and helps Bo up off the kitchen chair and stands him up in the tub on the dolly on the deck of the tugboat here at the very top of the Atlantic Ocean. Bo is shaky, he moans, his legs are buckling he lacks circulation and Irving calls to me, tells me to support Bo's other side, and oh this is just what I prefer not to do in my criminal training, exactly this, feeling Bo's palsy arm around me, smelling his hot breath, the sweat under his arm all the way through his black jacket on my neck, his hand fluttering grabbing my head like a claw, clutching my hair, his elbow drilling into the flesh of my shoulder, the man in his heat and animation resting his weight on me moaning over my head and his whole body in tremors. Here I am supporting the man I am helping to kill, we are his sole support, he holds on for dear life, and Irving says it's all right Bo, it's okay, and as calm and encouraging as a nurse, he kicks out the right stern shiv, we are facing the open deck you see, and commands me to do likewise with the shiv on my side, which I do quickly and accurately and we roll Bo on the dolly quite easily with the sea's help to the open hatch, where he lets go of us and grabs the framework standing now there alone his cement tub vehicle shooting back and forth like roller skates he can't quite manage yelling *ohh ohhoooooo*, his body twisting from the waist as he struggles to keep himself vertical and Irving and I stand back and watch this and all at once Bo learns the control, and manages to diminish the roll of the rubber wheels and with his legs locks his cement tub in some relatively governable slightness of motion and he trusts himself to look up and finds himself facing an open deck and a sea higher than he is and then lower than he is in a night of raging black wind, and his straining arms are being pulled out of the sockets and he takes great deep breaths of this awful wind and night and I see the back of his head moving and his shoulders and his head is up facing into this world of inexplicable terror and though I can't hear it for the wind I know he is singing and though I can't hear it I know the song, it is blown away by sea wind, his farewell chant, the song in his mind, all anybody ever has, and so Bo Weinberg was on his own in catastrophic solitude when the pilot engaged the engine and the boat suddenly shot forward and Mr. Schultz in his shirtsleeves and suspenders appeared and came up behind him and lifted one stockinged foot and shoved it in the small of Bo's back, and the hands broken from their grasp and the body's longing lunge for balance where there was none, careening leaning backward he went over into the sea and the last thing I saw were the arms which had gone up, and the shot white cuffs and the pale hands reaching for heaven.

TWELVE

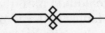

When I was through she didn't say anything. She handed me the wine bottle. I tilted my head up to drink from it and when I looked again she was no longer sitting beside me but had slid over the mossy bank and was by means of crevasses in the rocks and the small pine saplings growing from them lowering herself down the side of the gorge. I lay on my belly and watched. When she was two-thirds of the way down the mist enveloped her.

I wondered if she was going to do something really stupid. If I had told my story too well. I had not included everything, that for instance when Irving and the pilot were talking in the wheelhouse Bo Weinberg begged me to go below and see what was happening to her. I had done that and heard a little, not much, because the boat's engines were so loud down there. I listened for a few minutes outside the door of the cabin where Mr. Schultz had taken her and then I had gone back up to the deck and told Bo she was all right, that Mr. Schultz was pacing back and forth and explaining his point of view. But I had just wanted to make it easy for him.

"You wanted life?" I had heard Mr. Schultz shout. "Here, Miss Debutante, this is it, this is what it looks like!"

And then I couldn't hear anything for a while. I hunkered down in the passageway and just before I was about to give up I put my ear to the door and I heard his voice again: "You don't care for what's dead, do you? I'm telling you aside from the actual details he's dead. Can you understand that? You can forget the dead, can't you? I think you've forgotten already, haven't you? Well, I'm waiting, it's either a yes or a no. What? I can't hear you!"

"Yes," she said, or must have. Because then Mr. Schultz said: "Ahh, that's too bad. That's too too bad for Bo," and then he laughed. "Because if I thought you loved him I might have changed my mind."

I grabbed her skirt and shook it out and tossed it over the side and watched it float into the mist and disappear. What was I expecting? That she would find it, put it on, and climb back up? I was not acting sensibly.

I dropped over the side and turned my back to the gorge and went after her. It was harder than it looked, I found that out almost immediately with my head barely below the edge when the root I put my foot on broke away and I almost fell. I didn't like staring at rock face three inches from my nose. The rocks were scratching the shit out of my elbows and knees. I was in a panic of descent, I don't know what I feared, that she would just leave me there forever, that someone would find her, take her, do something bad to her. Some woods maniac just waiting for the opportunity. But it was more than that, that she would find him, that oblivious to the uses that could be made of her she would somehow hone in on him wherever he was skulking, in whatever foul den. Some of the pine saplings had stickum on them which glued up my hands and helped me to hold on. I felt the heat on my back, the farther I descended the hotter it was becoming. In one place there was a ledge and I stopped to rest: the sound of the water was mountainous, like coal pouring down a chute. Getting off the ledge was harder than getting on. Below it there were fewer and smaller saplings to hold on to. Soon there were none and I held on by sticking my sneakers in cracks and clutching outcroppings with my fingers. Then all at once it clouded up, it was chilly, and I realized there were boulders to stand on, and so, bit by bit I climbed down these piled boulders to the bottom and stood in a white mist with the sun high above me diffuse and pale.

The waterfall was to my right about twenty or thirty yards, it was the last and longest fall of the water and had not been visible from the top. It came home to me that falling water is what makes gorges, I mean this could not have been news to anyone but it was practically the first bit of nature I had ever seen in operation. I have read about dinosaurs too but that would not be the same as finding the bones of one. The water coursed swiftly past where I stood on a steeply tilted bank of sand and rock, the channel couldn't have been more than six or eight feet wide but it was the widest here of any place that I could see right or left. Her skirt lay on the ground where I had flung it. I rolled it up under my arm and I headed to the left away from the waterfall, and soon I was on boulders again, jumping from one to another with the water boiling beneath and around them, this was all in a generally downhill direction, I felt as if I was descending into a pore of the planet, and then I came around a bend and was looking down at a cantilevered ledge shaped like an enormous arrowhead, and piled on it were her clothes and shoes and socks. I leapt down and ran to the edge, I saw below me a clear black pool of water entirely still except for a silver rim of spill off at the far side.

It seemed to me I looked at this water until anybody under it would have to surface or drown. I was terrified, I pulled off my sneakers and shirt and prepared to jump in, I don't swim very well but I felt I could dive down in the water if I had to and at this moment the water shook and she broke into the air, her head and shoulders rising, and shouted or drew a great gasping breath that was like a cry of pain as the water poured off her shoulders, and then she threw her arms behind her and settled and floated on her back with her arms outstretched and lay there in the water with her chest heaving and her legs seeming to attenuate and wither as they floated downward in the black water.

After a while she was upright, shaking her head and smoothing her hair. She swam sidestroke out of my sight and appeared a minute later where I was not looking, climbing up onto the ledge with her body pale and wet and her teeth chattering and her lips blue. She looked at me without recognition. I rolled my shirt into a wad and rubbed her as she stood with her knees pressed together and her arms across her breasts, I rubbed her shoulders and back, the backs of her legs and after a moment's hesitation her backside and then the front of her legs while she stood and held her hands at her mouth and shivered herself warm. Then, for the second time in my life, I watched Mrs. Preston get dressed.

SHE SAID LITTLE ON THE WALK BACK. WE FOLLOWED THE GORGE TO WHERE IT WENT dry, and then widened on smaller rocks, and finally flattened out with the land. I was overwhelmed and could not speak on my own initiative and waited for her, and waited upon her, I felt we had an alliance of sorts, but it was conditional, as if I still had to grow up, I felt ignorant, I felt chastened and foolish and like a child. We walked again through the brown pine-needle forest and found the logging trail and came out into the meadows. She said, "Did he really ask you to protect me?"

"Yes."

"How very strange," she said.

I didn't answer.

"I mean that he would think I couldn't take care of myself," she said by way of clarification. She stooped where the sun shone through the trees to pick a small blue flower drooping over like a bell. "And you promised him you would?"

"Yes."

She came up to me and hung the flower over my ear and I found myself holding my breath till I no longer felt her touch. She sent out a very secret and indiscriminate beaming attraction, Mrs. Preston, as if it was always there whether you were or not.

"Oh don't move it," she said. "You're such a pretty little devil, do you know that?"

"That's what they tell me," I said and a few minutes afterward we scooted down a wooded embankment on our heels and came out to the dirt road and so eventually to the paved road leading down the hill to

Onondaga. I walked backward to look at her in the sun. Her hair had lost its wave and was dried sleek and off the forehead with the tracks of her fingers showing her careless attention to it. She had not a bit of makeup on her face but those full lips were their natural color now and her skin had regained the blush of her life. She was still not smiling though, and she had reddened, swimmer's eyes. Before we got back to the hotel she asked me if I had a girlfriend and I said I did, and she said whoever that girl was was lucky, but the truth was when she asked I felt guilty because I was no longer thinking of little Becky, who seemed to me now no more interesting than a child, but only of her. I was frightened by her, this woods guide, oh what she had shown me, like some counselor with a whistle on a lanyard, for the first time I understood what a match she made with Mr. Schultz, she took her clothes off to gunmen, to water, to the sun, life disrobed her, I understood why she went with him, this was not like mothers and fathers of ordinary existence, there was no consideration of love, it was not a universe of love they lived in, fucking and killing as they did, it was a large, empty resounding adulthood booming with terror.

I thought about her from the moment we went to our separate rooms and I lay on my bed in the late afternoon as dull-witted as the weather which hung hot and heavy in the Onondaga Hotel with the gauzy white curtains motionless in the open windows. The curtains grew gray, darkened, and were lit by a broad flashing and after an interval there was a muffled distant thunder. I now liked her far more than I had and knew in fact I might even be sweet on her, as how could a poor boy not after what she had put me through. Of course I had not entirely lost my wits and knew that whatever feelings I had I would suffer them in silence if I wanted to live on Earth a little while longer. I closed my eyes and watched her again climbing out of the pool at the bottom of the gorge with her nipples all crimped and blue and her pale pubic hair stringy with dripping water. I thought this time I was seeing someone who had tried to die, though of course I couldn't be sure because she lived an enlarged existence, it was not her nature to be contained by judgments. I wondered what would happen if her intimacy with Mr. Schultz prevailed over my confidences and she told him the things I'd reported. But I had the feeling she would not, that she had the character of independence, that she lived alone in some sort of mystery of her own making and that it was her integrity to be self-driven and self-communicating only, however alluringly close she might drift toward anyone at any given moment. I told myself that she had finally expressed some appropriate human grief and thought maybe that was a large part of my new liking for her, or tried to persuade myself of that anyway, even though it didn't quite jibe with the heavy tool I found in my hand with its own made-up mind existing, as she did, in the demonstrated inadequacy of my thought. I was resolved by the time I had had a cold shower in the big white bathroom all my own and had dressed for the evening in my suit and tie and glasses that no matter what my feelings they would not deter me from the justice my life demanded. I really had promised Bo Weinberg I would look after her and protect her, and now that I had told her, I would have to, but I hoped for my sake as well as hers that it wouldn't ever come to that.

THIRTEEN

By now in our stay at the Onondaga Hotel, as in any billet occupied for any length of time, the troops had been provided with a supplemental bill of fare that was more like home. Mr. Schultz had established a supply line from New York and once a week a truck came up with steaks and chops, racks of lamb, fish on ice, delicatessen, good booze and beer, and every couple of days someone went down to Albany, where an airplane landed with fresh New York rolls and bagels and cakes and pies and all the newspapers. The hotel kitchen was kept hopping, but nobody in there seemed to mind, as I thought they would, the implied judgment in all of this seeming to have escaped them. Everyone was without undue pride or umbrage or sensitivity, only too willing to cook and serve Mr. Schultz everything he provided them with, and in fact seemed to pick up in their own qualifications just being proximate to the big time.

Dinner became a ritual occasion as if we were all a family gathering at the same hour, though at different tables, at the end of the day. The dinners tended to go on awhile and were often the occasion for extended reminiscences on Mr. Schultz's part. He seemed relaxed at these times unless he drank too much, in which case he became surly or depressed and glared at one or another of us if we seemed to be having too good a time despite him, or eating too happily the food on our plates, which he liked to ask us to pass over to him for spite so that he could spear this or that morsel for himself before giving the plate back, he did this to me several times, which never failed to enrage me or cause me to lose my appetite, once he went over to the other table and took a steak from their platter, it was as if he couldn't be generous and hospitable without feeling at the same time that people were getting the best of him, and on these nights dinner was most unpleasant with Miss Drew excusing herself when she didn't like what was going on, it really took the heart out of you to think he begrudged the very food going into your mouth, it was demeaning to have your portion violated, and these evenings were not good evenings at all.

But as I say for the most part if he stayed sober he was even-tempered at dinner as if the days he spent showing Onondaga New York his sunny disposition and altruistic nature somehow actually made him feel right with the world. And on this particular evening I knew definitely I would get to eat everything I put on my plate because we had two guests at our regular table, Dixie Davis, who seemed to be staying past the hour of his return to New York, and the priest from St. Barnabas Catholic Church, Father Montaine. I like it that when the father arrived he stopped first at the table by the door to greet Mickey and Irving and Lulu, and Dixie Davis's driver who was seated with them, and to chat for a few minutes with a lot of jovial priestly banter. He was pretty lively for a man of God, he rubbed his hands with enthusiasm when he talked as if only good things could happen, he was brimming with ambitions for his small and not terribly well-off parish, St. Barnabas being a modest neighborhood church down by the river, where the streets were narrowest and the houses small and close together, and it was made of wood rather than stone like the Holy Spirit up on the hill, although the inside was just about as large and even more decorative with its painted plaster Christ and attendant saints hooked up along the walls.

On the menu was roast beef, served well-done the way I liked it, and fresh asparagus I was not wild about, and homemade french fries, big thick cuts of them, and salad greens, which I don't touch on principle, and there was real French wine I was learning to develop a taste for but did not indulge in for the same reason that Drew Preston was seated as far away as possible across the table from Mr. Schultz. I sat on Mr. Schultz's left and this Father Montaine on his right, and to my left was Dixie Davis, and Drew Preston sat between him and Mr. Berman. Dixie Davis chattered uncontrollably, perhaps he had been worked over a bit during the afternoon meeting, perhaps he had brought the wrong intelligence or his legal opinion had not met with favor, but whatever it was he couldn't stop talking, maybe it was just the fact of being seated next to the most beautiful aristocratic woman he had ever seen, who wore a plain black dress that set off her elegant neck, which was wound with a single string of pearls in each of which glowed a pinpoint of the light of the hotel chandelier, but he was telling Mrs. Preston how he'd gotten started in the legal profession, from what humble beginnings, reminiscing with hysterical self-satisfaction while she nodded her lovely head to keep him going and resolutely packed away everything in sight on her plate and downed several glasses of wine, which he poured happily for her while he continued to bask in her presence and entreated to impress her with the facts of his craven life. I know I wouldn't have boasted about hanging around the greasy spoons near magistrates court sucking up to bail bondsmen so that they would tip me off when some poor slob was arraigned and needed a lawyer. That's the way he'd got started, building up a practice from the daily court traffic of numbers runners at twenty-five bucks per rap of the gavel. "The rest is

history," he said with his toothy, downturned smile. I noticed too he sat
with a hunch and his head pushed forward toward its pompadour, so that
all his grooming and fine wardrobe was wasted on the posture of unctu-
ousness. I don't know why I had taken such a dislike to the man, I hardly
knew him, but I felt sitting next to him and watching him trying to look
down Drew Preston's dress that I should be sitting at the other table with
Irving and Lulu and the boys, not with this intellectual who did not once
address a remark to me or even appear to notice that I was sitting there to
his right.

And then he took a snapshot out of his wallet, it was of a woman in
a halter and sun shorts squinting into the sun with her hands on her ample
hips and her feet in their high-heeled shoes pointed outward, one before
the other, and he placed it in front of Drew Preston, who peered down at
it without touching it as if it was some object of natural curiosity, like a
cricket or a praying mantis.

"That's my fiancée," he said, "the actress Fawn Bliss? Maybe you've
heard of her."

"What?" Drew Preston said. "You don't mean it—*Fawn Bliss*?" she
said enunciating the name in tones of such incredulity that the lawyer
assumed she couldn't believe her good fortune in sitting next to him at the
dinner table.

"That's the lady," Dixie Davis said, grinning and gazing at the snapshot with insipid adoration. Drew Preston caught my glance and her eyes
glazed over and then crossed and I started to laugh, I didn't know she
could do that, and it was at this moment I became aware of Mr. Berman,
directly opposite, regarding me over the tops of his glasses, and he didn't
have to say a word or even tilt his head, I knew that I had been listening
to the wrong conversation. For all my resolve to stay alert I had been
unable to take my eyes off Mrs. Preston, a truth I felt in the bones of my
neck which actually creaked in their reluctance to swivel me around in the
direction of Father Montaine and Mr. Schultz.

"Ah, but you must make the spiritual journey," the father was saying
in his vigorous way, eating and drinking as he spoke so that the words
were like what he was eating, "you must ask for the catechisme, you must
hear the Gospel, you must purify yourself and prepare for election and
undergo the scrutinies. Only then can you undergo baptisme and have the
confirmahshun, only then can you receive the sacramahnt."

"How long does all that take, Father?"

"Oh well, this depends. A year. Five years, ten? How quickly you open
your heart to the mysteries."

"I can move faster than that, Father," Mr. Schultz said.

I didn't dare look at Mr. Berman because he would immediately see
that I had been caught unawares. Since meeting the father that time on the
sidewalk in front of his church we had gone one Wednesday to St. Barnabas's Bingo Night, and Mr. Schultz actually ran a few games, calling out

the magic numbers from the balls that popped into the cup, and making a big deal of it when someone won a dollar or two. Oh yes, and then he spoke into the ear of the father, who announced with great excitement Mr. Schultz's blessed generosity in putting up a special grand prize for the end of the evening of twenty-five dollars and there was a big round of applause, Mr. Schultz receiving it with a modest hand held in the air and a big sheepish smile, while all this time Mr. Berman and I sat in the back and thought about bingo cards, and he took a card and gave numerical values to each letter and showed me a possible way to handicap the lines after each number was called out, and then described to me several different ways an honest game could be rigged. But I didn't think how I could be faulted for not knowing the game of bingo was the first step in the conversion process.

The father put down his knife and fork and leaned back in his chair still chewing. He looked at Mr. Schultz, his heavy eyebrows raised in compassionate priestly skepticism. "From the Jewish to the Holy Church is a great revolution."

"Not so great, Father, not so great. We are in the same ballpark. Why else would all your big shots wear yarmulkes? I notice also you keep talking about our guys and reading our Bible. Not so great."

"Ah, but this is the point exactement, how we read, what we accept, this is the point, is it not?"

"I know guys, Catholic guys I grew up with, business associates, am I right, Otto?" Mr. Schultz said looking over to Mr. Berman, "Danny Iamascia, Joey Rao, guys like that. They think the way I think, they hold to the same virtues of right and wrong, they hold the same respect for their mothers, I have depended on Catholic businessmen all my life, Father, and how could I, and they on me, if we didn't understand one another like blood brothers."

With a deliberation matching these solemn sentiments he refilled the father's wineglass. Everyone had grown quiet.

Father Montaine gave Mr. Schultz a glance of Gallic reproach and then picked up the glass and drank it off. Then he patted his lips with his napkin. "Of course," he said very softly as if he was speaking of something better left unsaid, "there is in the special cases of the religious mature, another way."

"Now you're talking. The short form," Mr. Schultz said.

"In these case, I don't know, we must 'ave the confidahns that it is truly a beginning of the submisshun to the Lord Jesu Christe."

"I give you my word I couldn't be more sincere, Father. I brought it up, didn't I? I live a difficult life. I make important decisions all the time. I need strength. I see men I know take their strength from their faith and I have to think I need that strength too. I am just a man. I fear for my life like all men. I wonder what it's all for. I try to be generous, I try to be good. But I like the idea of that extra edge."

"I understan', ma son."

"How about Sunday," Mr. Schultz said.

Aᴼᴛᴇʀ coffee Drew Preston excused herself and a few minutes later the party broke up and Mr. Schultz invited Father Montaine to the sixth floor in the hotel, where they sat in his suite and drank from a bottle of Canadian whiskey on the table and smoked cigars and enjoyed themselves like fast friends. I thought looking in on them they even looked alike, both of them stolid and neckless and sloppy with their ashes. Dixie Davis was in there with them. The rest of the gang was in Mr. Berman's office, sitting around looking glum and not saying much. Finally the father went home and everyone moved to Mr. Schultz's suite, no one called a meeting or anything like that we all just wandered in and sat down, and everyone was very quiet while our boss paced back and forth and gave us his thinking. "Mickey, you understand, don't you, Mickey would understand after all, I've got to be ready, I can't take chances, I need all the help I can get. Who knows? Who knows? Years ago I remember being very impressed by that Patrick Devlin, you remember the Devlin brothers they ran most of the Bronx beer at the time, so we was just getting started and I wanted to teach him a lesson, he was the tough one, we hung him up by the thumbs, you remember, Lulu? but he didn't know what we had in mind he thought we were killing him and he screamed for a priest. Well that impressed me. Not his mother, not his wife, not nobody but his priest when he thought he was dying. It gave me a pause for thought. I mean you look to your strength in moments like that, am I right? Actually alls we did was smear some guts and shit from a dead rat on his eyes and tape it down with adhesive tape and we left him hanging there in his own cellar so's they would find him, although by the time they did, the stupid fucks, he'd lost the use of his sight. But I never forgot he wanted the priest. Those things stay with you. I like that little french-fried Canuck, I like his church, I'm gonna put a new roof on it so it don't leak during the sacred moments, it gives me a good feeling, you know what I mean? I get a good feeling every time I walk in there, I don't understand Latin, but I don't understand Hebrew neither, so why not both, is there a law against both? Christ was both, for christsake, what's the big deal? They push confession, I can't pretend I'm wild about that, no offense, but I'll deal with it when the time comes. This mustn't get to my mother—Irving, your mother neither, the mothers shouldn't know this, they wouldn't understand. I never liked the old men davening in the synagogue, rocking swaying back and forth, everyone mumbling to himself at his own speed, the head going up and down the shoulders rocking, I like a little dignity, I like everyone singing something together, everyone doing the same thing at the same time, I like the order of that, it means something everyone goes down on their knees the same time, it puts a light on God, is this too deep for you, Lulu? Look at that, he is so unhappy, Otto, look at his expression he's gonna cry, tell him I'm still the Dutchman, tell him nothing is changed, nothing is changed, you dumb Hebe!" And he gave his gunman a big bear hug, laughing and pounding him on the back. "You know how it is with a trial, don't you, you know we get a little nervous when we're on the docket. That's all. That's all. It's not the last rites for christsake."

Nobody said anything by way of reply except Dixie Davis, who kept nodding and smiling his vacuous uh-hums of encouragement, everyone else was stunned, all in all it had been a stunning day. Mr. Schultz kept talking, but when I judged the moment proper I quietly slipped out and went to my room. Mr. Schultz was excessive, anyone who worked for him should know that, he couldn't stop, he took things to extremes, so that what might have started out as business, like everything else up here, he would want to do to the limit, he would go overboard in these feelings just as he did in his angers. I hardly thought we were in any danger of losing him to the priesthood, he just wanted a little more coverage, like another insurance policy, he'd all but said so, and unless you were a religious person yourself who thought there was just one denomination of God, that God came contained in one denomination and one only, he made a kind of superstitious sense, he always wanted more of everything, and if we were up here much longer he'd probably become a member of the Holy Spirit Protestant church too, God knows he could afford it, this was his usual blithe everyday voracity, Mr. Schultz's urge to appropriate was stronger than his cunning, it was the central force of him, it operated all the time and wherever he happened to be, he'd appropriated speakeasies, beer companies, unions, numbers games, nightclubs, me, Miss Drew, and now he was appropriating Catholicism. That was all.

FOURTEEN

But now, not only was Mr. Schultz's trial due to start in the first week of September, his conversion was to precede it, in one blow he had doubled the critical ceremonies of his life for us all to think about. The following days were very busy, another lawyer appeared whom I had never seen before, a dignified portly white-haired gentleman clearly not a familiar of gangsters or their mouthpieces, as I could tell by his stately and solemn demeanor and his old-fashioned glasses, which were supported solely by his nose and were tied to a black ribbon, from which they dangled when not in use, and also the fact that he brought with him a young assistant, also a lawyer, who carried both their briefcases. These new arrivals entailed an all-day closed-door conference in Mr. Schultz's suite and a visit by everyone the next morning to the courthouse. The matter of preparations for Mr. Schultz's religious induction entailed meetings with Father Montaine at the church. In addition there was all the usual business, which seemed to send everyone off in every direction except Drew Preston and me.

So I found myself one morning on top of a living horse of the countryside holding very tightly to the reins, which seemed to me not enough in the way of structured support, and trying to communicate reasonably with this very tall and wide-backed beast who pretended he didn't understand me. I had thought horses were supposed to be dumb. When I said something to slow him down he broke into a canter, and when I urged him to go faster to keep up with Miss Drew on her gray filly, he stopped and dipped his head and began to eat the sweet and luxuriant grasses of the field. His back was my realm but it was his back. I either bounced along hunched over him so that I wouldn't fall, while Drew Preston beside me told me what I should be doing with my knees and how my heels should be hooked into the stirrups, fine points I wasn't quite ready for, or I sat there in the sun looking past this grazer whose neck sloped down at a precipitous angle until his head disappeared entirely and listened to him tear bunches of grass with his big teeth and grind the stuff up in his molars while the field opened up between me and the only other living human in sight. This horse was an ordinary-enough-looking bay going to black between the eyes and across the rump, but in perversity he was a champion. I thought it was cruel of Mrs. Preston to arrange it for me to be humiliated by a horse. I achieved a new respect for Gene Autry, who not only rode so that it looked easy but managed to sing pretty much on key at the same time. My only consolation was that nobody from the gang was around to see me, and when we put the horses away in the farmer's stable and walked back to town I loved the feel of the earth under my own two feet and thanked God and His sunny day for being alive, though slightly lame and sore-assed.

We had a late breakfast in my tea shop. Nobody else was there and the woman was back in her kitchen, so we could talk quite freely, Mrs. Preston and I. I was awfully happy to be alone with her again. She had not once laughed at my struggles atop the horse, she had seemed seriously interested in my instruction and thought I would be a good rider after a few more lessons. I agreed. She looked very fine in her pale silk shirt with its big collar and open neck, and with her blue velvet riding jacket with the elbow patches of leather; we ate our cereal and eggs and toast in leisure and drank two cups of coffee and smoked my Wings while she asked me questions about myself and looked at me with the most intense concentration and listened to my answers as if nobody in all her life had ever interested her so much. I knew she looked at and listened to Mr. Schultz in this same manner but I didn't mind. I thought having her attention was a great privilege and excitement, we were friends, intimates, and I couldn't imagine anywhere else I'd rather be than with her at this moment, in this shop out of sight of everyone, having breakfast together and talking in this natural way, although it wasn't that natural since the situation impelled me to perform at my brilliant best.

I told her I came from a criminal background.

"Does that mean your father is a gangster?"

"My father disappeared a long time ago. It means my neighborhood."

"Where is that?"

"Between Third Avenue and Bathgate Avenue in the Bronx. And north of Claremont Avenue. It's the same section Mr. Schultz comes from."

"I've never been to the Bronx."

"I didn't think you had," I said. "We live in a tenement. The bathtub is in the kitchen."

"Who is we?"

"My mother and me. My mother works in a laundry. She has long gray hair. I think she's an attractive woman or could be if she took care of herself. She's very clean and neat, I don't mean that. But she's a little bit crazy. Why am I telling you these things? I've never talked about her to anybody and I feel bad now saying this about my own mother. She's very kind to me. She loves me."

"I would think so."

"But she's not quite right. She doesn't care about looking her best, or having friends, or buying things or getting a boyfriend or anything like that. She doesn't care what the neighbors think. She sort of lives in her head. She's got the reputation of being a nut."

"I think she has had a hard life. How long has your father been gone?"

"I was very little. I don't even remember him. He was Jewish, I know that much."

"Isn't your mother Jewish?"

"She's an Irish Catholic. Her name is Mary Behan. But she'd rather go to temple than to church. That's the kind of thing I mean. She goes upstairs and sits with the women in the synagogue. She takes comfort from that."

"And what is the family name? Not Bathgate."

"Oh, you heard that."

"Yes, when you enrolled in Sunday school at the Holy Spirit. Now I know where you got it." She was smiling at me. I thought she meant where I got the name, from Bathgate Avenue, the street of plenty, the street of the fruits of the earth. But she meant the habit of ending up in the wrong church. It took me a moment. She was trying not to laugh at her own joke, looking at me askance, hoping I wouldn't take offense.

"You know that never occurred to me," I said. "That I was following in the crazy family footsteps." I laughed and then she did. We had a good laugh, I loved her laughter, it was low and melodious, like a voice under water.

Afterward, outside, with the sun burning down hot on the empty street, and without making a point of it, we naturally turned to stroll in the opposite direction from the hotel. She took off her jacket and slung it over her shoulder. I watched our reflections wavering in the empty store windows with their TO LET signs. Our reflections were black, very little color in them. Yet the street burned in light. I felt I knew Drew Preston this morning as she seemed to be in herself, without pretending anything or being afflicted with one of her large emotional wine-induced introspections, I felt I knew her under her brilliance of beauty, almost so that I forgot it, as she herself must looking out from it, and I thought I understood her as she must have understood herself, as someone maintaining her being while in the grasp of others. It was the kind of thing that would appear to the gang as slumming, which is why they had taken such offense, but was really more dangerous than that, more vulnerable of spirit, and I think what interested her about me was that I was in my way doing the same thing.

We walked for several blocks. She had fallen silent. Every once in a while she glanced at me. Then all at once she took my hand and held it as we strolled along. Just as I had been giving her credit for a kind of real basic sensibleness, she had to hold my hand in broad daylight like a girlfriend. It made me very nervous but I couldn't offend her by pulling away. I did look behind us to see if anyone we knew was on the street. I cleared my throat. "Maybe you don't appreciate the position you're in," I said.

"What position is that?"

"Well you're my governess."

"That's what I thought, but apparently all this while you've been looking after me."

"I have. But to tell you the truth," I said, "so far you seem to have done all right on your own." The minute I said this I thought it sounded snide. "But I guess I would keep my word if you got into a jam," I said by way of expiation.

"What kind of a jam."

"Well for instance it's not good if you aren't in this walk of life to have seen anything, to know anything," I said. "They don't like witnesses. They don't like it for people to have something on them."

"I have something on them," she said as if the idea was hard to understand.

"Just a little," I said. "On the other hand nobody outside the gang knows you do so that's a slightly better position than, say, if the D.A. knew you were on that boat and wanted to know what had happened on it. Then you might be in serious danger."

She was thoughtful. "You don't talk as if you're one of them," she said.

"Well I'm not. Not yet. I'm trying to catch on," I said.

"He has a high regard for you, he says only good things about you."

"What things?"

"Oh, that you're very smart. And that you have guts. That is not an expression I'm particularly fond of. He could have said you're bold, or feisty or fearless, he could have said you're stouthearted. Would you mind my asking how old you are?"

"Sixteen," I said exaggerating only slightly.

"Oh my. Oh my," she said as she glanced at me and lowered her eyes. She was silent for a moment. She removed her hand from mine, which was a great relief although I longed for her to put it back. She said, "Well you must have done something for them to have heard about you and chosen you above all the others."

"What others? It's not like getting into Harvard University, Mrs. Preston. I happened to catch their attention, that's all. I connected. This gang, they make things up as they go along. They use what's to hand."

"I see."

"I'm here the same way you are."

"I didn't understand. I thought you were even related in some way."

We went down the hill to the river and walked to the middle of the bridge and stood at the wood rail and looked down at the water coming down the wide shallows and breaking with rushing intent around all the rocks and boulders.

"If I have something on them," Mrs. Preston said, finally, "don't you?"

"If I don't catch on," I said, "yes, I will have something on them. If for some reason they decide against me. Yes. Nobody can tell what Mr. Schultz will do," I said. "I'll be a danger to them if he decides I am."

She turned to look at me. Her expression was troubled, there might even have been a glimmering fear in her though I could not be sure in this light that passed like waves of summer heat through those pale green eyes. If she was frightened for me I didn't want that, it was undermining, I thought if she had the reckless assurance of her own charmed life she should grant me mine. This may have been the dangerous moment of our alliance, when it was clear in its extent, that we actually cared for each other, I could not bear to be contemplated as overmatched, as a lamb among wolves, I wanted equality with her. I pretended to think she was in fear for herself.

"I don't really think you have to worry," I said, with a harsh peremptory edge to my voice. "So far as I can judge Mr. Schultz has every reason to believe you're trustworthy. And even if he didn't I think you can probably rely on the fact that he would do as little as he could to convince himself that you are."

"He would? Why?"

"Why, Miss Lola, I mean Miss Drew, I mean Mrs. Preston? Why?" I thought now I had hurt her and I felt bad. I was showing her I was a man with a man's crude judgments. But then I backed away from her on the wood bridge and she knew what I was up to and she was smiling again and I started to laugh, and now she lunged forward to grab my hand and as I tried to pull away she said, "Why, why, no tell me, tell me," like a little girl in her entreaties and she pulled me to her.

We stood there. I said feeling the heat of her on my face: "Because as everyone except you seems to know, Mr. Schultz is a pushover for blondes."

"How do they know?"

"Everyone knows," I said. "It was even in the papers."

"I don't read the papers," she whispered.

My throat had gone dry. "How can you know everything you need to know if you don't read the papers?" I said.

"What is it I need to know?" she said gazing into my eyes.

"Well maybe if you don't work for a living you don't need to know anything," I said. "But some of us trying to learn a trade have to be up on the developments."

I felt weak in the knees, overwhelmed, a little sick in the heat, I felt as if I was disappearing into her eyes. I wanted her in such totality of desire that it was diffuse, aching all through me, like my own blood heat, I wanted her in my fingertips and my knees and my brain and my face and in the little bones of my feet. Only the cock was not at this moment affected. I wanted her behind the palate, where tears begin, in the throat, where words crumble on the breaking voice.

"Here's the latest development," she said. And she kissed me on the mouth.

Oɴ sᴜɴᴅᴀʏ ᴍᴏʀɴɪɴɢ ᴇᴠᴇʀʏᴏɴᴇ ᴡᴀs sᴛᴀɴᴅɪɴɢ ᴀʟʟ ᴛᴜʀɴᴇᴅ ᴏᴜᴛ ᴄʟᴇᴀɴ ᴀɴᴅ shining in front of the Church of St. Barnabas, even Lulu, who wore a dark blue double-breasted suit that was tailored to make as discreet as possible the bulge of the shoulder holster and piece under his left arm. This would have to have been the last week in August, a new weather was creeping up on the days, like a different kind of light, on the hillside behind my room some of the leafy trees had turned pale with little yellowing patches, and here in front of the church a wind was blowing along the street from the river so that as women of the parish climbed the steps the hems of their Sunday dresses furled around their legs. My own summer suit felt air-cooled and as we stood waiting my careful haircomb ruffled up and began to break the crust given it by my Vitalis.

Drew Preston held on to a big holiday hat that hid her eyes from me. She had white lace gloves on her hands that just barely came up to the wrist. She wore a dark conservative dress and hose with the seams proper and straight down her calves and low-heeled black pumps, which made her almost invisible in this setting. At her side Mr. Schultz was nervous and kept picking at the little carnation pinned to his lapel, he unbuttoned the jacket of his gray pinstripe to yank up his trousers, and then he discovered the buttons of the vest were not in the right holes and tore open the vest and rebuttoned it, and then he reset his jacket on his shoulders and then brushed imaginary lint from the sleeves, and then he discovered his shoelace was untied and was about to bend down when Mr. Berman tapped him on the shoulder and pointed to a car that had just come around the corner and pulled up to the curb and sat there with its motor running. "He's here," Mr. Schultz said and a moment later another car, a coupé, came around the corner and drove past us and pulled up at the end of the block, and then a third car appeared and it moved very slowly along the street and came to a stop where we were, a black Chrysler with the wheels hidden by the fenders, I think it must have been a custom-made model, I had never seen one like it. Mr. Schultz moved forward and we all stood in rank behind him as two unsmiling men got out and looked at all of us in that way that only cops and mob men consider people, with an officious but expertly quick assessment, and they gave curt nods to Mr. Schultz and Lulu and Irving, and one of them went up the steps and peered into the church and the other looked up and down the street with his hand on the rear car door and then the first one nodded from the top of the steps and the second opened the car door and a thin dapper man, quite short, got out and Mr. Schultz who had been standing by patiently, almost humbly, embraced him with joy, and he was someone whose name I will not give even here and now these many years later, a man I recognized immediately from his pictures in the *Mirror*, the scar under his jaw, the one droopy eyelid, the wavy hair, in the instant I saw him I found myself instinctively moving behind someone just out of his line of sight. He had a dusky sallow coloring that was almost lavender, he was shorter and slighter than I had imagined, he wore a well-tailored pearl gray single-breasted suit, and he politely shook hands with Abbadabba Berman and Lulu and Mickey and warmly embraced Irving and then was introduced to Drew Preston and he said in a whispery voice he was pleased to meet her and he said looking up at the blue sky, "What a nice day this is, Dutch, I think you must already have an in with Il Papa," and everyone laughed, especially Mr. Schultz, he was so happy, so honored that a man of this position would agree to come all the way up from New York to speak for him as his godparent and present him formally to the priest for admission to the Church.

That's the way it works, a Catholic in good standing has to testify as a kind of character witness, I had thought it would be someone from inside the gang, like John Cooney or even Mickey if nobody else was convenient, because the gang was self-sufficient and whatever it needed it always arranged from its own resources, and I had no reason to believe it would not do the same in this circumstance. But I looked at Lulu Rosenkrantz, who stood behind Mr. Schultz with a beaming content, all of the gang were at peace in this moment, everything made sense now, they had worried about this conversion as they had worried about the girl, as if the Dutchman was going off half-cocked in every direction, but he had surprised them again, of course it figured that he would want the most eminent of men to get him in, not only so that that way there would be no hitch but because it was a political honor, it signified a certain recognition. I saw it was an obeisance on his part, perhaps, but also a degree of acknowledgment from a peer, I was gratified, I thought this is what Mr. Berman must have meant when he talked about the time coming when everyone would read the numbers, they were working on it already with this ritual of amity. In fact it was an imprimatur of a kind, in the stately morning shadow of the church, good faith was arraying itself in procession, these were the first representations of the new world coming, the guys had thought it was religion he was doing but it was the rackets after all, and all in all I thought it was a cunning move by Mr. Schultz, although probably not without Mr. Berman's help, to make such use of his own blind impulses, a man no more sophisticated than superstitious, and who had been using his unaccustomed time in the country learning to ride horseback from a blue blood with that same all-around three-hundred-and-sixty-degree enterprise.

I wanted very badly on this morning to believe in Mr. Schultz's powers. I wanted order in his sway, I wanted everything in its place where it belonged, it was a working tyranny he ran and I wanted him to run it well, without wavering. I didn't want him to make an error just as I didn't want myself to lose the harmonies of gang life, if a distortion of his vision was dangerous to the ruling order, so was my brazen sin of thought, my madness of usurpation stirring at the root. In my mind as I stood there I checked myself for weaknesses, unconscious revelations, errors of demeanor, losses of circumspection, and I found none. My patrolling mind found only the quiet, the peace of the unsuspecting.

At this moment the St. Barnabas Church bells began to ring as if confirming me in my hopes. My heart lifted and I experienced a rush of fierce well-being. While it is true I detest church organs I have always liked the bells that peal out over the streets, they are never quite on key but that may be why they suggest the ancestry of music, they have that bold and happy ginggonging that makes me think of a convocation of peasants for some primitive festivity such as mass fucking in the haystacks. Anyway not many emotions can be sustained, but self-satisfaction is one of them, and as I stood there with the air ringing I could review my overall position and feel confident that it was stronger now at this point of the summer than it had been at the beginning, that I was in the gang more firmly and seemed to have secured myself with varying degrees of respect from the others, or if not respect, acquiescence. I had a gift for handling myself with grown-ups, I knew which ones to talk to, and which ones to be clever with, and which ones to shut up in front of, and I almost astonished myself that I did it all with such ease, without knowing in advance what I was doing, and having it come out right most of the time. I could be a Bible student, and I could shoot a gun. Whatever they had asked me to do I had done it. But more than that, I knew now I could discern Mr. Schultz's inarticulate genius and give it language, which is to say avoid its wrath. Abbadabba Berman was uncannily perceptive, he had surprised me with my Automatic in that same manner of advanced thinking that allowed him to know exactly where I lived when he used the Bronx precinct cop to summon me. But I was no longer awed. Besides, he was so clearly given over to my education, how could I have gotten this far if he knew everything about me and could scan my mind, awake or dreaming, and know what inherited empowerment was looped in there, like my fate? Even if he knew about me exactly what I feared most, and I was still here, and not only here but growing and filling out to his hopes, then he had his own purposes for me, and my secret was good anyway. But I didn't really believe that he knew, I believe that in the most important knowledge I was now ahead of him, and that his inadequacy, finally, was that he would know everything except the crucial thing.

So I felt that things couldn't be better, I was elated just to be in the company I was in, there seemed to me no limit to the heights of which I was capable, Drew was right, I was a pretty little devil, as the eminent guest went up the steps and into the church with Mr. Schultz I even wished that someone had introduced me, or that I might have at least been noticed, though I had made a point not to be, but I was not put out, I knew that in the excitement of historic moments the niceties are sometimes scanted, I was directly behind these great men looking up at their haircuts, I was in a line of ascension with these famous gangsters of my yearnings, I was feeling generous and eager to give everyone the benefit of every doubt, even at the back of the line, at the bottom of the front steps, and the last in the procession that stopped now in the church entrance and waited while the regular service went on until it was time for Father Montaine to come off the altar and greet Mr. Schultz and usher him in to the church building as a symbol of his entrance to Catholicism.

As it happened this would take longer than anyone expected. Abbadabba Berman came back down the stairs to have himself a smoke on the sidewalk, I cupped the match for him against the wind, and then Irving came out to join us, and the three of us leaned with our backs against the visitors' glamorous streamlined Chrysler parked at the curb, and ignoring the other cars at each end of the block, we faced the edifice of St. Barnabas with its clapboard siding and wooden steeple. The bells now ceased with a little sequence of tapping afterthoughts, softer and softer, and I could hear faintly the different sound from inside the church of its organ. At this moment Irving came as close to a criticism of Dutch Schultz as I was ever to hear him utter.

"Of course," he said, as if he was continuing a conversation, "the Dutchman is wrong about one thing, he has no idea why the old Jews pray that way. Maybe if he knew he wouldn't say those things. Kid, you know the explanation of that?"

"I'm not big on religion," I said.

"I am not a religious man myself," Irving said, "but the way they nod and bow and don't keep still a minute, there's a very reasonable explanation for that. It's the way it is with candles, the old men praying in the synagogue are the flames of candles that sway back and forth leaning one way and another way, every one of them nodding and bowing like a little candle flame. That's the little light of the soul, which of course is always in danger of blowing out. So that's what that is all about," Irving said.

"That's very interesting, Irving," Mr. Berman said.

"But Dutch wouldn't know that. All he knows is it bothers him," Irving said in his quiet voice.

Mr. Berman held his elbow so that the hand holding the cigarette was up around his ear, which was his favorite position for thinking: "But when he says the Christians do everything in unison, he's right about that. They got a central authority. They sing together and they chant and they sit down and they stand up and they kneel and they do things in an orderly manner, everything under control. So he's right about that," Mr. Berman said.

WHEN THINGS FINALLY GOT GOING I FOUND MYSELF SITTING IN A PEW UP FRONT next to Drew Preston, which is where I wanted to be. I reminded myself that it was all right, that nothing had happened yet except that I had been admitted into the secret mysterious realm of her afflictions. That was all. She did not acknowledge me, which I both appreciated and agonized over at the same time. I blindly turned the pages of the missal. Her face in the church under her hat glowed in the soft colors of stained glass and suggested for me the more appropriate and ennobling role as her boy protector. But I wanted to fuck her so badly I could hardly stand. I didn't know if I would survive the service. Mr. Schultz had called this the short form and that made me wonder what the long form was like, in fact I understood for the first time the meaning of the word *eternal*.

I remember just a few things from the entire excruciatingly eternal service. The first was that Mr. Schultz went through it all, he was nominated, baptized, confirmed, and partook of the Eucharist, with his shoelace untied. The second was that when his honored godparent, standing just behind him, was directed by Father Montaine to place his hand on his shoulder, Mr. Schultz nearly jumped out of his skin. Maybe I fixed on these odd things because most everything else was going on in Latin and only when something actually happened did I really pay attention. I think Father Montaine was the only man in the world who would be allowed to pour a pitcher of water over Dutch Schultz's head not once but three times without suffering the consequences. He did this in a way I thought was lusty and full of liturgical enthusiasm as Mr. Schultz each time came up sputtering, with his eyes red and glaring while he tried to smooth his hair back without seeming to.

But the last thing I remember about that morning was the enigmatic presence at my side of my beautiful and amazing Drew, who became more innocent in my view the more devilishly I thought about her. She seemed to drink up the church music and become enameled in sanctity like one of the nun saints up in a niche on the wall. In the way my spinning world revolved now like some fiendishly juggled ball of God, her failure to acknowledge my presence beside her confirmed our conspiracy in my heart. I knew I could no longer deceive myself that I didn't adore her, and wouldn't destroy myself in submission to her, the moment, with the organ blasting away and the congregation singing at its most sacred pitch, she raised her white-gloved fingers to her lips and yawned.

PART THREE

FIFTEEN

The trial was almost upon us. I pulled my pistol practice and ran errands for Dixie Davis, who was by now in residence on the sixth floor. One morning when I had to deliver a letter for him to the courthouse clerk I stopped afterward to look through the little porthole windows of the doors to the courtrooms. None were occupied. Nobody said not to so I went into Part One and sat down. It was an open uncluttered kind of place, as opposed, say, to a precinct station: wood-paneled walls and big windows that were raised for the breeze and light globes hanging by chains from the ceiling. All the furniture in place for judge, jury, prosecution, defense, and audience. It was very quiet. I heard the ticking of the wall clock behind the bench. The courtroom sat there waiting was the impression I had. I had the impression that behind the waiting was a limitless patience. I understood the law had a prophetic utility.

I found myself entertaining a guilty conviction. I pictured Mr. Schultz being led off by the guards with the gang of all of us standing by not doing anything. I imagined him led away in an apoplectic rage, my last glimpse of his murderous being segmented by the diamond crisscross chain link welded across the rear windows of the Black Maria. I felt very bad.

Here I will say about Dutch Schultz that wherever he went he created betrayals of himself, he produced them perpetually from the seasons of his life, he brought betrayers forth from his nature, each in our own manner shape and size but having the common face of betrayal, and then he went murdering after us. Not that I didn't know, not that I didn't know. I took the elevator each night to the Schultz family dinner table and sat there aching in love or terror, it was hard to tell which.

A couple of nights before the trial a man named Julie Martin appeared who everyone in the gang knew except me. He was a stout man with jowls that shook as he talked, he was very much taller than Mr. Schultz or Dixie Davis, but he walked with a cane and wore a slipper on one foot. His eyes were very tiny and of indeterminate color and he needed a shave, he was gruff, with a voice even deeper than the

Dutchman's, and he was not at all well groomed, dark hairs curled off the back of his neck and his enormous hands had blackened fingernails as if he spent his time working on automobiles.

Drew Preston excused herself from dinner almost immediately and I was relieved she did. The fellow was trouble. Mr. Schultz treated him with a sardonic respect and addressed him as Mr. President. I didn't know why until I remembered Mr. Schultz's restaurant shakedown business in Manhattan, the Metropolitan Restaurant and Cafeteria Owners Association. Julie Martin had to be the man who ran it, that's what he was president of, and because most of the fashionable restaurants in the midtown area had joined the association, including Lindy's and the Brass Rail, Steuben's Tavern and even Jack Dempsey's, he was a pretty important man about town. He wouldn't be the one who actually threw the stink bomb through the window when the owner was reluctant to join the association, so I didn't understand why his fingernails were dirty or why he needed a haircut or why generally he didn't exude the confidence of a successful man of the rackets.

Apart from the occasional stink bomb, restaurant extortion was an invisible business, even more invisible than policy and almost as profitable. While diners were dining in the fine Broadway steakhouses, or while the old men were sitting in the cafeterias over their cups of coffee or sliding their trays past the hot table with its perpetual steam rising from the cooked carrots and cauliflower, the business went invisibly and brilliantly forward on the discreet conversation of men who were not ever, at the moment of their visits to any establishment, hungry.

Mr. Schultz was telling Julie Martin about his day of entry into the Catholic Church and bragging about who it was who had sponsored him. Julie Martin was not terribly impressed. He was a rude man and acted as if he had more important matters to attend to elsewhere. A bottle of whiskey was on the table, as there was now every night, and he kept pouring himself half tumblers of rye and drinking them down like table water. At one point he dropped his fork on the floor and called to the waitress, ''Hey you!'' as she was going past carrying a tray full of dirty dishes. She nearly dropped them. Mr. Schultz was by now fond of this girl, she was the one whom no generosity of tip or bantering small talk could persuade that she was not each night at dinner in danger of losing her life. Mr. Schultz had told me it was his ambition to lure her to New York to work in the Embassy Club, a great joke considering her all-consuming dread of him. ''For shame, Mr. President,'' he said now. ''This ain't one of your union help. You're in the country now, watch your manners.''

''Yeah, I'm in the country all right,'' the big man said in his basso. Then he delivered himself of a prodigious belch. I knew boys who had this ability, I had never trained in it myself, it was a weapon of the boor and implied a similar aptitude at the opposite end of the digestive system.

"And if I can get through this lousy dinner and you can get around to telling me what's on your mind that's so important I had to come all the way up here I'll be able to get the fuck out of your goddamn country and not too soon to suit me."

Dixie Davis sent a fearful glance in Mr. Schultz's direction. "Julie's a true New Yorker," he said with his down-at-the-mouth smile. "Take them out of Manhattan they go bananas."

"You've got a big mouth, you know that, Mr. President?" said Dutch Schultz looking at the man over his wineglass.

I didn't wait for dessert, even though it was apple cobbler, but went up to my room and locked the door and turned on the radio. Eventually I heard them all come out of the elevator and go into Mr. Schultz's suite. For a moment all their voices were talking at the same time in a kind of part song of diverse intent. Then the door slammed. In my peculiar state of mind I had an idea that seemed to me quite rational, that somehow I had invoked the argument, that my secret transgression had fired the metaphysical Dutchmanic rage, and that it happened only for the moment to be directed inaccurately at another of his men, and a valuable one too, as Bo was valuable. Not that I had any sympathy for the huge boor with the bad foot. I didn't know exactly what the fight was about except that it was serious enough and loud enough for me to hear the sound of it, if not the exact words, when I sneaked down the corridor and stood in front of the door. The exchange of angers terrified me because it was so close, like the loud close thunderclap of a lightning storm still some distance away, and I kept going back and forth from my room to the corridor to see if Drew's door was closed, to make sure she was not involved, and whenever the radio static crackled with extra snap I imagined I had heard a gunshot and ran out again.

This all went on over an hour or more, and then, it must have been about eleven o'clock, I did hear the real gunshot, there is no question what it is when it is that, the report is definitive, it caroms through the chambers of the ear, and when its echoes died away I heard the silence of the sudden subtraction from the universe of a life, and this time in the quaking reality of what I knew I sat on the side of my bed too paralyzed even to stand up and lock my room door. I sat there with my Automatic fully loaded and held it under a pillow on my lap.

What did I mean to have come with these men to their ferocious business in upstate hotels, was it to understand, only to understand? I had known nothing of their lives a few short months ago. I tried to believe they could have been doing all this without me. But it was too late, and they were so strange, they were all so strange. They all roiled up out of the same idea because they seemed to understand each other and make their measured responses accordingly, but I kept losing my fix on it, I was still to know what it was, this idea.

I can't say how many minutes passed. The door flew open and Lulu was standing there beckoning with his finger. I left my gun and hurried after him down the corridor into Mr. Schultz's suite. The furnishings were awry, the chairs were pushed back, this Julie Martin lay in his bulk across the coffee table in the living room, he was not yet dead but lay gasping on his stomach with his head turned sideways and a rolled-up hotel towel under his cheek and another towel rolled up neatly behind his head to take the blood, and both towels were reddening quickly, and he was gasping, and blood was trickling out of his mouth and nose and his arms hanging over the table were trying to find something to hold on to and his knees were on the floor and he was pushing back, pushing the tips of his feet with their one shoe off and one shoe on against the floor as if he was trying to get up, as if he thought he could still get away, or swim away, it was kind of a slow-motion breaststroke he was doing, whereas he was only lifting his broad back in the air and then slumping down again under its weight, and Irving was bringing more towels from the bathroom to put beside the coffee table where blood was dripping to the floor and Mr. Schultz was standing there looking down at this immense tortoiselike body, with its waving arms and eyes glazed blind like eyes from the sea, and he said to me, very calmly, quietly, "Kid, you got good vision, we none of us can locate the shell, would you be so good as to find it for me?"

I scrambled around on the floor and found under the couch the brass casing still warm of the thirty-eight-caliber round from his gun, which showed now under his belt with his jacket open, his tie was pulled down from his collar but somehow in this moment he glittered with a calm orderliness in all this mess of blood and unfinished death, he was still and thoughtful, and he thanked me courteously for the shell, which he dropped in his pants pocket.

Dixie Davis was sitting in a corner holding his arms around himself, he was groaning as if he was the one who had been shot. There was a soft knock on the door and Lulu opened it to admit Mr. Berman. Jumping to his feet Dixie Davis said, "Otto! Look what he's done, look what he's done to me!"

Mr. Schultz and Mr. Berman exchanged glances. "Dick," Mr. Schultz said to the lawyer, "I am very very sorry."

"To subject me to this!" Dixie Davis said, wringing his hands. He was pale and trembling.

"I am sorry, Counselor," Mr. Schultz said. "The son of a bitch stole fifty thousand of my dollars."

"A member of the bar!" Dixie Davis said to Mr. Berman, who was looking now at the agonized aimlessly repetitious movements of the sprawled body. "And he does this thing with me standing there? Takes out his gun in the middle of a sentence and shoots into the man's mouth?"

"Just calm down, Counselor," Mr. Berman said. "Just calm down. Nobody heard a thing. Everyone is asleep. They go to bed early in

Onondaga. We will take care of this. All you have to do is go to your room and close the door and forget about it.''

''I was seen at dinner with him!''

''He left right after dinner,'' Mr. Berman said looking at the dying man. ''He went away. Mickey drove him. Mickey won't be back till tomorrow. We have witnesses.''

Mr. Berman went to the window, looked out from behind the curtain, and pulled the shade down. He went to the other window and did the same thing.

''Arthur,'' Dixie Davis said, ''do you realize in a matter of hours there will be federal lawyers from New York checking into this hotel? Do you realize in two days your trial starts? In two days?''

Mr. Schultz poured himself a drink from a decanter on the sideboard. ''Kid, take Mr. Davis to his room. Put him to bed. Give him a glass of warm milk or something.''

Dixie Davis's room was at the far end of the hall, near the window. I had to physically help him, he shook so badly, I had to hold his arm as if he were an old man who could not walk by himself. He was gray with fear. ''Migod, migod,'' he kept muttering. His pompadour haircomb had collapsed over his forehead. He was soaking with perspiration, he emitted an unpleasant smell of onions. I sat him down in the armchair by his bed. Stacks of legal papers in folders were piled on the room desk. He looked at them and started to chew on his fingernails. ''I, a member of the bar of New York State,'' he muttered. ''An officer of the court. In front of my very eyes. In front of my very eyes.''

I thought perhaps Mr. Berman was right, there wasn't a sound from anywhere in the hotel as there would have been by now if the shot had been heard beyond our floor. I looked out of the corridor window and the street was empty, the streetlamps shone on stillness. I heard a door open and when I turned, there down the hall with the light behind her stood Drew Preston barefooted in her night shift of white silk, she was scratching her head and had a half-dopey smile on her lips, I will not speak here of the derangement of my senses, I pushed her back in her room and closed the door behind us and told her in urgent whispers to be quiet and go back to sleep, and I led her into her bedroom. In her bare feet she was about my height. ''What happened, has something happened?'' she said in her smoked-up voice full of sleep. I told her nothing and not to ask Mr. Schultz or anyone about it in the morning, just to forget it, forget it, and sealed my instruction with a kiss on her swollen mouth of sleep, and laid her down, smelling the lovely essence of her being gathered on her sheets and pillow like the meadows we had walked through, and put my hand on her small high breasts as she stretched and smiled in her moment, as always in her moment, and then I was gone and out the door, closing it quietly just as the elevator door opened at the other end of the corridor.

Mickey backed out of the elevator pulling a heavy wood-and-pipe-metal dolly, he did this as quietly as it could be done, I thought about the elevator boy and ducked behind the window drapes but Mickey had run it up himself and when he had maneuvered the dolly into the hall he turned out the light in the elevator and closed the brass gate not quite all the way.

The gang was in its element, the thing is when you're mob you move in the presence of violent death quickly and efficiently as a normal ordinary human being could not, even I, an apprentice, half-ill with dread and distraction, was able to follow orders and think and move in constructive response to the emergency. I don't know what they did to the body to make it still but it lay now quite dead across the coffee table and Irving was spreading editions of the New York dailies and the *Onondaga Signal* on the dolly, someone said one two three and the men rolled the immense cadaver of Julie Martin off the coffee table onto the newspapers, death is dirt, death is garbage, and that is the attitude they had toward it, Lulu wrinkling his nose and Mickey even averting his head as they handled this sack of human offal. Mr. Schultz sat in an armchair with his arms on the armrests like Napoleon and he didn't even bother looking, he was thinking ahead, planning what? convinced in his instinctive genius that however abrupt and sudden his murderous act had been, it had chosen the moment well, which is why the great gangsters don't get caught except by numbers and tally sheets and tax laws and bankbooks and other such amoral abstractions whereas the murders rarely stick to them. It was Abbadabba Berman who supervised the cleanup, pacing up and down in that sideways scuttle of his, his hat pushed back on his head, the cigarette in his mouth, it was Mr. Berman who thought to retrieve the cane and put it beside the body. He said to me, "Kid, go to the lobby and cover it so nobody notices the arrow."

I ran down the fire stairs three at a time, flight after flight, swinging around the landing posts, and got to the lobby, where the elevator boy sat dozing on the side chair next to the big snake plant with his arms folded across his tunic and his head on his chest. The clerk was similarly occupied behind his desk under the mailboxes. The lobby was empty and the street as well. I watched the indicator and in a minute the arrow began to swing around the circle, it came down around the one and kept going, to stop at the basement.

Out behind the hotel I knew they would have the car and that details I couldn't even anticipate would have already been thought through, there was a kind of comfort in that, I was an accessory after the fact, among my other problems, and when the elevator came back up to the lobby and the door opened Mickey put his finger to his lips and left the elevator as he had found it, lit, but with the brass folding gate pulled across, and he sneaked right back out to the fire stairs and after a minute I coughed loudly and woke the elevator boy, who was a Negro man with gray hair, and he took me up to the sixth floor and bid me goodnight. I might have congratulated myself for my essay in coldblood cunning except for what happened next. In Mr. Schultz's suite, Lulu had remained to put the furniture back in position and Mr. Berman came in the door with a set of keys and a pile of fresh white towels from the chambermaids' closet, I admired all the details of their professionalism, I thought of the crime as committed on one of those writing tablets for kids where the drawing disappears when you lift the page. Finally roused, as if from a slumber, Mr. Schultz stood and walked around the room to see that everything looked as it should, and then he stared at the carpet near the coffee table where there soaked in a dark black stain, with several drops beside like moons around a planet, the blood of the former president of the Metropolitan Restaurant and Cafeteria Owners Association, and then he went to the phone and woke up the desk clerk and said, "This is Mr. Schultz. We have an accident here and I need a doctor. Yes," he said. "As soon as you can. Thank you."

I was puzzled and somewhat alarmed, my mind struggled to understand what it knew only as something so enigmatic that it could not be good for me. Everyone else in the room was now deadly casual. Mr. Schultz stood looking out the window for several minutes and just as I heard the sputter of a car coming down the street he turned back to the room and told me to stand over by the coffee table. Mr. Berman sat down and lit a new cigarette from the old one, and then Lulu came over to me as if to adjust my position, because it was apparently not quite right, he positioned me and continued to hold my shoulders and just at the moment of my revelation but a moment too late I thought I saw him grin with a flash of one gold tooth, although maybe the slowness of my mind on this occasion was a blessing because actually as he swung I did not have the opportunity to reveal anything less than total sacrificial loyalty, it would not have done in this hierarchy of men to say why me why me, a blinding pain struck me dumb, my knees buckled, and a starlike flash exploded in my eyes, just the way prizefighters say it does, and an instant later I was crouched over, groaning and dribbling in my shock, holding both my hands over my poor nose, my best feature, bleeding profusely now through my fingers to the stained rug, and so I contributed the final detail of the Schultz gang's brilliant representations in matters of applied death, mixing my blood with the dead gangster's and suffering my rage of injustice as I heard the businesslike rap of our country doctor knocking on the door.

*   *   *

I REMEMBER WHAT THAT WHACK ACROSS THE FACE DID TO THE PASSAGE OF TIME, in the instant I felt it, it became an old injury and the rage it engendered in me was an ancient resolve to somehow pay them back, to get even— all this in the space of a moment's obliterating pain. While I had thought when I heard the gunshot that it could have been meant as appropriately for me, I thought the broken nose was uncalled-for. I was really upset and felt badly used, my courage flowed back with my anger and I was renewed in the heedless righteousness of my appetites. All night I kept an ice bag on my face so that the swelling would not disfigure me and make Drew Preston think I was no longer pretty. In the morning it was not as bad as I had expected, a certain puffiness, and a blueness under the eyes that might be attributed as well to debauchery as to a good sock.

I went out for breakfast as usual, I found that the act of chewing was painful, my lip was a little sore too, but I swore I would be as hardened and casual about the awful night that had just passed as anyone else. I put the image of that rising and slumping dead man out of my head. When I got back Mr. Berman's office door was open across the hall and I caught his eye and he motioned me to come in and close the door. He was on the phone, holding it under his chin with a raised shoulder and going over some adding-machine tapes with the person on the other end. When he had hung up he indicated a chair beside the desk, and I sat down like a client in his office.

"We are moving shop," he said. "We're moving out tonight and only Mr. Schultz and the lawyers will be in residence. The day after tomorrow begins the jury selection. It would not look good for the boys to be hanging around during a trial what with the press descended."

"The press will be here?"

"What do *you* think? It's gonna be like a hive of hornets has got loose in Onondaga. They'll crawl all over everything."

"The *Mirror* too?"

"What do you mean, of course, all of them. Newspapermen are the creeps of the earth, they have no sense of honor or decency and they are totally lacking in the ethics of behavior. If he was just Arthur Flegenheimer do you think they would find him worth the attention? But Dutch Schultz is a name that fits in the headline."

Mr. Berman shook his head and made a gesture, lifting his hand and letting it fall into his lap. I had never seen him so disconcerted. He was not his usual dapper self this morning, he was in working trousers and shirtsleeves and suspenders and bedroom slippers and he hadn't yet shaved that pointed chin. "Where was I?" he said.

"We are moving out."

He studied my face. "It's not too bad," he said. "A bump adds character. Does it hurt?"

I shook my head.

"Lulu got carried away. He was supposed to bloody your nose, not break it. Everyone is under a strain."

"It's okay," I said.

"Needless to say the whole thing was unfortunate." He looked around on his desk for his cigarettes, found a pack with one cigarette left, lit it, and leaned back in his swivel chair crossing his legs and holding the cigarette up around his ear. "It sometimes happens that there is more life than you can keep book on, and that is certainly true of up here, this is an unnatural existence, and why we got to get through this trial as quickly as possible and get back home where we belong. Which brings me to what I want to say. Mr. Schultz will be very busy from now on, he'll be in the spotlight, in court and out of it, and we don't want him to have anything on his mind except the problem to hand. Does that make good sense to you?"

I nodded.

"Well then why can't she understand that? This is a serious business, we can't afford any more mistakes, we've got to keep our wits about us. All I want is for her to take a powder for a few days. Go to Saratoga, see the races, is that too much to ask?"

"You mean Mrs. Preston?"

"She wants to see the trial. You know what will happen if she walks into that courtroom. I mean won't it bother her to have her picture taken as a mystery woman or some other goddamn cockamamie thing that they will cook up? That her husband will know? To say nothing of Mr. Schultz is a married man."

"Mr. Schultz is married?"

"To a lovely lady waiting for him and worrying about him in New York City. Yes. What do you keep asking all these questions for? We are all married men, kid, we got mouths to feed, families to support. Onondaga has been a tough son of a bitch for every one of us and it will all be for naught if love conquers all."

He was looking at me very intently now, not being sly in his study of my reactions or the thoughts that might be visible on my face. He said: "I know you been spending more time with Mrs. Preston than I or the boys, even from that first night when you walked her back to her apartment and kept an eye on her. Is that fair to say?"

"Yes," I said, my throat going dry. I could not swallow or he would see the rise and fall of my Adam's apple.

"I want you to talk to her, explain to her why laying low for a while is in the Dutchman's interests. Will you do that?"

"Does Mr. Schultz want her to go?"

"He does and he doesn't. He's leaving it up to her. You know, there are women," he said almost as if to himself. He paused. "There always is. But in all our years I have never seen him like this. What is it, he won't let himself admit he knows better, that she takes men down like bowling pins, what is it?"

At that moment the phone rang. "You haven't failed me so far," he said, turning in his chair and leaning forward to pick up the receiver. He gave me his look over the tops of his eyeglasses. "Don't fuck up now."

I WENT IN MY ROOM TO THINK. IT COULDN'T HAVE BEEN MORE PERFECT, LIKE AN affirmation of my wish for release from the life and task I had chosen for myself, and I knew exactly what I would do from the moment he told me to talk to her. Not that I didn't appreciate the danger. Were these my own thoughts of freedom or was I acting under his influence? This was really dangerous, they were all married people, willful and unpredictable mad passionate adults with God knows what depths of depravity, they lived hard and struck suddenly. And Mr. Berman hadn't told me everything, regardless of what he said, I didn't know if he was speaking for himself only or for Mr. Schultz as well. I didn't know if I was supposed to be working for Mr. Schultz in this matter, or conspiring to do what was in Mr. Schultz's best interests.

If Mr. Berman was shooting straight with me I could be gratified that he appreciated my utility as a superior brain in the outfit, he was handing me an assignment nobody else could handle as well, including himself. But if he knew what was going on between Mrs. Preston and me he could be telling me just the same things he had told me. If we were going to be murdered would it not be somewhere else than Onondaga? If Mr. Schultz could not afford her anymore? If he found me expendable? He murdered people who acted on his behalf at a distance from him. I knew for a possibility that if I left I was going away to die because either he knew my heart's secret in which case he would kill me, or my being gone from his sight would create the betrayal in his imagination that would amount to the same thing.

Yet what was any of this speculation but the symptom of my own state of mind? I would think of nothing like this if my conscience was clear and I was intent only to advance myself. I found myself starting to pack. I had a lot of clothes now and a fine soft leather suitcase with brass snaps and two cinch belts, I folded my things neatly, a new habit, and tried to think of the first moment when I would have the chance to talk to Drew Preston. I was feeling the first yawning intimations of the nausea I recognized as pure dread, but there was no question that I was going to make the best of the opportunity Mr. Berman had presented me. I knew what Drew would say. She would say she hadn't wanted to leave me. She would say she had big plans for her darling devil. She would say I was to tell Mr. Berman she was ready to go to Saratoga but wanted me to go with her.

* * *

THAT NIGHT, WHILE DREW ACCOMPANIED MR. SCHULTZ TO THE DISTRICT SCHOOL gymnasium, where he was throwing his big end-of-summer party for everyone in Onondaga, I moved out of the hotel with the rest of the gang, I didn't even know where we were going, only that we were going there, bag and baggage, in two cars, with an open truck following with Lulu Rosenkrantz sitting in the back with the steel safe and a stack of mattresses. The whole time in the country I had never gotten used to the night because it was so black, I didn't even like to look out of my window because the night was so implacably black, in Onondaga the streetlights made the stores and buildings into shapes of night, and out past the edges of town the endless night was like a vast and terrible loss of knowledge, you couldn't see into it, it did not have volume and transparency like the nights of New York, it did not suggest day was coming if you waited and were patient, and even when the moon was full it only showed you the black shapes of the mountains and the milky black absences of the fields. The worst part was that country nights were the real ones, once you rolled across the Onondaga Bridge and your headlights picked up the white line of the country road, you knew what a thin glimmering trail we make in that unmappable blackness, how the heat of your heart and your motor is as sufficient in all that dimensionless darkness as someone still not quite dead in his grave for whom it makes no difference if his eyes are opened or closed.

I was frightened to belong so devoutly to Mr. Schultz. I was made bleak in my mind by his rule. You can live in other people's decisions and make a seemingly reasonable life for yourself, until the first light of rebellion shows you the character of all of them, which is their tyranny. I didn't like for Drew to be back there with him while I was driven like the baggage. The distance would not be that great, only twelve miles or so as I was surprised to see from a surreptitious check of the mileage when we arrived, but I felt each mile attenuated my connection with Drew Preston, I was not confident her feelings could endure.

We pulled up to this house, who had found it, rented it or bought it, I was never to know, it was a farmhouse but there was no farm, just this run-down clapboard house with the leaning porch situated atop a dirt ramp rising suddenly up from the road, so that the porch looked over the road east and west from this bluff that was really not set back from the road but more like on top of it. Behind the house was a steeper hill of woods blacker than the night, if that was possible.

This was the new headquarters, which we were to see first by flashlight. Inside smelled very bad, the polite word is "close," which is the smell of an old unlived-in wood house, and the windows were rotted shut,

and animals had lived here and left their droppings now dried to dust, and
there was a narrow stairs going up from the entryway and what I supposed
was a living room through a door on one side of the entryway, and a short
hall going straight back under the stairs to a kitchen with an astonishing
thing in the sink, a hand pump for water, which came up in a trickle and
then a loud crashing rush of rust and muck that brought Lulu running.
"Stop fucking around and pull your weight," he told me. I went outside
to the truck and helped bring in mattresses and cardboard cartons filled
with groceries and utensils. We were doing everything by flashlight until
Irving got a fire going in the living-room fireplace, which improved matters not that much, there was a stiff dead bird on the floor who must have
come in through the chimney, oh this was terrific, no question about it, I
asked myself who would choose the carpeted life of hotels when he could
have this historic mansion of the American Founding Fathers.

Late that night Mr. Schultz appeared, in his arms were two big brown
bags full of containers of chow mein and chop suey that someone had
brought up from Albany, and while it was not the same thing as good
Chinese food from the Bronx it was much appreciated by all of us. Irving
found some pots to warm the stuff up and I got a fair share of everything,
the chicken chow mein over a mound of steaming rice and crisp roasted
noodles, the chop suey for the second course, litchi nuts for dessert, the
paper plates got a bit soggy but that was all right, it was a good satisfying
meal, except that it lacked tea, all I had to drink with it was well water,
while Mr. Schultz and the others washed it down with whiskey, which
they did not seem to mind at all. A fire was going in the front room and
Mr. Schultz lit a cigar and loosened his tie, I could tell he was feeling
better, and might even be feeling good here in this hideout where he was
not on display as he had been for many weeks in Onondaga and would be
as soon again as the morning, I think there was something bitterly comforting to him about being holed up again because it matched his sense of
his situation as someone surrounded on all sides.

"You boys don't have to worry about the Dutchman," he said as we all
sat around against the walls, "the Dutchman takes care of his own. Don't
think twice about Big Julie, he wasn't anyone you should concern yourselves. Or Bo. They were no better than Vincent Coll. They were the bad
apples. You guys I love. You guys I would do anything for. What I said
long ago, my policy still stands. You get hurt, you get sent up, or God
forbid you lose it all, you never have to worry, your families will be taken
care of as if you was still on the payroll. You know that. All the way down
to the kid here. My word is my bond. It's better with the Dutchman than
with the Prudential Life Assurance. Now this trial, in a few days we will
be clear. While the Feds have been fucking away the summer on the beach
we been up here sowing our oats. Public opinion is on our side. You
shoulda seen that party tonight. I mean it wasn't your or my idea of a
party, when we get back to town that will be a party, but this, the rubes

loved it. In the high school gymnasium with the crepe paper and the balloons. I had one of them back-hill fiddle-and-banjo bands playing their doughsee doughs and all the hands right. Hell I danced myself. I danced with my babe in all that crowd of washed and laundered hardship. I have become very attached to them. Not a wiseass will you find in the countryside, just hardworking slobs, work till they keel over. But they got one or two cards in their hand. The law is not majestic. The law is what public opinion says it is. I could tell you a lot about the law. Mr. Hines could tell you more. When we had the important precincts, when we had the magistrates court, when we had the Manhattan D.A.? Wasn't that the law? We got a man to argue for me tomorrow who wouldn't have me to dinner in his house. He talks on the phone with the president. But I have paid his price and he will be at my side for as long as it takes. So that's what I mean. The law is the vigorish I pay, the law is my overhead. The hondlers, they make this legal, they make that illegal, judges, lawyers, politicians, who are they but guys who have their own angle into the rackets except they like to do it without getting their hands dirty? You gonna respect that? Respect will kill you. Save your respect for yourselves."

He was speaking softly, modulating his resonant rasp even here twelve miles out of Onondaga in this house that could barely be noticed from the road in the daytime. Maybe it was the darkness of firelight that did it, the expression of the private mind in the intimacy of a fire, when you hear only your own thoughts in the night and see only shadows.

"But you know, it's a kind of honor, isn't it," he said. "After all, people have been counting out the Dutchman for quite a while now. And yet the whole world has followed me here, it's almost like Onondaga is another borough. Starting the other day with my new best friend from the downtown mobs. So I must be all right. See? I got my rosary. I carry it all the time. I will take it into court with me. This is a nice evening, this is good booze. I feel good now. I feel at peace."

Upstairs were two small bedrooms and after Mr. Schultz drove back to town I went to sleep in one of them in my clothes on a mattress on the floor with my head in the gable where I tried to believe I could see through the opaque windowpane to stars in the night sky. I did not question why with only two small bedrooms one was mine, perhaps I assumed it was my due as a boy with a governess. In the morning when I awoke two other guests whom I didn't recognize were asleep on their mattresses in their clothes except that they had hung their guns in their shoulder holsters from hooks on the wood door. I stood up, stiff and cold, and went downstairs and outside, it was barely dawn, there was some question in this moment as to whether the world would actually come back, it seemed in some sort of wet wavering drift as if it was not up to the task, but from this whitish blackness something detached itself, twenty yards down the road and at my eye level a man I recognized as Irving was at the top of a telephone pole and splicing a wire which was the same black wire that came up the dirt ramp and went past my feet into the front door. And then I looked across the road and saw down there a white house with green trim and an American flag hanging from a big pole in the front yard, and in a pine grove behind the house sprinkled among the trees were several tiny cabins of the same white with green trim and beside one of them the black Packard was parked pointed to the road with its windshield covered with frost.

I went around to the back of our hillside manse and found an ideal spot for a lengthy and meditative urination. I imagined that if I had to live here I could create a gorge as monumentally geographical as the one Drew Preston had found on our walk. Mr. Schultz seemed to have beefed up the firepower, if I understood correctly the two snoring strangers upstairs. I noted too of this ramshackle house on its bluff that it provided a good prospect of the road in both directions. And someone sticking a tommy gun out the window of his car couldn't just tear on past and shoot it up. All this was of technical interest to me.

But in a matter of hours I was leaving, although I didn't know for how long and to what end. My life was estranged from me, whatever my resolve I no longer was childish enough to feel it was commanding. Last night as we had sat in the firelight I had felt I was one of them in a way not just my own, not just of my own thinking, but in the common assumption of our meal shared in the empty hideout house, disguised by the bad light as a grown-up, a man in the rackets, once in never out, and perhaps this more than church bells ringing was the true quiet signal of the end of my provisional determination, the snuffingout of my unconscious conviction that I could escape Mr. Schultz anytime I wished. Now I thought this layout was more truly theirs, more like the real habitat of their lives, than any other place I had seen. I was impatient for people to get up. I wandered about, I was hungry. I missed my tea shop breakfast and I missed my *Onondaga Signal,* which I liked to read over breakfast, and I missed my big white bathroom with the hot water shower. You would think I'd lived in fine hotels all my life. I stood on the porch and looked in the living-room window. On a wood table was Mr. Berman's adding machine and the hot phone Irving was in the process of hooking up, there was an old kitchen chair with a tall back, and prominently in the middle of the floor, the Schultz company safe. The safe seemed to glow for me as the indisputable center of the upheaval of the past twenty-four hours. I thought of it not only as the repository of Mr. Schultz's cash deposits but as the strongbox for Abbadabba's world of numbers.

Irving saw me and put me to work, I had to sweep the floors and go around to all the windows and wipe them down so you could see out of them, I chopped wood by hand for the kitchen stove, which made my tender nose throb with pain, I hiked to a general store about a mile away and bought paper plates and bottles of Nehi for everyone's breakfast, I was as deep in nature as you could get, like a damn Boy Scout at a jamboree. Irving left in the Packard with Mickey and so Lulu was in charge then and he put me to work out in back digging a latrine, there was an outhouse there that looked perfectly usable to me though it tilted a bit, but Lulu found it offended his sensibilities to use a strange outhouse and so I had to take a shovel and dig this hole in a clear and level place in the woods above the house going into the soft earth around and around deeper and deeper with my hands getting blistered and sore before one of the men took over, I had thought I had imagined all the possible dangers attached to a life in crime, but death by excrement had escaped me. Only when Irving came back and resolutely built a small throne of pine boards for the hole did I remember what dignity lay in labor that was done with style, whatever the purpose, he was a model for us all, Irving.

I got myself into as clean and presentable shape as I could manage under primitive conditions and at about nine that morning I drove with Mr. Berman and Mickey into Onondaga and sat in the parked car across the public square from the courthouse. Almost every parking space was taken as the Model T's and A's and the chain-drive flatbeds came in from the countryside, and the farmers in their clean and pressed overalls and the farmers' wives in their unfashionable flowered dresses and sunbonnets climbed the steps and went through the doors for their impaneling. I saw the government lawyers with their briefcases walking up the hill from the hotel, I saw Dixie Davis looking very solemn beside the older portly lawyer with his rimless glasses dangling from their black ribbon, and then, slouching along in twos and threes, the fellows with the writing pads sticking out of their jacket pockets and the morning paper rolled under their arms and their little press cards like decorative feathers in the headbands of their fedoras. I studied the reporters very carefully, I wished I knew which of them was the *Mirror,* whether he was the one with horn-rim glasses who bounded up the steps two at a time or the one with his tie knot pulled down and his collar open at the neck, you could only guess about reporters, they never wrote about themselves, they were just these bodiless words of witness composing for you the sights you would see and the opinions you would have without giving themselves away, like magicians whose tricks were words.

Up at the top of the stairs news photographers with big Speed-Graphics in their hands stood around not taking pictures of the people going past them into the building.

"Where's Mr. Schultz?" I said.

"He snuck inside a half hour ago, while those jokers was still eating their breakfast."

"He's famous," I said.

"That's the tragedy in a nutshell," Mr. Berman said. He took out a wad of one-hundred-dollar bills and counted out ten of them. "When you're in Saratoga don't let her out of your sight. Whatever she wants, pay for it. This one has got a mind of her own, which could be inconvenient. There's a place called the Brook Club. It's ours. You have any problems you speak to the man there. You understand?"

"Yes," I said.

He handed me the bills. "Not for your personal betting," he said. "If you want to make a few bucks for yourself, you'll be calling me every morning anyway. I know something, I'll tell you. You understand?"

"Yes."

He handed me a torn piece of paper with his secret phone number on it. "Horses or women alone is bad enough. Together they can kill you. You handle Saratoga, kid, I'll believe you can handle anything." He sat back in the seat and lit a cigarette. I got out of the car and took my suitcase from the trunk and waved goodbye. I thought in this moment I understood the limits of Mr. Berman, he was sitting in this car because it was the closest he could get to the courtroom, he couldn't go where he wanted to go and that made him plaintive, a little humpbacked man with over-colorful clothes and Old Gold cigarettes the two indulgences of his arithmetized life, I felt looking back at him watching me from the car window that he was someone who could not function without Dutch Schultz, as if he were only an aspect of him, reflected into brilliance by him, and as dependent as he was needed. I thought Mr. Berman was the curious governor of this amazing genius of force, who if he one moment lost his spin would lose it forever.

SIXTEEN

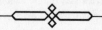

Amoment later a beautiful dark green four-door convertible came into the square, and it took me a moment to realize Drew was driving it, she didn't quite stop but drifted past me in low gear, I heaved my valise into the back, stepped on the running board, and as she put the car into second and picked up speed I vaulted over the door into the seat beside her and we were away.

I didn't look back. We went down the main street past the hotel, to which I said my secret goodbyes, and headed for the river. I had no idea where she had gotten this baby. She could do whatever she wanted to do. The seats were light brown leather. The tan canvas top was folded back on chrome stanchions so that most of it was recessed in a kind of well. The dashboard was made of burled wood. I sat with my arms on the door and the back of the seat and enjoyed the luxury of the sun shining as she turned to me and smiled.

I will say here how Drew Preston drove, it was so girlish, when she shifted she sort of leaned forward with her white hand on the gearshift knob, her slender leg draped in her dress rode down the clutch and she put her shoulders down and bit her lip in the concentration of her effort and shoved her arm straight ahead from the elbow. She wore a silk kerchief tied under her chin, she was happy to have me in her new car, we rattled across the wood bridge and came to the intersection where the road went east and west and she turned east and Onondaga was a church spire and some rooftops in a nest of trees, and then we went around a hill and it was gone.

We drove that morning down among the mountains and between lakes that lapped both sides of the road, we passed under canopies of pine and through little white villages where the general store was also the post office, she drove hard, with both hands on the wheel, and it looked like such pleasure that I wanted very badly to take a turn driving, to feel this great eight-cylinder machine moving under my hands. But one thing I hadn't yet had in my gang training was auto-driving instruction and I preferred to act to myself as if I knew how to drive and didn't care to than actually have her broach the subject, I wanted equality, the last and most absurd wish of this affection, I think now what an outrageous boy I was, with what insatiable ambition, but I had to have known it on this morning on our drive through the beautiful state of our wilderness, I had to have realized how far I had come from the streets of the East Bronx where the natural world was visible only in globules of horse manure pressed flat by passing tires, with dried seeds pecked at by the flittering flocks of street sparrows, I had to have known what it was to breathe the air of these sun-warmed mountains alive and well and well-fed with a thousand dollars in my pocket and the heinous murders of the modern world the inuring events of my brain. I was a tougher kid now, I had a real gun stuck in my belt, and I knew in my mind I must not be grateful but take what I was given as if it was my due, I felt there would be a price for all this and since the price would be in a currency too dear for life, I wanted to make it worth my while, I found myself angry at her, I kept looking at her imagining what I would do to her, I admit I entertained some mean and sadistic pictures born of my bitter boy's resignation.

Yet of course when we stopped it was because she stopped, she glanced at me and gave a bel canto sigh of capitulation and suddenly pulled off the road, bouncing along between trees and over tree roots, and jerked the car to a stop barely out of sight of any passing cars in a grove of tall high trees through which the sun flashed dappling us in moments of heat, moments of shade, moments of brilliant light, moments of dark green darkness, as we sat there looking at each other in our isolation.

The thing about Drew was she was not genitally direct, she wanted to kiss my ribs and my white boyish chest, she held my legs and ran her hands up and down the backs of my thighs, she caressed my ass and sucked my earlobes and my mouth, and she did all these things as if they were all that she wanted, she made small editorial sounds of approval or delectation, as a commentator to the action, little single high notes, whispers without words like remarks to herself, it was as if she was consuming me as an act of eating and drinking, and it wasn't designed to arouse me, what boy in that situation needed arousal? from the moment she stopped the car I was tumescent, and I waited for some acknowledgment from her that this was in fact part of me too but it didn't come and it didn't come and I flared through my need into an exquisite pain, I thought I would go mad, I became agitated and discovered only then her availability, that in all of this she was only waiting for me to find her absolute willingness to be still and listen to me for a change. This was so girlish of her, so surprisingly restrained and submissive, I was not artful but simply myself and this brought forth from her a conspiratorial laughter, it gave her the pleasure of generosity to have me in her, it was not an excitement but more like a happiness of having this boy in her, she wrapped her legs around my back and I rocked us up and down in the back seat of the car with my feet sticking out of the open door, and when I came she held her arms around me tight enough to stop my breath and she sobbed and kissed my face as if something terrible had happened to me, as if I had been wounded and she was, in an act of desperate compassion, trying to make it as if it had not happened.

Then I was following her stark naked through the brush into this noplace of such great green presence she had chosen arbitrarily or by happenstance, with her gift for centering the world around herself, so that it was all very beautifully central in my mind, the place to be, following her flashing white form around trees, under tangles, avoiding the whip of branches, with a brilliant chatter of communities of unseen birds telling me how late I was to have found it. And then we were going generally downward, and the ground became swampy and the air close and I found myself slapping at stings in my skin, I had wanted to catch her, tackle her and fuck her again, and she was doing this to me, taking me into furies of mosquitoes. But I came upon her squatting and ladling handfuls of mud over herself and we applied this cold mud to each other and then we walked like children into the sinking darkness of forest, hand in hand like fairy-tale children in deep and terrible trouble, as indeed we were, and then we found ourselves at this still pond as black as I had ever seen water to be and of course she waded in and bid me to follow and my God it was fetid, it was warm and scummy, my feet were in wet mats of pond weed, I treaded water to keep my feet from sinking and couldn't crawl back out fast enough, but she swam on her back a few yards and then came crawling out on all fours, and she was covered with this invisible slime, her body was slimed as mine was and we lay in this mud and I punched into her and held her blond head back in the mud and pumped slime up her and we lay there rutting in this foul fen and I came and held her down and wouldn't let her move, but lay in her with her breath loud in my ear, and when I lifted my head and looked into her alarmed green eyes in their panic of loss, I grew hard again right in her and she began to move, and this time we had the time, by the third time it takes its time, and I found the primeval voice in her, like a death rattle, a shrill sexless bark, over and over again as I jammed into her, and it became tremulous a terrible crying despair, and then she screamed so shriekingly I thought something was wrong and reared to look at her, her lips were pulled back over her teeth and her green eyes dimmed as I looked in them, they had lost sight, gone flat, as if her mind had collapsed, as if time had turned in her and she had passed back into infancy and reverted through birth into nothingness, and for an instant they were no longer eyes, for an instant they were about to be eyes, the eyes of soullessness.

Yet a few moments later she was smiling and kissing me and hugging me as if I had done something dear, brought her a flower or something.

* * *

WHEN WE STAGGERED UPRIGHT GLOBS OF MUD FELL FROM US, SHE LAUGHED AND turned to show me the back of her, absent in darkness, as if she had been cleaved in half, with the front of her shiny and swollen into sculpture. Even her golden head seemed halved. There was nothing for it but to go back into the pond, and then she swam further out and insisted I come after her, and the water grew cooler, it was deeper and it went on behind a bend, I swam with her stroke for stroke, giving her my best YMCA crawl, and we came out on the bank on the far side, washed clean of mud and somewhat less slick.

By the time we got back to the car we were dry, but putting clothes on was uncomfortable, as if we were covering extreme sunburns, we smelled of pond scum, we smelled like frogs, we drove off trying not to lean back in the seats and several miles down the road we came to this motor court and rented a cabin and we stood together in the shower and washed each other with a big cake of white soap and stood holding each other under the water, and then we lay on the top of the bed and she curled herself along my side with my arm around her, and perhaps created with that nuzzling gesture the moment of our truest intimacy, when by some shuddering retrenchment of her being she matched me in age and yearning for sophistication, like a boy's girlfriend, only two bodies between us and a long life ahead of terrible surprises. So I felt a kind of fearful pride. I knew I could never have the woman Mr. Schultz had had, just as he hadn't known the woman Bo Weinberg had known, because she covered her tracks, she trailed no history, suiting herself to the moment, getting her gangsters or her boys in transformative stunts of the spirit, she would never write her memoirs, this one, not even if she ever lived to an old age, she would never tell her life because she needed no one's admiration or sympathy or wonder, and because all judgments, including love, came of a language of complacency she had never wasted her time to master. So it all worked out, how protective I felt there in that cabin, I let her doze on my arm and studied a fly drifting into its caroming angles under the roof and understood that Drew Preston granted absolution, it was what you got instead of a future with her. Clearly she would not be interested in the enterprise of keeping us alive, so I would have to do that for both of us.

THE REST OF THAT DAY WE DROVE DOWN THROUGH THE ADIRONDACKS UNTIL THE hills softened, the land took on a groomed look, and in the early evening we rolled into Saratoga Springs and came down a street that had the insolence to call itself Broadway. Yet as I looked there was something appropriate too, the place looked like old New York, or as I imagined it must have looked in the old days, there were very civilized shops with New York names and striped awnings lowered against the evening sun, the people strolling in the street didn't look like Onondagans at all, there was not one farmer among them, there were lots of fine cars in the traffic, some of them with uniformed chauffeurs, and people clearly of the monied classes sat on the long porches of the hotels reading newspapers. I thought it odd at the height of the evening that nobody had anything better to do than read newspapers, until we checked into our own hotel, the Grand Union, the finest of them all with the longest broadest porch, a boy took our bags, another drove off to park the car, and I saw that the newspaper of choice was the *Racing Form*, at the front desk there was a stack of them with the next day's date at the top and the next day's card for the handicappers to go to work on. And there was no news in it except horse news, in the month of August in Saratoga nobody was interested in anything but horses, and so even the newspapers conformed, giving only horse headlines and horse weather and horse horoscopes, as if the world was populated only by horses except for the scattered few numbers of eccentric humans who gathered to read about their important doings.

As I scanned the lobby I did detect one or two persons whose interest in horses might not be sincere, a couple of badly dressed men sitting in adjoining armchairs and only glancing at their papers when I noticed them. The clerk recognized Miss Drew and was pleased she had finally arrived, they were getting worried about her, he said, smiling, and I realized she had rooms for the whole month of racing whether she used them or not, it was a place she would come to at this time of year whether Mr. Schultz said to or not. We got upstairs into this grand suite of rooms that immediately made me realize what small and modest resources the Onondaga Hotel had offered, a great basket of fruit lay on a coffee table with a card from the hotel management, and there was a side bar with a tray of thin-stemmed glasses and decanters of white and red wine and a bucket with ice and a cut-glass square-cornered bottle with a little chain hanging over it with a nameplate that said BOURBON, and another that said SCOTCH, and a big seltzer bottle of blue glass, and light streamed through these long paned windows that came practically down to the floor, and big slow-turning fans hanging from the ceiling kept the air cool and the beds were immense and the carpets thick and soft. Oddly enough all of this made me think not too highly of Mr. Schultz because none of it depended on him.

Drew took delight in my reactions to this luxury especially as I tested the bedsprings with a backward lateral body fling, and she fell on top of me and we rolled one way and then the other in a playful wrestle in the guise of which we really tested each other's strength. She was no slouch, though I pinned her by the arms soon enough so that she had to say, ''Oh no, not now please. I've planned this evening, I want to take you to see something marvelous.''

So we dressed for the evening in our summer whites, I in my slightly wrinkled linen double-breasted suit she had ordered for me from her store in Boston, and she in a smart blue linen blazer and white pleated skirt. I loved it that we dressed in our adjoining rooms with the doors opened between us, I loved the assumption of advanced relationship in our preparations to be seen together. We came down through the hotel lobby of evening idlers including my two shabby friends, and when we stepped outside the evening was warm with the heat rising from the pavement into the cool sky, so she suggested we walk.

We crossed the avenue and I noticed that the policeman directing traffic wore a white short-sleeved shirt. I couldn't take a police department seriously that dressed like that. I didn't know what it was, this marvelous place she wanted me to see, but I thought I had better stop drowsing in dreamland. It would have been lovely to be with her still in the deep woods, but we were going past stately lawns and in the shadows of big black shade trees with enormous homes behind them, this was a well-developed and serious resort, it was tempting not to look beyond her, so dazzled by her brilliant offering as to forget the circumstances, and not one person we passed on the street failed to notice her and to react to her, which made me foolishly proud, but we were holding hands and the warmth of her hand alarmed me, it suggested her pumping blood, it created in my mind visions of terrible retribution.

"I don't mean to be coarse," I said, "but I think we'd better remember what our situation is. I'm going to let go of your hand now."

"But I like to."

"We will again. Please let go. I'm trying to tell you something. My professional opinion is we are being shadowed."

"Whatever for? Are you sure? That's so dramatic," she said, looking behind us. "Where? I don't see anyone."

"Will you please not turn around? You won't see anything, just take my word for it. Where is this place we're going? The cops in this town, when the money comes up from New York, they can't be relied on."

"For what?"

"For the protection of law-abiding citizens, which you and I are pretending to be."

"What do we have to be protected from?"

"From the likes of us. From mob."

"Am I mob?" she said.

"Only in a manner of speaking. At the most you are a moll."

"I am your moll," she said, considering it.

"You are Mr. Schultz's moll," I said.

We strode through the quiet evening. "Mr. Schultz is a very ordinary man," she said.

"Did you know he owns the Brook Club? He's well connected in this town. You get the feeling he doesn't trust you out of his sight?"

"But that's why you're here. You're my shadow."

"You asked for me," I said. "That means they would watch both of us for good measure. He's married. Did you know that?"

After a moment she said: "Yes, I think I did."

"Well where does that leave you? Do you have any idea? I want to remind you he made a mortal mistake when he took Bo out of the restaurant with you there."

"Wait," she said. She touched my arm and we stood facing each other in the dark beside a tall hedge.

"You think he's ordinary? Everyone who's dead now thought he was ordinary. The night you came out of your room. Do you remember me putting you back to bed?"

"Yes?"

"They were getting rid of a body. That fat guy with the cane. He stole some money. Not exactly your salt of the earth. I mean I'm not suggesting it's a loss to the world. But it happened."

"You poor boy. So that's what that was all about."

"This nose: Mr. Schultz had Lulu slug me to explain the spots on the rug."

"You were protecting me." I felt her cool soft lips on my cheek. "Billy Bathgate. I love that name you chose for yourself. Do you know how much I love Billy Bathgate?"

"Mrs. Preston, I'm so nuts about you I can't see straight. But I'm not even talking about that, I'm not even beginning to think about that. It was not a good idea to come here. I think maybe we ought to get out of this town. The man kills regularly."

"We should talk about it," she said and she took my hand and we came around a corner past some tall shrubbery to a brilliantly lit pavilion with people streaming into it and cars pulling up as if to a concert.

WE STOOD UNDER A TENT LIT BY BARE BULBS AND WATCHED THESE HORSES BEING walked around a dirt ring, each horse had a small velvet blanket across his back with a number on it, and people standing with printed programs in their hands were able to read about its lines and specifications. They were young horses, they had never been raced, and they were up for sale. Drew explained things in a soft voice, as if we were in church. I was extremely agitated and almost hated her for bringing us here. She couldn't concentrate on what was important. Her mind didn't work properly. I noticed of the horses their coats were glossy, their tails combed, and some of them lifted their heads up against the leash or halter or whatever it was their handlers held them by, and others walked with their heads looking at the ground, but they were all incredibly thin-legged and rhythmically beautiful. They got led around by the nose, and were bred for business and trained and raced, their lives weren't their own but they had a natural grace that was like wisdom and I found myself respecting them. They produced a nice strawy tang in the air, the smell of them amplified their great animal being. Drew gazed at them with a kind of stunned attention, she didn't say anything but merely pointed when a particular horse attracted her as even more powerfully breathtaking than the others. For some weird reason this made me jealous.

I noticed of the people examining the horses that they were very nattily got up in horse-theme sporting wear, the men with silk cravats, more than one with a long cigarette holder like President Roosevelt's, and they all had a certain nose-in-the-air carriage that made me square my shoulders. No one was as beautiful as Drew but they were her long-necked people, all very straight and thin, with an assurance bred into them, and I thought it would be nice to have a program showing their lines and specifications. At any rate I began to relax somewhat. I calmed down. This was an impregnable kingdom of the privileged. If anyone from the rackets was here he would be highly visible. I felt from the one or two discreet glances given me that though I wore clothes of Drew's rich good taste and had taken the trouble to put my studious fake eyeglasses on, I just about pushed them to the limits of their sniffing tolerance. The thought passed my mind that Drew knew what she was doing in her own way of making the world, just as Mr. Schultz did, without sufficient thought.

After a turn or two around the ring, the horses were led out through a passageway into what appeared to be an amphitheater, as far as I could see from my angle of vision, with an audience in tiered seats and an announcer. Drew motioned to me and we went outside and around to the lighted front entrance, where the chauffeurs stood beside their cars, and came into the amphitheater and saw the same horses from a height under the stagey lights of the auction ring while the announcer or auctioneer proclaimed their virtues. And then they were held by the bridle in front of his podium while he directed the bidding, which came not as far as I could see from any of the people in their tiered seats but from employees like himself stationed here and there in the crowd who communicated the bids offered invisibly and in silence by the patrons on whose behalf they acted. It was all very mysterious and the sums were astonishing, going up in leaps and bounds to thirty, forty, fifty thousand dollars. These numbers frightened even the horses, many of whom saw fit to drop manure behind them as they were walked into the ring. When this happened a Negro man in a tuxedo appeared with a rake and shovel and quickly removed the offense from sight.

That was the whole show. I saw as much as I wanted to see in about three minutes but Drew couldn't get enough of it. Up behind the stands where we were, there was a constant traffic of people wandering around and looking each other over in a kind of unconscious imitation of the horses circling the ring below. Drew met a couple she knew. Then a man came over and soon she was in a small group of chatting friends and she made no reference to me whatsoever. This put me in the frame of mind of the shadow I was supposed to be. I was full of scorn, the women greeting one another appeared to kiss cheeks but in fact laid them together for a moment side by side and kissed the air beside each other's ear. People were glad to see Drew. I had a sense of an adenoidal group resonance. There was some giggling I imagined was directed at me, an entirely unreasonable assumption, which I also realized, but it made me turn away and lean on a railing and look down at the horses. I didn't know what I was doing here. I felt all alone. Mr. Schultz had held Drew for some weeks, clearly I was a strong enough novelty only for a couple of days or so. I had made a mistake to reveal my fears. Fears did not hold her interest. I had told her about Julie Martin's death and it was as if I had said I had stubbed my toe.

Then she appeared at my side and gave me a sideways hug and we looked together down at a new horse being led into the ring and in thirty seconds I was back in abject love. All my resentment dissolved and I reproached myself for questioning her constancy. She said we ought to have some supper and suggested we go to the Brook Club.

"You think that's smart?" I said.

"We will be what we're supposed to be," she said. "The moll and her shadow. I'm starving, aren't you?"

So we took a cab to the Brook Club and it was really an elegant place, with an awning all the way to the curb and beveled-glass doors and leather-padded walls, a horsey kind of place in dark green with little shaded lamps on the tables and prints of famous racehorses on the walls. It was somewhat larger than the Embassy. The host looked at Drew and wasted no time in showing us to a table right up front near a small dance floor. This was the man I was supposed to contact if I had to but he looked right through me and Drew did all the ordering. We had shrimp cocktails and aged sirloin steaks and hash browns, and chopped salad with anchovies, I hadn't realized how hungry I was. She ordered a bottle of red French wine, which I shared with her, though she had most of it. It was so dark in the club that even if friends of hers from her horsey set were there they couldn't have seen far enough in that low and heavily shadowed light to recognize her. I began to feel good again. There she was across the table from me, we were cocooned in our own light, and I had to remind myself I had had intercourse with her, that I had had carnal knowledge of her, that I had made her come, because I wanted to do this all over again, but with the same yearning as if it had never happened, with the same questions about her, and wonderings and imaginings of her physical quality, as if I was looking at an actress in a movie. This was the moment I began to understand that you can't remember sex. You can remember the fact of it, and recall the setting, and even the details, but the sex of the sex cannot be remembered, the substantive truth of it, it is by nature self-erasing, you can remember its anatomy and be left with a judgment as to the degree of your liking of it, but whatever it is as a splurge of being, as a loss, as a charge of the conviction of love stopping your heart like your execution, there is no memory of it in the brain, only the deduction that it happened and that time passed, leaving you with a silhouette that you want to fill in again.

And then musicians came out on the bandstand and they were my friends from the Embassy Club, the same group, with the same skinny lackadaisical girl singer who pulled at the top of her strapless evening dress. She sat on a chair to the side and nodded in time to the first number, an instrumental, and I caught her eye and she smiled and gave me a little wave, bobbing her head in time to the music all the while, and I felt very proud to be recognized by her. Somehow she communicated my presence to the other members of the band, the saxophonist turned to me and dipped his horn and the drummer laughed to see the company I was keeping and he twirled his sticks at me and I felt right at home. "They're old friends," I said to Drew, over the music, I was happy to be able to reveal the dimension in me of Man About Town, I felt in my pocket to make sure I hadn't lost Mr. Berman's thousand dollars, I thought it would be appropriate to buy the band drinks when they finished the set.

Drew toward the end of the dinner was a little bit looped, she sat with her elbow on the table and her chin propped in her hand and gazed at me with an aimless smiling affection. I was very comfortable now, the darkness of a nightclub is sustaining, it is a kind of shelter of controlled darkness as opposed to the open darkness of the real night with the weight of the whole sky of unfathomable possibilities, the music seemed so clear and figurative, they were playing standards, one after another, and every lyric seemed meaningful and appropriate and every melodic line of the solos had the clarity of a sweet truth. And as it happened one of the songs was "Me and My Shadow," which made us laugh—*Me and my shad-ow, strolling down the aven-ue* was its sly lyric, and it came to me that a kind of message was being sent of the conspiracy we all made together, I half expected Abbadabba Berman to scuttledance into the room, it was the old thing, as usual I never felt safe from Mr. Schultz when I was separated from him, Drew's idea to come here was a good one, if we were being watched we were doing the right thing having dinner in his club, getting the money back to him as loyalists would, this was his realm and because it made me feel closer to him to be here I wasn't afraid anymore.

I decided to worry no longer and make no decisions but trust our fate to Drew's impulses, to put myself at her disposal like a real companion in Mr. Schultz's interest, she knew more than I did, she had to, and what I perceived as her impracticality had the power of her nature. She really did know her way around, and for all her recklessness she was still alive. She was, in fact, quite safe in Saratoga. I was, in fact, looking after her for Mr. Schultz. I didn't know whose idea it had been that she come here, but I felt now that she could as easily have initiated this trip by claiming not to want to leave Onondaga as Mr. Berman could have by insisting that she should.

But then people began dancing on the little dance floor in front of our table and when she wanted to dance with me I strongly suggested that it was time to go home. I paid the bill but got her advice on the tips, and on the way out I left money with the bartender for the band's drinks. We took a cab back to the Grand Union Hotel and went prominently to the separate doors of our adjoining rooms and, once inside, met giggling at the open door between them.

BUT WE SLEPT IN OUR OWN BEDS AND WHEN I WOKE IN THE MORNING I FOUND A NOTE on my pillow: She had gone to have breakfast with some friends. She said I should buy a clubhouse admission and meet her for lunch at the track. She gave me her box number. I loved her handwriting, she wrote a very even line with round letters that were almost like printing and she dotted her *i*'s with little circles.

I showered and dressed and ran downstairs. The two men were not there. I found real morning papers in the lobby newsstand and took them with me to the front porch and sat and read them all in a big wicker chair. The jury had been chosen. The defense had used none of its peremptory challenges. The actual trial would begin today, and the prosecutor was quoted as saying he thought it would take a week at the most. The *Daily News* had a picture of Mr. Schultz and Dixie Davis conferring with their heads together in a corridor outside the courtroom. The *Mirror* showed Mr. Schultz coming down the courthouse steps with a big fake smile on his face.

I left the hotel and went along Broadway till I found a drugstore with a phone booth. I got a handful of change and asked the operator for the number Mr. Berman had given me. To this day I don't know how he was able to secure a number for a phone the phone company didn't know anything about, but he answered on the first ring. I told him we had gotten into town as scheduled, gone to the yearling sales, and were going to have a day at the races. I told him Mrs. Preston had met some of her friends here, silly people with whom she had nothing but silly conversation. I said we had had dinner at the Brook Club but that I hadn't felt the need to identify myself to the man there because everything was going fine. I told him the truth about these things, knowing that he would know it already.

"Good for you, kid," he said. "You want to parlay some of your expense money?"

"Sure," I said.

"There is a horse who will be the number-three position in the seventh race. That will be a good bet with handsome odds."

"What's his name?"

"How do I know, look at your program, just remember the number three, you can remember a three can't you?" He sounded testy. "Whatever you earn you can keep. You take it with you to New York."

"New York?"

"Yeah, get yourself on a train. We'll need you to do some things. Go home and wait there."

"What about Mrs. Preston?" I said.

At that moment the operator cut in and asked for another fifteen cents. Mr. Berman had me give him the phone number I was calling from and told me to hang up. I did and almost immediately the phone rang.

I could hear a match striking and then the exhaling of a lungful of smoke. "That's twice now you mentioned people by name."

"I'm sorry," I said. "But what do I do about her?"

"Where is the tomato at this moment?" he said.

"She's at breakfast."

"A couple of friends of yours are on the way. You'll probably see them at the track. Maybe one of them will even give you a lift to the train station you ask him nicely."

This is what I thought as I strode the streets of Saratoga, around the block and then around again, as if I was going somewhere, as if I had a purposeful destination: They had given me all that money, clearly more than I could use up in a day or even two, it was a week's big-time spending, hotel bills, restaurants, and paying for the play bets Drew Preston might want to make. Something was different. Either they really did need me in New York, a kind of advance man of the return to town, or they wanted me where I would not be in the way, but something had changed. Perhaps with Drew out of sight, Mr. Schultz had been persuaded of the danger she represented, perhaps his alienation was merely a reflection of hers, Mr. Berman seemed to think Mr. Schultz was perilously in love, but as I thought about it, after the first week or so when they were together in my company, Mr. Schultz ignored Drew more often than not, she became more like his display, an embellishment that added to his presence rather than someone he doted upon or squeezed the hand of, or seemed to deeply care about in the fond and foolish way people in love comport themselves. Whatever decision had been made, it seemed to me only expedient to assume it was of the nature of nightmare. I am proud of this boy I was, thinking through his cold dread, and you know the quickest thinking is the thinking of the body, and the body thinks surely, errorlessly, because it is not soaked in character as the brain is, and my best guess was of the worst that could happen, because I didn't remember coming in from the street or going through the lobby, but I found myself becoming aware that I was in my room and I was holding my loaded Automatic in my hand, I was holding my gun. So that was what I thought. The worst was he had turned against her, he needed more death, he was using up his deaths so quickly now he needed them faster and faster. What would she say, what would she do to him, if he wasn't able to protect himself, pinned down by the law, with the gang flying apart like a bomb had hit, and he abandoned and alone like one of those bombed screaming children of China, with the rubble falling down around him?

It was peculiar that Mr. Schultz knew everything about betrayal but the way it worked, in the freedom of the joyfully voracious spirit of all of us, or else why would his Abbadabba take the trouble to give me a horse? Mr. Schultz lacked imagination, he had a conventional mind, Drew was right, he was ordinary. Nevertheless I now faced enormous executive responsi-bilities, I had to bring things to pass, I had to engage people to do things I thought they ought to do and from a position of no authority whatsoever. As I thought about it, men in movies who got things done had assistants and secretaries. On a card right in front of me was the Grand Union Hotel's list of services, including a masseur, a barber, a florist, a Western Union office, and so on. I had an entire hotel at my disposal. I steeled myself and picked up the phone and in my lowest, softest voice, affecting the kind of nasality of speech of Drew Preston's friends, I informed the hotel operator that I wanted to reach Mr. Harvey Preston at the Savoy-Plaza in New York, and if he was not in residence to find out from the operator there his forwarding number, which might, perhaps, be Newport. When I hung up my hand was shaking, I, the juggler extraordinaire. I assumed it would take some time to locate Harvey, undoubtedly in bed somewhere with the company of his taste, so I called Room Service and they very respectfully took my order, which was honeydew melon and corn flakes and cream, scrambled eggs and bacon and sausages and toast and jelly and danish pastry and milk and coffee, I just went right down the menu. I sat in a wing chair by the open windows and tucked my Automatic behind the cushion and waited for my breakfast. It seemed to me very important to remain quite still, as one does in a very hot bath, so as to be able to endure it. Mickey would be driving and probably it was Irving with him because whatever they wanted to do would require precision in Saratoga, and perhaps patience, and something deft and sad in its effect rather than outrageous. I liked them both. They were quiet men and bore no ill will toward anyone. They didn't like to complain. They might inwardly demur but they would do their job.

I thought of what I would say to the elegant Harvey. I hoped he would be near a phone. It could even be white. He would hear me out having had the most perfunctory concern for Drew's safety over the summer because of the steady flow of charge account bills or canceled bank checks that had undoubtedly come to him in the mail. I would represent myself as transmitting his wife's wishes. I would be very businesslike. In my mind at the moment I had no personal interest at all in Mrs. Preston, certainly nothing that would tinge my voice with love or guilt. Not that I could ever feel guilty toward Harvey. But apart from that, I had lost in this situation any capacity at all for the eroticized affection, it wanes pathetically in terror, I not only could not remember making love with Drew, I could not even imagine it. She didn't interest me. There was a knock on the door and my breakfast was wheeled in and the very cart it came on was gatelegged out under its white linen cloth into a dining table. All the food was served in or under heavy silver. The melon was set in a silver bowl of ice. I had learned last night from Drew not to overtip and got the bellboy out of the room with aplomb. I sat feeling my gun in the small of my back and stared at this enormous breakfast as if I carried Bathgate Avenue where I went, with all the sweet fruits of the earth spilled on my plate. I missed my mother. I wanted to be wearing my black-and-white Shadows jacket. I wanted to steal from the pushcarts and hang around the beer drops and catch a glimpse of the great Dutch Schultz.

AT NOON, AFTER I PACKED MY BAG AND LEFT IT DOWNSTAIRS WITH THE BELL captain, I asked directions to the racecourse and made my way there on foot. It was about a mile from the hotel down a broad boulevard of dark three-story, deep-porched houses, one after another. In the front yards were signs that said PARK HERE and the residents stood in the street and tried to wave the passing cars into their driveways. Everyone in Saratoga was trying to make a little money, even the owners of these grand gabled houses. Most of the traffic was heading for the track's own parking lot, at every intersection cops in their short-sleeved shirts were waving it on. Nobody seemed to be in much of a hurry, the black cars moved at a stately pace and nobody blew their horns or tried to improve their position, it was the most mannerly traffic I had ever seen. I looked for the Packard even though I knew I wouldn't find it. If they set out in the early morning, even with Mickey driving it would take them to midafternoon to get here. All at once I saw the green roof of the grandstand, like some pennanted castle in the trees, and then I was on the grounds, and the day was festive with people streaming to the gates under their panama hats and sun parasols, they carried field glasses, men were hawking programs, the place was not as big as Yankee Stadium but grand of scale nonetheless, it was a wooden structure painted green and white, it had the air of a distinguished old amusement park with flower beds lining the paths. I stood on line for a clubhouse ticket and was told they would not let me in as an unaccompanied minor, I wanted to take out my Automatic and shove it up the guy's nose, but instead I asked an elderly couple to buy my ticket for me and walk me through the turnstile, which they were gracious enough to do, but it was a humiliating recourse for the trusted associate of one of the most deadly gangsters in the country.

Then when I climbed the stairs to the stands and came out to my first glimpse of the great oval track I felt immediately at home, it was that delicious shock of looking down from a deep shade to a green field in the sun, you got it from a baseball diamond or from a football gridiron, and now I saw the racecourse had it too, that sense before the sport begins of the glory of the day to come, the palapable anticipation of a formal strug- gle on a course as yet unmarked, with phantom horses racing to the finish line in a pristine brilliance of air and light. I felt I could handle myself here, I enjoyed the unexpected confidence that comes of recognition.

So there I was burdened with my deadly serious reponsibilities on this fine day when it seemed as if the whole society was coming to gamble, and the common people would do their betting on the grounds and stand in the sun by the rail to see what they could of the actual race, which was the homestretch, while the well-to-do bettors sat in the shade of the raked wooden stands so they could see somewhat more of the course, there were the boxes right at the front edge of the stands which had been bought for the season by politicians and men of wealth and fame, but if unoccupied on any particular day could be bought with a bribe to the usher to be used on a contingency basis, and finally, set back on a separate tier above the grandstand, was the expensive clubhouse where the truly sporting came to sit at tables and have their luncheon before the start of the day's races. I found Drew up there alone at a table for two with a glass of white wine in front of her.

I knew of course no matter what I told her she would not dream of leaving before she'd had her fill of the horses. I knew too that if I spoke of the danger she was in or acknowledged my fear her eyes would wander, her mind would wander, she'd drift away in her mind and spirit and the light I held in her eye would dim. She liked my precocity. She liked my street-tough self, she liked her boys gallant and bold. So I told her I had a sure thing in the seventh race and I was going to bet everything I had and make enough dough to keep her in bonbons and silk underwear for the rest of her life. It was supposed to be a joke but somehow it came out in a constricted voice, with more fervor than I intended, like a declaration of my childish love, and the effect on her depthless green eyes was to set them brimming. And now we both sat there in silence and great sadness, it was as if she knew from her own system of reckoning everything I didn't dare tell her. I couldn't look at her but turned my gaze to the track out there in the sun, a long wide beautifully kept raked-dirt oval track with white fencing, inside of which was an inner oval track of grass with obstacles for the steeplechase races, and inside that were plantings of red and white flowers and a pond with real swans paddling around, and all of it set in a vast verdant countryside with the foothills of the Berkshires far to the east, but I only saw oval, and ran my eyes around the closed track as if it were an endless bulkhead, as if I had not all the air of the world to breathe but the stifling diesel fumes in a tugboat deckhouse, and every moment that we had lived since that night was my hallucination, a moment's reprieve from the great heaving sea lunging up from itself to gulp at the night's prey, and people of my barest acquaintance who were dead had not yet died.

Little by little the tables filled up, though neither of us was hungry we lunched on cold salmon and potato salad, and finally the mounted men in red hunt coats came onto the track and the trumpet blew and the horses with their jockeys paraded at a slow pace past us to the far turn where the starting gate had been set up, and the first of the day's races went off, as they were to do thereafter every half hour, every thirty minutes or so a race went off, a mile or more or sometimes less around the broad raked-dirt track, you saw them perhaps for a few moments out of the starting gate and then unless you had glasses they became a rolling blur, as if one undulant individual animal was rippling around the far stretch of the track, and it was moving not all that quickly and only when it came into detailed view as horses again, in urgent and walloping whipped exertion, did you understand what a great distance they had run in what little time, and they were swift as devils as they galloped past you and crossed the finish line in front of the stands with the jockeys standing up then in their stirrups. And there was much excitement and importuning and shouting and screaming during the race, but it was not the kind of noise and cheering you got at a baseball game when Lou Gehrig hit a home run, it was not a joyous life sound and did not continue past the moment of the first horse's finish, but died off suddenly as if someone had thrown a switch, with everyone turning back to their charts to give the next half hour to the new bets, and only the winners still buzzing with happiness or gloating over their winnings, the flesh of the horse the least of anyone's concern, except perhaps the owner stepping into the winner's circle in front of the stands to pose for pictures with the jockey and the horse in its garland of carnations.

And I knew what Mr. Berman meant, what mattered were the numbers each animal carried around the track, the numbers on the big boards facing the stands that showed the odds at post time. The horses were running numbers, animated odds, even to the very wealthy squires who bred them and bought them at the yearling sales and owned them and raced them and won purses with them.

But all these impressions came to me through the corners of my eyes, as it were, and on the edges of my attention, as I left Drew and came back to her, and then took her down to her box and left her there, and went looking everywhere on all the levels for the hoods I knew and the hoods

I didn't know, because this was not the exclusive horse show of the night before, this was a grand convention of all the idlers of the world, I saw people pushing their two dollars under the grate who clearly were busted, people in the sun by the rail in their undershirts clutching their tickets that were the one way they could get out, whatever it was, to get out of it, I had never seen such pale faces come to enjoy a day, and everywhere on every tier, in every aisle, were the men who knew what others didn't and talked from the sides of their mouths and nodded the knowing nods of commerce, this was such a seedy stand of life, such a grubby elegance of occupation, with the drinkers of tall iced drinks or shots of neat all wanting too much from life and losing too much to it as they stood on the betting lines to try again in their democratic ceremonies of gain and loss on the creaking tiers of these old wooden stands.

All I asked of Drew was that she not go down to the paddock to see the horses before they came onto the track, that she sit in her box, which was numbered and known, just near the governor's box at the finish line, and content herself looking at them through her binoculars.

"You don't want me to bet?"

"Bet what you want. I'll go to the window for you."

"It doesn't matter."

She was very thoughtful and still and made a quietness around herself that I felt as a kind of mourning.

Then she said, "You remember that man?"

"Which man?"

"The one with the bad skin. The one he respects so."

"Bad skin?"

"Yes, in the car, with the bodyguards. Who came to the church."

"That man. Of course. How could I forget such skin."

"He looked at me. I don't mean he was forward or anything like that. But he looked at me and he knew who I was. So I must have met him before." She pursed her lips and shook her head with her eyes cast down.

"You don't remember?"

"No. It must have been at night."

"Why?"

"Because every night of my life I am a damn drunk."

I pondered this: "Were you with Bo?"

"I think I must have been."

"Did you ever tell Mr. Schultz?"

"No. Do you think I should have?"

"I think it's important."

"Is it? Is it important?"

"Yes, I think it might be."

"You tell him. Would you?" she said and raised her binoculars as the horses of the next race came at a walk onto the track.

* * *

A FEW MINUTES LATER A UNIFORMED MESSENGER CAME UP TO THE BOX WITH AN enormous bouquet of flowers in his hand and they were for Drew, a great armload of long-stemmed flowers, and she took them and her face colored, she read the card and it said *From An Admirer,* just as I had dictated, and she laughed and looked around her, up into the stands behind her, as if to find whoever it was who had sent them. I called to an usher and put a folded five-dollar bill in his hand and told him to bring a pitcher of water, which he did, and Drew placed the flowers in the pitcher and put them on the empty chair beside her. She was cheerier now, some people in the next box smiled and made appropriate remarks, and then another uniformed messenger arrived, this time with a floral arrangement so large it came with its own wicker stand, like a little tree with flowers like stalks of popcorn, and big green fan leaves mixed in and bell flowers of blue and yellow with little tails, and the card said *Ever Yours,* and now Drew was laughing with that shocked happiness of people who get Valentine's Day greetings or surprise birthday parties. I can't imagine, she answered when a gentleman leaned over and asked her what the occasion was. And when the third and fourth even larger deliveries were made, the last a display with dozens of long-stemmed roses, the whole box was transformed with flowers, she was surrounded by them, and there was considerable amusement and interest in the boxes around her and people stood up in their seats to see what was going on and there was a flurry of interest that spread through the stands and people started to come over from all directions to ask questions, to make remarks, some people thought she was a movie star, a young man asked her if he ought to be asking for her autograph, she had now more flowers around her than the winner of a cup race, she held them and was surrounded by them, and even more important, she was surrounded by the people who came up to see what all the excitement was about. Some of them were her friends from the horse set, and they sat with her and made jokes, and one woman had her two children with her, two little blond girls with bowl haircuts who were dressed in white dresses and bows and white anklets and polished white shoes, nice shy little girls, and Drew improvised little corsages for them to hold, and a photographer appeared from the local newspaper and took flash pictures, everything was going so well, I wanted those children to stay there, I asked the mother if they would like some ice cream and ran off to get some, and while I was at it I ordered from the clubhouse bar a couple of bottles of champagne and several glasses, flashing my roll and dropping Drew's name so that the bartender wouldn't give me a hard time, and soon she was entertaining right there in the box amid her flowers, and I stood back a step and saw that even some of the race officials on their horses glanced up from the track to where she was, it was as if the queen was present in her flower-bedecked box with little girl attendants and people lifting their glasses in her honor.

So all that was as good as it could be, still to come were deliveries of boxes of candy from the hotel chocolatier, I just didn't want her alone, I had other things up my sleeve if I needed them, I stood back and looked on my work and it was good, all I had to do was make it go on, how long I didn't know, another race's worth, another two, I thought it unlikely that members of the profession would want to perform at a crowded racetrack, that they would want to add to the history of a great track the story of an inexplicable assassination, and it would be clear to them if they checked the hotel first that her things were not packed, that she was not running, but how could I be sure of anything if I didn't know everything, I wanted a moving shield around her, like a fountain of juggled balls, like a thousand whirring jump ropes, like fireworks of flowers and the lives of innocent rich children.

So that was the situation, and I suppose it was during the fifth race, the horses were in the far stretch and all the glasses were raised, and how could I not know that among thousands of people one pair of binoculars down along the rail in the sun was turned the wrong way, how can you not know in the instant's deflected ray that you are looking down a tunnel into the eyes of your examiner, that through the great schism of sun and shade and over the cupidinous howl of the masses, you are quietly under the most intimate study? I turned and raced down the wooden staircase to the ground level and made my way past the tellers' cages, where a surprising number of bettors waited, listening to the public-address announcer's account of the race even though all they had to do was walk a few steps outside to see it for themselves. Everywhere on the ground was a litter of cast-off pari-mutuel tickets, and if I had been a few years younger I would probably have gone around and picked them up just because there were so many like things on the ground that could be collected, but the people who were hunkering here and there, turning the tickets over and picking them up and throwing them down again, were grown-ups, wretched pathetic losers scrounging around for that mystical event, the winning ticket mistakenly cast aside.

Out in front of the stands I immediately felt the heat of the afternoon, the light was blinding, and over the shoulders of shouting people I saw a blur of horses thundering past. You really heard them too, you heard the footfalls, you heard the whips in their sibilance. Did the horses run to win or to get away? I found Irving and Mickey at the rail looking for all the world like citizens of sport, with checked jackets and binocular cases hanging from their shoulders, and in Mickey's case a panama covering his bald skull and a pair of sunglasses masking his eyes.

"Faded badly in the stretch," Irving said. "All legs, no heart. You run a speed horse like that no more than six furlongs, if you're kind," he said and tore several tickets in half and put them in a nearby receptacle.

Mickey trained his glasses on the stands.

"Her box is just short of the finish line," I said.

"We can see that. All it lacks is the Stars and Stripes," Irving said in his whispery voice. "What is going on up there?"

"He's very happy to see her."

"Who is?"

"Mr. Preston. Mr. Harvey Preston, her husband."

Irving looked through his glasses. "What does he look like?"

"A tall man? Older."

"I don't spot him. What is he wearing?"

"Let me look a minute," I said and I tapped Mickey on the shoulder. He gave me his glasses and when I focused them she came into view so close in her anxious glance behind her that I wanted to call out I was here, I was down here, but the charm of my life held because as she stared, there indeed was Harvey coming down the stairs waving at her and a moment later he was in the box with his arms around her and she was hugging him, and they held each other at arm's length and smiled, he was saying something, she was genuinely happy to see him, she said something and then they both looked around them at all the flowers and he was shaking his head and holding his palms up, and she was laughing, and there was this milling crowd around them and one man was applauding as if in appreciation of the large gesture.

"Ain't love grand," I said. "In the madras jacket with the maroon silk foulard."

"The what?"

"That's what they call those handkerchiefs where the tie ought to be."

"I see him," Irving said. "You should have told us."

"How was I to know?" I said. "He showed up at lunch. This is their season here. How was I to know they practically own the damn town."

A few minutes later the whole box seemed to rise, a levitation of people and flowers, as Drew and Harvey proceeded toward the exit. He was waving at people like a politician and ushers hurried toward him to make themselves useful. I kept my eyes on Drew with her flowers in her arms, I don't know why but she seemed to move through the crowd with such care that I thought of a woman with child, that was my impression from this distance without the benefit of binoculars, that was my blurring impression. When they had disappeared down the passageway I moved with Irving and Mickey through the field crowd back under the stands past the betting cages and stood on the far side of a hotdog counter and we watched the party come down the staircase and Harvey had a car waiting right there, they had let it in through the gates where no cars were supposed to come, Drew turned and stood on her toes to look around, she was trying to find me, which was the last thing I wanted, but Harvey got her into that car fast, and jumped in after her, I had told him no cops, but a couple of state troopers stood there in jodhpurs and gun belts crisscrossed on their chests and those smart olive-drab felt scout hats complete with leather thong ties under their chins, these guys were on duty mostly for decoration, in case the governor showed up or someone like that, but they were large and incorruptible, I mean what could they give you in return, a highway? and the situation was ambiguous, I didn't like the frown I saw on Irving's face, if they had the idea that she was scared and running we were both in terrible trouble.

"What's this all about?" Irving said.

"Big-shot stuff," I said. "These guys have nothing better to do, that's all."

Moving quickly without running, Irving and Mickey left the park through a side entrance and moved to their own car. They insisted I come with them and I didn't feel I was in a position to argue. When we got to the Packard, I opened the door to get in the back and was shocked to see Mr. Berman sitting there. He was still up to his tricks. I said nothing and neither did he, but I knew now it was his passion I was dealing with. Irving said: "The husband showed up." Mickey got us into the traffic, and he picked up the car within a block and we followed it at a discreet distance. I was as surprised as anyone when it gathered speed and headed south out of town. They weren't even stopping for her things at the hotel.

Quite suddenly Saratoga ended and we were in the country. We drove behind them ten or fifteen minutes. Then I looked through the side window and realized we were abreast of an airfield, planes, single and double wings, were lined up parked like cars. Harvey's driver turned in there and we went past the entrance and pulled off the road under some trees where we could see the hangar and the runway beyond it. A wind sock at the end of the runway hung limp, just the way I felt.

There was a terrible silence in the car, the motor was left running, I could feel Mr. Berman calculating the odds. They had driven up to a single-engine plane whose door was open just under the wing. Someone already inside was extending his arms to help them climb in. Again Drew turned to look behind her and again Harvey stepped into her line of vision. She still had flowers in her arms.

"Looks like the little lady has pulled a fast one," Mr. Berman said. "You didn't see this coming?"

"Sure," I said. "Like I knew Lulu was going to bust me in the nose."

"What could she be thinking?"

"She's not scared, if that's what you mean," I said. "This is the way they travel in this league. The truth is she's been ready to move on for a while now."

"How do you know? Did she tell you that?"

"Not in so many words. But I could tell."

"Well that's interesting." He thought a moment. "If you were right that would certainly change the picture. Did she say anything about Dutch, was she angry at him or anything?"

"No."

"How do you know?"

"I just know. She doesn't care, it doesn't matter to her."

"What doesn't matter?"

"Nothing. Like she left a brand-new car at the hotel. We can take it, it won't matter to her. She's not after anything, she's not naturally afraid like most girls you'd meet or jealous or any of that. She does whatever she wants, and then she gets bored and then she does something else. That's all."

"Bored?"

I nodded.

He cleared his throat. "Obviously," he said, "this is a conversation that must never again be spoken of." The cabin door closed. "What about the husband. Is he someone who we should expect to give us trouble?"

"He's a cream puff," I said. "And in the meantime I have missed the seventh race and I didn't get to put a bet down on that sure thing you gave me. That was my paycheck, that was my big chance to make a killing."

A man came out of the hangar and grabbed one end of the propellor with two hands and spun it and jumped back when the engine turned over. Then he ducked under the wings and pulled the chocks from under the wheels and the plane taxied onto the runway. It was a lovely silver plane. It paused for a moment with its ailerons flapping and its rudder waggling from side to side, and then it took off. After a moment it lifted into the air. You could see how light and fragile it was rising and sliding and shuddering through the volume of the sky. It banked and flashed in the sun and then rose on its new course and began to be hard to see. As I watched it, its outlines wavered, like something swimming. Then I felt as if it was one of those threadlike things drifting across the ball of my eye. Then it disappeared into a cloud but I was still left with the feeling of something in my eye.

"They'll be other races," Mr. Berman said.

PART FOUR

SEVENTEEN

The moment I returned I realized the country had damaged my senses, all I could smell was burning cinder, my eyes smarted, and the clamor was deafening. Everything was broken down and falling apart, the tenements looked worn out by history, the empty lots were rubble, but what was most serious of all, what was clearly a sign to me of my brain damage, was how small my street looked, how miserably humble and wretchedly squeezed in among the other streets. And I came along in my rumpled white linen suit with the points of my collar curling up in the heat and my tie knot loosened, and I had thought I had wanted to look good for my mother, so that she would see how well I had done for myself over the summer, but I was instead wilted from the long trip, it was a hot Saturday in New York and I felt weak and washed out, with the leather valise a heavy weight on the socket of my arm, but the way the people looked at me I realized I was deranged in this sense of things too, I looked too good, I was not someone returning home but an absolute foreigner, nobody in the East Bronx had clothes like this, nobody owned a leather valise with two cinch straps, they all looked at me, the kids diverted from their games of skelly and box ball, the adults on the stoops forgetting their conversation, and I walked past them, stepping by in the damaged sense of my hearing, everything now hushed, as if the bitter acrid and stifling air had steeped me in silence.

But all of this was as nothing when I climbed the dark stairs. The door of our apartment was not entirely closed because the lock was broken, the first of a series of infinitesimal changes the universe had made in the downward direction while I was away, and when I pushed the door it swung open to a dismal low-ceilinged flat that was at the same time familiar and arbitrarily insane with slanting linoleum floors and furniture whose stuffing was hanging out, and a dead plant on the fire escape, and in the kitchen a whole wall and ceiling blackened where my mother's lights must have flared too hot. The kitchen table of burning drinking glasses was not now in operation, the tabletop was covered with hardened spires and globs and pools of white wax with small black craters and pits that made me think of a planetarium model of the moon. And there was no sign of my mother though she still lived here, I could tell that, her jar with the long jeweled hairpins was not moved, the photograph of her as a young woman standing next to my father, whose figure had been X'd out with a crayon and face carefully excised, that was still there, her few clothes hanging from the back of the bedroom closet door, and up on the shelf the hatbox I had sent from Onondaga, the hat still inside and wrapped in tissue just the way it had come from the store.

In the icebox were some eggs and a stale half a rye bread in a paper bag, and a bottle of milk that was curdled on top.

I turned on a light sat down on the floor in the middle of this domain of a lost woman and her lost son and from each of my pockets removed the folded bills of our wealth and smoothed them out and arranged them by denomination and straightened them into a stack, tapping them on all four sides with my stiffened palms: I had come down from the country with a little over six hundred and fifty dollars, the remains of my Saratoga expense account which Mr. Berman told me I could keep. It was an immense amount of money but it was not enough, nothing was enough to pay the bill for this high holy life of rectitude, faith, and bathing in the kitchen sink. I put the cash in my bag and the bag in the closet and found a pair of old knickers that were torn in the knees and a ribbed undershirt and my old Nat Holman lace-up sneakers with the soles worn away, and I changed into these things and felt a little better, I sat on the fire escape and smoked a cigarette and began to remember who I was, whose son I was, except that the prospect across the street of the brick-and-limestone Max and Dora Diamond Home for Children presented itself first to my eyes and then to my mind, I stuck the cigarette in the corner of my mouth, swung over the side of the fire escape, handed myself down the ladder, and hanging there from my hands dropped the last ten feet to the sidewalk, only realizing as I landed that I was not quite the flowing phantom of grace I had been, there was more of a shock to the knees in this hanging drop and to the little bones of the feet, I had eaten well in the country and perhaps filled out a bit, I looked up and down to see who was watching and walked across the street as slowly as I needed to in order to mask my inclination to limp, and went down the steps to the basement of the Diamond Home for Children, where my friend Arnold Garbage who had sold me my Automatic sat in his ashen kingdom and collected everything as it made its way down to us from the higher realms of purposefulness.

Oh my stolid friend, "Where was you," he said, as if I had been under a misapprehension all these years that he was dumb, the verbosity of the fellow, and he had grown too, he was going to be a giant fat man, like Julie Martin, he stood to greet me and tin pots fell from him clattering to the cement basement floor and he stood in his full height, this glandular genius, and he smiled.

So that was good, coming to the basement again, and sitting around smoking and telling lies to Arnold Garbage while he examined one mysterious unidentifiable inorganic item after another in order to make a determination as to which bin to throw it in, and the footfalls overhead of the Diamond orphans at their games thrupped and pounded the foundations and made me think of the sweet gurgling exertions of children as water springing from the earth. I actually wondered if perhaps I ought to return to school, I would be in the tenth grade if I did, Mr. Berman's favorite number, containing the one and the zero and capping all the numbers you needed to express any number, it was just a passing thought, the sort of idea you have when you're hurt and in a weakened condition.

But when I went upstairs to look in the old gym and see if I saw there anyone else I knew, a small black-haired girl acrobat, for example, I caused consternation, the rhythm of their games broke and that same silence came over them as when I walked into the block with my suitcase, the children, who now looked awfully young, stared at me in the sudden gymnastic hush, a volleyball rolled across the shiny wood floor, and a counselor I didn't recognize who was holding her whistle attached to a woven lanyard around her neck approached me and said this was not a public place and visitors were not allowed.

This was the first bulletin of the news that my assumptions were expired, that I could not reinsert myself, as if there were two kinds of travel and while I was moving upstate on roads over mountains, the people of my street were advancing in the cellular time of their being. I found out Becky was gone, she had been taken by a foster family in New Jersey, one of the girls on her floor told me this, how lucky Becky was because she had her own room now, and then she told me to leave, that I shouldn't come to the girls' floor, that it wasn't right, and I went to the roof where before I knew I loved her I had paid that dear little girl for her fucks, and the super was up there painting green lines for a shuffleboard court, and he stood up and rubbed the back of his hand that was holding the brush across his face where the sweat was itching, and he told me I was street trash and that he'd give me *three* to get off the property and that if he ever saw me here again he'd beat the shit out of me and then call the cops so that they could do it again.

Well all this as you can imagine was indeed an interesting homecoming, but really what angered me was how vulnerable I was, and stupid, to expect something, I didn't know what, from this neighborhood I hadn't been able to leave fast enough. In the days following I realized that wherever I had been, whatever I had done, the people knew about it not in its detail but in its fulfillment of their myth-knowledge of the rackets. My reputation had advanced. In the candy store on the corner where I bought the papers every morning and evening, on the stoops of hot twilight, and all the way over to Bathgate, I was known by sight, and who I was and what I did made this light around me as I walked, I understood

I was illuminated as one *in their midst,* it was a kind of infamy. I had
known those neighborhood feelings myself, there had always been someone like me to know about from the other kids, to hear mentioned only
after he had turned the corner, to be feared, to be told to stay away from.
Under the circumstances it was pretentious for me to wear my old kid
juggler's rags, I would go back to wearing the wardrobe of my success.
Besides, I didn't want to disappoint anybody. Once you're in the rackets
you can never get out, Mr. Schultz had told me, and he had said it not in
any menacing way but with a voice of self-pity, so that I thought, as a
proposition, it was suspect. But not now, not now.

Of course I am summarizing the rueful conclusions of some days, at
first there was only bewilderment, the worst shock was my mother, whom
I saw just a few hours after my arrival, she was coming down the street
pushing her brown wicker baby carriage and I knew immediately even
from a distance her lovely distraction had gone awry. Her gray hair was
uncombed and flowing, and the closer she got the more terribly sure I was
that unless I stepped in front of her and spoke to her she would pass me
by without a glimmer of recognition. Even at that it was touch-and-go, the
first emotion that registered on her face was anger, because the carriage
had met an impediment, then her eyes lifted and for a moment I felt as if
I was out of focus in her mind, that she saw me and knew just enough to
know it was important to make sense of me, and only then, after an
unendurable stop in my heart's beat, did I live again in the recognition of
stately, mad Mary Behan.

"Billy, is this you?"

"Yes, Ma."

"You've grown out."

"Yes, Ma."

"He's a big lad," she said to whoever it was who was listening. She
was staring at me now with such intensity that I had to move toward her
to get out of the glare, I hugged her and kissed her cheek, she was not fresh
and clean as I'd always known her to be, but had about her the acrid,
cindery redolence of the street. I looked down in the baby carriage and saw
there browning leaves of lettuce flattened neatly and spread like lily pads
over the inside, and corncobs, and the spilled insides of cantaloupe seeds
still attached in their mucusy webs. I didn't want to know what she
imagined she had there. She was unsmiling and not to be consoled.

Oh Mama, Mama, but once the carriage was in the house she overturned it and dumped the detritus on newspaper and rolled it up in a paper
bag and put it in the kitchen trash can, which waited as always for the
super's buzzer to signal when it was to be loaded onto the dumbwaiter. So
that was reassuring. I was to learn that she went in and out of her states
as if she suffered her own passing weather conditions, and every time she
cleared up I decided she would be all right for good now, that the problem
was over. Then she would storm over again. On Sunday I showed her all

the money I had, which seemed to please her, and then I went out and brought back the materials for a proper breakfast and she cooked everything up in the old way, remembering how we liked our sunny-sides up, and she had bathed and dressed herself nicely and combed and pinned her hair so that we were able to have a morning stroll to Claremont Avenue and up the steep stairs to Claremont Park and to sit in the park on the bench under a big tree and read the Sunday papers. But she would not ask me anything about the summer, where I had been or what I had done, not from any lack of curiosity, but from a knowledgeable silence, as if she had heard it all, as if there was nothing I could tell her that she didn't already know.

I felt by this time terribly guilty of neglect, she seemed so to enjoy being out of the immediate neighborhood, sitting in the peacefulness of the green park, and the possibility that she had been affected by my actions, that she had been made to feel estranged, as I was, in the general community misgiving of a bad family, a crazy woman who had of course raised a bad boy, was enough to make me want to weep.

"Ma," I said. "We have enough money to move. How would you like a new apartment somewhere around here, right near the park, maybe we could find a building with an elevator and we could look down into the park from every window. See, like those houses over there."

She gazed in the direction I pointed and then shook her head no over and over, and then sat and stared at her hands folded on her pocketbook in her lap and shook her head again as if she had to rethink the question and answer it again as if it kept popping up again and again and wouldn't stay answered.

I was so blue, I insisted we have lunch out, I was ready to do anything, take her to the movies, the thought of going back to our street was insupportable, I was so lost I could only think of living in public places, where something was happening, where I might be able to reanimate my mother, get her to smile, get her to talk, get her to be my mother again. At the edge of the park I flagged a taxi and had him take us all the way up to Fordham Road, to the same Schrafft's where we had had our tea that day she had come with me to buy clothes. We had to wait for a table but when we sat down I could see it pleased her to be back there, and that she remembered it and enjoyed its dainty pretensions, its suggestion of the dignity given to people from their patronage, though now of course I found it a dull place with very bland food in mincy portions, and thought to myself with a laugh of those heavily taken meals with the gang at the Onondaga Hotel and how they would all look right now if they were eating here at Schrafft's with the churchgoers from East Fordham Road, the expression on Lulu Rosenkrantz's face when the waitress served him his little cucumber-and-butter sandwich with the crust removed and the tall ice-cream glass of iced tea without enough ice. And then I made the mistake of thinking about my steak dinner at the Brook Club with Drew Preston and the way she looked across the table leaning on her elbow and drinking me in with her smiling tipsy dreaminess of expression and I felt my ears grow hot and looked up and there was my mother smiling at me in just the same way, in terrifying resemblance, so that for an instant I didn't know where I was, or who I was with, and it seemed to me they knew each other, Drew and my mother, by some imposition of one on the other that made them old friends, and that their full mouths matched and their eyes passed like rings through each other's eyes, and that I was cursed with an undifferentiated love that made them inseparable. This was all in the space of an instant but I cannot remember now when I have felt as catastrophically self-informed, I had molted and muscled out, skin and mind and wit, molted and muscled out again and again, except in the heart, except in the heart. I was all at once enraged, at what, at whom, I didn't know, at God for not moving as quickly, as adeptly, as I could, at the food on my plate, I was bored by my mother, I loathed the pathetic existence to which she had consigned herself, it was not fair to be dragged back into the hopeless boredom of family life, to be taken down this way after all the hard work of my criminal intentions, I was doing it, didn't she realize? She'd better not try to stop me. Let anyone try to stop me.

But you know, the waitress comes over and says will that be all and then you ask for the check and pay it.

On that first Monday morning after my return my mother went off to her laundry job as she always had, which suggested to me her madness was self-governed, which meant it was not madness at all but just a passing version of the distraction I had always known. Then I happened to look into the wicker carriage and saw there arranged as in a nest the eggshells from our Sunday breakfast. So for the first time but not the last, I went from confidence to despair in the space of a second. I wondered, as I would wonder over and over as part of the whole irresolute cycle, if perhaps I should stop fooling myself and come to grips with the truth that something had to be done, that I had better get her to a doctor, have her examined and treated, before she got so bad she would need to be put in an asylum. I didn't exactly know how to go about this, or whom to consult, but it seemed to me Mr. Schultz had an old widowed mother he took care of, perhaps he could help, perhaps the gang even had its doctors the way it had its lawyers. Anyway, who else could I turn to? I didn't belong here anymore, I didn't belong with the orphans or the people in the neighborhood, all I had was the gang, whatever my ultimate intentions and passing disloyalties, I was theirs and they were mine. Whatever desires I had—to abandon my mother, to save my mother—they all convened on Mr. Schultz.

But I wasn't hearing from him and I wasn't hearing from them and all I knew was what I got from the papers. I would not go out now except to get the papers or my packs of Wings, I read every paper I could get my hands on. I bought them all, all day and all night, it began late at night when I went up to the kiosk under the Third Avenue El and bought the early editions of the next morning's papers, and then in the morning I went to the candy store on the corner for the late editions, and then at noon I'd go over to the kiosk for the the early editions of the evening papers, and then in the evening I'd go to the corner and pick up the final editions. The government's case seemed to me inarguable. They had evidence on paper, they had accountants from the Internal Revenue Bureau explaining the income tax law, they were really laying it out. I was very nervous. When Mr. Schultz took the stand it seemed to me he was not persuasive. He explained that he had been given the wrong advice by his lawyer, that his lawyer had simply made a mistake, and that once another lawyer had explained the mistake he, Mr. Schultz, had endeavored to pay every penny he owed as a patriotic citizen, but this was not good enough for the government, which decided it would rather prosecute him. I didn't know if even a farmer would believe that lame story.

As I waited for the news I tried to see the good in either verdict as it might be handed down so as to try to prepare myself whatever happened. If Mr. Schultz went to jail we would all be safe from him for as long as he was put away. That was an undeniable good. Oh to think of being freed of him! But at the same time my faith in the quietly working clockwork of my given destiny would be shattered. If something as ordinary and mundane as government justice could tilt my life awry, then my secret oiled connections to the real justice of a sanctified universe were nonexistent. If Mr. Schultz's crimes were only earthly crimes with earthly punishments, then there was nothing else in the world but what I could see, and whereas I had been humming in the conviction of invisible empowerments, it was my own mind only making them up. That was unendurable. But if he beat the rap, if he beat the rap, I was back in my lines of danger and trusting with a boy's pure and shaking trust I would get through to the just conclusion of my chosen perils. So which did I want? Which verdict, which future?

In the way I waited I realized my answer, I looked every morning in the back of the *Times* at the passenger ship sailings, I just wanted to know which ships they were and where they were going and that there were lots of them to choose from. I trusted Harvey Preston had worked things out, I was beginning to like him, he'd certainly come through in Saratoga and I saw no reason why he wouldn't now. In my mind I watched her leaning on the railing with the moon out and staring at the silvery ocean and thinking of me. I imagined her in shorts and halter playing shuffleboard on the rear deck in the sun just the way the kids played it on the roof of the orphan home. If I had been wrong, if Mr. Berman and Irving and

Mickey had only come to Saratoga to take her back or to talk to her on behalf of Mr. Schultz, well then what, after all, had been lost except Drew to me, except my Drew to me?

In the Wednesday evening papers, the lawyers presented their summations, and on Thursday the judge gave his instructions to the jury, by Thursday evening the jury was still out and late Thursday night I went to Third Avenue and Mr. Schultz was the headline in Extras put out by both the evening and the morning papers: He was innocent of all charges.

I whooped and hollered and jumped up and down and danced around the kiosk while a train rumbled overhead. You wouldn't know from looking at me that I believed this was the man who just a week before had been intending to kill me. He was shown close up, broadly smiling at the camera in the *Mirror,* kissing his rosary in the *American,* and holding Dixie Davis's head in the crook of his arm and planting a big kiss on the top of it in the *Evening Post.* The *News* and the *Telegram* showed him with his arm around the foreman of the jury, a man in overalls. And all of the papers carried the remarks of the judge on hearing the jury's verdict: "Ladies and gentlemen, in all my years on the bench I have never witnessed such disdain of truth and evidence as you have manifested this day. That you could on hearing the meticulous case presented by the United States Government find the defendant not guilty on all charges so staggers my faith in the judicial process that I can only wonder about the future of this Republic. You are dismissed with no thanks from the court for your service. You are a disgrace."

My mother saved the front page of the *Mirror* with Mr. Schultz's smiling face and folded it so that just the picture showed, she laid it down in the carriage and brought a threadbare blanket up to its chin.

AND NOW I WILL TELL OF THE REVELS THAT WENT ON FOR THREE NIGHTS AND TWO days in the brothel on West Seventy-sixth Street between Columbus and Amsterdam avenues. Not that I knew at any given time whether it was night or day because the red velour drapes were pulled across every window and the lights were always on, the lamps with their tasseled shades, the cut-glass chandeliers, and the particular hour was not something very important after a while. It was a brownstone and one of the sights I remember is of a trembling slightly aged whore's puckered behind as she ran up the stairs shrieking in mock fear while this hood tried to catch her but fell on his face instead and slid down the flight of stairs face down and feet first and arms up. Most of the women were young and pretty and slender, and some of them got tired and left and were replaced by others. Also there were a lot of men I didn't recognize, this was supposed to be for the top gang members but word had gotten around and the unshaven faces kept changing, and on the second night or day I even saw a cop in his undershirt with his suspenders holding his blue pants up and a whore with his braid cap set awry on the back of her head kissing his bare feet, toe by toe.

Women were laughing and getting playfully pinched and tickled by fearsome men, but showing no fear and in fact going off with them up the stairs, like multiples of Drew in their fearlessness of taking killers into themselves. I was stunned by this transformation of the value of feeling into numbers, in a corner of a room I saw Mr. Berman's sly laughing face appearing through his cigarette smoke, and in the big downstairs parlor three or four women were draped all over Mr. Schultz, on the arms of his chair, in his lap, nibbling on his ears, begging him to dance, he laughed and fondled them and pinched them and handled them, there was a profusion of flesh and as I looked it didn't seem to be organized according to individual persons but was all jumbled together, profusions of breasts and constellations of nipples, cornucopic bellies and asses and tangles of long legs. Mr. Schultz saw me looking and appointed a woman to take me to bed, she reluctantly disentangled herself and led me upstairs, and there was a good deal of attendant merriment on the part of my colleagues, which turned the occasion into something unpleasant for me and for the woman too, who was seething with anger because she felt demeaned by my age and unimportance. Both of us could hardly wait to be finished, this was not the party, the party was elsewhere, it was appalling to me how unsexy sex could be humped up with such scorn and impatiently delivered, I had an actual Manhattan to drink afterward, it at least was sweet with a crunchy cherry at the bottom of it.

The madam who ran things stayed in the kitchen on the ground floor in the back, a very nervous woman whom I sat with and talked to for a while, I felt sorry for her because Mr. Schultz when drunk had slugged her for some imagined offense and had given her a black eye. Then he'd apologized and given her a new hundred-dollar bill. She was a tiny woman he called Mugsy maybe because she so resembled the little Pekingese she held in her lap, she had a little pug-nosed button-eyed face with highly curled but very thin red hair and a small skinny body dressed in a black dress and stockings which drooped a little at the knees. She had a low voice, like a man's. I talked to her while she held a slice of raw steak over her eye. In the oven of the stove were all the guns people had to turn over when they arrived. She would not leave the kitchen I think because she didn't want anyone to come in and get a gun and start shooting up her house, although what she could have done to prevent it, this little tiny lady, I can't say. She had a staff of Negro maids who kept things going, changing linens, emptying ashtrays, collecting empty bottles, and she had delivery boys, also colored, coming in the back door with cases of mixer and beer and booze, and cartons of cigarettes and hot dinners in metal containers from steakhouses and hot breakfasts in cardboard cartons from neighborhood diners, she was tense but had things very well organized, like a general who had planned well and deployed all his troops and had only to hear them report from time to time how the battle was going. I juggled some hard-boiled eggs in their shell and she was so sure I was going to drop them that she laughed with appreciation when I didn't, she took a liking to me, she wanted to know all about me, what my name was, where I lived, and I said yes, and how had a nice boy like me come to this sordid profession, which made her laugh again. She pinched my cheek and offered me chocolates from a fancy painted metal box which she kept by her side, it showed scenes of men in knee britches and white wigs bowing to ladies in big hoop skirts.

But this Madam Mugsy understood my inclination to linger in the kitchen for what it was, and with great delicacy and tact she suggested that she had something special for me, that most desirable item, a fresh girl, by which she meant a young one fairly new to the trade, and she made a phone call and within an hour I was up in a small quiet bedroom on the top floor with what indeed was a young girl, light-haired round-faced high-waisted and somewhat shy and rubbery to the touch, who lay with me through the night, or the quiet hours that passed for night, and fortunately needed as much sleep in her youth as I needed in mine.

I was too self-conscious and unsure of myself and sad to really enjoy these revels. Up in the Bronx as I'd waited for the trial to end I had the avid desire to reconnect with the gang, I felt love for every one of them, there was a kind of consistency to their behavior that made me feel grateful for their existence, but now that I was reunited with them the other side of that gratitude was guilt, I looked to the faces of Mr. Schultz and the others to see how I fared there, in a smile of gold teeth I read exoneration one moment, retribution the next.

But then, I suppose it was by the second night, I realized I wasn't the only one in a less than ecstatic state, Mr. Berman had entrenched himself in the front parlor and sat reading the papers and smoking and sipping brandy, he went out a lot to use public pay phones, and while Lulu was still exercising his uncouth being upon a selection of ladies not one of whom failed to complain to the management, Irving absented himself rarely, and only gave way to the joy of the occasion by taking off his jacket, loosening his tie, and rolling up his sleeves and serving as bartender to all the close and casual freeloaders of the criminal trades. I finally realized that Mr. Schultz's chief lieutenants were waiting, that is all they were doing, and that the celebration was by the second day not a joyful party of men who had been through something together but a sort of statement to the profession, a business announcement that the Dutchman had re-turned, and all the true merriment and joy and relief of victory had given way to the hollow gaiety of a public-relations event.

Even Mr. Schultz sought now the places in the house for the quieter pleasures of reflection, and I happened to pass one of the bathrooms where he was sitting in a hot soapy tub puffing a cigar into the steamy air and enjoying a back wash from the madam, Mugsy, who sat on a wooden stool beside the tub and talked and joked with him as if he hadn't slugged her the day before.

He glanced up and saw me. "Come in, kid, don't be shy," he said. I sat down on the lid of the toilet bowl. "Mugsy this here is my pro-to-jay, Billy, you two met yet?" We said we had. "You know who Mugsy is, kid? You know how far we go back? I'll tell you," he said, "when Vince Coll was on the rampage, gunning for me all over the Bronx, and going crazy looking for me where do you think I was all the time?"

"Here?"

"Except then I had my house on Riverside Drive," the madam said.

"Coll was so dumb," Mr. Schultz said, "he wouldn't know about the finer things of life, he didn't know what a high-class whorehouse looked like, and while he's going around shooting everything that moves, hitting bars and drops and clubhouses, the dumb fuck, I am snug like a bug in a rug at my Mugsy's taking pleasure and biding my time. Sitting in the bathtub and getting my back washed."

"That's right," the woman said.

"Mugsy's as square as they come."

"I better be," she said.

"Get me a beer, would you, doll?" Mr. Schultz said lying back in the tub.

"I'll be back," she said and dried her hands on a towel and left the room, closing the door.

"You having a good time, kid?"

"Yes, sir."

"It's important to get that clean country air out of your lungs," he said grinning. He closed his eyes. "Also to get your heart back in your balls, where it belongs. Where it's safe. Did she say anything?"

"Who?"

"Who, who," he said.

"Mrs. Preston?"

"I think that was the lady's name."

"Well she did tell me she liked you very much."

"She said that?"

"That you have class."

"Yeah? Comin' from her," he said and a pleased smile came over his face. He kept his eyes closed. "In a better world," he said. "If this were a better world." He paused. "I like the idea of women, I like that you can pick them up like shells on the beach, they are all over the place, little pink ones and ones with whorls you can hear the ocean. The trouble is, the trouble is . . ." He shook his head.

The steamy water and the tile did something to his voice, so that even as he spoke softly it hollowed out as if we were in a cavern. He was now staring at the ceiling. "I think you only fall for someone, what I mean is the only time it's possible is when you're a kid, like you, when you don't know the world is a whorehouse. You get the idea in your mind and that's it. And for the rest of your life you're stuck on her, and you think every time you turn around she's this one or that one who comes along and smiles like her and fills her in. We have that first one when we're stupid and don't know any better. And we walk away, and she becomes the one we look for for the rest of your life, you know?"

"Yes," I said.

"Hell, she was a dignified girl, Drew. Not ordinary ginch at all, nothing cheap about her. She had this lovely mouth," he said pulling on his cigar. "But you know the expression 'summer romance'? Sad to say it was no more than that. We both have our lives we had to go back to." He glanced at me to see my response. "I have a business to run," he said. "And I have survived in this business because of my attention to business."

He sat up in the tub, bubbles of soapy water caught in the black hairs of his shoulders and chest. "When you think who I have outlasted, what I have had to contend with. Every day in the week. The thieves, the rats. Everything you build up, everything you work for, they try to steal it from you. Big Julie. My dear Bo, my dear dear Bo. And like Coll, who I have mentioned. You know what loyalty is worth? You know what a loyal man is worth these days? His weight in gold. I was good to Vincent Coll. And he goes and skips bail I put up for him. Did you know that? I never start these things. I'm just this good-natured slob people think they can walk all over. And before you know it, I'm in a fucking war with this madman and having to hide out in a whorehouse. To tell you the truth I felt very bad about that, it was not the manly thing to do. But I had to bide my time. One day in the middle of everything Vincent is picked up and detained, he goes into temporary detention on some rap, and I figure this is my chance, so we lay in wait for him when he comes out except he knows we're there so he gets his sister to meet him and walks out holding his sister's kid in his arms. You see what I'm saying? We back off, we are not barbarians, he has us and we go away to fight another day. Just to show you. But the Mick he doesn't play by any rules of civilization, not a week later he comes rolling around the corner of Bathgate Avenue looking for me with the windows down as I happen to be in the neighborhood to visit my old mother and bring her some nice flowers. When I go see Mama I go alone, maybe that is stupid, I mean I know it is, but it is another life she leads and I don't want to offend it, so I am by myself with a nice bouquet of flowers I have just bought and I am on this crowded street nodding to this one or that who happens to know me, and I have that sixth sense, you know? or maybe I see something in the eyes of someone walking toward me, that he would look past me? I dive behind a fruit stall, the slugs fly and the oranges go up in the air and the peaches and watermelon busting like skulls spraying, and I am lying there under falling crates of grapefruits and plums and pears and all this juice, so I think I've been hit, it feels wet, it would be funny, I'm lying there with all this fruit juice leaking over me, except the screaming of the women and children, it is a family street for christsake, you know with all the pushcarts and the balabustas out doing their marketing, and then the car is gone and I get up and I see over the top of the stall people running the mother screaming in Italian and there is a baby carriage on its side with a baby spilled out, the baby nightie soaked in blood, blood all over his bonnet, the fuckers have killed the kid in its carriage, God help us all. And then someone starts pointing at me, cursing me, you know? like I have shot the kid! and I have to run for it with people shouting after me! Well when that happened I knew I would kill Vincent Coll if it was the last thing I did, I felt honor bound, I made a sacred vow. But the press gives me the rap, me, the Dutchman, because I am at war with this maniac madman, that is the joke of it, I am getting the blame for Vincent Coll, as if I didn't warn everyone, as if I didn't try to tell everyone to watch out for him, I get the blame for being the missing target, for not being shot instead of that murdered infant when the fact it was the Mick who did wrong from the beginning, jumping the bail of ten grand I put up for him, ten grand! and then hitting on my trucks and drops, it was a remorseful error of judgment I ever hired him in the first place, I had to get him, I swore to myself I would take him down, it was a matter of restoring the moral world in its rightful position. You know how I did it?"

There was a knock on the door and the little madam came in with a tray with two bottles of beer and a couple of tall glasses and set it down on the stool. "I'm telling about Vince," he said to her. "It was very simple, a simple idea, like the simple things are always the best. I remembered he and Owney Madden talked a lot, that was all."

"A gentleman, Owney," the madam said, lighting herself a cigarette.

"Exactly so," Mr. Schultz said. "Exactly the point, so I don't know, he must have had something on Owney because why else would a class guy like Owney have anything to do with him? So it wasn't that difficult. I send Abe Landau to Owney's office and he sits there with him all night in his office till the phone rings and Abe puts the gun in Owney's side, and he says just keep talking, Mr. Madden, keep him on the line, and we got this cop outside who gets the call traced, and the Mick is in a phone booth in the Excelsior drugstore on Twenty-third Street and Eighth Avenue. In five minutes I have a car there and he's got two guys sitting at the fountain to watch out for him but they look at the Thompson and out they go, running up the street as fast as their legs can carry them, no one has seen them since, and my guy, he stitches the rounds up one side of the phone booth and down the other, and Vincent he couldn't even get the doors open, he falls out only when they come off the hinges, and back in Owney's office Abe listens on the phone and hears it all and then there is silence on the line and he hangs up and says, Thank you, Mr. Madden, sorry to have been of inconvenience, and that was how we did in the Mick, may his gizzards boil in hell till the end of time."

Mr. Schultz fell silent and I heard him breathing hard in the exertion of his memory. He took a beer from the tray and guzzled it down. It gave me some comfort to see from his example that people can sustain any loss as long as they can go on being themselves.

THE NEXT MORNING I CAME DOWN THE STAIRS AND IT WAS IMMEDIATELY CLEAR TO me something had happened. There were no women in sight, the doors to the rooms were open. I heard a vacuum cleaner, I found Irving in the kitchen pouring mugs of coffee and I followed him to the front parlor and before he closed the door on me I saw that a meeting was going on, maybe a dozen or more men sitting around all dressed and every one of them sober.

I had been told to take a walk, which I did, I walked back and forth on the side streets of the Seventies from Columbus to Broadway, the town houses of brownstone and limestone, with their high stoops and basement doorways under the stairs, all stuck to one another from one end of the block to the other, not an alley in sight, no spaces, no views or vistas, no empty lots, just this continuous wall of residence. I felt closed out by these stone façades and shaded windows, and it was chilly too, I had not been out of doors for two days and three nights and it seemed to me true autumn had come in, a brisk breeze scuttled up the litter in the street, and the plane trees in their little fenced-in sidewalk plots were turning yellow, as if a tree blight of the north country had followed me, as if the cold was coming down after me no matter where I went. I felt at this moment as if I should never have left the city, I didn't feel at home in it anymore, from every crack in the sidewalk a weed grew, every corner had its cluster of puttering pigeons, squirrels ran the wires between the telephone poles like portents of lurking Nature, little spies of the encroachment.

Of course I was hurt to be shut out of what was clearly a serious business council, I wanted to know what I had to do to have my worth recognized, no matter what I did and how well, there were always these setbacks. I said fuck it and went back and I found that the meeting was over, the visitors were gone, and it was just Mr. Schultz and Mr. Berman in the front room, they were dressed for business in shirts and ties. Mr. Schultz paced while he twirled his rosary around his hand, not a good sign. When the phone in the front hall rang he ran out himself and took the call, and a moment later he was putting on his suit jacket and setting his fedora on his head and he stood in the hall inside the front door absolutely pale in his fury. I was standing in the doorway to the parlor. "What does a man have to do?" he said to me. "Tell me. To be deserving of a break, to be able to begin to reap the fruits of his labor. When does that happen?'' Mr. Berman at the window in the parlor called ''Okay'' and Mr. Schultz opened the front door and closed it behind him. I ran to the window and parted the drapes and saw him ducking into a car, Lulu Rosenkrantz was on the running board on the street side, and he looked up and down the street before he swung in next to the driver, and the car moved off smartly and was gone, leaving only the exhaust rising in the air.

The little madam, Mugsy, came in and she had under her arm a shoebox which she placed on the coffee table. It held all her receipts and invoices, and she and Mr. Berman went over them together like a stunty little couple in a fairy tale, an old woodcutter and his ancient wife puffing their magic white weeds of smoke and child mystification and having a conversation in their language of numbers. I picked some newspapers off the floor: Mayor La Guardia had warned Dutch Schultz that if he was seen anywhere in the five boroughs of New York he would be arrested, and Special Prosecuting Attorney Thomas Dewey had announced he was preparing an indictment of Dutch Schultz for state income tax evasion. So that's what it was. It all had to do with that verdict upstate, the editorial writers were outraged, I never read editorials but Mr. Schultz's name was all over them, everyone was calling for his scalp, and every politician who could be found and quoted was likewise outraged, borough presidents were outraged, controllers, members of the Board of Estimate, attorney generals, police commissioners, deputy commissioners, even a lieutenant in the Department of Sanitation was outraged, even the man in the street in the *News*'s Man in the Street feature. It was interesting, in the context of all this outrage, how Mr. Schultz's happy smiling face of exoneration looked so brazen and sneering and sinister.

''That is for damage,'' the madam was saying as Mr. Berman held up a slip of paper in query. ''Your boys broke a dozen fine dinner plates, you didn't hear that I suppose, when they was throwing my Wedgwood at each other.''

''And this?'' Mr. Berman said.

''General overhead.''

''I don't like estimates. I like factual numbers.''

''This overhead is factual wear and tear. Look, right there, the very couch you're sitting on, you see the stains? That don't come out, wine doesn't come out, I'll need new slipcovers, and that's an example. How shall I say this, Otto, it is not a YMCA crowd you run through here.''

''You wouldn't perchance be taking advantage, Mugsy.''

''I resent that remark. You know why Dutch comes to me? Because I am the best. This is a high-class establishment and it don't come cheap. You like the girls? You should, they are show girls, they are not whores from the street. You like the service and the furnishings? How do you think I supply them, by chintzing on everything? I get what I pay for and so do you. It'll take me a week to get this place to where I can reopen. That is time lost, but I still got to pay rent and the payoffs and the doctors' fees and the electric company. I'll tell you what, the black eye I give to you. On the house."

Mr. Berman took out a thick bankroll and removed the rubber band. He counted out hundred-dollar bills. "This and not a penny more," he said, pushing the money across the coffee table.

When we left the woman was sitting there on the couch holding her hand over her eyes and crying. A car was at the curb. Mr. Berman told me to get in and he got in after me. I didn't recognize the driver. "Nice and easy," Mr. Berman said to him. We drove down Broadway and then over to Eighth Avenue and down Eighth past Madison Square Garden and then west to the river and down past the docks, which frightened me for a moment until I realized what we were doing, we passed the landing of the Hudson River Day Line, where a paddle steamer was taking on passengers for an excursion, and then we headed east on Forty-second Street and then north up Eighth again, and so on, marking a big rectangle around the area known as Hell's Kitchen uptown and down, east and west, three or four times, until we finally came to a stop on a block in the West Forties not far from the stockyards. I saw Mr. Schultz's car parked maybe a half a block ahead of us on the south side of the street, right in front of a big brownstone church with an attached rectory and schoolyard.

The driver did not turn off the engine. Mr. Berman lit a cigarette and he said to me the following: "We cannot call the Chairman on the telephone. Nor will he speak to any of us on sight, not even Dixie Davis, who anyway is in Utica testifying at an inquest having to do with the lamentable death of a dear colleague of ours. My judgment is you are the only one who can get in the door. But you must dress nice. Wash your face and wear a clean shirt. You are going to have to see him for us."

All at once I was consoled. The crisis included me. "Is that Mr. Hines?" I said.

He took out a notepad and wrote down an address and tore off the page and handed it to me. "You will wait till Sunday. On Sunday he receives people in his home. You may tell him where we are in the event he has news for us."

"Where?"

"If I am any judge we will be residing at the Soundview Hotel in the city of Bridgeport Connecticut."

"What do I say to him?"

"You will find him charming and easy to talk to. But you don't have to say anything." Mr. Berman had removed his bankroll again. This time when he took off the rubber band, he unfolded the money the other way, where the thousand-dollar bills were, and he counted off ten and gave them to me. "Put these in a white envelope before you go. He loves clean white envelopes."

I folded the ten thousand dollars flat and shoved them deep in my breast pocket. But they felt very bulky, I kept pressing my side to make sure they were flat. We sat there in the car looking down the street at the black Packard.

I said: "I don't suppose this is a good time to bring up a personal problem."

"No, not too good," Mr. Berman agreed. "Maybe it's something you can take it up with the padre after he's through with Mr. Schultz. Maybe you will have better luck."

"What is Mr. Schultz doing in there?"

"He's asking for a safe harbor. He wants to be left in peace. But if I am any judge, although I'm not a religious man myself, they will give him confession and communion and all the things they give, but providing a hideout is not one of their sacraments."

We stared through the windshield at the empty street. "What is your problem?" he said.

"My mother is sick and I don't know what to do," I said.

"What's wrong with her?"

"Her mind is wrong, she acts crazy."

"What does she do?"

"She does crazy things."

"Does she comb her hair?"

"What?"

"I said does she comb her hair? As long a woman combs her hair you don't have to worry."

"Since I have come home she combs her hair," I said.

"Well then maybe it's not so bad," he said.

EIGHTEEN

Of course I would be lying if I said I didn't think about that ten thousand dollars in my pocket, and what I could do if I just went away with it, packed our bags and took my mother to the train station and got us on a train to go somewhere far away, migod, ten thousand dollars! I remembered the Business Opportunities section of the *Onondaga Signal*, how you could buy farms of hundreds of acres for a third of that, surely what was true of one part of the country would be true everywhere. Or we could buy a store, a little tea shop, something reliable, where we could work and keep ourselves decently and in my off hours I could scheme for the future. Ten thousand dollars was a fortune. Even if you just left it in a savings bank you made money.

At the same time I knew I would do nothing of the kind, I didn't know what I would do but I sensed that the nature of my own business opportunity was still to make itself known, life held no grandeur for a simple thief, I had not gotten this far and whoever had hung this charm over my life had not chosen me because I was a cowardly double-crosser. I tried to imagine what Drew Preston would think. She wouldn't even understand such small-mindedness, and it would have nothing to do with morality, she would just not understand backing off to the furtive edges of life like that because it was going in the wrong direction. What was the right direction? Toward trouble. To the agony of circumstance. It was the same direction I had been traveling since that first ride on the back of the trolley car to Mr. Schultz's policy business on 149th Street.

So while I had my larcenous thoughts I did not seriously consider them, my real problem was to keep this incredible amount of money safe, I had stashed my truly earned six hundred dollars in my suitcase on the top shelf of the bedroom closet, but that clearly wouldn't do, so I got down on the floor and stuck my hand up into the hole under the couch where the stuffing was falling out, and made a little cottony shelf in there and rolled the bills into a tube and wrapped a rubber band around them and shoved them in. Then for three days I hardly left the apartment, I thought that I might unwittingly betray my secret by the expression on my face, that people could read money in my eyes, but mostly I didn't want to leave the house unattended, I bought our groceries and ran home, if I wanted air I sat on the fire escape, and in the evening after my mother cooked dinner, I watched her very carefully when she lit one of her memory glasses because since my return she had taken to doing that again, one each evening, she was getting her lights going so she could understand what there was to understand.

On the second day I went to the candy store and bought a white business envelope for a penny, and early the next morning, bathed and combed and wearing a clean shirt, but not willing to risk a trip to Manhattan looking like a swell with money in his pocket, I wore only the trousers of my linen suit and topped everything with the black side of my Shadows jacket, and I took the Third Avenue El downtown. I would have given whatever odds you asked that nobody else on the train was carrying ten thousand dollars in his pants, not the stolid working men bobbing in unison on the cane seats, not the conductor opening the doors, nor the motorman in the front cab, or for that matter the people in the windows of the tenements we passed. I would have given odds that unless there was some smartass school kid in one of the cars nobody on the train would even know whose face was on a thousand-dollar bill. If I got up and announced that I was carrying that amount of money people would move away from me as from a crazy man. But these callow reflections finally had the effect of making me nervous, and rather than continue by train, I got out at the 116th Street station and invested my own money in a cab crosstown to Eighth Avenue and 116th, where the Chairman, James J. Hines, maintained an apartment.

It was interesting how slummy, run-down, and squalid his neighborhood was at the foot of Morningside Heights, with overflowing garbage cans and Negro men standing around on the corners and pitching pennies, but how grand and finely kept his apartment house, as if it was on Park Avenue. A doorman in a uniform politely answered my inquiries and a shiny brass modern self-service elevator took me to the third floor. But the squalid life had preceded me: I found myself at the end of a corridor of waiting men, they were standing in the dim light as if on a breadline. Men on a breadline stand close upon one another with their feet spread somewhat apart and their attention directed to the head of the line, as if only absolute concentration could move it along. But the line moved very slowly and when someone, having concluded his business, made his exit everyone stared at him as if to see in his face the success or failure he had had. It took me thirty or forty minutes to reach the open door of the great man's apartment. In that time I imagined myself living my whole life in destitution. Year after year, standing on lines and looking for a handout, shrinking in my clothes, my mind slowly polishing itself into the mind of a beggar. I carried money for the man, I was there to give him something, yet I had to stand there in that sweltering hallway and wait my beggar's turn.

Then I was in a foyer, or anteroom, where a few disconsolate men sat with their hats in their hands like patients in a doctor's office and I joined them, moving along chair by chair as I got closer to the inner sanctum, until finally I was admitted through double doors to a hallway where a man at a desk and another man standing behind him looked me over, I recognized them as of the same ilk I had been living among for some months, the kind you can hear thinking. Mr. Berman had felt no need to instruct me. I was not old enough to be a voter looking for a job, I was not a familiar of the neighborhood, I was a scrubbed boy trying to look his threadbare best. "I am the son of Mary Kathryn Behan," I said truthfully. "Since my father deserted us we have fallen on hard times. My mother works in the laundry but she is too ill to hold her job much longer. She says I must tell Mr. Hines she has always voted the Democratic ticket." The gorgons exchanged a glance and the standing one went off down a hallway. Maybe a minute went by and he came back and escorted me the same way, past a dining room with glass-doored china cabinets, and a living room filled with massive furniture, and some sort of game room with framed citations and a billiards table, and then I was shown into a carpeted heavily draped bedroom that smelled of apples and wine and shaving lotion, a very atmospheric habitat that did not appear to include any open windows. And there propped atop the covers on a grand bank of pillows, in a dark red silk robe, with the hairless legs of an old man protruding, was James J. Hines himself, the Tammany district leader.

"Good morning, lad," he said, looking up from his morning paper. He covered the whole length of the bed. His feet were large and knobbed and had thick callus on the bottoms, but other than that he was a handsome man, with silver hair combed down flat, a ruddy squarish face set with small features, and very clear light blue eyes, which looked at me amiably enough, as if he was reasonably disposed to hear whatever story I was about to tell, considering the stories he had already heard this morning and the stories still waiting in the corridor all the way to the elevator. I said nothing. He waited, and then grew puzzled. "Do you want to speak your piece?" he said.

"Yes sir," I said, "but I can't with this gentleman breathing down my neck. He reminds me of my truant officer."

That drew a smile until he saw the deadly serious expression on my face. He was not a stupid man. He dismissed the henchman with a wave and I heard the door close behind me. I stepped boldly to the side of his bed and removing the envelope from my pocket placed it on the coverlet beside his large meaty hand. His blue eyes fixed on me with alarm. I stepped back and watched the hand. First the index finger tapped in thought. Then the whole hand slid into the envelope, which was not sealed, and the fingers, spatulate though they were, deftly withdrew the crisp bills and fanned them out like cards, in what was, all in all, an impressive exhibition of an old man's dexterity of joints.

When I looked up, Mr. Hines leaned back on his pillow and sighed as if the burden of his life was suddenly too much to be borne. "So he has such cunning, still, as to use a lad to get through to me, the dirty bastard?"

"Yes sir."

"Where would he find such a trustworthy child?"

I shrugged.

"Then there is no Mary Behan after all?"

"Oh yes, she is my mother."

"I am relieved to hear that. Years and years ago I placed a fine young Irish woman in service who came to America by that name. She was the age of my youngest daughter. Where do you live?"

"In the Claremont section of the Bronx."

"That's right. I wonder if it's not the same person. She was a tall girl with a lovely carriage, and a quiet and modest way about her, the kind of girl the Sisters adore, I knew she would find a husband in no time at all, Mary Behan. And who is the scoundrel who would desert a woman like that?"

I didn't answer.

"What is your father's name, lad."

"I don't know, sir."

"Oh, I see. I see. I am sorry." He nodded several times and pressed his lips together. Then his expression lightened. "But she has you, has she not. She has raised a capable son with a bold spirit and a clear inclination to live dangerously."

"She has indeed," I said, slipping right into a mimicry of his lilting rhythms, it was hard not to, his speech was powerfully a part of him, he was a politician, the first I'd ever met, but I could tell by the way he made you translate yourself into his language that he was a good one.

"I was an adept fellow too, at your age. Perhaps a bit bigger in the bones, coming of a line of smiths. But with the same little man's gift for trouble." He paused. "You do not need my assistance, do you, to take your mother out of that laundry and see to her ease and comfort in the sadness of her life?"

"No sir."

"I thought as much but I wanted to be sure. You're a clever boy. Maybe you have some black Irish in you. Or Jew. Maybe that accounts for the company you keep." He grew silent and stared at me.

"Well if that is all, sir," I said, "I know you have people waiting."

As if he had not heard, he indicated a chair next to the bed where I should sit. I watched the big hand snap closed the fan of bills and insert them in the envelope. "Nothing makes me sadder I assure you than to turn back such a generous warrant of heartfelt feeling," he said. He pushed the envelope toward me. "They are fine crisp bills in the noblest of denominations. You understand I could accept them and he would be none the wiser. You understand? But I won't do that. Will you explain that to him? Will you explain that James J. Hines does not perform miracles? It's all too far along, Master Behan. There is that little Republican with the mustache. And he with not a touch of the poet in him.''

The blue eyes regarded me until I realized I was to pick up the envelope. I did and slipped it into my pocket. "Where did he discover the son of Mary Behan, on the street?"

"Yes."

"Well you tell him for me I am impressed, at least, with that. And as for you personally you know I wish you only a long and prosperous life. But I'm through with him. To hell with him. I thought he understood after that unpleasantness upstate. I thought I had made myself clear. You don't know what I'm referring to, do you?"

"No sir."

"Never mind, I don't have to give him chapter and verse. Just tell him I can have nothing to do with him. The business between us is over. Will you tell him that for me?"

"I will."

I rose and went to the door. "It is a momentous thing when the money won't flow," Mr. Hines said. "I had hoped never to see the day." He picked up his newspaper. "Not that our friend is a man given to introspection, but he had a highly regarded associate in Mr. Weinberg. Who knows if that was the beginning. Who knows, perhaps the day he found you was the beginning."

"The beginning of what?"

He lifted his hand. "Give my fondest regards to your dear mother and tell her I asked after her," he said, and he had resumed his reading by the time I shut the door.

WHEN I GOT BACK TO THE BRONX I WENT INTO THE CIGAR STORE ON THIRD AVENUE under the El and bought a pack of Wings and got a handful of nickels for the pay phone and put in a long-distance call to the Soundview Hotel in Bridgeport Connecticut. There was no Mr. Schultz registered, no Mr. Flegenheimer, no Mr. Berman. I went home and when I got upstairs the door was open and a man from the telephone company was there with that belt they wear with all the tools hanging from it, he was considerately installing a telephone just beside the couch in the living room. I looked out the window and, just as I had thought, there was no green phone company truck anywhere on the street, I hadn't remembered seeing one. He left as considerately as he had worked, without a word, and the front door ajar only slightly. The white hub of the dial where the number was supposed to be printed was blank.

I put the envelope with the Hines money back up inside the couch stuffing and sat over it and waited. It seemed to me that ever since catching on with Mr. Schultz I had been assailed by these advanced beings who were there before I was and knew more than I knew, they'd invented telephones and taxicabs and elevated trains and nightclubs and churches, and courtrooms and newspapers and banks, it was all quite dazzling to be inserted by birth into their world, to slide out raw through the birth canal to be christened with a great clop, as if from a champagne bottle upside the head, so that life was forever after dazzling, with nothing quite making sense. What was I now supposed to do with them all and their arcane dealings, what was I supposed to do?

Not more than fifteen minutes passed before the phone rang. It was a strange sound in our little apartment, it was loud as a school bell, I could hear it ringing up and down the hall stairs. "You got a pencil?" Mr. Berman said. "I'll give you your number. You can call your mama now from anywhere in the United States."

"Thank you."

He gave me the number. He sounded almost jovial. "Of course you can't call out, but on the other hand you won't get a bill neither. So? How did it go?"

I told him the result of my interview with Mr. Hines. "I tried to reach you," I said. "They said you weren't there."

"We're in Union City New Jersey, just across the river," he said. "I can see the Empire State Building. Tell it again with the details this time."

"He says it's more than he can handle. He says you can blame the man with the mustache. He says not to contact him anymore."

"What mustache?" It was Mr. Schultz's voice. He had been listening on an extension.

"A Republican mustache."

"Dewey? The prosecutor?"

"I guess that's who."

"That son of a bitch!" he said. It was amazing, most people's voices are skinned down by the phone, but I could hear Mr. Schultz's in all its rich tonality. "Do I need him to tell us Thomas E. fucking Dewey is on my back? The son of a bitch. The goddamn shiteating son of a bitch. Won't take the money? Suddenly after all these years my money's not good enough? Oh, I'm going after that cocksucker, I'll take that money and shove it in his teeth, I'll make him eat it, he'll choke on it, I'll cut him open and paper his insides with it, he'll shit money I get through with him."

"Please, Arthur. Just a moment."

Mr. Schultz slammed his receiver and my ear rang all the way to New Jersey and back.

"Are you there, kid?" Mr. Berman said.

"Mr. Berman, meanwhile I'm holding this envelope and it makes me nervous."

"Just put it in a safe place for the time being," he said.

I could hear Mr. Schultz yelling in the background.

"We'll have things organized in a couple of days," Mr. Berman said. "Don't go anywhere. We need you I don't want to have to start looking."

So that was my situation for those hot Bronx days of Indian summer and the Diamond Home sprinkler fixing a rainbow every morning like a halo over the wet street and the children running under it and shrieking. I was mournful. My mother every day got up and went calmly enough off to work, and there was a wobbly balance to our lives, but she didn't like the phone on the end table next to the couch and dealt with it by putting the framed photograph of her and my defaced father in front of it. I bought us an electric fan that swiveled back and forth through a hundred-and-eighty-degree arc, flaring up the candles in their tumblers in the kitchen, but bringing a cool blow periodically to my shirtless back as I sat and read the papers in the living room. I had a lot of time to think about what Mr. Hines had said. He was a very wise man, it truly was a momentous thing when the money wouldn't flow. I had counted off my time with Mr. Schultz by the killings, the gunshots and sobs and cracking skulls resounded in my memory like tolling bells, but something else had been going on all that while, which was the movement of money, it had come in and it had gone out all that time, as uninterrupted as a tide in its incoming and outgoing, as steady and unceasing as the quiet celestial system of the turning earth. I had naturally fixed on the coming in, it had always been the matter of most vociferous concern as Mr. Schultz struggled to maintain his control despite his being on the lam and his legal problems, despite the difficulties of running his business interests at a distance, and the thievery of lieutenants and the treachery of trusted associates, but the money that went out was just as important, it bought arms and food, it bought lawyers and cops and the goodwill of poor people, it paid for properties, it paid for salaries and the good times that assured the men he depended upon that he was of the magnitude of incandescence they expected of a bright burning star. As far as I knew Mr. Schultz didn't use the fortune he had undoubtedly made over the years, he surely had amassed it but there was no sign of it in his life, I supposed he must have a house or fancy apartment somewhere where his wife lived, I knew they must have nice things, but none of it sat on him like the mantle of their wealth on those people in the boxes at Saratoga. He did not live rich, he did not look it or act it or, from any evidence I had, feel it, up in the country he had an entourage whose daily living expenses he took care of, he went for the occasional horseback ride and flung his money about like he was expected to, but it was all for survival, there was no relaxed indolence of his right to it, ever since I had first seen him he had been on the run, he was a vagabond, he lived in hotel rooms and hideouts, he spent his money to make more of it, he had to make it in order to keep making it, because only if he kept making it would he live to make more of it.

So that was why Mr. Hines's refusal to take the ten thousand was such a monumental reverse: It didn't matter how the money stopped flowing, in or out, the result was equally disastrous, the whole system was in jeopardy, just as, if the earth stopped turning, according to what a teacher explained to us once in the planetarium, it would shake itself to pieces.

Now I found myself pacing the floor the way he did, I was truly excited, I knew now what Hines meant by the beginning, he meant the end, the fact of the matter was that I had never seen Mr. Schultz at the height of his powers, I didn't know him when he had a handle on things and everything was as he wanted it to be, I had come into his life when it had begun not to function in his interest, all I had ever seen him do was defend himself, I didn't remember a time when he wasn't embattled, everything we did, any of us, came of his concern to survive, everything he'd asked me to do that I had done was in the interest of his survival, collecting policy, going to Sunday school, even having my nose busted, even sleeping with Drew Preston and taking her to Saratoga and getting her out of his clutches was finally in the interest of his survival.

I couldn't have understood it that day on the cobblestones in front of the beer drop, when the third of the three silent cars pulled up to the curb, and all the boys came in awe to their feet and I juggled two Spaldeens, an orange, an egg, and a stone in adoration of our great gangster of the Bronx: He had risen and he was falling. And the Dutchman's life with me was his downfall.

AFTER A SILENCE OF A DAY OR TWO THE PHONE BEGAN TO RING REGULARLY. Sometimes Mr. Berman was my dispatcher, sometimes Mr. Schultz, and I went off to do errands the nature of which I didn't usually understand. The press was following the story, so every day going downtown on the subway I found myself trying to figure out what I was doing by reading in the newspapers what the Special Prosecutor's Office was doing. One morning I went to the Embassy Club, which looked in the daytime down on its luck with its faded canopy and tarnished brasswork, and a man I didn't know opened the door and shoved a Dewar's White Label box into my arms and told me to get moving. In the box were ledgers and loose adding-machine tapes and business letters and invoices and so on. As I had been instructed I went to Pennsylvania Station and put the box in a coin-operated locker and I mailed the key to a Mr. Andrew Feigen at a hotel in Newark New Jersey. Then I read in the *Mirror* that the special prosecutor had subpoenaed the records of the Metropolitan Restaurant and Cafeteria Owners Association upon the mysterious death of its late president, Julius Mogolowsky, alias Julie Martin.

On another day I run up a dank creaking stairs off Eighth Avenue to seek out the boxing trades of Stillman's at their work. This is the famous gymnasium, and I am thrilled to pay my admission, but I don't know what I'm supposed to do here except to give one of the thousand-dollar bills to someone I don't know the name of or what he looks like. I notice in the ring a shining black man with beautiful muscles and wearing leather armor about the head, punching punching while five or six men stand around shouting out advice, the same proportion as in the WPA pothole crews. Trow der right, Nate, dat's it, one two, give it toom. This is the race of men Mickey the driver comes from, the race of the raised ear, the flattened nose, the blind eye, they hulk about and skip and nod and spit in pails, and oh the whoppering bags and the resined sneakers squeaking, I understand the sweetness of this life, it is held in a small space, like a religion, it is all suspended in the thick smell of men's sweat, sweat is the medium of existence, like righteousness, they breathe one another's faith, it is in the old leather, it is in the walls, I can't resist, I grab a jump rope and give it a half a hundred turns. And as it happens I don't have to look for my man, it is very simple, he is the one who notices I am here. One of the men instructing the boxer in the ring, he comes over in his sweat-shirt that doesn't quite cover all of his hairy white belly and gives me the big long-time-no-see greeting, putting one stinking arm around my shoulder, which brings me in tight to the open palm he holds in front of me as he walks me to the exit.

There was nothing in the papers to help me with that one, only the feeling that it all went together, all the sweating exertions of the killer spirit.

Another thousand goes to a bail bondsman at magistrates court where Dixie Davis got his start, he is a little bald guy with a cigar stub that works its way from one side of his mouth to the other as he watches me remove the bill from my wallet. I reflect that John D. Rockefeller only gave away dimes. On Broadway and Forty-ninth at the august offices of Local 3 of the Window Washers and Building Maintenance Workers, a man who is to take another of the one-thousand-dollar bills does not happen at the moment to be in, and so I wait, sitting in a wooden chair by a railing across the desk from a woman with a black mole over her lip, and she is frowning about something, perhaps her loss of privacy, because I might see how little she has to do, the window behind her is tall and wide and entirely unwashed and stepping down through its plane of dirt are the legs of the monocled top-hatted Johnny Walker whiskey sign on the roof of the building across the street, these enormous rising and falling black boots walking in air over Broadway.

To tell the truth I loved this time, I sensed my time was coming, and it had to do with the autumn, the city in its final serious turn toward the winter, the light was different, brilliant, hard, it tensed the air, burnished the top deck of the Number Six double-decker bus with a cold brilliant light, I made a stately ride in anticipation of death, crowds welled at the corners under the bronze streetlamps with the little Mercuries, police whistles blew, horns blew, the tall bus lurched from gear to gear, flags flew from the stores and hotels, and it was all for me, my triumphal procession, I reveled in the city he couldn't enter, for a minute or two it was mine to do with what I would.

I wondered how long he could resist, how long he could control himself and not test their resolve, because they knew his haunts, they knew where his wife lived, they knew his cars and his men, and now without Hines there was no fix, not in the precincts, not in the courts, he could board the Weehawken ferry, he could come through the Holland Tunnel, he could cross the George Washington Bridge, there were a lot of things he could do, but they knew by now where he was and would know when he left, and that made New York a fortress, a walled city with locked gates.

After a week or so I had dispensed half of the ten one-thousand-dollar bills. As far as I could understand these were not payoffs I was making, for the most part they were warrants of continuity, little organizational stanchings because Thomas E. Dewey was drawing blood, he had found some Dutch Schultz bank deposits under false names and had had them frozen, he had subpoenaed records of the brewery the Dutchman owned, his assistants were interviewing police officers and others whose names they would not divulge to the press. But if there was money for this aspect of things, there had to be money to rebuild from the bottom, payoff by payoff, someone had to be doing it, there were ways after all, you're telling me Mickey couldn't shake a tail? Irving couldn't turn invisible? There were twenty, twenty-five men at the morning meeting in the whorehouse parlor, not all of them were in Jersey, the organization was functioning, twenty-five was not a hundred or two hundred but business was going on, stripped down, on hard times, its reach diminished, but mean and murderous and with plenty of money for lawyers.

So that's how I figured it to be, or how it would be if I was running things, I would be patient and bide my time and take no chances, and for a couple of weeks, maybe even into early October, that's the way it was. But I was not Mr. Schultz, he surprised you, he surprised himself, I mean why suddenly do I read that an entire floor in the Savoy-Plaza has been wrecked, that an unknown thief or thieves have broken into one of the residential apartments and done tens of thousands of dollars' worth of damage, cut up paintings, ripped down tapestries, smashed pottery, defaced books, and presumably stolen property of a value not known because the residents of the apartment, Mr. and Mrs. Harvey Preston—he is the heir to the railroad fortune—are abroad and cannot be reached?

THEN ONE NIGHT, FOLLOWING MY INSTRUCTIONS, I TOOK THE THIRD AVENUE EL TO Manhattan, and the streetcar all the way crosstown to the West Twenty-third Street ferry slip, and then I stood on the deck of the beamiest bargiest boat in the world, a boat that carried thousands of people every day in such unnautical stability as to suggest a floating building, a piece of the island of New York separated for the convenience of its citizens and let out on a line across the river, I stood on this boat that smelled like a bus or a subway car with chewing-gum wads pressed into its decks and candy wrappers under the cane seats and looped straps for standees to hang on to, and the same wire trash baskets you found on street corners, and I felt under my feet the tremors of the dark harbor, the lappings of the alive and hungry ocean, I looked back on New York and watched it drift away and I thought I was going for a dead man's ride.

I will say here too, at the risk of offending, that my arrival at the industrial landing on the Jersey shore, with ranks of coal barges lying at anchor and brick factories spewing smoke and the whole western horizon filled with the pipes and tanks and catwalks of hellish refineries, did not give me the assurances I sought from having land under my feet. A yellow cab was waiting outside the terminal and the cabby waved and as I approached he reached back and opened the passenger door, and when I got in it was Mickey who greeted me with an uncharacteristically effusive nod and a smart takeoff that threw me against the back of the seat.

You had to go through Jersey City to get to Newark, there was apparently some governmental distinction to be made between them, but I could see no difference, both cities together being just a continuous dreary afterthought of New York, a kind of shadow on the wrong side of the river, you could tell they thought they were the Bronx or Brooklyn, and they had the bars and the streetcars and the machine shops and warehouses, but the air stank in a different way, and the stores were oldfashioned and the width of the streets was wrong and the people all had that look of being noplace, they looked at up at the signs on the corners to remember where they were, it was a most depressing flatland, a monument to displacement, and I could tell Mr. Schultz would go out of his mind here trying to get comfortable prowling from Union City to Jersey City to Newark to find the best window where he could look out and see the Empire State Building.

It was a cemetery, no question about that, it was too ugly to live in. Mickey pulled up in front of this bar on a street paved not with asphalt but in whitish cement and with the telephone and streetcar wires hanging like a loose net over everything and let me off and drove away. The name of the place was the Palace Chophouse and Tavern. Now I will admit I had come to a tentative conclusion—that if Mr. Schultz was to all intents and purposes locked out of doing business in New York, and none of the trusted associates could take a chance either on going in for any prolonged length of time, I mean as the only one who had free rein, my value to the gang was increased and I thought I should be made a full-fledged member. I was doing more and more responsible work and I wondered why I had to depend on the odd handout that was thrown my way, no matter how munificent it happened to be. They were making advanced assumptions about me, counting on me in a really brazen fashion when you thought that I was not even being paid. I wanted a real wage and I thought if Mr. Schultz didn't happen to murder me I might be in a position to ask for it. But when I walked down the bar, turned a corner, and passed through a short corridor into the windowless back room where Mr. Schultz and Mr. Berman and Irving and Lulu Rosenkrantz were sitting at a table by the wall, the only diners, I knew I would not bring up the matter, it was peculiar, it was not a question of fear, which I was recklessly prepared to deal with, but of a loss of faith, I don't know why but I looked at them and I felt it was too late to ask for anything.

The room they were in had pale green walls, with decorative mirrors of tarnished metal, and the overhead light made them all look sallow. They were eating steaks and there were bottles of red wine on the table that looked black in this light. "Pull up a chair, kid," Mr. Schultz said. "Are you hungry or anything?"

I said I wasn't. He looked thin, peaked, his mouth was primed to its most undulant pout, he was sorely oppressed, and I noticed the collar of his shirt was curled at the corners, and he needed a shave.

He pushed his plate away with his dinner hardly eaten and he lit a cigarette, which was another thing because when he was feeling in control of things he smoked cigars. The others went on eating till it became apparent he had not the patience to wait for them to finish. One by one they put their knives and forks down. "Hey, Sam," Mr. Schultz called, and a Chinese man came out of the kitchen and took the plates away and brought cups of coffee and a pint bottle of cream. Mr. Schultz turned and watched him go back to the kitchen. Then he said, "Kid, there is a son of a bitch named Thomas Dewey, you know that, don't you?"

"Yes sir."

"You seen his picture," Mr. Schultz said, and he removed from his wallet a photo that had been torn out of a newspaper. He slapped it down on the table. The special prosecutor, Dewey, had nice black hair parted in the middle, a turned-up nose, and the mustache to which Mr. Hines had alluded, a little brush-style mustache. Mr. Dewey's dark and intelligent eyes gazed at me with a resolute conviction of the way the world ought to be run.

"All right?" Mr. Schultz said.

I nodded.

"Mr. Dewey lives on Fifth Avenue, one of those buildings that face the park?"

I nodded.

"I will give you the number. I want you to be there when he comes out in the morning and I want you to watch where he goes, and who is with him, and I want to know what time that is, and I want to know when he comes home from work and what time that is and who is with him then. He runs his show from the Woolworth Building on Broadway. You don't have to worry about that. It is only the comings and the goings from home to office and back. The comings and the goings is what interests me. You think you can handle it?"

I glanced around the table. Everyone, even Mr. Berman, was looking down. Their hands were folded on the table, all three of them like children at their school desks. None of them besides Mr. Schultz had said a word since I had walked in.

"I guess."

"You guess! Is that the attitude I come to expect from you, I *guess*? You been talking to these guys?" he said pointing his thumb to the table.

"Me? No."

"Because I was hoping someone in this organization still had guts. I could still rely on somebody."

"Aw boss," Lulu Rosenkrantz said.

"Shut the fuck up, Lulu. You're ugly and you're dumb. That is the truth of you, Lulu."

"Arthur, this is not right," Mr. Berman said.

"Fuck you, Otto. I am being punched out and you are telling me what is not right? Is it right my getting my ass handed to me?"

"This was not the understanding."

"How do you know? How can you tell?"

"The decision was to take it under advisement, they're looking into it."

"I'm looking into it. I'm looking into it because I'm gonna do it."

"We have a compact with these people."

"Fuck compacts."

"You don't remember he came hundreds of miles to stand for you in church?"

"Oh I remember. He came up showing me this attitude like he and the pope together was doing me this big fucking favor. Then he sits and eats my food and drinks my wine and says nothing. Nothing! I remember all right."

"Maybe not nothing," Mr. Berman said. "Maybe just the fact of his being there."

"You can't hear him half the time, like he has no voice box. You gotta lean over and put your face in that garlic mouth and then it still doesn't matter because you don't know what anything means, he likes something he don't like something, it's all the same, you don't know what he's thinking, you don't know where you stand with him. He's taking what under advisement! How do you know? Can you tell me what anything means with the son of a bitch? Me, if I like something I tell you, I don't like something I tell you that, I don't like someone he fucking well knows it, that's the way I am and that's the way it should be, not this secrecy of feelings each and every moment that keeps you guessing what the truth is."

Mr. Berman lit a cigarette and cupped it in his palm with his thumb and forefinger. "These are matters of style, Arthur. You got to look past these things into the philosophy. The philosophy is that their organization is intact. It is available to us. We have the use of it, the protection of it. We combine with it and together we make a board and we sit on the board with our vote. That is the philosophy."

"Yeah, it's a great philosophy all right, but have you noticed? I'm the one this dog-fucker Dewey is after. Who do you think sicced the Feds on me! It's my leg he has in his teeth."

"You have to understand they have an interest in our problem. It is their problem too. They know he knocks down the Dutchman it's their turn next. Please, Arthur, give them a little credit. They are businessmen. Maybe you're right, maybe this is the way. He said they would study it to see how it could be done but in the meantime they want to think about it a little while. Because you know as well as they do even when it's a lousy cop on the beat who is hit the city goes wild. And this is a major prosecutor in the newspapers every day. A hero of the people. You could win the battle and lose the war."

Mr. Berman kept talking, he wanted to calm Mr. Schultz down. As he went on to make each point of his argument, Lulu kept nodding and furrowing his brow as if he had been just about to say the same thing. Irving sat with his arms folded and his eyes lowered, whatever decision was made he would go along with it, as he always had, as he would to the day he died. "The modern businessman looks to combination for strength and for streamlining," Mr. Berman said. "He joins a trade association. Because he is part of something bigger he achieves strength. Practices are agreed upon, prices, territories, the markets are controlled. He achieves streamlining. And lo and behold the numbers rise. Nobody is fighting anybody. And what he has a share of now is more profitable than the whole kit and caboodle of yore."

I could see Mr. Schultz gradually relaxing, he had been leaning forward and holding the edge of the table as if he was about to turn it over, but after a while he sagged back in his chair and then he put his hand on top of his head, as if it hurt, a peculiar gesture of irresolution that as much as anything compelled me to pipe up as I did: "Excuse me. This man you mentioned, the one who came to the church. Mrs. Preston told me something about him.''

I will talk about this moment, what I thought I was doing, or what I think now I thought I was doing, because it is the moment the determination was made, I think about all their deaths and the manners of dying, but more about this moment of the determination, where it came from, not the heart or the head, but the mouth, the wordmaker, the linguist of grunts and moans and whimpers and shrieks.

''She knew him. Well not that she knew him but that she'd met him. Well not that she entirely remembered meeting him,'' I said, ''or she would have mentioned it herself. But she drank,'' I said looking a moment at Irving, ''she herself told me that and when you drink you don't remember that much, do you? But what she felt on the street in front of St. Barnabas,'' I said to Mr. Schultz, ''is that when you introduced them, she thought he looked at her as if he recognized her. She thought perhaps she must have met him before.''

It was so still now in the Palace Chophouse and Tavern that I heard Mr. Schultz's breathing, the magnitude of his respiration was as familiar to me as his voice, his thought, his character, it came in slowly and went out quickly in a kind of one two rhythm that left a silence between breaths that seemed like a consideration of whether to breathe at all.

''Where did she meet him?'' he said, very calm.

''She thought it must have been with Bo.''

He swiveled in his chair and faced Mr. Berman and sat back and stuck his thumbs in his vest pockets and a big broad smile came over his face. ''Otto, you hear this? You grope around and you grope around and all the time the child is there to lead you.''

The next moment he had jumped out of his chair and smashed me on the side of the head, I think he must have used his forearm, I didn't know what had happened, the room wheeled, I was suddenly confused, I thought there had been an explosion, that the room was falling in on me, I saw the ceiling lift and the floor jump toward me, I was flying backward over the chair, going down backward in the chair I'd been sitting in and when I hit the floor I lay there stunned, I wanted to hold on to the floor because I thought it was moving. Then I felt terrible pounding pains in the side, one after another, and as it turned out he was kicking me, I tried to roll away, I was crying out and I heard chairs scraping, everyone talking at once, and they pulled him off me, Irving and Lulu actually pulled him away from me, I realized that later when I began to hear in my mind what they had been saying, *it's the kid for christsake, oh Christ, leave off, boss, leave off,* all that urgent straining talk in the pinioning of violence.

Then as I rolled on my back I saw him shrug loose of them and hold his hands in the air. ''It's all right,'' he said. ''It's okay. I am all right.''

He yanked on his collar and pulled at his vest and sat back down in his chair. Irving and Lulu took me under the arms and put me instantaneously on my feet. I felt ill. They righted my chair and sat me in it and Mr. Berman pushed a glass of wine toward me and I took it with both hands and managed to swallow some of it. My ears were ringing and I felt a sharp pain on the left side every time I took a breath. I sat up straight, in that way your body instantly accepts what has happened to it, though your mind does not, I knew that if I sat straight and took only shallow breaths through the nose the pain was relieved somewhat.

Mr. Schultz said: "Now kid, that was for not telling me before. You heard what she said, that cunt, you should have come to me right away."

I started to cough, little hacking coughs that were excruciatingly painful. I swallowed more wine. "This was the first chance," I said, lying, I had to clear my throat to get my voice back, I didn't want to sound like I was sniveling, I wanted to sound offended. "I been busy doing everything you asked me, is all."

"Let me finish, please. How much of that ten grand is left that you been holding."

With trembling hands I took five thousand dollars out of my wallet and put it on the white tablecloth. "All right," he said. He took up all the bills but one. "That is for you," he said pushing it toward me. "A month's advance. You are now on the payroll at two hundred and fifty a week. This is what justice is, you see? The same thing you deserved a licking for you deserve this." He looked around the table. "I didn't hear nobody else give me the word on our downtown comparey."

Nobody said anything. Mr. Schultz poured wine in all the glasses and drank his own with a loud smacking of the lips. "I feel better now. It didn't feel right in that meeting, I knew it didn't feel right. I don't know how to combine. I wouldn't know how to begin. I was never a joiner, Otto. I never asked anybody for anything. Everything I got I got for myself. I have worked hard. And how I got where I got is I do what I want, not what other people want. You put me with those goombahs and suddenly I have to worry about their interests? Their interests? I don't give a shit for their interests. So what is all this crap. I'm not about to give it away, I don't care how many D.A.s come after me. That is what I was trying to tell you. I didn't have the words. Now I got them."

"It doesn't have to mean anything, Arthur. Bo liked a good time. It could have been at the track. It could have been in a club. It don't have to mean anything."

Mr. Schultz shook his head and smiled. "My Abbadabba. I never knew the numbers were for dreaming. A man gives me his word and it's not his word, a man works for me all those years and the minute I turn my back he conspires against me, I don't know, who has gotten to him? Who in Cleveland gets such an idea?"

Mr. Berman was very agitated. "Arthur, he's not stupid, he's a businessman, he looks at the choices and he takes the path of least resistance, that is the whole philosophy of the combination. He didn't have to see the girl to know where Bo was. He showed you a mark of respect."

Mr. Schultz pushed back from the table. He took his rosary out of his pocket and began to twirl it, around went the rosary in a tightening circle, it dangled for a pendulous moment and then spun the other way, looping out before snapping up tight again. "So who turned Bo? I see your precious combination, Otto. I see the whole fucking world ganging up on me. I see the man who takes me into his church, the man who makes me his brother and embraces me and kisses me on the cheek. Is this love? These people have no more love for me than I have for them. Is this the Sicilian death kiss? You tell me."

NINETEEN

And that's how I came to shadow Thomas E. Dewey, the special public prosecutor appointed to clean up the rackets, and future district attorney, governor of New York, and Republican candidate for president of the United States. He lived in one of those limestone-cliff Fifth Avenue apartment buildings that look over Central Park, it wasn't that far north of the Savoy-Plaza, in one week I became very familiar with the neighborhood, I idled lurked and strolled usually on the park side, across the street, along the park wall in the shade of the plane trees, sometimes diverting myself by trying not to step on the lines of the hexagonal paving blocks. In the early morning the sun came up through the side streets filling them from the east with light and shooting out like Buck Rogers ray guns across the intersections, I kept thinking of shots, I heard them in the backfirings of trucks, I saw them in the rays, I read them in the chalk lines made by the kids on the sidewalks, everything was shots in my mind as I shadowed the public prosecutor with a view toward setting him up for assassination. In the evening the sun went down over the West Side and the limestone buildings of Fifth Avenue glowed gold in their windows and white on their faces, and all up and down the stories maids in their uniforms pulled the drapes closed or let down the awnings.

In these days I felt very close to Mr. Schultz, I was the only one cooperating in the deepest spirit with him, his most trusted adviser deplored his intentions, his two most loyal personal attendants and bodyguards suffered grave misgivings, I was alone with the man in his heart, was what I felt, and I have to confess I was excited to be there alone with him in his cavernous transgression, he had slugged me and kicked my ribs in and now I felt a real love for him, I forgave him, I wanted him to love me, I realized he was able to get away with something no other person could get away with, for example I still did not forgive Lulu Rosenkrantz my broken nose, and in fact when I thought about it I didn't like the way Mr. Berman had lifted twenty-seven cents from me with one of his cheap math tricks that time in the policy office on 149th Street when I had barely caught on with the organization, Mr. Berman had been my mentor ever since, generously bringing me along, nurturing me, and yet I still did not forgive him that loss of a boy's few pennies.

You can't expect to shadow someone effectively unless you are an unremarkable figure appropriate to the landscape. I bought a scooter and wore my good pants and a polo shirt and I did that for a day or so, then I got a puppy from a pet shop and walked him along on a leash except people who were out early walking their own dogs kept stopping to say how cute he was while their dogs sniffed his wagging little ass, and that was no good, so I gave him back, it was only when I borrowed the wicker carriage from my mother for a couple of days and took it downtown by taxicab to stroll along with it like an older child watching his mother's new baby that I felt I had the right camouflage. I bought a doll from Arnold Garbage for two bits with a cotton bonnet to keep its face in shadow, people liked to get their babies out in the early morning, sometimes nurses in white stockings and blue capes pushed these elaborate heavily sprung lacquered perambulators along with netting to keep the bugs off of the little darlings, so I bought netting and draped it over the carriage so that even if some old lady got really nosey she couldn't see inside, and sometimes I walked and sometimes I sat on the bench just across the street from where he lived and pushed the carriage out and pulled it back and bounced it gently on its broken-down springs and in this manner learned that the early morning was the time with the fewest people and the most inflexible routine, without a doubt the morning appearance of Mr. Dewey was the preferred time to dispatch him.

And my mother liked that doll, she was pleased to have me enter her imagination with her, she rummaged through her old cedar chest to find the baby clothes there, my baby clothes, and to dress the doll in the musty little gowns and scalp caps she had dressed me in fifteen years before. But all this you see was the innocence of murder, I loved my mother for being innocent of the murders around her, as worried prophets are, I loved her very much for the stately madness she had chosen to suffer the murders in her life of love, and if I had any qualms for the work I was doing I had only to think of her to know that I was on the nerve of my innate resolve and so I could trust that it was all going to work out, that everything would end as I dreamed it would.

In fact I will declare right now that I knew while I held something of these events in my hands, I would not have them bloodied. I realize this assurance sounds self-serving and I hereby apologize to all of Mr. Dewey's relatives, heirs, and assignees for the revulsion they may feel, but these are confessions of a wild and desolate boyhood and I would have no reason to lie about any one of them.

Oddly enough the person I felt bad about was Mr. Berman, the moment I had chosen at the Palace Chophouse to reveal what Drew Preston had told me he must have perceived as an act of treachery, the moment of his ruination, it was the end of all his plans, when his man would not finally be brought along into the new realm he foresaw, where the numbers ruled, where they became the language and rewrote the book. He said to me once, apropos of this idea, this dapper little humpbacked man with the clawlike fingers: "What the book says, well let me put it this way, you can take all the numbers and stir them around and toss them up in the air and let them fall where they may and remake them back into letters and you have a whole new book, new words, new ideas, a new language you've got to understand with new meanings and new things happening, a new book entirely." Well that was a dangerous proposition, if you thought about it, was the proposition of X, the value he couldn't abide, the number not known.

But in his last glance for me over his glasses, the brown eyes widening to their blue rims, he saw everything instantly, with a kind of despairing reproach. What a tidy little thing the mind is, how affronted by the outlying chaos, he was game, this little guy, he'd made a brilliant life out of one faculty, and he'd always been kind to me, if deviously instructive. I ask myself now if my small word to the wise made that much difference, if it wasn't better for Mr. Schultz to go down knowing what his situation was, as Bo Weinberg had, if that honor wasn't due him; whereas he might never have known what hit him. And anyway I think now he knew all along, it was why perhaps he publicized his desire to assassinate the prosecutor, a suicidal act in any event, real or proposed, and it was as he said, I had just given him the words he was looking for all along for the feeling he had, that at the age of what, thirty-three? thirty-five? he'd run out of reprieves, the moment had long since passed when all the elements for his destruction had combined, and his life was attenuated, in the manner of a fuse.

But what I thought I was doing was delivering a message between intimates, a necessary message that could not be left undelivered, though I had tried, and he had understood that I had tried and so had thrashed me. I knew them both so well. She made me a boy again in the humming space between them: You tell him, would you? she had said, and lifted her binoculars so that I could see the parade of small horses curving around the lens.

AND THEN IT IS TIME FOR MY REPORT, AND IT IS LATE ONE NIGHT IN THE SAME BACK room of the Palace, with the pale green walls and the regularly spaced tarnished mirrors in frames suggesting with a few lines of hollowed-up tin the streamlined modernity of the skyscraper, their hierarchy of arches like a platformed chorus of pretty girls with raised knees, and we all sit sallow at the same back table with the impeccably clean cloth and it is so late by the time I get there, dinner is over, they have before them now not the thick plates and cups and saucers but the thinnest of adding-machine tapes, their eternal fascination, the time is midnight, I saw that on the neon-blue clock over the bar as I walked in, midnight, the moment of justice cleaved to the moment of mercy, Midnight, the best name for God.

And this is the moment I am finally with them, one of them, their confidant, their colleague. There is first of all the sense of craft that suffuses me, the sweetness of knowing one thing well. There is second of all the malign pleasure of conspiracy, the power you feel from just planning to kill someone who may at that moment be kissing his wife or brushing his teeth or reading himself to sleep. You are the raised fist in his darkness, you will fell him from his ignorance, it will cost him his life to know what you know.

Every morning he comes out exactly the same time.

What time?

Ten minutes to eight. There is a car there, but the two plainclothes get out of the car to meet him at the door and they walk with him while the car follows. They walk together to Seventy-second, where he goes into the Claridge Drugstore and makes a call from the phone booth.

Every day?

Every day. There are two phone booths to the left just inside the door. The car follows and it waits by the curb and the bodyguards stand outside while he makes his call.

They wait outside? Mr. Schultz wants to know.

Yes.

What's inside?

On the right as you walk in is the fountain. You can get breakfast at the counter. Every day is a different special.

Is it crowded?

I never saw more than one or two people at that hour.

And then what does he do?

He comes out of the booth and waves to the counterman and he leaves.

And how long is he in there altogether?

Never more than three or four minutes. He makes that one phone call to his office.

How do you know to his office?

I've heard. I went in to look at magazines. He tells them what to do. Things he's thought of during the night. He has a little pad and he reads from his notes. He asks questions.

Why would he leave his house to make a phone call? Mr. Berman says. And then on the way to work where he's going to see them in fifteen twenty minutes anyway?

I don't know. To get more done.

Maybe he's afraid of a tap? Lulu Rosenkrantz says.

The D.A.?

I know, but he knows from taps, maybe he just don't want to take the chance calling from his own house.

He's seeing witnesses all the time, Mr. Schultz says. He is very secretive, he gets them in there the back way or something so nobody knows who's squealing. I know that about the son of a bitch. Lulu's right. He doesn't miss a trick.

What about the return journey? says Mr. Berman.

He works late. It could be anytime, sometimes as late as ten. The car pulls up, he gets out and he's in the lobby in a second.

No, the kid's got it figured, Mr. Schultz says, the morning is when. You put two guys with silencers at the counter with their coffee. Is there a way out of there?

There's a back door leading into the lobby of the building. You can go down to the basement and come out on Seventy-third Street.

Well then, he says, putting his hand on my shoulder. Well then. And I feel the warmth of the hand, and the weight of it, like a father's hand, familiar, burdensome in its pride, and he is beaming his appreciation in my face, I see the mouth open in laughter, the large teeth. We will show them what is not allowed, won't we, we will show them how far you can't go. And I will be in Jersey all the time and will pull a long face and say I had no personal grief against the man. Am I right? He squeezes my shoulder and rises. They will thank me, he says to Mr. Berman, they will end up thanking the Dutchman for the caution I have instilled, you mark my words. This is what streamlining means, Otto. This.

He tugs on the points of his vest and goes off to the bathroom. Our table is in the corner in a right angle of pale green walls. I am facing the walls with my back to the doorway leading to the bar, but I have an advantage because the tarnished mirror allows me to see farther down the transverse corridor into the bar than someone sitting under the mirror and looking straight out. It is the peculiar power of mirrors to show you what is not otherwise there. I see the blue neon cast of the clock tube above the bar as it encroaches on the floor of the passageway to the dark tavern. It is like a kind of moonlight on black water. And then the water seems to ripple. At the same time I hear the bartender's rag suspended in its swipe over the zinc bar beneath the draft beer taps. I hear now that I heard the front doors to the street open and close with unnatural tact.

How did I know? How did I know? With the first wisp rising from the crossed wires of murderous intent? Had I believed of our conspiring that we had invoked images too powerful for the moment, as in some black prayer, so that they had inverted, and were flashing back on us to blow us sky-high? There is that earliest notion of leaning forward in the chair, the body getting ready from the base of the spine up.

Silencers, Lulu says, thinking of his life to come. Mr. Berman is just twisting around to look to the entrance and Irving's eyes rise with me as I rise to my feet. I notice how well-combed Irving's thin hairs are, how neatly in place. Then I am in the short passage leading to the kitchen at the rear. I find the men's room door. I am hit by the salt stink of a public bathroom. Mr. Schultz stands at the urinal with his legs apart and his hands on his hips so that the back of his jacket wings out, and his water arcs from him directly into the urinal drain, thus making the rich foaming sound of a proud man at his micturation. I try to tell him how, as an action, this is terribly obsolete. And when I hear the guns I think he has been electrocuted through the penis, that he made the mistake I have read about in the novelty books, of urinating in a thunderstorm when the lightning can hiss up from the ground in an instantaneous golden rainbow and flash you out like a bomb.

But he is not electrocuted, he is jammed with me in the small stall, I am standing on the toilet seat and his shoulder bangs into me as he fumblingly removes the pistol from his belt, I don't even know if he knows I'm there, he holds the gun cocked, pointed at the ceiling, and with his other hand he is doing an amazing thing, he is trying to button his fly, we don't listen to the explosions, we are rocked by them, they ring in the ears, they become a continuous erupting disaster in the ears, and I dig in the pocket of my Shadows jacket for my Automatic and it is twisted in the material of the lining, and I have to struggle with it, I am as graceless as Mr. Schultz, and now I smell the powder, the bitter sulfurous aftermath coming under the door like a poison gas, and at this moment Mr. Schultz must realize that he has no real protection in here, he will be killed in a toilet stall, he slams the door open with the heel of his hand and pulls open the bathroom door and I understand he is shouting, a great wordless scream of rage issues from him as he springs out and raises his arms to shoot, and through the two doors as they are held open by the wind of fire I see the black ovoid stain of sweat under his arm, I see him stumble forward and disappear, I see the pale green corridor wall, and I hear the deeper roar of the new caliber even as he spins back into view, and totters out again leaving sensational maps of the holes in him on the wall of the passageway as the doors slowly swing closed.

You don't know urgent life if you haven't heard a gun in your ears, it is the state of being able to do anything, defy all laws, a small window, like a transom, is at the back of the stall, just under the ceiling, I use the chain of the holding tank to haul myself to where I can reach it, it opens down into the room on a pair of elbow hinges, the window is much too small to get through, so I do it feet first, swinging them up and hooking them one at a time, and then twisting sideways and getting my legs through and then my hips then my painful ribs, and then I let go with my arms over my head like Bo going into the drink, I give myself a good crack as I slide out and fall to the ground, it is a ground of crushed cinders, like the bed of a railroad track, and it compacts my legs, I feel sharp pain, I have twisted my ankle, cinders are imbedded in my palms. And my heart seems to have gone awry, it pounds in furious broken rhythms as if it has gone off its shocks, it's sliding around my chest, lodging in my throat. It is the only thing I hear. I limp I scurry down the alley, holding my gun in my jacket pocket just like a real gangster in action, I peek around the corner of the Palace Chophouse and Tavern into the street and a speeding car without lights a half a block away fishtails and wavers a moment and in another moment it is lost in the shadows of the street, and I watch and wait but I don't see it anymore. I didn't see it turn, I step off the curb and stand in the gutter and the long back street is empty under its streetcar wires as far as I can see.

AND WHAT I HEAR NOW ARE MY OWN STREAMING SOBS. I OPEN THE DOOR TO THE bar and look in. The smoke lingers in the blue light and bottleshine. The bartender's head rises above the bar, sees me and appears to decapitate itself, and that is funny, fear is funny, I gimp my way to the back, turn, come down the short corridor of the visitation, and before I look into the room oh the air is bad burned air and humid with blood, I don't want to see this vealy disaster, I don't want to be contaminated by this terrible sudden attack of the plague. And I am so disappointed in them, I peek in, I almost trip on Irving, face down, a gun still in his hand, one leg drawn up as if he is still in the act of chasing them, and I step over him and Lulu Rosenkrantz sits blasted back against the wall, he never got out of his chair, it is tilted precipitously, like a barber's chair, and held fast against the wall by his head, Lulu's hair sticks up ready for the haircut and his forty-five caliber is in his open hand on his lap as if it was his penis and he stares at the ceiling as in the intense sightless effort of masturbation, my disappointment is acute, I do not feel grief but that they have died so easily, as if their lives were so carelessly held, this is what disappoints me, and Mr. Berman slumps forward on the table, his pointed back stressing the material of his plaid jacket in a widening hole of blood, his arms are flung forward and his cheek rests against the table and his glasses are pressed under his cheek on one leg the other standing away from his temple, Mr. Berman has failed me too, I am resentful, I feel fatherless again, a whole new wave of fatherlessness, that they have gone so suddenly, as if there was no history of our life together in the gang, as if discourse is an illusion, and the sequence of this happened and then that happened and I said and he said was only Death's momentary incredulity, Death staying his hand a moment in incredulity of our arrogance, that we actually believed ourselves to consequentially exist, as if we were something that did not snuff out from one instant to the next, leaving nothing of ourselves as considerable as a thread of smoke, or the resolved silence at the end of a song.

* * *

Mr. schultz lying flat on his back on the floor was still alive, his feet were turned slightly outward he looked at me quite calmly as I stood over him. His expression was solemn and his face was shining with sweat, he had his hand inside his bloodied vest like Napoleon standing for his portrait and he seemed to be in such imperial control of the moment that I hunkered down and spoke to him in the assumption that he was quite rationally aware of his situation, which he was not. I asked him what I should do, should I call the cops, should I get him to a hospital, I was ready for his orders, not mistaking the seriousness of his condition, but half expecting him to ask me to help him up, or to get him out of here, but in any event to be the one who decided what should be done and how. He gazed at me as calmly as before but simply did not answer, he was so extendedly suffering the shock of what had happened to him that he wasn't even in pain.

But there was a voice in the room, I heard it now like the wording of the acrid smoke, a whispering it was, too faint to understand, yet Mr. Schultz's lips did not move but he only stared at me as if, given the character of my feeling, his impassive gaze was commanding me to listen, and I tried to locate the sound, it was terrifying, fragmentary, where it came from, I thought for a moment it was my own breathy intake of stringed snot, I wiped my nose on my sleeve, I dried my eyes with the heels of my hands, I held my breath, but I heard it again and terror made my knees buckle as I realized, swiveling on my heels, that it was Abbadabba talking from his grimace alongside the tabletop, I cried out I didn't think he was alive I thought he was giving utterance from his death.

And then it seemed to me quite natural that their division would be expressed at this moment too, between the brain and the body, and that as long as Mr. Schultz was still alive, Mr. Berman would still be thinking for him and saying what Mr. Schultz wanted said, however corporeally dead Mr. Berman might be. Of course Mr. Berman was still himself alive, however faintly, but it was this other idea that presented itself as the logical explanation to my mind. It was perhaps some comfort for the thought that I had myself sundered them. I laid my head on the table alongside his and I will say here now what he said though I cannot suggest the time it took his voice to round itself for each word, with long rests between them as he sought for additional breath like a man searching his pockets for the money he cannot find. While waiting I stared at the blurred columns of numbers on his adding machine tapes that were strewn on the table. There were lots of numbers. Then, to make sure I was hearing correctly, I watched the words form in his teeth before I heard them. It is difficult for me to suggest the sense of ultimate innocence conveyed by his statement. Before he got through it I was hearing the distant sound of police sirens, and it was so arduous for him to speak it that he died of the effort: "Right," he said. "Three three. Left twice. Two seven. Right twice. Three three."

When I realized Mr. Berman was dead, or again dead, I went over to Mr. Schultz. His eyes were closed now, and he moaned, it was as if he was regaining consciousness of what had happened, I didn't want to touch him, he was wet, he was too alive to touch, but I put my fingers in his vest pocket and felt a key and I removed it, and wiped the blood on his jacket, and then I found his rosary in his pants pocket and I put it in his hand, and then, since the police cars were pulling up to a stop outside, I went back into the bathroom and went through the window again, again torturing my ribs and my ankle, and at the head of the alley the street was filling in with lights and people running and cars pulling to a stop, I waited a minute or two and slipped out quite easily into the crowd and stood for a while across the street in the doorway of a radio store and watched them bring out the bodies on stretchers covered with sheets, the bartender came out talking with police detectives and then they brought Mr. Schultz out strapped in a stretcher and with a blood plasma bottle held alongside by the ambulance attendant, and the Speed-Graphics flashed, and when the photographers dropped their used bulbs in the street they went off like gunshots, which made the neighborhood people jump back nervously who had come out to watch in their bathrobes and housecoats, and everyone laughed, and the ambulance with Mr. Schultz moved off slowly, its siren wailing, and men ran alongside a few steps to look in the rear window, murders are exciting and lift people into a heart-beating awe as religion is supposed to do, after seeing one in the street young couples will go back to bed and make love, people will cross themselves and thank God for the gift of their stuporous lives, old folks will talk to each other over cups of hot water with lemon because murders are enlivened sermons to be analyzed and considered and relished, they speak to the timid of the dangers of rebellion, murders are perceived as momentary descents of God and so provide joy and hope and righteous satisfaction to parishioners, who will talk about them for years afterward to anyone who will listen. I drifted to the corner, and then walked quickly down a side street away from the scene, and then made a two-block-wide circuit of the Palace Chophouse and Tavern, and when that yielded nothing, I went out two more blocks and made a bigger square, and by this means found the Robert Adams on Trenton Street, a four-story hotel of pale brick hung with rusted fire escapes. I sneaked easily past the clerk sleeping behind his reception desk and hobbled up the stairs to the fourth floor, and after reading the number on the key I had taken from Mr. Schultz's pocket I let myself into his room.

The light was on. In the closet, behind his hanging clothes, was a smaller safe than the one I remembered from the hideout in the house outside Onondaga. I was not able to open it right away. I could smell his clothes, they smelled of him, of his cigars and his rages, and my hands were shaking, I was not well, I was in pain that made me sick to my stomach, and so it took me a few minutes to work the combination, right to thirty-three, twice around left to twenty-seven, and two twirls to the right back to thirty-three. Inside the little safe were packs of bills in rubber bands, the real actual facts of all those numbers on the tapes. I shoveled them out and stacked them in an elegant alligator valise chosen for Mr. Schultz by Drew Preston in the early days of their happiness in the north country. The bills filled it full, it was very satisfying to build this solid geometry of numbers. A great solemn joy filled my breast, in the nature of gratitude to God, as I realized I had made no mistakes to offend Him. I snapped the hasps shut just as I heard the footsteps of several people running up the stairs of the old hotel. I relocked the safe, drew Mr. Schultz's clothes across the bar in front of it, let myself out the window and climbed up the fire escape, and I spent that night, it was October 23, 1935, on the roof of the Robert Adams hotel in Newark New Jersey, sobbing and sniffling like a wretched orphan, and falling asleep finally in the paling dawn, where to the east, I could see in the distance the reassuring conformations of the Empire State Building.

TWENTY

M r. Schultz had been mortally wounded and he died at Newark City Hospital a little after six the next evening. Just before he died a nurse's aide brought his dinner tray into the room and left it there, having had no instructions to the contrary. I came out from behind the screen where I'd been hiding and I ate everything, consommé and roast pork and cooked carrots, a slice of white bread, tea, and a trembling cube of lime Jell-O for dessert. Afterward I held his hand. He was by then in a coma and lay quietly with his broad, bare and badly sewn chest rising and falling, but for hours, all afternoon, in fact, he'd been delirious and talked constantly, he shouted and wept and issued orders and sang songs, and because the police were trying to find out who shot him they sent in a stenographer to put his ravings on record.

I found to hand behind my screen a nurse's clipboard with some pages of medical record forms attached, and in the top drawer of a white metal table, which I slid out very slowly, the stub of a pencil. And I wrote down what he said as well. The police were interested to know who killed him. I knew that, so I listened for the wisdom of a lifetime. I thought at the end a man would make the best statement of which he was capable, delirious or not. I figured delirium was only a kind of code. My version doesn't always match the official transcript, it is more selective, being in long-hand, there are words misheard, mistakes of my own emotion, I was also constrained not to be noticed by anyone who came at various times into the room, it was busy in there at times what with the stenographer, police officers, the doctor, the priest, and Mr. Schultz's real wife and family.

The stenographer's transcript made its way into the newspapers and so Dutch Schultz is remembered today for his protracted and highly verbal death, coming of a culture where it tends to happen abruptly to men who never had that much to say in the first place. But he was a monologist all his life, he was never as silent as he thought he was or as ill-equipped in speech. I think now, as one who linked my life to his, that whatever he did was of a piece, the murdering and the language for it, he was never at a loss for words, whatever he pretended. And while this monologue of his own murder is a cryptic passion, it is not poetry, the fact is he lived as a gangster and spoke as a gangster, and when he died bleeding from the sutured holes in his chest he died of the gangsterdom of his mind as it flowed from him, he died dispensing himself in utterance, as if death is chattered-out being, or as if all we are made of is words and when we die the soul of speech decants itself into the universe.

No wonder I got hungry. He went on for over two hours. I sat there and got to know that screen well, I think the material was muslin and it was laced taut on a green metal frame that could be rolled about on four little rubber casters, and his words seemed to paint themselves there on the translucent light of the cloth, or perhaps it was on my own unwritten mind, and I wrote them down, interrupted only by the wearing-down of the lead of the pencil, which I then had to reexpose by picking at the wood with my fingernails. Anyway I'll enter this here as I heard it delivered between the hours of four and six P.M. of October 24, until the moment before he finally but not for all time fell silent.

"Oh mama, mama," he said. "Oh stop it stop it stop it. Please make it quick, fast and furious. Please, fast and furious. I am getting my wind back. You do all right with the dot dash system. Whose number is that in your pocketbook, Otto: 13780? Oh oh, dog biscuit. And when he is happy he doesn't get snappy. Please, you didn't even meet me. The glove will fit what I say. Oh Kay Oh Kaioh, oh cocoa, I know. Who shot me? The boss himself. Who shot me? No one. Please, Lulu, and then he clips me? I am not shouting, I am a pretty good pretzel. Ask Winifred in the department of justice. I don't know why they shot me, honestly I don't. Honestly. I am an honest man. I went to the toilet. I was in the toilet and when I reached—the boy came at me. Yes, he gave it to me. Come on, he cuts me off, the beneficiary of his will, is that right? A father's son? Please pull for me. Will you pull? How many good, how many bad? Please, I had nothing with him. He was a cowboy in one of the seven days a week fights. No business, no hangout, no friends, nothing, just what you pick up and what you need. Please give me a shot. It is from the factory. I don't want harmony. I want harmony. There is none so fair, beyond compare, they call Marie. I'll marry you in church, please, let me just put it in a little way. Let me into the district fire factory. No no, there are only ten of us, and there are ten million somewhere of you so get your onions up and we will throw in the truce towel. Oh please let me up, please shift me, police, that is communistic strike baloney! I still don't want him in the path, it is no use to stage a riot. The sidewalk was in trouble and the bears were in trouble and I broke it up. Put me in control, I'll throw him out the window, I'll grate his eyes. My gilt edged stuff, and those dirty rats have tuned in! Please mother, don't tear, don't rip. That is something that shouldn't be spoken about. Please get me up, my friends. Look out, the shooting is a bit wild, and that kind of shooting saved a man's life. Pardon me I forgot

I am plaintiff and not defendant. Why can't he just pull out and give me control? Please mother, pick me up now. Don't drop me. We'll have the blues on the run. They are Englishmen and they are a type I don't know who is best, they or us. Oh sir, get the doll a roofing. For God's sake! You can play jacks and girls do that with a soft ball and play tricks with it. She showed me, we were children. No no and it is no. It is confused and it says no. A boy has never wept nor dashed a thousand kim. And you hear me? Get some money in that treasury we need it. Look at the past performances, that is not what you have in the book. I love the boxes of fresh vegetables. Oh please warden, please put me up on my feet at once. Did you hear me? Please crack down on the Chinamen's friends and Hitler's commander. Mother is the best bet and don't let Satan draw you too fast. What did the big fellow shoot me for? Please get me up. If you do this you can go and jump right here in the lake. I know who they are they are Frenchy's people all right look out look out. Oh my memory is all gone. My fortunes have changed and come back and went back since that. I am wobbly. You ain't got nothing on him and we got it on his hello. I am dying. Come on Missy, pull me out I am half crazy about you. Where is she, where is she? They won't let me get up, they dyed my shoes. Open those shoes. I am so sick, give me some water. Open this up and break it so I can touch you. Mickey please get me in the car. I don't know who could have done it. Anybody. Kindly take my shoes off there is a handcuff on them. The pope says these things and I believe him. I know what I am doing here with my collection of papers. It isn't worth a nickel to two guys like you and me, but to a collector it is worth a fortune. It is priceless. Money is paper too and you stash it in the shithouse! Look, the dark woods. I am going to turn—turn your back to me please, Billy I am so sick. Look out for Jimmy Valentine for he's a pal of mine. Look out for your mama, look out for her. I tell you you can't beat him. Police, please take me out. I will settle the indictment. Come on, open the soap duckets. The chimney sweeps. You want to talk, talk to the sword. Here is French Canadian bean soup on the altar. I want to pay. I am ready. All my life I have been waiting. You hear me? Let them leave me alone.''

SIMULTANEOUS WITH THE SHOOTINGS IN THE PALACE CHOPHOUSE THERE HAD BEEN attacks on known Schultz gang members in Manhattan and the Bronx, two were dead, including Mickey the driver, whose real name was Michael O'Hanley, three were seriously wounded, and the rest of the gang was presumed scattered. I had read about it in the morning papers while waiting for a train to Manhattan in the Newark station of the Pennsylvania Railroad. I was not mentioned in any of the accounts, the bartender's statement had not included reference to a kid in a Shadows jacket, which was good, but I put the valise in a pay locker and rolled up my jacket and disposed of it in a trash basket on the theory that not everything the bartender told the police might have found its way into the newspapers, and then I went out and got a taxicab to take me to Newark Hospital, having persuaded myself that Mr. Schultz's room was at that moment the safest place to be.

But now that he was dead, I was on my own. I looked at his face, it was the deep red color of a plum, the mouth was slightly open and the eyes staring up as if he had something else to say. For a moment I was fooled into thinking he did. Then I realized my own mouth was open as if I had something to say too, so that my mind flashed with an entire normal conversation between us, the one it was too late for, his confession and my forgiveness, or perhaps the other way around, but in either case the conversation you only have with the dead.

I limped away before the nurses came in and discovered him. I reclaimed my suitcase at the station and rode the train into Manhattan. It was a chilly night for a boy having no jacket. I took the crosstown trolley to the El, and I got back to the Bronx by about nine at night and did not go home directly but came around through the backyard of the Diamond Home for Children, and made my way into the basement where Arnold Garbage was listening to "The Make-Believe Ballroom" on the radio while looking through old *Collier's* magazines. Without going into details I told him I had to stash something and he found me a small space in the back of his deepest darkest bin. I gave him a dollar. Then I went back the way I had come, circled around to Third Avenue, and walked home the front way.

For weeks afterward I sat in the apartment, I couldn't seem to move, it was not that I was sore and aching, I could take aspirins for that, I felt as if I weighed a thousand pounds, everything was an enormous effort, even sitting in a chair, even breathing. I found myself looking at that black phone, waiting for it to ring, I even picked it up from time to time to see if anyone was on the other end. I sat with my Automatic stuck inside my belt, it was just the way Mr. Schultz had carried his gun. I was fearful that when I went to bed I would have nightmares but I slept the sleep of the innocent. Meanwhile the autumn began flying through the Bronx, winds rattled the windows and the leaves from God knows what distant trees came wheeling down our street on their crisp edges. And he was still dead, they were all still dead.

I kept thinking about Mr. Berman's last words to me and whether they meant anything more than the numbers of a combination lock. They were words to keep going, I could say that much, he was preserving something, he was passing it on. So they were trustful words. But trust could mean either of two things, not knowing any better or knowing full well, knowing all the time and never having let on, with those little looks over the tops of his glasses, the teacher, every act a teaching.

It was a strong powerful ghost they made in me, my dead gang. What happened to the skills of a man when he died, that he knew how to play the piano, for instance, or in Irving's case to tie knots, to roll up pant legs, to walk easily over a heaving sea? What had happened to Irving's great gift of precision, his just competence in everything, that I so admired? Where did that go, that abstraction?

My mother didn't seem to notice my state but she began to cook things for me that I liked, and she began to really clean the apartment. She snuffed the candles and threw out all her tumblers of lights, it was almost funny—now with someone really dead she was no longer in mourning. But I was only half aware of all of this. I was trying to figure out what to do with myself. I thought about going back to school and sitting in a classroom and learning whatever it was you learned in classrooms. Then I took it as a commentary on my sad state of mind that I would even consider such a thing.

I would from time to time take my transcript out of my pocket and unfold the pages and read again what Mr. Schultz had said. It was a disheartening babble. There was no truth of history in it, no message for me.

My mother found a store on Bathgate Avenue that sold seashells, and she brought home a brown paper bag full of these tiny ridged shells, some were no bigger than a pinky nail, and she began another one of her mad projects, which was to paste them to the phone using airplane cement she had found from an old balsa model I had never finished constructing. She dipped a toothpick in the bottle of dope and spread a glistening drop around the rim of the tiny shell and glued it to the phone. Eventually the entire phone, receiver and base, was covered in shells. It was rather beautiful, generally white and pink and tan, and rippled and gnarled, as if it was losing its form, as if the form of all things is lost in our attentions. She even attached shells to the cord, so that it seemed like a string of underwater lights. I found myself crying for my crazy mother when I thought of her as James J. Hines recalled her, a young and stately and thoughtful and brave young immigrant. I thought she must for a time have ennobled my father and that he had enlightened her in their undeniable love for each other before he had taken a powder. I had the money now never to have to send her away. I swore she would stay with me and I would take care of her for as long as she lived. But I couldn't seem to get going on anything, not even to the point of persuading her to quit her job. I suppose it was not a very gladdening prospect I saw before us. I was made very lonely by her strange use of objects, candles or pictures or remnants of clothing, broken dolls, and shells. One evening she came home with a fish tank, it was very heavy and she had trouble carrying it up the stairs, but her face was flushed and her expression happy as she put it on the end table beside the couch and filled it with water and then gently submerged the phone. How I loved my mad mother, how beautiful she was, I felt so bad, I felt I had failed her, I thought she had not changed because I had not gotten the final justice for us. The money in the valise across the street in the basement wasn't enough, I couldn't believe all the efforts of my intuitive scheming were fulfilled by it, of course, though I didn't know how much there was, even one month's weakened earnings of Schultz enterprises was enough to live on for several years, good God if I just drew from it twice my mother's salary from the laundry we would have everything we could possibly need, but I was terribly worried by it, we wouldn't be able to take it to a bank, I would have to think about it how to protect it all the time and use it in such dribs and drabs that it wouldn't draw attention to us and this seemed to me part of its skimpy insufficiency. I thought if it was going to change anything then it should have already, just the possession of it. But it hadn't. Then I realized that even though he was dead I felt about the money that it was still Mr. Schultz's. I had picked it up on instructions from Mr. Berman and now I found myself waiting for further instructions. I did not feel the calm I knew should come to me from the resolution of all my dreaming. I had nobody to talk to, nobody to know, in any event, to tell me I had done well. In fact only the dead men of my gang could ever appreciate as much as I had done.

And then late one night I was buying the papers at the kiosk on Third Avenue under the El when a De Soto pulled up and the door opened, and I was surrounded by men, two had come out of the cigar store at the same time as two came out of the car, and they had the impassive expressions on their faces of the criminal trades. All one of them had to do was nod toward the open door of the car and I folded my papers under my arm and got right in. They drove me all the way downtown to the Lower East Side. I knew it was important not to panic, or to imagine what might be happening to me. I thought back to all my movements of the past year and couldn't understand how he could know about me, I hadn't even let him get a good look at me in front of the church steps. I saw now that I had made one terrible mistake in not writing a letter to my mother with instructions to her only to open it if I didn't come home and didn't come home and died of not coming home to my mother.

They pulled up in a narrow tenement street, though naturally they didn't give me a clear look at it. I felt across my face the barred shadows of fire escapes in the dimly lit street. We climbed a stoop. We walked up five flights.

All at once I was in a kitchen under a bare ceiling-bulb and facing, as he sat at a little table covered with oilcloth like a rich visiting relative, the man who had won the gang wars. Here is what I saw: two mildly inquisitive eyes of no great intelligence and one of them drooped under a heavy hanging eyelid. And he really did have bad skin, I saw that now, and the scar under his jaw was whiter than everywhere else. All told he had a kind of lizardy look. His best feature was a good head of slicked-back wavy black hair. He was wearing a well-tailored topcoat over his businessman's ensemble. His hat was on the table. His nails were manicured. I smelled an eau de cologne. His was altogether a different style of malignity from Mr. Schultz's. I felt as you feel when you walk a few blocks into another neighborhood though it is not that far from your own. He gestured with an open hand very politely so that I would sit down opposite him.

"First of all, Billy," he said in a very soft voice, as if all conversation was regrettable, "you know how bad we feel what happened to the Dutch-man."

"Yes sir," I said. I was appalled that he knew my name, I didn't want to be in his registry of names.

"I had the greatest respect. For all of them. I knew them how many years? A man like Irving, you don't find his quality."

"No sir."

"We are trying to find out the cause of this thing. We are trying to get his boys back and put something together, you know, for the widows and children."

"Yes sir."

"But it is turning out to have difficulties."

The tiny room was crowded with the men standing behind me and behind him. Only now did I see, off to the side, Dixie Davis, the mouthpiece, slumped in a wooden chair with his knees pressed together and holding his hands locked between them to keep them from shaking. The underarms of Mr. Davis's expensive pinstripe suit had big dark sweat stains and his face was covered by a film of sweat. I knew these as signs of the extreme unction. I acknowledged him with the briefest of glances because I understood now who had identified me, which meant all I was giving away was the truth they already knew and I thought it might suggest I wasn't smart or devious enough to try to hide anything.

Then I turned back to my interrogator. It seemed important to me to sit straight and look at him clear-eyed. He would learn as much from my attitude as from anything I said.

"You were coming along nicely in their eyes is my understanding."

"Yes sir."

"We might have a job for a bright kid. Did you get out of it at least with something to show?" he said as casually as if my life wasn't in the balance.

"Well," I said, "I was just catching on. I was put on salary the week before and he gave me a month's advance because my mother's been sick. Two hundred dollars. I don't have it with me, but I can get it from the savings bank first thing in the morning."

He smiled, the corners of his mouth turned up for an instant, and he raised his hand. "We don't want your wages, kid. I'm talking about business affairs. They managed their business not always in a business way. I was asking if you could help us figure out about assets."

"Gee whiz," I said, scratching my head, "that is more in Mr. Davis's department. All I did was run out for coffee or if someone needed a pack of cigarettes. They never let me in meetings or where anything was going on."

He sat there nodding. I could feel Dixie Davis's eyes on me, I could feel the intensity of his stare.

"You never saw any money?"

I thought a moment. "Yes, once, on a Hundred Forty-ninth Street," I said. "I saw them counting the day's collection while I was sweeping. I was impressed."

"You were impressed?"

"Yes. It was something to dream about."

"Have you dreamed?"

"Every night," I said looking him in the drooped eye. "Mr. Berman told me the business is changing. That they will need smart quiet people with good manners who have been to school. I am going back into school and then I'm going to go to City College. And then we'll see."

He nodded, and grew very still and gazed into my eyes for a moment as he made up his mind. "School is a good idea," he said. "We may look in on you from time to time, see how you're doing." He lifted his hand, palm up, and I rose with it. Dixie Davis had put his hand over his face.

"Thank you, sir," I said to the man who had ordered the killings of Mr. Schultz, Mr. Berman, Irving, and Lulu. "It is an honor to meet you."

I WAS RETURNED SAFELY TO THIRD AVENUE, DRIVEN RIGHT BACK AND DROPPED OFF in front of the cigar store. Only then did I become terrified. I sat down on the curb. My hands were black where they had moistly picked up the newsprint of the papers I had been holding. I read fragments of headlines in my palms, pieces of words. I had no idea what might be going to happen to me. Either I was free or my days were numbered. I just didn't know. I jumped up and began to walk the streets. I found myself shaking, but not with fear, with anger at myself for my fear. I thought: Let them kill me. I waited for the sound of the engine of the specific killing car screeching around the corner with the windows rolling down. And then I tried to figure out what they would think I had done to make them kill me. They wouldn't kill me, they would watch me. That's what I would do if I didn't know where the money was.

The fact was I had learned something very interesting: The newspapers had estimated Mr. Schultz's fortune as anywhere between six and nine million dollars. Very little of it had been put in banks. The Combination hadn't found it, they were looking for it, they had the business but they wanted the money too, they wanted the business from its beginnings.

And it was odd but from one moment to the next I was exhilarated by the attentions of another great man, dangerous as they were, I thought it was indeed possible my days were numbered but my competitive spirit was reawakened, I realized I had been sharing the defeat of the gang in a morbid way, I had been dwelling on their deaths. But nothing was over, it was all still going on, the money was deathless, the money was eternal and the love of it was infinite. I waited a few days and then went down to Arnold Garbage's basement while he was out foraging, and I made a private space for myself in case anyone came in, and in the ashen air, with the footfalls of children over my head, I counted the cash in the alligator suitcase. I was a long time counting, it was far more than I had thought, I will mention the precise amount, it took me several hours to count it, it was three hundred and sixty-two thousand and one hundred and twelve dollars I had taken for my portion and stashed there under carriage parts and old newspapers and broken toys and bed slats and stovepipes, and paper bags of shoes, and clothing in bales, and pots and pans and panes of glass and machine gears and acetylene torches and screwdrivers without handles and hammers and saws without teeth and shoeboxes of bubble-gum cards, and bottles and jars and baby bottles and cigar boxes of rubber nipples and typewriters and parts of saxophones and the bells of trumpets and the torn skins of drums and bent kazoos and broken ocarinas, and baseball bats and ships in cracked bottles and bathing caps and Boy Scout hats and badges and campaign buttons and piggy banks and bent tricycles and molding stamp collections and tiny flags on toothpicks from all the nations of the world.

AND THEN OF COURSE I WENT BACK TO MY HANDWRITTEN STATEMENTS OF WHAT HE had said and studied them and found there my vision of living in flowering reward, I had been too impatient, a great charmed fate unfolds, unfolds, unfurls in waves, and floops out to the sun like the planet in flower, I heard Mr. Schultz's voice say *a capable boy, a capable boy* and oh I was! because I found stashes of money in his sentences, the money of his delirious passion locked away there like an insane man's riddle, I studied that transcript in my own handwriting and I learned from it what he had told me, he told me there would be money for Mrs. Schultz and his children somewhere they would know about, but the meaning of his life and his genius, why he would salt it about as his years went on so that you could find it in the periods of his criminal career as in his neighborhoods.

And to test this proposition I went one night with Arnold Garbage after I had sat for weeks in schoolrooms to prove myself not worth watching, and we broke open a lock in the old abandoned beer drop on Park Avenue where I used to stand around and juggle, and in the shudder of a passing train we went down into a darkness black as if the fires had gone out in hell, and with rats brushing against our ankles and in the dankness of the history of the old beer runs, found there in the shit and refuse of Arnold's dreams, by his faint flashlight, an unbunged barrel stuffed to the coops with the currency of the United States, and Arnold lugged it and rolled it home on a pushcart over the cobblestones while I went ahead of him and stood in the shadows of doorways, and from that midnight hour we became partners in a corporate enterprise that goes on to this very day.

But I don't mean to suggest I was satisfied that was all there was, the more he was beset the more he would gather it to himself, didn't I know him? I studied that transcript of his ghost's voice and I learned from it what he had told me, he had told me that as the world closed in he would pull his fortune to him, that the worse things got the more he would gather himself unto himself, he would call it in, like stocks like bonds like chips from the gambling table, keep more and more of it near him from day to day as he made the ever more perilous journey. And at the end he would stash it where no one ever dreamed he had been and if he never got back to it it would die with him if no one was smart enough to find it.

So now I knew everything, and everything brings with it an exacting discretion, I went back to school to stay, hadn't I been told it was a good idea? and though it was ordeal enough to quash the most resolute heart, I sat there in those classrooms alone with my education and for good measure worked prominently in a fish store after school for five dollars a week, and wore a white apron ornamented with normal daily splashings of blood, and managed to bide my time simply by assuming that all of it was being watched.

Within a year of Mr. Schultz's death the man with bad skin was himself indicted and tried by Thomas E. Dewey and sent away to prison. I knew enough of gang rule that as it accommodated itself to change, priorities shifted, problems were redefined, and there arose new issues of criminally urgent importance. So it would have been possible right then to go upcountry in safety. But I was in no rush. Only I knew what I knew. And something like a revelation had come to me through my school lessons: I was living in even greater circles of gangsterdom than I had dreamed, latitudes and longitudes of gangsterdom. The truth of this was to be borne out in a few years when the Second World War began, but in the meantime I was inspired to excel at my studies as I had at marksmanship and betrayal, and so made the leap to Townsend Harris High School in Manhattan for exceptional students, whose number I was scornfully unastonished to be among, and then the even higher leap to an Ivy League college I would be wise not to name, where I paid my own tuition in reasonably meted-out cash installments and from which I was eventually graduated with honors and an officers' training commission as a second lieutenant in the United States Army.

In 1942, the man with bad skin was pardoned by Governor Thomas E. Dewey, who as district attorney had sent him up, and deported to Italy in thanks for the assistance he was thought to have provided in making the New York City waterfront secure against Nazi saboteurs. But by then I was myself patriotically employed overseas, and so, what with one thing and another, I was not able to claim the treasure until I got home from the war in 1945. That is almost all I will say of this matter although the larcenous reader will be able figure things out for himself, for herself, in fact anyone can put two and two together, it's all right with me, because of course I did go and collect it, it was just where I knew it would be, Mr. Schultz's whole missing fortune which to this day and until now people have believed was never recovered. It was in the form of bundled Treasury certificates and crisp bills in the noble denominations of Mr. Hines's love and it was stuffed in a safe, packed in mail sacks. My veteran's self was moved by the prewar quaintness of it, it was like pirate swag, monument to an ancient lust, and I have the same feelings looking at it that I get from old portraits or the recordings of dead though still fervent singers. But none of these feelings discouraged me from taking it.

AND HERE I REALIZE I HAVE COME ALMOST TO THE END OF THIS STORY OF A BOY'S adventures. Who I am in my majority and what I do, and whether I am in the criminal trades or not, and where and how I live must remain my secret because I have a certain renown. I will confess that I have many times since my investiture sought to toss all the numbers up in the air and let them fall back into letters, so that a new book would emerge, in a new language of being. It was what Mr. Berman said might someday come to pass, the perverse proposition of a numbers man, to throw them away and all their imagery, the cuneiform, the hieroglyphic, the calculus, and the speed of light, the whole numbers and fractions, the rational and irrational numbers, the numbers for the infinite and the numbers of nothing. But I have done it and done it and always it falls into the same Billy Bathgate I made of myself and must seemingly always be, and I am losing the faith it is a trick that can be done.

I find some consolation, however, in having told here the truth about everything of my life with Dutch Schultz, although in some respects my account differs from what you will read if you look up the old newspaper files. I have told the truth of what I have told in the words and the truth of what I have not told which resides in the words.

And I have now just one more thing to tell, and I have saved it for last because it is the fount of all my memory, the event that doesn't exonerate the boy I was but may delay for a moment reading him out of heaven. I drop to my knees in reverence to think of it, I thank God for the life He has given me and the joy of my consciousness, I praise Him and give all reverent thanks for my life of crime and the terror of my existence. In the spring following Mr. Schultz's death my mother and I were living in a top-floor five-room apartment with a southern exposure overlooking the beautiful trees and paths and lawns and playgrounds of Claremont Park. And one Saturday morning in May there was a knock on the door and a man in a chauffeur's uniform of light gray stood there holding a straw basket by the handles, and I didn't know what I thought it was, laundry or something, but my mother came past me and took the basket as if she had been expecting it, she had great authority and confidence now, so that the chauffeur was very relieved, he'd had on his face an expression of the utmost anxiety, she was dressed in a real black dress that was appropriate to her figure and in fashionable shoes that fit her, and hose, and her hair was cut and combed in a comely manner to frame her serene lovely face, and she just took the baby, because that's of course who it was, my son with Drew, I knew the minute I looked at him, and she brought him into our apartment of morning sun and laid him in the holey brown wicker carriage that she had brought with her from the old apartment. At that moment I felt a small correction in the just universe and my life as a boy was over.

There was some confusion after that, of course, we had to go out and buy bottles and diapers, he didn't come with any instructions, and my mother was a little slow remembering some of the things that had to be done when he cried and waved his arms about, but we adjusted to him soon enough and what I think of now is how we used to like to go back to the East Bronx with him and walk him in his carriage on a sunny day along Bathgate Avenue, with all the peddlers calling out their prices and the stalls stacked with pyramids of oranges and grapes and peaches and melons, and the fresh bread in the windows of the bakeries with the electric fans in their transoms sending hot bread smells into the air, and the dairy with its tubs of butter and wood packs of farmer's cheese, and the butcher wearing his thick sweater under his apron walking out of his ice room with a stack of chops on oiled paper, and the florist on the corner wetting down the vases of clustered cut flowers, and the children running past, and the gabbling old women carrying their shopping bags of greens and chickens, and the teenage girls holding white dresses on hangers to their shoulders, and the truckmen in their undershirts unloading their produce, and the horns honking and all the life of the city turning out to greet us just as in the old days of our happiness, before my father fled, when the family used to go walking in this market, this bazaar of life, Bathgate, in the age of Dutch Schultz.

WORLD'S
FAIR

For R. P. D.

A raree-show is here,
With children gathered round . . .
                    Wordsworth
                    The Prelude

ROSE

I was born on Clinton Street in the Lower East Side. I was the next to youngest of six children, two boys, four girls. The two boys, Harry and Willy, were the oldest. My father was a musician, a violinist. He always made a good living. He and my mother had met in Russia and they married there, and then emigrated. My mother came from a family of musicians as well; that is how, in the course of things, she and my father had met. Some of her cousins were very well known in Russia; one, a cellist, had even played for the Czar. My mother was a very beautiful woman, petite, with long golden hair and the palest blue eyes. My father used to say to us, "You think, you girls, you're beautiful? You should have seen your mother when she and her sisters walked down the street in our village. Every head turned, they were so slim, their bearing so elegant." I suppose he did not want us to get conceited.

I was four when we moved up to the Bronx, a big apartment near Claremont Park. I was a good student, I went to P.S. 147 on Washington Avenue; when I was graduated from there I went to Morris High School. I completed all my courses and graduated, and reenrolled to take the program of commercial courses there and got enough credits to graduate all over again if I chose. I knew now how to type, how to keep books, I knew shorthand. I was very ambitious. I had paid for my own piano lessons by playing for silent movies. I watched the screen and improvised. My brother Harry or my father used to sit right behind me to see that nobody bothered me; movie houses were still primitive and they attracted a bad element. After my courses, I found a job as private secretary to a well-known businessman and philanthropist named Sigmund Unterberg. He had made his money in the shirt business and now spent a good deal of his time doing work for Jewish organizations, social welfare, that kind of thing. There were no government bureaucracies in social work, no programs as there are now, everything charitable came from individuals and the private agencies they created. I was a good secretary, Mr. Unterberg would dictate a letter to me and I could take it right on the typewriter, without an error, and so when he was finished I was finished and the letter was ready for him to sign. He thought I was wonderful. His wife was a lovely woman and used to invite me to tea with them, to socialize with them. I suppose I was by now nineteen or twenty. They introduced me to one or two young men, but I never liked them.

I by now was interested in your father. We had known each other since high school. He was extremely handsome, dashing, he was a good athlete; in fact, that's how I met him, on the tennis courts, there were clay courts on Morris Avenue and 170th Street and we were each playing there. You played tennis in long skirts in those days. I was a good tennis player, I loved sports, and that's how we met. He walked me home.

My mother did not like Dave. She thought he was too wild. If I went out with another boy he would ruin the date. He would hang around outside our house even if we hadn't arranged to do anything together and when he saw another boy coming to pick me up he'd do terrible things, he'd pick a fight, or stop us and talk when I was with this other boy. He would warn the other boys to treat me with respect or he would come after them. Naturally, he frightened a few of them away, it was very annoying, I was furious, but somehow I would not break off with him as my mother advised. In the winter we went ice-skating, in the spring he would surprise me with flowers, he was very romantic and over the course of these years I was falling in love with him.

Things were different then, you didn't meet someone and go out and go to bed with them one two three. People courted. Girls were innocent.

ONE

Startled awake by the ammoniated mists, I am roused in one instant from glutinous sleep to grieving awareness; I have done it again. My soaked thighs sting. I cry, I call Mama, knowing I must endure her harsh reaction, get through *that,* to be rescued. My crib is on the east wall of their room. Their bed is on the south wall. "Mama!" From her bed she hushes me. "Mama!" She groans, rises, advances on me in her white nightgown. Her strong hands go to work. She strips me, strips the sheets, dumps my pajamas and the sheets, and the rubber sheet under them, in a pile on the floor. Her pendulous breasts shift about in the nightgown. I hear her whispered admonitions. In seconds I am washed, powdered, clean-clothed, and brought to secret smiles in the dark. I ride, the young prince, in her arms to their bed, and am welcomed between them, in the blessed dry warmth between them. My father gives me a companionable pat and falls back to sleep with his hand on my shoulder. Soon they are both asleep. I smell their godlike odors, male, female. A moment later, as the faintest intimation of daylight appears as an outline of the window shade, I am wide awake, blissful, guarding my sleeping parents, the terrible night past me, the dear day about to dawn.

These are my earliest memories. I liked when morning came to climb down from their bed and watch my parents. My father slept on his right arm, his legs straight, his hand coming over the pillow and bending at the wrist against the headboard. My mother lay curled with the curve of her broad back touching his. Together under the covers they made a pleasing shape. The headboard knocked against the wall as they stirred. It was baroque in style, olive green, with a frieze of small pink flowers and dark green leaves along its fluted edges. On the opposite wall were the dresser and mirror of the same olive green and fluted edges. Sprays of the pink flowers were set above the oval brass drawer pulls. In my play I liked to lift each handle and let it fall back to hear the clink. I understood the illusion of the flowers, looking at them, believing them and then feeling the raised paint strokes with my fingertips. I had less fondness for the bedroom curtains of sheer white over the window shades and for the heavy draperies framing the curtains. I feared suffocation. I shied away from closets, the dark terrified me mostly because I wasn't sure it was breathable.

I was an asthmatic child, allergic to everything, I was attacked continually in the lungs, coughing, wheezing, needing to be steamed over inhalators. I was the mournful prodigy of medicine, I knew the mustard plaster, the nose drop, the Argyrol throat swab. I was plugged regularly with thermometers and soap water enemas. My mother believed pain was curative. If it didn't hurt it was ineffective. I shouted and screamed and went down fighting. I argued for the cherry-red mercurochrome for my scraped knees and I got the detested iodine. How I howled. "Oh stop the nonsense," my mother said, applicating me with strokes of searing pain. "Stop it this instant. You make a fuss over nothing."

I HAD DIFFICULTY WITH THE PROPORTIONS OF THINGS AND MADE REASONABLE spaces for myself in what otherwise was an unfairly giganticized home. I liked to sit in the shelter of the piano in the parlor. It was a Sohmer upright of black mahogany, and the cantilevered keyboard made a low-lying roof for me. I enjoyed the patterns of rugs. I was a familiar of oak flooring and the skirts of upholstered chairs.

I went readily to my bath in part because the tub was of reasonable dimensions. I could touch its sides. I sank walnut-shell boats in the tub. I swamped them in tidal waves and then I quieted the water.

I was also aware that for some reason my mother's relentless efficiency was suspended when I was in my bath. Other than calling in to me from time to time to make sure I hadn't drowned, she left me in privacy. The pads of my fingers would wrinkle before I rose from the bathwater to unplug the drain.

Of the wooden kitchen table and chairs I made a fortress. Here I had surveillance of the whole vast kitchen floor. I knew people by their legs and feet. My mother's sturdy ankles and large shapely calves moved about on the pinions of a pair of ladies' heeled shoes. From sink to icebox to table they went accompanied by the administrative sounds of silverware clattering, drawers sliding open and shut. My mother took confident solid steps that made the glass doors of the cabinets tremble.

My little grandmother inched her feet forward without lifting them from the floor, just as she drank her tea in tiny sips. She wore high-laced shoes of black whose tops were hidden beneath her long limp skirts, also black. Of all the family Grandma was the easiest to spy on because she was always in her thoughts. I was wary of her, though I knew she loved me. She prayed sometimes in the kitchen with her prayer book lying open upon the table and her old-fashioned shoes flat on the floor.

My older brother Donald could not be spied upon. Unlike adults he was quick and alert. Targeting him for even a few seconds before he knew I was there was a great triumph. I lingered one day in the hallway outside the open door of his room. When I peeked around the corner his back was to me, he was working on a model airplane. "I know you're there, Mr. Bubblenose," he said without a moment's hesitation.

I VALUED MY BROTHER AS A CONFIDENT ALL-AROUND SOURCE OF KNOWLEDGE AND wisdom. His mind was a compendium of the rules and regulations of every game known to mankind. His brow furrowed with attentiveness to the proper way of doing things. He lived hard and by the book. He was an authority not only on model building but on kite flying, scooter racing, and the care of pets. He did everything well. I felt for him the gravest love and respect.

I might have been daunted by his example, and the view I had through him of everything I had to learn, except that he had the generous instincts of a teacher. One day I was with our dog, Pinky, in front of our house on Eastburn Avenue, when Donald came home from school and put his books down on the front stoop.

He plucked a large dark leaf from the privet hedge under the parlor window. He placed the leaf between his palms and cupped his hands to his mouth and blew into the gap formed by his adjacent thumbs. This produced a marvelous bleat.

I jumped up and down. When Donald made the sound again, Pinky began to yowl, as she did also when a harmonica was played in her presence. "I want to try," I said. Under his patient instruction I chose a leaf like his, I placed it carefully on my palms, and I blew. Nothing happened. He arranged and rearranged my little hands, he changed leaves, he corrected my form. Still nothing happened.

"You have to work at it," Donald said. "You can't expect to get it right away. Here, I'll show you something easier."

The same leaf he had used for a reed he now split in half simply by pressing the heels of his palms together and flattening his hands.

My brother was very fine. He wore the tweed knickers and ribbed socks and shoes with low sides of a young man. A shock of straight brown hair fell over one eye. His knitted sweater was dashingly tied by the sleeves around his waist and his red school tie was loosened at the knot. Long after he had taken our maniac dog into the house, I conscientiously applied myself to the tasks he had set me. Even if I couldn't get the hang of them right away, I knew at least what had to be learned.

*   *   *

Donald was like my mother in applying himself resolutely to the demands and challenges of life. My father was a different sort. I thought he got to where he was by magic.

He would let me watch him shave because I rarely saw him except in the mornings. He came home from work long after my bedtime. With a partner, he owned a music store in the Hippodrome, a famous theater building on Sixth Avenue and Forty-third Street in Manhattan.

"Good morning, Sunny Jim," he said. He had noticed early in my life that each morning I woke smiling, an act of such extraordinary innocence that he had ever since commented upon it. When I was a baby he lifted me into his arms and we played a game: he puffed up his cheeks like a hippopotamus and I punched the air out, first one side of his face, then the other. No sooner was the job done than his eyes went wide and his cheeks refilled and I had gigglingly to do it all over again.

The bathroom was lined in squares of white tile and all the fixtures were white porcelain. An opaque crinkled window seemed to glow with its own light. My father stood in the diffuse sunlight of the white bathroom after he had partially dressed—shoes, trousers, ribbed undershirt, suspenders looping off his flanks—and brought his shaving soap to a lather in its mug. Then he applied the lather to his face with an artful slopping of his shaving brush.

He did this while humming the overture to Wagner's *The Flying Dutchman*.

I loved the scratchy sound the brush made on his skin. I loved the soap as it turned from a froth to a substantive lather under his rubbing. Next, he held taut from its hook on the wall a long leather strop about three inches wide, and upon this he wielded his straight razor back and forth with a twist of the wrist. I failed to understand how something as soft as leather could hone something as hard as a steel razor. He explained the principle to me, but I knew it was just another example of his magic powers.

My father did sleight-of-hand things. He could appear to remove the top joint of his thumb, for example, and then put it back. Behind the screen of one hand, you'd see the thumb of the other come apart and then the space between the two halves. Like all good tricks, it was horrifying. He'd lift the thumb off and then put it back with a little twist, and hold it out for my inspection and wiggle it to assure me that it was as good as new.

He was full of surprises. He punned. He made jokes.

As he shaved, here and there tiny springs of blood quietly leaked through the white foam and turned pink. He did not seem to notice but simply went on shaving and humming.

After he had rinsed his face and patted it with witch hazel, he parted his shiny black hair in the middle and combed each side back. He was always well barbered. His handsome pink face shone. He smoothed his dark moustache with the tips of his fingers. He had a thin straight nose. He had vivid sparkling brown eyes that sent out signals of a mischievous intelligence.

Assiduously he applied the lather remaining in his shaving mug to my cheeks and chin. In the medicine cabinet was one of my wooden tongue depressors; every time I required a visit from our family physician, Dr. Gross, I was given a new one as a present. My father handed me a depressor so that I could shave.

"Dave," called my mother as she rapped on the door. "You know what time it is? What do you *do* in there!"

He grimaced, ducking his head between his shoulders, as if we were, both of us, naughty boys.

My father always made promises as he went off to work.

"I'll be home early tonight," he told my mother.

"I have no money," she said.

"Here's a couple of dollars to tide you over. I'll have cash this evening. I'll call you. Maybe I can pick up some things for dinner."

I pulled on his sleeve and begged him to bring me a surprise.

"Well, I'll just see what I can do," he said, smiling.

"You promise?"

Donald was already at school. When my father left I'd have nothing to look forward to, so I watched him to the last second. He was portly, though trim enough in one of his suits with the vest buttoned tight. He checked the knot of his tie in the mirror in the front hall. When he set his fedora on his head at the stylish angle he affected, I ran into the parlor so as to be able to see him as he came out the front door. Down the steps he skipped, and turning to wave, and smiling at me as I stood in the parlor window, he strode off down the street in that brisk jaunty gait of his. I watched him turn the corner and from one moment to the next he was out of sight.

I understood the reach of his life. I understood him as living by nature as a sojourner. He went forth and returned. He covered ground. His urges and instincts even on his one day off pointed away from home.

He rarely kept his word to return in time for dinner or to bring me something. My mother could not abide his broken promises. She was forever calling him to account. I saw that this did no good. By way of compensation he brought me things when I least expected them. A surprise surprised. It was a kind of teaching.

T W O

My mother ran our home and our lives with a kind of tactless administration that often left a child with bruised feelings, though an indelible understanding of right and wrong. As an infant I was bathed with brisk, competent hands and as a boy fed, clothed and taken through unpleasant events with strong admonitions to behave myself. I was not to express dissent. I was to stop the nonsense.

She was a vigorous buxom woman in her late thirties. A strong will beamed in her clear blue eyes. There was no mistaking her meaning—she was forthright and direct. She construed the world in vivid judgments. She felt strongly that even little boys bore responsibility for their actions. For example, they could be lazy, selfish, up to no good. Or they could be decent, kind, truthful, honest. However they were, so would their fate be decided.

All about in the air were the childhood diseases—whooping cough, scarlet fever, and, most dreaded of all, infantile paralysis. She believed children were at risk to the extent that their parents lacked common sense. "I saw that Mrs. Goodman at the Daitch Dairy," she said coming in from her shopping one day. "Poor woman, I don't envy her. Her daughter wears a brace on her leg and will for the rest of her life. She cried telling me this. But she let the child swim in public pools on the hottest days of the summer, so what else could she expect?"

Her stories dazzled me. Their purpose was instruction. Their theme was vigilance.

In the mornings, with my father and brother Donald out of the house, my mother threw open the windows, she plumped up pillows and quilts and laid them across the windowsills in the sun. She washed dishes and put clothes to soak in the laundry tub. She swept and ran the Electrolux vacuum cleaner. Everything she did was a declarative act. Her mastery of our realm was worth my study.

My mother wanted to move up in the world. She measured what we had and who we were against the fortunes and pretensions of our neighbors.

That my brother and I were properly clothed; that my father was self-employed; that we paid the rent on time, the telephone bill, the electric light bill: these were the elements of a composition she wanted the world to understand as the quality of our family.

When she was ready to do her marketing, she changed into a belted dress and shiny black shoes and put on a straw hat whose brim she turned up on one side. A little ribbon ran around the crown. She applied red lipstick and went off with her pocketbook tucked under her arm.

At the end of an afternoon she sometimes rested on the sofa for a few minutes and read the newspaper. In contrast to my father, who held the paper open at arm's length at the breakfast table, my mother, reclining, held the paper at the spine with one hand and slapped the pages left and right with the back of the other.

"I don't trust that doctor," she said of the physician attending the Dionne quintuplets. "He likes the limelight too much."

In the evenings, after dinner, with everything quieted down, she sat in the living room and read a novel from the rental library while she waited for my father to come home. I sometimes watched her when she didn't know it. After a while she would close the book in her lap, her legs would be tucked under her, and she would stare at the floor. She worried a lot about my little grandmother, who was sickly and had spells. But I think she worried mostly about my father.

My father was not a reliable associate, I was to gather. Too many things he said would come to pass did not. He was always late, somehow he would suppose he could get somewhere or accomplish something in less time than it actually took him. He created suspense. He was full of errant enthusiasms and was easily diverted by them. He had, besides, various schemes for making money that he did not readily confide to my mother. She seemed most of the time to be aroused to a state of worry regarding his activities.

When he was late my father was evasive, which seemed to justify her anger. He had a weakness for cards, I heard my mother tell her best friend, Mae. He liked to gamble and could not afford to.

I understood that my father seemed to elude my mother's ideas for him. He did not comport himself appropriately, given the hard times we were living in. I knew he was unreliable, but he was fun to be with. He was a child's ideal companion, full of surprises and happy animal energy. He enjoyed food and drink. He liked to try new things. He brought home coconuts, papayas, mangoes, and urged them on our reluctant conservative selves. On Sundays he liked to discover new places, take us on endless bus or trolley rides to some new park or beach he knew about. He always counseled daring, in whatever situation, the courage to test the unknown, an instruction that was thematically in opposition to my mother's.

The conflict between my parents was probably the major chronic circumstance of my life. They were never at peace. They were a marriage of two irreducibly opposed natures. Their differences created a kind of magnetic field for me in which I swung this way or that according to the direction of the current. My brother seemed to be more like my mother in his love of rules and a disposition for the proper doing of things. I, a quieter, more passive, daydreaming sort of child, understood my father with some sympathy, I feel now—some recognition of a free soul tethered, by a generous improvidence not terribly or shrewdly mindful of itself, to the imperial soul of an attractive woman.

My mother's one indulgence was to play the piano, which she did with authority, as she did everything. She had paid for her own lessons as a girl by working as an accompanist for silent movies. She was very good. What I liked, when she sat down to play, was that her rigorous thought was suspended. Her expression softened and her blue eyes shone. She sat with her back very straight, like a queen, her arms outstretched, and she filled the house with beautiful music that I thought of as waterfalls or rainbows. She could sight-read any score placed before her. When Donald brought home a new lesson from the Bronx House Music School, he would ask her to play it through just to hear how it was supposed to sound.

Donald was up to "Für Elise," by Beethoven. He had already mastered Schumann's "The Wild Horseman."

I expected someday to take piano lessons too. In the meantime I toyed with the keys, experimented with sounds, with the moods and feelings I could produce in myself by arranging my fingers on several keys at once and hammering away.

Under the glass counter near the cash register in my father's store downtown were shelves of toy instruments for children. I had one of every kind. I tooted a penny whistle, I blew a Hohner Brothers Marine Band harmonica, I got sounds from an ocarina, known also as a sweet potato because of its shape.

The easiest thing to play was a kazoo, not an instrument at all, but an oval tin tube with a piece of waxed paper screwed taut in a hatch halfway down its length. The paper vibrated as you hummed into the kazoo, and "Voilà," as my father said, you were a musician.

I liked to march down the hall all the way from my room at the back of the house to the front door while playing the kazoo with one hand and waving a flag with the other.

THREE

We lived at 1650 Eastburn Avenue. We occupied the ground floor and our landlords, the Segals, the second or top floor. To distinguish our way of living from that of the families who tenanted the apartment houses prevalent in the Bronx, we called ours a "private house." It was of red brick and had a flat roof. A stoop of eight white granite steps led down from the glass-pane doors to the street. To one side of the stoop, under the windows of our front parlor, was a little square of earth contained on three sides by a privet hedge. Here I built roads and dwellings—a whole city, in fact—for a society of small brown ants, whose reluctance to inhabit it never discouraged me.

I remember the light on Eastburn Avenue. It was a warm and brilliant bath that bleached the brick houses of red and of yellow ocher, the ruled sidewalks, the curbstones of blue Belgian block, into a peaceful and forbearing composition.

I imagined houses as superior beings who talked silently to each other.

At noon the sun shone from the top of my favorite toy, a Railway Express truck like the ones that occasionally made deliveries in the neighborhood. My truck was dark green, with solid matching green wheels and tires of hard rubber, and red frontier-style Railway Express lettering on the sides. The two rear doors unbolted and swung open exactly in the manner of the real ones. The steering wheel, which actually worked, was mounted at the correct angle, an undeviatingly horizontal on an absolutely vertical shaft. The sound of the motor, an electric whine, I supplied myself. I liked to push my truck over the cracks in the sidewalk and the obstacles of pebbles and sticks.

The sun baked the sidewalk so that it felt good on the knees and the palms of one's hands.

Across the street was a six-story apartment house, and two more private houses like ours, with droopy, heavy-leaved trees in front; up at the corner of Mt. Eden Avenue, the south end of the block, was the tile-roofed red brick mansion of Mrs. Silver, the widow of Judge Silver, a state Supreme Court Justice. My mother had told me that. This mansion was on a raised lawn behind a retaining wall of round stones cemented together. I never saw Mrs. Silver up close, but my mother assured me she was a fine woman who did not think she was better than anyone else.

I could see past the corner of Mt. Eden Avenue to the plane trees of the Oval, a small park with benches circling the garden beds of tulips, where the mothers and children gathered in the afternoons. A string of such ovals bisected the width of Mt. Eden Avenue all the way up the hill west, to the Grand Concourse.

On the far side of the Oval was the beginning of Claremont Park, or the big park, as we called it; from my vantage point it was a great swatch of forest where the land went green.

If I turned in the other direction, I saw the north end of the block, 173rd Street. Here there was no greenery, but another apartment house whose entrance was around the corner, and, across the street, the enormous schoolyard with its chain link fence of P.S. 70. This was Donald's school and I would go there too.

Everything we needed was close by. Beyond P.S. 70 was 174th, where all the stores were. I had been born in a small lying-in hospital at the corners of Mt. Eden and Morris avenues, just a block west. The Mt. Eden Center, the temple where my old grandma went on Friday nights to pray, was also on Morris Avenue.

Most of these buildings and parks and houses were not more than ten or fifteen years old. It was a new neighborhood. I think the light was so clear and broad because of all the open space that allowed the sun to come down evenly. There were no big buildings or narrow alleys to make sharp angles and deep shadows and block out the blue of the sky, as was the case downtown in Manhattan, at my father's store.

IN THE STREET I PREFERRED MY OWN COMPANY TO WHATEVER MISERABLE WRETCH of a child wanted to pit his ideas and requirements for me against my own. Alone, I could be happy. I assumed everyone's will was stronger than mine. This attitude may have come of my situation as a severely younger brother.

Because I was eight years younger than Donald I was something of a novelty among his friends—like a puppy or a kitten. I grew up being instructed, led about and mauled by older children. There were great numbers of them. As an infant I had held on to the sides of my carriage in terror as one or another of these louts pushed me along the street as fast as he could. They would have contests, a sort of Eastburn Avenue Olympics in occupied baby-carriage racing. Their tender ministrations poked ice cream pops into my face, or, in winter, pulled my hat down over my eyes so that I would not suffer from the cold. They were not cruel, merely dangerously boisterous. Their names were Seymour, Bernie, Harold, Stanley, Harvey, Irwin, and so on. In my mind they are like a chorus of noisemakers. Not faces or voices I recall, but horns, bladders, ratchets, and wheezing party favors that someone blows into your face.

In my own consciousness I was not a child. When I was alone, not subject to the demands of the world, I had the opportunity to be the aware sentient being I knew myself to be.

BUT I DID HAVE A COMPANION OF SORTS, THE FAMILY DOG PINKY. MY FATHER HAD brought her home without warning. We had named her for the color of the inside of her pointed ears. She was a long-haired dog, a sort of terrier, white, with a thin snout and dark bright eyes. She was smart, she seemed to understand words. She had a good trick, which was to drink water from the fountain in the Oval: she stood on her hind legs and held the pedestal basin with her front paws.

But when my mother put Pinky out with me, she tied her leash to a root branch of the privet. This was because the dog was totally untrained and ran away whenever she had the opportunity. And she was fleet. My mother was not fond of her. My father was. Donald, of course, loved her. I loved her but could not control her. If I held her leash, she pulled me all over the place until I fell. She got away from me almost every time. I didn't like that.

As I played in front of the house Pinky sat and watched me or barked at passing cars and lunged against her restraint. This particular morning we both heard a roar from the north end of the block. The dog barked furiously. Around the corner came the Sanitation Department water wagon. An enormous cylindrical tank was mounted on the flatbed of a Mack truck. The entire equipage was painted khaki, suggesting perhaps its origins during the World War. As it turned into our street two fanlike jets of water shot out of the nozzles suspended under the tank. Oh what a sight! An iridescent rainbow moved like a phantom light through the air, disintegrating as millions of liquid drops of sun and forming an instant torrent in the gutters at the curbstones. The water wagon rolled by with a fearsome roar and hiss. I ran along the sidewalk to feel the driest edges of the great spray. Behind me Pinky was barking and rearing against her collar. Then, from one moment to the next, the nozzles shut off, the truck went into another gear and turned the corner at Mt. Eden Avenue, and was gone from sight. But the air was cool and fresh. The street was black and shining. In the raging course of water flowing swiftly along the curb I tossed a Good Humor ice cream stick. Other children had appeared and dropped in their sticks and twigs. We followed our boats back down the block as they turned and twisted in the current, followed them down the gentle incline of Eastburn Avenue to their doom, a waterfall pouring into the sewer grate at the corner of 173rd Street.

I COULD COUNT ON SEEING THE WATER WAGON IN WARM WEATHER EVERY COUPLE of weeks. Less frequent appearances were made by the coal trucks. They came in early autumn, usually, while the temperature was high.

These trucks were of great interest to me. They were so heavy, so massive, especially when loaded with their mountains of coal, that only a clanking chain drive could turn their wheels. They were like rolling houses. One day a delivery was made to 1650. The coal truck backed up to the curb, parking almost at right angles to the sidewalk. It was the lawless arrogance of the mighty. The driver jumped out, bare to the waist, heavily muscled, like the truck. He was whiter in the chest than in the arms and he had a red bandanna around his neck. I recognized him as brother to the men who held the jackhammers and swung the picks and axes in the street-repair gangs. He disdained even to hear the barking dog. He threw a lever and the truck bed rose, tilting back on its hydraulic lifts so slowly, and with such grinding protest, as to transform itself in my mind into a screeching rearing dinosaur. When and only when the loaded bed stood at a dangerously slanted angle, almost at the vertical, did he bring it to a stop and throw open the sluice gate at the back: the great smoking avalanche of black stone poured itself onto the sidewalk.

Now, I had anticipated the event by untying Pinky and moving back with her to see things from a distance. There was a garage next to our house with a double set of folding doors. It belonged to the adjoining private house whose entrance was around the corner on Mt. Eden Avenue. It was set farther back than our front steps and so made a kind of playing area. I had looped Pinky's leash to the broken handle of one of the doors. The great tumbling slide so terrified her that she snapped her leash and ran off.

I did not realize this. I was too intent on watching the driver, who now climbed into the truck, straddling the side of the bed with a flaunted animal daring, and with a long-handled broom pushed the lingering chunks of coal out the chute. When this was done, he leaped nimbly to the ground, brought the truck bed back to the horizontal with a resounding clang, and drove away, sprinkling a thin trail of coal in the street behind him.

I contemplated the pyramid of slag in front of my house, in wonder for the weight of it, with some increased sense of the hierarchy of being, how the mass of it had been manipulated to do human bidding. I felt its substance keenly. I felt through my feet the earth as gravity.

I waited for the coming up from the alley with his shovel and wheel-barrow of Smith, our black janitor, who inhabited the basement.

He appeared. He didn't seem to notice me, which I counted as my good fortune.

Smith was a huge man, bigger and more muscular than the coal-truck operator. His slow gliding walk and slow speech, as resonantly basso as the voice at the bottom of a cavern, was to me consistent with the size of him. He wore overalls in winter or summer. He smelled of coal dust and ashes and whiskey. His hair was grey. His skin was black with a rich purple tone, he had raised scars on his face, his eyes were bloodshot, and he was now, as always, regally, imperially angry.

Piece by piece, he was going to move the coal to the coal bin.

He shoveled not from the top, where I would have, but from the bottom. When he filled the barrow, he stuck the shovel like a spear into the coal pile, lifted the handles and, his arm muscles tensing, rolled the wheelbarrow down the alley to the cellar. When he came back out again, he did not look at me, but I was the only one he could have been talking to when he said, "That dog done gone."

At this same moment I realized I had not for some time heard Pinky barking. Of course I ran into the house and got my mother. We went looking. We went from one end of the block to the other. Pinky was nowhere to be seen. The calamity of her loss panicked my small heart. As we half ran, half walked, my mother questioned me: had I noticed which way she'd run? how could I not have seen her break away? and so on. The judgment was explicit. My mother was sorely put out with me. At the same time she expressed the hope that Pinky might finally have run away forever. "With luck she'll never come back," my mother said.

This was her way—to express concern from opposite sides of the crisis.

I was ready to cry. Then I saw her. She was crossing Mt. Eden Avenue from the Oval to the big park. Her leash trailed behind her. "Pinky!" We ran across the street. "Pinky!" I shouted.

She ignored us. At this moment a car bore down on her. She had never understood cars. Now she froze in the middle of the street. She flattened herself head to tail, pressing her snout between her front paws, and the car passed over her.

"Oh my God," my mother said. We ran across the Oval and into the street. The car, a Nash or Hudson, I wasn't sure which, did not stop. The driver hadn't even seen her. Pinky was where she had hunkered down, she had not moved. She looked up at us with her dark eyes shining in terror. A big chunk of hair was gone from her back. She whimpered. "Oh Pinky," my mother said and got down on her knees and hugged the dog she despised. Pinky stood up trembling. Other than her skinning she was no worse for wear. She trotted home obediently behind us, I holding the remainder of the leash with both hands.

Cars were built high off the ground and so the dog survived. We were all to praise her for her instructive reaction before the oncoming car; we did not tell each other how stupid she was for having gotten in front of it in the first place. My mother put Vaseline on Pinky's scrape, and within an hour it was as if nothing had happened.

And I went back to watching Smith. He was working slowly and steadily in that way of skilled laborers. After the last barrowload was put away he came back out and hosed the sidewalk. The big penumbra of black dust dissolved. Then, everything clean and fresh again, Smith slowly went back to his basement.

I sat alone in the silence on the front stoop. My dog was safe. I sat there on the steps and looked into the peaceful shining street. In the passage of this sun-filled afternoon, it was as if the monumental event of the coal truck had never occurred, and that weightless light, and the iridescence of sprayed water, were, after all, the reigning forces of the universe.

SOME BLACK-AND-WHITE EIGHT-MILLIMETER FILM RECORDS A MOMENT WHEN I WAS commissioned by my brother to hold the spring-wound Universal movie camera that our father had brought home to us. The camera was not much larger than a pack of cigarettes, though much heavier. My job was to press the button and photograph Donald and his friends grouped around Pinky in the sun in front of the double folding garage doors alongside our house. First you see a sedate composition of boys standing and kneeling like a team around its mascot. Pinky barks and strains at her leash, which Donald has trouble holding. The group is waving, smiling, but then Pinky jumps, knocks over one of the kneeling boys, and soon the whole company are falling over themselves, laughing and shouting and mugging for the camera while the dog gets loose among them. They bang into each other grabbing for her. As you watch this scene the film seems to waver, the subjects career out of frame and back, and Donald, disengaging himself from the extras, advances toward me with a frown. He shakes his head, waves his hands, and indicates with his characteristic expression of intense concern that I am doing something wrong. His scowl looms into the shot—I was determined to keep the button pressed as long as I could.

ROSE

By the time the war started, World War One, I had through Mr. Unterberg gotten interested in social welfare work. He had said to me watching the way I dealt with people who came into the office, that I had greater abilities than secretarial. I was very sensitive to poor people, and sometimes going to the settlement house on some errand of Mr. Unterberg's I would see these people in need and talk to them and try to help them. So he got me a job working for the Jewish Welfare Board, dealing with immigrants and their problems. The Board had set up a model tenement apartment up on 101st Street and First Avenue—up near the vinegar works. I taught the immigrant women and men how to live in the modern world. How to keep clean, store food, make beds, all that sort of thing. It was astonishing how little people knew, how uneducated and green they were. It was touching, you could not help being moved to see the struggles they had to understand, to learn, their desire to make good in America. I, having been born here, had no idea of my own parents' struggle, they too had come as young people not knowing the language, the ways of the new world, but at least they had skills, my father had a profession, he had work the day he landed, he was always very proud of telling us that. My father always knew how to make a living, and he worked till the day he died. He was extremely responsible, for him the family was everything, he not only got himself work but other musicians too, he became a sort of booking agent for musicians in addition to working himself. I learned ambition from him.

At any rate, working for the Jewish Welfare Board, when the war started I was naturally involved with that. Teams of us used to travel to the armories to serve coffee and doughnuts and talk to the soldiers and maybe dance with them at their functions. It was all chaperoned, all proper. Your father by then was in the Navy, he was training to be an ensign at the Webbs Naval Institute on the Harlem River, and as usual, he was devilish; he would each night climb over the fence and sneak out to see me without official leave. He did things like that. He would come to wherever I was

265

working—we did this work in the evening—and there he would be in his blue sailor suit, one sailor among hundreds of soldiers and it could be quite a problem for him, the rivalry between soldiers and sailors being what it was, and he was totally outnumbered and still he'd take me away from these other boys with whom I'd been talking or dancing. He was lucky not to be killed.

Then in 1918 we had the terrible flu epidemic, and my two older sisters, my dear sisters, one twenty-three, the other twenty-four, they each contracted the flu and within months of each other they both died. To this day I don't like to think about it. I saw my poor mother turn old before my eyes. It was never an easy life, she was the hardest-working person I had ever seen, and how they had struggled the both of them to make a good life, and bring us up properly and see to it that we had some prospects for our own lives, some promise. It was not easy raising six children on the wages of a free-lance musician, however responsible he was; and in those days, of course, there was nothing that made running a home easy; you washed clothes with a washboard, you scrubbed them by hand in the sink. I used to do that myself, and you shopped every day because there was no refrigeration, and you cooked from scratch, there were no conveniences in cooking any more than in anything else. She had never had help. And these two beautiful young women got sick and died. She lost her two oldest daughters! I've blocked it all out, I don't remember the funerals. I try not to picture those girls. I don't remember any of it, only that that time in my mind is blank, a grey space, an emptiness.

When I was twenty-three I eloped with your father. We went to Rocka-way Beach and we got married. What had happened is that my brother Harry, who was always very protective, went to Dave and he said, "You and Rose have been going out for eight years. She's twenty-three and she wants to get married. She would like to marry you, but if you won't she doesn't want to see you anymore. You either marry her or stay away." Well, you remember your father. He had a most unusual mind. He didn't think the way other people thought, he was unconventional, his ideas were different. Even then. I knew he wanted to marry me. But he didn't like to be told what to do, he never liked that. So the answer was to marry in this scandalous way, to elope, and get married by a justice of the peace rather than formally in a synagogue with a bridal veil and a celebration with the families' blessing. He disliked religion, your father. He was very modern, interested in the new ideas—just as he loved new gadgets he loved new ideas. He believed in progress. He'd learned some of this from his father, Isaac, a wonderful man, very scholarly, but not pious. For Isaac religion meant superstition and poverty and ignorance as it had in the old country. He was a socialist, your grandfather Isaac, he believed the prob-lems on earth in life—food, shelter, education—should be solved on earth. The promises of Heaven didn't interest him. So your father had a background in these sorts of ideas. We went out to this remote beach

community and married and set up house there. Both families were outraged and hurt. We lived a block from the ocean away from everyone else.
I loved it there, it was very beautiful. Every day Dave took the train into
the city. He worked for a man named Markel, who was in the phonograph
business. After World War One, phonographs—Victrolas we called
them—became popular. Markel liked Dave and taught him the business.
That is how he got into it, through that man. For a while before we were
married, I worked for Markel too, keeping the books, running the office.
Dave had gotten me that job.

At any rate, though it was sometimes lonely in Rockaway, that was
more than compensated for by the ocean and the sky and the privacy. We
didn't have our families on our backs. You don't know what that meant.
To have come from a large family living together, to have grown up in
apartments and city streets. Now we were alone and we had privacy and
we had space. It was a wonderful time in our lives. When we went out we
went down to the Village, Greenwich Village. It was very much the thing
then. Your father had a gift for making friends, meeting people, and he
naturally gravitated to people of intelligence, people with fine minds and
radical ideas. Well, in the Village that's the way things were, lots of young
people thinking new thoughts and living differently from everyone around
them. We had artists for friends, and writers. We read the latest books,
listened to poets reading their poems in living rooms, in garrets in the
Village. We knew Maxwell Bodenheim, who was then a very well known
Village poet, we even met Edna Millay, who was already well known
outside the Village. We ate in restaurants where actors and playwrights
ate; I remember one, you walked down a few steps from the street, Three
Steps Down, that was the name of it, and there we found ourselves sitting
at a table next to Helen Hayes. How young and beautiful she was.

George Tobias, the actor, was a friend of ours. He was a young man
then. He later went to Hollywood. And Phil Welch, a reporter for the *New
York Times*. Phil admired your father very much. We had wonderful
friends. Only now do I see that our lives could have gone in an entirely
different direction.

FOUR

Winters, with their short and darkening days were difficult. When it stormed, snow got down my collar, inside my galoshes and under my sleeves. Despite my mother's bundling me in several layers of clothes, all sealed in by my snowsuit, I was wet and freezing in a discouragingly short time considering everything I had had to go through to get out the door. I moved lurchingly, stiffly, breasting the snow like some tiny golem.

But the season had its revelations. I stood one afternoon at my front steps with a gale blowing and immense drifts of snow filling the block, banking against the parked cars, and making dunes of the stone stoops of the private houses. It was awesome, furious, but afterward, the sky clearing, the stars appearing in the dusk, I breathed the sharpest coldest air as some draft of incredibly clear and delicious water. In a moment my senses were alert and settled me in a stillness of perception as quiet as the snow. No cars moved, no people were in sight, and then, silently, the streetlamps came on like the assurance of survival of the buried.

Another day, a Saturday, with the sun shining and two feet of fresh snow on the ground, I discovered Donald and his friends in the backyard. Inspired perhaps by the legendary Admiral Byrd, they had undertaken to build an igloo. I did not usually venture into the backyard. It meant first of all going down the alley past Smith's door. And it was an enclosed space with stone retaining walls on three sides. It was a place to be trapped. At the rear our house and the one across the alley were three stories high and included car garages at basement level. Not that anyone had a car. Over a wood fence on the retaining wall at the back of the yard loomed a tenement with clotheslines strung from all the windows to an enormous creosoted pole planted just behind the wall.

But with Donald in the backyard, I ran right down. Talking, chattering, arguing, working away with their jackets thrown off, shirttails hanging, woolen watch caps askew, the friends were cutting blocks of snow with one of Smith's coal shovels and laying out a circular foundation. Their faces were red and their breaths were spouts of steam. As they slowly built the igloo up on an ever-decreasing circumference, I watched with a sense of the anti-material oppositeness of the thing; bit by bit, it was eliminating itself as an idea from the light of the sun. I felt that what was being built was not a shelter but some structured withdrawal from the beneficence of the lighted day, and my excitement was for invited darkness, the reckless enclosure, as if by perverse and self-destructive will, of a secret possibility of life that would be better untampered with. I jumped up and down in a kind of ecstasy of my own being, inducing deliberately from my frame a series of spasms of shivers of concentrated awareness. Little by little the light was being blacked out, and when the final block of wet snow was installed at the apex of the hemisphere, my brother, who had been working as the inside man, disappeared entirely.

I was very impressed. It was a marvel of an igloo for anyone to have built, let alone five or six arguing, pushing, shouting boys. Donald dug his way carefully out the side and then they all built a crawl-through entrance, a kind of hemicylindrical foyer. Then a hose was brought out to play water over the igloo so that it would freeze up hard. Then they punched an air hole in the top with a length of broomstick and the thing was done.

By the next day the igloo had become the talk of the neighborhood. Not only children but adults came down the alley from the street to have a look at it: Dr. Perlman, our family dentist and friend, who lived in the apartment house across the street; Mrs. Silver's chauffeur, who lived over the garage of the late Justice's mansion on the corner; Lieutenant Galardi of the Sanitation Department, who lived on 173rd Street; and several other mothers and fathers I didn't know by name.

My mother had donated a square of old carpet and a candle and the five builders had settled in, only sometimes deigning to respond to the importunings of the children outside who wanted a turn. Actually, they soon grew bored of occupying the thing, learning fast enough that the real excitement had been the building of it; but it was almost as good lording it over their friends and those who were younger, designating this or that one to take a turn, and instructing him as to the rules of deportment once he was admitted. For a while they had considered charging admission, but settled instead for barter offered in bribe—one child paying with a small American flag on a stick, which they embedded in the top like Peary at the North Pole, another a candy bar, another a half-eaten peanut butter and jelly sandwich, and so on. As younger brother of one of the founding architects, I had a special relationship to the igloo, being one of the first guests permitted entrance and, thereafter, more or less free to enter and exit at my own judgment at such moments as the crowd inside was not too great. It was a source of considerable amazement to me how, in this hemisphere of snow, my house, my yard and the Bronx, New York, disappeared in space and time. I was further engrossed by the paradox of the warmth of a structure made of solid ice. You sweated in there, it was so hot. You took off your hat and snowsuit jacket or you were, almost immediately, glisteningly hot as on the hottest day of summer.

The igloo lasted physically long after the builders and everyone else grew bored with it. Inside a week it was almost totally forgotten. It began to shrink, but maintained its geometry even as it grew smaller and greyer and less interesting. I had discovered this about ice cream cones too—that they maintained their original proportions even as they were consumed. Long after I had lost any interest in sitting inside the igloo I nevertheless took pleasure from its integrity of form, almost as if my brother and his friends had used the magic of an ethereal idea as something to hand—like the most skillful magician.

Eventually I joined some other children working at the igloo and kicking it down into a pile of solid snow. It seemed as important to do that as it had been to go inside and sit down when the thing was in its fresh, crystal glory and all the world was reduced to the cold and silent space of an Arctic night, and the faces of your fellow humans looked at you, red and expectant, with the light of the candle flame filling the centers of their widened eyes.

FIVE

As my birthday, January 6, approached each winter I anticipated it with the conviction that the number six was sacramental, my number, the enumeration of my special being. It was like my name, which was mine alone. The holiday season and the New Year seemed to me just a lighting of the way, an advance fanfare for the culminating event, like all the motorcycle policemen in their slouch caps and riding boots, and with their captains in the sidecars, roaring down the street ahead of the President.

My mother inadvertently confirmed my feeling by considering my birthday, as she did every ritual, in its historical context.

"Can you imagine not wanting this golden little boy?" she said to her friend Mae as they sat in the kitchen having tea. We were waiting for the first of my party guests.

In my white shirt and tie and my short pants held up by attached suspenders, I stood by my mother's side leaning my elbows on the table and indolently eating a cookie. She combed her fingers through my blond hair and I shook my head as a horse shakes his mane.

"Give him to me if you don't want him," Mae said, who was an unmarried woman. She winked at me. Unlike my round-armed mother, Mae was skinny. She wore thick eyeglasses that made her eyes small. And she smoked cigarettes, which my mother did not do. With her elbow crooked, Mae held the cigarette between her index and middle fingers and she pointed it at the ceiling.

"Oh, we like him now all right, I suppose," my mother said. She pulled me up on her lap. "Now that he's here, we'll keep him."

More than once my mother had told me that I was a mistake. What this meant I both knew and did not know, in that way children have for getting just enough of the sense of something not to want to pursue it in detail. The idea that I was not expected or striven for did not injure me, however. I felt assured of my mother's love, as troublesome as I may have found it.

"He's always been difficult," she said proudly. "Full of surprises, from the day he was born. A breech birth no less."

"An acrobat," Mae said.

"I'll say. Except the acrobat didn't walk till eighteen months. And you remember the trouble I had weaning him?"

"Maybe now that he's a big four-year-old fella he'll take it easy on you," Mae said, smiling at me through the smoke.

At that moment the doorbell rang, and in anticipation of my first guest I wriggled out of my mother's arms, slid my arched spine over her knees, and landed on the floor under the table, and crouched there. "Aren't you going to answer the door?" my mother asked. But I had no intention of doing that; I only wanted to hide.

The day was momentous, but parties were mixed blessings. You got presents, all right—pick-up sticks, or crayons, or flat boxes of modeling clay in many colored strips—but they were the lesser presents of party admissions. And we all had to sit at the table with ridiculous pointed paper hats, and paper plates and noisemakers and popping balloons and pretend to a joyful delirium. In fact, a birthday party was a satire on children directed by their mothers, who hovered about, distributing Dixie Cups and glasses of milk while cooing in appreciation for the aesthetics of the event, the way each child was dressed for it and so on; and who set us upon one another in games of the most acute competition, so that we either cried in humiliation or punched each other to inflict pain.

And it was all done up in the impermanent materials of crepe paper, thin rubber and tin, everything painted in the gaudy colors of lies.

And the climax of the chaos, blowing out the candles on the cake, presented likely possibility of public failure and a loss of luck in the event the thing was not done well. In fact, I had a secret dread of not being able to blow out the candles before they burned down to the icing. That meant death. Candles burning down to the end, as in my grandmother's tumblers of candles, which could not be tampered with once lit, memorialized someone's death. And the Friday-night Sabbath candles that she lit with her hands covering her eyes, and a shawl over her head, suggested to me her irremediable grief, a pantomime of the loss of sight that comes to the dead under the earth.

So I blew for my life, to have some tallow left for the following year. My small chest heaved and I was glad for my mother's head beside mine, adding to the gust, even though it would mean I had not done the job the way one was supposed to, with aplomb.

* * *

GRANDMA LIVED IN THE ROOM NEXT TO MINE. SHE WAS A DESICCATED ASTHMATIC little woman who wore high-laced shoes and all manner of long old-fashioned dresses, and shawls, usually black. She lived a very private life, which made me wary of her. She stayed in her room for hours on end, and often came out in such a thoughtful, brooding state as not to notice what was going on around her.

She was very slender and tiny with delicate features. But her face was all wrinkled and her complexion was sallow. She wore her long wavy grey hair neatly braided and coiled when she was feeling well, and uncombed and flying when she was unwell. Like my mother, she had the palest blue eyes. But they looked at me, these eyes, either with great smiling love and animation, or with no recognition in them at all. I never knew on any given day whether Grandma would know and love me, or stare at me as if she had never seen me before.

Had I known precisely what her trouble was, it might have helped to remove some of the terror of her in my mind. My mother only told me what a sad hard life she had had. She had lost two children many years ago. And the year before I was born, her husband, who would have been my grandfather, had died. In this view Grandma's behavior was appropriate. But then why did she insist that my mother taste everything she put before her on the table? Grandma would not eat anything if my mother did not taste it first. She believed my mother, her own daughter, was trying to poison her. She sat with her hands in her lap and stared at her food. So now, whether Grandma was feeling that way or not, my mother tasted everything conspicuously before she served it. And she did that with everyone, even me. She sipped from my glass of milk and set it down before me, a practice I came to regard as normal.

Sometimes, when everything was all right, Grandma helped my mother with the cooking. In fact, she was a good cook, and knew things my mother didn't know. "Oh Mama," my mother said, "why don't you make your wonderful cabbage soup." I could tell my mother loved Grandma—she lost her self-assurance when Grandma was not well. She worried about the old woman terribly. She could not get her to go to a doctor. My father was kind to Grandma, but was not around her enough to worry about her. Donald, I suspected, was as shy of her as I was, though he tried not to show it. He sometimes gave Grandma his arm so that she could descend the front steps more easily when, the weather being mild, she was persuaded to get some air. Grandma negotiated steps the baby way, bringing both feet together on each level.

She spoke mostly in the other language, the one I didn't understand. When she felt all right she blessed me and kissed me on the forehead and produced pennies from her change purse and pressed them into my hand. "For a good boy," she said. "So he should buy something." She pulled me to her, and with my face lodged in her skeletal shoulder she muttered an instruction to God as to the good health He must always assure me. Since these love words were in the other language, as her curses were on her bad days, they made me similarly uneasy.

I knew the name of the other language: Jewish. It was for old people.

Grandma's room I regarded as a dark den of primitive rites and practices. On Friday evenings whoever was home gathered at her door while she lit her Sabbath candles. She had two wobbly old brass candlesticks that she kept well polished. She had brought them many years ago from the old country, which I later found out was Russia. She covered her head with a shawl, and with my mother standing beside her to keep the house from burning down, Grandma lit the white candles and waved her hands over the flames and then covered her eyes with her wrinkled hands and prayed. The sight of my own grandma performing what was, after all, only a ritual blessing seemed to me something else—her enacted submission to the errant and malign forces of life. That an adult secretly gave way to this sentiment I found truly frightening. It confirmed my suspicion that what grown-ups told me in my life of instruction was not the whole truth.

Grandma kept her room clean and tidy. She had a very impressive cedar hope chest covered with a lace shawl, and on her dresser a silver hairbrush, and comb. There was a plain slat-back rocking chair under a standing lamp so she could read her prayer book, or Siddur. And on an end table beside the chair was a flat tin box packed with a medicinal leaf that was shredded like tobacco. This was the centerpiece of her most consistent and mysterious ritual. She removed the lid from this blue tin box and turned it on its back and used it to burn a pinch of the leaf. She applied a match and blew on the leaf as my brother blew on punk, to get it started. It made tiny sputtering pops and hisses as it burned. She turned her chair toward it and sat inhaling the thin wisps of smoke—it was a treatment for her asthma. I knew it helped her breathing, and that it was scientific, having been purchased from Rosoff's Drugstore on 174th Street. But the smell was pungent, as if from the underworld. I didn't know, nor did any of my family seem to know, that this medicinal leaf my Grandma burned was marijuana. Even had they known, it would have held no significance, since it was readily and legally available without prescription. But to this day the smoke of grass produces in me memories of the choking harsh bitter rage of an exile from the shtetl, a backfired life full of fume and sparks, like a Fourth of July held in an open grave and projecting on the night a skull's leer and a clap of crossed bones.

ONE OF MY FAVORITE WAYS TO SPEND GRANDMA'S PENNIES CAME ALONG EASTburn Avenue in the afternoons: Joe the Sweet Potato Man. He pushed a small unmarked cabinet on wheels. Inside the cabinet was a kind of oven of homemade design, the fuel being charcoal. Joe raised the hinged top lid and reached down practically to his armpit to withdraw one of his roasted sweet potatoes. He was an impassive man who wrapped himself in sweaters and coats, obviously scavenged, and a watch cap over which was a peaked khaki hat of rough wool. He wore old Army shoes, cracked and splitting. Over all his clothing he had tied a shoulder-to-ankle waiter's apron not recently washed. This costume suggested great authority to me. With his large hands, dirt uniformly running under his nails, Joe slapped the potato on the cart, pulled an enormous knife from its wooden sheath and sliced the potato in half lengthwise. He then stuck the tip of the knife into a can and withdrew a slab of butter, which he inserted in a slit made almost simultaneously in the meat of the potato, and, after sheathing the knife, wrapped the purchase like a cornucopia in a torn half sheet of the *Bronx Home News* so that you could hold the potato and eat it without burning your fingers. For this golden, sweet, steaming hot feast I gave up two pennies. Another, and I could have the potato whole.

Joe went along his impassive way as, with dusk descending on the cold blue-grey sky over the Bronx, I sat on my stoop and ate his remarkable cuisine. It was not only something to eat but something to warm my hands against, as if I had plucked a tiny hearth from an elf's house.

Sometimes when my mother was going shopping I went along so that I could spend my money at the candy store on the corner of Eastburn and 174th Street. Many different things were to be had for a penny, candies of various kinds, Fleer's Double Bubble gum, or some shoe leather, which was what we called a pounded sheet of dried apricot, or Indian nuts that fell from the chute of a glass canister after you deposited the coin and twisted the key, or, what I usually went for, a shot-glassful of sunflower seeds poured into my hands by the proprietor.

I put the seeds in my jacket pocket and followed my mother from store to store as I cracked the shells one at a time between my front teeth and withdrew each seed with the tip of my tongue. I did this without missing a thing that was going on around me. In fact, the steady and relentless crunching of Polly seeds brought my gaze to sharp focus. One next to another, stores were built at street level in the sides of apartment houses. The street was astir with cars, trucks and horse-drawn wagons. It interested me that horses could, without any reduction in speed, raise their tails and leave a trail of golden dung.

The old Italian who repaired shoes managed to conduct his business without speaking English. His shop was a dark little basement store throbbing with the running motors and looped and slapping belts of leather trimmers and buffing wheels. Each wheel was stained with shoe polish of a different color. My mother held out a pair of my father's shoes. ''Heels and tips,'' she said, and the old man, barely looking up from a shoe he clutched to his chest while he carved its sole to size, nodded and grunted something in Italian. My mother asked him the cost and when the shoes would be ready. She addressed him in English and he replied in Italian, and the negotiation was completed to everyone's satisfaction. As we left he grabbed a handful of nails and put them in his mouth: he was about to attach the sole.

A few doors down was the Atlantic and Pacific Tea Company, where a man in an apron stood behind his wooden counter and ground up coffee to order and collected the items you asked for from the shelves behind him. If what you wanted—a box of junket, for example, or Cream of Wheat—was too high for him to reach, he grabbed it with a long pinching stick whose ends he could contract by squeezing the handle. The box flew through the air and he caught it. Then, with the purchases stacked in front of him, he wrote the cost of each on a brown paper bag with a small pencil he took from behind his ear and totaled the row of sums smartly, and then used the same bag to pack everything. I liked this store because of the coffee smell and the sawdust on the floor. I liked sawdust as long as it was dry.

In Irving's Fish Store, the sawdust was often wet. Irving's had a kind of swimming-pool atmosphere about it. The walls were bare of shelves. Everything was white. Two holding tanks of live fish were along the wall where the customer came in. Water ran in them continuously. Irving's apron tended to be wet and red with fish blood. He was a big jovial man. "Hello, Missus!" he said to my mother as we walked in. He was scaling a big brown fish. Fish scales flew through the air, some sticking to his glasses like snow. "How are you, sonny boy?" he said to me. "I want some salmon, Irving," my mother said, "but only if it's not expensive." Irving came around from behind his counter, took a short-handled net from the wall and ran it around the dark tank, where I could see the shadows of several fish slithering in panic. They looked elusive to me, but in a second or two Irving had raised one twisting and curling in the net and dripping water on the floor. "I saved this beauty for you," he said to my mother. He slapped the salmon down on the counter and held it pressed against the wood block with one hand while with the other he banged it on the head with a heavy wooden mallet. The fish went still. I admired Irving's fast hands. My mother turned away, but I watched as he sliced off the salmon's head with one of his large knives, eviscerated it, washed it under the faucet, and sliced it up in steaks. I recognized the salmon now.

Our last stop was Rosoff's Drugstore, on the corner of Morris Avenue. Large glass jars of red and blue liquid stood on display in the window; what they were meant to suggest I had no idea, but I liked the way the sunlight went through them and lit the colors. Also on display was a brass mortar and pestle, whose function I understood because my grandmother had one just like it to use in the kitchen to pound nuts and seeds. There were also various mysterious items made of red rubber. Inside the store I breathed an atmosphere of sweet soaps and bitter medicines, rolled bandages and anodynes, sodas, salts and pungent tinctures. Along the walls were glass cabinets that went all the way up to the patterned tin ceiling. Mr. Rosoff reached the upper levels by means of a railed ladder, which he rolled along the wall. He climbed the ladder for the implement of porcelain or the bottle, box, packet or tin the customer called for. He was a tiny sweet-tempered man with a round face and a soft voice. He politely inquired about the health of everyone in the family, particularly my grandmother. He shook his head in sympathy as my mother told him. He wore a starched white short-sleeved tunic buttoned to the neck, like a doctor's, and could offer such medical services as taking out things that had gotten into your eye—rolling your eyelid back and dabbing off the offending mote with a bit of cotton. He had done that for me.

My mother made a purchase, a box that Mr. Rosoff placed precisely in the middle of a sheet of dark green wrapping paper, which he had torn from a big roll on his counter. His pudgy hands flew about the box like bird wings and in a matter of seconds the green wrapping had been folded over, tucked in at the corners, triangulated at the ends, and tied around with white string from a spool hanging from the ceiling above his head. To break the string he looped it around each hand and gave a smart tug.

When we left I asked my mother what was in the box. She didn't want to tell me. "It doesn't concern you," she said. But I persisted. I had no more Polly seeds and no more pennies. "What did you buy," I said. "Tell me." She strode along. "Tell me," I whined.

"Oh stop it, they're sanitary napkins. Are you satisfied?"

I was not satisfied because I didn't know what sanitary napkins were, but I knew from her tone that I had used up my allotment of questions and so pursued the matter no further.

S I X

It was early spring when my uncle Billy came to live with us. He was an
older brother of my mother's, a gentle ineffectual man down on his luck.
Claremont Park was beginning to turn green. Uncle Billy moved into
Donald's room, and Donald came down the hall to stay in my room, which
was actually a bit larger. I was thrilled by this arrangement but Donald was
deeply affronted. "It's only for a little while," my mother told him. "Till
Billy gets back on his feet. He has nowhere else."

Donald lay on his bed and threw a hardball toward the ceiling and
caught the ball in his first baseman's glove, one-handed. He did this over
and over. Sometimes the ball hit the ceiling. A polka-dot pattern of black
marks began to appear there. Sometimes the ball missed his glove and
thudded on the floor and under the bed. I retrieved it for him.

Uncle Billy was a divorced man, something quite rare at this time, and
he had the further distinction of having been a successful bandleader in
the nineteen twenties. He was not insensitive to the disruption caused by
his joining the household. Before he had finished unpacking his suitcase,
he came into our room with a rolled cloth under his arm. His vest was
unbuttoned. "You boys ever see this?" He gave the cloth a flap and spread
it on the floor. It was a rectangular banner of purple velvet with gold
lettering, all in capitals, and a border of gold. On the floor it was like a
room rug. Before I could work it out Donald said, " 'BILLY WYNNE AND
HIS ORCHESTRA.' "

"That's right," Uncle Billy said. "You hung that over the bandstand
everywhere you played— 'Billy Wynne and His Orchestra.' That was me
in the good old days."

Donald and I were awed. We hadn't known he was that famous. He
leaned against the doorjamb with his hands in his pockets and began to
tell us about the hotels he had played, the nightclubs. "We were booked
for two weeks in the Ambassador," he said. "And we stayed for thirteen."
He had a reedy voice, up in his head. I was too shy now to look at him

directly. But he had the hurt blue eyes of that side of the family, though smaller and closer together than my mother's or grandma's. He had a double chin and had thinning hair combed carefully sideways to hide his scalp. His nose was red and bulbous. When he laughed he had teeth missing.

I felt the velvet with my fingertips. "You boys keep it," he said.

"Don't you want it?" Donald said.

"Naah, take it. It's a nice souvenir of the good old days."

We thanked him. He turned to go. "You know the first orchestra ever to broadcast over the radio?"

"Billy Wynne?" Donald said.

"That's right. WRPK Pittsburgh, 1922."

How Uncle Billy had lost his orchestra was never made clear to me, but it seemed to have had to do with a crooked business manager as well as his own ineptitude. He'd had numbers of jobs in the years since. He fit into the house easily enough—in a matter of a week or two it felt as if he had always lived with us. He was a decent, kind man. My mother appreciated his help in dealing with Grandma. Uncle Billy talked to the old woman and pacified her. She was glad to see him, but she also shook her head and cried, seeing how poor he'd become. "Mama," he said, "don't you worry about a thing. I've got a coupla aces up my sleeve."

In fact he was now working for my father in the Hippodrome music store downtown on Sixth Avenue. They went off to the subway together every day. My father's theory was that Billy would bring customers into the store. Some of them might even remember his name. The salary wasn't much, but he could earn commissions on the big items. Uncle Billy was grateful. He was not an educated man and regarded the books in my parents' house with great respect. I saw him once pick up a book and squeeze it and riffle its pages and put it down and smile and shake his head. When my father talked to him about politics, or history, he felt honored. "Dave," he'd say. "You should've been a professor."

"Thanks, Willy," my father said. I noticed both my father and my mother used the names Billy and Willy interchangeably as if there were no difference. Later I found out my mother's family's name was Levine. So Billy Wynne was Willy Levine. After I worked that out I always called him Uncle Willy.

Uncle Willy sometimes did tricks for us, and I remember one trick in particular that was my favorite and that he did very well. He'd stand in the doorway to my room and make it appear that a hand belonging to someone else just hidden from view was grabbing him by the throat and trying to drag him away. He would choke and gasp and his eyes would bulge and he'd try to tear at the clawlike hand; his head would disappear and reappear again in the struggle, and sometimes it was so realistic that I'd scream and rush to the door and beg him to stop, jumping up and swinging on the arm of the malign killer hand, which, of course, was his own. It didn't matter that I knew how the trick was done, it was terrifying just the same.

WITH THE LENGTHENING OF THE DAYS I STAYED OUT LONGER. WARM BREEZES BLEW into the evening. The new leaves of the privet were pale green. People opened their windows and came out of doors, women with their baby carriages, children at games. I studied the more difficult or daring games against the time when I would be old enough to play them: hit and span, which took you into the gutter and was waged with one's best marbles; the infernally difficult paddle ball, in which a small red ball connected to a paddle by a long single strand of rubber was hit so that it would fly off and return to the face of the paddle to be hit again. (Rhythm was everything.) And the variations of baseball, including stoop ball, punch ball and stick-ball; and also the ball games utilizing the sides of buildings or the cracks in sidewalks, such as slug or hit the stick.

Of course the ice cream vendors appeared—going very slowly and jingling their bells till a child came running. The Bungalow Bar truck was roofed like a fairy-tale house. A Good Humor pop, at a dime, was twice as expensive, but if your stick had the words GOOD HUMOR burned into it you'd get a free one. Competing with these motorized corporations was the swarthy steadfast Joe. The Sweet Potato Man was now dressed for the spring in a strawhat with the top punched out and his pushcart retooled to sell ices. Impassive as ever, Joe gave you for your two cents a scoop or ball of shaved ice over which he pumped the vile syrup of your choice—cherry, lemon or lime. The concoction was served in a small pleated paper cup that was so porous it soon took on the color of the syrup.

The mothers themselves came out for Harry's vegetable wagon, the fruits and vegetables displayed in their wooden crates in tiers, steeply raked, and the prices of things scrawled on paper bags still folded flat and stuck over slats in the front of the crates. A spring scale hung from three chains. Harry was a thickset, red-faced man with a gravel voice and an incantatory salesmanship. He packed up the purchases of one customer while calling up to the windows the catalogue of what he had for sale, how good it was, and how fairly priced, in a kind of double mode of communication, the soft voice for the already sold customer, the loud voice to broadcast for the customer still to come. I liked Harry's horse too, an ancient flea-ridden creature with sores on his back who chewed the oats from his feed bag in a way to capture my interest, slowly but tirelessly, with the glassy eyes of a superior contemplation.

Less frequent visitors were the knife and scissor sharpeners who worked on the trucks with their noisy footpedal grinding wheels that sent sparks off the steel, sparks being to me the most suggestively volatile phenomena, so quickly self-consuming as almost not to exist; and peddlers wearing derbies who bought used clothes and carried them in enormous packs on their backs; and junk dealers who pushed two-wheeled carts piled high with newspapers and rags and flattened tin cans and broken chairs and beds and boxes of dishes; and men ringing doorbells to sell cartons of fresh eggs, or magazine subscriptions, or red paper poppies from the American Legion; and bearded men in black hats and black winter coats who came begging at the door with coin boxes and letters of credentials from yeshivas. "My God," said my mother one day, closing the door after still another transient had rung the bell, "is there no end to this? When my father brought us to the Bronx when I was a little girl, he didn't know the whole Lower East Side would follow."

These itinerant peddlers, beggars and entrepreneurs were often unwholesome-looking or shabby or dirty and had dull blackened eyes from which all light had departed, but I don't ever remember feeling threatened by any of them.

One day a Department of Public Works crew appeared to repair a pothole. Their truck carried tar pots and towed a two-wheeled cart that was a kind of stove for heating their asphalt. The stove made a roaring sound as it fired. The crew raised and dropped long-handled flat-irons to flatten the smoking asphalt fill. One of the workers wore a pin-striped suit and vest, and a grey fedora. He was dressed just like my father. But his suit was creased and dirty, and because he was warm his tie was loosened. His hat was pushed back. I was alarmed. I had hoped he was the boss, but the boss was sitting in the truck and reading the newspaper.

When the job was done, this man in the suit swung his long-handled tar iron over his shoulder, just like the others, and followed the truck up the street as it slowly went looking for the next pothole.

LATE EACH SPRING A PARKS DEPARTMENT TRAVELING FARM EXHIBIT ENCAMPED IN the big park, Claremont. With great excitement of her own my mother took me to see it one day. We crossed Mt. Eden Avenue and the Oval, and the other direction of Mt. Eden Avenue, and then we were at the foot of the park's retaining wall of rounded stones. We raced up the flight of stone stairs. It was a huge wonderful park, with playgrounds and fields and tree-shaded paths. It was cool compared with the street. In a wooded meadow were the tents and trucks of the traveling farm. There was no gate, no entrance. Suddenly we were among the sheep and their lambs, cows and calves, horses with their foals, all of whom seemed to lend themselves in gentle patience to the touches of city children. Only an occasional bleat or whinny suggested they would rather be somewhere else. But the geese and ducks squawking about in clipped-wing panic would not let us get near them, which seemed to me a logical reaction, a mark of their intelligence, in fact. I was invited to hold a rabbit, which I did. Animals were warm. I touched a foal's back too lightly and the hide twitched, as if I were a fly. A wooden pen, about the size of a sandbox, held a rippling of peeping chicks, as if a bright yellow flag of the sun was waving over the ground. Hay was played out to the animals in their pens; I smelled the hay, and the manure, and it was not entirely unpleasant, it was a forceful array of smells that alerted you, somehow, to an insistence on more life than you knew. Smiling suntanned young women in light green dresses lectured from the back steps of trailers. We were guided with our mothers' blessings amid the animals in their fecundity, and invited to enjoy the reality of them, which I fervently did.

But the truest and most daring expeditions of spring were mounted by my father, whose restlessness drew us ever outward. Usually on Sundays he preferred to visit his mother and father, my grandma and grandpa, who lived north of Kingsbridge Road on the Grand Concourse. But in this season he was too much with the fullness of himself and his good feeling to do the ordinary thing. And so one Sunday we went to the tennis courts on Morris Avenue and 167th Street—a good walk—and he played tennis first with my mother, hitting the white ball back and forth over the net, and later with Donald, whom he instructed in the forehand and backhand strokes. "That's the way," he said. "Good. Good one." I was too small to hold the wood racket with one hand. When my turn came, I hit with it as if I held a baseball bat. I didn't want to do it long because I was afraid of hitting the ball into another court and disturbing someone. "Don't worry about that," my father said. I thought he looked splendid in his white ducks and shirt and tennis shoes, his dark eyes flashing as he lunged this way and that to stroke the ball. It seemed effortless as he did it, he was always where the ball was. "You've got to bend your knees," he said. "You've got to anticipate. Keep your side toward the net. Bring the racket back, and when you swing, follow through." I was having too good a time to listen carefully. My mother played well; although she didn't move quite as fast as my dad, she hit the ball smartly and it flew right back to him. She was not awkward as you would expect a girl to be. She wore a white dress and a sunshade tied around her hair, and white ankle socks with her shoes.

There were many courts. I counted twelve. Around the entire compound was a fence of chicken wire. The courts were red clay and made the bottom of my socks red. The white lines were whitewashed on with lime and had to be redone by the court attendant because they were rubbed out by the players' shoes.

My father was always rousing us up to do things. It was his idea to persuade his friend Dr. Perlman, the family dentist who lived in the apartment house across the street, and who owned a car, that the two families should have a picnic in the country. And so we did. I did not relish the drive sitting on my mother's lap in the back of Dr. Perlman's black Plymouth. I didn't know if it was true of all Plymouths, but it certainly was of Dr. Perlman's, that it seemed designed to lurch and jerk and drift and lurch again but never to travel at a steady rate. Somewhere on the Saw Mill River Parkway north of the Bronx, my green color was noted, and I was dumped over the back of the front seat to sit up there with my father and Donald, the little front swivel window pushed out wide to give me the breeze.

But then we were out in the country, as far out as I had ever been in my life. The country was an endless pathless park. We were in a broad meadow of millions of buttercups. We ran races in the sun, Donald and I and the Perlmans' boy, Jay, who was a bit younger than I but taller and stronger, which did not endear him to me. My father called the races with a newspaper rolled up as a megaphone and my beret on the top of his head. His vest was open, his jacket lay on the ground. My mother and Mrs. Perlman, a woman with a limp, and Mae Barsky, sat on blankets in the shade of a tree and set out the sandwiches and fruit and lemonade. Donald took home movies with our Universal camera. My father throws a ball at the camera. My father bats. My father stands facing Dr. Perlman, a big horse-faced man with rimless glasses, and he waves his arms in a hocus-pocus circle and points his two index fingers and Dr. Perlman disppears. Someone has produced ice cream and I am eating a Melorol happily, smears of it all over my mouth. I smile and wave at the camera.

This was a place called Kensico, an Indian name. The field we played in was at the foot of a high sheer bluff covered with bushes and trees and vines. The tracks of the New York Central ran along the top of the bluff. Trains came along, but they were so high above the meadow and the trees they seemed no bigger than toy electric trains. Whenever we heard the whistle of the locomotive, we stopped what we were doing and stood still in the grass before we saw it. And then it appeared, the tiny train, and we waved and the engineer, who was too small to be seen, blew his whistle in greeting.

But the spring had its maniac leer, some dissolving smile of menace that I couldn't quite catch sight of. The whole earth was pushing up, everything was turning out and open. My arms and legs hurt, and my mother told me I had growing pains. I thought I would rather not feel myself growing. I felt my heart banging and understood life as something that lived itself in you, an irresistible animating power that was mindless enough to go out of control, like the spring in a windup toy that without warning would run amok and bust itself to pieces.

A genial man from the neighborhood whose name was Ziggy walked past my house every day. His head was the size of a watermelon; the little features, including the tiny smiling mouth, were way up front. Ziggy walked with mincing steps, shuffling, his knees bent, his too-heavy head bobbing this way and that so that it appeared it might topple him over at any moment. Ziggy laughed and clapped his hands like a baby when he saw something that pleased him. My mother told me she'd heard he was a mathematical genius.

Even among children, people of my own ilk, there were some who didn't act right or were tremblingly uncoordinated or had half-grown limbs or clubfeet. I knew a pair of twin boys my age—they came to my first few birthday parties; one was normally nasty and verbal, the other a saint of retardedness. They were identical twins and when little had sat side by side in one of those double strollers of brown wicker.

From the tenement behind my backyard all sorts of urgent and enraged cries rose on the spring night. My room was in the rear of our house, just over the garage. The clotheslines were strung from tenement windows to the creosoted pole like the cables of a bridge. I saw things I wasn't looking for, people in the lighted windows in their underwear, women pulling themselves out of their corsets. Prowling about, sometimes at dusk, or on cold mornings of rain when everyone still slept, strange youths not from the neighborhood came vaulting over the fences into our yard. They climbed the retaining wall and disappeared. These were boys who hated boundaries and straight lines, who traveled as a matter of principle off the streets, as if they needed to trespass and show their scorn of property. They wore felt hats with the brims cut away and the crown folded back along the edge and trimmed in a triangle pattern. They wore undershirts for shirts and high-top sneakers without socks. They carried cigarettes behind their ears. Slingshots stuck out of their back pockets. They were the same boys who rode the backs of the trolley cars by standing on the slimmest of fenders and holding on to the window frames with their fingertips. They wrestled sewer covers off their seats and climbed down in the muck to find things. They were the ones, I knew, who chalked the strange marks on our garage doors.

I had noticed these chalk marks one day while in the yard. Donald and his friends were building a Ping-Pong table. It was to be a marvel of a table, hinged in the middle and painted regulation green with ruled edges. It was to rest on sawhorses. Donald and his friends were quietly and cooperatively building their table for a contentious Ping-Pong tournament full of shouting. I caused them to look up from their work by pointing out the sign on the garage doors. I wanted to know what it was.

I hadn't expected their complete attention. They stopped what they were doing and stood and looked at the chalk scrawl. Donald stepped up and raised his arm, and used the sleeves of his sweater as an eraser. The other boys were equally solemn. They took the whole thing seriously. "It's bad," Donald told me. "Whenever you see one of these, make sure to erase it. Use your shoe sole, spit on it, rub it with dirt, do anything. It's a swastika."

My mother added to this intelligence later the same day. "The next time you see one of those boys you tell me," she advised. "If you see someone who obviously is not from this neighborhood and doesn't belong here, don't stand around, but come inside and tell me. Or tell Donald. These boys think they're smart. They'd like to be Nazis. They're disgraceful. They carry knives. They confront Jewish children and say they killed Christ. They rob. You come inside if you see them."

And so my horizons were expanding. As I understood it, beyond Eastburn Avenue, on the far side of Claremont Park and down the hills, were the East Bronx neighborhoods, pockets of Irish and Italian poverty, that were the source of these depredations. These Irish and Italian neighborhoods were far below us, in valleys that rang with trolley-car bells and shook with the passing of elevated trains, where people lived in ramshackle houses with tar-paper siding amid factories and warehouses.

I had the good fortune to be living in this neighborhood, but its borders were not inviolate. That my house was of red brick, which I knew was essential from the tale of the three little pigs, evoked in me feelings of deepest gratitude. However, in bed at night, after the light was out, I heard outside in the dark sometimes the kicking over of ash cans, or a police siren, and then closer to my ear but somehow less audible, the breath of someone watching me. And in my sleep figures would loom in threatening gesture and just as suddenly recede into colored swirling points, as if I myself had been spread-eagled on a wheel spinning so fast that the colors melted together and became a target.

ROSE

Only now do I see that our lives could have gone in an entirely different direction. We were young and energetic. But little by little the two families were accepting us. The shock was wearing off. This began when Donald was born. Another generation! Donald was born at St. Joseph's Hospital in Rockaway Beach. A Catholic hospital. The nurses there were lovely to me, the nuns. It was a wonderful hospital and they took everyone in, it didn't matter to them. The only thing was the nurses wore habits and in the front lobby on the wall was an enormous gold cross, and in each room was a crucifix that was quite specific, with a painted Jesus on the cross. Well, you can imagine, when it was time for the birth my whole family traveled all the way from the Bronx, and for them the occasion was to be celebrated in the traditional way, with cake and wine and a little whiskey, so there were, in addition to my mother and father and sister Bessie and my brothers Harry and Billy, my aunts and uncles and cousins. Here they came dragging all the way from the Bronx, which was quite a trip then, nobody had cars, nobody could afford them, you took buses and the elevated train and then the real train, it took hours. And they had bags and shopping bags and gifts. And when they walked into St. Joseph's and saw that big cross on the wall, they were stunned. One of my uncles, an extremely religious man, a ridiculous pompous man, took one look and turned around and walked out and went right home—Aunt Minnie's husband, Uncle Tony, he was English, he wore homburgs, he had a very high regard for himself. Then Minnie followed him, of course, she always let him lead her around, and one or two of the others, but my mother, a blessed dear woman, she and my father stayed, they were no less religious than Uncle Tony. The crosses on the walls were a profound offense to them, but they didn't let it faze them, they knew what was important, and what was important was that they had a new grandson and that their daughter wanted them there.

The circumcision was done by a regular doctor in an operating room, that was the way we wanted it, we didn't want a mohel; and the Sisters

286

had set aside a room where we could all gather and have our cake and wine. They were what they were, and we were what we were, and it all worked out fine. Even the Mother Superior came in and had a sip of whiskey. I had gotten along very well with all the Sisters and I liked her very much and I was honored that she came.

Your father was very funny. He was in the city working when Donald was ready to be born. Donald was not expected for another week or two. I went to the hospital alone, and by the time they called Dave I had given birth. He came rushing out and the first thing he said to me was "Why didn't you wait!" Can you imagine? He was so excited, so solicitous. Donald was a tiny baby and had jaundice the first few weeks of his life and we were very worried about him, Dave was worried. When we brought him home, all wrapped up, a tiny little face peering out of his blankets, you should have seen how proud his father was, how excited!

But that was the beginning of the return to the families. With the baby we were respectable in their eyes. Or it seemed that way. My mother-in-law in particular kept urging Dave to bring us back to the Bronx. "You're so far away," she said, "we're all here, it's not right both families so close to each other in the Bronx and you and Rose and the baby so far away." Then too it was a matter of having help, of being able to call on someone; Dave had a good job, but we couldn't immediately afford nurses or live-in maids, I needed my mother. I needed her to tell me how to do things, I didn't want to make mistakes. It was so much work, washing and boiling diapers, sewing clothes, our old family doctor Dr. Gross was in the Bronx, and so on. These were all considerations. But I think I would have stuck it out in Rockaway if Dave had wanted that. He seemed to give in, maybe he was scared by the responsibility, maybe he felt it would be easier commuting to Manhattan from the Bronx than from Rockaway; he could leave later and be home earlier; but who knows what he thought, in many ways he was very mysterious, very secretive, your father; and in those days husbands didn't help out particularly, the division of labor was very clear-cut and everyone abided by it, so who knows what he felt. But somehow the decision was made. We found an apartment on Weeks Avenue and Mt. Eden Avenue next to Claremont Park, it was right back in our old neighborhood. So back we went, and my heart sank, I had loved it so in Rockaway. I loved the salt air, I loved the sea and the sky. Everything was so bright and fresh. It wasn't till we were ensconced in our new apartment that I realized how sorry I was.

SEVEN

You learned the world through its dark signs and also from its evil devices such as slingshots, punchboards and scumbags. I found a slingshot one day that was beautifully made. Someone had taken great pains with it. The Y-shaped frame was a shaved piece of tree branch with close to symmetrical arms. The sling was a heavy band of rubber in the absolute center of which was strung a pouch of soft leather. The key stress points were tightly and evenly wound with kite string. I immediately placed a small round stone in the pouch and let fly. It didn't go very far. I tried again, this time pulling back on the rubber as hard as I could with my right hand and holding my left arm stiff, my hand clenching the frame handle. The stone went like a bullet, pinged a car door, leaving a dent, and then bounced off the carriage of a child sitting in the sun next to my house.

The mother was furious. She went up the steps of my house and rang the doorbell. But even before my mother came to the door I had dumped the slingshot in the ash can. It was powerful magic, it had some animating force of its own, well beyond the strength in my child's arms. No wonder it was, with the springblade knife, the weapon of choice of the swastika youths.

One day I was sitting with Pinky on the steps and an older boy stopped and offered me a chance on a punchboard, a cardboard packet with a grid of little holes fitted with white paper plugs. At the top was a cartoon of a girl in harem pants dancing with her arms over her head. For a nickel I might win a dime, fifty cents, or even five dollars. The nickel in my pocket was for ice cream, but I turned it over to him. Punchboards were made in Japan, a country specifically known to all children as the source of cheap toys and novelties that broke very quickly. With the punch key, a miniature version of the kind of key used to open a sardine tin, I pushed out my chance, a tightly folded accordion-pleated piece of paper a half-inch long. I unfolded it with the seller looking over my shoulder. I felt his hot breath on my ear. The chance was blank. I experienced the loss of my nickel.

Later Donald questioned me. "Was the punchboard full?"

"Yes, I was the first."

"If the punchboard is honest," Donald said, "and you have only the kid's word on that, then when you buy your chance affects the odds. Do you know what odds are?"

"No."

"Well, look, if the board is half punched and the kid tells you the prize money is still unclaimed, then you have a better chance of winning. Do you get it? Your odds are better."

I strove to understand.

"Well, you'd better forget it anyway," Donald said. "It's gambling. Gambling is illegal. You can get caught. Mayor La Guardia took the slot machines out of the candy stores and now he's after the punchboards. It's in all the papers. So you might as well forget the whole thing, if you know what's good for you."

I was prepared to do that. A couple of years later I would overhear some boys in school describing an older girl as a punchboard. I was unable to make the metaphorical leap, though understanding something bad was being said.

But the scumbag, ah the scumbag, here was an item so loathsome, so evil, that the very word itself was too terrible to pronounce. There was a seemingly endless depth of dark meaning attached to this word, with intimations of filth, and degradation, touching on such dark secrets as the young prince of life that I was would live in eternal heavenly sunlight not to know. In order to learn what a scumbag specifically and precisely was, beyond the foul malevolence of the sound of the word, you had to acquire knowledge of sick and menacing excitements to a degree that would inflict permanent damage to your soul. Yet of course I did learn, finally, one summer at the great raucous beach of crashing waves and sand-caked bodies known as Rockaway.

THE BEACH WAS SOMETHING MY MOTHER AND FATHER COULD AGREE ON. WHY THEY favored Far Rockaway at the sea edge of Brooklyn I did not quite understand. It was an enormous journey getting there. Perhaps my memory is faulty, perhaps we never made a day trip to Far Rockaway but rented a bungalow there for a week, in the summer, in the years when my father was doing comparatively well. But I remember, after a subway ride downtown, standing in the cavernous waiting room of Penn Station. We had with us bundles and blankets, newspapers and picnic baskets. High above was the vaulted roof of steel and translucent glass. The steel ribs that buttressed the roof were curved as delicately as scrollwork. Holding everything up were slender black-steel open columns taller than the columns that supported the elevated tracks on Jerome Avenue. The sun came through the roof on planes of dust, giving everything a pale greenish color and hushing the vast babble of all the people waiting for their trains, and the redcaps with their baggage dollies, and the echoing public address system announcements.

Yet even after the train trip to the seaside there was a long walk in the sun through blocks of one-story bungalows and across streets half filled with sand.

· Rockaway might be overrun with sunbathers, the boardwalks jammed, not a place to lie down, but with my father leading the way we encamped miraculously enough in a space that hadn't been seen as possible by anyone except us. And there we were on a ridge of wet sand, facing the Atlantic Ocean.

My mother grew happy, the characteristic expression of concern lifted from her face, which now shone with a blissful contemplation as she tugged on her rubber swim cap and waded into the surf. It was as if she was alone, and not another human being around her. My father, who was more accustomed to relaxing and enjoying himself, reclined on the blanket and read his newspapers, interrupting himself every now and then to lie back on one elbow and point his face into the sun.

The trouble was, I had difficulty with the idea of changing into or out of a bathing suit in public. My father swam way out past the breakers, and when he came back he thought nothing of letting his black wool tank suit dry right on him in the sun. Donald too wore his belted bathing trunks through many swims. But my mother insisted that when I was wet, if I wasn't going into the water again, I had to change out of my suit into a pair of dry shorts.

I didn't understand the logic of this—that it was all right to be wet in the water but not on land. My father tried to arbitrate. "Why be uncomfortable," he said. "You put this blanket around you and slip off your suit underneath, and put your pants on. Nothing to it, one two three."

I was not persuaded. I saw other children changing this way and I knew their shame when they saw me watching. My mother thought I was being ridiculous. Yet I had never seen her change her clothes in public, nor my father, nor anyone but another child. I had heard it said of a little girl I knew how silly she was to refuse to wear a simple pair of cotton briefs for a bathing suit. "You have nothing up there to hide," her mother told her, pointing at her chest. "Nobody cares." What could she have possibly revealed to the world but that she lacked what she was supposed to have? We were not equipped as adults; we were small and without hair. That was the reason for modesty. Yet our dreams and desires were great shadows on the sun, enormous looming fearful attacks of unnamed chaos of the heart. To be undressed was to seem to be a child, a degrading state.

So I was taken to the public bathhouse behind the boardwalks—I suppose our bungalow was too many blocks away—and in the hot still air of a box of dark wood, a rented key for ten cents on an elastic loop attached to my wrist, I hurriedly changed. The air was motionless, woodsmoked. I had latched the door but someone could get down on his knees and peek underneath because the door did not reach the ground. People were changing in the other cubicles. I heard voices from all directions. I peeked through the cracks to make sure no one on either side was watching me: I was looking at monumental square inches of naked flesh. I heard the snap of elastic. I heard distant giggling. I heard a slap. I heard an urgent female demand to be let alone.

And then I found, stuck to my big toe, a flattened tube of whitish rubber. Instinctively repelled, I flicked it off with a shake of my foot.

The beach at Rockaway in 1936: Monoplanes with enormous wings slowly pulled banners of the alphabet through the sky. Washed in on the surf were dead jellyfish and the shells of horseshoe crabs, upside down, like shallow bowls. In the cold dark sand under the boardwalk I came upon a veritable garden of those flattened rubber things. They were stiff, not pleasant to touch, they lay pasted together and they smelled bad. Everything from the sea smelled bad—bulbous oily pods of green weed, jellyfish, half-eaten shellfish and those white rubber things under the boardwalk. I picked one up. ''Don't touch it!'' my brother said. ''Don't you know what that is, you dope?''

Oh what a roaring sun-blasted life on the beach! Tiny piping holes bubbling in the sand. Birds with legs like toothpicks scurrying in front of the wavelap. Gulls hovering in windplanes off the sandbank. Donald and I ran to the shaded precinct of the boardwalk arcades. Sea winds blew through the open game rooms. We stood in our bare feet and bowled wooden balls down chutes, we spun the wheel to make the miniature steam shovel in the glass case clutch the prize. We wanted the real penknife, the silver cigarette lighter. We got only the gumballs.

Sand is in my crotch. I am turning red, the sun is inflating me. I eat sandwiches on the blanket, I drink cherry Kool-Aid, which is like liquid Jell-O. All speech is shouted, the surf crashes, I fear only two things, the water crashing up at my feet and the desert hordes of human beings among whom I may get lost. Crying children are walked by fully dressed policemen among the families on their blankets. Life is raw here; more policemen in their dark shirts and trousers and garrison caps, and with their heavy belts and guns, stand on the boardwalk overlooking the masses of bare bodies. Behind them big clown faces smile down from the false front of the amusement park. They are not fooled. Bad things are happening everywhere. Lifeguards bring in an exhausted child. An ambulance backs up to the steps of the boardwalk leading to the beach. I dig banks of sand around me. I create structures to support me, I bury my own leg to the knee. I am in the salt and the sun and the sea of voices. It all crashes over me, but I am not drowned.

It seems to me now that in this elemental place, these packed public beaches in the brightest rawest light of day, I learned the enlightening fear of the planet. Everywhere I looked men stood on their hands or climbed to other men's shoulders. Women of flesh slept ground into the sand. Beyond any name's recognition, under the shouting and teeming life of the world's public on their tribal Sunday of half-nude ceremony, was some quiet revelation in me of unutterable life. I was inspired in this state of clarity to whisper the word *scumbag*. It was as if all the sound had stopped, the voices, the reedy cry of gulls, the sirens and the thunderous surf, for that one word to be articulated to illumination. I felt through my fingers the sand pour of bones, like some futile archaeologist of a ground-up mineral past. I recognized the heat in the sand as some invisible power of distant light. And from the glittering blue water I took its endless motion and unimaginably frigid depth. All of this astonishingly was; and I on my knees in my bodying perception, worldlessly primeval, at home, fearful, joyous.

EIGHT

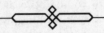

It must have been that summer or not long after that my little grandma's mental condition worsened. She took to running away. I was outside the house one afternoon when the front door opened and down the steps she came. She cursed and shook her fist at me. Her hair was uncombed. I backed away, but when she reached the bottom of the stoop she wandered off in the opposite direction, giving me the distinct impression that she had cursed me only because I was in her line of sight. She turned the corner at 173rd Street and was gone.

I ran and got my mother, who was at the laundry sink scrubbing clothes. She hadn't even known Grandma had left. Wiping her hands on her apron, my mother ran after her. She found the old woman and brought her back, but that was only the first of several episodes in which Grandma, crying and calling curses down on our house, wrapped a shawl around her shoulders and ran off.

In her curses she suggested that it would be a good thing if cholera were to kill us all. My mother numbly translated for me when I asked her what was being said. Another eventuality Grandma hoped for was that a company of Cossacks on their horses would ride us down. My mother cautioned me not to take these remarks at face value. "Grandma loves us," she said. "Poor Grandma doesn't know what she's saying. She's remembering her life as a little girl in her village in Russia, when these things happened. Cholera killed people when they drank water that was contaminated. The Cossacks were horse soldiers of the Czar, who mounted pogroms against Jewish settlements. She never forgot, poor thing."

I understood and did not take Grandma's madness personally. In fact, I tried to be friendlier to her when she was sane, to show her I loved her. I took to bringing her her tea in the morning when she got up. She liked that. My mother might look in on her to see that she was all right and then in the kitchen pour her tea for her in a glass, and put the glass in a saucer, with two cubes of sugar next to it, and in my two hands I would carry the glass of tea down the hall.

But now we all had this additional worry of Grandma disappearing at any hour of the day or night. We worried that she would be hit by a car, because she wandered in the street so intently involved with her inner rage that she paid no attention to cars. When Grandma fled, if Uncle Willy was home, he would go get her. He was the best at it. He sighed, and put on his shoes, and went out and followed after her with mild consoling words of the gentlest reproach. "Oh Mama," he said, "come back, it's getting chilly and you'll catch cold. Come, Mama, no you don't mean that, don't say that, you know how sorry you feel afterwards when you talk that way. Come home, *Mamaleh*," he said and held his hand out with the palm up, like a man extending an invitation to dance; and many blocks from Eastburn Avenue with her rage vented, and her curses cursed, she turned and allowed herself to be escorted home.

Naturally, the neighbors knew of our trouble. Children in the street got out of Grandma's way, but were so fascinated they followed her at a safe distance. My mother's mortification was intense. With Uncle Willy out in the middle of the street trying to lead Grandma back inside, my mother waited in the shadows beside the parlor window where she couldn't be seen. She cried and shook her head and bit her lip. "What did I do to deserve this?" she muttered, not unlike Grandma. "God in heaven, what have we done to deserve this!"

And one night Grandma disappeared entirely and no one could find her. My father finally called the police. Hours went by. Nobody went to bed, not even me. Then a green-and-white police car pulled up to the curb in front of our house. Two policemen got out and opened the rear door, and gently assisted Grandma out of the car and up the front steps as if they were her footmen. She was quite docile. They told my father they had found her on a street bridge overlooking the New York Central tracks all the way over on Park Avenue.

THERE WAS SOME MESSAGE TO ME IN ALL OF THIS THAT DID NOT ADDRESS ITSELF TO my rational being as a good boy. But all I knew consciously was that I was making mistakes of recklessness and getting into trouble. I was wild. I tore up my knees from running too fast and falling. My knees or my elbows recorded these events with scabs. I was rarely clear of them. One afternoon in my room I heard my brother coming home from school; I ran the length of the house down the hall to the front door. Donald was ringing the bell, I saw his shadow on the curtain; the door was glass-paned from its top to its bottom. Running, my hand outstretched for the doorknob, reaching, reaching, what could account for my excitement? Did I have something to tell him? Did I have some story about Pinky? Or was it only that I knew Donald coming home from school commenced the day's action? My hand missed the knob and went through the glass door. I felt the slash of an inanimate evil. Without so much as the caesura of a drawn breath I was first shouting in joy, then screaming in shock. Pain tore through my hand, and the mess of my own red substance was on the curtain. My mother running from the back of the house, my brother calling her, the door opening, glass falling to the floor, I stood looking at my palm, blood pouring down my arm. Ripples of terror went through the community of my home, as each person had in turn to learn and respond to the awful event. I was being tourniqueted, washed, soothed, but at the same time an investigative procedure had been initiated, my mother searching from my brother's answers to her questions the possibility of his having been responsible for this event, while he defended himself right- eously, loudly and adeptly, and my grandmother was with her hand on her cheek coming along down the hall and shaking her head and saying "*Gottenyu, Gottenyu,*" thus suggesting the cosmic forces once again assail- ing us all. Pinky was furiously barking, and Uncle Willy, awakened from a nap on his day off, was simply trying to get the news of how this had happened, since nobody had taken the time to stop and tell him. Eventu- ally, from the center of all of this, sobbing fitfully as I stood, hand ex- tended for the operation over the bathroom sink, and winced as my mother removed shards of glass with a tweezer, I nevertheless found an inner certitude and calm, perhaps in advance of my willingness to stop crying or feeling sorry for myself. Everyone stood around me and watched. Thus the element of performance added itself to my behavior and I real- ized the advantage to my small being—the smallest lowest ranking voice in the family, in constant attendance to any one of this pantheon of powerful creatures I lived with, each with a different strength and call upon my loyalty, each entitled to tell me what to do and how to do it— I could not fail to realize the power residing in me at this moment. I was an instrument of fearful prophecy. More than that, I knew I had found the weakness of their adult strength and resolution—that misfortune could reach them through me. Even my grandma was diverted to total attention.

It is a heartening knowledge that comes sooner or later to all children that they can achieve parity. I had seen time and again in the streets a child hurting himself and then being spanked by his mother for hurting himself—pain added upon pain, which seemed cruel or stupid until it became clear that the mother intuited the malign exercise of the child's act. She was being hurt and so she responded in kind. My mother did not ever hit me for hurting myself, not having the sufficient distance from me or cynicism to do so; there was too fine an appreciation in her for the eternal hazards given to consciousness, poor woman, here she was in the Depression, with her sick mother, her improvident brother, her two chil- dren, a yapping dog, and maintaining an entire family while in economic dependency to her unpredictable husband. To her my injury might save me from worse if it could be seen to be a lesson.

"All right," she said, "stop that whimpering. It's not so bad. Maybe you'll know now not to run through the house like a maniac."

IN SOME EMBLEMATIC MEASURE OF THIS SENTIMENT MY MOTHER DECIDED TO TAILOR a wool suit for me. I endured many fittings before the thing was done. Early one afternoon of an autumn Sunday I emerged from our house all decked out in a camel-colored tunic and matched leggings and on my head a color-coordinated beret of dark brown. I could feel the grip of the elastic band on my forehead. The buttons on my tunic went all the way up to the neck, the top one tightly fastening the military-style collar. I felt contained. At the ankles of the leggings was a row of snaps, simulating spats. The leggings came down over the tops of my new tightly laced shoes of brown leather.

I rode up and down the sidewalks for a while on my tricycle. My father joined me a few minutes later and we had a catch in front of the setback garage doors next to our stoop. I lurched after the ball when I dropped it. I couldn't move that well. Also I didn't want to forget myself and fall and tear the new suit or get it dirty. As soon as my mother came out, we would head past P.S. 70, across 174th Street, and up the Eastburn Avenue hill to the Concourse, where we would take the bus to visit my father's parents, my grandma and grandpa, who lived north of Kingsbridge Road. Donald was old enough not to have to go. It was a beautiful cold sunny day and I had to squint to see the ball coming at me. My father wore an overcoat open over his dark double-breasted suit and tie. His hat was set at the usually jaunty angle. We were waiting for my mother and then would be on our way.

At this moment an itinerant photographer came around the corner and walked toward us with a box camera on a tripod over his shoulder, and with a small pony trailing behind him. My father's face lit up. "You've got a customer!" he called, waving at the man, and from one moment to the next my day turned bad, as if the sky had suddenly filled with dark clouds.

I didn't want my picture taken. I didn't want to get on the pony. It was a shaggy dull-eyed thing and I could see the breath coming out of its nostrils. I knew immediately it was a badly used animal with a cynical spirit. But this was the kind of fortuitous event that made my father happy. Life declared itself in him. "It's just the thing, just the thing!" he said. I disagreed. We exchanged views. The unctuous photographer felt privileged to join the argument on my father's side, saying the pony loved to have children sit on his back. I knew his game. Finally my father could contain himself no longer. He lifted me under the arms and set me on the pony's back, my legs split wide over the saddle. I felt the pony stomp and stir about. The saddle seemed to me loose and creaking. The pony whinnied and took a step or two. My father was holding one hand on my back and holding the reins with the other while the man busily set up his camera. I felt the shuddering animal life of the pony between my legs, I had never sat on a horse before and I would not stick my feet in the stirrups. "Get me down!" I shouted, and I put up such a fight, squirming and sliding and threatening to fall by my vehement twistings and kickings, that the pony started to clip-clop about, turning in circles on the sidewalk. The photographer now tried to soothe him, patting his neck and gripping his mane, and my father, holding me under the arms and not lifting me off, said, "You're all right! Don't you see you're all right? This little pony is more frightened of you than you are of him. Stop shouting so, stop screaming, you're all right, nothing to be afraid of, come on, you can do it, give it a try."

There I was, buttoned down and collared in the tight, almost suffocating fit of my mother's vision, and my father was urging me to heights of daring and adventure.

I thought in my desperation of a compromise. I would permit my picture to be taken, but on my tricycle, not on the pony.

I still have that picture. My little hands clutch the handlebars. My feet rest on the block pedals of the oversized front wheel. I am in my matching jacket and leggings of stiff wool. The beret is only slightly askew. I am allowing my adorable self to be commemorated in his new outfit. I am a good-looking open-faced towheaded child and I am smiling as I have been instructed; but it is a tentative wary little smile, my deportment in life, ready to placate, appease, if that will work, but my foot on the pedal, ready to fly me away, if it doesn't.

It wasn't as if I weren't eager to learn their ways and take the instruction I was given and assume my place in life. But each of my deities spoke from a different strength and to different aspirations. All around me was the example of passionate survival, but I could never be sure, as I held in me the conflicting arguments of how it was done, what was the margin for error, the tolerance for wrong moves.

NINE

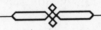

Extending from my mother and father were two family wings, unequal in strength, making our flight erratic. My grandma and grandpa on my father's side were not people of means, living in a three-room apartment a few miles to the north of us. But they were whole, complete, they took pride in themselves and their children—my father being one of three, the others my aunts Frances and Molly—and they had clear views on most things. We rode up there on the red-and-black Concourse bus, which had a long engine hood and doubled rear wheels and spare tires chained to the back and torturously shifted gears. I enjoyed the ride, but once it was over, I had the visit to get through. Not that I didn't love my grandma and grandpa; they were warm little old people who beamed at me and pressed food upon me, and kisses. But there was danger there.

My grandma liked to put out a lace tablecloth on the big dark table in their dining-living room. She served tea in her good china with its pale green and white sliced-apple motif, and also Uneeda crackers and home-made plum jam with cloves in it and a big cut-glass bowl of fruit, and a smaller bowl of pistachio nuts. Most often too we brought cake from a bakery. And everyone sat around the table and talked. My grandfather had a wonderful way of paring an apple, with his own pocketknife, so that the peel came off in one continuous strip. Sometimes, one or the other of my aunts was there but without my cousins, who, like my brother, were old enough to get out of such visits. So there was nothing to do. I stared through the double windows into the courtyard. My grandparents lived in the back of a house, off the street, and I found myself looking at opaque lace curtains or drawn shades. I sat under the big table radio in the corner of the room next to my grandfather's favorite chair and tried to find something interesting to listen to—not too easy in the middle of a Sunday afternoon when the New York Philharmonic seemed to be the brightest choice. Or I wound up the big console Victrola in their bedroom and put pennies or nutshells on the spinning turntable and watched them fly off. Sometimes I leafed through a picture book I had brought along, sometimes I browsed through my grandfather's bookcase in the foyer beside the front door. He owned many books, some of them in Russian. They were stuffed in, every which way. Each shelf had its own glass door that lifted up from the bottom and slid back under the shelf above. But there were so many books the doors wouldn't slide. From my grandfather I first heard the names Tolstoy and Chekhov. He owned sets too—uniform editions, such as *The World's Great Orations* and the *Harper's Picture Encyclopedia of the Civil War*. I liked to look at the steel engravings of the Army of the North doing battle with the Army of the South. Each scene was protected by the thinnest sheet of paper.

Another diversion was the dumbwaiter in the kitchen. My grandmother let me open the little door in the wall and poke my head into the black air shaft. Odors of ash and garbage rose on the cold black air. A thick rope bisected the column of darkness. I could pull on this rope and bring into view the wooden box on which the tenants delivered their garbage to the superintendent.

My grandmother hobbled busily about, she was a bent woman with glasses and thin yellow-white hair, which she kept parted in the middle, braided, and tightly coiled in a bun. Her eyes watered and her hands were palsied, but her afflictions didn't seem to daunt her. She bustled around to great effect and never sat still. She was in charge. My grandfather by contrast was a very slow-moving, slow-talking, gentle, slight man, with thick grey hair cut close; he was partial to a tan cardigan sweater, which he wore always over a white shirt and tie, brown pants and house slippers. He smoked odd oval-shaped cigarettes, Regents, which came out of a grey-and-maroon box. He liked me to press my palm against his and measure our hands; this was the way he kept track of my growth, he said. My growth was a matter of enormous pleasure to him. Invariably he was encouraged to find my hand had increased in size since our previous measurement. He patted me on the back of my neck. He was a retired printer. He had emigrated from Russia as a young man from the Minsk district—this had been the old country too of my grandmother. Apparently they had known each other as children, but only after they had come separately to America did they renew their acquaintance, conduct a courtship and marry. It was a matter only of momentary fascination to me to imagine my dear old grandfather Isaac as an erect black-haired young man, even younger than my father; to imagine him, for instance, lifting my father in his arms as my father sometimes did me. My father called him Papa. I did not dwell on these paradoxes. I think I did not entirely believe in them. Besides, my grandfather spoke so philosophically from such thoughtful distances of wisdom that no fanciful illusion could be maintained for very long about his being anything else but a grandfather. He told me that three times, in three separate presidential elections, he had cast his ballot for someone named William Jennings Bryan. Yet he was a socialist and came of a generation of enlightened Jewish youth who understood, as Bryan did not, that religion was a means of holding people in ignorance and superstition and therefore submissive to impoverishment and want. I did not really understand what he told me; but as he repeated these ideas and phrases over time, I was comfortable with their sentiments and was finally able to identify him as a critic of prevalent beliefs. He was in opposition—that I understood. In his bookcase were authors whose names were familiar to me before I knew who they were or what they stood for: Ralph Ingersoll, Henrik Ibsen, George Bernard Shaw, Herbert Spencer. Although my grandmother was pious, and kept a kosher home, my grandfather was an atheist. He treasured a book by Thomas Paine called *The Age of Reason,* and used its arguments, and some of his own, to tease my grandmother and point out to her the absurdities and contradictions in her literal readings of the Old Testament. " 'My own mind is my own church,' " he said, quoting Paine. Yet, as she proudly told us even in her irritation with him, he had read the entire Bible many times and knew it better, God help him, the atheist, than she did.

So this was a substantive household, an establishment in history next to which my mother's poor dependent half-mad Mama in her widow's weeds was no match. Nor my hapless, self-effacing formerly famous uncle Willy. You had to go see my father's mother and father. They had a home. They were progenitors not only of my father but his two sisters—the elder, my aunt Frances, and the younger, my aunt Molly. And each of these ladies in her way had much to contribute to my sense of this family's complexity. My aunt Frances was married to a successful lawyer and lived in Pelham Manor, in Westchester County, a Christian community over the city line. Aunt Frances not only owned a car but knew how to drive it, which was quite unusual for a woman. When she drove she wore white gloves. She was very gracious and soft-spoken and naturally dignified, like my grandfather; her two sons were at Harvard. My father's younger sister, Molly, by contrast had her mother's earthy practical ways. Molly was in addition a comedienne, an irreverent, brassy, unkempt woman, as blowsy as her sister was well groomed. Molly smoked cigarettes, whose ashes invariably dropped on the bosom of her dress. She squinted in the cigarette smoke. She read a newspaper my father thought a terrible rag— the *Daily Mirror*—because its coverage of horse racing was the best in the city and because it featured a columnist, Walter Winchell, whom she adored. She played the horses, as did her husband, Phil, a cabdriver. They had one daughter, my older cousin Irma. When the whole family was gathered in my grandparents' small apartment on a Sunday afternoon, the two old people spoke English with strong inflections of Yiddish, Frances spoke in the cultivated tones of an upper-class Westchester matron, and Molly in a heavy Bronx accent. Somewhere in the middle of this mélange of styles and meld of social intention stood my father. His older sister had done well, and his younger had rebelliously married beneath her. His was the fate not yet decided. When it came to my father the stakes were high.

He was the one son. Would Frances turn out to be the family exception or would Molly? It was not only his own destiny that was at issue but the final judgment still to be made of all of them.

How did I know this? On those darkening Sunday afternoons I only half heard the conversation. It would start quietly enough, filled with pleasantries, and then, almost imperceptibly, go bad. On this day my grandmother Gussie picked up my new hand-tailored camel tunic to examine my mother's sewing. "Very nice," she said, her eyebrows rising, her mouth turning down at the corners. "And lined too, no less. My daughter-in-law stops at nothing."

Behind this remark was my grandmother's penury. She took the position that my mother was impractical and careless with my father's money. My mother knew this was untrue. It was a terrible slander and it hurt her deeply. It hurt her that my grandmother Gussie felt privileged to give her opinions as to the way my mother dressed her children, how she ran her house, and whether or not she took proper care of her husband. Though Grandma's tone was sweet, her style was sly and indirect. She could bring my mother to tears, as she had now done. My tempestuous mother started to yell and my father told her to lower her voice. I looked for the pictures in books. I wound the Victrola and let the turntable spin. My grandparents maintained two goldfish in a bowl; I stared at the goldfish, studying their ways.

The visit was clearly over. My mother would not say good-bye. She put on my coat and buttoned it, and she took my hand and walked out of the door. My grandfather came after us in his slippers. "Rose," he said in the hallway. "Forgive Gussie. That's the way she is, she means no harm, she has the greatest respect for you."

"Oh Papa," my mother said. "That is not respect. That is not even civility. You are a compassionate, kind man, perhaps too kind." She hugged Grandpa, and we went down the stairs to the lobby and waited for my father. She could not sympathize with whatever anxiety of universal judgment, or perhaps God's, led my grandma on. The old woman made her regularly understand that she was not good enough to be married into this family, that she was not good enough for my father, that she was not what he needed.

I lived in the weather of my mother's spirit, and at these times, after these visits, the sky grew black. My father came down the stairs and he was whistling, as he did when something bad had happened and he was trying to be cheerful about it. We stood in the dusk at the bus stop. "Why do you let her talk to me that way?" my mother said. "Don't you care how I feel? Nothing I ever do is good enough, nothing is ever right enough. If I wash one of her dishes she will wash it after me. And you like that behavior. You like that viciousness. Never once have you defended me from dear sweet Gussie."

But the argument between my mother and father didn't really begin until they got home. Here the sight of the pathetic remnants of her own ancestry magnified the injustice she felt: Did anyone on my father's side ever inquire about her mama's health? My father's whole and thriving family treated her like dirt and her poor mother like a social pariah. Did they ever invite Mama on a Sunday? Did they ever invite Billy? I went into my room and closed the door, but it was no good, it was too interesting. It was as if my father had caught my grandma's point of view, just as my mother insisted.

But then he offered a criticism of my mother that I knew, in part, to be accurate. "You always think the worst," he said. "You're suspicious and distrustful." She told him to go to hell. He called her a fishwife. Mythic realms were indeed the territories of these disputes. Ascriptions of good and evil flew back and forth like furies, like phantoms, to take shape as sweet truths or malign imputations. Truth hovered above everything waiting to alight, and as I grew older I saw that it never did anywhere, for any length of time. I felt guilty that I preferred the company of my grandma and grandpa up on the Concourse to my sick little grandmother in the room next door. I sometimes saw my grandma Gussie as truly mischievous, jealous and up to no good. But I could not believe anything bad about any one of these people for very long, because they all seemed to love me so much.

TEN

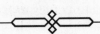

In fact, love was what it was all about. However painful it might be, as sure as heat or freezing cold or storms were in the nature of weather, the daily tempest of my life among these elemental powers—the screams, demands, disagreements—was the nature of love. But they had their sly ways: I secretly grieved for the dark mysterious things my parents did in the privacy of their relationship. I didn't know quite what these things were, but I knew they were shameful, requiring darkness. They were never referred to or acknowledged in the light of day. This aspect of my parents' life lay like a shadow in my mind. My mother and father, rulers of the universe, were taken by something over which they had no control. How problematical that was, how unsettling. Like my little grandma with her spells, they were afflicted in the manner of some kind of possession, and then afterwards they seemed to be normal again. I could not talk about this to anyone, certainly not my brother. If he didn't know about it he was lucky. The devastating truth was that there were times when my parents were not my parents; and I was not on their minds. It was not a subject to dwell upon. I resented the early hour of my bedtime, in part because it was earlier than anyone else's bedtime, in part because it brought on that vast period of darkness when those things happened about which I had insufficient knowledge; I could only make do, like a detective with the barest of clues, inaudible words, an indefinable sound of panic, a dim light, going on and off, all of it enfolded and obscured in my sleep-drugged state.

But I was coming to rely on my brother in some way that my parents' vehemently intense life together did not allow me to rely on them. Donald was steadfast. He lived his earnest life as one human being, not as half of two. He was still within reach. He taught me card games, easy ones like War and Go Fish, and a hard one, Casino. We played on the floor, where I was comfortable. He held my hand as we walked to the candy store. He was at home when my parents went out at night. The sight of Donald doing his homework suggested to me the clear and purposeful intention of life and its march to a visionary future. He would soon be graduating from P.S. 70 and going on to high school. He was now thirteen or so. Painstakingly, with his characteristic frown of concentration, he constructed airplane models of balsa wood, as light as feathers, and hung them on sewing thread from the ceiling of our room—snub-nosed racing planes, and a Ford Trimotor. The skins on the wings and fuselage were thin colored papers stretched taut by dampening. He was also building a solid wooden Strom-Becker model of the China Clipper. He read *Popular Mechanics* and pulp detective-story magazines, and in a magazine called *Radio Craft,* which my father had brought him, he found instructions for the building of a crystal radio set at a cost of sixty-five cents. He was saving his money.

Of course we had our problems. When his friends were around he tended not to want me to be with them, but I understood that, even as I complained and pestered him. It was a matter of principle with me to pester Donald and his friends. Of course they were not without resources in dealing with this. They knew my weaknesses, that, for instance, if anyone around me cried, I cried too. It was true, I caught crying as if it were a communicable disease, I couldn't help it, I was a walking dust mop of emotions. Donald pretended to cry to get rid of me. In fact, he had refined the art of it by only threatening to cry, holding his arm up to his eyes and issuing one preliminary sob and peeking out from under his arm to find me biting my lip, my eyes filling, ready to bawl for no reason, not even knowing what the matter was, the pain, but only that whatever it was, it was overwhelming and impossible to endure. I was burdened with this terrible affliction, just as my friend Herbert from Weeks Avenue had crossed eyes, or a little boy who played in my park had inward-turning feet. There was nothing to do but hope to grow out of it, this awful teariness. First it would hit me in the throat. Then it affected my ability to see, I had to close my eyes. It was a form of shyness or sorrow for the world's hard life. Sometimes my brother and his friends Bernie and Seymour and Irwin would, all together, pretend to cry; and I would be made so tearful by this mass assault that even knowing they were teasing me and even after having them emerge from their pretense laughing and jolly, I would find myself uncontrollably sobbing, as if a substantive wrong had taken place, like a bashed thumb or a cut, or the loss of something precious. And then, of course, it took forever to wind down, a trail of heartbreaking hiccuppy sobs issuing from me for several minutes as I went about my business.

Weakness and insufficiency seemed always to be my lot. I suffered from dust and pollen, colds, coughs, flus. At times of seasonal change I more or less lived in bed. All of this led, without my understanding it, to a crisis in my relationship with my brother. My parents concluded one day that Pinky, our dog, would have to be gotten rid of because I was allergic to her.

* * *

IT WAS HER HAIR THAT WAS THE PROBLEM, NOT HER CHARACTER. SHE SHED HER white hair on the rugs and on the furniture. Donald would not believe this was a reason for losing his dog forever. "You don't like her," he said to our mother. "That's what this is all about. You never have liked her."

"That's a false charge," my father said, coming to my mother's defense. "On occasion she has saved Pinky's life." He had us there. One day the dog had come up from the basement and my mother had noticed, as none of us did who were Pinky's champions, that she was dragging herself about with uncommon listlessness. My mother saw a speck of something green on the tip of Pinky's nose. "Oh my God," she said, "this stupid dog has eaten rat poison." Quickly she whipped up a couple of raw eggs in a bowl and put the dog and the bowl in the grass yard, a tiny patch on the south side of the house under the windows of Donald's room. Pinky slurped up the eggs and vomited, as my mother had expected she would, and thus her life was saved.

But the argument continued for several days. During this time we had reason to reflect on our history with this dog. She had been run over several times, and was no worse for wear. The green-poison story had become famous, although, as my mother told it to our neighbors, she did not want to admit that anything resembling a rodent could have needed the serious attention of a poison in our basement, and so she had represented that Smith had left open a can of some sort of janitorial substance of industrial strength and this was what the stupid dog had gotten into. Pinky had also enlightened our lives one day by giving birth to three or four puppies on Donald's bed, an event I peeked in at from the doorway and could accommodate with brief glimpses. Little squirming pups were coming out of her backside. She attended to everything with her tongue. Her ears were flat and her demeanor uncharacteristically solemn, and as each moving creature emerged she licked it and licked it and, in the same manner, herself and the bedspread, like the most responsible and decorous of dogs. Something my brother called the afterbirth she consumed in its entirety. I had not quite worked out the concept of procreation. It was not a matter in which anyone in my family thought I needed instruction. I was amazed that my mother was not angry at the mess Pinky was making. In my mind materials from the inside of the body were abhorrent to one degree or another; I included puppies. Yet a big shallow box was found and made into a nursery with shredded newspaper, and the dog Pinky, now given the astounding title of Mother, retired there to nurse; and eventually the puppies were placed.

All of this was in the nature of a lifelong commitment, my brother argued. Pinky to us and we to her. How could we kick out our dog at this point in all our lives together? Was nothing sacred? Other less drastic measures might be taken. Perhaps he could vacuum the entire house every day. Yes, he would be prepared to do that! Maybe Pinky could spend more time out of doors. He could train her not to run away. She might be kept in the cellar. And so on.

Donald was skilled in disputation, he was a good student and was able to call up all manner of appeals from the fields of science, ethics, and psychology, but none of them seemed to work. "It's not fair," he said in what I thought was his most trenchant remark, "it's not fair that an entire family should lose its dog just because one baby pipsqueak gets a runny nose." Nevertheless he seemed to believe that there was still time, still room for negotiation, and perhaps my parents did somehow give that impression. Even as he rehearsed me to make a passionate protest of my own, which I was earnestly prepared to do between sneezes and eye-watering coughs, Donald was talking to his friends to try to get one of them to keep Pinky. His idea was that with the dog gone, were I to show continuing signs of allergic hysteria, then it would be proven not to be Pinky's fault and she could be brought back home. In any event, he went off to school one morning, and while he was gone my parents struck: With the help of our family friend, the dentist Abe Perlman, who lived across the street, my father took time off from work so as to transport Pinky to a place he insisted was the closest thing to an ideal existence for a dog, a place called the Bide-A-Wee home. Here Pinky would be cared for and have other dogs for friends. After a day or so she would not even miss us. I was very nervous about this and insisted on hugging the dog even though that might bring on an asthmatic attack. I asked for full particulars about the Bide-A-Wee home, I wanted to accept its credentials at face value because I didn't want to be a sniveling wheezing sissy all my life. I did not miss the heavy meaningful glance between my father and Dr. Perlman, nor the barely concealed smirk on that man's face as he assured me the dog would be loved even more where she was going than in our house, but I decided to believe everything would be all right. I did not think that was possible, but still stood, irresolute and uneasily pacified, on the sidewalk as they drove away in Dr. Perlman's Plymouth with Pinky sticking her head out of the window because Dr. Perlman's driving made her carsick, just as it did me.

When Donald got home from school and found no Pinky, and heard my report to him, he became enraged. His green eyes grew large. "You believed that baloney about the Bide-A-Wee home? They took her to the ASPCA! They put her to sleep! You let them trick you! Pinky is dead and it's your fault!" He threw down his books, grabbed his fielder's mitt and began to pound the pocket. He paced up and down. "I hate you!" he said. "I hate Mom and I hate Dad and I hate Dr. Perlman, but most of all, I hate you, because you caused the problem in the first place. You're a little shit.

Get out of here! Go on. Get out,'' he said. He pushed me into the hallway and slammed the door.

I went outside. The more I thought about the situation, the worse I felt. A panic of grief rose in me. Implicit in what my brother said was the truth, I knew, that adults could be loved but never trusted; only Donald could be trusted. He had always told me the truth, he was passionately attached to reality and could always be relied upon to tell me exactly how things were. He showed me how to do things, and when I did them the way he said they should be done—you hold the bat this way, you catch the ball so—they worked out just as he predicted. Donald was never wrong. I had failed him, I had betrayed him, I had let them take our dog off to be killed. Our Pinky dead! I was to blame. I sat on the front stoop. I was stunned and sick. I knew the most terrible of states, irremediable damnation. I had done something fainthearted and it could not be made right, it was a disastrous act, irreversible. Some terrible chord of self-knowledge rang in me. Pinky, now invested with my moral soul, had fled and for the last time. She would never come back, running in that fleet abandoned fur-flattened way of hers, across streets, through yards, through tunnels, over bridges, under cars, but farther and farther from me, far past any range of my calling, heedless of my despair.

I WAS NOT AS ADVANCED A BEING AS MY BROTHER. IN MY ANGUISH IT NEVER occurred to me to be angry at my parents. I could perceive their characters, but I could not go on to make moral judgments of them. All my wit was spent in avoiding their critical judgments of me.

Yet now, here, I surely must have resented the clear evidence of the adult's crass disregard for the feelings of children. It was so devious of them to have gotten rid of Pinky in this way. Evading confrontation with his thirteen-year-old son and conning his five-year-old, my father had spirited away the family dog. Was it difficult for him? I knew he liked Pinky. When he walked her he took her off the leash and knew how to talk to her to keep her with him. Perhaps he regretted the decision to get rid of her. The urgency to do it would have come from my mother. But he was charming, my father. He did not raise his voice, he cajoled. He did not give commands, he appealed to reason. He rarely used physical force, unlike my mother who would swing away at the drop of a hat. I recognized the evasive style of the kidnapping as his.

*   *   *

My father loved tricks, gentle practical jokes, "now you see it, now you don't" kinds of things. He loved word games, riddles. I first heard Zeno's paradox from him, the runner halving the distance to the finish line, and halving it again, getting closer and closer but never reaching it. He loved puns and limericks.

> A queer old bird is the pelican
> His mouth holds more than his belly can
> He can hold in his beak
> Enough food for a week
> And you wonder how the hell he can.

He could not resist buying a volume of light verse if he happened to see one in a bookstore. He liked Sir Arthur T. Quiller-Couch:

> The lion is the beast to fight,
> He leaps along the plain.
> And if you run with all your might
> He runs with all his mane.

He relished the lore of the trickster in song or story. He had great appreciation for the legendary entrepreneur P.T. Barnum. He told me how Barnum had had a problem keeping people moving through his exotic animal exhibits so that more paying customers could be admitted. Barnum's solution was to put up a sign at the exit that said THIS WAY TO THE EGRESS. And the people poured through thinking an egress was another rare animal.

My father in his early forties was vigorous, ambitious, and struggling to make a go of things. He lived zestfully the code of the insider. He sold radios, Victrolas, sheet music. The stock of records in his store was vast, thousands of shellac records in brown paper sleeves and great heavy albums of operas and symphonies, European recordings as well as American, classical, jazz, swing. He even carried the records of obscure black folksingers from the South. He really knew his business, and some of the artists on labels he carried came into his store to buy the records from him. He was always very proud of knowing and dealing with famous musicians. "Stokowski came into the store today," he would tell us when he got home. Or, "Rubinstein's secretary called and gave me an order worth fifty dollars." I understood the value of the inside position. On those exciting Saturdays when I went downtown with Donald to my father's store, I saw how the people came in, I saw how he controlled what they bought by his advice and counsel, I was proud of him. He wore a blue pin-striped suit and vest and a red tie. His skin was pink and his brown eyes bright and alert. I didn't like his partner, though, Lester, a tall, unctuously hearty man with blond hair combed in a pompadour. He was in charge of the radio section. Lester had discovered that a certain percentage of customers could be counted on to bring radios in for repair that had nothing wrong with them. The residential hotels in the neighborhood were equipped with direct current. Usually the plug had been inserted in the power outlet the wrong way; by simply reversing the prongs of the plug, Lester could get the radio to work. Instead, he told the customer that the repairs would take several days; he would dust the innards, polish the cabinet, and write up a bill, having fixed a radio that was in perfect working order. "Oh, by the way," he would say as the customer was leaving with his radio, "just reverse the plug if nothing happens when you turn it on. It works fine now." My father had a kind of aesthetic appreciation for his partner's larceny. He said he held Lester down to reasonable amounts so that no one customer was stung for very much. But he told us of this practice expecting us to appreciate its humor. It was in the nature of being in the know, on the inside.

He took great pleasure from a book he brought home, an anthology of mistakes made by schoolboys on their exams and in their compositions. The mistakes were called "boners" and he read them to us. The chief animals of Australia are the kangaroo, larkspur, boomerang, and peccadillo. Medieval cathedrals are supported by flying buttocks. Shakespeare lived at Windsor with his merry wives. The two most important rivers of Scotland are the Firth and the Forth. In Pittsburgh they manufacture iron and steal. Four animals belonging to the cat family are the father cat, the mother cat, and two kittens. Acrimony, sometimes called holy, is another name for marriage. . . . Some of these made everyone laugh, some of them just my father laughed at. It was under his guidance that I would send away for my first Little Blue Books at five cents each, from the E. Haldeman Julius Company in Girard, Kansas: *Ventriloquism Self-Taught* and *Tales of Hypnotism and Revenge*. He was teaching me the available recourses in a universe run by humorless women. He himself had a mother he loved and must contend with, just as I did. My grandmother Gussie up on the Concourse had strong opinions and liked to control things. My grandfather Isaac was a bookish, peace-loving man with an intellect, like my father. So there was some cosmic scheme behind my father's puns and limericks and love of language games, a representation of the moral universe grounded in the archetypal male and female relation. Where had it come from? It was a peasant vision, a thing of funny papers and dialect jokes. It cut across all borders. It had come from the old country. In the street I heard from children its darker vulgar representations: A wife is something you screw on the bed and it does all the housework.

ROSE

Things went along smoothly for a while. My mother was an enormous help and comfort. Every day at lunch I'd wrap up my baby and put him in his carriage and go to my mother's house for lunch. I loved my parents. My brother, my older brother, Harry, was staying with them temporarily while looking for a job. So it was like old times for me, my family right around the corner. My mother was a dear sweet woman, so quiet, a very religious woman. She was one of the original members of the synagogue and the Sisterhood, she was there when they laid the first brick. I was close to her and I was happy taking care of my tiny child and making a nice home for my husband. He was making good money then. He worked for a man named Markel in the record business. That is how he got into it. Markel was some sort of jobber or distributor of phonographs and phono-graph parts. This was a very good business in the 1920's—before radios, before anything else. People bought those old phonographs with big horns and they bought records to play on them and to dance to, and it was the first home entertainment besides playing your own music. Windup Vic-trolas first, then electric ones. It was a revelation to people accustomed to hearing music only at the concert hall. So that was the business. I didn't like Markel, he had shady ways, I had worked for him myself for a while as secretary and bookkeeper. Dave had gotten me the job. But then I saw what Markel was like and I left. He used to order things from the manufac-turers, Victor, Edison, all of them, and then he wouldn't pay his bills. The office was a loft in the East Twenties. He had a whole floor with his office and the stockroom, and there was a fire escape at the window behind his desk. People in those days sent the sheriff around when they couldn't collect money due them. When he heard the sheriff coming up the stairs, this terrible man Markel would run down the fire escape. Your father was out selling all over the city. And so I was left to deal with the problem. I didn't like that. That's when I quit and found work with Sigmund Unter-berg, and then through him with the Jewish Welfare Board. Now I think

Markel was a bad influence on your father. True, he taught him a good business. But what else did he teach him? It was at this time, I think, that your father got interested in gambling, in card playing, and I think that was Markel's doing. Dave had a zest for adventure, he always dreamed of a big killing. It made him vulnerable. As fine as he was, as refined and cultured—and he loved good music, he loved opera—he indulged in bad things. And I never knew what was happening, he never told me anything, he gave me an allowance and that was that.

At any rate Dave's younger sister, Molly, had her baby prematurely after she and her husband, Phil, the cabdriver, had separated. So there was Molly with this sickly little baby and what was her mother Gussie's response? She wouldn't have anything to do with her. And her fancy older sister, Frances, up in Westchester had washed her hands of her. The thing about Molly was that she was the rebel in the family, the black sheep. She never finished high school, she went with riffraff, and she married someone beneath her. Phil was a decent fellow but not too smart. He spoke badly. But that wasn't the problem. The problem was that Molly after marrying him had taken up with another man. Bob, I think his name was. So it was a terrible mess. Molly begged to come and stay with us. She had no place to go. I went to the hospital to see her and she wept so. I liked Molly. She was the only one in that family besides Papa, besides Grandpa, that I felt comfortable with. She did not put on airs, she did not give me the feeling that I was not as good as she was. So I said to her come stay with us. And Dave agreed.

Now, we only had a three-room apartment at that time on Weeks Avenue. So it was quite a sacrifice. It was a light, large, airy apartment, but there was only one bedroom. So Molly slept in the bed with me and Dave slept on the couch. I had not expected her to stay long. I thought she would make some arrangement, put her life together, and after a week or two she would be gone. But that was not to be. She stayed for months. I had a girl in to help me clean and wash Donald's diapers. Donald was maybe a year old then. But the girl would not wash Molly's baby's diapers. So I had to do that myself, for this little infant girl, Irma. And where was Molly? She was out running around. This Bob kept coming to the house and taking her out on dates. Her husband, Phil, would come at night and start raising hell and shouting. The neighbors complained. It was the scandal of the whole house. I was going out of my mind. Your father had come to like having Molly in the house. He said to his mother one day, "Mama, I was thinking of increasing Rose's allowance." He asked his mother about everything. And there I was, taking care of Molly and her child, paying for everything out of the ordinary family budget, and the old lady said—I heard her right in the next room, we had gone there for a visit—"No, it's enough, she has enough, it's quite sufficient." Can you imagine? That terrible woman? I am taking care of her own daughter, she

and her other daughter have done nothing, and she says that? Dave belonged to them. He never consulted me, he told me nothing. His mother
was his consultant.

As you can imagine, I was very unhappy. My life was not good. I was
not sleeping with my husband, it was very upsetting. There was no privacy. I tried to get Molly to leave, but he would stop me—it was as if he
wanted her there. He wouldn't even talk about it. I think it was during this
time that he began to look around for other women. At lunchtime I would
take my baby boy and run to my mother's and cry. "Mama," I said, "I
want to leave him. I can't go on. I can't live this way. I'm so unhappy I
want to kill myself." And my mother would soothe me, and hug me and
caress me, but she was very old-fashioned and most conservative in her
ways. "You are a married woman," she would say. "You must make the
best of things. You must take care of your child and keep a home for your
husband. No matter what."

So I went back. If not for my mother I would have left and gotten a
divorce, but I could not disobey her, I wouldn't think of it. But finally I did
do something. One day this boyfriend of Molly's who had caused all the
trouble came around when she was out and I spoke to him. Bob. I didn't
dislike him. And I said to him, "Listen, Bob, you're a nice enough young
man. You're getting yourself into such a mess here. Aren't you ashamed
of yourself, to come calling on a woman who is married, who has just had
a baby, a woman whose mother has thrown her out, and whose sister
won't have anything to do with her because of this? And here she is living
with me, my husband has given up his bed so that she can stay here. Do
you think that's fair? You're too nice a young man to get mixed up in a
mess like this."

Well, that little talking to must have had some effect. I don't know
quite what happened, but one day Phil rang the bell and took Molly and
her baby and her bags and baggage away with him. And Bob was gone and
Molly and Phil were back living together. And I had my husband back. But
it was not easy to forget. What would happen next time? If it was not
Molly with her shenanigans, what would it be? I had this family on my
back. They controlled my husband, he belonged to them; whenever there
was a conflict he was on their side. I counted for nothing. When you were
born, and with two children we needed more space, that's when I met
Mrs. Segal and we moved to the private house on Eastburn Avenue. And
now Dave was doing well. He felt confident enough to go into business on
his own and he was making a go of it. He sold sound boxes and then took
the record concession at Vim's, a sporting goods and appliance store, part
of a chain. It was on Sixth Avenue and Forty-second Street. He had the
balcony at the back, overlooking the main store. He paid Vim's a percentage of his profits. We had money, we bought some furniture, it was 1931,
'32, and everywhere people were out of work, but somehow, in the heart

of New York, there was still life. Then when you were an infant, about a year old, my father died suddenly, and my poor mother came to live with us. This was the last straw for her. She prayed in her room, her health declined. And her mind was affected, my poor sweet mama.

ELEVEN

Death was on my mind, I thought about it, brooded about it and studied its representations. I had an old book of nursery rhymes that I hadn't looked at in a while. The letters were large, the drawings tinted in pale orange and pale green. The children and other beings in nursery rhymes were peculiar, ethereal, they inhabited nations, worlds, with which I was not familiar. Their characters were a source of uneasy imaginings. Little Miss Muffet: I would not call any girl of my acquaintance Miss anything; this one was so prissy and girlgood as to be insufferable, fully deserving her fate. I did not like Humpty Dumpty, who lacked all manly definition and was so irrevocably fragile. Georgie Porgie, Jack Horner, Jack and Jill, all seemed to me unnatural abstractions of child existence; there was some menacing propaganda latent in their circumstances but I couldn't quite work out what it was. It was a strange planet they lived on, some place of enormous fearful loneliness and punishment. Or it was as if they were dead but continued to be alive. Whatever happened to them kept happening over and over, good or bad, and I perceived a true moral in this repetition of fate, this recurring inevitable conclusion to the flaws in their beings. They suffered humiliation, damage, and shame, all forms of death or the feeling of death. They were like my dreams—birds flew out of pies, children ran with kings and queens, sheep, those most docile and slow-moving of animals, ran away, whereas the sheep in the Farm exhibit in Claremont Park in the spring didn't even move when you touched them. No human, animal or egg acted quite right in these stories. My final unalterable judgment was that nursery rhymes were for babies and I would not suffer hearing them again.

There was another kind of damage and death in the front-hall bookcase, in a set of art folios bound in flexible covers tied with colored string. Each folio had several color reproductions of the work of a great artist. I was very interested in bodies, and bodies were what these paintings showed: plump flying infants holding bows and arrows or trumpets; and naked moonfaced ladies with long blond hair and small breasts, not at all like my mother's; and scraggly bearded men almost naked and looking very pale with their eyes rolled up in their heads and their arms stretched out on wooden posts and with nails in their hands and feet. Or the same bearded, very pale, sad-faced men lying in the arms of several women who wore long veils and layers of gauzy dress and were crying, and with more of those flying babies hovering in the air above them. There were pictures of clouds with old grandfathers sitting in them with their arms extended and rays of sun shooting from their fingers, or of those scraggly bearded men again, there seemed to be an awful lot of them, they were like brothers in the same family, or members of a tribe, this time riding into little stone villages on the backs of donkeys whose eyes and facial expressions were as mournful and weary as their riders'. I wanted to paint but found the crayons I had for my use could not produce the lines and shapes or even gradations of color that I saw in those strange paintings. All pictures seemed to tell a story if you looked long enough, but these were truly mysterious events. They seemed to describe death. These pale, unhealthy-looking yellowish men with the nails in them and their eyes rolled up sometimes died in the desert, sometimes in grand palaces, they were either the fathers of those flying babies or the husbands of the crying women, it was hard to tell. They had been punished and killed but I didn't know why or by whom. How many there had been! I felt slightly queasy when I put the pictures back in the covers, I felt I had seen something I shouldn't have. They conveyed to me, whatever their intent, a kind of mental coercion which I felt as the mildest of nauseas, the slightest intimation of a need to rest.

In BED WITH A COLD, I CALLED LOUDLY TO MY MOTHER TO BRING ME SOME ORANGE juice. I heard her rustling about. Slam of refrigerator door. Footsteps coming down the hall. I threw myself half off the bed, my head back, my eyes staring wide, tongue extended and hands dragging on the floor. Screech. A shattering of glass. I sat up and laughed. Eventually, after sitting down on my bed to catch her breath and recover, she laughed too. "What a terrible thing to do," she said. My mother had been trained in death and disaster. She was vulnerable. She had lost two older sisters and her father. She had grieved and mourned three times, an experience I could only wonder about. She looked at Grandma every day with frowns of concern. Her blue eyes went dark. She played the piano, when she had time, almost as a form of prayer. Big chords, dashing arpeggios. My mother sat regally at the piano. Her arms reached wide.

* * *

ONE MORNING, AFTER MY BREAKFAST OF OATMEAL AND MILK AND TOAST AND jelly I took Grandma her tea. Carrying the glass and saucer carefully with two hands, I walked slowly down the hall to her room, next to mine, at the back of the house. In the saucer beside the glass were two white cubes of sugar—the same size Donald marked with a fountain pen to make homemade dice for one of his games. I tapped on her door; I waited for her to call "Come ahead" in Jewish so that I could push open the door with my foot and set the tea on the stand beside her bed. Grandma was interesting to me at these morning meetings. In bed she would not yet have dressed her hair—it lay in long grey braids on her pillows. She looked like a girl. Her light blue eyes were rested, and in the sun coming in the window the thin, fair skin of her face was quite smooth and you could see a little freckle here and there. She did not fear being poisoned in the morning. I enjoyed her approval. I basked in her love. In the back of my mind was also the idea of building up some reservoir of good feeling so that if she became unhappy during the day and started cursing and screaming, she would look at me and remember how she had loved me earlier and take it easy on me.

I thought now I heard her call to come in. I pushed open the door and saw immediately that something was wrong. "Grandma?" I said. I whispered, "Grandma?" She was lying in bed on her back with the blanket pulled up to her chin and her hands clutching the blanket's edge. She emitted a strange sound—like marbles spilling on the floor. Clumps of the blanket were gathered under her fingers. She was very yellow. The sound stopped. Her eyes were neither closed nor open—as if the lids were between sleep and awakeness. Her chin looked collapsed somehow, the mouth was slack. Now I felt the overall stillness of her, a declared inanimateness, the monumental event of death recorded here for me as another kind of life, a superseding condition with more visible torment than I could have imagined was possible. I put the tea down on the bureau far from her bed. I ran down the hall to the kitchen, where my mother and father were having breakfast. I thought Grandma was behind me and coming to get me. My parents saw me in the doorway and I said, "I think Grandma has died." I had not yet in my brief life been thought of as a reliable witness of anything. My parents exchanged glances as if looking for each other's assurance that what I had said could not possibly be true. But they knew something of her precarious health, and the edge of despair on which she lived and often tottered. My father pushed his chair back and hurried to the back of the house; my mother stared at me and put her hand to her cheek.

* * *

Later with the thing offically acknowledged and phone calls made and the visit of the doctor, I felt better. That the adults had taken charge was comforting to me, and no moment since my discovery of my grandma had been quite as bad. Everyone talked in whispers. I had not yet begun to think of her as dead, only that she had died. These seemed to be two separate ideas in my mind. She still lay in her room. It was still her room. I peeked through the half-closed door and saw Dr. Gross examining her with a stethoscope. He was our family doctor, a short, round jowly man with greying black hair and a moustache who wore looped across his vest a chain with a membership badge of some sort depending from it. I had studied that little badge many times as he attended me through my wheezes and hacks and earaches. His office was only a few blocks away. He had removed the covers from my grandma and taken off her gown. She lay white and slender; I could not see her face, but her body, the female whiteness of it, was dazzling to me, not at all wrinkled and not bent but straight. I had just a glimpse before my mother saw me and told me to go about my business and shut the door firmly. I wondered if it was a thing about death that made grandmas into girls.

The next day my mother and father and Uncle Willy, all of them dressed in dark clothes, went off to the synagogue, which was around the corner and one block down on 173rd Street and Morris Avenue. Donald stayed home from school, but neither he nor I was allowed to go to the services. But we were drawn there somehow, and so we walked with my hand in his to where we could stand across the street from the synagogue and hear what traces of the music and prayer could be heard. It was a large square synagogue faced in a pebbly texture of concrete. I had touched it many times. It had white granite steps in the front that narrowed toward the top, and curving brass handrails. It had stone columns on either side of the front door, like a post office, and a translucent dome for a roof. At the very top, where pigeons sat, were two tablets connoting the Ten Commandments. Around the side where we stood, stained-glass windows were tilted open in a way that didn't allow you to see inside. We heard singing.

"Poor Grandma," Donald said. "The only fun she had was going to services."

We saw the black hearse, and another black car behind it, move slowly to a stop in front of the synagogue. "People will be coming out in a minute," Donald said and we walked back home.

I had the distinct impression death was Jewish. It had happened to my grandma, who spoke Jewish, and everyone had immediately repaired to the synagogue. A memorial candle in a glass now stood flickering on the kitchen table for Grandma, whom I had seen light similar candle glasses for her own dead. Hebrew letters were on the glass label as on the window of the chicken market where dead chickens hung on hooks by their feet, some plucked, some half plucked, some with all their feathers. Chickens, I knew, were Jewish. For days after Grandma's burial, the mirrors were covered in our house and my mother walked around in stockinged feet. We were visited by friends, who brought many white bakery boxes tied with string and put them on the kitchen table. Pots and pots of coffee were made, and women I didn't know, friends of my mother, stood strangely at the kitchen sink and washed dishes. My mother hugged me in front of visitors, drew me to her and hugged me till it hurt. She was tearful, sentimental, easy to deal with. She complimented me and told everyone how bright I was. "This is the boy who knew before any of us," she said. "He came to tell us and he knew exactly what had happened." But she also spoke Jewish to these people, just as she had to my grandmother. I went to my grandmother's room. The bed was stripped, the closet had been emptied. But in her cedar chest there were still her treasures, shawls of lace and folded dresses, and wool sweaters and knitted things all wrapped in thin white paper and with mothballs between the layers. There were also old sepia pictures of her family when she was a child, many little girls and boys standing and reclining around old men with white beards and black hats who sat stiffly in chairs, behind which stood several stern-looking women with their hands on the old men's shoulders. The little boys and girls were dressed oddly and all seemed to have drawn faces and dark hair hanging over their ears and enormous staring dark eyes. On the top of the chest was my grandma's prayer book, her Siddur, and the cover had those Jewish letters on it that looked to me like arrangements of bones. In my room I played with my pick-up sticks to see if I could arrange them in Jewish letters, but they lacked bony width, they lacked the knobby thickness even of chicken bones.

Now it was my mother who, on Friday nights at the kitchen table, placed white Sabbath candles in the wobbly old brass candlesticks, and drew a kerchief over her head and lit the candles and prayed with her hands over her glistening blue eyes.

TWELVE

More frequently now there came to the front door the old men in black who wore their prayer shawls under their coats and carried letters from rabbis and credentials from yeshivas. Now they were invited in. My mother sat them in the parlor and gave them tea. They told their stories in hushed tones or spoke only in Jewish, and so my eavesdropping didn't yield anything that specific. But I was getting the gist of things. And finally one man spoke enough English to make it clear. ''The *kinder* from the schools are pushed, so now they can't go. And the business of the fathers are taken from them. Little by little. And in the street they revile them, the brownshirt heathen, and spit on them. And to the *polizei* they must report. Thousands are leaving, Missus. Their homes, their livelihood is gone. All of it gone. To Palestine, on boats, but anywhere! Where can they go! What can they do!''

My mother produced two crumpled bills from her purse, folded them, and pushed them into the old man's coin box. It was a blue box with white stripes and a white six-pointed star.

My mother joined the Sisterhood of the synagogue and began going to services on Saturday morning. She had never been religious before. ''I never had the patience,'' she told her friend Mae. ''When I was a girl, I gave Mama such a hard time because I wouldn't go. I thought it was all so old-fashioned and unnecessary. We were bohemians, Dave and I. And look at me now.''

One Saturday I went with her just to see what it was all about. The women sat upstairs in the synagogue. The men, who were the bosses, sat downstairs. Sometimes there was crying, sometimes singing, but mostly Jewish death words. Jewish death was spreading.

I left and ran home by myself. Through a grate in the sidewalk on the 173rd Street side of the synagogue I could see into the basement windows. Another synagogue was down there where the poor people prayed.

I was familiar with the texture of sidewalks and the embellishments in brick at the sides of buildings. Most brick was red and of a pocked cracked surface that scraped the finger; some brick siding was yellow and was smoother. The steps of my front stoop were worn white granite, very smooth to the touch.

After this summer I would be going to school. This had been discussed several times by my parents. They were pleased about it. I was ready for school—eager, in fact—but now my mother was saying that I would also go to Hebrew school twice a week in the afternoons. She said this as a kind of declaration and she put her hand on my head. I secretly resolved to fight the edict. It seemed to me a reckless, even insane act of public exposure. I already knew that if I found myself in the wrong part of Claremont Park I could be knifed and robbed for being Jewish. I knew from the old men's whisperings in the front parlor that similar things, though even worse, were happening in Europe, especially Germany. A little boy who went to Hebrew school would live in endlessly concentric circles of danger, beginning with my park, and rippling out over the globe. Everything connected in a circle of being that, unfortunately, had assigned to us the life of prey, as on the steppes, or the veldt, where the herds of beautiful zebra or wildebeests were run down and this or that animal isolated and slaughtered for the evening meal of the predator cats. I could not have reasoned consciously that European culture took revengeful root in the New World, to which it had been transplanted. Yiddish-speaking households were not foreign to me, they were American. I did not speak the language, but I understood bits of it as spoken by my grandmother to my mother or in less purist fashion by my father's parents to him. In my comic books purchased at the candy store on the corner of 174th Street, or on the faces of the bubble gum cards, stories were told of wars between gangsters or wars between countries. Planes dive-bombed the agonized faces of screaming civilians, tanks rearing like horses on their hind legs loomed over Oriental babies crying for their mothers, and G-men and crooks, who were dressed alike, drilled each other with tommy guns. It all seemed of a piece to me, and insofar as it had something to do with the strategy of survival, I attended to it. I understood that one had as resources oneself, one's brother, one's parents and then perhaps President Roosevelt.

Of course I knew virtually nothing about religion, beyond a few of the major Bible stories and the holidays associated with them. I knew so far that most of the Jewish holidays were not as much fun as the regular ones. There was some forced insistence behind them. This was not true of the Fourth of July or New Year's or Thanksgiving. Purim, where you got apples and raisins and noisemakers and little blue-and-white flags, was sort of fun; and Chanukah, of course, where you got presents. But spinning the wooden top, to see which Hebrew letter would fall, like a gambler in death, was not to my liking. And the Purim story seemed to me not as victorious as it was made out to be. One bad man was shamed and deposed, but the king was still there who was the real problem.

Passover was the giant of the Jewish holidays and had much to say for it. The story was good and the food was good. Technically it lasted eight days, but the fuss was made for only one. It came along in the spring, but with that peculiarity of Jewish holidays of being very casual about the date of its arrival. I noticed when adults talked about Passover they said either that it was late or that it was early, but never that it was on time. This year it was late. My mother bought flowers for it, tulips and daffodils. Passover involved getting dressed up and taking an enormous journey with packages and flowers.

W E WERE MOST OF THE DAY GETTING READY. EARLY IN THE AFTERNOON, AN unusual time for me to be so clean and well groomed, we set off—Donald, my mother and I—walking east on 173rd Street over the Topping Avenue hill, and descending by degrees to the valley of Webster Avenue. This was the East Bronx of mythological dangers; surrounded by my family I was not concerned, although it would have been better still were my father with us. But he was required to work most of the day and would be meeting us later.

We boarded a red-and-yellow streetcar with rush seats, all occupied. It was the W car, headed north. It went clanging up Webster, a wide thoroughfare of gas stations, warehouses, lumberyards and auto repair shops. The farther north we rode, the longer the stretch between stops. One by one we found seats. My mother, sitting first, kept all the bundles on her lap. At 180th Street the car swung sharply right, the wheels screeching loudly and all the passengers tilting in unison. At this point, Donald began a sharp lookout. He was our navigator. We rode to the stop under an elevated station that he had been waiting for, and got off to transfer to another trolley, the A car. Now the Bronx flattened out in blocks of empty lots, with schools in the middle of dirt fields, and spired churches, and even an occasional wooden house with its own yard. Finally, after a turn or two, we broke into the peaceful suburban avenues of Mt. Vernon. Here the car ride was smooth and we were practically the only passengers. We sat together. I liked the brown wood decks of streetcars, the walls and window frames and ceilings were of wood too; it must feel like this in a bunkhouse or a riverboat, I thought. And it all rested on steel carriages. It appealed to me that fast or slow, barreling along or creaking around corners, the trolley car could go only as directed by the tracks; it was all planned, all the motorman could do was crank up the power and the flanged wheels had dutifully to go the way they were led. Of course, occasionally the motorman stopped the car, got off and, with a crowbar, moved the track switch one way or another, but the principle held.

The air was cool. The streets were not of cobblestone but of smooth cream-colored seamless paving. Green parks and fields were on either side of us. Then near the end of the line, the conductor already walking down the aisle and yanking the seat backs forward for the return trip, the car reached a certain corner in Pelham Manor, where, to my mind, began the quietest, most elegant block in the world. And here we disembarked, and made our way along the beautifully named Montcalm Terrace, after a general in the French and Indian War. This was where Aunt Frances lived, on a street of raised lawns and grand homes. Her house had a sharply raked tile roof, and casement windows, and dark wood beams impressed in the grey stucco siding.

AUNT FRANCES GREETED US WITH A SMILE AT THE DOOR. BEHIND HER WAS HER full-time maid, Clara, a tall, angular black woman who wore a white uniform with matching white shoes. Clara took our coats and bundles. To our surprise and delight, my habitually late father was already there. He had come up from Grand Central Station on the New York Central. "You're late," he said. "What took you so long!" And everyone laughed. Then the master of this house appeared, Uncle Ephraim, horse-faced, very proper, a bit pompous, in fact—a portly man who spoke always as if delivering a speech. He gazed down at me, with critical intelligence coming like sparks of light off his eyeglasses. He had enormous teeth. "And how is Edgar?" he said. I could tell he felt superior to his wife's family. He had a patronizing air. On the second night of Passover they would have a seder for his family; the two families never met. And it was true, we were a raucous crowd. Uncle Ephraim conducted the seder down at the end of the table. Beside him sat my atheist grandfather, who was equally proper about the form of the thing. Together they prayed and directed the sacramental moments for us all, while we, our attention wandering, talked and whispered, Donald and my cousin Irma trying to step on each other's feet under the table, and my father getting into a political argument with Uncle Phil the cabdriver, who did not believe the cabdrivers should be unionized. Uncle Phil wore not the ceremonial black skull cap supplied by the house but the same felt hat with the front brim turned up in which he drove his cab. Irreverent Aunt Molly kept up a patter of remarks that made us laugh. She always looked disheveled, even in holiday clothes, with wisps of her hair not quite tucked in, face florid, bosom crooked, dress sticking to her from its own static. "Where do you suppose the Duke and Duchess of Windsor are having *their* seder tonight," she said. Even my grandmother Gussie laughed, who was pious and God-fearing and tried to shush everyone before she laughed again. When things got too noisy, Uncle Ephraim, without looking up, slapped the table with his open palm, and for perhaps thirty seconds everyone was chastened until someone broke out in the giggles, usually me, because of the funny faces Aunt Molly was making to get me to do just that.

And here we were all of us sitting around the long table in the dining room, a room where you only ate, imagine that, and even the animosity between my mother and grandmother was suspended as the sweet holiday wine, sipped at the requisite times in the ceremony, began to bring color to people's faces. The candlelight shone in everyone's eyes. There was a splendid chandelier of many crystal lights. I was asked to open the front door for Elijah, the prophet, for whom a place setting was laid and wineglass filled. It was a heavy wooden door, with a cathedral arch and black cast-iron fixtures. I peeked into the darkness of Montcalm Terrace to make sure Elijah was not there. I pictured him as one of the old bearded men who came to the door with terrible stories and a collection box in his hand. I was relieved that he hadn't come. The night sky was filled with millions of shining stars.

My brother was prevailed upon to ask the four questions the youngest male asks at the seder. He protested, was overruled and, scowling, turned to me and said, "This is the last time I do this, next year you better know how." He felt demeaned—a student at Townsend Harris High School asking why this night was different from all other nights. The answers in Hebrew to the four questions seemed, not only to me but to most everyone at the table, interminable. "Listen to them down there," Molly said of Grandpa and Uncle Ephraim. "The Jews are the only people in the world who give you a history course before they let you eat." Finally the big moment arrived—the actual dinner. Aunt Frances rang a little bell and a moment later Clara appeared from the kitchen and began to serve. I had nibbled at the bitter herbs and barely sniffed at the hard-boiled egg in salt water. Now my time had come. The chicken soup with *knaydl,* how good that was! The fish I passed over. That was my father's joke that made everyone laugh: "No thank you, Aunt Frances. I'll pass over that." Then roast lamb, baked potatoes, I even ate the string beans. Honey cake and watered wine for dessert. Then, after a brief reprise of the impenetrable ceremony, the time for singing, at which point everyone with great gusto, as much in gratitude for the finish of this exhausting event as in praise of God, sang the traditional songs as loudly as possible. The song I liked best was one of those add-on songs, like "There Was an Old Woman Who Swallowed a Fly." This song described a father buying a kid, meaning a goat. Then a cat devoured the kid, then a dog came and bit the cat, a staff came and smote the dog, and a fire came and burned the staff and then water came and extinguished the fire, then the ox came and drank the water, and finally, by the last verse you got the whole causal sequence— the slaughterer came and slaughtered the ox, which had drunk the water, which had put out the fire, which had burned the staff, which had smitten the dog, which had bitten the cat, which had eaten the kid, which my father had bought for two coins—one only kid, one only kid. I had no idea what any of this meant and I didn't want to ask for fear of being answered, but it pleased me very much.

When the time came to leave, Aunt Frances stood talking to my mother about her poor mother, and then the two women hugged. Uncle Ephraim had a gold toothpick that he kept on a fob. He held up a hand to cover his mouth while he picked his teeth. We all piled into Uncle Phil's De Soto taxi, which had jump seats. It was crowded but we fit. I sat on my father's lap and fell asleep as we went back down to the Bronx. First Phil dropped off the old folks. Then he drove us to our door. My father carried me up the front steps, I half asleep in his arms, the cool night air of spring blowing gently around my ears like an echo of the Passover songs in my mind.

THIRTEEN

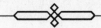

School was just a half block from my house, across the corner of 173rd Street, but my whole life changed once I began there. I was six—no longer a child. I wore a white shirt with a red tie. In the morning my time was as important as anyone else's. I had to be turned out at a certain hour just like my brother and father; I ran home for lunch at twelve and back at twelve-forty-five, and when I got home from school in the afternoon I had just a few hours before I'd have to start thinking about homework. I enjoyed the seriousness of my calling. Reading came to me effortlessly. I had in a subliterate way been making sense from books for some time. The moment I began competently to read was imperceptible to me. Numbers were more difficult.

My teacher Mrs. Kalish asked me on my first day in her class if I was Donald's brother. He had been a brilliant student, she said, her favorite student at the time. This sort of comparison would eventually disturb me. Now I smiled with pride at the identification. I was a confident scholar. School held no terrors. I did not once vomit in the classroom. The janitor had a surefire system for dealing with such disasters. He appeared with his pail of ammoniated water and his mop, and a shovel and a garbage can and a bag of sawdust. He would spill the sawdust on the offensive pool, shovel it up, and then mop the whole thing with ammonia and drive the smell away. Why did children vomit so much at P.S. 70? Bathroom accidents were oddly less frequent, perhaps because the rules about going to the bathroom were fairly relaxed.

The materials of school interested me, the stiff colored paper, the jars of white paste, the sticks of chalk, the erasers larger than bars of brown soap that had to be taken outside and pounded against each other to get the dust out. To be chosen to do that, to be authorized to leave the classroom and go out in the closed yard in the sun, all alone, was an honor. Another honor was to be designated monitor of the window shades, which needed adjustment all during the day as the sun went across the sky and the light shone in our eyes or in the teacher's. Honors seemed to fall my

325

way in school without my having to do much to get them. I was liked by the other children and they elected me class president, although neither I nor they had very much idea what the class president was supposed to do. Yet I enjoyed being president. The stair monitor had more power, but that was all right.

In the spelling bees I was the best of the boy students and invariably wound up the last of my kind to face three or four of the girls on the other side of the room. Girls were devilishly good at spelling. I might defeat almost all of them, but just as I was the boy champion, Diane Blumberg led the girls, and inevitably, when the showdown came between me and Diane, she would win. She was good at math too, and taller than I was, with fat little squirrel cheeks and a mouth perpetually primed in contemptuous judgment. Diane Blumberg was in all ways smug and insufferable.

A watercolor portrait of President Roosevelt hung above the blackboard in the front of the room. On the window ledges were various things we did for Nature, one of the best of subjects—bulbs growing in pots, or a frog in a terrarium. We had a bowl of turtles, who sunned themselves on stones, and for one or two days in spring an Easter rabbit donated by one of the mothers. Abraham Lincoln was shown on a poster and over his figure was printed the Gettysburg Address. In the long closet with sliding doors at the side of the room, on rainy days steam seemed to come from our rubber slickers and galoshes. I loved anything that got me out of the classroom. We would in two-by-twos trek downstairs to the big auditorium for the weekly movie, never something as good as we'd expect to find at the real movies, but something old and tame, like *Mrs. Wiggs of the Cabbage Patch* or *Tom Sawyer*. After each reel the lights would come on and we would be noisy and throw spitballs at one another—the discipline was less exacting at these times. The best breaks in the routine were the fire drills, because then we could march outside and stay there for mysterious endless amounts of time, the whole school standing quietly in ranks in the breeze, all the apartment buildings of the neighborhood surrounding our yard, while seemingly secret and troubled school administrative selfexamination took place. On mornings of fire drills lunchtime always came quickly.

I had discovered in myself the double personality engendered by school: the good attentive boy in class, the raucous, unsprung Dionysian in the schoolyard at recess. It was a matter of expressing the dominant force—order or freedom. Other boys in the class were bigger, rougher in the mold, and their wildness was a model to us all. The quiet teacher's child in me went and sat down somewhere in the back of my brain while the hellion ran about shouting and punching. You found weaknesses and went chasing after them, like the cheetah, which I knew was, for short distances, the fastest animal in the world. The weakness of girls was their underpants. To see these or mention them or allude to them brought red embarrassment to their faces, or glances of fear, or hisses of hatred. They had an awful way of half bending their knees, holding their hands in their skirts, protecting *something*. I knew to stop, always, short of the flying fanged leap. One or two boys did not know, they had some ungoverned crudeness of spirit that did damage, bent arms back, humiliated their prey, and turned themselves into the despised among all of us, girls and boys. They were feared and detested, and went on living that way in rude derision of their unpopularity, for months at a time. When I went back into class I became serious, as if my character could only be maintained by alternations of opposites. I tried out different Edgars in the class, in the schoolyard. In transit from school to home and back in that short half block, I ran from one of my beings to another aware only of the sound of the racing breath in my ears, the scent of cold air in my brain, some pungent essence of winter and the momentary revelation of my own lengthening limbs.

School made me hungry. For lunch I loved a baked potato with butter and salt and a glass of milk. Or cabbage soup with potatoes in it and sour cream. Under my father's advice, I was developing a taste for tart things, a taste, he claimed, that was far more enduring than one for the sweet things. I was bought my first pair of knickers. They were corduroy and worn with long argyle socks. I liked my looks in the mirror, a young knickered student in his fall wool sweater, and a shock of blond hair over one eye. I liked to see my softness going away, the leanness of cheekbone emerging, a line of jaw.

There was in my second-grade class the smallest of girls, Meg. She had grey eyes and very light straw-colored hair worn short, and her mother favored more doll-like versions of the skirt and middy that girls customarily wore—skirts with stiff outward-spreading understuff and white knee socks and white-and-brown strap shoes polished clean every morning. She was the shortest person in the class, and as she was extremely quiet as well, she was clearly too delicate and inconsequential to excite the envy or malice of the other girls or the desire of the boys to inflict torture and torment. She had no apparent wish to use what she had or what she came from to make her place in our society. We all knew what a spoiled child was and she was not one. She demanded no obeisances as any of us would on the basis even of the ownership of a new pencil box. Our social life was competitive, we made alliances and broke them with the cunning of nations, but she was clearly not one of our coarse breed. She did her work well and throughtfully, without ostentation; she never volunteered an answer but always knew it when she was called on. When the school day was over she did not linger in the yard, but with her books stacked and held against her chest in that way of girls, she walked through the school-yard gate and to the corner, and looking both ways before crossing 173rd Street, made her way along Eastburn, right past my house to the corner of Mt. Eden Avenue, where she crossed the Oval, turned left and went along the Claremont Park wall to her apartment, overlooking the park up the hill near Monroe Avenue. Although the theatricality of her mother's taste made Meg's underpants easier to see than most, she did not suffer from this. No one bothered her, least of all me. Perhaps her size made her the baby in our minds. But for the same reason, size, I may have seen in her an assumption of that titled babyhood for which I had less and less desire in myself. I was grateful to her. I was glad no one bothered her because then I would have had to reveal myself as her defender. And then it would have been said I loved her, which would be unfortunate. She had a full, inflamed-looking upper lip, which I found attractive. I was not yet bold enough to walk beside her even though her path took her right past my stoop, but her quietness, and a quality of inner certitude she had, conveyed, in the brief moments I watched her or thought about her, a similar central silence to me, and I felt as if I were looking ahead down a still corridor into my calm and resolute manhood.

SCHOOL BROUGHT ABOUT AN ENLARGED SOCIAL LIFE, GENERALLY, FOR I WAS NOW permitted on Saturday to go out for lunch and then spend the afternoon at the movies with one or more of my school friends. My expeditions were funded with a weekly allowance of twenty-five cents. Two hot dogs with mustard and sauerkraut and a bottle of Pepsi-Cola cost fifteen cents at the delicatessen on 174th Street; and the dime in change was exactly the price of admission to the Surrey Theater on Mt. Eden Avenue just the other side of the Concourse. The Surrey showed a cartoon, a newsreel, either a travelogue or a short, such as one of Lew Lehr's monkey pictures, where the monkeys rode bikes and wore diapers and sat in high chairs to eat baby food, one or two chapters of a serial like *Tim Tyler's Luck* or *Buck Jones and the Phantom Rider,* and finally, a double feature, an A picture and a B, the A usually about gangsters and G-men, the B a Laurel and Hardy comedy or perhaps a Charlie Chan mystery. At the end of the afternoon I came out of the theater staggering. I was shocked to see that it was still daylight, that mankind did not live in eternal darkness lit only by flashes of gunfire or the flames of car crashes, and in fact was going about its ordinary business in no visibly dramatic manner. This letdown, or perhaps it was the light, or that my skull still resounded with the unmodulated screams of joy of a theaterful of children, invariably brought me home with a headache, which, however, I could not confess to my mother lest I be reminded of it the following Saturday.

Sometimes this routine was varied with a trip downtown, if we could persuade one of the mothers or an older brother or sister to go with us. We did not choose places that were chosen by our teachers for trips on a bus during school hours—the Museum of Natural History, for instance, or Fraunces Tavern, where Washington said farewell to his troops. We liked to see radio shows. One day we got into the Babe Ruth program, where the great man himself stood in front of the microphone, although not, disappointingly, in his baseball suit but in an ordinary double-breasted suit and tie, and read from a script haltingly and ran a quiz with lucky kids picked from the audience. In fact he was past his prime as a player. But there were prizes up to five dollars and a lot of advice about clean living from the Babe. His voice was hoarse at the end, his tie loosened, his hair rumpled, but he got through it. We didn't have to be cued by the director with his placards to cheer; stopping our throats was more difficult.

On expeditions such as these I liked to drop in at my father's store, if it was within range, and show it off to my friends. "Hey, young fellow," my father would say as I walked in. Donald would be there putting stock on the shelves, Uncle Willy might be taking an order on the phone. I cautioned my friends not to make noise. I gave them a guided tour in hushed tones as we passed among the customers.

Downtown was my father's realm. In my mind it belonged to him. Every day he went to it on the subway as a diver in a big iron bell descended to the depths of the ocean; and he found things there and brought them back. His restless mind lapped our house every night like the evening tide and brought to our shores the treasures of his escapades— opera tickets, art books, magazines, papers, little badly printed magazines of radical thought, a new electric clock with an illuminated dial, a wonderful set of silver electric trains. When he took me downtown to spend the day with him, that was the best trip of all. I could then open my mind to the chaos of adult civilization, knowing that he would find the order for me. He pointed out buildings and named them and told me what was done in them, he instructed me on the difference between streets and avenues, he described the routes of the trolley cars by the letters they displayed on the front, he knew flawlessly how to get from one place to another, he knew the best shops for this or that, the best values, he knew everything. My father was an expert jaywalker walking us boldly across the streets of traffic with unerring grace. When my mother brought me downtown, she deferred uncharacteristically to his decisions, he was the master in this realm. He loved the great city of stone—it made him catch his breath and laugh. I understood, studying him, that his mind made a design of it. There was the appearance of it, which I knew, a dazzle of noise and disparate intention, jackhammers punching holes in the street, cars and trucks flowing past obstructions, yellow cabs with their skylights, double-decker buses, the great liners in the harbor blowing their basso horns; but in reality all of it was somehow arranged, it was a place of accommodation for human desire, it supported the diverse intentions of millions of people simultaneously, and he knew that and gave me the confidence to understand it and not be afraid. The heels of thousands of people drummed the sidewalk. He had been born on the Lower East Side. New York was his home, he loved its music, and through a speaker over the front door of Hippodrome Radio he sent the sound of symphonies and swing bands into the street like his own voice.

Yet when I walked from our home to the subway station on 174th street and entered that cool catacomb through the tightly sprung turnstile, it was usually in the company of my mother, herself no mean guide. She too was a native. Holding my hand tightly, she brought me to spectacles designed for children—theatricals, puppet shows, Thanksgiving Day parades. It was to my mother I would turn in the huge air-cooled cathedral of Radio City when Snow White ran through the woods and the trees came alive to grab at her tresses and scratch her clothes into tatters; my mother was the sponsor of all that looming animated surreality.

One day she took me to the Ringling Brothers and Barnum & Bailey Circus at Madison Square Garden on Fiftieth Street. My father had gotten the tickets free. It was a weekday matinee and he could not come. My school was over, but Donald still had his high school exams, and so it was just the two of us. Far below me on the tanbark of the center ring a sad-faced clown swept the spotlight into a smaller and smaller circumference until finally it went out altogether. Another clown strode along with half a dozen baby pigs trotting after him. He pressed a button and his nose lit up. Someone doused him with water, so he opened a tiny umbrella the size of a saucer and held it by its long handle high over his head. I watched the great swinging teams of fliers doing somersaults in the air. I saw the march of elephants.

It interested me particularly that in the circus there was one wistful clown who climbed the high wire after the experts were done, and scared himself and us with his uproariously funny, incredibly maladroit moves up there. Slipping and sliding about, losing his hat, his floppy shoes, and holding on to the wire for dear life, he was actually doing stunts far more difficult than any that had gone on before. This was confirmed, invariably, as he doffed his clown garments one by one and emerged from the woeful little potbellied misfit as the star who headlined the high-wire act. In his tights and glistening bare torso he pulled off his bulbous nose and stood spotlighted on the platform with one arm raised to receive our wildest applause for having led us through our laughter, our fear, to simple awe. I took profound instruction from this hoary circus routine. It was not merely that I, the sniffler with the red nose, would someday in my good time reveal myself to be a superman among men. There was art in the thing, the power of illusion, the mightier power of the reality behind it. What was first true was then false, a man was born from himself. All the problems of my own being were not the truth of me, I knew. In my own eyes I was a man no matter what daily evidence was thrown in my face to the contrary. But that there were ways to dramatize this to an unsuspecting world was the keenness of my understanding. You didn't have to broadcast everything you knew all at once, but could reveal it suspensefully, and make them first cry out in fear, and make them laugh, and, above all, make them applaud, when they finally saw what an achievement had been yours by taking on so well and accurately the comic being of a little kid.

Of course that was a hard illusion to maintain once the show was over and the lights went on. I aspired to the power of myself. My struggle went on every day but not always in my consciousness of it. School assisted me because I did well there, I was among peers and I was proving out. But the odds at home were against me; no matter how I grew and what I learned, I couldn't seem to better my position. Invariably there were ceremonies of my helplessness that caused me to revert to the child I had been and thought I was no longer—as, for instance, when my mother decided it was time for still another excursion downtown, but to a place I despised and detested, S. Klein's on Union Square.

I could not subscribe to whatever value it was that plunked me down, semiannually, at S. Klein's. She hated it too, or so she said, but she went about her preparations to leave the house with an energy that suggested happy anticipation. It was possible for us to communicate sensibly sometimes but not when she wouldn't admit her true feelings. So I knew all was lost, I was helpless before impending disaster, and nothing could console me, neither the long trip in the subway in which I got to stand at the window next to the engineer's cab nor the promise of lunch out. I went immediately into my passive-resisting sulk, in which my feet didn't seem to work properly, my wrist had to be held and I was by this means shaken and yanked forward, shoetips scuffing the sidewalk, or dragged in a kind of sideways lurch and stumble, all the way to the 174th Street subway station.

"Walk properly, Edgar," she would say. "You want me to leave you behind? Don't think I wouldn't! Oh, you foolish boy, who do you think I'm doing this for? You grow out of things as soon as I put them on. Do you know how lucky we are to have a few dollars? Other children wear castoffs and they're happy to have them."

If I persisted she would say, "I warn you, my patience is wearing thin," and give me a particularly vehement yank. I always admired my mother's metaphors. Even as they were familiar to me from much usage, they held up nicely. Patience wearing thin was very fine. A little later she would say, "If you don't walk like a human being I'm going to knock the spots out of you." That was good too, although I never quite understood the etymology of it. Some people had freckles, but I didn't, and, of course, chicken pox and measles brought spots, but no one would beat a sick child and expect to cure him in this manner, not even my mother. Besides which the phrase was *out of you,* she didn't say I'm going to knock the spots *off you,* she said *out of you,* and so that was totally mystifying. I had seen her pounding pillows or shaking blankets out the window before laying them across the windowsill; maybe it was a dust metaphor. Not that I had much time to reflect on it, because there followed almost immediately the ultimate assurance: that I would be murdered in cold blood. I never had the leisure to think about that one. Uttered in a voice loud enough to make people on the street turn and stare, it meant that unless I wanted to be physically abused, I had no recourse but to give in and allow myself to be pushed through the turnstile.

But I would not forgive her. To walk out of a brisk autumn day into a Klein's fall sale was an unimaginably perverse act even for an adult. Greeted by blasts of hot air whooshing up through the floor grates between the outer and inner doors, we passed into a harshly lit wasteland of pipe racks and dump bins hung and piled with every conceivable kind of garment for every gender, age and shape, from infants and toddlers to boys, young misses, juniors, men and women. And every single one of these garments seemed to be undergoing the imperial scrutiny of the released population of an insane asylum. Some sort of frenzied mass rite was taking place, the Flinging of the Textiles. As if in a state of hypnosis, my mother immediately joined in while I held on to her, for my life. Wriggling and elbowing her way through communicants three and four deep around a counter of sweaters, say, or scarves, she immediately began tossing them up in the air, just as everyone else was, altogether creating a kind of fountain of rising and falling colors. She did this for a while and, shaking her head to show her dissatisfaction, fought her way outward into the great flow of wandering shoppers passing across the ancient wooden floors of the place like a tumultuous migration of buffalo, hoofbeats thundering on the plain, only to find another counter to stop at and press her way toward so as to go through the same fountaining behavior all over again. Little by little as we made our way on this endless pilgrimage I slowly peeled off my clothing, like a foreign legionnaire stumbling under the merciless heat of the sun over dune after dune, my hat first, then my mackinaw, then my sweater. I held on to these items in some attempt to keep from losing them, but it was a law of life at S. Klein's that even as you were establishing loyalties to new items of apparel your old ones tried to flee from you in a kind of poltergeist of moral rebuke. Time after time I would find the cap or the sweater gone, or the jacket slipping away from me. I'd have to buck the current to find my hat under someone's foot— dangerous work: if I slipped and fell it was sudden death, there was no question about that. Or I'd find the sweater in the hands of some *other* mother looking around with a compassionate and pitying expression on her face for the owner; and then I'd have to *thank* her and suffer my mother's smiling theatrical scolding for the sake of this woman. And on we'd pass, driven like ceremonial dancers to the *plink plink* of those odd bells peculiar to department stores and to hortatory shoppers' advisories delivered like sermons over the public address systems. Stock clerks in grey jackets pushed and spun wheeled bins of clothing through the crowd with brutal élan, like the drivers of Dodgems in an amusement park. Long lines of people wound through corridors and around counters well out of sight of the cashier posts to which, arms filled with piles of ticketed clothes, they had committed themselves. And mothers were telling children to stand still and children were hanging on to their mothers' skirts and coats, and they were whining and dribbling snot from their noses, and staring at one another in slack-mouthed fascination. And people were shouting, and the occasional clerks who could be seen were denying customers whatever satisfaction they sought, and my mind was being obliterated by this population, everyone desiring in competition what we desired; I felt they were multiples of us, we had disintegrated into thousands of restless constantly moving people, a fun-house mirror of enraged and threadbare gentility, and these masses were sending up a great planetary music, harsh and dissonant like a sea wind, and it was blowing me away, eroding me, chunks of myself were flying off, soon I would be no more than a grain of sand. And then that would be swept up.

But my mother strode on. The more the scene whirled around us like a roaring inferno of human pretensions, the more steadfast she became, taking this and that, discarding one thing for another, and so gradually accumulating what she had come for. And somehow she would find some haven, some alcove, perhaps on a higher floor, where the population was thinned out and the atmosphere was quieter; and we would encamp and examine what we had. Her technique was to take from the racks several things of each kind—several shirts or coats or pairs of knickers or sweaters—and try them all on me to see which were best. So now I endured the Try-On. "Try this," she would say, and a pullover would come down over my head. "No, it's too small, try the size larger," and off would come the pullover and down come another. My role in this rite was to lift my arms on command or lower them, to endure having my head swaddled for terrifying moments in a sweater until she had found the neck hole and brought me back into light. I would have to turn around and have things held up to my back, and turn back around and have them held up to my front, or, most hideously of all, repair to some grim cubicle and behind a flimsy curtain that anyone might open, take off my pants and try on new ones. There is a kind of exhaustion that comes over you in the Try-On that is like no other. It is as if having been turned into a hothouse vegetable you have now gone into vegetable decline, or wilt. "Stand up straight, Edgar, how can I tell if something is right if you slump this way." But at this point of the ordeal it was not resistance I was offering, or intransigence, or any willfulness of any kind, because I had none; I was without volition, like a marionette whose strings are slack.

Somehow we would go through everything and come up with the selection. And then would come the Standing on Line, and lo, I was one of those miserable little children hanging on to their mothers and staring at the other beings their own size, or conspicuously ignoring them, as we moved with agonizing slowness to the register. Except that now I was sound and whole again, my mother's triumph in her purchases having reestablished in my soul the conviction that we were, after all, special human beings in all this mob, with our own secrets and superiorities. ''This sweater is a wonderful buy, and it's just the right size, you'll be able to wear it with the sleeves turned up, and grow into it and wear it some more. And you'll like the knickers. They're made of the finest wool, I think they made a mistake and underpriced them, they were the only ones in the whole store. Isn't it lucky they fit? Maybe I'll take it in a bit at the waist and then let it out when it needs it.'' And so on. Without doubt, she had done it again, found in this emporium of rags and seconds, and badly made and cheap clothing, just those few things that were worth buying.

And we would get out of there and find a luncheonette or a Nedick's and I would have a grilled cheese sandwich and an orange drink, and she would have a cup of chicken noodle soup; and I'd be miraculously restored, my eye keen for New York and its excitements, which usually came to a point as a new *Flash Gordon Big Little Book* at the newsstand. We took the Lexington Avenue IRT home, a subway in Manhattan that ascended into the light just south of Yankee Stadium in the Bronx, and then rocketed along northward on elevated tracks over Jerome Avenue. I sat next to her in this train, whose seats ran under the windows all the way down the side of the car, and leaned against her, my tormentor and redeemer, as she sat in her stolid thought with her ankles crossed and the Klein's bags gathered on her lap. I drew up my knees and read of the latest depredations of the wily Oriental despot Ming the Merciless, ruler of the planet Mongo, and of Flash Gordon's tough, resourceful, but sportsmanlike response. I liked Flash, and Dale, his girlfriend. They flew about the heavens in rocket ships without wearing much of anything, but they never caught cold.

FOURTEEN

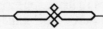

I suppose I was at this time in the second grade. I was becoming more aware of my mother's unhappiness, in part because it was more explicit. Before going to work one morning my father put in her hand two fifty-cent pieces. He left and she sat down at the kitchen table. "With this," she said, indicating the coins, "I am expected to maintain a family, keep a house running, put food on the table." She was a strong woman but she wept easily. I patted her. She washed clothes using a washboard angled into the laundry sink in the kitchen. Her arms went up and down in the suds. "I used to have the most wonderful maid," she told me. "When you were an infant. A woman from Jamaica, Carrie was her name. She adored you, took you out in your new carriage and would shoo anyone away who got too close. Carrie guarded you as if you were the Prince of Wales."

Coming home from school, now I often smelled cigarette smoke, which told me my mother's friend Mae was visiting. Mae worked as a bookkeeper part time, in the mornings. It was the best work she could find. She lived with her old mother and father around the corner and got out of the house in the afternoon by visiting her friend my mother. But my mother had also come to rely on Mae, who listened to her concerns, injecting a question here or a wry comment there. Mae sat leaning forward, with her legs crossed and her hand with the cigarette up in the air. She was totally attentive and sympathetic. I liked the sound her stockings made when she crossed her legs. She understood that I found her attractive and would pinch my cheek, but not so that it hurt, or rub her hand in a circle on my back. One evening she was wearing a silk see-through blouse with a lace bow at the collar. Her shoulders and arms were visible and also her brassiere. "What are you looking at, Buster?" she said with a laugh.

I heard a lot when my mother talked to her friend Mae. "I have exactly three dresses that I wash and iron and wash and iron," my mother said. "And I will go on washing and ironing them until there's nothing left. I haven't bought a stitch of clothing in years. And he plays cards. He knows we need every penny and he plays cards." Mae shook her head. My mother wondered where the rent was coming from. She was jealous of her mother-in-law and her sisters-in-law. "Whenever he has a spare moment he's with them," she said. "And they're always asking him to do things for them, as if he had no responsibilities of his own. They like things wholesale. Does Frances, who lives in Pelham Manor in a beautiful home and sends her sons to Harvard, need things wholesale?"

I remember hearing my mother say something that I felt like a sudden weight in the chest: "He keeps the store open till nine—all right, he may have to—but what does he do then? He comes home at one, two in the morning. Where has he been? What has he been doing! I'm struggling here all by myself, trying to keep things going. . . . And when he *is* home he runs to Mama." She had stood now, I was in the hall just outside the doorway to the kitchen. She paced back and forth, "I'm a good wife," she said. "I can make do with nothing. I've got a good mind. I know what's going on in the world. I know music. I've kept my figure. I don't think I'm all that bad a person to be with." Her voice broke and she was crying, which brought me forward into the doorway. My mother's back was turned to me and she had lifted the corner of her apron and was dabbing her eyes. Mae, seeing me, said with a wink, "Well, that's a pretty kettle of fish."

On a Saturday my mother decided that we would go downtown and visit my father in his store. "And we'll get him to take us to the Automat for lunch," she said. She put on her blue hat, a sort of Robin Hood model, which she set on her head at an angle and checked in the mirror. "Do you think it looks smart?" she asked me. I said it did, it looked very smart. She was wearing her grey wool dress with a belt and shoes that she called pumps. She tucked her purse under her arm and we were off. We were taking the Sixth Avenue subway. Our station was at 174th Street, where it tunneled under the Concourse. We walked past my school and turned left and went along past the shoemaker, the Daitch Dairy, the bakery. Mr. Rosoff was in the window of his drugstore and waved to us and smiled. Ahead was the dark enormous arch of the Grand Concourse overpass. The Sixth Avenue line ran north and south under the Concourse, and so from the 174th Street tunnel we actually had to walk up to get to the subway platform.

At my urging we sat in the first car so I could stand at the window at the front end of the car right next to the motorman's cab. The train clattered through the black tunnel. The stanchions flashed by. The train headlamps cast light on the rails ahead that looked to me like two continuously shooting stars. Up ahead the next station came into view as a box of light. Closer and closer it came and suddenly the white tiles of the new station blazed forth, everything was bathed in brilliance, and we were grinding to a halt but still whizzing past the people waiting on the lighted platform. The engineer knew where to stop according to the number of cars in the train. In Manhattan at 125th Street, we became an express all the way down to Fifty-ninth. This was the best part of the trip, passing the lighted stations from the middle track, the lights rippling by, the train going so fast it rocked from side to side, banging against its own wheel carriages.

"Hello, young man," my father said when we walked into the store. Several customers were at the racks of sheet music, two were talking to Uncle Willy in the back. Lester waved at my mother. He was selling someone a radio. My father was unpacking a carton of ukuleles behind the counter near the front door. "We're having a run on these," he said. I sat down behind the counter to try one for myself. They were not serious instruments, I knew, because they were sold up here rather than in the back, where the horns and banjos and drums were. I asked my father where Donald was, because on Saturdays Donald worked at the store.

"He's out on a delivery," my father said.

My mother said to my father we were hoping he would take us to lunch. "That is entirely possible," he said. He was waiting for some calls. There was a man at Carnegie Hall he might have to meet. "Wait awhile and we'll see," he said. He did not like to be pinned down. He answered the phone and went to the back to check on some stock. Up and down the walls behind the counter were rows and rows of record albums, with dark green spines and gilt lettering, thick, heavy albums of operas, symphonies, which I hesitated to withdraw because I didn't want to break anything. Lester had sold a small radio. He saw the customer off and came to the cash register and counted several bills carefully; then he rang open the register and put all the bills inside. Then he removed a bill and put it in his pocket and closed the register. He found my mother looking at him and smiled. He adjusted his tie and patted his hair. Clearly he knew he was handsome. He took his hat from a hook behind the counter. "Tell Dave I had to go out. I'll be back in a while."

My mother had been reading some sheet music. "Did you see what Lester did?" she said to me. I had not known how to tune the ukulele properly, I could not peg the strings taut. Other people came into the store. My father moved around constantly, he was on the go. Every time the door opened the street noise flowed in as if cars and buses and thousands of pedestrians were about to come into the store. As suddenly as it had started, the sound stopped. I felt safe behind the counter. "I'm hungry," I said to my mother.

"We're waiting for your father," she said. This was a very familiar situation. He had said neither yes nor no.

When my mother spoke up he said, "You run ahead and get a table and I'll be there shortly."

"While we cool our heels?" my mother said. "Not this time." We sat and waited. Somehow my father needed pressure applied. He could not be counted upon except when pressured.

Finally, at a quiet moment, Uncle Willy said to my father, "For God's sake, Dave, I'm here and Lester will be back in a few minutes. Take your family to lunch."

The Automat was on Forty-second Street, a great glittering high-ceilinged hall with murals on the walls and rows and rows of tables. I dropped three nickels in a slot, I worked the little knob next to the glass door, and the sliced cheese and baloney sandwich on white bread was mine. One nickel got me a turn of the chocolate milk lever. This was quite fine. My parents had soup and bread and coffee. Strange people sat all about. Some of them peered at us: a little old woman with odd bumps on her face, wild red hair and a crocheted hat, and several men with unpressed clothes and stubble on their chins. The lady in the change-making booth rang the nickels on the marble counter. The busboys slapped the trays together. Because there were three of us, we thought we'd have a table to ourselves, but it was crowded and a man sat down at the fourth chair and ate his lunch from his tray. He wore his homburg tilted back on his head, he had on a dark shiny suit with cigarette ash rubbed into the lapels, his shirt collar was creased and dirty. All hunched over, he ate spaghetti and sucked in the strands like Charlie Chaplin, with little flooping noises.

My father seemed oblivious to all of this, but my mother stopped eating and dabbed her mouth with a napkin and pushed her chair back and sat with her purse in her lap, ready to go. She looked at the murals on the walls. She asked my father where Donald had gone on his delivery to be away so long. He said Donald had gone to Brooklyn.

"He agreed to do that?" my mother said.

My father laughed. "We gave him a choice. Did he want to go to Brooklyn or New Jersey. He chose Brooklyn." My mother's eyes narrowed. "Under the circumstances," my father said, "he thought he was getting a good deal." He looked at me: "Everything is relative," he said.

My father decided he wanted dessert. "How about some fresh fruit salad," he said. "No thank you," my mother said.

I went with him to the food counter. "They have red Jell-O, your favorite," he said. I didn't want to disappoint him because I knew the Jell-O was hard, it was cut in cubes; I liked it as it was made at home and I was able to spoon it up while it was still shimmery and easily liquefied between the teeth. That was the way I liked my desserts. I liked to take a Dixie Cup and stir the ice cream around until it was soup and drink it off. My mother tapped her fingers on the table. The old man had left. She had put her tray on another table. She said, "I saw Lester take money from the register."

"That couldn't be," my father said.

"But I'm telling you he did."

"If he did, he'll put it back," my father said.

"No wonder the store isn't making a dime, if one of the partners skims the cash register," my mother said. "I've seen consoles disappear off the floor too. You won't listen to me. The man is a thief."

"Rose," my father said. "That's why I don't like to have you in the store. You're a suspicious person, you're always thinking the worst of people. You know nothing about business, why don't you just let me take care of it?"

"I know more about business than you do," my mother said.

She was very unhappy now. Icy, furious. Right in front of my eyes the day had turned bad. I knew it would be worse when my father got home. Then the true argument with the shouting and the name-calling would begin. I thought now I had probably realized everything would go this way before we ever set out the door. I was not surprised. In my mind I had traded a good subway ride for the desolate afternoon ahead, which now commenced, my mother taking my hand and walking out, leaving my father smoking a cigarette at the table. In the swinging door I went around twice while she waited outside. I saw my father still sitting in the Automat. He smiled and gave a sad little wave.

FIFTEEN

The next day my mother refused to come on the visit to Grandma and Grandpa. Donald chose to exercise his right not to go to family things if he didn't want to, so I was the only one to accompany my father. I felt guilty doing this because it was far more fun than staying home with my glowering silent mother. She would listen to the New York Philharmonic broadcast and read and sew. That was hardly festive.

Eastburn Avenue was empty as it tended to be on Sundays once past the lunch hour. In the morning there was always a big softball game in the schoolyard, but when it was over, the whole neighborhood grew quiet. My friends had to go visit their relatives too, or stay upstairs to receive relatives visiting them. To journey up the broad Concourse with my father was to be somehow in the proper rhythm of the day, like everyone else. He cheered up, too, outside the house. He loved to be going somewhere. He insisted we get off the bus two stops early to get a walk in. He walked with a jaunty stride. He claimed a brisk pace was the only way to get anywhere and was, besides, less tiring than walking slowly. I struggled to keep up, half running when I fell behind. "Throw your shoulders back," he said. "Breathe in. Hold your head up. That's the way. Look the world in the eye!" I understood this as a spiritual instruction. But I couldn't have understood it as a self-urging, which I see it now to have been—in that way of the parent who expresses for the child in imperatives the prayers he makes for himself. From the same religion of health and hygiene, he insisted that I turn the water all cold at the end of my showers; I was still working on that, practicing by putting my head under the cold water first, then my shoulders, and so on. But I hadn't got much beyond a few seconds. He had shown me too how to rub myself down with a towel afterward, using it on my back the way a shoeshine man used his strip of cloth to buff the shoes. "Rub hard," he had said. "Bring the blood to the skin."

Immediately, when we arrived, my grandmother said, "So where's Rose?" Without embarrassment my father said she was not feeling well.

Clearly my grandmother understood the situation. She shook her head. My benign grandfather was sitting in his chair by the radio. We held our hands out palm to palm and he said, "You have grown since the last time." Grandma bustled about setting out the tea things. My father had stopped at the Sutter bakery near Fordham Road. The babka he had bought was the centerpiece, a plump cinnamon loaf shaped like a baker's hat.

We stayed late into the afternoon, it was always this way with my father—to arrive late, and to stay late. The light faded, I grew bored. My grandfather smoked his Regent ovals and my grandmother, without my mother to contend with, was very happy, relaxed, freely prying into the finances of my family. She offered my father advice on running the store. My father adored her, calling her *"Mamaleh,"* which means little mother. Then he and my grandfather talked about the war in Spain. They agreed it was tragic that President Roosevelt was not helping the Spanish government fight the Fascists. My father grew heated. "Hitler sends dive-bombers, Mussolini sends tanks. I have to wonder, Pop. In the South there is still a poll tax. Negroes are lynched. Who is Roosevelt, anyway? What do we *think* he is?"

My grandfather was more stoic: "You cannot expect of a President that he should not be a politician," he said. "Even our revered Roosevelt."

Now it was late enough to hear *The Shadow*, on the radio. The Shadow was Lamont Cranston, a wealthy man-about-town, who possessed the power to cloud men's minds and become invisible. By this means he fought crime. "Who knows what evil lurks in the hearts of men?" he said in his invisible voice at the beginning of every program. "The Shadow knows." And then he laughed a sniggling nasal laugh that made *him* sound evil. That had always slightly bothered me. When the Shadow went into his invisible mode, you could tell because his voice sounded as if it were coming through a telephone; this made sense because you couldn't see people in real life either when they were talking to you on the telephone. But there was something stunted about the Shadow's adventures. They were no contest. Typically, in a Shadow story, it would take Lamont Cranston a while to realize he was faced with a severe enough crisis to change into the Shadow. Sometimes it would happen that his girlfriend Margo was threatened. The criminals were always stupid and talked either with foreign accents or in rough gravelly voices with the diction of the Dead End Kids. They would have guns and shoot wildly, but to no avail. The Shadow would laugh his sniggling laugh and tell them they had missed. Actually I knew that with a tommy gun a smart crook could hold his finger down on the trigger and spin around in a 360-degree circle spraying bullets up and down and so have a fair chance of hitting the Shadow whether he was invisible or not, and no matter how far he threw his voice. His invisible blood would run. But they never thought of that.

Listening to programs, you saw them in your mind. From the sound effects you were able to imagine what things looked like and tell from the sound of its engine if a car was sleek and streamlined, or big like a taxi with lots of leg room and a running board. I thought of Margo, Lamont Cranston's friend, as looking like my mother's friend Mae but without her glasses, and without Mae's little jokes. Margo was an attractive woman, but lacking in humor. Cranston himself I thought a little slow-moving to take as long as he did to go into action; he was fairly sedentary, as compared, say, with the Green Hornet, who could probably lick him in a fight if they went at it visibly. I didn't think of the Shadow as being able to jump rooftops or climb ropes or run very fast. On the other hand, why should he have to? Also, I wondered about his restraint when he could become invisible anytime he chose. I wondered if he ever took advantage of women, as I surely would. Did he ever watch Margo Lane go to the bathroom? I knew that if I had the power to be invisible I would go into the girls' bathroom at P.S. 70 and watch them pulling their drawers down. I would watch women take their clothes off in their homes and they wouldn't even know I was there. I wouldn't make the mistake of speaking up or making a sound, they would never even know I had been there. But I would forever after know what they looked like. The thought of having this power made my ears hot. Yes, I would spy on naked girls but I would also do good. I would invisibly board a ship, or, better still, a China Clipper and I would fly to Germany and find out where Adolf Hitler lived. I would in absolute safety, with no chance of being caught, go to Hitler's palace, or whatever it was, and kill him. Then I would kill all of his generals and ministers. The Germans would be going crazy trying to find the invisible avenger. I would whisper in their ears to be good and kind, and they would thereafter be thinking God had been speaking. The Shadow had no imagination. He neither looked at naked women nor thought of ridding the world of dictators like Hitler or Mussolini. If his program hadn't been on a Sunday afternoon, I would probably not have listened to it.

Hitler was on my mind a lot lately. I had heard his voice on a radio broadcast, he shouted in German, which I heard as a language full of spitting and gulping and galumphing, almost as if the words were broken in the teeth; it sounded as if he were shattering glass in his mouth, as if he breathed fire and made the air explode in front of his face. He would say something and you'd hear his fist pounding the speaker's platform and then a great roar go up from the crowd, like some shrieking wind, and then it would begin to pulsate and radio static would crack through it, and the announcer, speaking calmly in English, would describe what was going on at this rally, the way everyone's right arm extended straight in the air as the crowd chanted and did this salute taken from ancient Rome, arms shooting up and big red-and-black Nazi flags with swastikas fluttering everywhere.

I tried that salute in front of the mirror in my room, throwing my arm forward with the elbow stiff, and trying at the same time to click my heels. Donald marched around my room holding a small black comb under his nose like Hitler's moustache and chanting German gibberish. He brushed his hair down over his forehead. It was funny. It was easy to imitate Hitler. Actually, when I had first seen his picture in a magazine I had confused him with Charlie Chaplin. Everyone seemed to notice the resemblance, they both wore these little black moustaches, and had black hair and heavy eyebrows. Charlie Chaplin himself had noticed the resemblance and Donald told me Charlie was making a movie about Hitler that was going to be really great because Charlie hated Hitler. I resolved to see that movie when it came out.

I found it disturbing, however, that they resembled each other. I loved Charlie Chaplin. We had the same taste in women, like the blind flower girl, whom we both found very beautiful and kind. He had helped her, as I would have. He was a wonderful little guy, he never got as mad at other people as they did at him, even when they were fighting, although he was often hurt by them. He just picked himself up and swung and ran. In *Modern Times* big voices telling him what to do came from speakers in this shining modern factory, but he himself, Charlie, never spoke, no matter how bad things got, he never made a sound: like the time he went after the loose nut on the assembly line and got picked up by the moving machinery and was sent winding through the gears. When he had his lunch a machine wiped his mouth for him. It seemed to me an unfortunate coincidence that he and Hitler looked alike. My father had a moustache too, they all three had moustaches. I dreamed one night my father sat with Charlie on one knee and Hitler on the other; he held on to them by the backs of their necks as if they were ventriloquist dummies, and made their mouths clack open and shut and held out each of them to me in turn, one with his floppy little legs dangling in baggy trousers and a cutaway coat, the other in a brown Army uniform with leather boots. And then my father laughed.

DONALD

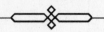

Sure, I remember when we moved to Eastburn Avenue. I pushed you there in your carriage. It was great moving to a larger place. I had my own room. I was eight, a big fellow. The responsible older brother.

It's only natural that we remember things differently. I had Mom and Dad to myself for all those years before you joined us. We were prosperous. Before he got into the retail end of things Dad was in the sound box business. In those days record players, Victrolas, had spring motors, you cranked them up like you cranked cars, and the critical element was the sound box at the end of the tone arm. It was a metal cylinder, about an inch wide, three inches in diameter, with a convex grille face, and inside was a diaphragm that vibrated. You stuck a steel needle into a socket on the rim, and tightened it with a fixed screw, and put the needle on the record and that was how you got sound. Dad ran the business from an office in the Flatiron Building.

The day Lindbergh was welcomed up Fifth Avenue we saw it from the office window. I was very young, maybe four, and I stood on the windowsill and saw Lindbergh in an open car, all the confetti falling, the crowd going wild. I was so excited I leaned too far out and almost lost my balance. Dad had to pull me back in.

You say he didn't use force. Maybe he'd mellowed a bit by the time you came along. With me he was very strict and didn't hesitate to haul off when he felt it was necessary. My first day of school I refused to go. No amount of cajoling, imploring or bribing by Mom could budge me. Dad lost his temper. He picked me up and carried me to school under his arm. I'll never forget it. He carried me right up the steps and down the hall, and opened the door to my classroom and dumped me on the floor, in front of everyone.

There was another time, in Rockaway. You and I were staying with Grandma and Grandpa. They had a bungalow for the summer. The folks shipped us out there to get us out of the heat, but they didn't come themselves, Dad had to work and Mom couldn't leave her mother. So you and I were on our own with the old people. We ran around all day on the beach and played in the penny arcades, and in that time I don't think either of us bathed. So on the second weekend the folks came out to see us. Mom will tell you the story. She saw these two children walking toward her in the street, I was holding your hand, and your pants drooped and my socks were around my ankles, and our faces were dirty, she thought at first we were a pair of street urchins, she didn't realize she was looking at her own sons. She was furious that Grandma, with her vaunted cleanliness, had let things get so out of hand. There was a big argument. Dad asked me to go into the bathroom and have a shower. I refused. He was mad, everyone was mad, he picked me up just as he had my first day in school, and turned on the shower and threw me in, clothes and all.

He was a terrific athlete. He spent a lot of time with me, teaching me to play tennis, or to skate or swim. He urged me to excel. Always I was made to know what his expectations were for me. I think this explains somewhat why we had a difficult time with each other in later years. After you came along it was made clear to me that I was to help with your upbringing, and put in time with you as he had with me. And so I did. A lot of the things I taught you he had taught me. One passed things on. One worked for the family. You know that picture of Dad and me walking together stride for stride on Sixth Avenue on some business matter— where is that picture, do you have it?—I was all of thirteen at the time. I started working for him very young. Take a look at that picture when you have the chance. I have on a suit and tie just like his, but I'm wearing knickers. It's a tinted photograph, our faces are washed in this rosy color, Dad has a cigar in his mouth, he has a packet of business papers under his arm, his shoulders are back, he looks happy, we both look happy, healthy, energetic, full of beans, and the street photographer picked up on this father and son, and snapped the picture and sold it to us.

Dad liked to patronize street people. You would be walking along with him and he'd suddenly veer over to a pushcart, or stop to buy a pamphlet from someone. He did that as a matter of principle. He idealized the little man. He had a political consciousness. He rode the train to Boston for a rally for Sacco and Vanzetti. He wanted to take me but Mom wouldn't let him. The case obsessed him. He brought home Upton Sinclair's novel about it—*Boston*—it was in two volumes. He was very much a man of his time. He devoured the papers. Maybe everyone was more radical in those days. Nowadays when people protest something, they're looked on as oddities. But, for instance, Dad was talking about Hitler very early. He was onto him. That doesn't sound so unusual now, but you'd be surprised how little was known about Hitler, it took the establishment in America a long time to understand what was going on. Dad was an antifascist. He was a leftist, like our grandpa, but more of a fighter. In the big strikes—steel, coal, automobile—he was on the side of the unions. He didn't believe in minding his own business, his brain was always working. You could be sure he'd come up with another slant on things. Like when King Edward of England abdicated the throne to marry his girlfriend Wally Simpson. Well, Mom loved that story. You know, a king giving up his throne for love. It was in all the papers and magazines, the King's abdication speech was on the radio, carried shortwave from London. Everyone loved that story. But not Dad. He got angry because Mom took it so seriously. "Don't you realize," he said, "the idea of a king in the twentieth century is ridiculous? The English king is a fossil. Like all of them in Europe now, a bunch of useless dimwits who strut around and indulge themselves at public expense. This romantic king of yours lives on the tax revenues taken from working people. I can see why the upper classes of England would find him useful, but why the American press treats this as serious news, and you fall for it, is another matter." Mom was quite miffed. "Don't you ever relax about anything?" she asked him. "I'm not the intellectual you are—all right?" They disagreed about politics as about most things.

I don't know much about Dad's life as a boy. I know he was born on the Lower East Side. Grandma and Grandpa were both from the Minsk district, they emigrated in the 1880's, I know that. They were young and married here. But where they lived, where Dad went to school, you would have to ask Aunt Frances, she would know. Dad was almost thirty when he got married. He'd already missed out on a couple of major opportunities. One was when he was training to be an ensign in the First World War. He was stationed at Webb's Naval Institute on the Harlem River. He loved the water, he used to tell me how he swam in the East River as a kid. He loved ships. He was desperate to go to sea, but the war ended before he got his commission. So that had to be a great disappointment. And then you know the story about *The Perils of Pauline*. He was a handsome fellow, and they were casting for this series, and came into the bank where he worked as a teller. I don't know, he must have been twenty-one, twenty-two at the time. And this man came into the bank who was directing the movie, I don't remember his name, but as I heard it he had a beret and a pince-nez and wore riding boots. And he looked at Dad and asked him to take a screen test. He wanted him for the male lead. Dad refused. I don't know why. Maybe he thought he had a surer thing in banking. Who knows, he might have become a big actor in the silents or he might not. But the point is, it was unlike him to back away from a challenge. He liked to gamble, take risks, he liked what was new and different. No one had a record store to match Hippodrome Music. Dad stocked black singers from down South, race records, as they were called, blues bands, ethnic music, jazz, he was really informed and it didn't matter to him that some of these things were commercially risky. One day I came back from a delivery and he motioned to me and took me into the booth and put on a record. "Listen to this," he said. "It's something new." And it was, a wonderful bouncy music, with a great clarinet solo that made you want to dance. It was Benny Goodman's first record. "Isn't that fine?" Dad said. "It's called swing."

SIXTEEN

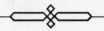

Donald now had materials from his Townsend Harris High School courses that were beyond my understanding: slide rules, calipers, T squares. He brought home mechanical drawings that he had done and gotten good marks for, little 95's and 90's in red ink at the top corner of each drawing. They were like blueprints and showed cylinders and cones, and machine parts in three dimensions, each line measured by another that indicated its length. He explained the concept of scale to me. He knew all this and was confident with it. He had special fountain pens for drawing. All I had was one fountain pen, which I was not even supposed to use in school. But I liked to open my bottle of Waterman's blue-black ink and fill my pen by opening the little .spring clip on the side and closing it slowly. You could hear the ink being sucked up. There was a thin rubber tube inside the pen that was attached to the point—that's what filled up. I borrowed his sticks of charcoal to draw with. He was generous. But if I was careless with something of his, misplacing it, or damaging it, he acted as if I had committed a great crime. Sometimes it wasn't worth the care I had to take when I borrowed something, so I didn't.

I had to acknowledge the fact that my brother was changing. He spent less time with me. High school took up a lot of his time, and then on Saturday he had his job with my father. I was left more and more on my own.

There was a candy store near Rosoff's on 174th Street—not the one I frequented, but one where the older boys gathered to horse around and talk about girls. Sometimes girls gathered there too. My brother and his friends Harold and Bernie and Irwin attached themselves to this society, sometimes stopping there in the afternoons after they got off the train. Gambling went on, boys pitching pennies against the wall or matching nickels. Inside they sold policy, a word familiar to me, though I didn't know what it meant. My brother did not talk about these things. When my mother found out why he was coming home late from school, she was alarmed. She had strong opinions about Donald's friends and never failed to deliver them. "So now they've turned into sidewalk cowboys," she said. "I don't wonder. You hang around that store and you'll end up with them in the criminal class," she said.

Donald was hurt by her remarks but did not change his ways. His green eyes showed defiance. I didn't stop to think, nor did my mother, what an estimable life Donald was leading—he was doing well in school, knocking out good grades, he worked all day Saturday, and he was studying music. Yet from my mother's vivid testimony I imagined him going to jail. I circumspectly went to see the infamous store one afternoon, being careful to do my surveillance from across the street, from the vantage point of the Morton bakery.

I saw my brother and his friends in a crowd of older boys and girls. The crowd moved about constantly. They leaned against the newsstand in front of the candy store, or sat on the fender of a car parked nearby. One boy grabbed a girl from behind and wrestled with her and put his arms around her and she screamed and laughed too. Two boys were having a boxing match but without really hitting each other. I saw Donald talking to a blond girl while ostentatiously smoking a cigarette. At that moment, for some reason, his eye caught sight of me, just a flickering glance. But even across the street I knew from the look I got that I was never to tell on him or my life would be over.

So all of this made me thoughtful. I could see my brother changing, but in no way detected any difference in myself. I didn't look taller in the mirror, I didn't feel older or anything like that. Meanwhile a thin moustache appeared above Donald's upper lip. His voice became deeper. He was moody, and his passion for music increased. He began to collect records in lieu of wages from my father. He practiced the piano now every day and without being asked. He was a better pianist, there were not those agonizing delays I remembered from the old days when in the middle of a piece all life would stop while we waited for Donald to find the keys for the next chord. When he was through practicing his lesson, he took out his music copybook in which he'd written out swing tunes borrowed from my father's stock of sheet music, and he played those. Uncle Willy had moved out of our house after Grandma died; he had taken a small apartment on the West Side of Manhattan not far from Hippodrome Music. So Donald moved back into his old room and hung Uncle Willy's banner on the wall, the purple and gold of BILLY WYNNE AND HIS ORCHESTRA taking on some suggestion of defiance or irrepressible intent, as if Donald were saying to the world that it had better get ready for him.

One New Year's Eve my parents arranged to go out and there was a big family fight because Donald no longer wanted to stay with me as he had on past New Year's Eves. He wanted to go to a party with his friends. My father wore his tuxedo this particular night, and my mother a long pale blue dress with lacy sleeves. Their eyes were alight with excitement and I felt gloomy and neglected watching them prepare themselves. My father tied a black satiny cummerbund around his waist. He let my mother carry on the argument with Donald. I enjoyed the special buttons for his shirt front and cuffs, which he showed me how to operate. But this was not compensation enough for their leaving, and putting me in the charge of my resentful brother with a moustache. "All right," Donald shouted as they were heading for the door, "but I warn you, this is it. I swear I will never, never stay home again on New Year's Eve." My mother in her long pale blue dress and her hair newly marcelled, her lips painted red, a little beaded bag in her hands, soothed Donald and with uncharacteristic gentleness agreed that this would be the last New Year's he would be called upon to take care of his little brother.

Although I would have enjoyed a game of war, or battleship, I diplomatically chose to stay in my room and play by myself. I did leave my door open to hear what I could hear. Donald was on the phone in the front hall a good deal of the time. Then he turned on the console radio in the living room to listen to the dance music being broadcast from some hotel downtown. I secretly wanted to stay up to see in the New Year but knew better than to ask. Instead I got into my pajamas and pretended to go to bed. I had my own windup clock. It had a radium dial. I could see it in the dark. At midnight I tiptoed down the hall to the living room and I found Donald asleep on the sofa in front of the radio, which was still playing. The broadcast was from Times Square. Crowds cheered, horns blew, and the announcer interviewed people who shouted their greetings into the microphone. It was 1937. I looked out the window. Eastburn Avenue was dark. I hoped my parents would be home soon. Happy New Year, I said to myself, and went back to bed.

As WINTER MOVED INTO SPRING I BEGAN TO HEAR FROM THE FRONT PARLOR, IN THE late afternoons, not only Donald's swing piano but the honks and squeaks of Seymour Roth's saxophone, and the earsplitting blasts of Harold Epstein's trumpet. There was also a snare drummer, Irwin. In the kitchen my mother said, "If those boys had conspired to drive me crazy, they couldn't be doing a better job of it." The band met not only after school but on Sunday afternoons. My mother wanted to know why Harold's mother or Seymour's couldn't sacrifice themselves and their households for at least one day a week. Donald said, "We're the only ones who have a piano," and that was that. At night he listened to *Make Believe Ballroom* on the radio, where the announcer, Martin Block, played his records while pretending to be broadcasting from an actual bandstand. Of course, it was not an illusion too emphatically insisted upon. It was not, for example, as scrupulous in its representations as the broadcast baseball games in which the announcer in the studio, using sound effects of the bat cracking and the crowd roaring, pretended to be at the ballpark. Martin Block kept lists of the most popular songs of the week, and Donald wrote down the titles and made a note to get them copied.

Finally I learned what was going on. Donald and Seymour, the saxophone player, had put their first names together and invented a fictitious bandleader, Don Seymour. Don Seymour's band was known as the Musical Cavaliers, and they were preparing to audition for a summer job at a resort hotel in the Catskills, the Paramount. They had not yet decided which of them would pose as Don Seymour if they ever reached the lofty heights of the Paramount Hotel bandstand. They were too busy rehearsing. As day after day I heard them go through their repertoire I learned every song by heart. "Deep Purple" was one: "In the still of the night, once again I hold you tight, Tho' you're gone your love lives on when moonlight beams, And as long as my heart will beat, Lover we'll always meet, here in my Deep Purple Dreams." They played that well, I think, because it was slow. They were better with slow songs. "I Must See Annie Tonight" was one of their rare fast ones, and sometimes they created a double-time effect with it because Irwin's downbeat on the drums was often dissynchronous with Donald's on the piano. It was not uninteresting. And then that peculiar "Stairway to the Stars": "Let's build a Stairway to the Stars, and climb that Stairway to the Stars, with love beside us to fill the night with a song." That part of it was all right, although it was not a terribly appealing idea as I thought about it—a long climb, in fact, in cold black space. But then it went: "Can't we sail away on a little dream and settle high on the crest of a thrill, Let's build a Stairway to the Stars. . . ." and at that point I was always made nervous, just as I was when I read *Alice in Wonderland,* because sailing is what you do on water, not on stair treads, and the crest of a thrill made me think of some sort of jungle bird, the Crested Thrill, so they would all be sailing up these stairs and ending up perched on the head of a bird. But it was "Japanese Sandman" that gave me the worst time, the idea of a sandman who could put you to sleep as he chose had always bothered me, that casting of grains that made your eyelids heavy and robbed you of volition was a magic I didn't like to contemplate. Added to that, the fact that the Sandman was Japanese was especially worrisome. On my bubble gum cards very toothy leering Japanese soldiers in green uniforms were machine-gunning Manchurian civilians. They were leaping over trenches with bayonets affixed to raised rifles. They cast not magic sleep grains but pure red and orange flame from the mouths of flamethrowers.

*   *   *

WITH THE INCLUSION OF A STRING BASS AND ANOTHER SAXOPHONE PLAYER, Frankie, the band had grown to six pieces. On a Sunday afternoon, instead of going with my father and mother to see my grandparents, I was permitted to stay home and hear the Cavaliers rehearse. In a moment of inspiration I ran back to my room and took one of my pick-up sticks and came back and led the band with it. I stood in front of the Cavaliers and conducted. Maybe I could be Don Seymour. The light coming through the parlor windows turned the leaves of the potted snake plants a brilliant green. Donald thumped away happily at the upright, his back to the rest of the band. Next to him was Sid the string bass man, playing with eyes closed in transports of head-shaking self-approval; Sid liked to hum one octave higher than the bass notes, like Slam Stewart, a famous jazz bassist, who was his hero. Next to Sid was Irwin the drummer, now endowed with a snare, a tom-tom, cowbells, and a bass drum resting on its side, which he played with an attached pedal that catapulted a big bulbous hammer up against the drum skin. And sitting side by side in the front row of the band, just like the men of Paul Whiteman's orchestra, were the two saxophonists, Seymour and Frankie, and the trumpet player, Harold. First they played "I Have Eyes to See With," then a rousing rendition of "Bei Mir Bist Du Schoen," which Donald thought was their best number. Standing in front of the band, I waved my baton and tapped my foot. It didn't seem to bother anyone. But then I saw that the new saxophone player, Frankie, seemed not to be exerting himself. There was some hesitancy about him. I watched him closely without being obvious about it. When the moment came in the sheet music to go on to the next page, Seymour and Harold leaned forward simultaneously and turned the pages sitting on their music stands, but Frankie waited a split second before he did the same thing. Then I saw that his fingers did not depress keys on his saxophone, they only touched them. And that most of the time they weren't the same keys Seymour was pressing on *his* saxophone. Frankie was a tall, long-faced boy with sad, deep-set eyes and the shadow of a dark beard on his face. He did not live in the neighborhood. He glanced nervously at me over his saxophone. Clearly I was a danger to him. The others were making their music, and loudly. The Cavaliers were not always exactly on key but had a lot of enthusiasm. I felt the same excitement as when a parade band passed close to me on Memorial Day along the Grand Concourse, that same vault of the heart in the blare of performed music. But I knew the band members were intensely occupied with keeping up with Irwin, the drummer, who tended to go faster and faster with each passing bar, and that none of them was secure enough as a musician to really hear the others. None of them, not even Donald, knew that Frankie was making no sound.

When the number ended, Donald said, "Let's go through it one more time, and try to make the opening attack crisper and to build a little higher for the ending." As the bandleader, he had that responsibility of critique.

I asked to see him, pulling at his arm as he stood in front of them. He shrugged me off and kept talking. I persisted. Finally he said, "What is it, pest!" I pulled him into the living room and closed the parlor doors. "Donald," I said, pulling again on his arm as he looked at me with that frowning wary expression of his. A shock of hair habitually fell over his forehead, his light green eyes were the eyes of an adult, his face had not a bit of fat on it, he was a lean, not very tall, wiry big brother, a good athlete, a brain at high school, a fellow with many plans and responsibilities at age fifteen and a half. But he had hired a musician who couldn't play. He bent over and I whispered in his ear: "Frankie is faking."

He looked at me incredulously and I nodded affirmation of what I had said. "You stay here," he said and went back into the parlor and closed the door after him. I heard them go into "Bei Mir Bist Du Schoen" again, but after a bar or two they stopped. Then I heard my brother's voice. He sounded angry. Soon they were all talking. An argument began. "Shit," I heard Irwin say, and then it was quiet and I smelled cigarette smoke. A few minutes later the parlor door opened, and Frankie came out carrying his saxophone case. His shoulders hunched and he didn't look at me as he passed into the hall and went out the front door.

Nobody felt that I had been, in essence, a tattletale. The hapless Frankie was, first of all, much older than I and therefore not in the same moral universe. In the second place, he was an impostor, a fraud, who stood to gain from his imposture at the expense of the other members of the band. What would it have done to the credibility of their audition had the booker for the Paramount Hotel noticed that one of them couldn't even play? My brother was delighted with me. Everyone was. The story was told within the family and around the neighborhood how the little kid brother had turned out to be more perceptive than the musicians themselves. I was a hero. For once I had proven useful to my older brother, I had done something for him. I could make a fair claim now to be taken seriously. There was also a new awareness in me that size wasn't everything, that wit was a strength in the world, the exercise of one's brain.

Nevertheless a shadow lay on my mind. My mother now wondered why a boy—meaning Frankie—would be so desperate as to pretend to be able to play the saxophone. Did he so badly need a job? Where did this Frankie come from? she wanted to know of my brother. Where did he live? What did his father do? These questions and my doubts were overwhelmed, fortunately, by the news of a successful audition just a few days later: Don Seymour and the Musical Cavaliers had been hired for the following summer. Five dollars a week per man, plus room and board. For this they would also have to do lake duty as lifeguards, in the afternoons.

SEVENTEEN

Happy with my brother's accomplishment I was slow to think of the result—that he would be gone for the whole summer. I would be alone with my parents. Things were changing, and, as usual, in the spring, a season I was beginning to appreciate as the mysterious menacing time of the cycle, I became uneasy. Almost in confirmation of my feeling, we were told that we had to move. Our landlords, the Segals, who lived above us, had sold the house. The people who had bought it, German refugees named Loewenthal, wanted the ground floor for themselves. The Segals had been genial friendly landlords, generous with the heat in winter. The new owners were a dour couple, not gracious at all. My father said they lacked style. There were arguments about painting the upstairs apartment and replacing the antiquated refrigerator with the gas cylinder mounted on top of it, and, after we moved upstairs, about the piano playing and even the noise we made walking across the floor. I didn't like their daughter either, a small, skinny dark-haired child, a spy and a snitch who whispered in her girlfriend's ear as I walked by. On a particularly raw day when my mother asked Smith to put some more coal in the furnace, Mrs. Loewenthal stopped him and told my mother to wear a sweater if she was cold.

My mother declared to me that German Jews, even newly arrived ones, were arrogant and heartless. We were descendants of Eastern Europeans, a more natural, more humane people, who knew what suffering was. "They thought they were Germans," she told me, "and look what's happening to them now. With their snobbish highfalutin ways. You'd think, barely getting out with their skins, they would change."

But the apartment upstairs was clean and light. I looked down at the backyard now from a safe distance, I was above the clothesline strung across to the back fence, and the sheets on washdays flew in my mind like pennants below the king's tower. From the corner of the window of my room in the back I could see over our side yard and through a tantalizing window of an alley to a rhomboid of green grass in Claremont Park. The

354

whole apartment did seem smaller. Because of the front stairs there was
one less room. On the other hand, with Grandma gone and Uncle Willy
moved to Manhattan, the family had shrunk. In some way the new light
in these rooms illuminated for me the degree of our family's struggle. The
Sohmer upright had to be hauled upstairs by piano movers with block and
tackle hanging from the roof; the piano came in through the living room
window. That was exciting, but I saw now the chips in the lacquered
mahogany I hadn't seen before. My parents' bedroom furniture with its
romantic olive color and frieze of rosebuds looked old and scratched.

At P.S. 70 WE WERE NOW DEEMED OF AN AGE TO BE SENT ONCE A WEEK TO THE
below-ground swimming pool, a vast chlorinated cavern of tile, where
first the boys and then the girls were set to swimming if we could, or
taking instruction in waving our arms and holding our breath. The boys'
teacher was old Mr. Bone, the Poseidon of the place. He didn't speak, he
roared. His deep voice bounded over the water in echoes of itself. He was
the school's swimming coach and lord of this underworld, a fat bald man
with steel-rim spectacles who wore a white cotton undershirt stretched
taut over his enormous belly, and white ducks and rubber sandals. He also
had a gimpy leg. But that he was fit we all understood by the size of his
arms, rounder and thicker, even, than my father's. And that he was
dedicated, there was no question—he spent his sunless life down here,
whereas we had to endure the pool and showers only once a week.

The girls were instructed by his associate, Mrs. Fasching, as skinny as
he was fat, with red hair curling from under her bathing cap, and in a
black-skirted swimsuit, which successfully hid her person except for the
freckled legs and arms. It was common knowledge that the girls wore
bathing suits to swim, while we did not. Even during their showers they
wore suits, which seemed unjust. How could you take a real shower while
wearing a bathing suit? Brown soap was available at each position, big
hard cakes of it, and if we were not seen by Mr. Bone to be adequately
scrubbing ourselves, he would warn, in that voice like a whale's call, that
we had better get to it properly or he would come into the shower and
show us how.

That weekly visit to the realm of water tested my courage. I was not
ready to swim and didn't care to shower in public. There was no air to
breathe down there, only a fetid mist that seemed to turn to oil on your
skin. It did no good to tell Mr. Bone you had had a bath the night before,
or that you bathed at home twice a week: under the shower you went.
And it's true, for some children the P.S. 70 shower was the only water
they saw from one week to the next. It was because of those same children we had to endure health checks in the nurse's office, where our

scalps were examined for lice and ringworm. The nurse also turned up the children who were discovered to need eyeglasses. It was my mother I always went to for explanation of the complexities of money and class. "Some children are from families too poor to have their own doctors," she said. "They don't come from good homes and school showers are the only water they see. They are the same children who need to stay in school for lunch because there is no lunch waiting for them at home."

On the other hand, she told me, some of my teachers were getting quite rich. "They've kept their jobs in the middle of the Depression," she said. "They have done quite well on their salaries. Prices have gone down and they can afford things no one else can who hasn't that security. Some of them are buying cars and houses. They've become landlords."

I appreciated this information but found it of no use in dealing with my fear of swimming underground. There was one exercise in which we boys were sent into the pool to hang with our hands on the pool's tiled rim while we let our bodies drift backward and then kicked our feet. Since that didn't involve putting my face underwater I could handle it all right. But we were a string of fifteen or so boys along the edge at intervals of three or four yards, and some of us were inevitably in water that we couldn't stand up in. My friend Arnold was next to me and he lost his grip and went under. I looked for Mr. Bone, but he was down at the end of the line yelling at someone. Arnold came up gasping and went under again and was flailing, so that he was putting himself farther and farther from the edge. He was getting out of reach. His arm came up. Letting go the edge with one hand, I grabbed his arm and pulled him toward me and put his hand on the tile. Arnold came up red and sputtering and spitting water. His eyes were red. We looked at each other, too terrified to acknowledge the seriousness of what had happened. You came up, you went down, you took in water like air, and in a few quiet moments you could die.

THE SCHOOLYARD, ALSO, WAS A REALM OF MYTHIC DIMENSIONS. IT WAS THE SITE of games and ceremonies of enormous meaning. It was an immense yard fenced in chain link. The Eastburn Avenue end was level with the street, but since 173rd Street went uphill, the Weeks Avenue end was a couple of stories below street level. On Sunday mornings I watched grown-up softball games with such towering Ruthian hitters as could power the ball from home plate, at the Eastburn Avenue end of the yard, over the fence atop the concrete wall two stories high a block away. I rarely played in the yard after school, it was too vast, an enormous concrete plain with that high fencing around it and beyond the fence the attached apartment houses looking down through their windows. I always thought of windows as eyes, I always saw animate intelligence in them; I saw cars that way too, cars had faces when you saw them from the front, they had eyes and noses and mouths with teeth.

On a school day a Chevrolet coupe ran up the sidewalk on Weeks Avenue and knocked a woman through the chain link fence atop the high wall. With her bag of groceries she fell the two stories to the schoolyard below. She had been carrying bottles of milk. They had broken and the milk spread in pools about her body. Then her blood seeped into the milk. The front half of the car stood pushed through the fence, its wheels hanging over space and spinning. One of the children happened to be at the window of our classroom. She cried out. Everyone, including the teacher, ran to the window. I saw the thing in that moment of peace and stillness when the disaster has occurred but not yet resounded.

Then all at once the street was in a commotion. I heard a scream. Cars screeched to a halt. My teacher ran out the door to the principal's office. As we watched, the mixture of milk and blood spread over the concrete. In moments people were running from every direction, as if the street had never been empty and the event had occurred in front of an audience. Our teacher had called the police, but others had too. Two green-and-white police cars arrived. Police attended to the driver. Then one of the cars raced down 173rd Street to the Eastburn entrance of the yard. The police drove right into the yard. An ambulance from Morrisania Hospital came. This was our morning's class. The ambulance could not get into the schoolyard, and so the two attendants in white came on the run. They examined the woman. She was quite still. They put her body on a stretcher and put a blanket over it. It lay there while police and doctors consulted. Then the attendants carried the body to the ambulance. I watched the woman's arm, which had slipped off the edge of the stretcher: it bobbed in rhythm with the unhurried pace of her stretcher bearers.

All of us jostled about the windows and looked. I felt the vibrancy of the heated bodies around me.

I would have been glad then to go back to work, but my teacher was too upset. She let us out a few minutes early for lunch. Everyone was talking about the accident. I went home the regular way but saw up on Weeks Avenue a crowd of children standing looking at the Chevrolet coupe, which had still not been extricated from the fence. The police were keeping them back. The schoolyard itself was closed off in case the car fell into it. When I arrived home my mother was on the phone; she had heard the news. She was quite shaken when she came into the kitchen, where I sat over my tomato soup and peanut butter sandwich. She knew the family. The dead woman was the grown daughter of a member of the Sisterhood of the synagogue. My mother sat down across from me. "Right there in the schoolyard where children play," she said. She was pale. She ran her fingers through her hair. "What a terrible thing. How awful. That poor woman."

Yet from my vantage point high over the schoolyard, in the sunlit classroom windows, I had felt not fear but enlightenment. Air was like water. You could fall into it. From this height the spectacle of the event was magnified, the whole field of circumstance could be seen. The human figures were small.

At night, before sleep, I remembered the arm of the dead woman bobbing up and down as she was carried in the stretcher, the hand limp, palm up, as if the dead arm were pointing to the schoolyard, indicating it repeatedly—so that I should not forget—as a place of death. For weeks afterward the stain of her blood was visible on the schoolyard ground, a darkening of meaningless shape on the sun-bleached cement.

I FOUND IT VERY PLEASURABLE TO RUB COLOR COMICS ONTO WAXED PAPER. YOU LAID the waxed paper over the comic and rubbed back and forth with the edge of a ruler or a wooden tongue depressor. The color would attach to the waxed paper like a decal. It was never as vivid as the original but was all there, quite legible, the characters and the words they spoke. I had resumed another practice, soap carving, which I had learned from my brother. This required my mother's cooperation because soap cost money. But if you could cadge a bar of white soap, you could work at it, shave away at it with a kitchen knife or a pocketknife, and carve animals or human figures. I made a man in a bowler hat. The shavings could be wet and molded into a kind of vestigial soap bar.

A peach pit could be hollowed out: if you did it right, and left the seed inside intact, you could make a real whistle. But it took a while. If you started in the summer you'd be finished in a year, because it was dreary work.

Donald was busy all the time, but I could still get him to help me build a model airplane, because it was really exacting work. He couldn't resist. You taped the diagram to a table and then built the wings or fuselage, pinning the struts of balsa to the paper. You cut them to size with a single-edged razor blade, and then attached one strut to another with a drop of clear airplane dope. Predrawn templates of flat balsa automatically provided the curves. If I made a mistake and ruined a piece, Donald could make a template copy out of a blank piece of balsa scrap. When I had all the parts constructed—wings, fuselage, rudders and elevator—he took over the assembly and then the covering of thin colored paper.

I had my eye on one model advertised in a hobby company catalogue: it wasn't just a plane, it was an airship. To me airships, or zeppelins, were the most amazing things in the sky. You saw them occasionally from a distance. They were so big they could be seen even on the horizon. They floated gently, like clouds. They moved so slowly they were visible for a long time, as airplanes were not. One evening on the radio, the newscaster said that the largest airship ever built, the *Hindenburg*, was sailing from Germany to New York. Its route would bring it to the eastern seaboard over Long Island. It would head due west to a landing tower in New Jersey, which meant it would be visible over the city sometime in the afternoon. I might then be through with school. Yet I didn't dream I would see it, it did not occur to me that something on the news would be something I would witness. I didn't think of the Bronx as a place where anything happened. The Bronx was a big place with miles of streets and six-story apartment houses attached one to another, up hills and down hills it went, every neighborhood had its school like my school, its movie, its street of shops built into the sides of the apartment houses; it was tunneled with subways and bound together with trolley lines, and elevated lines; but for all of that, and for all of us who lived here, myself included, it was not important. It was not famous. It was not central to the world. I thought the *Hindenburg* would more naturally fly over Manhattan, which was central to the world. I talked on the phone to my friend Arnold, who lived in the apartment house across the street. Would his mother let us go on the roof after school? I thought from Arnold's roof, six stories high, it might be possible to catch a glimpse of the *Hindenburg* way downtown, over Manhattan the next day, if it was flying at a high enough altitude.

But Arnold's mother said no one was allowed on the roof, so I gave up thinking about it. When I woke up the next morning I had all but forgotten about the *Hindenburg*. I went to school. It was a warm clear day. I walked home after school with my friend Meg. Then I played stoopball. I flipped bubble gum cards. The leaves were pale green on the hedges. Harry, the fruit and vegetable man, pulled up along the curb with his wagon. He called out to the windows. He tethered the reins to the big brake on the side of the wagon. Harry had a wrench for opening fire hydrants. He opened the fire hydrant in the middle of our block and filled a pail with water and put the pail on the street in front of his horse. The horse drank. The wooden poles that connected him to the wagon dipped toward the ground. For good measure a leather harness was chained from its braces to the front of the wagon. The leather went around the horse's hocks and up over its back. The harness itself looked enormously heavy, like a big leather tire around its neck. The wagon had spoked wheels rimmed in steel. Leaf springs sprouted from the axles. All the fruits and greens were wet. Harry had sprayed them with a hose to make them clean and shining. I could smell the wet greens. He twisted off the green stalks of a bunch of carrots for a lady and fed the greens to his horse.

I went to the small park, the Oval, in the middle of Mt. Eden Avenue. Here, as it happened, one had a clear view of a good deal of sky. I don't remember doing much of anything. Perhaps I bought a Bungalow Bar. Perhaps I was looking for Meg, who sometimes came to the Oval with her mother. Over the roofs of the private houses that bordered the north side of Mt. Eden Avenue, across the street from the park, the nose of the great silver *Hindenburg* appeared. My mouth dropped open. She sailed incredibly over the housetops, and came right toward me, just a few hundred feet in the air, and kept coming and kept coming and still no sight of the tail of her. She was tilted toward me as if she were an enormous animal leaping from the sky in monumental slow motion. Some sort of line lagged under her, like a halyard, under the cupola. Then, as I blinked she was visible in her entirety, tacking off some degrees to the east, and I saw her in all her silver-skinned length; the ribbed planes of her cylindrical balloon, thick in the middle, narrowed at each end, reflected the sunlight, flaring sunlight in striations, as if a deck of cards were being shuffled. I heard her now, the propellers alongside her cupola whirring like fans in the sky. She did not make the harsh raspy snarl of an airplane, but seemed to whisper. She was indeed a ship, a real ship in the sky, she moved like an airship. The enormity of her was out of scale with everything, out of scale with the houses and the cars on the street and the people now shouting and pointing and looking up; she was like a scoop of sky come down to earth, or a floating building, or a populated cloud. I could see little people in the cabin, they were looking out the window and I waved at them. The *Hindenburg* was headed over Claremont Park now, toward Morris Avenue. I was not supposed to go there alone. I looked both ways and ran across the street, and up the stone steps into the park. Cars had stopped in the street and drivers had gotten out to see. Everyone was looking at her. I ran through the park following the *Hindenburg,* she was going so slowly, so grandly, I felt I could keep up with her without trouble. I saw her through the trees. I saw the length of her passing through an opening of blue sky between the trees. I waved at the people in the cupola, which was the size of a railroad car. She was going over treetops. I ran into a grass meadow to get an unobstructed sight of her, but now I realized she was going faster than I thought, she seemed to drift in the wind, I heard a rising pitch of her engines, she was changing course, she was over the street, over the trees, and slipping behind the apartment-house roofs of Morris Avenue. I waved and called. I wanted her back. I had been laughing all the while, and now, as the tail of her disappeared, she was gulped up by the city as if she had been sucked out of the sky. I ran as far as the park wall, smiling and red-faced and breathless, unable to believe my good fortune that I had seen the mighty *Hindenburg*.

I hurried home to tell my mother. When Donald came home he said he had seen the ship too. He had still been in school for some special exam and had looked out the window and seen her. Everyone taking the test and the teacher, too, had run to the windows. "We should get a model of the *Hindenburg*," he said. "We should save up and get it."

And then in the evening she crashed. We did not hear the radio broadcast describing this, it was the hour for *The Answer Man* and *I Love a Mystery*. But then a news bulletin came on. At the mooring tower in Lakehurst, New Jersey, she had caught fire. She collapsed, the steel twisting and curling up like paper. I could not imagine something the size of a flying ocean liner going up that way. Many people had died. They fell out of the sky in flames. I didn't understand how it could happen. "You see," Donald said patiently, "airships are really lighter-than-air ships. They couldn't fly unless the gas inside the balloon weighed less than air. You see that, don't you?"

"Sort of," I said.

"The gas they use is hydrogen, because its density is so much less than the density of air. On the other hand, it's a very volatile gas, which means it ignites easily. That's what happened. Maybe someone lit a cigarette. I don't know, it might even have been static electricity." I was impressed with his explanation. So was my mother. She beamed at him. He was taking chemistry at Townsend Harris. He had a chemistry set in a wooden box—not a toy but a real set, with vials of powdered chemicals stoppered with corks and their scientific names on the labels, and beakers and test tubes, and rubber hoses and clamps and measuring spoons, and a little scale with two dishes.

I did not think of the dead people, I thought only of the fall of the *Hindenburg*. My mother had said she was a German ship, sent over by Hitler for his own glory, and that if those people had to die she hoped they were Nazis. But none of that mattered to me. All I could think of was that the ship had fallen out of the sky. They were not supposed ever to touch land, they were tethered to tall towers, they were sky creatures; and this one had fallen in flames to the ground. I could not get the picture of that out of my mind. In the Saturday cartoons, one, about Popeye, showed Popeye's ship sinking. He swam away and the ship stuck its nose up in the air and went straight down, like a knife, making a funny *glub glub* sound and sending up a stream of bubbles. But a real ship going down, I knew, was a terrible sight, like a great animal fallen; she would lie on her side, or maybe turn upside down, and go under by degrees, faster and faster, creating a terrible whirlpool in the sea as she went. My father had told me he had once seen newsreels of an ocean liner foundered on a beach in Jersey. She lay in flames on her side. Even on water ships could burn. Everything around me was going up and down, up and down. Joe Louis hit Jim Braddock and Braddock went down. I had seen paintings in books of knights fallen from their horses, or horses fallen, and in *King Kong* there was the terrible shaking of the earth by the falling of the great dinosaurs in battle. And, of course, Kong himself had fallen. Just recently I had seen an old man in the street suddenly drop to his knees for no reason at all, and then topple to one side and sit on the sidewalk leaning back on one elbow, and I had found that terrifying. In bed, trying to sleep, I imagined my father stumbling and crashing to the ground, and I cried out.

EIGHTEEN

Of course I fell all the time, but that was different. I lived in proximity to the pavement, in front of my house I knew the topography of the stoop and the cement sidewalk, and the cracks in the sidewalk and the chips in the grey blocks of the curb. I had a best friend now, Bertram, who lived a block away on Morris Avenue and took clarinet lessons. He was short, and tubby. I directed our games. Pretend I'm this. Pretend you're that. Pretend I say this and you do that. The latest serial in the movies was *Zorro*, a kind of Lone Ranger in black with a black horse, and in our games I was Zorro and Bertram was everyone else in the cast. I was more agile than he, and therefore the hero. We had laths we had found in the ash can which we used for swords. Bertram, in our duels, represented many soldiers or a whole posse, and I'd no sooner stab one of them and see him fall, than another would pop up and challenge me. I leaped up on the stoop, I raced past him down the brick stoop and jumped to the ground. I fell and dueled with Bertram while on my back. He danced around me. Our game was a long-running serial and took us down the alley and into the backyard. Here, as Zorro, I now had the daring to climb the stone wall patched with cement that divided my yard from the back of the apartment house on the other side of it. The wall held up a rotting wooden fence that tilted over it and impeded passage. The cement was cracked and crumbling. Colonies of brown ants lived in the holes. My friend couldn't quite handle this wall. I raced along my dangerous parapet and he ran alongside, below me, in the yard. Loyally, he huffed and puffed. He could never win these adventures because I was always Zorro. He died and died again. He might, during our dueling, touch me with the end of his sword and say he'd gotten me, but I always insisted it was a flesh wound even if his sword hit me square in the middle of the chest. He'd try to argue but I'd draw him back into the duel, lifting my sword, nicking him and dancing backward with a merry laugh. He'd start to chase me and we'd be back in it. Truly we were not playing. It was understood life was cheap. People fought. Blood flowed. Honor and justice were at stake. We went on with it hour after hour. The invention was endless. I told him what to say, then I answered. We replayed the scenes when I thought of something better. The dirt and grit of crushed stone was embedded in the flesh of our palms. Our eyes glistened from exertion, our cheeks were red. Once or twice a day Bertram cried real tears and I was close to them. When we reached some grim exhausted end to all this, with someone's mother calling, dusk sending a chill down our sweated backs, we emptied our pockets of the things we had collected in the course of the day's adventures—clothesline, flinty chips of rock, empty cigarette packages, ice cream sticks—and went each to our home.

After the last day of school Bertram and I had all day to fight it out. But then his mother took him away for the summer to a cottage in the Catskills. Donald left for his job at the Paramount Hotel. My father was away at work most days and nights, and so my mother and I were each other's companion a good deal of the time. Once, I reflected, our house had been full and something was always going on. Now there were just the two of us and it was not much fun.

My mother sat at the window of the sun parlor and looked out. I understood it was not something she preferred to do. It was what she did. She sat there, with her arms on the windowsill. Sometimes she drank a cup of coffee, sometimes a cup of tea. She was not so strict with me. I could stay out after supper. The exact hour of my bedtime was not now of the utmost importance to her, perhaps because I didn't have school in the morning and could sleep late, perhaps because she had other things on her mind. I took advantage of the situation readily enough. I listened to programs that would have been unthinkable during the school term: *Gang Busters,* the crime-story show written by Colonel H. Norman Schwarzkopf, which came on at ten o'clock; *The Kraft Music Hall* with Bing Crosby and Bob Burns, and even *Jimmy Fidler's Hollywood Gossip* at ten-thirty. Adding these to my regular shows, which I had won from hard and protracted negotiations—*Easy Aces,* and the *Chase and Sanborn Hour* with Charlie McCarthy, and *The Royal Gelatin Hour* with Rudy Vallee, and the *Green Hornet,* of course, and *Jack Benny,* and *Eddie Cantor, Mr.Keen, Tracer of Lost Persons, Horace Heidt and his Musical Knights,* plus all my afternoon adventure shows—I pretty much had free rein with the airways. Listening to a full day's radio programs exhausted me, but it was a nervous sort of exhaustion, lacking real physical discharge, and my limbs hurt and my mind clamored. Bed at night was a stale place, the pillow grew clammy despite my plumping it and turning it so that I could feel its cold side. I reheard bits and pieces of the radio programs in my mind. I concentrated on the serials. I analyzed how they achieved the realistic sounds of horse hooves at a gallop, airplanes in dogfights, chairs breaking over people's heads, creaking ropes at quayside in mysterious Oriental ports, and so forth. Mostly I imagined the geography I had been taught, the backgrounds of these programs being barely indicated by a descriptive line, or a remark in the story or a trace of a sound effect, but which shone in my mind in colorful detail. There was a West, there was a vast deep sky to fly, there was the Orient, there was Europe, and dangerous seas between. Occasionally I realized that the pillow under my head was one of the very malefactors who populated these exotic realms; somehow he had gotten to the Bronx. I wrestled him, punched him, grunting and grinding my teeth in appropriate fashion; sometimes it looked as if he had me, but with my last bit of strength I flung him from me up into the air, and took him out with one beautiful sock as he came down.

Oddly, on those rare evenings when my father was home some discipline was reinforced. He felt most of the shows I liked were trash. "You'd be better off reading a book," he said, although he knew I read books all the time. He himself listened to the news commentators, like H.V. Kaltenborn, although I couldn't see why he did, they irritated him so. He turned them off in anger when he could no longer stand what was being said, but he always tuned in again the next time.

The only program the whole family could agree on was *Information Please*, the quiz show in which the questions were really hard and the board of experts who answered them were really learned. The joy of the show was in hearing questions asked the answer to which no one could possibly know, and then hearing one or another of those fellows answer in a shot, and make it all sound simple. Each of them had fields of expertise the others did not, and altogether it was pretty hard to trip them up. If you did, if the question that you sent in *did* stump the experts, you were awarded a set of the *Encyclopaedia Britannica*. We all sat and listened to this program. Sometimes, if the subject was music or politics or history, my father guessed the answer before the experts did.

I loved it when the three of us all did something together. If my mother and father were fighting, our going out and doing something was the way they called a truce. Everyone could be angry and not talking, and I would nag each of them in turn until I got them up and out, my father going along with what he pretended was my mother's idea, and my mother pretending it was my father's. But it was mine. I'd get them to the movies this way. Going to an air-cooled movie on a hot evening was a necessity. It didn't even matter to me what the films were, my mother seemed to like love stories and musicals, my father dramas. I would sit through Jeanette MacDonald and Nelson Eddy singing to each other just to be cool and just to know that in the dark on either side of me sat my parents and that they might actually talk to each other afterwards on the way home. Most times they did, but sometimes even the evening out wouldn't do any good; I would have heard my mother laughing during the movie, but when we came out she still wouldn't talk to my father. Sometimes my father fell asleep during the movie, sometimes when he was restless he went out for a while. He knew how to leave the movie house and go have a soda or smoke a cigar and then get back into the theater without paying another admission. I myself would never try that.

His business was not good and this seemed to make him quieter and more serious. He did not bring home surprises as often.

M<small>Y ONE RELIABLE FRIEND THIS SUMMER WAS THE LITTLE GIRL MEG, WHOSE FAMILY,</small> like ours, had no vacation planned. I played potsy with her in the Oval if I had previously checked to see no boys I knew were in sight. This was a girl's game of hopping around in numbered boxes and it was quite easy. You threw your skate key or something into a particular box you had to reach, and if it stayed in, you hopped and jumped your way over to it, picked it up while standing on one foot, reversed your direction without touching a line, and hopped your way back. Certain boxes had to be avoided if the other person had previously claimed them. Sometimes it got complicated. My mother thought Meg a sweet child, that's what she called her, a sweet child, although she was critical of her name.

"What kind of name is that," she said.

"It's short for Margaret," I said. "But everyone calls her Meg."

"Well, that's no name for a girl, that's a scullery maid's name. I fault the mother."

She did not look approvingly on Meg's mother. I couldn't understand why. The woman had always been nice to me, she was a pretty woman, slender, with short reddish-blond hair and a nice smile. She seemed always to be listening to a pleasant song inside her head. Her name was Norma. I knew this because this is how Meg addressed her, it was very unusual not calling your mother Mother, but Norma did not seem to mind. She had a good way of making a cold chocolate drink, she took a spoonful or two of cocoa, and added milk and sugar; then she crushed some ice cubes in a dish cloth with a hammer; then she poured the ice cubes into an Orphan Annie Ovaltine Shake-up Mug, which was a cup with a domed lid; and she shook it up till it was cold and served it with the crushed ice. "I'd make a good bartender," she said. She did nice things like that.

They were not particularly well off, this family. They lived in a tenement house without an elevator, on the fifth floor, a long walk up. The stairs were dark, the hallways were tiled in little six-sided tiles, like a bathroom. Their apartment was small, but very light, since it overlooked Claremont Park at Monroe Avenue. In the basement of the building was a little grocery store with a window that looked up at the front sidewalk. In that store you saw people's legs as they went by, as if they were chopped off in the middle. I sometimes went there for my mother.

Meg did not have her own room. There was only one bedroom, so she either slept in her mother's bed or in the living room on the sofa. Things were broken down in the living room, the sofa's springs were coming out the bottom, and a standing lamp with one of those upside-down glass shades to direct the light to the ceiling had a piece of the shade missing as if chomped out by something that ate glass. It was not a clean house by my mother's standards. The bedroom was overpacked with things, bureaus piled with folded clothes and perfume bottles, boxes stacked in the corners, newspapers and junk everywhere. It was just those two rooms and a kitchen. On the kitchen ceiling was a wooden rack with clothesline strung up on it; you let it down like a shade by means of a rope attached to the wall, and you dried your clothes that way. So pink silk underwear always hung from the kitchen ceiling. There were roaches in the bathroom, and a red rubber hot-water bottle and a trailing enema tube hung from the shower rod over the bathtub. There was a bathroom tray for a cat, although Meg told me their cat had fallen out the window and died. I remember this apartment so clearly because I spent so much time there, especially on rainy days. It was interesting to me that from the mess of this house both Meg and her mother could come out looking so clean and nicely dressed, as they always did. Meg's white summer one-strap shoes were always newly polished. She had very many of the latest toys and games. Of course, they would be of more interest to girls; she had several dolls, for example, including a Shirley Temple model complete with different outfits to dress her in. These were contained in a miniature trunk, just like the trunks people took with them on ocean voyages. Inside, on hangers, were a Shirley Temple nursing uniform with a red-and-blue cape of satin, a horseback-riding outfit with riding boots, coats, sundresses, shorts, and so on. Meg loved Shirley Temple. I myself could not abide her, but said nothing. I had seen Shirley Temple in just one movie—I knew that kind of spoiled girl. Buttery, overly cute, a teacher's pet, a real show-off. Meg herself was not like that or I wouldn't have been her friend. She was a serious, thoughtful child, very quiet and trusting. She never got mad and never left the game no matter how badly it was going for her. We were playing in the park one day and it began to rain. I went to her house and called my mother to let her know where I was. "You're up there?" my mother said. "You come right home." "But it's raining," I said. "It's letting up," she said. "This minute!"

When I got home I was angry. My mother said I was not to go into that house ever again and I said I would if I wanted to. She called me a foolish child. "But what's wrong?" I said over and over. "I will not discuss it," she said. I had to reason this out for myself. I knew she liked Meg and never put up an objection when she came to our house. So it had to do with her house. Or her mother. In the mysterious way of our family conversation, whenever something was not quite right I was left in the dark about it, although smartly feeling its consequences. When my mother was angry at my father, I could never exactly pin down her reasons. It was like that.

I would learn more by listening to them argue at night when I was supposed to be asleep. Now I eavesdropped on a phone conversation my mother had that evening with her friend Mae. Our phone was in the front of the house, and I was in the kitchen having supper. I heard just one phrase: *ten cents a dance*. I don't know how, but I knew my mother was talking about Norma. I didn't know what she meant, exactly, but it was such a weighted comment, delivered in her tone of moral authority, part disgust, part sarcasm, that I immediately decided it was unjust. I resolved to continue to go to Meg's house. I was not willing in this case to accept the humiliation of being told what to do. My mother had a way of telling you what to do that left you with no honor. Once I showed her an advertisement on the back cover of a comic book, it was for an air rifle that shot BB's. I wanted it and proposed to save up for it. "Don't be ridiculous," she said. "Stop bothering me with such nonsense."

But the episode did suggest to me something I had not been prepared before to recognize. When I went upstairs to Meg's I always hoped Norma would be there. I had to acknowledge that to myself now, and with a weird feeling in the chest, some breathable excitement, as if I had done something terribly wrong although I didn't know what it was. When the mother wasn't home, or when she went out while I was there, I was disappointed. The visit became less interesting. She always smiled when she saw me. She had large eyes, widely spaced, and a wide mouth. She was very kind. Sometimes she joined us in our games. She would sit on the floor with us, and we three would have a good time.

NINETEEN

W̲e received our first letter from the Paramount Hotel in the mountains. "Dear Mom, Dad, and Edgar," wrote my brother in his orderly way, assigning to each the places we had in his mind. I admired Donald's handwriting. He wrote in ink on unlined paper, and there were no blots and the lines were straight. One of my bad subjects in school was penmanship, and so I studied his letter and copied it out. I could hear his voice as I read, he was very good at explaining things—and I heard him now explaining how things were at the Paramount Hotel so that we would understand. He told us he was working hard and enjoying it. Some of the guests had requested tunes other than the ones the Cavaliers knew how to play—that was the biggest problem. People were getting tired of hearing the same songs every night. Could my father send up sheet music for a list of songs that was attached to the letter as quickly as possible? He would try to find time to rehearse, although it would be difficult because the management wanted them down by the lake during the day. Anyway the food was good, and he was getting a nice tan. It was a characteristic of the mountains that no matter how hot the day was the evenings were cool. My parents laughed over the letter, although I didn't find anything particularly funny in it. My father said he would mail up some sheet music immediately, before the Cavaliers heard the gong. This was a reference to the *Major Bowes' Original Amateur Hour*, a radio program. Aspiring musicians were contestants on the program, and if they were no good, Major Bowes would ring a bell to stop their performance. It made you laugh even though it could not have been funny to whoever it was who might have been rehearsing for weeks to be heard on the radio and hoping to win a professional contract from the appearance. But it was funny. People played glasses of water each filled to a different height to make a different note; they played big ripsaws by bending the blade and stroking it with a violin bow; they played spoons, and even made music by tapping their teeth and slapping the sides of their face while their mouth was open. They always got the gong. One-man bands, my favorite, always got the gong. But I thought some of them were amazing—strumming guitars while blowing on harmonicas held on neck braces, or cornets affixed to their chairs, and beating bass drums with their feet, and playing organ chords with their elbows, and hitting cymbals with sticks taped to their foreheads. It was not real music they produced, these one-man bands, but something else, a mechanical not-quite-in-tune-music, like calliopes or music boxes; whenever I had the chance to listen to a one-man band I did.

My father explained to me that in the old days of vaudeville on the Lower East Side there was a fiddler named Romanoff who was famous for playing "The Flight of the Bumblebee" while holding the violin behind his back. "The immigrants loved Romanoff, they thought he was the best violinist in the world because he could play the fiddle behind his back," my father said. "Not even the great Heifetz could do that. Not even Fritz Kreisler." He looked at me with a big smile on his face, his eyebrows poised while waiting for me to get the point. I understood what he was saying, but I still liked one-man bands.

A more serious matter arose regarding my brother when our former landlady, Mrs. Segal, came by to visit. As it happened, Mrs. Segal and her husband had gone to the Paramount Hotel for a week's vacation and had been delighted to find Donald there. "But you wouldn't believe the hovels they have those boys in," she said. "Shacks, with mattresses on the floor, like dirt farmers. No running water, they have to use the outside shower beside the boathouse."

My mother was speechless.

"Ordinarily I wouldn't say anything," Mrs. Segal said, "but I know how particular you are."

"He didn't tell us," my mother said.

"Of course not," Mrs. Segal said, "You know boys, it doesn't matter to them. They wouldn't bathe if they lived in Buckingham Palace." Mrs. Segal held my chin in her hand as she said that. She thought the whole situation very funny. "Of course Donald is having the time of his life," she assured my mother. "He's a big shot. All the girls adore him."

When my father came home my mother told him what Mrs. Segal had said. "I want him home this instant," she said. "He's living in filth. Send him a telegram. I'll go up there myself if that's what it takes to get him out of that pigsty."

"Rose," my father said, "if you bring that boy home in the middle of the summer, he'll never forgive you."

It was difficult for my mother to control herself. After a day or two she wrote Donald a letter and said she had heard from Mrs. Segal about the living conditions of the staff. "Stand up for your rights," she told him. "You're just as good as the finest guest. Professional musicians have a right to expect sheets on the beds, at least."

TWENTY

I had a theory about death in its various forms—for instance, drowning, being run over or burned alive, which were death by accident, or something like infantile paralysis, which was death by germ: It was simply that if I thought of it, if I imagined it, it would not happen to me. I would be guarded against it, made immune, merely by an act of thought, foiling this or that particular death with a mental inoculation against it. And it didn't matter how the thought entered my mind, if I had heard of something terrible happening to someone else, or seen something bad, or just idly dreamt of the word describing it, I was safe. Perhaps it was not so much theory as a working hope, but it was holding up nicely.

In the fall of my eighth year I woke up one morning with one of my stomachaches. I was pleased to be allowed to stay home from school. I had a new comic book about Frank Buck, a real person. Frank Buck went to Africa and Asia and trapped big game; he didn't kill animals, he brought them back by ship to the zoos and circuses. He was kind to the animals, which I liked. He had wild adventures.

My illness brought no theoretical thoughts to my mind. It didn't seem at all consequential. Exhibiting the same aplomb with which I handled death, I regarded myself as an expert on illnesses, at least as they made their appearance in me. I knew my colds, my grippes, my earaches. I knew their characters and the courses they might take and the treatment they called for. They posed no fears for me, although they did for my mother. I had learned how secretly to avoid the worst treatment. Mustard plaster for chest colds for example: once it was applied and my mother had left the room, I would insert a towel between my skin and the brown bag paper in which the clammy English mustard had been spread. Then I would pull the covers up to my chin so I didn't have to breathe the acrid fumes of the cursed detestable stuff. When I heard her coming back, I would remove the towel and suffer the burning sensation for as long as it took her to leave again.

This time I had a low fever, which was no particular inconvenience. I just didn't eat very much. Everything was fine. But on the second day the mildly annoying ache was still there and I stayed in bed more of the time, a fact noted by my mother. In the late afternoon Dr. Gross came over and had a look at me. As usual he made me a present of some tongue depressors. He pressed my stomach and looked down my throat and in my ears while his vest chain swung with its hanging badge.

"Well," he said in his genial growly voice, "it doesn't appear to be much of anything. Let's wait another day or two and see what happens." This was not my mother's usual inclination in the face of illness, she liked to know what it was and to deal with it firmly. But the symptoms were vague and I seemed to be active enough even though in bed. I drew, listened to my programs, I demanded tea and toast and Jell-O with annoying regularity, and so she acceded to the doctor's advice.

A couple of days later my stomach was still hurting and was tight as a drum. I went to bed early. When I awoke the next morning my stomach hurt no longer. I told this to my mother with a smile. She regarded my flushed cheeks. "I don't like the way you look," she said. When she read my temperature on the thermometer she gasped. It was a hundred and five degrees.

My mother cursed the name of Dr. Gross and called Aunt Frances in Westchester. As a well-to-do matron, Aunt Frances knew numbers of specialists. At her behest we received a phone call very soon afterward from a Dr. London, a friend of her family's. I heard my mother describe the situation to him. She came back to my room with an alarmed expression on her face. "Dr. London is a Manhattan doctor," she said. "He's sending around an associate of his who has an office near here. He said you are not to move but to lie quietly with a pillow under your knees." She placed the pillow very gently as she spoke. She was pale.

A short while later the associate arrived. I did not get his name. He scared me. He was not genial like Dr. Gross, but severe and unsmiling; he did not prod me about in Gross's friendly way, kneading this and that, but touched me gingerly with the tops of his fingers and peered at me with a worried frown. He wore a dark blue pin-striped suit and vest. His hair was grey. "Dr. London's suspicion was correct. This child must immediately go to the hospital," he said to my mother. She put her hand to her cheek. They went out of the room together. I resented being left like that when it was me they were talking about. I heard them in the hallway.

The strange doctor spoke on the phone in the front hall and then spoke to my mother outside my room door. "You are not to waste time calling for an ambulance. Get a taxi. Take him to Poly Clinic hospital. It's on West Fiftieth Street. Here is the address. Dr. London will be waiting."

He explained to my mother how I should be carried, wrapped in a blanket, in a folded position, with as little room for movement as possible. Then he left.

My mother called her friend Mae for help. "His appendix has burst," she said.

I was alarmed now because in my registry of self-protective thoughts I had never entered a burst appendix. How could I have, not knowing what it was! I felt light-headed. My fear dissolved and I became angry. The pain was gone and *now* was when I had to go to the hospital. I decided I would not go to the hospital. I complained bitterly while my mother put me in fresh pajamas and wrapped me in a blanket. She was uncharacteristically gentle but simply ignored what I had to say.

By this time Mae had arrived and was ringing the bell. A yellow De Soto cab was waiting at the curb in front of the house. My mother carried me down the steps and Mae ran ahead to hold the cab door. To my mortification there was the landlady's little girl from downstairs, whom I hated. She was there in front of the house carrying her schoolbooks, watching the whole thing. She had no regard for my feelings but kept looking and looking, she hadn't the decency to go about her business. I ignored her, but was furious with this wretched brat. Oh my awful luck, to be seen carried wrapped up in this way just at lunchtime when the children were coming home from school. How she *knew*. She would tell her mother. And my humiliation would be public knowledge.

That was the reason I cried in the taxi, not because I was feeling ill. "Shh," my mother said. "Don't worry. Everything will be all right." I could tell she was not entirely sure this was so. The cab was going very fast. The driver blew the horn repeatedly. I knew where we were, we were going down the Grand Concourse. I saw the tops of the trees on the center islands, the framed blue-and-white street signs attached to the lampposts, I saw the tops of the apartment houses. I was seeing the Bronx upside down. We kept going and crossed the bridge into Manhattan at 138th Street. I smelled the cracked leather of the cab's upholstery. I saw the back of the driver's head, his soft cap. I heard the ticking of the meter and tried to count the clicks, to keep time with them in my mind. I must have dozed. We were coming down Madison Avenue now from Seventy-ninth Street, there is a hill there and I twisted to look out front at the cars and buses. The driver blew the horn. The cab turned into Central Park and headed to the West Side of Manhattan.

I FOUND MYSELF ON A STRETCHER IN THE HOSPITAL. MY BLANKET WAS TAKEN AWAY. I was very thirsty. I twisted my head looking for my mother but I could not see her. I was being wheeled down a hall, the overhead lights ticking past like the ratchets of the taxi meter. "I am very thirsty," I said, "I want some water, please." Someone said, "In just one minute we'll give you water."

And then I was in an elevator with several people smiling at me and saying reassuring things. I didn't know them. I didn't believe them. Then we were out of the elevator in some dark room, and many people were there, indistinct shapes in the darkness, and the stretcher was being positioned in some way, and the movement back and forth was nauseating me. I was terribly thirsty and asked for water. Instead, straps were fastened around each of my wrists and my ankles and chest.

A doctor with a white cap on his head and a long white apron like Irving the Fish Man's, appeared. I couldn't see his face, he had on a mask covering everything except his eyes. He was saying something but his voice was muffled by the mask. He wore rubber gloves. I realized he was saying I was going to be all right. How could I trust him! I had no control over what they were doing to me. They had tied me down. They did not seem to hear when I said I wanted something to drink.

Another doctor in a white cap sat down next to my head and said he was going to put a mask over my face and he wanted me to breathe very deeply when he did. "Let me see the mask," I said. He held up not a white cloth mask such as he wore, but a conical rubber device, colored black, whose sides were collapsed on each other, the narrow end attached to a tube. It looked more like a balloon than a mask. I knew beyond question that I wanted nothing to do with it. He saw the alarm in my eyes. He lifted the mask toward me and turned away at the same time and turned a wheel on some kind of machine I had not noticed before that was sitting next to him. I heard a hissing sound. The mask as it came toward me was now a perfect circle. I knew I could not avoid it but turned my head from side to side anyway. I wanted a moment to compose myself. "Just breathe deeply," he said. "Can you count? Count from one hundred as you breathe, but backwards, see if you can, ninety-nine, ninety-eight and so on," and he clasped it over my face. I was shaking my head no. I tried to tell him I was thirsty. I wanted two things, a glass of water and a moment to compose myself, but I could not speak because the hideous rubbery mask was clamped over my face and held there. I couldn't breathe, I was trying to tell him. A cold sweet poisonous gas was what this man wanted me to breathe. I tried to get him to stop. I had something to say. I began to struggle and felt hands holding me down. Whichever way I turned my head the cold sweet suffocating poison stuck to me. I was breathing it, I couldn't help it, I tried to hold my breath but it was impossible, and with each breath I took, more of this unbreathable sweetness was coming into my lungs and choking me. I gagged. It was not air. It was cold, it smelled like the hiss of gas in a cellar, it had echoes in it, it rang like metal footsteps, it hissed, cell doors clanged shut, I heard my voice calling to me down long stone corridors, I could not breathe. I knew I must not lose consciousness. I fought. I shook my head, I could not free myself.

And now great swirls of colored light advanced toward me, spinning like pinwheels, revolving so fast they seemed to scream. And then the light was splintering and flying toward me, needles of it stinging me, flying past me, yellow and red stings, and now a roaring sound filled my head and began to pulsate. And all this swirling light and roaring screaming noise popped into Donald Duck looming up from a point, and he spoke and clacks came out of his mouth, and then Mickey Mouse loomed up in front of me and made horrible faces, and spoke in clacks or roars, and they were laughing at me and shaking their fists and showing their teeth. And I couldn't help it, now I was breathing in this terrible gas in a white tiled swimming pool or corridor whose walls moved in toward me and then outwards. I was falling through my *Compton's Picture Encyclopedia* article on the sea and these underwater animals were laughing in my ears, but the laughter pulsated like a machine, and I couldn't stop breathing even though I knew it was the machine breathing. The smell was cold, the hiss grew softer. I felt as if I were under the sea but breathing under the sea somehow this air that was the only thing left to breathe in all this cold floating. And then, with a certainty that made me scream, I knew I was being cut, I felt the knife go into my belly and cut downward. I tried to tell them to stop, but water hissed into my mouth and I saw myself drifting away and they cut and cut, and I wanted to cry but could not, the tears remained in my throat and in my throat I grieved, and felt such despair of death that I gave up and I let it come floating. And it all floated away.

THEN, MUCH LATER IT SEEMED, I SAW THINGS FOR A WHILE AND THEN NO LONGER saw them. It was quiet. I heard voices but could not distinguish words. My mouth was dry. When I called for water, a wet piece of cotton was brushed across my cracked lips. I was angry and came into consciousness kicking. That they would tie me to a table and force me to breathe what I couldn't breathe! I was held down, Donald was holding my hand, he was saying, "Take it easy, take it easy!" I went to sleep and awoke, quite clear in the head now. I was in some sort of room with curtains. Others were outside the curtains. They had their own concerns. Children were crying. The curtain was pulled back and a nurse showed me how I could have water. She took a tongue depressor with cotton wrapped around one end and dipped it into a glass of water and then let me suck the water from the cotton. It was not enough, but she would only give me it that way.

I felt very bad, as if things were sticking in me so that I could feel the insides of me, what my insides felt like. I was told to lie still, which I was glad to do because of this wet sticking feeling in my stomach. Then my mother stayed with me awhile. She was angry at the nurse about something. She told me I had my feelings under the covers like that because I had drains in me, the operation was over, I didn't have to worry that that would ever happen again, but meanwhile where they had made the incision there were rubber drain tubes to see to it that all the poison left my body. The idea was to keep those drains in me for a while and not to close things up to make sure all the poison came out. That was all. I didn't want to know about it. I didn't want to see.

Whenever the doctors changed the dressing I kept my eyes closed because I didn't want to see. I was not well. I was not happy. I was very tired and injured, I felt I had been badly treated, I had been cut, I had stitches in me and drains, and at night when no one was there and I woke, I heard another child crying and I couldn't help it, I wept too.

Then my grandma came to visit me. She walked through the curtain. So she hadn't died after all. I was glad the curtains were pulled around my bed because none of the others could see her, she embarrassed me speaking in Yiddish and looking very old and shabby in her black dress, and with her grey hair pinned up in her braids but scraggly around the edges, she was not as neat as she usually was and she smelled of her sour grass. But I was thirsty and explained to her how to do the water, and she did this properly. Then she felt my head with her dry ancient hand and she thought I was too hot, she found a washcloth at the foot of my bed and went outside the curtains to the sink along the wall and rinsed the cloth in cold water and came back and put the folded cloth over my forehead. "You are a dear precious boy," she said to me and I understood this clearly even though it was in Yiddish. She took a penny from her old change purse of cracked leather. In her forefinger and thumb she held this penny and with her other hand opened my hand and pressed the penny into my palm, just the way she always did. "I bless you, my beloved child, I pray for good health for you. You are a good boy and I love you," she said. "God will protect you."

WHEN MY MOTHER AND FATHER ARRIVED, I TOLD THEM GRANDMA HAD COME TO see me. They exchanged looks. My mother excused herself and left the room holding a handkerchief to her eyes. My father sat down at the side of the bed.

"I brought you some books," he said. "It's something new. They have these pocket-sized books now, wonderful books for twenty-five cents. I know you like Frank Buck, don't you?"

I nodded. He was very serious. Dark circles were under his eyes.

"Here is his own book about going after big game," my father said. "Bring 'Em Back Alive. It's not just a comic book. It's his autobiography. And here is a story about a young deer called Bambi, by Felix Salten," he said. "Just to get the animal's point of view."

That didn't interest me as much, but I didn't say that to my poor father. I realized how worried he was, how I had worried them all with my burst appendix.

"And here is a famous book, a classic that you might not find interesting just now but you may in the future. It's a wonderful book, *Wuthering Heights,* by an English writer, Emily Brontë."

"Thank you," I said, although I was too tired to do more than look at the covers.

"I'll put them here on the table next to you. You see them? You can just reach over when you want to look at them."

Much later I found out what happened at the end of the hospital corridor outside my room. After visiting me, my parents met with Dr. London, who had performed the surgery. He told them I had a fifty-fifty chance of pulling through. Then he left to go about his rounds and at that point my mother attempted to throw herself out of the hospital window. The odds the doctor had quoted did not seem to her favorable. My father held her, wrestled with her at the open window. He held her until she went limp in her despair and broke down crying.

If they had only asked me, I could have told them I wasn't going to die. I knew I would not because of my theory. My theory held that if I thought of something before it happened, it wouldn't happen. I had experienced a ruptured appendix before I had thought about it and that was unfortunate, but I had thought about dying from it before it had had the chance to kill me, so now it couldn't. It was very simple.

I was no longer frightened. I may not have liked the drains in me, the profoundly uncomfortable foreignness of tubes lolling about in my guts, but I did not fear for my life. The time of terror for me was before I was put under as I wrestled the deadly sweet ether that filled my throat and my lungs with its terrible chemical chill. But it is apparent to me now that my parents interpreted the visit from my dead grandma as a sign of my own impending death. That particular day I was very close to death. Nobody could have persuaded me that it was not a palpable visit Grandma had made, a real event, and that was the point. My dear hollow-eyed family, these great framers of my existence and gods of my thought, had a way of coming into my room so hesitantly, with grim and fearful glances from the door, and lips pressed tight in pale faces as if awestruck by what they saw; I had to turn my head and smile at them before they would come in, before they were satisfied that I was still alive. They would suppose, in the delirium that produced my occult meeting with my Grandma, my own terrible passion,with my eyes turned into the past as if rolled up in my head, and I seeing what was dead and gone in the disconnection from my own forwardness through time, as if, becalmed and drifting to stillness, to inanimation, the mind sees death as life.

These horrors of meaning were for my family to understand. I was only ill with peritonitis. My conviction was not shaken even when I was moved into another room, a bigger room, with no curtains around my bed, but with a kind of railing, like a crib's. I was very insulted. It was a children's ward, and there were many such crib beds, each with a child either younger than I or older, and there were many of us now regardless of age in these humiliating beds and all of the others were looking at me. Some of the little ones stood up to look at me. I still had to lie down. I could see out a big window to a windowless building across the street. It was the north side of Madison Square Garden, which pleased me. At night I imagined I could hear a sports crowd cheering at a basketball game.

When Donald came to visit he was angry because nobody had told him that I had been moved to this special ward.

"I went to your old room and the bed was empty and the mattress was rolled up," he said. "Nobody I spoke to knew anything. I ran all over the place trying to find out what had happened."

He sat down beside my bed and rubbed his eyes with the back of his hand. "Can you imagine a hospital full of doctors and nurses and not one of them knew where you were?" He began to laugh with tears in his eyes. "Finally, I saw one of your nurses, and she told me you were here." He shook his head. "Jesus, what if I had called Mom when I couldn't find you!"

I introduced Donald to the other children nearby. There were four or five of them. I wanted them to know I had an older brother. He waved and some of them said hello but most just stared. They were all dying. I knew that, it was clear to me. One girl, Miriam, who was several years older than I, had had her leg sawn off. She was on the bed next to mine. A couple of kids were in wheelchairs during the day and had to be helped into their beds at night. One of them was very yellow and skinny. They were all dying. I knew that because I had heard the doctors and nurses talking. Also the toys here were very elaborate, the toys and games these children had were the most glorious I had ever seen, but they didn't seem to care; each day their parents or grandparents came and brought more toys and games but they were not thankful. Some of the children had been here for months. They did not enjoy visits, they only enjoyed talking to one another, and teasing one another. I was not one of them, I could see that. Though I had been put in among them, I didn't think that I was dying. They didn't think I was either, because none of them wanted to be my friend. Except Miriam, the big girl in the bed next to mine. She liked me. "Your brother's very handsome," she told me after Donald had left at the end of the visiting hour.

* * *

WHAT PULLED ME THROUGH WAS A NEW DRUG, SULFANILAMIDE. MY IMPRESSION then was that it was a kind of yellow powder that had been sprinkled all around inside me before I had been sewn up. I think now it was administered after the operation as well. In a few weeks I was released from the hospital and brought home wrapped in blankets. It was winter. In the early spring I was allowed to get out of bed for a while each day, and after that I was taken to the country for my convalescence, the country being Pelham Manor, on Montcalm Terrace, the home of Aunt Frances and Uncle Ephraim, hosts of the yearly Passover dinner.

Their three children were grown and away at college, two boys at Harvard and the youngest, a girl, Lila, at Smith. Here, in the stillness of this elegant home, with its low ceilings, carpeted stairs, casement windows and wine and velvet smells, I stayed for a week and took my ease. There was a backyard with a large rock and a profusion of forsythia in bloom. Aunt Frances had undoubtedly saved my life by finding for my parents a doctor who understood what had happened to me. She really liked me and I liked her, she was gracious and kind, a very pretty woman with prematurely white hair and a quiet aristocratic bearing, like a good queen in a fairy tale who still bears some of the loveliness of the princess. She did not raise her voice, which endeared her to me. I was given the bedroom of her daughter, Lila, a single room, with Lila's awards and honors all over the walls. She had raised dogs in her early youth, and various ribbons, many of them blue, testified to her skill. Her champion dog, Vicky, a Kerry blue terrier, was still in residence. I was invited to browse through her books, a largely disappointing collection of science texts and dog-training manuals and, from her childhood, Nancy Drew mysteries. But she did have all the Oz books, by L. Frank Baum, and I read these and found them to my taste.

I was still slightly afraid of my uncle Ephraim. He was the kind of intimidating adult who thinks of children as naturally imperfect beings that have to be constantly instructed against their own worst natures. He had a deep voice and he asked questions that awaited answers. An oil painting of himself stood over the mantel in the large living room. I studied that painting in the day, when he wasn't home. It portrayed him as thinner and handsomer than he was, it showed him without his glasses. He was a portly man, with frameless eyeglasses and large teeth, a big nose and a double chin, and he wore dark suits and went off to take the New Haven line to his lawyer's office with the somber mien of a cabinet minister proceeding to affairs of state. At dinner once I put a green pea on my knife and received a ten-minute lecture on why this was not right. I was asked if I understood the points he had made and was then asked to repeat them. I thought he liked me but that I had a long way to go before he could respect me or admire me. He looked on our family, all of us, I thought, as woefully flawed and probably tempered his judgment with the reflection that not many people could be expected to achieve life's heights as he had.

He was a right-wing Republican and liked to argue with my father in a Socratically baiting manner that was condescending.

Yet, of course, he was kind. He had assumed the role of overseer of the entire family's legal welfare, even though we were connected to him by marriage only. He was everyone's lawyer, without fee, charging neither my uncle Phil the cabdriver, when Phil needed to be incorporated for his protection as a medallion owner, nor presumably my father, who probably had needed some legal work in starting up his record business. Uncle Ephraim had more money than anyone else in the family and so probably contributed greatly to the support of my grandma and grandpa. I couldn't have known that a man as proper and august as this had his own deferences: he had not been allowed to marry Aunt Frances until he had given up his job running a magazine subscription business and gone to law school and gotten his degree. That ruling had come from my grandma and put him in her debt for the rest of her life. His three or four years studying law at night while he supported himself in the day taught him a discipline for which he was grateful; the frustration of going unmarried until he proved himself able to support the woman he loved brought him out of the Jewish lower-middle class into a life of wealth and self-determination. Money, propriety and responsibility were his and he wore them all like a judge's robes.

I knew my father detested Ephraim's politics, and his conservative values and pomposity. I assumed my uncle Ephraim disapproved of my father's leftist politics, his impulsiveness, his impracticality, his romanticism. They were like the Aesop tale, the ant and the grasshopper, and I could not for long decide for either existence because I would find it by itself insufficient, though I was all for my father. I always wanted him to win. I did not want that carefree singing grasshopper to come begging when snow covered the ground and he had nothing to eat. This feeling governed me in the week or so I stayed at Pelham. It was like Heaven for a good child, muffled and beautiful. I sat wrapped in a blanket, the sun coming through the parlor windows behind the kitchen; outside was a composition of grass and flowers and trees. Everything was in its place, even the Japanese beetles, which dutifully flew into the lamplike trap to quietly crawl over one another and die. Aunt Frances made her will known quietly, and courteously; even her live-in housekeeper, Clara, the tall black woman with a stony face and a sweet, low mellifluous voice, had a stately grace. Everyone in this house seemed to move in a kind of self-assured regal calm. I contrasted this with the chaos of my home, the intensity of our lives, the extremity of our emotions. In the mornings I drove with Aunt Frances and Uncle Ephraim in their enormous black Buick Roadmaster to the Pelham Manor railroad station. There at exactly the same time each morning the train came along its gravel bed—not a subway but a real train pulled by a locomotive—and chuffed to a stop, and Uncle Ephraim climbed aboard and waved to us. There seemed to be no errors in this life, it moved with a picture-book perfection, at least as it was presented to me in my convalescence.

But I disliked the charitableness of it, it was a life of dangerous propaganda, the more so because it was so quiet. I felt guilty for enjoying myself and the peace of this privileged household. I had to be someone else here, I couldn't whine or complain or make demands, but only show my gratitude. I felt coerced here in Heaven, and I was happy when at last it was time to leave.

Now I RECALL THE PRESENT DONALD BROUGHT ME WHEN I WAS STILL VERY ILL AND lying in the children's ward. It was actually a gift from one of his friends, Seymour or Irwin, or Bernie, I don't remember which. It was a lapel pin shaped like a pickle. It was funny. It was a Heinz 57 pickle, which people got for visiting the Heinz Dome at the New York World's Fair.

"When you're all better," Donald said to me as I turned the pin over in my fingers, "we'll go to the World's Fair."

"Have you been yet?" I said.

"No," my brother said. "We wouldn't go without you, you know that. We'll all go together. Mom and Dad and you and I. The whole family."

AUNT FRANCES

I don't know what to tell you about your father. He was a free spirit. As children we were not that close. I was older, I had different friends, different ideas. I spent my time at the downtown Ethical. The downtown branch of the Ethical Culture Society was for Jews. The Upper West Side Ethical was for the Irish. I learned table manners, music, how to behave, all the better things. The Ethical made my life.

But Dave was not interested in that. He was wild. He was handsome and bright but very trying. He teased my friends. He chased them when they came to visit us. Or he held the door closed against them. One day one of my friends was wearing her first pair of heels and he was chasing her down the stairs of our building and her heel caught on a step and snapped right off. How she cried. He was sorry then, although he pretended not to be.

One of my friends was Felix Frankfurter's sister. The Frankfurters were poor too, as poor as we were.

We lived on Gouverneur Street. Every week, with my group of girls, I walked from the Lower East Side to the Academy of Music opera house on Twenty-third Street. We each had fifty cents for the occasion. Seats were twenty-five cents. The other twenty-five cents were for carfare, but instead we bought bunches of violets, so we walked both ways and sang the songs we'd heard on our way home, with our pretty violets. I remember seeing *Babes in Toyland* at the Academy, but that must have been later, when I was in high school.

Dave was a dreamer, he was always late to school. When he was getting dressed in the morning he'd be putting on his shoes and socks and he'd forget what he was doing and sit there, he'd forget he was supposed to be pulling on his sock.

As a teenager he spent most of his time at the Socialist headquarters. That was our father's influence. Your grandpa was a wonderful man. He read three papers a day. He was a great reader, he loved books, the Russian authors were his favorites. He had a remarkable memory, he remembered books he'd read thirty-five years before, he could quote from a book and talk about it as if he had it in front of him. He was a dyed-in-the-wool Socialist. But he never pressed his ideas on us. He would explain things and let us make up our own minds. Dave loved him, he adored him.

When my father first came to America, this would have been 1886 or 1887, he was a young man not yet married. In fact he and Mama had not even met. He worked at whatever they gave him, they made him a cutter, but he was terrible at it, he was terrible all his life at business, he had no head for it. Years later he became a printer. He had a little shop on Eightieth Street east of Third Avenue. Before that he worked for your father in the sound-box business. But as a young man he immediately enrolled in school and learned everything he could. He went to the East-side Alliance every night after work to learn English. And he studied socialism. Morris Hillquit was his teacher, the famous lawyer. And at the end of the year Morris Hillquit gave my father a dictionary because he was the best in the class.

My mother was better at earning a living than my father. She did piecework. For a while she had a tea shop. Later she ran a resort, a kind of boardinghouse, in the country. I was fifteen or so. The resort failed. She was strict with us girls, with me and Molly, the baby. But Dave could do no wrong. Dave she adored. Dave was the apple of her eye. And he loved her.

From Gouverneur Street we moved all the way up to 100th Street, where the hospital is now. Then there were tenements. There was a farm on Park Avenue at Ninety-eighth Street. My mother would hand me ten cents and I'd go to the farm and pick the things we needed. Everything was a penny. A bunch of radishes, a penny, a cucumber, a head of lettuce. One penny.

Dave and I were not close until many years later when we were each married, with children. I married much earlier. When he married Rose they made the handsomest couple I had ever seen. Rose was a beautiful girl.

Ephraim and I began to court when I was sixteen. Dave was thirteen or fourteen. There is a family story that Dave threw Ephraim down the stairs, but that is not true. What he did was lock him out, hold the door to keep him from visiting me. Dave made Ephraim's life miserable. There was friction between them. They never liked each other.

Ephraim and I had a wonderful marriage. We never argued. He was a conservative Republican, a member of the Liberty League. He knew I felt differently. I voted for Norman Thomas one year and simply didn't tell him and he didn't ask. He trusted me to handle all the household accounts and make the domestic decisions while he attended to his law practice. He never questioned my judgment. The system worked beautifully. Ephraim was a remarkable man. You know, by the twenties we had a household staff of five—housekeeper, cook, maid, a nurse for the children, and a chauffeur. But when the stock market was booming, Ephraim advised many of his clients to take out second mortgages on their homes and invest in the market and so after the crash in '29 he felt responsible to those people and made good on every one of those mortgages. He didn't have to, but that's the way he was. He wiped out his fortune. We had to let the staff go, except for Clara. We had to struggle to put our boys through college.

Dave should have done better than he did. But he was a dreamer. When we lived on the Lower East Side, he liked to go down by the docks and look at the sailing ships. In those days the ships came right up to the street. The prows extended over the sidewalks. You could hear the ropes flapping in the wind, you could hear their masts creaking. He loved that. he stared at the sailors. My mother told him not to go there. She thought he would run away to sea. He was unpredictable. He was a trial to us all. Papa had a wonderful sense of humor! When they were retired and living up on the Concourse, Dave would call on the phone and say he was coming to visit on Tuesday, for example. Tuesday would come and he wouldn't appear, and wouldn't appear, and my mother would fret and Papa would say, well, he didn't say *which* Tuesday.

I loved Dave, we all did. When he was so sick, the last year of his life, I drove him around Manhattan to his accounts, to the stores he sold to. He could hardly walk, he was on crutches, but he couldn't afford to stop working.

I do remember one story about your father when he was a little boy. There was a wonderful family, the Romanoffs, who had taken my mother and father under their wing when they were first married. They were an older couple with no children. Mr. Romanoff enrolled me in school because at that point my parents' English was not that good; he knew English and could speak to the authorities. Anyway, they were delighted with us. Mr. Romanoff had a successful business, a drugstore up in the hundreds somewhere. That was the country. And he especially loved Dave. So the Romanoffs invited Dave to stay the weekend with them, they had no children of their own, you see, and so my mother, wanting to show her little boy at his best, bought a beautiful new suit for him with a hat. Dave turned red when they dressed him up for the visit. He hated the new suit. The hat was a little top hat, I think. When Mama brought him to the Romanoffs, Dave went upstairs and while the adults were downstairs on the street in front of the house, the suit came sailing out the window and landed at their feet. He would not wear it. And to emphasize the point he came outside in his underwear, this four-year-old, and came down the steps and in front of everyone threw the hat down in the dirt and stomped on it. He jumped up and landed with both feet on the hat again and again. Stomped it into the dirt. So they would know what he thought of it.

TWENTY-ONE

For several months I would sleep badly. I was afraid to go to sleep: in my dreams I smelled ether and felt a knife cutting into my belly.

When I went back to school, I was for a day or so treated as a returning hero. We all smiled shyly at each other. My classmates had sent me a big homemade get-well card with everyone's name painstakingly autographed. My friend Meg's hand was very clear and round and firm, which had not surprised me—as a girl she would be good at penmanship. My friend Arnold wrote like a spider.

All along my teacher had been sending me the lessons and I was almost caught up.

At home I learned that my father was moving his store to another location. The Hippodrome theater was being torn down and all the businesses there had to leave. He had found another site a few blocks north on Sixth Avenue, up near the new Radio City Music Hall between Forty-sixth and Forty-seventh streets and was hopeful about it. It was a large space, which meant he could display more stock; on the other hand, the rent was more and there would be inevitable losses of sales from the move. So everything was at a risk, including the money he and his partner had borrowed to build the shelves and the cabinets for the display of merchandise. There would also be a loss of selling time while this work went on.

One day my mother took me downtown to see the new store as it was being renovated. We found my father in his shirt sleeves, which was unusual, he always wore his coat and vest and tie, even at home on weekends. He was running around with a cigar in his mouth and stacks of records in his arms; he and Donald were stocking the shelves with albums. Lester, his partner, was unpacking radio consoles, and in the back a man on a ladder was still painting the wall and two carpenters were building the listening booths, of which there were to be three. I was tremendously excited by what was going on. The store was much bigger than the old one, half again as wide. The floor was carpeted. A wide staircase halfway back and in the middle of the floor led to a basement level that was to be devoted entirely to musical instruments. Uncle Willy was to be in charge of this section. My father's face was flushed with excitement. He put his cigar down on a counter for a moment and his partner, Lester, said, "Dave, don't you know better than to put a lighted cigar on a new piece of furniture? We haven't even opened the store yet!" We all stopped what we were doing. My father said very firmly, "Lester, this cigar won't burn the counter. Don't you know anything about tobacco? A cigar is a rolled leaf, it is not shredded like cigarette tobacco. A cigarette will continue to burn, a cigar goes out when you put it down." He was very scientific in his explanation, and I was relieved. "Put that in your pipe and smoke it," he said to Lester, and everyone laughed.

Outside, crowds of people moved along the sidewalks. I was excited that my father's new store was so close to the Radio City Music Hall. Only a block away was the Roxy. We were at the heart of things. Occasionally people stopped to peer through the locked doors. They pressed their noses up against the windows. They were very curious.

Some days later the store opened, and the following Saturday we again went down to see it. Everything was finished now and shining. Red, white and blue bunting was draped across the top of the windows and the front door. In the windows were displays of radios and electrolas, and photographs of Paul Whiteman and George Gershwin, Benny Goodman and Fats Waller, and Arturo Toscanini and Josef Hoffmann, as if somehow they all knew my father and had gathered to celebrate the new store. The inside was hushed and remarkable. Standing on slightly raised platforms were the latest models of console radios, all the famous makes, like Stewart-Warner, Grunow, Maytone, Philco, and Stromberg-Carlson. Attached to each was a small tag with the price and description of the radio's feature. I liked particularly the RCA Victor model in heart walnut that went for $89.95. It had eight tubes, two of glass, a magic eye, an edge-lighted dial and a phono connection. Also there was a Crosley with fifteen tubes, five of them glass, an autoexpressionator, a mystic hand, and a cardiamatic unit for $174.50. Smaller table radios were grouped on counters and shelves behind the counters in the radio section. I liked very much a new-model Radette that featured telematic dial tuning. It was a telephone dial set right over the circular station indicator so that you could dial your station as you dialed a telephone. I thought that was really fine for only $24.95.

There were many different kinds of phonographs as well, and one or two units that combined radios and record players, although these were very expensive. A glass cabinet held packets of steel needles and books on musical subjects, including *The Victor Book of the Opera*. We had that at home. The walls were lined with shelves filled with record albums, and in the listening booths there were standing ashtrays and record players built into the counters with electric pickup arms, the kind you didn't have to wind, and soundproofing panels on the side walls and ceiling. I liked the way the doors to these booths clicked shut.

Downstairs all the musical instruments shone in their cabinets, golden saxophones and black clarinets, and silver trumpets, and accordions with gleaming ivory and black keys. There was even a card with batons of different sizes with tapered cork tips. A set of drums sat on a pedestal lit with special spotlights. Uncle Willy let me sit up behind this rig and play for a minute or two, but with the brushes only, so that nobody would be disturbed. Of course, there were no customers down here, so it didn't matter that much. And when I went upstairs just one or two people were on the premises, one in a listening booth, the other studying the rack of sheet music. Lester stood behind the radio counter, his arms folded, a cigarette in the corner of his mouth. My father awaited customers at the classical music counter. Behind him was a whole wall of record albums of symphonies and operas and concertos. Their bindings were dark green. He stood with his hands flat on the glass countertop, he was dressed in his blue serge suit with the vest and his dark red tie, he looked impressive to me standing there leaning slightly forward, attentive to the occasion and awaiting for whoever it was would come in needing assistance.

We had not yet been to the World's Fair, but all around were signs that it was going on. Kazoos and ocarinas in their cards had World's Fair emblems. Next door was a souvenir shop where Trylon and Perisphere pins were on sale, and banners with pictures of them painted on the cloth. The Trylon was a skyscraping obelisk; the Perisphere was a great globe. They stood side by side at the Fair, and together they represented the World of Tomorrow, which was the Fair's theme. Almost every day in the newspaper was a picture of Mayor La Guardia welcoming some dignitary or movie star to Flushing Meadow, the site of the Fair. I did not pester my parents, I knew we would go eventually. Everyone was very busy. Besides, the truth was I had misgivings about it, it seemed so vast, such an enormous place, with so many things going on simultaneously, shows and exhibits and people from foreign countries, that I did not know where I wanted to go first. It was difficult to visualize. I was not even there yet but had fallen into the habit when I thought about the World's Fair of worrying that I would miss the best things. I didn't know why I felt that way.

My father had predicted the Fair would be good for business. He explained that people were coming to see it from all over the country. They would have to stay in hotels, they would have to have dinner, they would spend money going to Radio City and they would pass the shop and see records and electrolas they wanted and they would come in and buy something. People on trips always set aside money to buy things. Besides, in his store they could find things you couldn't find anywhere else. He was very optimistic.

Nevertheless, as the year moved into the winter, and the year 1940 began, the Fair closed for the season and business had not been what he had hoped.

At home in the evenings earlier now, my father was in the habit of listening to all the news commentators to find out what was going on in Europe. I knew, even before it was discussed in my class during current events, that a terrible war had begun—Hitler and Mussolini against England and France. He listened to every one of those news commentators; they didn't just read the news bulletins, but analyzed them too. Then my father analyzed their analyses. His new theory was that you had to listen to them all to figure out what the truth was. He liked Gabriel Heatter and Walter Winchell because they were antifascist. He detested Fulton Lewis and Boake Carter and H. V. Kaltenborn because they were against the New Deal and against unions and made comments verging on fascist, America First sympathies. He hated Father Coughlin, who said the Jewish bankers were to blame for everything. I grew to recognize the voices of these men and the products that sponsored them. Gabriel Heatter talked about gingivitis, which was a fancy name for bleeding gums; he passionately described the advantages of Forhan's toothpaste for this condition in the same fervent tones with which he described democracy's battle against fascism. If you didn't listen carefully, you might think that fascism and bleeding gums were the same thing.

My father sat in a chair near the radio and the newspapers opened in his lap to news stories with maps about the very same events being discussed by the commentators. He bought most of the papers—the *Times,* the *Herald Tribune,* the *Post,* the *World-Telegram,* even the *Daily Worker.* He would not read the Hearst papers.

In the movies on Saturday afternoons, after the cartoons, the Fox Movietone newsreels showed scenes from the war in Europe: big cannon muzzles afire in the night, German dive-bombers with angled wings coming out of the clouds. You saw the bombs falling. You saw burning buildings in London. You saw people swinging bottles of champagne against the sides of ships and diplomats getting out of cars and walking hurriedly up the steps of palaces for meetings. The war was talked about everywhere and shown in pictures. I liked to draw, I had made up my own comic-book stories and drawn them and colored them with crayon. I had a hero modeled after Smilin' Jack, the comic-strip pilot. I called my man Daring Dave. He had a moustache and wore a leather helmet with goggles and a lumber jacket and he had flown racing planes—like Smilin' Jack. I loved to draw these planes, snub-nosed daring little machines with checkerboard designs on their wings and ailerons. I drew them trailing exhaust in the sky so you could see what looping maneuvers they were capable of.

They flew around courses measured by pylons. They flew over hangars decorated with wind socks. I wasn't sure exactly how something as vast and immeasurable as air could be used for a closed race course but I trusted that it could. I drew all sorts of those racing planes, some with cylindrical engine cowlings, some with enclosed cowlings pointed like index fingers. I drew cockpits that were open to the wind and cockpits that were enclosed with Plexiglas covers, but whatever the plane, whatever the design, I always put those streamlined wheel covers on them that were like raindrops coming along the window sideways in a windy rain. I liked streamlining, I liked those Chrysler cars that looked like beetles because their wheels were almost completely covered over and all their surface was rounded to get through the wind more easily, and for the same reason I liked those rear tapered airplane wheel covers. But now that World War Two had come to Europe I decided to get Dave into a fighter plane. I put him into a Spitfire flying over London for the Royal Air Force. The English insignia was a bull's-eye colored red, white and blue. I liked the colors but wondered if it wasn't a mistake to paint brightly colored targets on the wings and fuselage of your planes for the enemy to shoot at. I showed Nazi Messerschmitts going down in smoke.

I did not think the war was anything but far away. I did not feel personally threatened. But my mother talked about the war with worried references to Donald. He had graduated from Townsend Harris High School under a rapid advance program and now, age seventeen, he was enrolled at City College. My mother was afraid Donald would draw a low number in the Selective Service registration and be drafted into the Army and taken off to fight in Europe. This seemed to me an outlandish worry, inasmuch as America wasn't even in the war. I could not quite make the connections adults around me were making. One day I saw a headline in my father's copy of the *Post:* WAR CLOUDS, it read. The article went on to speculate about how and when the United States might have to become involved in the war against Hitler.

In the same Madison Square Garden where I had seen the Ringling Brothers and Barnum & Bailey Circus with that family that rode bicycles on high wires and the little clown who swept the spotlight at his feet, the American Nazis, called the Bund, had held a rally. They had put up a flag with a swastika next to an American flag, and marched in their brown shirts and with belts like Texas Rangers going from their shoulders down slantwise to their waists. They gave the fascist salute. There were thousands of them. Charles Lindbergh and Father Coughlin had spoken to them and they shouted and screamed just as the Germans did when Hitler spoke to them. "They are everywhere, this rabble," my father said one night at dinner. "Two of them came into the store today and I kicked them out. Can you imagine the temerity—coming into my store in their uniforms to try to sell me a subscription to their magazine?"

Donald told us about one of the boys who had been in his junior class at Townsend Harris. His name was Sigmund Miller. He lived in Yorkville, the German neighborhood on the Upper East Side of Manhattan, and he was a fascist. "Considering that the school was almost one hundred percent Jewish, he was pretty brave about it," Donald said. Sigmund Miller would explain in class discussions why he was for Hitler. He got beat up repeatedly after school. But Donald was telling this because of what happened subsequently. Donald and Bernie and Irwin and Harold Epstein and Stan Mazey all went together to high school every morning. They met at the corner and walked across the Concourse and down Mt. Eden Avenue to the Jerome Avenue El. One morning on the train a man was reading the *Daily News*. Sigmund Miller's picture was on the front page. He had murdered his girlfriend. He had made a suicide pact with her, but after he killed her he had not been able to keep his part of the bargain. "Excuse me," Stan Mazey said to the man reading the paper, and yanked it right out of his hands. "I think a friend of ours just killed someone."

"Why would they want to commit suicide, your friend and this girl?" I asked at the dinner table.

Donald looked at my mother. "She was pregnant," he said.

My mother said, "I don't think this is appropriate conversation for dinnertime."

I was offended. "You think I don't know what pregnant means?" I said to her. "I can assure you, I know exactly what it means!" Then I was doubly offended because everyone laughed, as if I had said something funny.

TWENTY-TWO

It was winter now and the sky grew dark early in the afternoon. My father came home from work in the darkness with the cold blowing off him like the breath of his coat and hat. Donald came home each night with his books under his arm, his nose red and his eyes glittering with the cold. Even now I had pains where my scar was—lesions, the doctors called them. I played out of doors very little. I was not supposed to exert myself. My scar was long and I examined it every day. It was a thick raised welt slanting from my side down toward my testicles. At the top of the scar and at the bottom were depressions, dips in the skin, where the drains had been placed. These were the tenderest spots of all, and when I touched them I could feel my insides cringe. So people who went out into the world of German war, fearless of the Nazis on the dark streets of New York, had my admiration. I had changed physically since the operation; I had been a lean wiry little boy, very well coordinated, I was never a fast runner but I could throw gracefully and catch and get some fair hits in punchball or stickball. All that was gone. I was shaped like a pear, I was overweight from all those weeks in bed, and physically shy of my own movements. I was always afraid of tearing something, I did not like to jump around or leap down from the wall in the backyard as I had once done in my Zorro games with my friend Bertram; it was as if I still had stitches in me, I could sometimes feel them, and the terrible awful feeling when they had been removed, I could feel them as they had been snipped by the doctor and I could feel the gut string pulling through my flesh. I had nothing to counteract my tendency to fat. If I wasn't afraid to run around, my mother was afraid for me. She had very quickly gone grey at the temples. She looked at me worriedly and fed me as if I were still convalescing even though I had long since gone back to school. I ate lots of junket desserts and lots of eggs and slices of buttered bread and thick soups of chicken stock and beef with potatoes and cabbage and vegetables of all sorts. I drank lots of milk, it came now homogenized, which meant you didn't have to shake the bottle to distribute the cream evenly. I had to eat hot cereal in the

390

morning, Cream of Wheat or oatmeal, even though I preferred Post Toas-
ties or Kix. And since I didn't move around very much, my whole being
was changed, I had grown taller and bulkier, I still had a sunny smile and
a handsome countenance, but also a double chin. I tried to compensate for
this by combing my hair in a way Donald combed his, with a pompadour
in the front. Mine didn't stay up for very long, I was never allowed to let
my hair grow long enough to make it really work. Donald as a college
freshman grew his hair longer and combed it carefully each morning and
in the evening too when he came home from school. In fact, when he
didn't have anything else to do, Donald went to the mirror to comb his
hair, running the comb through it, and propping it and patting it with his
other hand till it was the way he wanted it. He was these days dignified
and soft-spoken and serious, as befitted a college student. He no longer
wore knickers, he wore long trousers pleated and with slightly pegged
cuffs. He wore a chain from his belt to his side pocket. Outside the house
he affected a straight briar pipe, which he clenched in his teeth on one side
of his mouth. He never smoked it, that I knew, he just clenched it. Our
relationship was changing. At seventeen he now hovered at about twice
my age, and took on the coloration of a father rather than an older brother.
He showered every day. He offered me less instruction because our interests no longer coincided, but appeared more and more in my eyes as a
model to be emulated and studied. In the evening, when he got home, he
listened to the fifteen-minute sports broadcast of Stan Lomax, who with
great thoroughness rattled off all the minutiae of collegiate sports with
heartening references to the New York city colleges and institutions that
were disdained by the other sports news authorities. Stan Lomax dealt
with the football fortunes of Brooklyn and City colleges with the same
judicious objectivity as he mentioned the University of Michigan or the
Minnesota Gophers or the Duke Blue Devils. Donald liked that. He had the
fervent pride of the assimilationist, as we all did. Listening with him, I
envisioned gothic campuses of idyllic rusticity, as if the sports scores were
stories being told. Elegant young football players with names like Tommy
Harmon strolled across tree-lined quadrangles in their slacks and argyle
sweaters and two-toned shoes with pretty coeds in pleated skirts and
angora sweaters by their sides. In their conversation they quietly admitted
to having scored the winning touchdown. There were no books and no
lectures in these visions of mine. What was essential to them was that
same dusk of winter, that late afternoon of cold hard air and leaves
spinning down from the plane trees of the Bronx streets, produced by the
clouds of World War Two. I liked in my house circles of lamplight surrounded by rings of darkness that grew in depth the farther out they went.
I liked the shelter of a desk lamp, feeling toward it Bomba the Jungle Boy's
affection for his campfire in the roars of the dark surrounding night.

TWENTY-THREE

Yet actual football, as opposed to the symbolic game, we preferred, as it was performed by professionals. This was a trait we learned from our father, who had discussed how much better and livelier the pro game was than the collegiate version. There were two teams in New York, the Giants and the Brooklyn Dodgers. They had the same names as the baseball teams but were not related. For some reason my father liked the Dodgers, he admired their quarterback, whose name was Ace Parker, and two linemen, Perry Schwartz, an end whom he thought almost as good a pass catcher as Don Hutson of the Packers, and a terrific tackle named Bruiser Kinard. Donald and I made the Giants our team. We had Tuffy Leemans in the backfield, along with Ward Cuff, Hank Soar, and the passer, Ed Danowski. On the line was the iron man Mel Hein, at center, and two great ends, Jim Lee Howell and Jim Poole. That was a team. Everyone played both offense and defense, Mel Hein usually played the whole sixty minutes without a substitute, Ward Cuff dropkicked field goals and Hank Soar could be counted upon for at least one interception when he was back at Safety on defense. When the Giants played the Dodgers, fans of both teams showed up at the park.

One Sunday at about one o'clock my father decided to take us to a Giants-Dodgers game. Donald said, "We'd just as well not even try, we'll never get in, people started lining up for seats early this morning."

"Let's just give it a shot," my father said. My mother made us sandwiches and a thermos of hot chocolate. She claimed she was tired and would not mind being by herself for a few hours by way of placating Donald's and my guilt at leaving her alone on a Sunday. We knew Sunday was the only day my father was at home. For his part he seemed to have no cares leaving her.

Wrapped up against the cold November day, the three of us boarded the subway and rode down to 155th Street, and came upstairs in the shadow of the El outside the great steel-girded Polo Grounds. My heart sank. The streets were packed. The game was less than an hour from kickoff and immensely long lines of people were in front of the ticket kiosks. My father told Donald and me to get in line, just to keep a place, even though we knew it was likely the game would be sold out before we ever got to the booth. Saying he would be right back, my father disappeared.

All around us hawkers were selling pins and pennants, and bags of roasted peanuts. I really wanted one of those football pins, miniature footballs painted golden brown with painted laces attached to a ribbon with each team's colors, blue for the Giants, silver and red for the Dodgers; but I didn't want to be thought of as a baby. The footballs were made in Japan and you could pry them, like walnuts, in half at the seams. We could hear the crowds roaring inside the stadium as the teams warmed up. Occasionally we heard the sound of a punt. Our line inched forward with tormenting slowness. What could be worse than being on the outside and hearing cheers rise from behind the ballpark walls? The El pulled into the station overhead, and people came running down the stairs. The side-walks overflowed; people ran and walked in the streets between the cars. I developed that specific prayerful longing that went with these situations: If we got into the game, I said to myself, I would do my homework every day for a week the minute I got home from school. I would help my mother when she asked. I would go to bed when I was told to.

Taxis kept pulling up and discharging passengers. Occasionally I saw a limousine polished to a black shine, with one of those open driver's seats and with white sidewall wheels and glittering chrome radiators and head-lamps, and a running board trimmed in new grey rubber. The chauffeur would run around to the sidewalk door and out would step elegant women in fur coats and men in belted camel-hair coats, the collars turned up. They carried leather cases, which I understood were filled with flasks of whis-key and picnic delicacies, and they carried plaid blankets to keep warm, and some of them were recognized by people in the crowd, who called to them. They waved, smiling, as they passed through the gates. One or two older men in black coats and homburgs were saluted by policemen on guard. I saw in these sportsmen, I derived from them, information of a high life of celebrity, wealth, and the careless accommodation of pleasure. I understood that these people were politicians and gamblers first and sportsmen second. Something in their attitude appropriated the occasion. It was theirs. The team was theirs, the ballpark was theirs, and I, standing with my runny nose and muffled to invisibility in a buffing crowd of heavy-coated football fans on the outside and waiting to get in—a mo-mentary swatch of color at the edge of their field of vision—I was theirs too. I felt all this keenly and became angry. Someone jostled me and I pushed back with my elbow.

Then there was a commotion in the street. One of the ticket booths had closed its window and put the SOLD OUT sign behind the little iron bars protecting the opaque window glass. The crowd at this kiosk dissolved noisily, there was shouting, and people invaded the lines at the other windows not yet shut down. Policemen were running toward us from the street and from under the concrete stands. Another elevated train thundered in.

"It's almost game time," Donald said, and just then another roar went up and our line dissolved into a swirling pushing angry mass. He was exasperated. "Where's Dad," he said. "We've come here for nothing."

At this moment, as we stood bewildered and feeling bruised with disappointment we heard a voice—"Don, Edgar, over here!" My father was waving to us at the edge of the crowd. We pushed our way toward him. "This way," my father said, his eyes alight. In his hand he held three tickets spread out like cards. "What!" we said, finding it hard to believe. He'd done it! From one moment to the next he led us from despair to exhilaration through the turnstiles and up the ramp into the bright sunlight of the stadium.

Ah, what a moment, coming out into the raked tiers, seeing with my own eyes the green grass field, the white stripes, the colors of the two helmeted teams deployed for the kickoff. Tens of thousands of people roared with anticipation. Pigeons flew into the air. The game was about to begin!

Incredibly, my father had gotten tickets for the lower stands on the 35-yard line. We couldn't believe our good fortune. It was magic! His face was flushed with delight, his eyes widened and he pursed his mouth and puffed his cheeks like a clown. We were no sooner seated and the game was under way than he looked around and spotted an usher; five minutes later we were in even better seats, farther back in the section, where with some altitude we could now see the whole field clearly. "What do you think of this," my father said, smiling at us in triumph. "Not bad, eh?" He loved this sort of situation, the suspense of getting in just at the last moment. The game meant more now, more than it might have if he had purchased the tickets a week in advance.

There was no question we were witnesses to a momentous event. The two teams struggled back and forth on the field. We groaned or cheered as the pass was caught or the punt dropped.

Donald and I followed the game intensely, cracking peanut shells and chewing and frowning and offering each other extended critiques of the action. My father was more calm. He smoked his cigar and every now and then closed his eyes and turned his face up to the afternoon sun.

The Giants were in blue jerseys and the Dodgers in red and silver, and both wore the sectioned leather helmets that came around the ears, and the buff-colored canvas pants, and the black high lace-up shoes. When the sun went below the roof level of the upper stands, long shadows fell across the field and across our faces. The changing color of the day brought new moods to the game, new fortitude and desperation to the embattled lines, as the backs slashed off tackle or did their line bucks, as the centers hiked the ball and the backfield ran in box formation and compacted into their handoffs and laterals and blocks, and ran and threw from their scattered single wing. They were well matched, you could feel their effort, you heard the thudding leather of their shoulder pads. The dust flew up in the planes of sunlight as they fought on the dirt part of the field, the baseball diamond. My father did not passionately root for the Dodgers. It seemed more important to him that the score remain close. Donald and I wanted the Giants to pull ahead and win without any equivocation. Something happened to the sound of the game; the dimming light seemed to give it distance. Ace Parker punted the ball for the Dodgers and it rose in a looping spiral high over the tops of the stands; then I heard the sound of his shoe hitting the football.

In the late afternoon, dusk falling, the game ended, with the Giants winning by one touchdown. Everyone cheered. The two teams walked together toward the small bleachers at the end of the field and climbed the stairs under the scoreboard into their locker rooms. They held their helmets in their hands. Fans leaped over the bleacher walls and called to them. People flowed onto the field. We made our way down. It was awesome to tread in the black grass, with the marks of the cleats visible like traces of battle. It seemed to me a historic site. It was a hard cold ground. A wind blew in from the open backs of the stands, which now stood silhouetted, a great horseshoe-shaped shed, little light bulbs glittering dimly in each section of the upper and lower tiers. The air down here on the field was pungent with the cold. It smelled electric. I apprehended the awesome skill and strength of the football player. Boys ran through the crowd, dodging and dashing about like halfbacks, with invisible balls under their arms. I walked with my brother and father to the field gates, passing under the scoreboard and out to 155th Street. Here the milling crowds, the gabble, the horns of taxis, the rumble of trains, and police on horseback blowing their whistles brought my mind back to the city. We were hoarse and tired. The day was over. We pushed our way down the subway steps into the crowd on the station platform. We jammed into the train, the three of us forced together, packed tight in the train and barreling toward the dark Sunday night, when even the arguing stopped and there was stillness, and a cessation of all striving, my night of unnameable dread, that most mysterious night of the day of rest.

TWENTY-FOUR

The winter was to be a bad one. I woke up one night to hear my mother and father arguing. They were all the way at the other end of the house but I could hear her clearly. She was saying he had lost the store. I heard his voice then, but not the words, only the tone of earnest entreaty. He spoke a long time.

"Undercapitalized, my eye," she answered. "You've gambled it away. When you should have been taking care of business, you were out playing cards, running around and being a big shot. And Lester meanwhile was stealing from you."

"You don't know what you're saying, Rose," my father said.

"I know full well," she said. "Yes, of course these are bad times, but other people survive. They're competitive. They pull in their horns. They cut costs, they do not give credit, they buy on consignment—don't tell me how to run a business. If I were in charge you wouldn't be in the trouble you're in now."

I fell asleep while the argument went on. But in the morning everything was as it had always been. My father went off to work. Donald went off to school. My mother gave me my breakfast and asked me if I had done all my homework.

The issue I understood as the way each of them thought. Something was wrong, but my father seemed to think he could set it right and my mother was telling him it was too late to make things right. I heard pieces and bits of this argument over several weeks, sometimes late at night, sometimes allusively, right in front of me at the dinner table. My mother's voice rang with prophecy. She spoke as if something had already happened when it hadn't. This I resented especially, as I knew her to be more realistic. He still had hope. He insisted things were to be done and I couldn't entirely believe him, but I resented that she would not honor his intentions, she would not take them seriously. "Don't hand me any of your cock-and-bull stories," she said. "What bank is going to lend you money with the books you've kept."

This terrible event loomed larger and larger as it did not happen. It was the subject of all our lives. Donald continued to work in my father's store on Saturdays, just as he had since the age of thirteen. He was not paid, it was his family responsibility, which he dutifully met. I campaigned to help too. On Saturdays I went downtown to be Donald's assistant. As I grew stronger I accompanied him on his delivery rounds. Stores on Sixth Avenue adjoined residential neighborhoods. All the little brownstones and residential hotels between Sixth Avenue and Ninth, on both sides of Broadway, provided a small town's population for any shop or service. Donald delivered records that people ordered by phone, and radios and phonographs that they had left for repair. Sometimes he journeyed south to the Fourteenth Street area, where one or another of my father's jobbers supplied him with spare parts or record stocks. These were interesting trips for me, my courage held in tremulous tension by the presence of my older brother at my side. We walked in the dappled shadows of the El on Third Avenue, under the structure of black steel trestles that shook and sounded into the depths of the street bed the thunderous but unseen passage of the trains. There was no louder noise. It was like a tornado of sound; you could not, as the train passed overhead, hear what was said to you. You could see in some places the crossties laid under the tracks with nothing but air between them. People lived in tenements whose third- or fourth-floor windows looked out on the tracks, so close they could jump right onto them if they chose, so close the headlamps of the clattering trains would shine into their windows at night. We passed Christian missions with men in soft caps and shabby black coats standing about gazing at everyone who walked by, we passed electric tattooing parlors and barbershops that advertised fifteen cents for a shave and haircut, there were pawnshops with wooden Indians out front, and shooting galleries, ten shots for ten cents. Men with sandwich boards hung over their shoulders and flyers in their hands walked along advertising "Best Price for Old Gold," "Gaiety Follies." We stood under the marquee of a theater showing a triple bill with movies and movie stars I had never heard of. Men sat in there all day for ten cents, Donald said, just to have somewhere to sleep. Pushcart peddlers at the curbs sold everything—shoes, notions, fruit, even books. Men slept on their sides in the doorways, their hands under their heads, they were grown men but they slept curled up as I did. The doorways were their homes. How could I not with these sights in my eyes understand the meaning of a business? It was not an obscure lesson. Donald took us through gatherings of people poised at the corners waiting for the lights to change, he jaywalked us between jams of yellow cabs and trucks, streetcars running in the shadows of the elevated lines rang their bells at us, and he got us unerringly to our destination, into lofts or offices where we were expected and where packages marked with my father's name were waiting for us. My father still existed in business, and this encouraged me. My brother knew his way around town. Back at the store, people were buying things. Hippodrome Music looked busy. Why was all of this not sufficient?

I thought neither my father nor my mother was the one to whom this question should be put. I asked Donald.

"It's hard to understand," he said. "But it's not your problem. It is not anything a kid should worry about."

"Everyone's always hiding things from me," I said. "We weren't allowed to go to Grandma's funeral, which was really stupid when I was the one who found her dead."

"What are you talking about that for?" Donald said. "This is business. When the store moved they lost customers. It's taken them longer to build a clientele. Reliable customers who come in again and again are called a clientele. They can't get enough money from what they're selling to pay their salaries, and their bills, and to buy more things to sell too. Now, do you understand?"

Then while all this was going on Donald quit college at the end of his first term. He told me it was boring and that was why he was getting out. But that didn't make sense. He had joined a fraternity and I knew he loved spending time with his frat brothers, as he called them. They even owned their own house. They all smoked briar pipes there. Snooping around Donald's room when he was out, I found a letter from the college in his bureau drawer and it gave his marks, two D's and two F's. I knew what these grades meant, he had explained to me that in college they didn't mark with numbers, they marked with letters. I could not believe that my wonderful brother, who had been held out to me all through grade school as a wonderful student, was failing courses at City College. He was becoming like my parents—an adult to be observed and worried about. All these strange things were going on, everyone was unhappy and the three of them got into all sorts of arguments now, nobody liked what anybody else in the family was doing, my father was angry at my brother, and my mother was furious with both of them. All of it together pushed me down into myself, I wondered if I was to blame because of my operation; people didn't just leave the house, they slammed the door, dinners were silent, I felt small. I felt my ears were flattened along the sides of my head. My friend Arnold, from my class, had ears that grew that way, tight against his head and very tiny, and that's the way I felt my ears were now. I was feeling all hunched up into myself.

IN THIS TERRIBLE TIME SOME BASIC PRACTICES WERE MAINTAINED, INCLUDING THE Sunday afternoon visit to Grandma and Grandpa's house on the Concourse north of Kingsbridge Road. Once again I was the only representative of the family to accompany my father on these visits. It was

Grandma's feeling that extravagance at home had contributed to the financial fix he was in; Rose had not been as economical as she might have, she was careless with a dollar, she liked good things too much.

"Please, Gussie," my grandfather said. "The man is talking business. If you have nothing intelligent to say, say nothing."

Even my father was piqued by his mother's inability to think of anything but his wife's spending habits. "Papa," he said, "why are all women like this? It's as if we don't exist. Whether they love or they hate, they think only of each other, they are alone in the universe," he said with exasperation.

"You talk," my grandma said in an ugly spiteful voice, hobbling across the room with the tea things, and slamming them down. "And she spends."

On one of these trips our visit coincided with the visit of Aunt Frances, who for the first time heard all the details of our family's troubles. She looked very fine, with a dark blue suit and a black hat and a white blouse. She wore white gloves and put them down on top of her leather handbag when she came in. She took off her hat and ran her fingers through her beautiful white hair. She calmed everyone down, she could do that, calm people down because she spoke so softly and with such grace. "I will talk to Ephraim," she said.

I respected Aunt Frances because she was so soothing. My parents had relied on her to get the right doctor for me. My mother hated my grandma but disliked Frances only on occasion. However, she liked Aunt Molly, the funny one who was so sloppy, and she felt they were friends. My father loved both his sisters as well as his mother, but disliked Frances's husband, Ephraim, although he would not tell me that, I knew it for myself.

But Frances and her husband Ephraim had powers over us all. I didn't know why. I knew they were wealthier, but I didn't know if they were wealthier because they had these powers, or if they got them from being wealthy, but they were not troubled people, as far as I could tell; even when they had had troubles such as my cousin Lila's getting polio when she was a little girl, before I was born, they would not have doubted their powers to do something to save her, as they did, or to know what to do to save me, which they knew. It was hard for me to understand exactly what I perceived of my aunt and her husband, but they were a degree or two above us, although I couldn't have said what I meant by "above." People wouldn't talk to them in a way they wouldn't want to be talked to. They had power over situations, they could command things, they could run things, and especially impressive in my beautiful aunt's case, they could do so without raising their voice.

Donald had been looking for any kind of a job he could get, he did not want to work for my father now because he would not be paid. He would put in part-time hours while he was looking, he said, but he wanted a real job of his own. One of Uncle Ephraim's connections, it turned out, was the

owner of a large printing firm, B. J. Warriner. This firm was so important it printed the ballots for all the elections held in the City of New
York. It printed documents of all kinds for the city and the state, and the
man who owned this firm was Uncle Ephraim's friend and legal client.
One day Donald received in the mail a letter from Uncle Ephraim and
another letter under it addressed to the Employment Manager of the B. J.
Warriner firm. I studied this letter over Donald's shoulder as he sat in
the kitchen. "Be careful," my mother said, "or you'll get it wet. Keep it
off the table." At the top of this letter, which looked almost like parch-
ment, was the name *Ephraim Goldman* in raised letters, you could feel
them with the tips of your fingers—*Attorney at Law*. In the letter Uncle
Ephraim called the attention of the Employment Manager to Mr. Donald
Altschuler of 1650 Eastburn Avenue, The Bronx, as a young man known
to him for many years, whom he could recommend as being of sterling
character, commendable intelligence and great promise, and who was
now looking for suitable employment.

Donald got a job with the Warriner firm as a messenger boy for fifteen
dollars a week. It was not a job he could take satisfaction in, he found it
demeaning after having led a band and attended college. "Uncle
Ephraim's influence isn't what he thinks it is," Donald said. He left every
morning very early, because Warriner was far downtown, on Hudson
Street, and the subway ride was very long. When he came home he
smelled faintly of ink. He said the presses were interesting to watch. He
said he liked the men in the pressroom but not the executives in the office.
They sat at phones and sold people printing and thought they were hot-
shots. He liked getting out and making the deliveries. Regularly he took
proofs of things to police headquarters on Centre Street and to the Munici-
pal Building on Chambers Street. He liked the far downtown; when he had
a free minute he liked to go to the piers. He could steal a few minutes from
delivering something on Whitehall Street to watch the ferries at Battery
Park. Or if a delivery ran into his lunch hour he could go to the Aquarium.

But his disposition had changed, he didn't see his friends now, he
didn't want to play with me at all; when he got home from work, he didn't
talk to anyone but threw himself across his bed and went to sleep.

In my memory I now think of this time as sunless. It was a harsh winter
with snow always in the street, accumulating through several snowfalls
despite the Department of Sanitation snowplows, which were really water
wagons with plows attached, and despite the sanitation men who with
long-handled flat-bladed shovels pushed the slush and snow into the
sewers. Snow built up in banks along the curb, and lay against the sides
of buildings grey and crusted. The sun never seemed to come out and light

left the sky not long after school was over for the day. I huddled near my radio and listened to my programs. I read my Richard Halliburton book that Mae Barsky had brought me in the hospital: *The Complete Book of Marvels*. Richard Halliburton went around the world exploring its marvels. He swam the length of the Panama Canal, and climbed to the top of the George Washington Bridge while it was being built. He slept secretly one night in the Taj Mahal, and he had his picture taken sitting at the top of the biggest pyramid in Egypt. He climbed the mountain to Macchu Pichu, the ancient hidden site of the Incas of Peru. He went places by ship and sometimes flew the flying boats.

I also found myself deeply attentive to movie serials. It was a matter of serious discussion with my friends how closely the heroes of the movie serials resembled the originals of the comic strips. *Dick Tracy* was one of the more effective in bringing the comics to life. I believed Tracy was Tracy, his chin wasn't as pointed as I'd hoped but he had that look about the eyes. *Don Winslow of the Navy* was another good one. Don Winslow got into fights on speedboats as they were running along out of control. At one point he was captured and taken by motorboat into a secret cave hidden inside a cliff; there were landing docks in there and steel doors in stone walls and sailors in black sweaters under the command of an evil Oriental. Anything with caves fascinated me. The caves in Missouri that Mark Twain describes in *Tom Sawyer* I had never forgotten: When Tom and Becky got lost in those caves, and they shared their pitiful piece of cake and Becky lay down to die and Tom went on in the narrow lightless passageway with only a string to bring him back to her, I could almost not bear to read. The worst moment of all was when they heard the voices of rescuers come closer and closer only to recede and leave them alone once again, in the silence. I could not breathe reading that. I thought in that situation I would not be as brave as Tom or resigned, however piteously she cried, as Becky. In sheer terror, like someone buried alive, I would exhaust myself screaming and trying to break through the cave walls with my bare fists, I would run around in circles and stumble into deep clefts in the rocks, I would gasp and moan and die of apoplexy. But Don Winslow, who habitually found himself imprisoned in caves, did not worry me. They were very well lit caves, they were electrified, steel doors rose and fell silently, a mark of civilization, and it was far preferable to be a prisoner of someone, no matter how evil, than to be alone in the darkness miles underground. In fact, it wasn't until Tom Sawyer saw Injun Joe's candle around the corner in one of the dark rock corridors that I knew the children would escape. As mean and frightening a villain as he was, Injun Joe was life. For me he was a sign of the way out, a hint from the author that he would relent and give his children back to the ordinary concerns of good and evil.

But, generally speaking, the movie versions of comic book heroes were great disappointments. Flash Gordon, for example, was too thick around the middle. He didn't seem to be as quick-witted as he was in the panel drawings, there was some sinuous capability lacking there. Of course, Zorro was better on the movie screen than in the original. And *The Green Hornet* was best of all on the radio. My friends and I were thoughtful critics of these conversions of life forms. Arnold—the boy with the peculiar flattened ears and handwriting like a spider, in addition to strangely large eyes behind his eyeglasses and a wet sort of speech that produced a kind of spray when he was excited—was the most astute of all of us. He knew everything about serials, he could tell us who produced them—Republic Studios or Universal or Monogram—and the names of the actors who played in them. He even knew the genealogy of Britt Reid, the Green Hornet: Britt Reid, he said, was none other than the Lone Ranger's grand-nephew. We were skeptical, and hurt Arnold's feelings by laughing at him, but he drew himself up and marshaled his facts. "One, the Lone Ranger's real name was Reid, and he had a nephew, Dan Reid." We gave Arnold that—Dan Reid was in several of the radio stories. "Two," said Arnold, "Britt Reid, who is the Green Hornet, has a father named Dan Reid. Three, this Dan Reid who is Britt Reid's father is an old white-haired man, which proves enough years have passed for him to be the same Dan Reid, the boy, whose uncle was the Lone Ranger. Four—Britt Reid is the Lone Ranger's grandnephew!"

Wiping my face, I grudgingly accepted Arnold's analysis. I thought privately that if it was true, it was disappointing. The Lone Ranger was one thing, the Green Hornet was another. One rode horseback, the other drove a Lincoln Zephyr with custom wheel covers. The Green Hornet moved about the city, a modern city, he wore a hat with a snap brim and a belted raincoat with the collar up. I didn't want to know that he was related to the Lone Ranger. Also I didn't like to believe that families through genera-tions tended to wear masks and dedicate their lives to fighting crime. Each of them would be presumed to eliminate all crime forever. There was a loss of the idea of perfection. The Lone Ranger was *lone,* and that was the way he should have been.

But then one night when *The Green Hornet* radio program came on, my mother happened by and heard the opening theme music. It was very fast and full of tension. " 'The Flight of the Bumblebee,' " my mother said. "Why do you suppose these junky programs all use classical music for their themes?" She was thinking also of *The Lone Ranger,* which used the overture from *William Tell,* an opera by Rossini. That led to my revelation. In school the next day I sought out Arnold. "Arnold," I said, "it's not that the Green Hornet and the Lone Ranger are related. It's that their writers are related! I bet you we will find out that both stories are written by the same person. Both programs use classical music, both the heroes wear masks, the Lone Ranger has Tonto at his side, and the Green Hornet has Cato driving his car."

Arnold looked at me. His favorite subject was Science. He wanted to be a scientist when he grew up. He already had the objectivity of the scientist, which is the willingness to give up one hypothesis for another that is more reasonable. His eyes widened. "And they both leave calling cards!" he shouted.

"A silver bullet!" I cried.

"A hornet pin!" he screamed. And we pounded each other and jumped up and down and laughed.

I FOUND OUT THAT MY FATHER HAD LOST HIS STORE ONE MORNING WHEN I MET HIM at the breakfast table. He was cheerful. "How are you, young man," he said. He had brought home a radio that you didn't have to plug in. It worked on a battery. It was covered in alligator skin and had a leather carrying handle. It was like a small suitcase and you flicked the switch and it lit up on the dial just like a regular radio. You could carry it anywhere, to the beach or picnics, but I found it heavy. Then I noticed a cardboard box with many packets of needles and also a microphone, the kind used by radio stations, except that it wobbled on its base. And finally there was a pack of records in green envelopes. Some of them were old with grooves only on one side. "These are rare recordings by Caruso and Gigli," my father said. "If we hold on to them long enough they'll be valuable." While I ate my oatmeal he opened his newspaper. I saw the headlines. The other bad news was that France had fallen to Hitler.

DONALD

I didn't actually flunk out of City College, although I was called before the dean—the late Dean Morton Gottschal. He said I would have to improve my grades or I would be out. But I wasn't ready for a full-time college career, I knew that. I quit City and enrolled in night school and went to work as a messenger at Warriner during the day. I wouldn't go back to school full time till after the war, when I racked up straight A's and got my degree in two and a half years. At Warriner I made twelve dollars a week, not fifteen, as you said, although I could hope to supplement that with what I could clip on the expense account. You'd charge for a bus ride, a nickel, but you walked—that sort of thing. You walked fast. I didn't feel I was cheating. They paid me nothing. I worked hard, I did what I was supposed to. Maybe they paid so low because they knew all messenger boys padded the expense account. But anyway I worked all day and then went to night school. I was still seventeen and a half. I was a kid. I'd always worked. I started working for Dad when I was thirteen or fourteen. I know I was that young because I couldn't go to lunch myself, he had to take me. I still wore knickers. Now, maybe eighteen, I was keeping the family going. Dad had lost his store, he was out of work, and my crummy twelve dollars was keeping the household in food. I turned my pay envelope over to Mom every week. I was the breadwinner. I was very disturbed by that. It didn't last long, a couple of months till Dad got a job as a salesman with Home Appliance Distributors. But it wasn't good. I was tied down to them, I was doing what he should have been doing. Mother always complained about not being given enough to run the household, although there was never any time when we didn't have food or clothing or were threatened with eviction. But that was the big problem in the family, never having enough money. We all lived with that idea, it was the thirties, it conditioned everything—teenage kids were expected to help out, there was no question about it. But it was getting to me, I suppose. Harvey Stern, whom I'd known since first grade, had found out about an interesting opportunity. The Signal Corps was accepting applications for a civilian trainee program. They taught you how to be a radio operator, how to transmit and receive in Morse code, work a transmitter, repair radios, all of that; and they paid you besides. When Dad got his job at Home Appliance and began to bring money into the house, the folks didn't need my salary anymore. The great thing about this job was that it wasn't even in New York, it was in Philadelphia. Harvey and I went down and took the exam and a few weeks later we were told we had passed, and we were hired. We would live in a dormitory there and study radio and get paid and be on our own. So that was a big break for me. The folks gave me permission, it seemed the wisest course for several reasons. We all knew I would be drafted. When the time came it would be better to enlist. If I had experience in radio, I could hope to get a technical rating in the Signal Corps.

So I was free. I was leaving the house. I would not come back for several years, until after the war. I went down there and started to live for myself. It was a remarkable feeling. In Philadelphia we met some girls and went to bed with them. That was the first time for me. Life was speeding up. Everyone believed war was coming, nobody knew how or why, but everyone felt it. People wanted to live and enjoy themselves while they could. It was a strange feeling living for myself, on my own, with nobody to tell me what to do, and with nobody's welfare to worry about except my own. I did well in the Signal Corps school, in fact I finished first in my class. I was a very good radio operator. I bought my own bug. That's what the telegraph key in its modern form was called. It was semiautomatic. You could transmit faster than you could with an old-fashioned key. We each had our bug and developed our sending styles so that they were as recognizable to other operators as our handwriting or our voice. I wanted to go into the Signal Corps when I enlisted and become a radioman on airplanes, I wanted to get an assignment to the Army Air Corps, which is what the Air Force was called then, it wasn't a separate branch, it was part of the Army. The word "radioman" had glamour attached to it. You were on the leading edge of technology. I thought I was getting out, getting away from that intense family life we lived, I couldn't have realized it or articulated it but we were all too close and everything was terribly intense. There was no letup. Partly it was everyone's struggle for survival, partly it was the enormous difference in the personalities of Mom and Dad. Dad went off in all directions, he was full of surprises, some of them were good, some not so good. But it kept everyone on edge, Mother especially. You know, once I was working in the store when it was at the Hippodrome, and, you remember, Dad kept these record catalogues on the counter by the cash register, catalogues, and invoices, all that sort of paperwork. And stuck among these one day I found a photograph of a woman. A very glamorous woman, it showed her head and shoulders, it was a formal portrait theatrically lit. She had long hair flowing over her shoulders, which were bare, she was wearing some sort of costume, I suppose she was some kind of singer, I don't know why I thought that. But, anyway, in ink at the bottom she had written, *To Dave, Always*. And it was signed *Irene*. I didn't say anything, but I was enraged. I found it unforgivable that he was fooling around. He was the kind of man to fool around, to philander. He was errant. He had a wild streak in him. He was generous to us and we all lived together as a very close knit family relying on one another, and that was all true, but he had his secrets and they came out of the same part of his character that made him dream big impractical dreams that he couldn't realize. I mean he was a scrapper and he kept us going somehow. But something really broke for me when he accepted my messenger's salary for Mom's allowance. Why didn't he say something about that? Why didn't he say he'd pay me back? Why didn't he say he'd keep an accurate record, and account for every dollar and make sure I got it back when he was on his feet again? But he didn't. And Mom came to depend on me. I mean I think of it now, I started working very young, I always did something, I was always trying to get ahead, get myself a summer vacation by putting together a band with my friends. That wasn't a bad thing to do, at age sixteen, posing as a nineteen-year-old professional musician. Where did I learn that enterprise? It was part expediency, of course, partly the spirit of the time, but I had some drive to bring to it that was all my own. Dad was a good model in one way—he didn't like working for anyone else, he liked to be on his own, he had ambition, he was always cooking up deals, even though most of them didn't come through. But that would have impressed me. He was a good salesman too, and knowledgeable about what he sold. Even though he wasn't really the hustling salesman type, he had a refinement about him that would not let him hard-sell. But he was never satisfied to be what he had chosen to be. Do you know what I mean? You could not define him by what he did. There was no security in him of definition. You could never imagine his finding one thing to do and making a success of it and not try to do anything else. I don't think he ever found what it was that would make him say, "This is me, Dave Altschuler, and I am forty-eight years old and I live at such and such address and I do such and such for a living and I am satisfied with my life and my work." You couldn't pin him down. And the funny thing is I thought I was getting away from him. And what did I go and do but get into a radio business of another sort, just like my father, riding the airwaves for a living.

TWENTY-FIVE

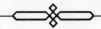

still had my Heinz pickle pin from the World's Fair; lots of people had them, there was a currency in these things and some kids didn't care for them, they went from hand to hand; and so I now had not only the Heinz pickle but the Planters nut company's Mr. Peanut, who wore a top hat and monocle, and I had a DC-3 charm from the aviation exhibit. I found out that my friend Meg's mother had a job at the World's Fair, although she didn't say doing what. But as a result Meg made me a present one afternoon of a full-color map of the Fair, and it was the kind of map I liked, with the drawings of the buildings in three dimensions, and in color, as if you were looking down from an airplane, but it was like a cartoon too, with little flags and people walking, and the very clear overhead view showed you immediately where the attractions were and named each one right on the roof. Meg had already been to the Fair several times and was able to tell me what was good. I got a hang of the layout this way, and by studying the map carefully—it had an index, which located things for you by means of a simple grid, A to K and 1 to 7—I was able to plan just how I would go about seeing the Fair, where I would start, and the best way to proceed, step by step, until I felt that I knew what to do, I could see everything I wanted to see and not become confused or miss anything. That had been a worry of mine.

It was peculiar living in the house without Donald, it was not the same as his being away for the summer, I felt the distance of our ages keenly, that I was a boy and he was now a grown man. Somehow I had not kept up to my original rate of lagging behind. When he did come home from Philadelphia for a weekend, I found I was shy, I didn't know what to say. And he was reserved too, he asked me about school as if he didn't remember what it was like.

He had a snapshot of himself standing in front of a car with his arm around a dark-haired girl in a belted wool coat and they were both smiling at the camera. Behind the car was a red brick building, which was the apartment house where he lived.

And then as time went on Donald came home less and less on the weekends and the house was very still. I couldn't seem to make the noise to fill it up, even when I asked a friend over. When I came home from school my father would not be there, of course, he worked now for a distributor, selling appliances to stores around Manhattan. As often as not my mother would be out shopping, or doing work for the Sisterhood, and so I would be alone in the house. I would have instructions from my mother to turn on the light under the three-sided iron pot in which she baked potatoes. Or there would be some change for my ice cream. Alone in my house after school, I sometimes became desolate. On one afternoon of rain my mother was late coming back and I began to imagine she had been hit by a car. Maybe she had fallen on the subway track. I cried. I don't know why her absence affected me so.

When she came home I hugged her, which made her laugh with surprise.

There was some sort of chastened peace between my mother and father having to do with the changed circumstances of our lives. Donald would be called into the Army if war came. That was very much on their minds. And then this new job of my father's had done something to his spirit. He had not worked for anyone else for many years, he had become used to being his own boss, he did not easily acclimate to his setback. On the occasions when I stayed home from school with one of my colds I saw that he did not leave the house eagerly. He found excuses not to leave, he would clean up the kitchen or offer to do some shopping for my mother before he left for work. He claimed that, as a salesman calling on accounts, he had to give the stores time to open their doors and get going on their day. This reasoning did not persuade her, she felt he was losing out to his competitors. But my father could not be budged, he took a long time over breakfast and then washed all the dishes, and then even on the way to the subway stopped to do errands.

He was not attentive to me, at home he read the newspaper or listened to music. He was thoughtful. He was always a robust man but now seemed to be stolid and portly and losing his joy of things. I would not think of mentioning the World's Fair to him. Nor to my mother, who was out of sorts most of the time and afflicted with various aches or pains. Her shoulder was giving her trouble, she had some sort of inflammation of the shoulder and sometimes wore her arm in a sling. She rested on the sofa a lot; she could not easily play the piano with her bad shoulder.

AND THEN I WAS TOLD THAT WE WOULD BE MOVING OUT OF OUR HOUSE. THE reasoning was that, with Donald not living at home anymore, the three of us didn't need such a large place. The landlord was intending to raise the rent when the lease was up, and it just wasn't worth the money.

My mother had found just the apartment for us and she took me to see it while it was being painted. It was up on the Grand Concourse. She met me after school. North of 174th Street, Eastburn Avenue became a hill. We trudged up Eastburn past apartment houses of the walk-up variety, four or six stories around small courtyards and with dingy front halls. Our new house was at the top of the hill where Eastburn met with the Concourse and also 175th Street—a six-story edifice of ocher brick triangularly shaped to the corner it was on, like the famous Flatiron Building in Manhattan. My father had made this comparison by way of encouragement when he knew I'd be going to have a look.

The apartment was on the second floor, one flight up. You entered a narrow windowless corridor that led into a foyer. The foyer opened in one direction into the living room and in the other to a small kitchen and dinette. A painter was on his ladder in the kitchen. A second painter was doing the bathroom next to the dinette. Then down another narrow hall, exactly at the triangulated end of the building, was the bedroom. There were three big windows, one on each wall. We overlooked the stop where we had always waited for the bus going up the Concourse to my grandma and grandpa's house.

"You see," my mother said as I looked out the window, "it's a wonderful view. When there's a parade on the Concourse you can stand here and see the whole thing. Everything's so light and airy. You're not much farther from school than you were. A nice wide street, with trees, the Grand Concourse. This is the place to be. We're very lucky."

But I knew what she felt. It was painful to me that she was making the best of things, finding reason to be thankful about this and that when I could tell she was miserable. We no longer had the means to maintain ourselves as we had. It was a degree of the seriousness of our decline that she would not articulate it. "The only thing is, we'll be a little bit pressed for closet space," she said. I liked my mother to be tough and realistic and to call a spade a spade, as she always had. As she went around now, pointing out why this tiny apartment would be such a wonderful place to live, I was truly glum. It felt as if you could barely turn around in it. I had never lived anywhere but in a private house near the park. The Concourse was a wide six-lane thoroughfare with pedestrian islands to help one cross, the outer lanes being for local traffic, the four inner lanes for express traffic. The pedestrian islands were planted with trees. Way over on the far side was an unbroken bank of apartment houses, north and south, as far as the eye could see. I didn't know anybody who lived in them, or if there were any children.

*   *   *

WHEN THE MOVE ACTUALLY OCCURRED, I WAS IN SCHOOL. THAT MORNING I HAD gotten up from my own bed in my own room as usual, I had my breakfast in the kitchen, where I'd always had it, the morning sun coming in the windows that looked on the alley, the old wooden table with the oilcloth, and the wooden chairs with the spoked backs, just where they'd always been in the middle of the large kitchen. On one wall the refrigerator with the cylindrical motor on top; on the other, the big enameled cabinet my mother called a "Dutch kitchen" with a slide-out ledge, lots of little closet doors and a flour sifter built in. "Here's your lunch," my mother said, handing me a paper bag. "Tuna salad sandwich, which you like, and an apple. Here's ten cents for your milk. At the end of the day, don't come back here. Come to the new apartment. Look both ways before crossing."

I left the house walking over bare floors and through cardboard cartons of packed things. Pulling up to the curb was a moving van.

At the end of the school day, as instructed, I turned right as I came out of the schoolyard, crossed 174th Street, and took the long walk up the Eastburn Avenue hill to the new apartment on the Concourse. It felt strange. I kept turning around to look down the hill. I saw children coming out of school and going my old way home.

The door was open. My steps resounded on the bare floor. I found my mother sitting alone among many of our things, which now looked strange in these new rooms painted cream, the latest color, she had told me. She sat on the sofa and looked exhausted. She gave me a wan smile. She had managed the whole move herself, my father having gone off to work as I had to school.

In the new kitchen I drank my milk as I always had. The refrigerator was a new model with round corners and the motor hidden in the rear. White metal cabinets hung from the walls over the sink. Everything was very close together. The kitchen floor was little more than a space between the fixtures. It was all neat and compact. The kitchen was divided by partitions that came to my shoulders. The partitions created the dinette. We had a new oval table with a shiny, marbleized top and four matching chairs.

The modernity of everything was what we talked about; that and the reasonable rent and the concessions given by the landlord as a reward for our having moved in.

The new living room was filled to capacity with our upright Sohmer and sofa and chairs and lamps, and console radio and record player and carpet and end tables and knickknacks. Against the wall at right angles to the old sofa with its curved Empire back was a new square two-cushion sofa with high square arms that could be converted into a bed. My parents would sleep here. Gone was the olive bed with the frieze of flowers on the headboard. I would have the triangular bedroom looking out over the bus stop. There were two new single beds here. When Donald came home, he would share the room with me.

Each day when I returned from school I explored more of the neighborhood. The Concourse, I saw, was actually built along a ridge; if there were no buildings, if all the land were returned to early times, the Concourse would be a plateau overlooking valleys to the west—that would be Jerome Avenue—and, less precipitously, those to the east. The light was different on the top of the plateau. A bit colder. There were no green hedges or plots of grass. We were suspended one story above a great impersonal street, with a lot of sky visible, and the constant hum of traffic. Across 175th Street, on our side of the Concourse, was the Pilgrim Church, whose bell rang on Sunday. And directly on the other side of the Concourse and one block down, was the new Junior High School that I would be going to when I finished the sixth grade, at P.S. 70. And so my last connection with Claremont Park and with my old street and schoolyard would be gone.

Understanding the isolation I felt, my mother relaxed the rules about my coming home immediately after school was out. She even consented to my visiting my friend Meg. I had only to advise her in the morning if I intended to stay on in the old haunts with my friends and play. I played stoopball or punchball in the same clothes—white shirt, red school tie— I wore for my classes. I came home with shirttails hanging, my sweater tied by the sleeves around my waist, and my knickers drooping. My mother, who had to scrub the clothes on a small washboard in the sink in the little kitchen, did not complain. She missed Donald and had softened her discipline of me. She too found things to do in the old places, taking on the direction of the Mt. Eden Synagogue Sisterhood choir two afternoons a week.

TWENTY-SIX

In the spring, with the days getting warmer and the light lasting, I spent as little time at home as I possibly could. On rainy days I went invariably to Meg's and drank milk with her. Meg had grown a bit, she was still petite, but she had filled out some. I was aware of the faintest golden down on her forearms and legs. She was very graceful and held her head high when she walked, her hair was thicker, which made her look older; and I happened to notice at times when I was behind her that her skirt moved in the rhythm of her moving backside, which was round enough now to push out the cloth that way. I couldn't have said what I felt, but all the children in the class now considered me Meg's boyfriend and believed that when we grew up we were going to get married. If someone teased me about this, I had to throw my books down and jump him. But most of the time I was not directly confronted in this manner and so did not have to deny anything. She and I never discussed these things, recognizing the danger of entrusting such delicate matters to words. If either of us had said anything, the other could no longer have sustained the relationship. It could only continue unarticulated, tacit, in the pretense of ignorance. We felt loyal to each other and calm in each other's presence. We shared things: she gave me cookies and, outside, I would buy two ice creams with my money. We played in Claremont Park a lot, where we were by ourselves. I sometimes found her looking at me with a grave expression on her face. I liked her mouth, especially the upper lip, which flourished in a thickened curve toward its corners so that at any moment you would think she was about to cry. She had light grey eyes, which had grown larger. We were nine years old now.

Meg's mother, Norma, worked every day at the World's Fair from four in the afternoon to closing time. This meant she went off to the subway in the early afternoon, before we were out of school. Norma had to take a subway to Manhattan and then transfer to the Queens IRT. When I saw her she was very weary, but said she was lucky to have the job. But that meant Meg and I were left alone most of the time. We did our homework together. She still liked to play with dolls, to serve them an imaginary tea on little tin plates and cups, and talk to them. One of her dolls was a very popular model called a Didy-Doll, as ridiculous a bit of cutesyness as everything else having to do with girl culture. The feature of this doll was that a small nippled bottle of water could be applied to its mouth and a moment later the water would come out of a hole between its legs. I found my friend's attentions to this doll embarrassing. One rainy afternoon we were sitting on the floor in her living room and she insisted that I administer the water. I didn't want to. The doll was lying there on its back with its legs spread out and no clothes on. Meg insisted that I push the little nippled bottle against the doll's painted mouth. The blue glazed-button eyes of the infant doll stared up at me. Meg kept saying, "Go ahead, she's thirsty, can't you see she's thirsty. Please, do it, she is very thirsty." Her voice grew constricted as she repeated these words, and my own pulse was loud in my ears and I felt my face flushing. The intensity of her belief, as if this toy were really alive, I found both disgusting and thrilling at the same time. But I was determined not to give in, but to torment these feelings of hers and be cruel to them. I jammed the rubber nipple not into the doll's mouth but at the hole between the legs. I pushed down until water spilled over the doll and onto the floor. Meg cried out and threw her small self at me, knocking me backward from my sitting position. In the next moment she was on top of me and using her whole body to pound me, rearing up and dropping down flat, as if trying to pound the breath out of me, doing that again and again while I lay there on my back. Each time she fell on top of me I could feel her warm breath chuff in my ears. I felt the warmth of her, I smelled her sweet soap smell, I put my arms around her and found myself holding her backside with my hands. Her dress was up around her waist and I felt her thighs and her cotton underwear. She tired suddenly and lay still on top of me. Then she became aware of something that was not too familiar to her, although it was to me—my stiffening. She struggled back from it in alarm, the prod of it was uncomfortable to her. I wouldn't let her go but pushed up and rolled her over and lay on top of her as she struggled. Her eyes were lowered. Just for a moment I held her pinned like this and then got off and sat up, as she did, and a moment later we were playing as if nothing had happened. The little puddle of water became spilled tea in her game and she sponged it off the floor with a paper napkin. Later we did our homework and then I went home.

In a confusion of thought I saw my friend in my mind as I went to sleep that night. I was restless. I could not get the pillow right. Finally I lay on my side, curled, with the pillow turned lengthwise so that it was between my legs. I experienced a diffuse sense of urgency all through my body, my limbs, my fingers and toes. I found that I was angry. And then all at once I was feeling sorry for myself. I heard no sound in the house. My father was not home. My mother was reading in the living room. The corner street light shone on the ceiling. I heard a steady hum of traffic. I didn't know where I was. We had new venetian blinds, of which my mother was proud, but no matter how they were adjusted the bright light of the Concourse shone through.

Yet it gradually came to me that i now had a private life. nobody in my family saw Meg and Norma, only I did. I liked that. Living in a new neighborhood had made me independent. I ranged now. I did not run right home after school. I could see Meg without even telling anyone. This was an unusual household, this mother and daughter. It had no father. It brought out in me a certain feistiness. My loins stirred with protective feelings. This was my secret life of adventure. Norma was nothing like other mothers I had known, including my own. There was some carelessness of spirit about her, which I perceived in the way she pushed at her hair with her fingertips, or looked at herself in her living room mirror over the sofa. She did not represent authority in my mind. Once, on her day off, she and Meg and I sat down to play a board game. I started to read the rules just as Donald always did. "Let's not bother with that," Norma said. "Let's just play."

I could not envision my mother sitting down with Meg and me on the floor and playing one of our games with us. Maybe that was the sort of thing that made my mother dislike her. Both daughter and mother had got down on their knees, and sat back on their legs the way girls do. Except that Norma was wearing a housecoat and it fell back over her thighs, which looked very white and soft to me; she kept pulling the material over herself and it kept falling away, and I noticed that. Then she noticed me noticing and she smiled and tousled my hair.

With my new freedom I was developing a certain confidence. I was reading more than I ever had, three or four books a week, sea stories and boys' stories, and sports and adventure novels; and I began to feel hampered having to wait for an adult, my mother particularly, to find the time to accompany me to the library. The library was in the East Bronx, on Washington Avenue. It was quite far. I applied now and received permission to go to the library myself. After the first or second time, I had no fear of getting lost. I went every Saturday morning. It was May, the weather was warm, and I walked along in the sun of the season holding two or three books in each hand at my side. I developed a modest shortcut or two, walking east on 176th Street past an old people's home, where they sat on rockers on a porch and looked at me, and then down a steep grade curving to a junction with Tremont Avenue, a main thoroughfare, just at the site of an Eye Hospital. At the bottom of the hill was Webster Avenue, with its trolley cars and cobblestones of Belgian block. Crossing Webster at

Tremont could be dangerous, trolley lines bisecting and branching off, trucks rumbling along, you had to keep your wits about you. Then I passed over the New York Central tracks at Park Avenue, and with the Third Avenue El in sight, I turned right on Washington Avenue and only one block away was the library. It was an Andrew Carnegie branch library. Across the street was a company that sold stones for cemeteries. A big display room was filled with these immense granite monuments with names of imaginary dead people carved in them. Around the corner was the Pechter Bread Company. The whole neighborhood smelled of delicious bread baking. They baked those hard-crust rye breads with the little postage-stamp union labels stuck on them. Our family bought the Pechter breads and here was the very place they were made.

I never made this trip carelessly. These were still dangerous precincts. The East Bronx turned out not only criminal boys but, as I now knew from the kind of history children collect in schoolyards, major big-time gangsters. My library was not far from the late Dutch Schultz's old beer barns. He'd owned taverns on Third Avenue, under the El. I knew I had more to fear from the boys than from the grown-up gangsters, but altogether there was a culture here that was not mine. No, the East Bronx was not a place to take lightly. I had to admit to myself to being slightly relieved when I reached the front steps of the Washington Avenue branch and passed into the quiet rooms with the oak bookshelves.

IT WAS AT THIS LIBRARY THAT I LEARNED ABOUT THE CONTEST FOR BOYS SPONSORED by the New York World's Fair Corporation. An essay contest. A poster on the bulletin board told all about it. The topic was the Typical American Boy. You had to write in two hundred and fifty words or less what you thought were the qualities that best exemplified American boyhood. You had to submit a signed photograph of yourself and you had to write the essay clearly in your own hand and on one side of the paper. The paper could be lined or unlined but it had to be eight by eleven in size.

I had a keen eye for contests. Many were false and ridiculous, and only the innocent would enter them. They usually required you to say what you liked about a product in twenty-five words or less and send in your remarks with a boxtop or label. The contest was really designed to get you to buy the product. My friend Arnold had made up a contest for Castoria, the laxative. "I like Castoria because it's foul-tasting and gives you terrible diarrhea, and we all know what fun that can be."

But this was different. This was run not by a company but by the World's Fair. I read the rules carefully. They wanted original thought. Whoever won would have a statue made of him by a famous artist, and the name of the statue would be "The Typical American Boy." There were other prizes too, including free trips to the Fair, all expenses paid. My mind began to race.

In the old days Donald and I had collected coupons from newspaper promotions of various sorts. Enough coupons and you collected your premium—in one memorable instance the *New York Evening Post* offered a set of ten volumes called *The World's One Hundred Best Short Stories*. That had taken a year of coupons. We had been very methodical and efficient, cutting the coupons out on the dotted line, keeping them in order in packs, slipping rubber bands over them and storing them in a cigar box. But there were contests too of an intellectual sort, puzzles, rebuses, tests of vocabulary and grammar. With success you could earn subscriptions to magazines or even money. All these were means of entry in my mind to a just and well-regulated world of carefully designed challenges to boys. By accepting these challenges you advanced yourself. So I recognized this World's Fair essay contest. I recognized it. In my early days I had joined secret organizations run by Tom Mix and Dick Tracy, among others. I had in the depths of my desk drawers numerous artifacts of entry, a Jack Armstrong whistle ring, little lead Buck Rogers rocket ships with wheels, water pistols, magnifying lenses, badges, secret code cards, and so on. For each of them I had once eagerly awaited the mail. The mail was very much a part of all this. There were rules of postmark to consider and specifications as to format. Wherever you were, at whatever far edge of the world's consciousness, one three-cent postage stamp could vault you into the heart of things.

Under the printing of the contest rules were the palest, most meaningful shadows of the Trylon and Perisphere. Only gradually did I perceive them. They emerged in my mind as a message just for me, a secret summons, wordless, indelible.

I fully understood why our family hadn't gotten to the World's Fair. Nobody had said anything, but I knew. Boldly I asked the librarian if I could borrow a pencil. I asked also for a piece of paper. I didn't care if she smiled. I copied down the information on the poster. My heart was beating wildly. I worried that the old people trying to read their periodicals would hear it and the derelict men nodding in their hard chairs would wake up, and all of them would give me dirty looks.

Setting out for home, I thought past the sentences I would compose for my essay, and saw my own noble head in bronze gazing into the sky over the New York World's Fair. One day Meg and her mother would arrive at the Fair and see it prominently displayed. Their mouths would drop open.

I decided not to return home the way I had come but to walk past the

Pechter Bread Company to Park Avenue and go north along the railroad tracks to Tremont. I wanted to see the trains in their wide trench below the street. This was the line my stately uncle Ephraim rode to and from his mansion in Pelham Manor. Park Avenue was split down the middle by the tracks and each narrow half was cobblestoned, barren of people, bordered on one side with windowless red-brick warehouses and on the other by a fence of black iron spears. I walked along this fence in weeds strewn with garbage and imagined myself doing a tightrope act on the grid of electrified wires over the tracks.

At this moment I was confronted by two boys with knives.

They were on me before I even saw them. They pushed me up against the fence, prodding me with the tips of their knives until I was pressed fast. I felt the fence imprinted on my back.

My terror afforded me a stunned clarity of mind. These boys were big, they were my brother's age. The thinner one had the lightest, deadliest eyes I had ever looked into; they were close together in a narrow, lopsided face. There was a loutish droop to the small mouth, the lip turning outward at one side, the lower teeth showing.

The heavy one was taller and he had very black hair combed back in a pompadour, and he had pimply skin and a roundish jowly face with a snout for a nose. His black nostrils made almost perfect circles. His knife was not held as precisely to my stomach as the other's. He was nervous and looked up and down the street.

"You Jewish?" the thin one said.

"No," I said.

He grinned, reached forward with his free hand, and stripped my books from me. The books lay in the weeds. "Jewboy," he said, "I'm going to cut your ears off. What do you say at confession?"

"What?"

"Let's see you cross yourself." I did not know what this meant. "You're a Jewboy," he said. He pushed the knife point into me. I could feel it. One shove and it would go right through me.

"Where's your money."

"Come on," the fat one said. "Hurry it up." He was really nervous. I produced my money, a dime and two pennies. The fat one scooped the coins out of my palm. "Let's go," he said to the other one.

"First I'm gonna slice up this lyin' Jew."

"My father's a cop," I said to the larger boy. I stared at him as resolutely as I could, knowing him to be scared. "He works in this precinct," I said. "In a patrol car."

They were both staring at me now. I gave no more evidence. In an instant I could be dead or free as the deadly shorter one casually drifted from one side of his impulse to the other. I felt the point of the knife. The pressure increased.

"Come on, let's go," the fat one said.

The thin one grabbed my jaw and banged my head against the fence. "Fuck you, Jewboy," he said.

They ran across the street, laughing. They turned the corner and were gone.

I picked up my library books. The sheet of instructions I had copied had fallen out of a book and lay crumpled in the grass with a footprint across it. I could still feel the knife point. I pulled my shirt up to see if it had drawn blood. There was the smallest red dot, like a pinprick, just at the top of my scar.

I DECIDED NOT TO TELL ANYONE WHAT HAD HAPPENED. I WALKED HOME QUICKLY, turning every block or so to see if they were following me. The affront increased with every step I took until I was hard pressed not to cry. I found myself trembling.

Why had I mentioned my father! He existed now in their minds. I thought this put him terribly at risk, even if I had portrayed him in a uniform. A policeman! It was the weakest of ploys, if they had been any smarter they would have remembered how infantile a claim it is: My father is a policeman. It is what four-year-olds say to one another.

I was supposed to be on guard in the East Bronx. I had smugly assured myself that I was. All my life I had known about boys like this, and here I had foolishly wandered into their lair. I had come to their attention. If I hadn't been busy daydreaming, I would have had the sense to stay away from the railroad tracks. Edgar, I heard my mother saying, your head is always in the clouds. Come down if you know what's good for you.

The last block to my apartment house I ran. I stood inside the street door, in the shadow, and waited for them to appear. When they came in the door I would run out again. I did not want to lead them to my mother.

No one came. Standing in the dark hallway, I played and replayed the scene over in my mind, looking for some small moment of honor, something I could find for the pain. But it came out the same way every time: "You Jewish?" "No." Humiliation broke over me in waves, like sobs. I was enraged. At this moment if those boys had appeared I would have killed them. I felt ill. Then I began to sweat and grew suddenly cold. I leaned against the wall. A film of cold clammy sweat covered my face and neck and back.

For weeks afterward, whenever I went out, I looked for those two boys, and the fact that I never saw them did not remove them as a threat from my mind. I could go about my business only by the accident of their not being there, a matter entirely of their choice, and so even when absent they had me. But at the same time I knew it wasn't even these two in particular, because Christian boys were like this all over, and you were free only at their collective whim, only if they happened not to walk down your street or lope through your backyard or otherwise see you. I struggled to understand Christianity as something that would shove a knife into my belly.

I WAS NOT TO RESUME MY SATURDAY TRIPS TO THE LIBRARY FOR SOME TIME. BUT my resolve to enter the World's Fair contest for boys was unshaken. In fact, writing an essay on the Typical American Boy had now the additional appeal of an act of defiance. I, not those miserable louts, would propose the essence of American Boyhood. They were no models for anything. I doubted they could even read. If, by some accident, they were to hear of the contest, they wouldn't know the first thing about how to go about writing for it. The best they could hope for was to go along the streets and stick up someone who had written for the contest and to steal what he had written. Well, it wouldn't be me.

I knew I was in for a lot of work. I had not only to compose the essay and copy it out neatly, but to find an envelope and buy the stamps for it. I decided to write my essay in secret, at night, after I did my homework. I would confide in no one. First of all, the writing was supposed to be done without help. But also I didn't want anyone confusing me with advice. I especially didn't want anyone telling me what the odds were against my winning. The age limit was thirteen, which meant I was competing with people in the eighth grade.

I was now engaged in an enterprise that was more interesting to me than anything else in my entire life. I felt good again. When my mother was out of the house, I searched everywhere for a good picture of myself to enclose with the essay. I assumed they wanted a picture for two reasons—first, to help make sure you were the writer; second, so that if the essay was good they could look at the picture, and the artist who was doing the sculpture would tell them if you were handsome enough for his purposes. If two essays were equally good, they would choose the better-looking boy.

I found the gold Pickwick Chocolates tin where the family snapshots were kept. The best, most good-looking picture was one taken before my operation, when I was leaner and with a firmer jawline. Donald had snapped it with my father's Kodak. It was not the newest of photos, it was from a few summers before, when my father had money and had taken us to the country for a vacation on a real working farm in Connecticut. But it had been shot fairly close up, so that you couldn't see how short I was then. I knew the picture had to go with the words and that the words would be good, so I couldn't send a picture that suggested that this boy, whoever he was, was too young to write so well. But this would do: it was a clear black-and-white photo, just the right size, and the sun lay across my face so that I squinted in a friendly attractive way. Behind me was an open field.

The evening I finally sat down to write my essay I propped my picture on the table in front of me. I thought of being in the country. My bold father liked the unusual, even in vacations, so together with our friends across the street, Dr. and Mrs. Perlman and their son Jay, we had all driven in the Perlman car to this farm. Connecticut was even farther out than Pelham Manor. At the time I thought of our going there as a foray into Christianity. Perhaps my mother did too. She was leery of the idea and would have preferred a place like White Lake, in the Catskills, at a real resort hotel with dancing in the evenings.

Instead of writing my essay, I fell to dreaming about our vacation. But it was really interesting. The farm was immense, with crops growing up everywhere in the sun. The farmer was a skinny buck-toothed man who laughed a lot and sat at the end of a long table as the boarders and the farmer's family and the farmhands in their overalls all had dinner together. Fresh corn grown right there, fresh milk from his own cows, eggs and chickens from his own coops. There were big soft tomatoes and sweet peas and chunks of hand-churned butter, and bread baked in the kitchen by the farmer's wife. She was a big woman who wore an apron all the time, her grey hair was bound behind her head in a bun, she had fat red hands that passed under my face as she put the bowls of food on the table. She had two daughters, who helped serve, and one of them who had hair the color of hay caused my father and Dr. Perlman to glance at each other when she came to their attention. My father was now inspired to recite the shortest poem in the English language. "It's called 'A Dissertation on the Antiquity of Microbes,'" he said, and cleared his throat. Everyone looked at him in alarm. "'Adam had 'em,'" my father said. Everyone laughed.

Hanging corkscrews of flypaper turned slowly in the breeze coming in through the screen doors. Flies were stuck to the paper, clumps of them, some of the hanging swirls were all black. My mother could not look at them. There were two kinds of milk in pails on the table: milk the farmer's wife had boiled and raw milk straight from the cows. Of course my father wanted us all to try the raw milk. My mother gently suggested she would prefer the pasteurized for Donald and me.

"But these are certified cows," my father said. "Isn't that so?" he said to the farmer.

"Yes sir," the farmer said, smiling his buck-toothed smile. "Ain't nothing wrong with these cows," he said, but then, unfortunately, went into a coughing spell that turned his face red and shook his skinny chest. He cleared his throat and smiled.

"Well," my mother said as diplomatically as she could, "we're used to the pasteurized, if you don't mind."

My father continued to argue the point. He had no shame in discussing private feelings in public places; he did this too at restaurants, embarrassing everyone in the family by talking with the same directness as when we were home alone. "There probably isn't one TB bacillus left in New England," he said. My mother gave him a look, but it did no good. He seemed oblivious to the fact that the farmer and the two farmhands at the table were enjoying the discussion. My mother ladled the milk that had been boiled into our glasses. My father dramatically held his glass up to the light and poured the raw milk, lifting the ladle farther and farther away so that it made a rich froth in the glass and sounded delicious. He then drank off the milk in one draft, smacking his lips and putting the glass down on the table with a rap. He looked at us and spread his arms. "I'm still alive," he said. He was having a good time. Meanwhile, my mother quietly pushed from her place a soft-boiled egg in which she had discovered a blood spot.

One of the farmhands let us come haying with him. Donald and I rode the wooden wagon, you could feel the horse's exertion in the creak and lurch of the wagon over the rutted road. The wagon stopped and hay flew up in our faces and we laughed. Then I started sneezing and had to get down. The cows in the fields swished their tails about and flies rose from their flanks. Cow flop looking like disks of chocolate pudding was everywhere in the stony field. Down at the lake we rowed a boat about and found the water choked with weeds. My father and another guest found some chains, and from the rowboat we dragged these chains through the water and pulled up the weeds until we had made a clear place in the lake near the shore. Here we swam, or, rather, Donald and my father swam. I splashed about for a while and then left them swimming and went up the hill to play by myself. The sun shone, and what amazed me was the fact that no one paid attention to the animals and nevertheless they didn't run away. Pinky had always run away if you took her off the leash. The animals in the Farm in the Park had been in pens or corrals. Here the cows stood about in the open as far as you could see. Horses grazed in the field and they weren't hitched to anything. Chickens ran in the yard and a dog who didn't even have a collar lay asleep at the foot of the porch where the women guests sat. I had never seen animals left alone before. The sun and the sky seemed untethered too, I felt the freedom of things at this farm, and I could run everywhere I wanted and watch everything and still be on the farm. At night the air became cool, we wore sweaters after dinner and I went to bed under a soft eider quilt on starchy scratchy sheets. I became drowsy listening to the adults talking softly on the porch below my window. The crickets and the frogs of night grew louder in my ears, like my own pulse. I kept my face under the top sheet because of all the mosquitoes in the room. I might have complained and caused a disturbance except for what my father had said when I'd shown him my first mosquito bite on this day of our arrival. "Quick, Henry, the Flit" is what he said, smiling. That's what I said under the covers hearing the mosquito buzzing just above my ear, "Quick, Henry the Flit," although there was no Flit near, no spray can to put it in, and no Henry.

TWENTY-SEVEN

This is the essay I sent to the World's Fair on the theme of the Typical American Boy.

The typical American Boy is not fearful of Dangers. He should be able to go out into the country and drink raw milk. Likewise, he should traverse the hills and valleys of the city. If he is Jewish he should say so. If he is anything he should say what it is when challenged. He roots for his home team in football and baseball but also plays sports himself. He reads all the time. It's all right for him to like comic books so long as he knows they are junk. Also, radio programs and movies may be enjoyed but not at the expense of important things. For example he should always hate Hitler. In music he appreciates both swing and symphony. In women he appreciates them all. He does not waste time daydreaming when he is doing his homework. He is kind. He cooperates with his parents. He knows the value of a dollar. He looks death in the face.

Once I had done it, I copied it out in my best penmanship. I had to copy it twice because just as I got to the end the first time my pen leaked and I got a big blot in the margin. I mailed it according to all the rules, and then I stopped thinking about it. I had given the American Boy contest everything I had, but now it was out of my hands and so I wanted it out of my mind as well. I knew these things took a very long time. Even when you sent away for something you had to allow six weeks for delivery. I had never understood why, but there it was.

* * *

OF COURSE, SINCE I HAD THOUGHT THAT THE ESSAY REPRESENTED MY LAST AND only chance to get to the World's Fair, it was inevitable that an opportunity to go would arise immediately. It came by way of the shy soft voice of my friend Meg. "I go every Saturday," she told me. "Norma doesn't like to leave me alone all day, so she takes me with her. But I have to stay close by where she works and so it isn't much fun. If you came with me, we could take care of each other and Norma wouldn't worry. Edgar, we could see everything!"

Oh my dear friend—this was the longest statement she had ever made to me! She tucked her hair behind her ears and smiled her ambiguous smile. I could see her lovely slender neck. She had small hands and the largest, clearest grey eyes. We were sitting after school in the swings at Claremont Park. Our feet were on the ground and we were pushing ourselves back and forth in small arcs. I couldn't believe my good fortune, but I pretended to think about it very soberly. "It's a good idea," I said, finally. "Everyone would benefit."

As soon as I could, but without unseemly haste, I left Meg and ran home to talk to my mother. This would take some doing. A rill of disloyalty opened up in me. But Donald no longer lived at home and nothing could be further from the thoughts of my mother and father right now than the World's Fair. I had waited patiently and without making a pest of myself. So maybe it would be all right.

I marshaled my arguments over a glass of milk and two Oreo cookies. When my mother came home from shopping, I helped her put the groceries away and then I told her about the invitation. "Who invited you?" she said, sitting down with a cup of coffee. "Is it your friend's idea or the mother's?"

This was the tough question. Either answer was a calculated risk. The mother was not looked on favorably. But a child's invitation lacked substance. "It's the mother's," I said. "She asked Meg to ask me to ask you."

My mother gazed at me, not unkindly. "I suppose everyone has gone by now," she said. "How much would it cost?"

"That's the beauty part. We get in free, Meg's mother works at the Fair."

"Doing what, may I ask?"

"I don't know exactly," I said. "But it must be a good job because she has a discount pass for the rides. Most of the exhibits are free anyway. The souvenirs, I suppose, would cost something. But who needs souvenirs?" I said stoutly. "They're for children."

I saw the indecision in my mother's eyes. This was better than I had hoped for. "I'll talk to your father," she said. "Now go do your homework."

That evening it was time for bed, and my father had not yet come home. I turned off the light and decided to wait up in the dark. I watched the lights of the Concourse traffic on the ceiling. A light would hover in the corner of the room and then flare outward and disappear just as the sound of the engine became loudest. Then the sound would recede. I must have fallen asleep because I awoke to a conversation already under way.

"The phone bill," my mother was saying. "Consolidated Edison. Today I didn't even have the money to get your shirts out of the Chinese laundry."

"I have some money for you."

"You've been saying that for three days."

"I drew something against my commissions this morning. I don't like to do that, since it puts me in the hole."

"I'll tell you what puts you in the hole. Your card playing puts you in the hole."

"Does this go with dinner? What course is this?"

"Tell me of any other wife who waits to twelve o'clock to serve dinner? Where have you been? What have you been up to?"

"If you don't let me eat in peace, I'm going to walk right out of here."

"Walk. You don't frighten me. Do I ever have your company? Would I know the difference?"

But it was quiet for a while. I heard the sounds of silverware on a plate. The kitchen faucet ran.

"You want anything else?"

"No, thank you."

"I have another matter to discuss," my mother said. "Edgar has been invited to go with that little girl Meg to the World's Fair."

"Well?" my father said. "Why not?"

"Of course, you know whose child she is," my mother said.

"Whose?"

At this moment a bus pulled up to the curb under my window and the doors hissed and the engine idled loudly. The doors closed and the bus drew away, its gears grinding.

"I hate gossip," my father was saying. "In fact, that's worse than gossip, that's slander. How would you feel if people went around telling stories about you?"

"These are not stories, these are facts. Everyone knows. It's common knowledge in the neighborhood."

"Well, supposing it's true. That was years ago. The man is dead."

"How has she gotten by all these years?" my mother said. "Do people change that much?"

"I'm not interested," my father said. "She sounds like a nice enough woman to me. I've seen his little friend. She's a sweet girl. Let him go. He can take care of himself. I've been meaning for us to go to the World's Fair."

"One of your promises."

"Yes, one of my promises. And I will make good on it. In the mean-time, if he has the chance he should go and enjoy himself. There's little enough for anyone to enjoy these days."

"You're telling me," my mother said.

WHEN THE DAY CAME, I WAS READY. I DRESSED IN A SHIRT AND TIE AND WORE MY school knickers and my new low shoes, of which I was very proud. I had until recently worn the old high lace-up kind. Folded in my pocket were two dollars that my father had given me with instructions that I didn't have to spend all of it if I didn't need to; but that if I needed to, then I had it to spend. I understood this instruction. It was a great morning of the spring. I raced down the hill from the Concourse, crossing Eastburn at 174th Street, and ran along past the schoolyard, crossed at 173rd, went right by my old house, turned left at Mt. Eden Avenue and ran through the Oval, and up the hill to Meg's house overlooking Claremont Park. My mother had wanted to walk me here so as to "thank" Norma, as she said, but I knew that wasn't a good idea and talked her out of it. She would have let Norma know what a great responsibility it was to take care of another woman's son for a whole day. I didn't think Norma needed to hear that. However subtle my mother believed herself to be, however delicately suggestive in her statements, she was in fact brutally direct. It was a characteristic I had come to rely on, knowing in no uncertain terms where I stood—that was her phrase, *no uncertain terms*—but it took getting used to. I didn't want Norma to hear from my mother in no uncertain terms.

I rang the bell and Meg opened the door. She stood there smiling. She wore a white dress and white shoes newly polished and a blue-ribbon bow in her hair. Behind her, Norma in a flowered dress was putting on her hat while looking at herself in the mirror. She stood tugging at it until she found the right angle. It was one of those hats with a wide brim that throw shade on the face. As I stepped in the door and Meg closed it behind me, their phone rang and Norma answered. "Oh, hello," she said, "this is she." Norma threw a glance in my direction, and I realized that my mother, not to be deterred, was on the other end of the line. "Oh, it's my pleasure," Norma said, and smiled at me. "We love having him, he's a joy to be with." She paused. "Well, fairly late, I should think. Yes. Right to the door. Of course." She listened some more. "No, I quite under-stand," she said, "I would make sure too. It does get a bit cool in the evening. I see he has his sweater with him. That should do him fine, I think."

My mother went on for a while and Norma sat down on the sofa and lit a cigarette as she held the phone cradled in her shoulder. She blew smoke and looked at me through the smoke. I was embarrassed about this but didn't know what to say. When Norma hung up she said, "Your mother likes you a lot, Edgar." I agreed. "But why would anyone like a monkey face like you?" Norma said, and we all laughed.

TWENTY-EIGHT

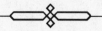

Even from the elevated station I could see the famous Trylon and Perisphere. They were enormous. They were white in the sun, white spire, white globe, they went together, they belonged together as some sort of partnership in my head. I didn't know what they stood for, it was all very vague in my mind, but to see them, after having seen pictures and posters and buttons of them for so long, made me incredibly happy. I felt like jumping up and down, I felt myself trembling with joy.

I thought of them as friends of mine.

We came down the stairs right into the fairgrounds. Banners flew from the pavilions. The wide streets were painted red, yellow and blue. They were absolutely clean. The buildings were mostly streamlined, with rounded edges, as I supposed buildings of the future should be. We walked on Rainbow Avenue. The day was fine. Thousands of people were here. They smiled and chatted and pointed things out and consulted their guidebooks. We walked along Constitution Mall. Brilliant tulip gardens were in bloom. The Fair had its own buses. It had its own tractor trains, and Norma decided we should have a ride. An orange-and-blue electric-powered tractor pulled a dozen rubber-wheeled cars behind it, and when the driver blew his horn it played the opening measures of "The Sidewalks of New York": "East side, west side, all around the town." Norma wanted us just to look around and get our bearings. We sat on the last car of the train, so that it whipped around a bit at the corners. Of course it was very tame, nothing like the roller coaster we could see in the distance in the amusement area; it had to go slow because it moved among great crowds of strolling people. Everywhere people walked in family groups and stopped to take their pictures in front of exhibit buildings. There were lady guides in grey uniform jackets and hats. The shuffle of feet was like a constant whispering in my ears, or what I imagined a herd of antelope would sound like going in great numbers slowly through high grass. We went around Commerce Circle and through the Plaza of Light and right around the Trylon and Perisphere, which, up close, seemed to fill the sky.

The pictures of them hadn't suggested their enormity. They were the only white objects to be seen. They were dazzling. They seemed to be about to take off, they looked lighter than air. A ramp connected them, and I could see a line of people silhouetted against the blue sky. We passed the statue of George Washington. I had my map, which I consulted. But with Norma it wasn't really necessary. She knew everything. "Let's make our plans," she said. She had been so happy to have me with them that she'd arranged to join the fun. "I don't have to go to work yet, so I thought we'd start with a little education. I thought we'd look, for instance, at the interesting foreign pavilions like Iceland or Rumania." My heart sank. Meg said, "Norma, stop your kidding!" and I looked up and saw Norma laughing and realized she was funny for a mother, and she knew what children liked and what they hated. I laughed too.

We rode across the Bridge of Wheels and got out, of course, at the General Motors Building. That was everyone's first stop. We took our places on a long line that went up a ramp and turned a corner and up another, alongside this great streamlined building of rounded corners and windowless walls. It reminded me of the kind of structure I would make by turning over a pail of wet sand at the beach and pounding the bottom of the pail and lifting it off the sand mold. The General Motors exhibit was the most popular in the whole Fair, and so I didn't mind the long wait we had, practically an hour. We inched along. Meg held my hand, and Norma just behind us smoked her cigarettes and fanned herself with her hat. We were quiet. In the momentousness everyone was quiet. It was the quiet World of Tomorrow, everyone all dressed up.

Finally we got inside. My stomach tightened and my heart beat as we prepared for the exhibit. We ran and took seats, each of us in a chair with high sides and loudspeakers built into them, they faced the same direction and were on a track. The lights went down. Music played and the chairs lurched and began to move sideways. In front of us a whole world lit up, as if we were flying over it, the most fantastic sight I had ever seen, an entire city of the future, with skyscrapers and fourteen-lane highways, real little cars moving on them at different speeds, the center lanes for the higher speeds, the lanes on the edge for the lower. Cars were regulated by radio control, the drivers didn't even do the driving! This miniature world demonstrated how everything was planned, people lived in these modern streamlined curvilinear buildings, each of them accommodating the population of a small town and holding all the things, schools, food stores, laundries, movies and so on, that they might need, and they wouldn't even have to go outside, just as if 174th Street and all the neighborhood around were packed into one giant building. And we passed bridges and streams, and electrified farms and airports that brought up airliners on elevators from underground hangars. And there were factories with lights and smoke, and lakes and forests and mountains, and it was all real, which is to say, built to scale, the forests had real tiny trees, and the water in the tiny lakes was real, and around it all we went, at different levels, seeing everything in more and more detail, thousands of tiny cars zipping right along on their tracks as if carrying their small beings about their business. And out in the countryside were these tiny houses with people sitting in them and reading the paper and listening to the radio. In the cities of the future, pedestrian bridges connected the buildings and highways were sunken on tracks below them. No one would get run over in this futuristic world. It all made sense, people didn't have to travel except to see the countryside; everything else, their schools, their jobs, were right where they lived. I was very impressed. No matter what I had heard about the Futurama, nothing compared with seeing it for myself: all the small moving parts, all the lights and shadows, the animation, as if I were looking at the largest most complicated toy ever made! In fact this is what I realized and that no one had mentioned to me. It was a toy that any child in the world would want to own. You could play with it forever. The little cars made me think of my toy cars when I was small, the ones I held between my thumb and forefinger, the little coupes and sedans of gunmetal whose wheels spun on axles no thicker than a needle as I drove them along the colored tracks of my plaid carriage blanket. The buildings were models, it was a model world. It was filled with appropriate music, and an announcer was describing all these wonderful things as they went by, these raindrop cars, these air-conditioned cities.

And then the amazing thing was that at the end you saw a particular model street intersection and the show was over, and with your I HAVE SEEN THE FUTURE button in your hand you came out into the sun and you were standing on precisely the corner you had just seen, the future was right where you were standing and what was small had become big, the scale had enlarged and you were no longer looking down at it, but standing in it, on this corner of the future, right here in the World's Fair!

That dazzled me. Perhaps it might only have been the sudden passage from darkness to daylight, but I actually wobbled on my feet. I had the feeling that I too had changed size, and it only lasted a moment but it was quite strange. It alerted me to the sizes of everything at the Fair. Norma took us to the Railroads Building. We sat in an auditorium facing a stage with a scenic diorama of O-gage trains and locomotives rolling through hills and valleys and over rivers and through cities. So we were big again. A model freight train would disappear around a bend just as a model passenger train came over a bridge. An announcer told us they had laid the tracks for this exhibit on seventy thousand tiny railway ties that were fastened with a quarter of a million tiny spikes. And then outside, in the daylight behind the exhibit hall, was a real railroad yard with ancient steam engines on display, "The General," the "Daniel Nason," and the newest most modern locomotive of all, a sleek and monumental monster of dark green whose wheels were taller than a man. So there it was again!

And then at the Consolidated Edison exhibit, again everything was shrunk—it was a diorama of the entire City of New York, showing the life in the city from morning till night. We could see the whole city and across the Hudson River to Jersey, the Statue of Liberty in the harbor. We could see up in Westchester and Connecticut. I looked for my house in the Bronx, but I couldn't see it. Norma thought she saw Claremont Park. But below us were the great stone skyscrapers, the cars and buses in the streets, the subways and elevated trains, all of the working metropolis, all of it sparkling with life, and when afternoon came there was even a thunderstorm, and all the lights of the buildings and streets came up to deal with the darkness.

Everywhere at the World's Fair the world was reduced to tiny size by the cunning and ingenuity of builders and engineers. And then things loomed up that were larger than they ought to have been. The Public Health Building had an exhibit showing the different parts of the body, each of them depicted many times their real size. An enormous ear, and nose, with their canals and valves and cellular bone marrow exposed—big pink plastic organs, bigger than I was. The eye was so big you walked into it! You walked into this eye, saw through its lens, which changed to make you nearsighted or farsighted. We all grew dizzy with that one. And then an enormous man made of Plexiglas, I suppose, with all his giant internal organs visible, but no visible penis, a mistake in representation about which I said nothing to Meg and Norma, thinking it was not polite.

And everywhere outside were stone statues of men and women in various poses, wrestling dogs, or bulls, swimming with dolphins, or standing on one foot, or carrying farm tools. They wore stone dresses or stone pants, or they were naked with stone breasts and backsides. You could see the muscles in their legs or arms, you could see their ribs and spinal columns of stone. They stood or lay about in pools or atop pylons or rose up from shrubbery. Some of them were pressed into the sides of buildings, so only the front halves of them showed, sculptures of concrete pressed in like sand molds. The same kinds of expressionless people were painted on the sides of buildings, enormous murals of them holding beakers of chemicals or blueprints in their hands. They looked like no one I knew, parts of them were immense, other parts were small. They intermingled, so you didn't know which arms belonged to which bodies. I was made light-headed by the looming and shrinking size of things.

We wanted to go everywhere, do everything. ''Whoa, whoa, hold your horses,'' Norma said. We were getting wild. She took us to a dairy counter and we sat down and had egg salad sandwiches on white bread and malted milks, an excellent lunch. We sat at a little metal table under an umbrella and ate and drank while Norma leaned on an elbow and smoked a cigarette and watched us. She had bought a buttermilk for herself. When we had finished, she leaned forward and gently wiped with a paper napkin the malted milk around Meg's mouth, who lifted her chin and closed her eyes while this was done.

Then we were off again. It was late afternoon. We saw a rotating platform on which real cows were milked by electric pumps. The cows stared at us as they turned past. They were like the cows on that farm in Connecticut. That they had to be milked by machines while they were rotated I did not question. I thought this was a new discovery; perhaps it kept the cream from rising. We saw in the General Electric Building hall an artificial lightning generator. This was truly fearsome. Bolts of lightning shot thirty feet through the air. Meg screamed and people around us laughed. You could smell the air burn, the thunder was deafening. This was part of the exhibit showing General Electric Appliances for the home. There was so much to see and do. We watched Coca-Cola being bottled and Philadelphia Cream Cheeses wrapped and we saw France and Spain and Belgium. In the Radio Corporation of America Building, which was shaped like a radio vacuum tube, we saw a demonstration of wireless telegraphy saving a ship at sea, and a new invention, picture radio, or television, in which there were reflected on mirrors tilted over a receiver actual pictures of people talking into microphones at the very moment they were talking from somewhere else in the city, not the World's Fair.

We were tired now and stopped to rest on a bench, and to watch the people walk by. All you had to do was turn around and wherever you were you could see the Trylon and Perisphere.

"OK, kids," Norma said, "now I've got to go to work. I have it all planned out. If you're going to make it through this evening, you've got to rest awhile."

She took us on another tractor train to the section of the Fair where she worked. The Amusement Zone. This was very familiar to me. It looked like the boardwalk at Rockaway, with the same penny arcades and shooting galleries and scales to stand on while the concessionaire guessed your weight. But there were big rides too and showplaces like Gay New Orleans and Forbidden Tibet. Meg tugged my arm. "Look, Edgar!" We were going past what I had thought was only another building. But on the roof was a truly amazing sight, a gigantic red revolving National Cash Register, seven stories high. It showed the day's Fair attendance as if it were ringing up sales. Clouds floated peacefully behind it.

NORMA'S PLACE OF WORK WAS A WOODEN THEATER BUILDING WITH A PLATFORM and a barker's lectern in front. The doors were still closed. It was some sort of nautical show. An underwater scene with an octopus was painted on a curtain. Nothing was going on. Behind this building, in a little backyard with a broken-down fence, with towels and women's underwear hanging on a clothesline, was a canvas tent. The flaps were down. Norma found us deck chairs and told us to rest. When she raised the flaps and went into the tent, I saw women sitting at dressing tables.

The afternoon was turning dark now, a chill was in the air here in the shade behind the wooden building. I put on my sweater. Meg sat in her chair all asprawl with her legs hanging over the sides. She looked at me as her eyes glazed over. These chairs were old. The colored stripes were faded. Even two light children sank back into the old canvas—I saw the outline of Meg's back in her chair, the weight and roundness of her in the chair sling. It was very quiet here behind the World's Fair. I heard the murmur of voices but couldn't hear the actual words said. I heard a woman's laughter. I heard calliope music—a circus march that I recognized and that at any other time would have made my heart pound with excitement. I closed my eyes.

TWENTY-NINE

Norma's job was to wrestle with Oscar the amorous octopus in a tank of water. First she stood outside with five or six other women on the platform stage in front of the building. The women wore bathing suits and high-heeled shoes and stood up there while a barker, in a straw hat and holding a cane, told the people who had gathered what they would see inside. Norma looked down and smiled at us. Her bathing cap was turned up on the back of her head. Her one-piece woolen bathing suit was dark blue.

When the doors were opened we pushed inside and got right in front of the glass tank; it was like a small swimming pool made of glass. People pushed behind us. Inside the tank, on the floor, was an octopus. I could tell immediately it was not real. First of all, I had read that octopuses were smaller than people generally believed, their heads were not much bigger than grapefruits; their tentacles were seldom more than a few feet long. This was a rubber model, with a head the size of a sack of potatoes; the tentacles rippled along the floor of the tank in a kind of mechanical way. The eyes ogled us, and the creature moved to the glass and pressed against it as if it wanted to get at us. The audience laughed. He had eight tentacles, and they swished around in more or less independent searching patterns. Occasionally one of the tentacles curled back and touched his mouth, as if he had found something to eat and was eating it, the way an elephant will bring its trunk to its mouth. But it was always the same one. I didn't believe the octopus was real. The little suckers at the end of each tentacle looked molded. The whole thing was the amber color of a rubber nipple.

We could see the women now. They were kneeling at the back edge of the tank on a kind of deck or standing with their hands on their knees and peering in. They were in shadow. The light was in the water where Oscar was. He lifted that one tentacle and curled it back toward himself, like someone saying "Come here" with his index finger. The crowd appreciated this. Then music began, an electric organ playing "The Blue Danube Waltz," and Oscar began to sway in time to the music. One of the women dove in smartly and rose up past the tank window and looped over herself neatly and touched Oscar on the top of his head and then hoisted herself out of the tank. Another dropped in and Oscar grabbed for her, but she eluded him and swam past us, smiling with her eyes open, even though she was underwater, kicking her legs right past us, and she too climbed out of the tank just before the octopus almost grabbed her foot. They were all playing a game with him. Norma dove into the tank now, she dove well. She did the bravest thing of all, she actually allowed Oscar to put his tentacles in her hands and they did an underwater dance together, swaying in time with the music, an underwater ballet, although Oscar looked out at us while he danced and one tentacle came up behind Norma and attached itself to her backside while he ogled at the audience, rolling his eyes, and his mouth curled back in a kind of leer. The audience laughed.

But Norma got away, up the ladder, and now two by two the women jumped in and flirted with Oscar and touched him and swam away before he could get his tentacles on them, although sometimes he did. And soon they were all in the tank with him, and their white legs flashed by, or their arched backs, or they came up from the bottom along the glass front with their hands over their heads, their palms pressed together and their bathing suits stretched taut over their bodies. I couldn't tell anymore which was Norma.

All this time underwater lights were playing through the water, turning it different colors, light blue and green and dark green and red that at first looked black. Now the music had changed, and it was hard to see what was going on, it was dark and foreboding music, like the music of *Inner Sanctum*, a horror-story radio program, very dark music. A white body pressed up to the glass and was tugged back into the murk. And then I felt Meg's hand in mine. She pulled me through the crowd to the door. I understood why. We let the crowd flow around us. It was mostly men, a few women, we were the only children that I could see.

Norma had told us we could wander as we wished around the Amusement Zone, she had even given us money so that we could do what we liked. The only condition was that we had to check back with her every half hour or so during the time when she was offstage. Meg had pulled me back from the tank because we were losing valuable time watching her mother when we could be seeing the Fair.

Yet as we ran along not knowing what to do first, it became clear that we would have to be organized. There were lines everywhere at the big important rides. If we had to show up back at Norma's tent every half hour or forty minutes, it was clear we would have only one thing each time around; we should plan what that was beforehand.

"What is your absolutely essential ride?" I said.

"Parachute," Meg said after a few moments of thought.

I dreaded going up in the parachute, but couldn't let on. "Me too," I said. "Now, what is the absolutely most important exhibit as far as you're concerned?"

"The babies in the incubators," she said. That was a keen disappointment.

"I thought you saw that already."

"I know," Meg said. "So what?"

"I'd rather see Frank Buck's Jungleland," I said. Nevertheless we were getting somewhere. Neither of us was interested in Little Old New York or the Winter Wonderland, despite its contingent of penguins brought back from Antarctica by Admiral Byrd. And we both could do without Merrie England. And we agreed that if we had time, we would like to visit the Odditorium, which was supposed to have amazing freaks of all kinds, according to my friend Arnold.

So with our agenda set, we ran into the night. In front of the Infant Incubator building was a giant thousand-pound sculptured stone baby on its back with its arms and legs waving in the air. But inside, behind glass partitions, attended by nurses in white, these real ugly little scrawny ratlike babies jerked their hands around or slept. How they could sleep in bright light I didn't know, although I understood that babies this age are still blind. Before the invention of the incubator, babies born too early would not have lived. Meg pressed her face against the glass. A nurse saw her and wheeled over an incubator so that she could see it more clearly. The little kid inside was all hooked up to things. It had the face of a wrinkled nut or peach pit. But Meg thought it was cute.

We ran back to Norma. She stood in front of her tent behind the Octopus building. She wore a terrycloth robe and her hair was combed back, all her makeup was gone and her face looked very white, and her eyes red, from swimming in the tank. She smiled when she saw us, she had been awaiting us anxiously. We hugged her. I put my arm around her lower back. I could feel the swell of her hips under my forearm. She wore pink mules on her feet.

Almost immediately we were off again, running down the Midway to Frank Buck's Jungleland. At last! It was a zoo technically, he had lots of different animals, but the railings were wood and the cages were portable, so it was more makeshift than a zoo, more in the nature of a camp. There were three different kinds of elephant, including a pygmy, and there was a black rhinoceros standing very still, as still as a structure, and who obviously understood nothing about where he was or why; there were a few sleeping tigers, none of them advertised as a man-eater; and tapirs, an okapi, and two sleek black panthers. You could ride on a camel's back, which we didn't do. On a miniature mountain, there lived, and screamed and swung and leaped and hung hundreds of rhesus monkeys. We watched them a long time. I explained Frank Buck to Meg. He went into the wilds of Malaya, usually, but also Africa, and trapped animals and brought them back here to zoos and circuses and sold them. I told her that was more humane to do than merely hunt them. In truth, I had worshiped Frank Buck, he lived the life I dreamed for myself, adventurous yet with ethical controls, he did not kill. But I had to confess to myself, though not to Meg, that I had now read his book twice and realized things about him I hadn't understood the first time. He complained a lot about the personalities of his animals. He got into scraps with them. Once an elephant picked him up and tossed him away. An orangutan bit him, and he nearly fell into a pit with a certified man-eating tiger. He called his animals devils, wretches, pitiful creatures, poor beasts and specimens. When one of them died on the ship to America, he felt sorry for it, but he seemed sorrier to lose the money the specimen would have brought. He called the Malays who worked for him in his camp "boys." Yet I could see now in the Malay village in Jungleland that these were men, in their loincloths and turbans, and they handled the animals in their care quite well. Frank Buck himself couldn't have been more impressive. They laughed among themselves and moved in and out of their bamboo shacks with no self-consciousness, barely attending to the patrons of Jungleland. I looked around for Frank Buck, knowing full well he wouldn't be here. I understood his legendary existence depended on his not being here, but I looked anyway. The truth was, I thought now, Frank Buck was a generally grumpy fellow, always cursing out his "boys" or jealously guarding his "specimens" or boasting how many he had sold where and for how much. He acted superior to the people who worked for him. He didn't get along with the authorities in the game preserves, nor with the ships' captains who took him on their freighters with his crated live cargo, nor with the animals themselves. I saw all that now, but I still wanted to be like him, and walk around with a pith helmet and a khaki shirt and a whip for keeping the poor devils in line. The Jungleland souvenir was a gold badge, with red and yellow printing. I pinned Meg's to her dress and mine to my shirt.

We wandered up and down. We bought jelly apples, the good kind with the hard clear red casing. There was a strolling jazz band and we followed it along the Midway. As the evening wore on I forgot everything but the World's Fair. I forgot everything that wasn't the Fair as if the Fair were all there was, as if going on rides and seeing the sights, with crowds of people around you and music in your head, were natural life. I didn't think of my mother or my father or my brother, or of school or the Bronx or even of keeping my wits about me and watching my step. After each of our forays we returned to Norma in her robe and damp hair. We were in the rhythm of the thing. She received us sitting in one of those striped canvas beach chairs with her knees up and her arms around her knees, or with her legs crossed and a dreamy thoughtful look as she smoked one of her cigarettes.

We went to the Odditorium, where the freaks were shown, terrible-looking poor beasts, some of them looking worse for wear than the animals in Jungleland: a half-bearded man/lady wearing half of a bathing suit on one flank and half of a dress suit on the other; something that had fur all over its body; male Siamese twins joined at the hip; a man with enormous webbed feet; a man who claimed to be made of rubber and proved it by suspending heavy weights from rings in his chest—when he stood up, his skin came out toward the weights like bat wings; a woman in a basket who had no arms or legs, just little flippers at the shoulders and hips, which were covered with woolen pink gloves and pink booties; and so on.

Meg didn't like any of this, which I could understand. She perked up in Little Miracle Town, the community of midgets. The midgets were grown-ups, they acted with all the assurance and confidence of grown-ups—they really ran things all by themselves—except that they were tiny, with tiny voices as if they talked through telephones. They had little pug faces, like Mickey Rooney. They looked up in your face and patronized you. They had their own cars and railroad line, their own theaters and stores and toy and doll factory. They sang and showed you around, there were many of them, they showed you their city hall and let you peer in the windows, and some of them were even dressed as soldiers and they stood guard at their bivouac of tiny tents.

Typically of the Fair, almost next door to the midgets was a genuine human giant who sold rings from his finger for fifty cents. He had an English name, Albert something. He was real, all right, every few minutes he stood up to prove it, though most of the time he was seated because in actuality to be that large puts a great strain on the heart. He didn't speak. A card said he was eight feet tall and came from the English Midlands. He had heavy eyebrows, large facial features, his teeth were not good, but he seemed a kind man, if bored by what he was doing. Of course if he got too bored he might become angry. His hair was black and nicely combed. His hands were enormous. He wore a baggy suit. The ring was cheap stuff, I could tell. Each time he sold a ring he got another one from a cardboard box and put it on his finger for the next customer. The price was steep. Nevertheless, I decided Meg should have a ring.

She didn't want one. She was shy. I pulled her by the hand till we were right in front of him. I held out one of my dollars. The large hand gently took it from me. I was surprised at the humanity of this commerce. The giant hand deposited a half dollar in my palm. Some sort of sound, like distant thunder, issued from him, and then found tone. He was chuckling. Meg's eyes went wide and she held her breath. The giant removed a ring from his enormous finger and lifted her arm and slipped the ring over her hand and onto her wrist. We ran off.

ALL NIGHT MEG HAD BEEN WAITING FOR THE PARACHUTE JUMP. I'D HELD OFF AS long as I could. I saw no way out of it. We took our place on line. The Jump was sponsored by the Life Savers candy company. I looked up. Big Life Savers of every color were affixed to the metal lacework of the parachute tower. That was consoling. The line moved quickly. People were pulled up into the black night under the large circular frame that was like a mushroom cap at the top of the tower. Then they floated down, their parachutes billowing. As we were buckled in I noticed that rigid guy wires kept us from swaying and would keep the parachute from actually falling. This was not a true parachute jump, but more like the feeling a fireman would have sliding down a brass pole. That was fine with me. There was a lurch, and we began our rise. My heart beat furiously. I went rigid and held my breath. Up we rose, higher and higher, I could see the whole Fair dropping away under us, the shining white Trylon and Perisphere were bathed now in pale blue light. I saw the Lagoon of Nations, its fountains lit in many colors. I saw the Aquacade. I heard music from a dozen directions, and then, as we rose the breeze added itself to the music like a string section, but in a mocking way of fluctuating sound, as if we would never stop rising from the earth and were bound now for another realm of fierce winds and darkness, a sky life, and we would be blown about in it forever.

Meg was holding my arm so tightly it hurt. "Edgar," she shouted. She held on to my arm with both hands. Her eyes were wide with panic. "I'm scared! Let me down, tell them to let me down!"

"Close your eyes!" I shouted. "Close them!" I was terrified she would squirm so, she would slip right through the harness and fall to her death. "Don't move! Hold on to me! We'll be back down in a few seconds!"

"I'm scared!" she wailed and buried her face in my neck.

"This was your idea!" I shouted as the wind blew about our heads. It was not a gracious thing to say but I couldn't help myself. I saw out over the world now, over the Fair. I saw Manhattan, I saw clouds over the city lit from below by electric light. I grew dizzy. I closed my own eyes and held on to Meg as tightly as she held me. I swore that if I came out of this alive, never again would I go up in such a contraption.

Then we jerked to a stop. And for one moment hung there like pendants from the neck of the night. That is what I thought, that is what went through my head. That we were jewels on the breast of an enormous giantess. My eyes were closed but the bright bulbs of the parachute tower lit my lids, and gave me the illusion of a shelf of white flesh behind me. Then we were falling, gliding, and shouting in our terror; but it was thrilling too. I looked up and opened my eyes, and over our heads a beautiful red parachute streamed up like an immense flower and gathered the wind into itself and flooped out to its fullness. I laughed. We were floating to the earth, I heard the calliope again, I heard the insouciant horns of "The Sidewalks of New York." I was shouting and laughing. Meg had pressed her face against me and I was telling her to look up, but she wouldn't. I had one more scare as I saw the ground rising toward us at an alarming speed, but then we were braked, gently, and dropped the last few feet in a mechanical way, as an elevator comes to a stop; and a few moments later we were on the ground again.

Now Meg permitted herself to look up at where she had been. She was very pale. Her hand in mine was moist. "It was fun, wasn't it," she said as we walked quickly back down the Midway to Norma. "I liked it." And I nodded and didn't say anything. I was too pleased with my own courage, and quietly surprised by it, to tease her or make her feel bad.

I THINK BY NOW WE WERE BEYOND EXHAUSTION. OUR EYES SHONE UNNATURALLY. Norma put her hands on our cheeks and insisted that we not do anything else but sit and wait for her while she finished the last show. A man was with her. He wore a leather jacket, and trousers that were like pipes on his legs. He wore a soft cap with the peak pulled down at an angle. He jiggled the change in his pocket as he looked at us. He had broad shoulders and a friendly face but he needed a shave. Pinned to his cap just over the peak was a button with a number printed on it. He smiled as Norma introduced us, Joe was his name, but I could tell watching him watch her as she tucked her hair up under her bathing cap and then folded back the earflaps that he was her boyfriend.

Norma said to us that she had to go to work. Joe said to us, "And my job is to watch from out front." Norma smiled, removed her robe, and put her arm in his as they went through the alley to the Midway.

I wanted very badly to see those women in the water with the octopus. It seemed to me important. Meg was slumped in a deck chair. She had wrapped Norma's robe around her legs. She examined her collection of badges and pins from the different things we had done. I felt she knew what I wanted and by studiously ignoring me was telling me she had no objection. I ran down the alley to the side door and got into the crowd just as it was filing into the theater. Taking advantage of my size, I squeezed between people and crawled under their legs till I was in the first row, by the rail.

There was Oscar. I thought I could make a pretty good guess now which of the two tentacles had a man's real arms inside them and which two had his legs. The legs were easier. As the women swam by or drifted past him he seemed to rear himself off the floor of the tank, and after the place in the act when the water grew dark and the music mysterious, he seemed more loomingly agile than he had before, a kind of suspended potato sack with ogling eyes that caught what small light there was and shone eerily through the ink. His tentacles waved sinuously. Now when the lights brightened again, Oscar the Amorous Octopus had caught one of the swimmers and had pulled her to him under the water, and as she struggled he pulled her bathing-suit straps off her shoulders and down her back. She got away finally, shooting upwards, but for a moment her breasts were visible, as Fay Wray's had been when after she took the steep dive off the cliff while Kong was occupied with the pterodactyl she came up in the water right past the camera. It was this way now. The audience was not laughing anymore as Oscar seemed to be able to catch the women who swam with him and turn them upside down and pull at their suits. Some of them flailed their arms and legs, some were quite still, as if playing dead, but the music got faster, and Oscar's tentacles more efficient, and soon he was chasing all the women at the same time. They did not climb out of the tank now, but swam about, you could see their legs underwater. One after another they were caught by the monster and dragged under and exhibited. He turned them around and over and upside down, and feigning a clumsy curiosity, he pulled off their bathing suits. Light began to suffuse the water, until it was a pale green. The women were all naked now and came up to the glass of the tank and drifted upwards like dancers, lifting their arms and scissor-kicking their legs right in front of us. They all did this holding hands now, swimming down to the bottom of the tank, coming forward and floating up past us. I needed to know which was Norma, and I found her, her face was blurred by being underwater, but she was the only blond lady, and that became clearer as the light became white. She was the most beautiful. She floated up past me, breasts and thighs, and kicked her legs open and did a somersault. After that the women left the tank one by one until only Norma was left. Oscar went after her. He had been lying exhausted on the bottom of the tank, with his tongue hanging out, as if octopuses had tongues, but now he seemed revived by the sight of her. He chased her and caught her. Now he was doing something she really seemed not to want him to do, one of his tentacles went between her legs and up her back, she had to push him off and dismount the tentacle, rolling around with him in the process, all bent double and rolling around up past the glass and the eyes of all of us. I couldn't breathe. I felt a thrumming kind of heat between my legs but I felt sick too, as if I were going to faint, my ears rang and I was hot and my mouth had gone dry; but my stomach felt cold as if it were filling with the cold water in that tank after the lights had faded and it turned to ink. There was a scattering of applause.

* * *

A WHILE LATER WE WERE ON OUR WAY HOME IN JOE'S TAXI. HE WAS A CABDRIVER, like my uncle Phil. Because he was Norma's friend, Joe had not put down the flag on the meter.

Meg and I had the back to ourselves. We had lots of room to sprawl in. I leaned against a corner and she lay across the seat with her head in my lap. Joe drove with his arm around Norma and she sat huddled against him. Her hair was still damp. I could see it shining in the light of the World's Fair.

We made our way slowly past the fairgrounds. "Look!" Norma said, and we sat up. The big fireworks show had begun over Fountain Lake. We watched it on our knees in the backseat, first through the side window, then through the rear. Great cascades of booming color, showers of red and green and white, pops and swirls and parachutes of color firing the sky and exploding in our ears. It was a most terrible racket. The World's Fair stood in separate instances of daylight. The cab seemed to shake and shudder under the concussive explosions, sparks whirled in circles over our heads, as if we were under attack. We turned a corner, now hearing more than we saw, only the highest rocket showers visible through the window.

Meg sank down on the seat and I joined her. We lay again as we had been. Soon everything was quiet once more.

Meg had said nothing to me about her mother nor acted as if anything unusual had happened under water this evening. She was used to this. I tried to put the images of Norma out of my mind. I knew no one like her. She acted free. I did not think of her as a bad woman but as someone who probably took a different view of things. Otherwise she would not be this way. I could not talk to her about this, of course, but I wondered what she would say. I thought about the casual recklessness of her life. There she was sitting in the front seat of the cab with her boyfriend's arm around her and they were like some new mother and father still in love. I again saw her body in its underwater ballet. I didn't want to think about it. I felt queasy thinking about it, the picture of it produced the faintest illness from somewhere under my stomach, something between nausea and an ache; I knew, though it was there for everyone at the World's Fair to see, I shouldn't have seen it. Norma's freedom made life more thrilling and more dangerous. I felt the danger now. Meg had been born to the thrilling freedom that I only now suspected was possible. The burden of it made her quiet and beautiful. I loved her. The weight of her small body against me now I took as some natural condition of my life, as if we were joined and we shared the same blood, like those Siamese twins, although the twins had been men. Or perhaps we were like swimmers under water, undulating and drifting over each other, rolling about around each other's limbs. I was very sleepy now, and could not distinguish the hum of the taxi on the streets from the resonance of my own thoughts. The fireworks echoed in my mind as a kind of congratulations to me for what I knew. I saw once again Norma's body, the tremors of the muscles of her inner thigh as she swam through the water, the extension and contraction of musculature under the quivers of flesh of her buttocks and belly. And the other women too, that revolving underwater dance of them in their exertions with Oscar. I found now if I held myself the nauseating ache was bearable. Then I pressed Meg's head against myself. I knew everything now, the crucial secret, so carelessly vouchsafed. After all, I had not intended this, it had come to me without my bidding, without any planning or calculation on my part, presented, in fact, as an accident of the adventure. It was not my fault. I had worried before, all the time in this enormous effort to catch up to life, to find it, to feel it, comprehend it; but all I had to do was be in it and it would instruct me and give me everything I needed. As I fell asleep the fireworks went off over and over again like me pounding my own chest and sending my voice to the heavens that I was here.

THIRTY

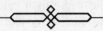

A few weeks later I found out that Norma and Meg were moving to Brooklyn as soon as the school term was over. Norma was going to marry Joe the hackie, as she called him, and they were going to live in a private house in the Bensonhurst section, wherever that was. "Oh, Edgar," Norma said to me one day, "the only bad thing is how we're going to miss you!" I affected nonchalance. Meg, too, seemed undisturbed by the prospect, we both left it to Norma to express the regrets of the matter.

But then we had the last week of school, with its half days, and then a class party, and then school was out and Meg was gone. I went to the park across the street from their house and I looked up at the windows. The shades were up. I could see sunlight on the walls, it was obviously a vacant apartment. My mother asked me after a day or two if I missed my friend, by which she meant to show sympathy, I suppose, but which sounded to me like a tactless annotation of my pain. I denied that I did. "Well, that was nice of them anyway to take you that day to the World's Fair. What did you say the mother's job is?"

"She's one of the guides," I said. "They have these guides in uniform and she is one."

Norma had said that as soon as they got settled they would get in touch and invite me to their new home. This was not a promise I took seriously, Brooklyn being so far from everyone's experience as to be a foreign country. I knew it had the baseball Dodgers but I was not fond of the Dodgers. People liked their pugnacity, as if they were a street gang. Sports cartoons showed them pitching and batting with black stubble on their faces, and cigar butts in their mouths. The whole borough offered itself in that characterization—raucous, rowdy, proud of its lack of manners, like the Dead End Kids. That was all right, except that they meant to claim for themselves the essential New York spirit. I was a Yankee fan myself. I liked the quiet brilliance of Joe DiMaggio, the derring-do of Tommy Henrich. Bill Dickey was a solid professional, strong and fair-minded. All the Yanks were like that—Red Ruffing, Joe Gordon. They were good players who concentrated on what they were doing, who were modest about their tremendous skills and never argued with umpires or played to the crowd. When things were going badly for them, they did not complain but bore down harder. They were civilized and had a naturally assured way about them. That was the true New York quality of spirit. Not bumhood.

Meg did write a letter and then another, but I couldn't bring myself to answer. I kept promising myself that I would write but I didn't. Baseball was a new passion of mine and I didn't think she would be interested. I liked to listen to the games on the radio. Even when the Yankees were out of town, the game circumstances were telegraphed to the studio in New York and the announcer described the game from the telegraph wire, but as if he were on the scene. That interested me more than the game itself. Crowd background noise, the bat hitting the ball, crowd cheering noise. You could hear the telegraph clicking, but the announcer could make you picture the field all the same. ''Joe McCarthy's going out to the mound now with that duck's waddle of his. The manager takes the ball from Lefty and waves to the bullpen. So that's all for Lefty Gomez. He walks slowly to the dugout. The Boston fans give him a good hand. He tips his cap.''

I played my own baseball games with cards or dice. Aces were home runs, kings triples, queens doubles, jacks and tens were singles, there being more of these in a game. I kept scoreboards and made up player names and kept the batting averages. Before my friend Arnold went away to camp, we played strikeouts in the schoolyard. This was a hard game for us but we changed some of the rules to make things easier. We brought the pitcher's mound closer to the schoolyard wall. One out per team per inning, otherwise first man up would bat all day. Hitting was much easier than fielding. We played for hours in the sun inside the chain link fence on the great concrete expanse of the schoolyard.

I didn't know anybody who lived on the Concourse, and by July, when I went down the hill to my old street, there was rarely anyone there. Most families had gone for the summer. My father struggled to make good in his job—he could not afford to give us a vacation. My mother was glad we had moved away so that none of the neighbors would be aware of this. We went to the movies a lot, sometimes the three of us, but most often just my mother and I. I was bored by the movies she liked, which were usually about love, except if they were funny. She didn't have favorite movie actors, she thought most of the leading men were dopes. But she liked and admired actresses. She liked elegance, and wit. She liked women who spoke well and stood up for themselves. She made a point of seeing a movie if Loretta Young or Margaret Sullavan or Irene Dunne or Rosalind Russell was in it. My favorite actresses were Fay Wray and a beautiful woman I had seen only once or twice, but whom I loved, named Frances Farmer. In one picture Frances Farmer played both a mother and her daughter. That reminded me of Norma.

My father when he came with us couldn't sit still for a whole double feature. The newsreel always interested him. He told me that sometimes when he had a free hour during the workday he would go to one of the Trans-Lux newsreel theaters and watch the news and maybe a travelogue. He always wanted to know what was going on, keeping up with the world was what mattered to him more than stories.

Donald came home once or twice on the weekend and he took me to the beach or the movies. He was very relaxed and happy and was a sport with his money. He bought me lunch in a Chinese restaurant. He showed me his bug, an intricate-looking technical device in a black box. He removed it and gave me a demonstration. It was like a tuning fork laid on its side. You didn't tap down, as with an old-fashioned telegraph key, but rattled the key between your thumb and forefinger, thus doubling the rate of clicks. I gave him a sentence from a book and he clicked it out almost as fast as I read it. He explained that every operator developed a sending style that was as recognizable over the air as his signature on paper. That interested me. I resolved to learn the Morse code. You could write it out in dots and dashes. A dot followed by a dash was an *a*. Maybe I would send Donald a letter all in Morse code.

In the heat I lay around a lot and read. My mother wanted me to go out, but I had no place to go. I was very lazy. I thought about the World's Fair. I came upon the Little Blue Book no. 1278, *Ventriloquism Self-Taught,* that I had ordered through the mail long before but had never read. I had always been attracted to ventriloquism. It was a powerful magic, throwing your voice and fooling people, although the author warned that the expression "throwing the voice" was misleading: "A large part of the otherwise intelligent public still labor under the delusion that the ventriloquist is endowed by nature with the power of throwing his voice . . . but what the ventriloquist really does is to imitate as exactly as possible a sound as it is heard by the ears after it has travelled some distance. . . ." I got past this nitpicking and into the training. The most difficult consonants to say without moving your lips were *b* and *p*. But in the context of a sentence you could get away with "vhee" for the *b* and "fee" for the *p*. Thus, a big piano would be a vhig fiano. But before I could even work on the letters, I had to master the *ventriloquial drone*. "To acquire this," the manual said, "take a long deep breath and, holding it, make a sound at the back of your throat as though you were trying to be ill. . . ." This I did, over and over. I was aiming for the resonant drone tone that the author assured me I would recognize as soon as I found it vibrating in my vocal organs. But what kept coming out was a very liquid gurgle that attenuated, as my breath ran out, to the sound of someone choking to death. "Edgar," my mother said, "what is the *matter* with you!" She fervently wished for the end of the summer when, by law, I would have to return to school.

*   *   *

AND TO MY DELIGHT AS WELL AS HER GRATITUDE, SEPTEMBER DID ARRIVE AND I reported for the fifth grade in my first pair of long pants.

I had always loved the beginning of the school year. All the children looked older and more serious. There was a shyness among us for the leaps in height we had made over the summer. Growth required us to become reacquainted. We were older and wiser, and had put childhood behind. Even the louts and fools appeared at their best for the first few days of the term. Everyone arrived with combed hair, clean shirts or middies, and new pencils and erasers. Some of the girls wore stockings instead of socks. We listened to our teacher outline the planned course of work and realized we were respected for the responsible scholars we had become. It was all very engrossing.

Best of all was the equipment our advanced studies required. New notebooks with more lines per page, compasses, protractors. Thicker text-books than any we had known. And new subjects, such as Civics. I was always eager to do my assignments at the beginning of the school year. I liked having a fresh Composition notebook, whose binding of pressed cardboard layers had not begun to separate at the corners and whose black-and-white marbled design was still shiny with varnish. I had not drawn on the inside of the covers yet, no airplane dogfights, no masked and booted avengers, no block letters that made my name appear hewn in stone. That would all come later, with boredom.

One evening as I was doing my homework on the living room floor I looked up and found my father peering at me over the edge of his newspaper. His eyes blinked. He kept staring at me and so I was not able to avert my gaze. I might have thought something was wrong, except that his eyes had no concern or anger in them. When he lowered the page to reveal his face, his mouth was set in the faintest of startled smiles.

"How many boys with your name, do you suppose, live at 1796 Grand Concourse, The Bronx?"

"Just me," I said. In fact there were no other boys of any name in this house that I had ever seen.

He consulted his paper for a moment. "Well then, this must be you," he said.

I got to my feet. "What must be me?"

"It must be you who won honorable mention in the World's Fair essay contest for boys."

"What now?" my mother said, standing in the door and wiping her hands on her apron.

"Our son entered a contest and won," my father said.

I was peering over his shoulder at the news story. I was one of six honorable mentions. The winner was an eighth grader from P.S. 53.

"Not exactly," I said. I was trying to appear casual about the whole thing, but there was my name in black and white in the newspaper. My mother had sat down on the couch. "When did this happen?" she said. "I knew nothing about a contest."

"My name is in the newspaper!" I shouted. "I'm famous! I'm in the newspaper!"

Then we were all laughing. I hugged my father. I ran across the room and hugged my mother. "You're full of surprises, aren't you?" she said.

My father read the entire news story aloud. Included in the account was an excerpt from the winning essay. " 'The typical American boy should possess the same qualities as those of the early American pioneers. He should be handy, dependable, courageous, and loyal to his beliefs. He should be clean, cheerful and friendly, willing to help and be kind to others. He is an all around boy interested in sports, hobbies, and the world around him. . . . The typical American boy takes good care of public property he uses. He enjoys the comics, the movies, outdoor games, pets, and radio programs. He is usually busy at some handicraft or hobby and is always thinking up something new to do or make. That is why America still has a future.' "

I folded my arms across my chest. "It's not that good," I said. "It sounds like the Boy Scout pledge. A Scout should be courteous, friendly, clean and all that drivel."

"Now, Edgar," my mother said.

I was upset. I had had sports in mine too, and kindness. He had pioneers. Why hadn't I thought of that? And he had brought in the future of America. He was right—the typical American boy mentions America.

"Shouldn't they inform the winners directly?" my mother said. "Supposing we didn't happen to read the *New York Times*?"

"Has anyone checked the mail recently?" my father said.

"I'll go," I said. "Where's the key?"

"Before you do," he said, "bring me your essay, I'd like to read it if I may."

I brought out my first copy, the one I couldn't send because I had gotten an inkblot in the margin, and gave it to my father. Then I went out and ran down the stairs to the bank of mailboxes in the front hall at the bottom of the stairs.

Inside the box was a long white envelope addressed to me with the word "Master" in front of my name. A small blue-and-orange Trylon and Perisphere were stamped on the back flap. The letter was from Grover Whalen, chairman of the Fair Corporation. I knew him from the newsreels, he had a moustache and liked to cut ribbons and congratulate people. Now he was congratulating me. He said that by merely presenting this letter at the gates I and my family would be entitled to a free day at the Fair with privileged access to all exhibits and events and free admission to all shows and rides. He said that I was a fine boy, and a good citizen. And he congratulated me again. I wouldn't have known who he was if he hadn't typed his name, that's how badly written his signature was.

"We can go to the Fair!" I shouted as I came into the apartment. "The whole family! It's free!"

But my father held up his hand. My father was reading my essay aloud to my mother.

" 'He should be able to go out into the country and drink raw milk. Likewise, he should traverse the hills and valleys of the city. If he is Jewish he should say so. . . .' "

It sounded good in my father's voice. He read it with feeling. He read it better than I could have. I was thrilled that he thought it worth reading aloud in his own voice. As he reached the end he spoke almost in a whisper.

" 'He knows the value of a dollar. He looks death in the face.' "

Neither of them said anything. They were staring at each other. I realized my mother was crying. "What's the matter?" I said. "Ah, Ma," I said and felt that old despicable thing in me in which tears came to my eyes at the least provocation. She shook her head and lifted the hem of her apron to her eyes.

"Nothing's the matter," my father said. "She's very proud of you, that's all. Come here."

I went to him and he opened his arms and pulled me to him and he held me. It was awkward for me but I did not protest. When he released me, he stood up and fished around in his pocket for a handkerchief and blew his nose.

I still didn't like it that my mother was crying. "Come on, Ma," I said. "We have free tickets!" She laughed through her tears.

My father said, "Don't be disappointed that you didn't get first prize, Edgar. You are not a typical American boy and that's all there is to it." He cleared his throat. "Let's celebrate! What do you say? Let's go out for the evening!"

"Won't that get him to bed very late?" my mother said.

"We'll go to Krum's," my father said.

"He has school tomorrow," she said.

"Rose," my father said, "this boy has done something wonderful. Come along, don't dally, get dressed. The night is young."

She gave in readily enough, it was what she wanted too. And so a few minutes later we were on our walk up the Concourse, my mother and my father and I. He was in the middle. My mother's arm was in his and on the other side I held his hand. They looked very nice. She wore her flowered sundress with a matching jacket and a smart hat with the brim pulled over on one side, and he wore his double-breasted grey suit and his straw boater tilted at a rakish angle. I had put on a clean shirt and tie and had washed my face. "Don't we look swanky!" I said. We were all very happy. Krum's was up near Fordham Road. At their fountain were devised the best ice cream sodas in the Bronx. Perhaps in the world. The evening was balmy, the sun had set but the sky was still blue. The Concourse was alive with cars and people strolling in the early evening. The trees on the road dividers were in full leaf. The streetlamps had come on, and some of the cars drove with their parking lights, but the underside of the passing clouds in the sky were sunlit. My father strode along as he did when he felt good, his shoulders moving from side to side, it was almost a dance. His head bobbed. "Shoulder back," he said to me, "chin up, eyes straight ahead. That's it. Look the world in the eye."

"We should call Philadelphia and tell Donald the good news," my mother said. "We'll do that when we get home," she said after a moment. "He's probably out for the evening anyway. And where did you *get* that stuff," she said to me, leaning forward across my father to catch my eye. "Appreciating all women, indeed. You're a chip off the old block, all right," she said, and when we laughed she laughed with us.

I thought to myself that I was, too, in another way. Perhaps what so pleased my father—beyond my essay, beyond my enterprise—was that I had gotten us into something, in the least likely way I had come up with the tickets.

THIRTY-ONE

The following Friday night Donald came home, and the next day we all went to the Fair. Donald enjoyed very much the way it had happened that the family was finally going. He claimed not to be able to believe it. He hit his forehead with the heel of his hand.

The minute we entered the fairgrounds I felt at home. Everything was there just as I had left it. It was even more amazing to see the second time. We were admitted just as the letter promised, each of us was given a special pass to pin like a badge to our clothes. I was proud, I enjoyed it when people looked at us and then looked again.

We stood in the shadow of the Trylon and Perisphere, and I felt these familiar forms, huge and white, granted some sort of beneficence to my shoulders. It was hard to articulate, but it was as if I were in some invisible field of their guardianship.

I was eager to show my family what I knew. The first thing I wanted them to see was the General Motors Futurama. They all pored over the guidebook. Donald planned the itinerary. Futurama would be on it, of course, yet it made more sense first to see Democracity, the diorama inside the Perisphere. So that is what we did. We rode an escalator up inside the Trylon and walked across a pedestrian bridge into the Perisphere. It was a strange globelike room. We stood on a moving belt that went 360 degrees around the inside of the shell. We were looking down at a totally planned planetary city of the future. Everything had been designed to eliminate all problems and difficulties. A recorded narration told us about it. "In this brave new world," said H. V. Kaltenborn, my father's not terribly favorite radio news commentator, "brain and brawn, faith and courage, are linked in high endeavor, as men march on toward unity and peace."

"M'God," said my father, "he's here too."

The music of an orchestra and choir directed by André Kostelanetz rose from the background. Everyone stared intently at the display, but I was not terribly impressed because nothing moved except us. It was not quite as exciting as a merry-go-round, which is itself fairly dull. My mother was made slightly dizzy moving sideways in this manner. My father pointed out that he knew the music, the score was by a Negro composer named William Grant Still. It was available on records, and he had sold quite a few copies when he had his store.

We left via the Helicline, a ramp leading from the Perisphere to the ground. From this close both structures could be seen in their texture, the sunlight illuminating the gypsum board of their siding. The rough siding made dimples of shadow on the Perisphere. At one point the whiteness turned silver and I could imagine it as the flank of a great airship. Then I could see where the paint was peeling, which was discouraging. But then as we neared the ground the two structures loomed in their geometry, gradually becoming more and more monumental and revealing more of their familiar form, until everything was all right again.

Even though it was Saturday, the Fair was not as crowded as it had been on my first trip, and with fewer people filling the avenues it wasn't as pretty a place. With fewer people in their dress-up clothes the Fair wasn't as clean-looking or as shiny, I could see everywhere signs of decay. Perhaps this was just in my mind; I knew that in only a month the World's Fair would close forever. But the officials who ran the exhibits seemed less attentive to the visitors, their uniforms not quite crisp. Many empty stroller chairs stood about in banks, their operators in their pith helmets talking to one another and smoking cigarettes. Now the tractor-train horn playing ''The Sidewalks of New York'' seemed plaintive because so few people were aboard. I hoped my family didn't notice any of this. I felt responsible for the Fair. However, it all seemed interesting enough to them, they were intent on the main things.

At the Westinghouse building, before we entered the Hall of Science, where Electro the Robot was the star, we stopped at the Time Capsule—or rather the site of its burial. I had seen it before it was put in the ground, because one Saturday afternoon at the Surrey Theater it was shown in the Movietone newsreel, a polished steel cylinder suspended from a crane, twice as tall as a man and pointed at both ends, like a double-headed bullet. The president of the Westinghouse Company spoke into micro-phones from all the radio stations that were set up there, and then they sank the Time Capsule into this hole they had dug that was just a bit wider than the capsule itself, and into which a slightly larger casing had been sunk so that the capsule would not be eroded by water in the soil and so on. And down it went into its Immortal Well, as the hole was called, and the audience applauded and then workmen screwed a cap over the whole thing and then they built a sort of concrete observation platform around it and that's where we were now, peering down at the cap and reading the descriptive material they had posted.

The Time Capsule had been devised to show people in the year 6939 what we had accomplished and what about our lives we thought meaningful. So they had put articles of common use in there, like a windup alarm clock, a can opener, and a toothbrush and a can of tooth powder and a Mickey Mouse plastic cup, and a hat by Lilly Daché; and they had put in material like asbestos and coal, and messages from scientists, and a U.S. silver dollar and the alphabet in hand-set type, and an electric wall switch; and they had put in the Lord's Prayer in three hundred languages, and a dictionary and photographs of factories and assembly lines, and assorted comic strips and *Gone with the Wind*, by Margaret Mitchell, which I had not yet read; and finally newsreels of President Roosevelt giving a speech, and scenes of the United States Navy on maneuvers and the Japanese bombing of Canton in the war with China, and a fashion show in Miami, Florida.

My father wondered aloud what the people five thousand years from now would derive from these things collected in the Time Capsule. "They will think we were good engineers for a primitive people," he said, "and had in our religion only one prayer, which we spoke in a babble of tongues, and that we wore odd hats and murdered each other and read abominable books."

"Not so loud, Dave," my mother said. Other people were standing there and listening. One man laughed but my mother didn't want my father to offend anyone. Of course her reaction only provoked him into even more embarrassing comments. He asked my brother and me why we thought there was nothing in the capsule about the great immigrations that had brought Jewish and Italian and Irish people to America or nothing to represent the point of view of the workingman. "There is no hint from the stuff they included that America has a serious intellectual life, or Indians on reservations or Negroes who suffer from race prejudice. Why is that?" he said as finally we edged him away from the Immortal Well and into the Hall of Science.

It wasn't as if my father couldn't have a good time. On the contrary, he was enjoying himself tremendously. He could be critical of something and admire it at the same time. He just liked to use his mind. By contrast, my mother lacked any capacity for irreverence. She could be bitter, but never disrespectful. When we went through the Town of Tomorrow, a sample community of modern detached houses, each in its own new yard, she became incensed. "What's the point of showing such houses," she said, "when they cost over ten thousand dollars and no one in the world has the money to buy them?"

I was happy when it was time to eat. We sat in the sun and ate waffles with different kinds of topping, which we shared, and not a voice was raised in criticism.

I thought when I got them all to the Futurama, even they would be impressed. And as we rode sideways in our speaker chairs, the whole splendid panoply of highways and horizons before us, all lit up and alive with motion, an intricate marvel of miniaturization, they oohed and aahed as anyone else would. I felt better. It was exhausting to use your mind all the time, education was exhausting, particularly when it was administered by one's parents.

My father understood that I had a proprietary interest in the occasion. So afterwards, outside, he was very gentle and said many things to show his appreciation and his delight. "It is a wonderful vision, all those highways and all those radio-driven cars. Of course, highways are built with public money," he said after a moment. "When the time comes, General Motors isn't going to build the highways, the federal government is. With money from us taxpayers." He smiled. "So General Motors is telling us what they expect from us: we must build them the highways so they can sell us the cars."

Even I had to laugh at that. Everyone did, we were having a good time.

"That may be so," my mother said a moment later to me as my father and brother walked on ahead. "But it would be very nice to own a car."

I CAN'T RECALL MUCH MORE OF THAT FINAL DAY AT THE FAIR. MY PARENTS, growing tired, decided to concentrate their energies on the foreign pavilions. My mother wanted earnestly to see the Jewish Palestine pavilion. She was proud that Jews had a place among other countries. She had contributed a bit of money to the building of it. "They show how the Jewish farmers have made Palestine fertile again, with irrigation and forestry programs," she said. "They show that Jews can be like everyone else."

My father was interested in the Czechoslovak pavilion because of what had happened in that country. "Chamberlain betrayed them to Hitler," he said. "I want to go there and pay my respects. Also the Netherlands, now also lost. They have a carillon—those bells we heard a while ago? That's the Netherlands."

Donald and I had no particular interest in these things. We agreed to split in two groups and arranged when and where to meet. My parents rode off in a hand-pushed chair, like children in a stroller. "I'm sorry they tore down the Soviet pavilion," my father said to no one in particular. "I'd like to have seen it." He turned and waved to us the hand that held the cigar.

Donald and I took the bus down Rainbow Avenue, across the bridge and into the amusement section. Here it was more crowded. I didn't let on I knew about the amazing Oscar, but secretly I hoped to see my friend Meg. I imagined her sitting in the back, in a faded deck chair. I strolled along with Donald and just happened to bring him to the place. But there was no more Oscar the Amorous Octopus, the building was occupied by jugglers and fire-eaters. So we rode a Dodgem electric car with rubber bumpers, in a great mad crackling horde of similarly equipped drivers, all murderously intent. We bumped them and they bumped us, and we laughed hysterically. Donald let me drive, his arm over my shoulders, as we spun about crashing and banging into people and being bashed in return, everyone's head threatening to fly off. Donald yelled over the din: *"This* is the Futurama!" Then we went to a fun house and watched ourselves bend and flatten and elongate in the mirrors, our recognizable selves disappearing into nothing, and looming over us a moment later. We ended up at the Savoy, a place where swing was played and people danced to a band on the bandstand. Donald was entranced, the Jimmy Lunceford band was on the stage and we stayed for two whole shows while Donald shook his head in time to the music and closed his eyes and rapped his fingers on the tables like drumsticks. The dancers jitterbugged and did the Big Apple. It was good music.

Later it rained, and I remember seeing the fireworks go up in the black night and lighting the rain as if some battle were being fought between the earth and the sky.

My winning honorable mention in the essay contest brought me a degree of celebrity for a few days at P.S. 70. The detestable Diane Blumberg, whom I had yet to beat in a spelling bee, looked at me with a new respect, I thought. The principal, Mr. Teitelbaum, saw me in the hall and stopped to shake my hand. "That's the kind of student we turn out at Seventy," he assured me in case I had thought the credit should be mine. Perhaps my sense of accomplishment is what kept the World's Fair in my mind, a kind of dwelling in secret amazement at the boy I was for having boldly done the job; or perhaps it was the recollection of those clean and painted streets, red and yellow and blue, and the flower gardens and the whiteness of the future as it expanded in my mind perispherically and thrust its needle into the sky. One day in October I decided to make up my own time capsule. I think the idea came to me when I found a cardboard mailing tube my father had brought home. I lined the tube inside and out with tinfoil I methodically collected from the insides of cigarette packs and gum wrappers. My friend Arnold found out what I was up to and joined in. And one day after school he accompanied me to Claremont Park, the place I had chosen as the burial site.

I led us fairly deep in the park where there was a little clump of bushes. Here the ground was soft, and also one could dig something and be circumspect about it. Meg and I had played close by here. Arnold helped dig the hole. We measured it with the tube itself until finally it could be slipped down and not show.

Ceremoniously I showed Arnold the items I had chosen to represent to the future my life as I had lived it: my Tom Mix Decoder badge with the spinner shaped like a pistol. My handwritten four-page biography of the life of Franklin Delano Roosevelt, for which I had gotten a grade of 100. This had to be rolled like a cigar. My M. Hohner Marine Band harmonica in its original box that was Donald's but which he had given me when he got the larger model. Two Tootsy Toy lead rocket ships, from which all the paint had been worn, to show I had foreseen the future. My Little Blue Book, *Ventriloquism Self-Taught*, not because I had succeeded but because I had tried. And finally something I was embarrassed to let Arnold see, a torn silk stocking of my mother's, badly run, and which she had thrown away and I had recovered, as an example of the kind of textiles we used— although it was true I had heard that women no longer wore silk stockings in protest against the Japanese, but now wore cotton or that new nylon stuff made of chemicals.

Arnold had brought something too and he asked if he could drop it in the tube. "It's my old prescription pair of eyeglasses," he said. "The frame is cracked but they might understand something about our technology when they look through the lenses." I said OK. Once, long ago, Arnold had showed me he could start a fire in dry brush with those glasses. He dropped them in and I screwed the cover on the tube and slipped it into the ground.

Then I pulled the tube back up and unscrewed the cap and removed the ventriloquism manual. It seemed to me a waste of a book to bury it like that.

I dropped the tube back down in the hole. Looking around to make sure that we hadn't been seen, we filled in the hole with dirt, and stood up and stamped the ground to make it as hard as it was everywhere else. I think we both felt the importance of what we were doing. We brushed some leaves and crumbs of dirt over everything for camouflage.

I remember the weather that day, blustery, cold, the clouds moving fast. The dead leaves flew in the gusts, and the great trees creaked in Claremont Park. My way home headed me into the wind. I put my hands in my pockets and hunched my shoulders and went on. I practiced the ventriloquial drone. I listened for it as I walked through the park, the wind stinging my cheeks and bringing a film of water to my eyes.

LOON LAKE

To Helen Henslee

They were hateful presences in me. Like a little old couple in the woods, all alone for each other, the son only a whim of fate. It was their lousy little house, they never let me forget that. They lived on a linoleum terrain and sat in the evenings by their radio. What were they expecting to hear? If I came in early I distracted them, if I came in late I enraged them, it was my life they resented, the juicy fullness of being they couldn't abide. They were all dried up. They were slightly smoking sticks. They were crumbling into ash. What, after all, was the tragedy in their lives implicit in the profoundly reproachful looks they sent my way? That things hadn't worked out for them? How did that make them different from anyone else on Mechanic Street, even the houses were the same, two by two, the same asphalt palace over and over, streetcars rang the bell on the whole fucking neighborhood. Only the maniacs were alive, the men and women who lived on the street, there was one we called Saint Garbage who went from ash can to ash can collecting what poor people had no use for—can you imagine?—and whatever he found he put on his cart or on his back, he wore several hats several jackets coats pairs of pants, socks over shoes over slippers, you couldn't look at his face, it was bearded and red and raw and one of his eyes ran with some yellow excrescence oh Saint Garbage. And three blocks away was the mill where everybody in Paterson made the wages to keep up their wonderful life, including my father including my mother they went there together and came home together and ate their meals and went to the same bed together. Where was I in all of this, they only paid attention to me if I got sick. For a while there I got sick all the time, coughing and running fevers and wheezing, threatening them with scarlet fever or whooping cough or diphtheria, my only power was in suggesting to them the terrible consequence of one mindless moment of their lust. They clung to their miserable lives, held to their meager rituals on Sundays going to Mass with the other suckers as if some monumental plan was working out that might be personally painful to them but made Sense because God had to make Sense even if the poor dumb hollow-eyed hunkies didn't know what it was. And I despised that. I grew up in a dervish spin of health and sickness and by the time I was fifteen everything was fine, I knew my life and I made it work, I raced down alleys and jumped fences a few seconds before the cops, I stole what I needed and went after girls like prey, I went looking for trouble and was keen for it, I was keen for life, I ran down the street to follow the airships sailing by, I climbed firescapes and watched old women struggle into their corsets, I joined a gang and carried a penknife I had sharpened like an Arab, like a Dago, I stuck it in the vegetable peddler's horse, I stuck it in a feeb with a watermelon head, I slit awnings with it, I played peg with it, I robbed little kids with it, I took a girl on the roof with it and got her to take off her clothes with it. I only wanted to be famous!

And the coal trucks releasing their fearsome anthracite down the sliding chutes to the dark basements, and Ricco the Sweet Potato man putting into your hand a hot orange potato in a half sheet of the *Daily News* for three cents, the filthy black snow lying banked in the streets, the wind smelling of soot and machine oil blowing down Mechanic Street and you are holding your hands on the sweet heat, cupping it holding it up to your red face. The taking humbly, almost unconsciously of goodness by little kids who took it all, the rage of parents, the madness of old women in the dank stairwells, murder, robbery, threat in the sky, the unendurable prison of schoolrooms. In the five-and-ten was the cornucopia of small tin cars with wind-up keys made in Japan and rubber cops on motorcycles, and rubber chiefs in sidecars from Japan there were tin autogyros and tin DC-3s! You went for the small things, the molded metal car models that would fit in your palm, you watched the lady in her green smock and the eyeglasses looping from a black string around her neck, and when she turned, out came the white hand like a frog's tongue, like a cobra's, and down the aisles you went, another toy of goodness, bright-painted toy of gladness in your pocket.

But I was alone in this, I was alone in it all, alone at night in the spread of warmth waking to the warm pool of undeniable satisfaction pissed from my infant cock into the flat world of the sheet and only when it turned cold and chafed my thighs did I admit to being awake, mama, oh mama, the sense of real catastrophe, he wet the bed again—alone in that, alone for years in all of that. I don't remember anyone's name, I don't remember who the gang members were, I don't remember the names of my schoolteachers, I was alone in all of it, there was some faculty of being alone I was born with, in the noise of life and clatter of tenement war, my brain was alone in the silence of observation and perception and understanding, that true silence of waiting for conclusions, of waiting for everything to add up to a judgment, a decision, that silence worse than the silence of the deaf and dumb.

And then one day I am caught breaking the lock on the poorbox, the fat priest in his skirts grabbing my neck with a hand like pincers, not the first time slapping my head with his flat hand and giving me the bum's rush back to the sacristy behind the stone Christs and Marys and the votive candles flickering like a distant jungle encampment and I conceive of what a great vaulting stone penitence this is, with its dark light quite deliberate and its hard stone floors and its cathedral carved space intimating the inside of the cross of man the glory of God, the sin of existence, my sin of existence, born with it stuck with it enraging them all with it God the Father the Son and That Other One really pissing them off with my existence I twist turn kick the Father has balls they don't cut off their own balls they don't go that far the son of a bitch—spungo! I aim truly and he's no priest going down now with eyes about to pop out of his head, red apoplectic face I know the feeling Father but you're no father of mine he is on his hands and knees on the stone he is gasping for breath You want your money I scream take your fucking money and rearing back throw it to heaven run under it as it rains down pennies from heaven on the stone floor ringing like chaos loosed on the good stern Father. I run through the money coming down like slants of rain from the black vaults of heaven.

I LIVED IN NEW YORK FOR A COUPLE OF MONTHS. IT SEEMED TO ME AT FIRST AN incredibly clean place with well-dressed people and washed cars and bright-painted red-and-yellow streetcars and white buildings. It was a stone city then, and in midtown the skyscrapers were white stone and the sanitation men went around pushing big cans on two-wheeled carts and they'd stop here and there and sweep the gutters, that seems incredible to me now, they wore white jackets and white pants and military style caps of khaki. And in Central Park, which I thought of as the country, the park men came along with broomsticks with a nail on the end of them and impaled cigarette wrappers and ice cream wrappers on these sticks and then wiped the sticks off in these burlap bags they carried over their shoulders. The park was glorious and green. The city hummed with enterprise. It was a wonderful city! I thought, a place where things happened and where everyone was important even streetsweepers just from being there not like Paterson where nothing mattered because it was Paterson where nothing important could happen where even death was unimportant. It had size it had magnitude, it gave life magnitude it was one of the great cities of the world. And it went on, it was colossal, miles of streets of grand famous stores and miles of streetcar tracks, great ships bassoing in the harbor and gulls gliding lazily over the docks. I rode the clattering elevated trains that rocked and careened around the corners and when the weather was cold I stayed aboard making complete circles around the city keeping warm on the rush seats set over the heaters. I got to know the city. It calmed me down. Off on its edges you could always get a place to flop, there were still shanties on the hillsides below Riverside Drive, there were mission houses where you could get a bed down at the Bowery and be fumigated and there was a whole network of welfare places where you could get soup and bread if you weren't proud. But I looked for work, I tried to stay clean and present myself at employment agencies crowds of pushing shoving men staring at jobs described in chalk on blackboards at employment agencies it was very difficult to persuade yourself you and not any of a hundred others were the man for the job.

One day I got wise. I saw a fat kid delivering groceries. He was wearing an apron over his clothes and pushing a cart, one of those wooden carts with giant steel-banded wheels. The name and address of the grocery was painted on the slats. His arms full, he went down the steps to the trade entrance of a brownstone, rang the bell and disappeared inside. The cobra strikes! I raced down the street clattering the cart over the cobblestones, I tore around the corner, I went down a side street made dark by the gridwork shadows of industrial firescapes and dark green iron fronts, I felt like Charlie Chaplin, turning one way, braking, doing an about face, scooting off another way, I think I was laughing, imagining a squad of Keystone Kops piling up behind me, I thought of the fat kid's face, even if he knew where to look he couldn't catch me. I sat down for a while in an alley and caught my breath. Eventually, like the most conscientious grocery boy in the world, I trundled my cart back the way I had come and delivered every last one of the orders. Each bag and box had a bill stuck inside with the name and address of the customer. I took tips and cash receipts. I was polite. I pushed my cart back to Graeber's Groceries Fancy Fruits and Vegetables and found Graeber himself loading up another cart grumbling and saying things in German and making life hell for his clerks. No fat kid among them. Graeber was angry, suspicious, skeptical. He didn't believe I found the cart abandoned at a tilt in an alley. And then I turned over into his hands the cash receipts. To the penny.

And that's how I came to be a grocery delivery boy in the rich precincts of Murray Hill. I wore the long white apron and pushed the wooden cart and I earned three dollars a week and tips.

At one home in Gramercy Park I made the acquaintance of a maid she had an eye for me she liked my innocent face. She was an older woman, some kind of Scandinavian wore her hair in braids. She was no great shakes but she had her own room and late one night I was admitted and led up all the flights of this mansion and brought to a small bathroom top floor at the back. She sat me in a claw-foot tub and gave me a bath, this hefty hot steaming red-faced woman. I don't remember her name Hilda Bertha something like that, and she knows herself well before we make love she pulls a pillow over her head to muffle the noise she makes and it is really interesting to go at this great chunky energetic big-bellied soft-assed flop-titted but headless woman, teasing it with a touch, watching it quiver, hearing its muffled squeaks, composing a fuck for it, the likes of which I like to imagine she has never known.

Come with me

Compose with me

Coming she is coming is she

She was very decent really and for my love gave me little presents, castoff sweaters and shoes, food sometimes. I tried to save as much of my wages as I could. My luxuries were cigarettes and movies. I liked to go to the movies and sit there you could see two features and a newsreel for a dime. I liked comedies and musicals and pictures with high style. I always went alone. In my mind was the quiet fellow trying to see himself, hear what he sounded like. He fitted himself out in movie stars he discarded them. I was interested in the way I instantly knew who the situation called for and became him. For Graeber, who wore a straw hat and a bow tie, a stubblehead German with an accent you better not laugh at, I was the honest young fellow who wanted to make something of himself. For Hilda the maid I was the boy who thought he was lucky to have her. When I went along after work with my tips in my pocket I was John D. Rockefeller. I came to make the distinction between the great busy glorious city of civilization on the one hand, and the meagerness or pretense of any one individual I looked at on the other. It was a matter of the distance you took, if you went to the top of the Empire State Building as I liked to do seeing it all was thrilling you had to admire the human race making its encampment like this I could hear the sound of traffic rising like some song to God and love His Genius for shining the sun on it. But down on the docks men slept in the open pulled up like babies on beds of newspapers, hands palm on palm for a pillow. Not their dereliction, that wasn't the point, but their meagerness, for I saw this too as I stood at the piers and watched the ocean liners sail. I watched the well-dressed men and women going up the gangways, turning to wave at their friends, I saw the stevedores taking aboard their steamer trunks and wicker hatboxes, I saw the women wrapping their fur collars tighter against the chill coming up off the water, the men in sporty caps and spats looking self-consciously important, I saw their exhaustion, their pretense, their terror, and in these too, the lucky ones, I understood the meagerness of the adult world. It was an important bit of knowledge and no shock at all for a Paterson mill kid. Adults were in one way or another the ones who were done, finished, living past their hope or their purpose. Even the gulls sitting on the tops of the pilings had more class. The gulls lifting in the wind and spreading their wings over the Hudson.

I distinguished myself from whomever I looked at when I felt the need to, which was often, I felt I could get by make my way whatever the circumstances. I would sell pencils on the sidewalk in front of department stores I would be a newsboy I would steal kill use all my cunning but never would I lose the look in my eye of the living spirit, or give up till that silent secret presence grew out to the edges of me and I was the same as he, imposed upon myself in full completion, the same man with all men, the one man in all events—

I remember this roughneck boy more whole than he knew. Going down the dark stairs of the mansion on Gramercy Park one night trusted to let myself out by the drowsy spent maid, I lifted a silver platter a silver creamer and teapot and a pair of silver candlesticks from the dining room. Even now I see the curved glass cabinet doors in the streetlight coming through the French windows. I hear my breathing. I catch sight of my own face in the salver. Loot-laden I tiptoed over the thick rug I half walked half ran through the streets clutching my lumpy lumberjacket. I had a room on the West Side in a rooming house fifty cents a night no cooking. In the morning going to work from across the wide cobblestone street the cars going past, the streetcars ringing their bells horns blowing trucks ratcheting along with chain-wheel drive I see in Graeber's Groceries Fancy Fruits and Vegetables an officer of the law in earnest conversation with my employer.

Come with me
Compute with me
Computerized she prints out me

Commingling with me she becomes me
Coming she is coming is she
Coming she is a comrade of mine

Sometimes around those fires by the river a man would talk a war veteran usually who had a vision of things, who could say more than how he felt or what was so unfair or who he was going to get someday. And invariably he was a socialist or a communist or an anarchist and he'd call you brother or comrade this fellow and he was always contemplative and didn't seem to mind if anyone listened to him or not. Not that he was wise or especially decent or kind or even that he was sober but even if none of these in those fitful flashes of lucidity like momentary flares of a dying fire he'd say why things were as they were. I liked that. It was a kind of music, I lingered by the edges of the city with the hobos and at night that grand and glorious civilization now had walls all around it we were on the outside looking up at this immense looming presence, a fortress now it was a kind of music to point to the walls and suggest why they would come down. And if you didn't have a true friend, someone in the world as close to you as you were to yourself, this kind of music was interesting to hear. At night you smelled the river in daylight you didn't, I smelled the river scum and felt the mosquitoes and followed the shadows of the great rats who butted right through the tar-paper shacks and dove into the shitholes, and some poor tramp on Sterno would suddenly present with incredible grace an eloquent analysis of monopoly capitalism. It would go on two three minutes he'd take a swig eyes would roll up in his skull and he'd pass out falling backward into the fire and he'd roast his brains if we didn't pull him out his hair smoking his singed burned hair. Wide awake again he'd tell us more.

But it was here I also learned about California. In California you could eat the oranges off the trees, along the seaside boulevards the avocados fell when they were ripe and you found them everywhere and peeled them and you ate them on the seaside boulevards. When you were sleepy you slept on the sand and when you were hot you went wading in the warm Pacific surf and the waves lit up at night off the shore with their own light. And off beyond the waves was a gambling ship.

I decided to go to California.

Armed only with his unpronounceable last name, he went down to the freight yards to begin his journey. He confuses this now in his mind with the West Side slaughtering plant such atomized extract of organic essence, such a perfumery of disembowelment, that in the fetid blood spumed viscera mist above the yards helplessly flew flights of gulls schools of pigeons moths bats insect plagues all swirling round and round in a great squawking endlessly ejaculative anguish.

I found a door that slid open, got it wide enough to slip through, climbed in, pulled the door almost shut behind me stood in the darkness breathing triumph. The car lurches again, almost stops, begins to roll, I was thrown into something that moved. I look around my private car my eyes accustoming themselves to the darkness, soot and pungent cinder begins to flow through the boards, that railroad tang, my eyes see all around the perimeter of my private car a cargo of youths. We are the shipped manufacture of this nation there must have been thirty or forty of us in that car gradually my eyes made out fifty sixty sitting on the floor by the dawn in eastern Pennsylvania at a siding in the chill frosted morning a hundred of us jumped and ran when the bulls came shouting ahead from the engine. Later alone in the tall weeds of another crossing a toot and leisurely around the bend bell-clanging another stately red ball my chance I make for it all around me from the weeds a thousand like me leap I thought I was alone.

I let it go. All my gaunt brothers in my own rags carrying my roped valise hopped the freight. I watched it go. I put up my collar pulled my cap down on my head stuck my hands in my pockets and headed north up the road.

Come with me
Compute with me
Computerized she prints out me

Commingling with me she becomes me
Coming she is coming is she
Coming she is a comrade of mine
Comrades come all over comrades
Communists come upon communists
Hi. Hi.

We are here to complete our fusion
We are here to create confusion
Do you confuse coming with confession?
Do you fuel for nuclear compression?
I'm for funicular ascension.

Decline all word temptation
Define all worldly tension
Deride all prayerful intervention
Computer nukes come pray with me
Before the war, the war, after the war
Before the war the war after the war the war before the war
Disestablishes human character.

Computer data composes World War One poet
Warren Penfield born Indianapolis Indiana
City of Indians in the Plains Wars after the peace
City of Indians going about their business
Indian poets in headbands walking on grid streets
Secure in their city of Indian architecture of cool concrete
Bernard Cornfield Investors Overseas Securities

Data linkage escape this is not emergency
Before the war before the last war
A boy stood on the dirt street in Ludlow Colorado.
The wind of the plain blew the coal dust under his eyelids
The wind blew the black dust down the canyons of the Sangre de
Cristo. The clothesline stretching across the plain
The miner's cotton swung its arms and legs wildly in the wind.
A miner's wife stepped from a tent with an infant girl
suspended from her hands. She held the child beyond
the edge of the wood sidewalk over the dirt the dust blowing
back along the ground like hordes of microscopic creatures running.
The infant's girl's dress raised under her arms
she hung from her knees and underarms
so as to have her hairless child's fruit expressed
for the purpose indicated by the mother's sibilant sound effects
punctuated with foreign words of encouragement.
The boy standing there happening to be there remained to watch
shamelessly and the beautiful little girl turned upon him a face
of such outrage that he immediately recognized her
willing white neck companion of the old monk it's you
and with then saintly inability to withstand life she closed
her eyes and allowed the thin stream of golden water to cascade
into the dust where instantly formed minuscule tulips
he beheld the fruition of a small fertile universe.

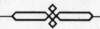

When the nights were bad, when the uncanny sounds in the woods kept him awake, when the crack of a twig in the pine forest was inexplicable or some distant whimpering creature sounded in his mind like a child being fucked he swore it was still better than going with the red ball. Whowhoo. Better to take alone whatever came. Soft web of night threads across the face. Something watching breathing in the dark a few feet away. He had heard of people having a foot cut off for the dollar in their shoe. It was still better. It was still better to take alone whatever came. Better to die in the open. Whowhoo. Lying in a city mission flop in the great stink of mankind was worse. Arraigned in the ranks of the self-deluding in their bunkbeds was worse.

It was the bums of the commonest conversation who angered him the most, the casuists of misfortune who bragged about the labels inside their torn filthy coats, or swore there was some brand of alcohol they wouldn't be so low as to drink. Or the ones who claimed to be only temporarily down on their luck, en route to some glorious destination not where they had a job waiting or a family, but where they were *known*, where what they were did not have to be proved.

I didn't want these mockeries to my own kingship of consciousness, with all the conquests of my life still to come. How could I hope or scheme however idly in a flophouse with a hundred others, a thousand others, a hundred thousand others where the dreams rise on the breath and dissolve one another in a precipitate element not your own—and you are trapped in it, a dark underwater kingdom fed by springs of alcoholic piss and sweat, in which there live and swim the vilest phantoms of God.

And strangely enough each morning I woke up still alive. In the lake villages and the small towns of old mills, I was moved along by the constable but a shade more gently. I didn't feel like a tramp when I asked for work. I even had a certain distinction. We were like birds or insects, pestilential, when we buzzed or flocked in great numbers, but one sole specimen could be tolerated with a certain scientific interest. Sometimes

I washed dishes for a meal. Sometimes I stole my food. Sometimes I found a day's work at some farm.

Then in one town, walking down the main street in a manner that suggested I had someplace to go, I saw coming out of the drugstore three midgets and a heavyset dwarf who huddled over them like their father. They took their quick little steps down the street, all talking at the same time, the muscular torso of the dwarf jolting from side to side with each step. I followed them. Even when they noticed me following them I followed them. They led me to the edge of town. In a grass lot between two stands of trees was the Hearn Bros. carnival, a traveling show of tattered brown tents, old trucks, kiddy rides and paint-peeled wagons. I heard the growl of a big cat.

Ah, what I felt standing there in the sun! A broken-down carnival— a few acts, a few rides and a contingent of freaks. But the sight of it made me a boy again. I was going backward. Those ridiculous bickering midgets had called up my love for tiny things, my great unslaked child's thirst for tiny things, as if I had never held enough toys that were small to my small hand. Holy shit a carnival! I knew it was for me as sure as I knew my own face in the mirror.

I hung around. I made myself useful. They were still putting it together. I helped lay the wooden track for the kiddy cars. I heaved-ho the tent ropes, I set the corral poles for the pony ride. There were three or four tired stiffs doing these things. I recognized them for what they were, everyone of them had a pint of wine in his pocket, they were no problem at all. I thought the Hearn Bros. were lucky to have me.

But nothing happened. Nobody paid attention. At dusk the generator was cranked, and the power went on with a thump. The string lights glowed, the Victrola band music came out of the loudspeakers, the Wheel of Fortune went ratatat-tat, and I saw how money was made from the poor. They drifted in, appearing starved and sucked dry, but holding in their palms the nickels and dimes that would give them a view of Wolf Woman, Lizard Man, the Living Oyster, the Fingerling Family and in fact the whole Hearn Bros. bestiary of human virtue and excellence.

The clear favorite was Fanny the Fat Lady. She sat on a scale that was like a porch swing. Over her head a big red arrow attested to six hundred and eight pounds. Someone doubted that. She responded with an emphatic sigh and the arrow fluctuated wildly, going as high as nine hundred. This made people laugh. She was dressed in a short jumper with a big collar and a bow in her hair, just like Shirley Temple. Her dyed red hair was set in waves over her small skull. The other freaks did routines or sold souvenirs and pamphlets of their life stories. Not the Fat Lady. She only sat and suffered herself to be gazed on, her slathered legs crossed at the ankles. I couldn't stop looking at her. Finally I caught her attention, and her little painted mouth widened like the wings of a butterfly as if it were basking on some pulpy extragalactic flower. The folds of her chins rising in cups of delicate hue, her blue eyes setting like moons behind her cheeks, she smiled at me and unsmiled, smiled and unsmiled, sitting there with each arm resting on the base of a plump hand supported by a knee that was like the cap of an exotic giant white mushroom.

I realized she was slow-witted. Behind her and off to the side was a woman who was keeping an eye out, maybe a relative, a mother, an aunt. This woman looked at me with the alert eyes of the carney.

And as I went about I saw those eyes everywhere behind the show, alert carney eyes on the gaunt man with a white shirt and tie and sleeve garters, on the girl in the ticket booth, on the freaks themselves staring out from their enclosures. What were they looking for? Life! A threat! An advantage! I had that look myself. I recognized it, I knew these people.

But I wasn't getting anywhere with them. By midnight the crowd had thinned out. The lights were blinked in warning and the generator was turned off. The last of the rubes drifted back into the hills. They held Kewpie dolls. They held pinwheels.

I saw the acts going into their trailers to find some supper or drink some wine. I sat across the road with my back against a tree. I wanted a job with the carney. It seemed to me the finest possible way to live.

A while later a truck came along running without headlights and it turned into the dark lot. I sat up. I heard the truck doors slam. A few minutes later an old car and three men got out and walked into the carney. Other men arrived on foot, in jalopies. A few lights had gone back on. I crossed the road. There was some kind of renewed commerce, I didn't understand. I saw the belly dancer standing in the door of her trailer her arms folded a man at the foot of the steps tipped his cap. I saw the girl who sold tickets outside her booth she was looking into a hand mirror and primping her hair. At the back end of the lot in the shadow of the trees a line of men and boys outside a trailer. I went there and got on the end of the line. A man came out and talked in low tones to the others. I heard something moaning. Another man went in. From the trailer came these sounds of life's panic, shivers and moans and shrieks and crashings and hoarse cries, the most awesome fuckmusic I had ever heard. I got closer. I hadn't seen before sitting on a chair at the foot of the trailer steps that same woman attendant from the afternoon who kept a close and watchful eye on the crowd in front of Fanny the Fat Lady.

I LED HER FROM THE TRAILER TO THE TENT IN THE AFTERNOON AND BACK TO HER trailer at the end of the night. She placed her hand on my shoulder, and walking behind me at arm's length with a great quivering resettlement of herself at each step, she made her stately trustful way down the midway.

Once she hugged me. She was surprisingly gentle I did not share the popular lust for her I was embarrassed and maybe frightened by that mountainous softness I pulled away. Right away I saw I'd made a mistake. Fanny had a cleft palate and on top of that the sounds she made were in Spanish but I could tell her feelings were hurt. I moved to her and let her hug me. She put her warm hand on the small of my back. I thought I felt the touch of an astute intelligence.

She was truly sensitive to men, she had a real affection for them. She didn't know she was making money, she never saw the money. She held out her arms and loved them, and it didn't matter what happened, if they came in the folds of her thighs or the creases in the sides of her which spilled over the structure of her trunk like down quilts, she always screamed as if they had found her true center.

I decided that between this retarded whore freak and the riffraff who stood in line to fuck her some really important sacrament was taken, some means of continuing with hope, a ritual oath of life which did not wear away but grew in the memory of her around the bars and taverns of the mountains, catching her image in the sawdust flying up through the sunlight in the mill yards or lying like the mist of the morning over the clear lakes.

On the other hand it was common knowledge in the carney that fat ladies were the biggest draw.

I got along with all the freaks, I made a point to. It was as if I had to acclimate myself to the worst there was. I never let them see that I had any special awareness of them. I knew it was important not to act like a rube. After a while they stopped looking at me with the carney eyes and forgot I was there. Some, the Living Oyster for instance, were taken care of by members of their families who lived with them and probably got them their jobs in the first place. There was about them all, freaks and family, such competence that you almost wondered how normal people got along. There was a harmony of malformation and life that could only scare the shit out of you if you thought about it. The freaks read the papers and talked about Roosevelt, just like everyone else in the country.

But with all of that they lived invalid lives, as someone in the pain of constant hopeless bad health, and so their dispositions were seldom sunny.

The Fingerlings were mean little bastards, they were not really a family but who could tell? They all had these little pug faces. They used to get into fights all the time and only the dwarf could do anything with them. They used to torture Wolf Woman. What she had done to arouse their wrath I never knew. They liked to sneak up on her and pull out tufts of her hair. "That's all right," they screamed, scuttling out of her way. "Plenty more where that came from!"

And every day the rubes paid their money to see them and then went off and took a chance on Fortune's wheel.

I had great respect for Sim Hearn. He was the owner of the enterprise.

He was pretty strange himself, a tall thin man who walked with a stoop. Even the hottest days of the summer he wore an old gray fedora with the brim pulled way down, and a white-on-white shirt with a black tie and rubber bands around the sleeves above the elbows. He had stick arms. He was always sucking on his teeth, alighting on a particular crevasse with his tongue and then pulling air through it. *Cheeup cheeup!* If you wanted to know where Hearn was on the lot, all you had to do was listen. Sometimes you'd be doing your work and you'd realize it was you he was watching, the *cheeup cheeup* just behind your ear, as if he'd landed on your shoulder. You'd turn and there he'd be. He'd point at what he wanted done with his chin. "That," he'd say. He was a stingy son of a bitch even with his words.

I was fascinated by him. Sucking his teeth and never speaking more than he had to gave him an air of preoccupation, as if he had weightier matters on his mind than a fifth-rate carney. But he knew his business, all right. He knew what towns to skip, he knew what games would go in one place but not another, and he knew when it was time to pull up stakes. We were a smooth efficient outfit under Sim Hearn. He'd go on ahead to find the location and make the payoff. And when we drove into town he'd be waiting where we could see him sitting behind the wheel of his Model A with one arm out the window, the rubber band around the shirt sleeve.

His real genius was in freak dealing. Where did he get them? Could they be ordered? Was there a clearing house for freaks somewhere? There really was—a theatrical agency in New York on lower Broadway. But if he could, Sim Hearn liked to find them himself. People would come up to him and he'd go with them to see what was hidden in the basement or the barn. If he liked what he saw, he named his terms and didn't have to pay a commission. Maybe he had dreams of finding something so inspiring that he'd make his fortune, like Barnum. But to the afflicted of the countryside, he was a chance in a million. I'd go to work one morning and see some grotesque I hadn't seen before, not necessarily in costume at show time but definitely with the carney. Sometimes they didn't want to display themselves in their own neighborhoods. Sometimes Hearn's particular conviction of their ability was lacking or maybe he hadn't figured out how best to show them. They required some kind of seasoning, like rookie ballplayers, to give them their competence as professionals. One would be around awhile and disappear just as another would show up, I think they were traded back and forth among the different franchises of this mysterious league.

But when a new freak was introduced, that evening everyone would shine, the new one would tone them all up in competitive awareness, except for Fanny, secure and serene in her mightiness.

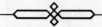

Herewith bio the poet Warren Penfield.
Born Indianapolis Indiana August 2 1899.
Moved at an early age with parents to southern Colorado.
First place Ludlow Consolidated Grade School Spelling Bee 1908.
Ludlow Colorado Boy of the Year 1913.
Colorado State Mental Asylum 1914, 1915.
Enlisted US Army Signal Corps 1916.
Valedictorian US Army Semaphore School Augusta Georgia.
Assigned First Carrier Pigeon Company Seventh Signal Battalion
First Division, AEF. Saw action Somme Offensive
pigeons having the shit shot out of them feathers falling over
trenches blasted in bits like snowflakes drifting through the
concussions of air or balancing on the thin fountain of a scream.
Citation accompanying Silver Star awarded Warren
Penfield 1918: that his company of pigeons having been
rendered inoperable and all other signal apparatus including
field telephone no longer available to him Corporal Penfield
did stand in an exposed position lit by flare under enemy
heavy fire and transmit in extended arm semaphore the urgent
communication of his battalion commander until accurate and
redemptive fire from his own artillery indicated the message
had been received. This was not true. What he transmitted
via full arm semaphore under enemy heavy fire was the first
verse of English poet William Wordsworth's Ode Intimations
of Immortality from Recollections of Early Childhood as follows
quote: There was a time when meadow grove and stream the
earth and every common sight to me did seem apparelled in
celestial light the glory and the freshness of a dream. It
is not now as it hath been of yore—turn wheresoe'er I may by
night or day the things which I have seen I now can see
no more endquote.

So informed Secretary of Army in letter July 4 1918, medal
enclosed. Incarceration US Army Veterans Psychological
Facility Nutley New Jersey 1918. First volume of verse
The Flowers of the Sangre de Cristo unpaged published by
the author 1918. No reviews. Crosscountry journey to
Seattle Washington 1919. Trans-Pacific voyage 1919.
Resident of Japan 1919–1927. Second volume of verse *Child
Bride in a Zen Garden* unpaged published in English
by Nosaka Publishing Company, Tokyo, 1926. No reviews.
Deported Japan undesirable alien 1927. Poet in residence
private mountain retreat Loon Lake NY 1929–1937.
Disappeared presumed lost at sea on around-
the-world airplane voyage 1937. No survivors.
Third volume of verse *Loon Lake* unpaged published
posthumously by the Grebe Press, Loon Lake NY 1939.
No reviews.

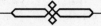

You are what? said Jack Penfield, leaning over the table to hear better. His brow lowered and his mouth opened, the face was poised in skeptical anticipation of the intelligence he was about to receive. Or had he received it? In his middle age he no longer wanted to be the recipient of good news of any kind. And if some was forthcoming he quickly rendered it ineffective, almost as if it were more important that the world be grimly consistent at this point than that it would offer a surprise. You are what?

The boy of the year, his son said.

What does that mean?

Oh Warren, his mother said, isn't that fine. She sat down beside her son, pulling the wooden chair next to his, and she faced her husband across the table. He would have to work on both of them now.

I don't know, Warren said. You get a certificate and five dollars at the spring ceremony.

Jack Penfield leaned back in his chair. I see. He got up and went to the mantel and took his pipe and tobacco tin and came back to the table and fixed up for a while while they watched. The large flat fingers tamped the tobacco in the bowl. The hand of the lifelong miner with its unerasable lines of charcoal in the knuckles and under the nails. He lit his pipe. You know, he said, when I come up this evening there was a man with a rifle on Watertank Hill.

Please Jack his wife said.

What you going to do with the money lad?

I don't know.

That's moren a day's wages. Are you proud?

I don't know.

You won't make four dollars when you come below. Did you know that?

Yes.

If there still is a mine. Are there any other english-speaking there aren't are there?

I don't think so.

Well then you had to be boy of the year didn't you.

Please Jack.

Didn't you.

I suppose.

The only one they can call up to the platform and trust to say thank you properly. No polack wop or damned greek knows to say thank you for makin me boy of the year does he?

I don't know.

And your ma's going to find a clean shirt for you that day won't she. And she'll comb her hair back and put the comb in it and go with the tears of thanks in her eyes for the company school and the company supply and the company house and the company boy of the year.

You poison everything Neda Penfield said. You make everything bad, you make a child feel bad for being alive. There's nothing worse than that. There's no evil worse than that.

But he minded less than his mother thought he did. He wanted his father to talk this way. It was very helpful to him. The consistency of their positions was all he asked, that his pa be unyielding and full of anger, that his ma be enraged or worse frightened by her husband's spiritual tactlessness. Warren knew they were poor and lived lives the color of slag. He knew there was nothing beautiful in Ludlow but he was eager to get up each morning and test the day. He knew the real evil was his own, the eye and ear that took in everything and suffered nothing. He accumulated meaningless useless data that nevertheless bewitched him. The thick bulbed vein in his father's hand, for instance, in contrast to the thin greenish vein in his mother's. The characteristic smell of the house and the privy were noted and recorded. There were certain objects he liked very much. His mother's tortoise-shell comb, the teeth broken off in several places. The coal stove, whose shape was like a naked woman, her long neck disappearing through the roof. He liked to see underwear drying on the line the wind animating it to a maniac dance. Sometimes he thought of the flapping long johns as a desperate signaling of imprisoned or tortured people. He was absorbed by the sun rising and the sun setting or the rain when it fell from rock to rock. He was excited by any kind of violence, a parent hitting a child a man hitting a woman. When he happened to see such things he would be suffused with a weird heat. His heart would beat furiously and then he'd feel sickened and would feel like throwing up. Until he broke into a cold sweat. Then he would feel all right again. He listened now with eyes downcast but in some contentment to their argument, enjoying the words of it, the claims and counterclaims, agreeing with each in turn they were so well matched and spoke so well the images that flew through his mind on their words.

I got out of bed and rolled my clothes and shoes into a bundle. I grabbed the money from the bureau. I unlatched the door quietly and closed it behind me. There were no other guests at the Pine Grove Motor Court. A thin frost lay on the window of her car. The wind blew.

I threw the bills into the wind.

I found a privy up the hill behind the cabins and next to it an outdoor shower, the kind you pumped the water for yourself. I stood in the shower of cold spring water and looked up at the swaying tops of the pine trees and I watched the sky turning gray and heard through the water and the toneless wind the sounds of the first bird waking.

I dried myself as best I could and put on my clothes. Shivering, stipple-skinned, I struck off through the woods. I had no idea where I was going. It didn't matter. I ran to get warm. I ran into the woods as to another world.

All morning I went up and down the hills of timber. Sometimes I'd hear the sound of a truck or a car and it would shock me. I'd veer off to get as deep in the woods as possible. It was difficult to keep my sense of direction, difficult to put life behind me. I'd come along into a clearing and find the remains of a fire or an empty wine bottle. Traces of human life everywhere: stone fences, old trails, dirt roads grown over. I found a busted inner tube, yellowed sheets of newspaper with dates on them from the early summer.

But I saw no one: any stiff in his right mind would get out of the Adirondacks before autumn.

By the late morning I was so hungry I changed course and went downhill till I found a paved road. I walked along the tree line for several miles and came to a country store with a gas pump and some chickens in a coop. Stood in the trees and waited to see a black Model A or perhaps a carney truck or even a state police car. The odds were against it, but I was not thinking odds. The carney was a territory in my mind. It loomed out further than I had gone or maybe could go.

There were no cars. I slid down the embankment of loose earth behind the store and went around front and stepped in the door like any customer. I had my savings of the summer, twenty-six dollars, in my shoes; in my wallet I carried three dollars more. I bought a loaf of wax-papered bread, some slices of baloney, a bottle of Grade A milk and a package of Luckies. The store lady, short and wide and with thick dirty eyeglasses, treated me as if it were the most normal thing in the world for someone to come along from nowhere, as maybe it was.

I went down the road till it curved out of sight of the store, and then I ran back up into the woods and found a tree in a spot of sun and sat there and made my lunch. Then I went to sleep for a while, while the woods were still warm, but it was a mistake because I suffered terrible dreams of indistinct shapes and shadows and awful sounds of violence. Someone was crying, sobbing, and it turned out to be me. I jumped up and got going again.

I went deeper and deeper into the woods and sometime at the height of the afternoon wandered into a stand of ancient pine with a porous forest floor of brown pine needles that was so soft you couldn't hear your own footsteps. It was dark in here, there was an umber twilight in lieu of the day, and there seemed to be no usual busy life at all, no birds, no insects, just this dark place of unnatural quiet. Looking up, I could hardly find anything green. Yet it was not threatening, the solitude was so complete, the stillness so perfect that I felt as if I had come into some vast, hushed cathedral of peace. Not even a Father. I stopped walking and stood very still and listened for I don't know what. And then, right in my tracks I sat down and for a while was as still as everything else.

I thought of Fanny the Fat Lady's warm hand on the small of my back.

By early afternoon I was traveling again on roads, only jumping off to the side when I heard a car coming, or taking to the woods in order to skirt a town. I went along that day with no destination in mind, no plan of action except to follow the rise, and go for the altitude. I had no food left and did not feel I needed any. I came out to a broad plateau and looking out ahead of me realized I had gone past the region of towns and now, for my arrogance, had no hope of supper unless I found a farmhouse some-where.

The open ground was uncultivated, mile after mile. I was on a crum-bling two-lane road with grass growing in the cracks and this suggested to me the unlikelihood of a ride coming along. Still I kept going.

And then with the sun turning red as it dropped toward the evening, I saw to my left, perhaps fifty yards into an open space of tall weed and tangled brush, a single-track railroad embankment. Behind the embank-ment was a curved outcropping of shiny flaked rock. I got up on the embankment for a professional survey: I had happened upon a one-track spur line of some sort. I figured that as it curved in an arc around the rock hill, there was a fair chance it would be going slowly enough to hop.

Coming down from the roadbed, I found a bare patch of ground spotted with oil. And beside the charred remains of a fire I saw a flask of clear glass and a lady's shoe with the heel torn off. So others had stopped here in their great study of the outdoors—it was a station of sorts.

I gathered a great bundle of kindling, but I was too tired to build a fire. I lay on my back with my hands behind my head and I watched the sky. The sun had gone down but the sky was still blue, a very pale blue, with a few high clouds still golden with sunlight. Soon I was lying in the dusk and feeling the chill of the evening but the sky was sunlit and blue and so far away in its warmth that I felt I was looking at it from a grave.

I fell asleep that way and sometime during the night was aroused by a train whistle. I lay there listening for it again in case I had only been dreaming. Again I heard it, this time somewhat closer. I stood up and tried to pound some circulation into my stiff hulk. The train was coming without question now. I had no idea what time it was, the sky was black, starless. I thought I could hear the locomotive. I moved toward the embankment and waited. I could hear the engine clearly now and knew it was moving at a slow speed. The first I saw of it was a diffuse paling of the darkness along the curve of the embankment. Suddenly I was blinded by a powerful light, as if I had looked into the sun. I dropped to my knees. The beam swung away from me in a transverse arc and a long conical ray of light illuminated the entire rock outcropping, every silvery vein of schist glittering as bright as a mirror, every fern and evergreen flaring for a moment as if torched. I rubbed my eyes and looked for the train behind the glare. It was passing from my left to my right. The locomotive and tender were blacker than the night, a massive movement forward of shadow, but there was a passenger car behind them and it was all lit up inside. I saw a porter in a white jacket serving drinks to three men sitting at a table. I saw dark wood paneling, a lamp with a fringed shade, and shelves of books in leather bindings. Then two women sitting talking at a group of wing chairs that looked textured, as if needle-pointed. Then a bright bedroom with frosted-glass wall lamps and a canopied bed and standing naked in front of a mirror was a blond girl and she was holding up for her examination a white dress on a hanger.

Oh my lords and ladies and then the train had passed through the clearing and I was watching the red light disappear around the bend. I hadn't moved from the moment the light had dazzled my eyes. I'd heard of private railroad cars but was not prepared. I was under the impression I would see it again if I waited. I waited. I heard it going down the track and listened until I couldn't hear it anymore. Into my vacated mind flowed all the English I never knew I'd learned at Paterson Latin High School. Grammar slammed into my brain. In an instant this vision of incandescent splendor had left me more alone and terrified than I knew it was possible to be.

I got a fire going and made it as large as I could, I threw everything I could find into it, it was a damn bonfire and I crouched beside it trying to get warm I made an involuntary sound in my throat for my dereliction, my loneliness, the callow hopes of my life. Who did I think I was? Where did I think I was going? What made me think it was worth anything to stay alive?

The fire blazed up. I wanted to get in it.

At the first light of the morning I climbed the embankment and set out down the tracks in the direction the train had gone.

Compare the private railroad car sitting on the Santa Fe siding one night in 1910 in front of the mine near Ludlow Colorado whose collapsed entry was being dug away by rescue crews. Late at night by the glow of torches they began to bring out the dead hunky miners, some so impregnated by coal dust they looked like ancient archaeological finds of considerable significance. Some had been blown to pieces and were assembled on the cold ground by thoughtful colleagues who matched the torn halves of pants legs or recognized what head went with what trunk. The boy followed these deliberations and remarked on the sepulchral interest of assembling pieces of bodies matching and discarding, trying this arm here that foot there on the dark ground, the chill of the October night on the slag hills, the black mineral mountains looming darker than the night sky, the boy noticing the darkening stains around the bodies as blood blacker than coalwater. Some miners were brought out intact, uninjured and looking only slightly stunned to have breathed all the available air until there was no more. Some faces had the look of irritability that comes when something small has gone wrong. Others had eyes rolled into their heads in exasperation others had sorrowed into death and by some curious self-embalmment of the skin left the tracks of their tears like shining falling stars through their grizzled faces. The rescue work was commanded from the private railroad car, a property like the mine and like the miners of the Colorado Fuel and Iron Company, and in the car a self-sufficient unit with bedrooms kitchen small library and a row of partners' desks were three or four officers of the firm some in gartered shirt sleeves efficiently dealing with the wives making settlements pushing waivers across their desks proffering pens matching the tally sheets to the employment records and in general dealing so efficiently with the disaster that the mine would be back in action within the week. The only thing that threatened this work performance was the occasional embittered woman who would come in screaming and tearing her hair and cursing them in her own language. They would nod to one of the private peace officers and the troublesome woman would be removed. Gradually in his inspection of the disaster the boy found his way into the car and in the moment before he was ejected he observed one of the company officers, a stolid man impassively wiping the spittle from his cheek. The brass plate at his desk informed the boy of F. W. Bennett Vice President for Engineering. Warren felt the rough hand of the armed guard on his neck and then the coolness of the night air as he flew from the top of the rail-car step to the graveled ground. His knee was embedded with bits of stone as the miners had been peppered with coal fragments, so he understood that feeling. To understand what it meant to be buried alive in a mountain he sat later with his eyes closed in the night and his hands over his ears and he held his breath as long as he could.

Every day to school she wore her faded dress of flowers, horizontal lines of originally cheery little tulips row upon row. It came below her knees and there the cast off shoes, boots practically, hook-and-eye boots all cracked and curled, there the boots began, and so nothing of her was uncovered except the neck above the high collar of frazzled lace, and the wrists and the hands and the incredible face that struck my heart like a jolt every time I raised my eyes to look at it.

Migod. When it was possible to feel that way.

Wasn't it. I used to wake up before dawn and wait impatiently for the light to come into the window so that I could jump out of bed and get ready for school. I would sit on the front wooden step and wait for her to come down the canyon. She would smile when she saw me.

Were you her best friend?

We were each other's only friend. Her English was very bad. The theory of the teacher with all these immigrant kids was that if you spoke English loudly enough they would eventually understand. They all sat there with their immense eyes and watched her every move. They never smiled, even when she scratched her head with her pencil and her wig moved up and down on her forehead. She taught them the pledge of allegiance phonetically.

I would like to have known you then.

You would not believe it, Lucinda, but I was very sensual.

I believe it.

No, you're smiling. But I was, I really was. I lived in such an alerted state that even the daylight sifting through a cloud would give me enormous shuddering response. My friend and I used to play after school in the hills above town. The sun would go down behind the Black Hills but we'd see it to the east still on the plains, moving away from us on the flat plains, racing away in a broad front like an army losing territory on a map. In the shadow in some gully or behind some rock she'd lie in my arms and look at me with her dark eyes, frightened and speechless by our strange intimacy, frightened but not spooked. She could say my name but not much else. She rolled the *rr*'s. Wadden.

Light me a cigarette, will you?

Is this boring?

No, it makes me sad, though. I know what happened.

I have in my life just three times seen faces in dark light, at dusk, or at dawn, or against a white pillow in which the fear of life was so profoundly accurate, like an animal's perfect apprehension, that it encompassed its opposite and became the gallantry to break your heart.

Go on.

One day I remember late in the summer, before we all had to leave Ludlow for the flats, we were playing up there at some run-off. Some black-water run-off falling off the rocks somehow, so filthy with coal dust that just putting your hand in it was enough to dye yourself black. She didn't want to get her one and only dress wet, she'd get a beating for that, so she tied it up around her waist and hunkered there by the stream to play. She wasn't as old as I. She was a younger person. She wore nothing underneath. It was very lovely. Because I had become still she became still. She let me touch her. She let me run my hand over her small back. I could feel the bones in her ass. I could feel the heat under her skinny thighs.

Was this when you became lovers?

Perhaps so. I mean I know we were at one time or another, I remember that it happened, but I don't remember the experience of it. What is that up ahead, Lucinda? It looks very dark.

It's nothing. A line squall.

HEAVE SAID HIS FATHER AND THEY SWUNG THE WOODEN CHEST UP ON THE WAGON bed. Now make it fast. He pushed up with his hands landed lightly on one knee and stood up beside the chest and worked it firmly between the bureau and the slatted side gate. He glanced up the canyon. They were coming along steadily now, mule-drawn wagons like his own or the two-wheeled handcarts which required the woman to throw her entire weight stiff-armed on the handle to keep it from rising and the man around the front braking with his bootheels dug into the ground.

She was nowhere in sight.

The sky was heavy almost black, it felt like evening although it wasn't yet noon. A fine drizzle misted on the skin and made everything slippery to hold. Each drop of rain seemed to contain a seed of coal dust. If you rubbed the water on the back of your hand it smeared black. Hey his father shouted keep your wits boy! He nearly fell backward as a cardboard box hit him in the chest. He grabbed it. His mother came out of the house with her arms full of pots and pans. His parents went in and out of the door bringing him things which he found a place for on the wagon bed. Gradually he realized he was constructing the model of a city. Seen from a distance, the boxes and headboards and chairs and chests were the skyline of some glorious Eastern city, the kind he had seen in the rotogravure, New York maybe, or St. Louis.

I have a comment here: I note the boy Warren Penfield's relentless faculty of composition. Rather than apprehend reality he transforms it so that in this case, for example, in the eviction of the striking miners from the Colorado Fuel Company's houses, the pitiful pile of his family's belongings on the wagon bed is represented as a vision of high civilization. No wonder his father is angered by his constant daydreaming. Jack Penfield perceives it as mental incompetence. How he wonders will his son survive the harshness of this life when he the father and she the mother are no longer there to protect him? As to book learning, Warren can do that passably well, but as to plain good sense the character of his mind is not reassuring.

Neda Penfield takes a different view but not without some irritation that the boy doesn't give her more support for it. Her view is that he is a rare soul, a finer being either than herself or her husband. By some benign celestial error he was born to them and to their life of slag who would more properly have been the child of a wealthy family going to the finest schools and with every material and intellectual advantage. He gives her qualms of course but she nourishes a private and barely articulated conviction that he is not deficient only latent, that his strength is there but still wrapped up in itself still to unfold in its fullness when the time is ripe. When will the time be ripe? His hands and feet are large and clumsy, he looms next to her sometimes like a giant he is at that stage of life when the largeness of him seems to wax and wane according to his own rhythms of confidence. She is aware as mothers are of the changes in him the manhood beginning to shine and she is comforted. But the wisdom of him has still to appear. Sometimes the light will hit his amber eye and she will feel ill at ease, as if she is living with two men rather than a man and a boy. Perhaps Jack Penfield feels this too and anticipates the revolt of his son, the loosening of his power over him, the freeing of his son from himself till he has nothing but himself and then inevitably he will be subjected to his son's power over him. Yet he is secretly proud too and likes the boy's good looks. Warren is gentle and distracted as ever only his ears and elbows and wrists and ankles show the power of him still to come.

Neda Penfield would like Warren to win some sort of scholarship and go away to the city to study. She wants this desperately even though she knows her life with her husband then would be hell. Jack Penfield wants Warren in the mines. He wants him in the mines to establish such rage that he will finally be in contact with the circumstances of his life, he will wake up to it. And then see what happens, then see what glorious flights of power and genius the boy has in him perhaps to become an organizer a great union orator a radical a leader of men out of their living graves of coal. Let the boy work in a crouch for ten hours hacking coal in the chilling blackness of the earth, crouching with his feet in brackish water, not knowing which bite of the pick will bring the roof down on him. Let him work for his three tons a day and bring them up to be short-weighted by the company. Then my son will justify me and sanctify my name and fulfill the genius of my line.

The wagon loaded, Warren gives a hand up to his father and after a moment the two of them teetering on the gate, he nimbly leaps down and suffers the inspection of his work. The father pushes this adjusts that but says nothing, which is the highest approval. Together they tie everything in a web of stout rope, Warren running around from one side of the wagon to the other hauling tight looping knotting and he thinks of a wonderful bridge with granite towers and steel suspension cables what bridge is that.

And then his mother comes out of the house her hands empty but for a summer straw hat, a wide-brimmed straw with a round crown, and not seeing any place to put it she places it on her head. It is such a gallant gesture, so incongruous with the rain and the state of their fortunes that the two men look at her startled and she pulls her shoulders back and defies them with her glance, her face peculiarly shadowed by the brim as if the sun was oddly proven, but they wouldn't laugh because both have perceived in one shimmering instant before the fact of her wearing that hat is established, the still alive girl and the undefeated kingdom of their family.

She took her place on the bench and looked straight ahead over the mule's rump. Jack Penfield went into the house and came out with the last thing, his new bolt-action Savage whose stock was oiled smooth and whose barrel was blue steel, and he placed this across his lap as he sat up behind the mule and took the reins.

And so with a lurch of the wheels they turned into the traffic of wagons winding down through the canyons. In front of the Colorado Supply Company two sheriff's deputies stood on the porch to watch the procession. They had Winchesters cradled in their arms. Some of the families passing them made loud remarks. Some of them sang their union song. Most of them looked straight ahead and went on down the street into the descent of the prairie, too cold or too realistic to bother with the trappings of the spirit.

The rain was changing its nature, getting heavy turning hard, and Warren sitting cross-legged on top of a bureau felt the sting of ice, like steel pellets. He held out his hand and received a particle of hail. He put up his denim collar. He was facing forward but for some reason swiveled on his rump and looked back at the street just as the wagon behind picked up the pace to fill in the slack in the parade and it was she in her dress of tulips faded sitting up on her wagon on a stool like a princess borne in her palanquin, her body moving forward and back, her head moving in the lag of her body's rhythm and he smiled and raised his hand and she smiled and raised hers, and they stared at each other their bodies gently bending and straightening in the rhythm of the mules' pace, the wheels creaking in the mud the traces rattling like ancient music of fanfares and the two of them staring at each other like royal lovers in a procession toward their investiture under the hardening rain through the canyon of slag going down to the plains.

Thinking about that girl standing in front of the mirror and holding up the white dress on the train gliding past me out of sight, I came along the track before I even knew it into the main street of a mountain village.

It was noon on the church tower. A pretty lakeside village with a general store a gas pump a white hotel with rocking chairs on the porch, a bait-and-tackle shop. I wanted to keep going but there was a cop on the corner. Casually I crossed the street and went into a diner and ordered the baked ham and brown beans in a crock and coffee. When I finished I ordered the same thing again. The waitress smiled and the chef himself looked out through the porthole of the kitchen door to see this prize customer.

I got out of that village without trouble resuming my walk just beyond the station crossing, following the rails that forked off into a narrower cut of trees. The track went through some woods circled around a small mountain lake and then it started up a grade a long slow winding grade, I was not already in love with her but in her field of force, what I thought I felt like was some stray dog following the first human being it happened to see.

In the late afternoon I came to a miniature station house of creosoted brown logs complete with ticket window and potbellied stove. It was empty. Out the back door was the sidetracked private railroad car.

I climbed aboard. Each room had a narrow door with brass handle opening onto the corridor going down one side along the windows.

Here was the room of grand appointments where the men were drinking a card table of green baize and leather with receptacles for poker chips, a bar with bottles and glasses in fitted recesses, a Persian rug of rich red tone, paneling of dark wood, books in the shelves The Harvard Classics. A faint odor of cigar smoke. I brushed the tassels of the lampshades with the back of my hand.

Everything in this room, unlit and still, seemed more awesome than from the distance of the night, for it was quite clearly owned. That was the

main property of the entire car, not that it was handsome or luxurious but
that it was owned.

In the girl's bedroom I sat on the plump mattress newly made up with
fresh sheets thick quilt of satiny material there was no sign of her of course
not a thread not a bobby pin but as I thought about it the faintest intimation of a scent, a not unfamiliar scent, I inhaled deeply, a variety common
enough to have previously informed the nostrils of a derelict somewhere
before in his wandering one summer night in the carney perhaps.

The afternoon light came through the window at a low angle between
the trees it suddenly faded the car darkened I left. Outside, the sky was
showing stars as it does earlier than you think it should in the last of the
summer.

I was so blue. I was sorry I'd found the car, if I hadn't found it I could
have thought about it for the rest of my life. If any. But now I felt let-down
stupid at a loss what to do. The breeze had a chill and I supposed I couldn't
do better going back as I'd come, so I followed the one road from the small
station as it ran uphill into the woods.

Long before I got there, probably from the moment I left the village, I'd
been on private property. They were the same hills and forest and stone of
the natural world, they looked like the Adirondacks, but I was walking in
fact on a map of fixed color, crimson perhaps.

The road inclined gradually around the side of a mountain, one side
dropping away to show the darkening sky.

And then, below, a broad lake came into view, a lake glittering with
the last light of the day. I stopped to look at it. Something was moving,
making a straight line of agitation, like a tear, in the surface.

A moment later a bird was rising slowly from the water, a bird large
enough to be seen from this distance but only against the silver phosphorescence of the water. When it rose as high as the land it was gone.

The rest of my survey I made in darkness, by the light of stars. I had
come on some isolated reservation, and its center was a cluster of buildings on the mountain overlooking this same lake: a lodge of two stories,
and several smaller outbuildings, barns, stables, garages. Even in darkness I could tell that the buildings, like the little station house at the
bottom of the trail, were uniformly of log construction.

My vantage point was from the land side, a rise in an enormous rolling
meadow beside a tennis court fenced in wood and mesh. I did not try to
move closer to see in detail what was in the light of the lodge windows,
all ablaze everywhere, as if great crowds were inside. I knew there were
no crowds. The wind amplified in gusts the strains of a dance band. When
the song was over, it began again. It was a Victrola record of a tune I
recognized, "Exactly Like You."

The perverse effect of this music and the lighted windows was of a
repellent and desolate isolation.

Now the wind came up stronger across the meadow, it was off the lake and carried the water's chill. I looked up to the treetops of the wood behind me and saw them prancing and bucking in the way of a hard life of eminence. I was fixed by my own pride from going to the back door of this establishment and asking for a place to stay or a meal. I didn't know if I had the stamina for a night on these grounds, but it was as if I was reflecting the clear arrogance of whoever owned this place and traveled to it by imperial railroad, for I was goddamned if I would ask him or them for anything.

I didn't want her to see me like this!

I remember squatting behind the little tennis shack and keeping myself company with my cigarettes. I smoked one after another and made a community around their glow.

Now I'll tell what I don't remember. I don't remember the sound they must have made, the uncanny sound as it separated itself from the wind in the trees, of group exertion, breath chuffing across twenty or thirty hanging tongues, yelps of murderous excitement. Was the moon out? I rose from my crouch seeing something like an earthwave coming toward me, as if the ground were advancing in a sort of rolling quaking upheaval. This gradually distinguished itself as the furred musculature of shoulders and chests and legs, and I think now I must have seen the face of the lead dog, flung into moonlight, its maddened red eyes like the tracers of those launched fangs. If I didn't see it I've dreamed it a thousand times.

Goddamnit, if city boys knew any animals at all it was dogs. But these were like nothing I'd ever seen. Not that I had the leisure for contemplation. I held up my forearm and his teeth tore it like a piece of paper. Together we rammed into the side of the tennis shack. And then the others were up, tossing themselves at me in their fury but with great inefficiency, they turned on each other snarling for getting in each other's way though they were effective enough to my pain and screaming terror. I was kicking at them and flinging them off going for the throat trying to tear my throat out, I was kicking and waving my arms and fists and howling like a dog myself and knowing that if I went down I faced something more than the end of my life—shit—the extenuated appreciation of its end, piecemeal, my life taken from me chunk by chunk drop by drop every nerve shrieking.

I think I can imagine some faint memory of the odor of those dogs, feel the closeness of their life, their wild heartbeat! I hear their snorts and the snaps of teeth on air, I remember the toothtumblers lock once the flesh is found, the quick release and regrip down to the bone.

I recall without difficulty the intimate apprehension of prey in the jaws of a maniac life beyond all appeal.

Somehow I was vaulted or inspired upward in some acrobatic backward tumble through the unframed shack window. I took one of the dogs with me, slamming it fixed in my wrist against the inner wall of the shack while the heads of the others appeared outside the window, a fountain of faces leaping and falling back in rage in frustration. But then one gripped the sill with its paws and began to pull itself up till its own weight would get it inside, I grabbed a tennis racquet hanging in its press and swung toward that head down on those paws. The dog fell out of sight and the other, who had come in with me, stunned loose from its slam against the wall, I now caught on the back with the racquet edge in its heavy press and broke its spine. They were not uniformed pedigreed hounds, they were every kind and make, and this one, a smaller mongrel, I lifted howling and threw to the others.

Things immediately got quiet. I heard the yelps and moans and grunts of appeasement, the soft sound of flesh being fanged. The small moonlit square of night I saw from the floor of the shack was peaceful with stars. Maybe I heard human voices, or the firing of a rifle or a gun, but I'm not sure. I lay there and as the blood flowed from me I lost consciousness.

Adirondacks.
Region first known for wilderness industries trapping hunting.
Earliest roads were logging trails out came the great trees
chained to sledges. In the winter blocks of ice were sawn
from the frozen lakes and carried in procession on funicular tracks
uphill to the railroad depots for shipment to the cities.
In early spring the tapping of the huge sugar maples
and the sap houses sweet blue smoke hanging over the green valleys.
In summer the natives grew small corn and picked wild berries
and grilled trout on open fires by the edge of rock rivers.
But one summer after the May flies painters and poets arrived
who paid money to sit in guide boats and to stand momentously
above the gorges of rushing streams.
The artists and poets patrons seeing and hearing their reports
bought vast tracts of the Adirondacks very cheaply
and began to build elaborate camps there thus inventing
the wilderness as luxury.
Loon Lake a high mountain retreat cratered as purely cold and
clear in the mountains as water cupped in your hands.

IN THE MORNING THE OLD MAN, BENNETT, GAVE THEM ALL WOOLEN PONCHOS AND took them for a speedboat ride on the lake. She sat up front between him and Tommy. Tommy put his arm around her but she preferred to lean forward in the lee of the windshield where she avoided the wind if not the cold space it left as it blew by.

The little flag in the stern flapped like a machine gun. In the back seat there was no protection at all and they were truly unhappy. The cigarette was whipped out of Buster's mouth and taken in the air over the wake by

494

a black-and-white bird, some sort of gull. She saw that, having turned to smile back at them, her knee just touching the old man's pants leg, and Buster, looking startled, saw it too. It seemed to fall away into the sky. He faced her stupidly, his mouth still open and a piece of cigarette paper pasted on his lower lip.

She knew Bennett was showing off for her, rearing the mahogany speedboat through the waves as if it were Buck Jones' Silver. The sky was very low and the tops of the hills around the lake were shrouded in clouds. The clouds drifted through the trees and she was startled by that intimacy. She thought clouds should stay up in the sky where they belonged.

They had come to the closed end of the lake. The old man throttled down and the boat settled flatter in the water. There were marshes here and dead striplings poking out of the water. He headed straight for the trees and she felt Tommy clench up until a notch appeared in the shoreline. They went into a channel at slow speed and rode serenely by a beaver lodge of wet dark sticks and mud. The old man pointed it out.

She imagined the beaver pups inside their lodge lying on shelves just out of reach of the wavelets lapping their feet.

Then they were out in an even bigger lake with the hills somewhat farther away and a broad stretch of sky higher over everything. It turned out the old man owned this lake too. She wondered if he trained the crazy bird who came down from the sky for a cigarette.

Later, in the boathouse, Buster was so relieved at having survived travel on water that he told everyone about the bird.

That was a loon, the old man said, a kind of grebe. They all respectfully considered this intelligence.

You knew that didn't you Buster, Tommy said.

They put their ponchos back on the wall pegs and reclaimed their fedoras. There were other speedboats in the boathouse, each in its own berth. There were racks with wooden canoes. It was a brown log boathouse with casement windows in the same style as the big house up the hill.

There was a man there to take care of everything.

Bennett led the way. She noted how easily he moved up the path, his back straight, beautiful white hair. These people knew as no one else how to take care of themselves. He was dressed for the outdoors, with boots and a red plaid flannel shirt.

She held Tommy's arm and enjoyed the warmth of the land on her back. It looked as if the sun might burn through the clouds. She felt good. She felt like dancing. She watched her own feet walking in their strap shoes. They were grown-up-looking feet. She was arm in arm with Tommy, pulling him in close, trying to match strides up the hill. She watched his small black wing-tipped shoes pacing along, their shine ruined, and the cuffs of his pin-stripe flapping dust from the ground.

Up ahead the party was met by a fat guy. He saw her and stood as if

struck by lightning. He had been coming down to the lake but turned now
with another glance at her over his shoulder and ran along behind the old
man.

She held Tommy's arm, held him back and let them all go out of sight
up the hill.

You've got to be joking, Tommy said.

She rubbed against him. She kissed him and ran her tongue over his
lips and leaned back from him holding her groin against him and looking
into his eyes right there in the mountains of the Adirondacks.

Well the kid's impressed, Tommy said.

She nodded while looking into his eyes. The tip of her tongue appeared
in the corner of her mouth. He disengaged her arms and stood back from
her.

That's how much you know, he said.

IT'S WHO SHE IS, THINKS WARREN, DEFINITELY, NOW DRESSED IN FLIMSIES AND
struggling with the torments of her class but it's her, the same girl, returned to my life, changed in time, true, changed in place, changed let us
be honest in character, but how can I doubt my feelings they are all I have
I have spent my life studying them and of them all this is the indisputable
constant, the feeling of recognition I have for her when she appears, the
ease with which she comes to me regardless of the circumstances, for I
have no particular appeal to women, only to this woman, and so the
recognition must be mutual and it pushes us toward each other despite our
differences, and our inability to understand each other's language, and
here it has happened again though I am indisputably older fatter and more
ridiculous as a figure of love than I have been before. Always I am older.
Always we do not understand each other. Always I lose her. Oh God who
made this girl give her to me this time to hold let me sink into the
complacencies of fulfilled love, let us lose our memories together, and let
me die from the ordinary insubstantial results of having lived.

WHAT HE INTUITS FROM THE COOLNESS OF HER CONVERSATION OR THE MOODS THAT
come over her is that she did not expect to find herself in her present
situation. She is not devious and did not plan this. She seems to take each
day as it comes and is clearly forged in her being by the race of men she's
had to deal with. In short, they are equals. The realization sends him to
the bottle with a shaking hand.

Naturally she would think he was part of the old man's retinue. It was a natural assumption. At drinks that evening they're alone. Can I tell you a story? he says. Outside, the rain is heavy, the kind of rain that tamps down the wind. Smoke from the big fireplace drifts into the room like a wisp of cloud come in from the mountains.

I've lived here for six years. I'm a poet and the Bennetts are my patrons. But I found this place on my own and when I came here it was to kill him.

The old man?

Yes.

She has to this point only half listened but now he is rewarded by her direct gaze. She sips her Manhattan. She is wearing pleated linen slacks and a thin blouse half buttoned. She likes to show herself.

I swear to the lordourgod I will make her see who I am.

People I loved died because of the policies of one of his companies. He owns lots of companies.

You know what he's worth?

Worth? What can it matter. I haven't got a dime myself, he says conscientiously, as if he'd made it his life's achievement. Millions, billions, the power over people. So I was going to kill him. I got through the dogs with just a tear or two and introduced myself out on that terrace there through the dining room one morning with my knife in my pocket.

She turns and looks through the big bay windows. She turns back.

But you didn't, she says.

ONE NIGHT WHEN THE DOGS ARE IN THE NEIGHBORHOOD HE TAKES TWO WINE-glasses and a bottle of his table red and closes his door and half walks half runs over to her cottage.

I thought you might need some company, he says.

He follows her inside. She wears a robe. She is barefoot. He realizes she answered the door without breaking stride. She is pacing the room. Her arms are folded across her breasts.

The doors to her terrace are closed and locked. The curtain is pulled shut. The room smells of cigarettes. He pours the wine.

Later they are sitting on the floor beside the bed. He has been telling her about his life. He has recited some of his work. She has listened and smoked and held out her glass for wine.

Listen, he says holding his hand up, forefinger pointed. The dogs are gone. She smiles and accepts this as something he's done. Sitting Indian style, she leans forward and touches his face. Her robe has fallen open over her thighs like a curtain rising. He kisses her hand as it is withdrawn. I've loved three times in my life, he says. Always the same person.

I don't know what that's supposed to mean, she says. But I see I've got a live one here.

Then she is lying on the floor in his arms reading his face with judicious solemnity, her eyes gathering up the dim light of the room so widely open that he feels himself pouring into them. Because her spirit is strong he is surprised by the frailty of her. She is a small person. Her breasts are full and her thighs rather short. He can feel her ribs. Her buttocks are hard with a thin layer of sweet softness over them, like a child's ass. Her mons hair feels lightly oiled. He touches her cunt. She closes her eyes. A queer bitter smell comes off her body. He kisses her soft open mouth and it's just as he knew, she is here and he's found her again.

Like many large overweight men he has surprising agility. She is obviously entranced. But the lack of practice is too much for him.

She says with characteristic directness: Is that the whole show?

He laughs and one way or another maintains her interest. Eventually he is ready again. Later he will try to remember the experience of being in her and will find that difficult. But he'll remember them lying on their backs next to each other and the feel of the hard nap of the carpet on his sweaty skin. He'll remember that when he turned on his side to look at her the silhouette of her body in the dark was like a range of distant hills.

Yes, she said, as if their fucking had been conversation, sometimes nothing else will do but to drive as flat out hard and fast as you can.

Annotated text *Loon Lake* by Warren Penfield.
If you listen the small splash is beaver.
As beaver swim their fur lies back and their heads elongate
and a true imperial cruelty shines from their eyes.
They're rodents, after all.
Beaver otter weasel mink and rat
a rodent specie of the Adirondacks
and they redistrict the world.
They go after the young trees and bring them down—
whole hillsides collapse in the lake when they're through.
They make their lodges of skinned poles, mud and boughs
like igloos of dark wet wood
and they enter and exit under water and build shelves
out of the water for the babies.
And when the mahogany speedboat goes by
trimmed with silver horns
in Loon Lake, in the Adirondacks,
the waves of the lake inside the beaver lodge lap gently
against the children's feet in the darkness.

Loon Lake
was once the destination of private railroad cars
rocking on a single track
through forests of pine and spruce and hemlock
branches and fronds brushing the windows of cut glass
while inside incandescent bulbs flickered
in frosted-glass chimneys over double beds
and liquor bottles trembled in their recessed cabinet fittings
above card tables of green baize
in rooms entered through narrow doors with brass latches.

If you step on a twig in a soft bed of pine needles
under an ancient stand of this wilderness
you will make no sound.
All due respect to the Indians of Loon Lake
the Adirondack nations, with all due respect.
What a clear cold life it must have been.
Everyone knew where he stood
chiefs or children or malcontents
and every village had its lover whom no one wanted
who sometimes lay down because of that
with a last self-pitying look at Loon Lake
before intoning his death prayers
and beginning the difficult business of dying by will
on the dry hummocks of pine needles.
The loons they heard were the loons we hear today,
cries to distract the dying
loons diving into the cold black lake
and diving back out again in a whorl of clinging water
clinging like importuning spirits
fingers shattering in spray
feeling up the wing along the rounded body of the
thrillingly exerting loon
taking a fish
rising to the moon streamlined
its loon eyes round and red.
A doomed Indian would hear them at night in their diving
and hear their cry not as triumph or as rage
or the insane compatibility with the earth
attributed to birds of prey
but in protest against falling
of having to fall into that black water
and struggle up from it again and again
the water kissing and pawing and whispering
the most horrible promises
the awful presumptuousness of the water
squeezing the eyes out of the head
floating the lungs out on the beak which clamps on them
like wriggling fish
extruding all organs and waste matter
turning the bird inside out
which the Indian sees is what death is
the environment exchanging itself for the being.
And there are stars where that happens too in space
in the black space some railroad journeys above the Adirondacks.

Well, anyway, in the summer of 1936
a chilling summer high in the Eastern mountains
a group of people arrived at a rich man's camp
in his private railway car
the men in fedoras and dark double-breasted suits
and the women in silver fox and cloche hats
sheer stockings of Japanese silk
and dresses that clung to them in the mountain air.
They shivered from the station to the camp
in an open carriage drawn by two horses.
It was the clearest night in the heavens
and the silhouettes of the jagged pines on the mountaintop
in the moonlight looked like arrowheads
looked like the graves of heroic Indians.
The old man who was their host
an industrialist of enormous wealth
over the years had welcomed to his camp
financiers politicians screen stars
European princes boxing champions and
conductors of major orchestras
all of whom were honored to sign the guest book.
Occasionally for complicated reasons
he received persons strangely undistinguished.
His camp was a long log building of two stories
on a hill overlooking Loon Lake.
There was a great rustic entrance hall
with a wide staircase of halved logs
and a balustrade made of scraped saplings
a living room as large as a hotel lobby
with walls papered in birch bark
and hung with the mounted heads of deer and elk
and with modern leather sofas with rounded corners
and a great warming fireplace of native stone
big enough to roast an ox.
It was a fine manor house lacking nothing
with suites of bedrooms each with its own shade porch
and the most discreet staff of cooks and maids and porters
but designated a camp because its décor was rough-hewn.

Annotate old man who was their host as follows: F (Francis) W (Warren)
Bennett born August 2 1878 Glens Falls New York. Father millionaire
Augustus Bennett founder of Union Supply Company major outfitter army
uniforms and military accessories hats boots Springfield rifles insignia

saddles ceremonial swords etc to Army of the United States during Civil War. FW Bennett a student at Groton thence Massachusetts Institute of Technology Boston graduating with a degree in mine engineering. Bought controlling interest Missouri-Clanback Coal Company St Louis upon graduation. Took control Missouri & Western Railroad 1902. Founding partner Colorado Fuel Company with John C. Osgood Julian Kleber John L Jerome. Surviving partner associate of John D. Rockefeller Colorado Fuel and Iron Company, vice president of engineering. Immense success Colorado and Missouri speculative coal-mining ventures suggested use of capital abroad. Took over National Mexican Silver Mining Company. Founder Chilean-American Copper Company. Board of Directors James Steel Co., Northwest Lumber Trust, Baltimore, Chicago & Albuquerque RR Co., etc. Trustee Jordan College, Rhinebeck N.Y. Trustee Miss Morris' School for Young Women, Briarcliff Manor NY. Member Knickerbocker, Acropolis, New York; Silks, Saratoga Springs; Rhode Island Keel, Newport. Marriages Fanny Teale Stevens, no issue; Bootsie van der Kellen, no issue; Lucinda Bailey, no issue. Died 1967 Lausanne Switzerland.

And this party of visitors were really romantic gangsters
thieves, extortionists and murderers of the lower class
and their women who might or might not be whores.
The old man welcomed them warmly
enjoying their responses to his camp
admiring the women in their tight dresses and red lips
relishing the having of them there so out of place
at Loon Lake.
The first morning of their visit
he led everyone down the hill
to give them rides in his biggest speedboat
a long mahogany Chris-Craft with a powerful inboard
that resonantly shook the water as she idled.
He handed them each a woolen poncho with a hood
and told them the ride was fast and cold
but still they were not prepared when under way
he opened up the throttle
and the boat reared in the water like Buck Jones' horse.
The women shrieked and gripped the gangsters' arms
and spray stinging like ice coated their faces
while the small flag at the stern snapped like a machine gun.
And one of the men lipping an unlit cigarette
felt it whipped away by the wind.
He turned and saw it sail over the wake
where a loon appeared from nowhere

beaked it before it hit the water
and rose back into the sky above the mountain.

Annotate boat reared in the water like Buck Jones' horse as follows: Buck
Jones a cowboy movie star silents 1920s and talkies early 1930s. Others
of this specie: Tom Mix, Tim McCoy, Big Boy Williams. Buck Jones' horse
palomino stallion named Silver. Others of this specie: Pal Feller Tony.

The old man rode them around Loon Lake, its islands
through channels where beaver had built their lodges
and everything they saw the trees the mountains
the water and even the land they couldn't see under the water
was what he owned. And then he brought them in throttling down
and the boat was awash in a rush of foam
like the outspread wings of a waterbird coming to rest.
Two other mahogany boats of different lengths
were berthed in the boathouse
and racks of canoes and guide boats upside down
and on walls paddles hanging from brackets
and fishing rods and snowshoes for some strange reason
and not a gangster there did not reflect
how this dark boathouse with its canals
and hollow-sounding deck floors
was bigger than the home his family lived in
when he was a kid, as big as the orphan's home in fact.
But one gangster wanted to know about the lake
and its connecting lakes, the distance one could travel on them
as if he was planning a fast getaway.

Just disappearing around the corner out of sight
was the boathouse attendant.
And everyone walked up the hill for drinks and lunch.
Drinks were at twelve-thirty and lunch at one-thirty
after which, returning to their rooms,
the guests found riding outfits laid across their beds
and boots in their right sizes all new.
At three they met each other at the stables
laughing at each other and being laughed at
and the stableman fitted them out with horses
and the sensation was particularly giddy when the horses
began to move without warning ignoring them up there in the saddle
threatening to launch with each bounce like a paddle ball.

And so each day the best gangster among them realized
there would be something to do they could not do well.

The unchecked walking horses made for the woods
no one was in the lead, the old man was not there.
They were alone on these horses who took this wide trail
they seemed to know.
They were busy maintaining themselves on the tops of these horses
stepping with their plodding footfall through the soft earth
of the wide trail.
By and by proceeding gently downhill they came
to another shore of the lake, of Loon Lake,
and the trees were cut down here and the cold sun shone.
They found themselves before an airplane hangar
with a concrete ramp sloping into the water.
As the horses stood there the hangar doors slid open
there was a man pushing back each of the steel doors
although they saw only his arm and hand and shoetops.
And then from a gray cloud over the mountain
beyond the far end of the lake an airplane appeared
and made its descent in front of the mountain
growing larger as it came toward them
a green-and-white seaplane with a cowled engine and overhead wing.
It landed in the water with barely a splash
taxiing smartly with a feathery sound.
The horses nickered and stirred, everyone held on
and the lead gangster said whoa boy, whoa boy
and the goddamn plane came right out of the water
up the ramp, water falling from its pontoons
the wheels in the pontoons leaving a wet track on the concrete
and nosed up to the open hangar
blowing up a cloud of dirt and noise.
The engine was cut and the cabin door opened
and putting her hands on the wing struts a woman jumped down
a slim woman in trousers and a leather jacket and a silk scarf
and a leather helmet which she removed showing light-brown hair cut
    close
and she looked at them and nodded without smiling
and that was the old man's wife.

Annotate old man's wife as follows: Lucinda Bailey Bennett born 1896
Philadelphia PA. Father US Undersecretary of State Bangwin Channing
under McKinley. Private tutoring in France and Switzerland. Miss Morris' School for Young Women. Brearly. Long Island School of Aviation

practicing stalls tailspins stalled glide half-roll snap roll slow roll rolling eight wingovers Immelmann loops. Winner First Woman's Air
Regatta Long Island New York to Palm Beach Florida 1921. Winner
Single-Engine National Women's Sprints 1922–1929. First woman to
fly alone Long Island–Bermuda. Woman's world record cross-country
flight Long Island to San Diego 1932, twenty-seven hours sixteen minutes. First woman to fly alone Long Island to Newfoundland. Winner
Chicago Air Meet 1931, 1932, 1933. Glenn Curtiss National Aviatrix
Silver Cup 1934. Lindbergh Trophy 1935. Member President's Commis-
sion on the Future of Aviation 1936. Honorary Member US Naval Air
Patrol 1936. Lost on round-the-world flight over the Pacific 1937.

She strode off down the trail toward the big house
and they were not to see her again that day
neither at drinks which were at six-thirty
nor dinner at seven-thirty.
But her husband was a gracious host
attentive to the women particularly.
He revealed that she was a famous aviatrix
and some of them recognized her name from the newspapers.
He spoke proudly of her accomplishments
the races she won flying measured courses
marked by towers with checkered windsocks
and her endurance flights some of which
were still the record for a woman.
After dinner he talked vaguely of his life
his regret that so much of it was business.
He talked about the unrest in the country
and the peculiar mood of the workers
and he solicited the gangsters' views over brandy
on the likelihood of revolution.
And now he said rising I'm going to retire.
But you're still young said one of the gangsters.
For the night the old man said with a smile
I mean I'm going to bed. Good night.
And when he went up the stairs of halved tree trunks
they all looked at each other and had nothing to say.
They were standing where the old man had left them
in their tuxes and black ties.
They had stood when he stood the women had stood when he stood
and quietly as they could they all went to their rooms,
where the bedcovers had been turned back and the reading lamps
        lighted.
And in the room of the best gangster there

a slim and swarthy man with dark eyes, a short man
very well put together
there were doors leading to a screened porch
and he opened them and stood on the dark porch
and heard the night life of the forest and the lake
and the splash of the fish terrifyingly removed from Loon Lake.
He had long since run out of words
for his sickening recognition of real class
nervously insisting how swell it was.
He turned back into the room.
His girl was fingering the hand-embroidered initials
in the center of the blanket.
They were the same initials as on the bath towels
and on the cigarette box filled with fresh Luckies
and on the matchbooks and on the breast pockets of the pajamas
of every size stocked in the drawers
the same initials, the logo.

Annotate reference the best gangster there as follows: Thomas Crapo alias
Tommy the Emperor. Born Hoboken New Jersey 1905. Hoboken Con-
solidated Grade School 1917. New Jersey National Guard 1914–1917.
Rainbow Division American Expeditionary Force 1917–1918. Saw action
Château-Thierry. Victory Medal. Founder Brandywine Importing Com-
pany 1919. Board of Directors Inverness Distribution Company. Founding
partner Boardwalk Amusement Company 1920. President Dance-a-dime
Incorporated. Founder Crapo Industrial Services Incorporated, New York,
Chicago, Detroit. Patron Boys Town, March of Dimes, Police Athletic
League New York, Policeman's Benevolent Society Chicago. Present
whereabouts unknown.

Annotate reference his girl as follows: Clara Lukaćs born 1918 Hell's
Kitchen New York. School of the Sisters of Poor Clare, expelled 1932. S.S.
Kresge counter girl (notions) 1932–1934. Receptionist Lukaćs' West 29th
St Funeral Parlor 1934. Present whereabouts unknown.

The gangster's girl was eighteen
and had had an abortion he knew nothing about.
She found something to criticize, one thing,
the single beds, and as she undressed
raising her knees, slipping off her shoes
unhooking her stockings from her garters
she spoke of the bloodlessness of the rich not believing it

while the gangster lay between the sheets in the initialed pajamas
arranging himself under the covers so that they were neat and tight
as if trying to take as little possession of the bed as possible
not wanting to appear to himself to threaten anything.
He locked his hands behind his head and ignored the girl
and lay in the dark not even smoking.

But at three that morning
there was a terrible howl
from the pack of wild dogs that ran in the mountains—
not wolves but dogs that had reverted
when their owners couldn't feed them any longer.
The old man had warned them this might happen
but the girl crept into the bed of the gangster
and he put his arm around her and held her
so that she would not slip off the edge
and they listened to the howling
and then the sound nearer to the house
of running dogs, of terrifying exertion
and then something gushing
in the gardens below the windows.
And they heard the soft separation
together with grunts and snorts and yelps
of flesh as it is fanged and lifted from a body.
Jesus, the girl said
and the gangster felt her breath on his collarbone
and smelled the gel in her hair, the sweetness of it,
and felt the gathered dice of her shoulders
and her shivering and her cold hand on his stomach
underneath the waistband.

In the morning they joined the old man
on the sun terrace outside the dining room.
Halfway down the hill a handyman pushing a wheelbarrow
was just disappearing around a bend in the path.
I hope you weren't frightened, the old man said, they took a deer
and he turned surprisingly young blue eyes on the best gangster's girl.
Later that morning she saw on the hills in the sun
all around Lake Loon
patches of color where the trees were turning
and she went for a walk alone and in the woods she saw
in the orange and yellowing leaves of deciduous trees
the coming winter
imagining in these high mountains
snow falling like some astronomical disaster

and Loon Lake as the white hole of a monstrous meteor
and every branch of the evergreens all around
described with snow, each twig each needle
balancing a tiny snowfall precisely imitative of itself.
And at dinner she wore her white satin gown
with nothing underneath to ruin the lines.
And the old man's wife came to dinner this night
clearly younger than her husband, trim and neat
with small beautifully groomed hands and still young shoulders and
    neck
but brackets at the corners of her mouth.
She talked to them politely with no condescension
and showed them in glass cases in the game room
trophies of air races she had won
small silver women pilots
silver cups and silver planes on pedestals.
Then still early in the evening she said good night
and that she had enjoyed meeting them.
They watched her go.
And after the old man retired
and all the gangsters and their women stood around
in their black ties and tuxes and long gowns
the best gangster's girl saw a large Victrola in the corner
of the big living room with its leather couches and
grand fireplace
the servants spirited away the coffee service
and the gangster's girl put on a record and commanded
everyone to dance.
And they danced to the Victrola music
they felt better they did the fox trot
and went to the liquor cabinet and broke open some Scotch
and gin and they danced and smoked
the old man's cigarettes from the boxes on the tables
and the only light came from the big fire
and the women danced with one arm dangling holding empty glasses
and the gangsters nuzzled their shoulders
and their new shoes made slow sibilant rhythms
on the polished floors
as they danced in their tuxes and gowns of satin at Loon Lake
at Loon Lake
in the rich man's camp
in the mountains of the Adirondacks.

He was a whistling wonder with his face and arms and legs in bandages and bandages crisscrossed like bandoliers across his chest. Every now and then they looked in on him with the same separation of themselves from the sight as rubes looking at the freaks. They all wore green.

They told him the dog packs were well known in the region, several of them told him that, as if it were a consolation. He had difficulty speaking through his pain and swollen tissue, so that they could not be exactly sure what he thought of them and their fucking dogs.

The elderly country doctor was eager to see what complication might set in to try him beyond the resources of his medicine.

There were pills for the pain but I took as few as I could. It seemed important to me to stay awake, to know what was going on. Maybe I thought the dogs would come back. The room was damp. There was a small window high on the wall. I was in the basement of one of the log buildings I'd seen and it seemed to me not a very safe place to be. Also it was as bad as the original event to dream of it again drugged in a kind of dream prison and struggling for consciousness. Pain was better. It came in spasms and with the sharp point of imprinted teeth, it tore along in clawing sweeps down my chest and seemed sometimes to raise the bandages from the skin. I tried to consider it objectively, like a scientist sitting in a white coat looking through a microscope. Ahh, peering at each little cellpoint of pain. Remarkable!

And since I was in pain, I thought of my mother and father. I thought of myself bedridden in Paterson. They look at me lying there flushed and wheezing, a boy impossibly exercised just by the act of living, and go off to work at their machines.

A man looked in on me each morning and made a grunt of disgust or scorn just like my father had although heavyset not at all like my thin and gaunt father but in the same role, with the same wordless eloquence. He wore a kind of uniform of dark green shirt and matching pants.

And for my mother a woman in pale green uniform and white shoes and opaque brown hose with a thick seam down the back. An impassive porky being with hands that worked at high speed setting down trays pounding pillows carrying off urinals while she thought her own thoughts.

I could tell that each of them felt badly used to be taking care of some tramp who had wandered onto the grounds. It was an affront to the natural order which made service to people bearable because they were higher than you, not lower.

I responded with a pride of my own which asked for nothing and gave as little indication of need as possible. And I never thanked them for anything. As I felt better I grew contemptuous as if, coming into this province of wealth, I had adopted its customs. Or perhaps it was more serious, perhaps it had been injected in the saliva of the dogs.

On the other hand I had only the word of these people that the dogs didn't belong to the owner of this place. And even if they didn't, they certainly ran to his advantage. My rage flared as if it were the last wound to be felt and the slowest to heal.

As time went on I understood that I lay in a room of the staff house where perhaps fifteen or twenty people lived who wore the green livery, forest-green for the outdoor workers, the paler shade for the indoor. They all looked somewhat stolidly alike, as if related.

I was alert to find a friend and I did. She was a girl of the pale green set, a young maid in the big house who shyly looked in on me, advancing each time a little farther into the room until finally she showed up in mid-morning one day when everyone else was working. She had seen we were the same age and that was enough.

Her name was Libby. She didn't think of not answering any question that occurred to me.

This place was called Loon Lake. It was the domain of the same F. W. Bennett of the Bennett Autobody Works. Did I know the name? He was very rich. He owned thirty thousand acres here and it was just one of his places. He owned the lake itself, the water in the lake, the land under the water and the fish that swam in it.

"But not the dogs," I said.

"Oh no," she said, "those are wild-running, those dogs. It's the fault of the people who own them and can't feed them anymore. And then they go off and forage and breed wild and hunt in packs."

"The people?"

"The dogs. All through the mountains it's like that, not just here. Does it hurt?" she asked.

"It don't tickle."

A tremor went through her. She held her arms as if she was cold.

"Tell me, does your F. W. Bennett have a wife?"

"Oh, sure! She's famous. The Mrs. Bennett who wins all the air races. Her picture's in the papers. Lucinda Bennett?"

"Oh, her," I said. "The one with the blond hair?"

"No, she's a brunette." Libby touched her own hair, which was brunet too. Like all her features it was ordinary. She was possessed of a sort of plain prettiness that caused you to study her and wish this feature or that might be better.

"Brunettes are my favorite," I said.

She blushed. She was a simple innocent person, she granted me her own youthful face on the world without knowing who I was or where I came from. In five minutes I had her whole history. Her uncle, one of the groundkeepers, had gotten her the job. She made twelve dollars a week plus room and board. She was fervent in her gratitude. She spoke in what I could tell was the communal piety of the staff. How nervously lucky they would have to feel, how clannish in their good fortune exempt in these mountains from an afflicted age. Mr. Bennett and Mrs. Bennett came or went separately or together or had guests or didn't, but the place was maintained all year round including the dead of winter.

"Don't you get lonely up here?" I said.

She thought a long time. "Well, I send six dollars to my father in Albany."

Not realizing this was enough for me to feel chastened, she frowned and cast about in her mind for justification. "You'd be surprised who comes here," she said. She brightened "You get to see famous people."

"Who?"

"Why, big politicians, and prime ministers from England. And Jeanette MacDonald? She was here in the spring! She's beautiful. I saw her clothes. She gave me five dollars!"

"Who else?"

"Oh well, I never saw him, it was before I came. But Charlie Chaplin."

"Sure," I said. "On roller skates."

She looked then suddenly frightened. Who would doubt her word? She turned and left the room, and I thought to myself well that's that. But a short while later she returned, softly closing the door behind her. She held a large leatherbound book to her chest and looked at me over the gilt edge with bright excited eyes. "I better not get caught," she said.

It was the Loon Lake guest book. She fixed the pillows so I could pull myself up and she sat on the side of the bed and opened the book to a page marked "1931." Her index finger ran down a list of signatures and stopped and she turned her eyes on me as I saw whose signature it was: Charles Chaplin had made an elegant scrawl, and next to it, where there was a space for comment, he had written: "Splendid weekend! Gay company!"

Vindicated, Libby watched with pleasure as I became absorbed by all the names, right up to the present: signatures of movie stars, orchestra leaders, authors, senators, all famous enough to be recognized by me, but also signatures I recognized only vaguely, or only sensed as names of magnitude, like the name F. W. Bennett, names that had been given to things, names painted on the big signs over factories or carved in the stone over the entrances of office buildings. I couldn't stop looking at them. I felt I could learn something, that there was something here, some powerful knowledge I could use. But it was in code! If only I could understand the significance of the notations, I'd have what I needed I'd know what I'd always dreamed of knowing—although I couldn't have said what it was. I touched the signatures, traced them trying to feel the ink. It was some mysterious system of legalities and caste and extended brilliant endeavor—all abbreviated into these names and dates of proud people from all over the world who had come here to this secret place in the mountains.

I became aware of this girl Libby in her pale green uniform. She sat very close to me, the starched front of her uniform rose and fell with her breathing. When I glanced up from the book I found her face near mine, her head bowed and her eyes on the page, but her consciousness all directed to me. Her full lower lip was impressed into a suggestion of voluptuousness by her front teeth. She had thick wavy hair. What sweet appropriate modesty of being. Her trust was part of it, or so I understood— the willingness of the others of us to find a place and live our lives within it, making our trembling alliances and becoming famous and powerful to each other.

I turned back to the book. Some of the people there were such big shots they needed only one name to identify themselves. Leopold, one of them had written. Of Belgium.

I said to Libby, "Hey, how long have I been here, anyway?"

"We were taking off the summer covers and putting the rugs down," she said. "It was that night. I never hope to hear what I heard that night."

"Well, when was it, please?"

"Two weeks ago."

"Wasn't someone here then? Didn't you have visitors?"

She looked at me and then looked away. She glanced at the book. She wanted it back.

"I saw the train, Libby. People were on it. Is anyone here now?"

She shook her head.

"Well, how come I don't see anything that recent in the guest book?"

She was silent a long while. I knew I was extending her loyalty. I gazed at her and waited for my answer. She looked discouraged. "Not just anyone gets to sign," she said finally.

"Is that right?" I said. She wouldn't look at me now.

"I think someone's calling you, Libby."

"Where?" She went to the door, opened it and listened. I leaned over with a painful lunge to the bedside stand. In the little drawer was a fountain pen. I unscrewed the cap, shook a blot on the floor, spread open the guest book and signed my name with a flourish.

"What are you doing!" Libby said. Her hand was on her cheek and she stared at me in horror.

"Joe," I wrote. "Of Paterson. Splendid dogs. Swell company."

I fell back on the pillow. By signing the guest book, did I mean to be going on my way? I felt the pretense, as well as any other, washed away in a wave of weakness and despair.

The girl grabbed the book and ran.

She had a friend, as it turned out, a man who lived on the grounds as a kind of permanent houseguest. He came to look at me later that day, peering in the door with an expression of wonder very odd in a full-grown middle-aged adult.

He was a large heavy man. He was bearded. His hair was overgrown and unkempt. His eyes were blue and set in a field of pink that suggested a history of torments and conflicts past ordinary understanding. His weight and size seemed to amplify the act of breathing, which took place through his mouth. His nose looked swollen, a web of fine purple lines ran up his cheeks from the undergrowth, and all the ravage together told of the drinker.

He said his name was Warren Penfield. He wanted to speak about moral responsibility.

He padded around the room in a pair of old tennis sneakers. He wore baggy trousers belted below his stomach, and an ancient tweed jacket with patches at the elbow. Beneath the jacket was what seemed to be a soft graying tennis shirt part of the collar folded under he didn't seem to be aware of this.

"I can understand your feeling better than you can, young man. I spend my life understanding feelings, yes, my own and others, that's what I do, that's what poets do, that's what they're supposed to do."

"You're a poet?"

"I'm the poet in residence here," he said, drawing himself up slightly trying to tuck his shirt in glancing then at me from the corner of his eye.

I thought I would never know the end of the subtle luxuries with which the wealthy provided themselves.

"So I can understand your feelings. But I also understand poor Libby's, good God she's one of the few decent people around here, and now she's in fear for her job. Do you realize what it would mean for her to lose her job? Of course I'll do what I can, the Bennetts aren't here right now, fortunately, I'll think of something, yes, I'll speak to Lucinda, I suppose I can, but that's not the point. You should have realized the girl was responsible for anything you did. She was nice to you, she made you her friend, she shared something she knew, and that's how you repaid her."

I liked him enormously. I was smiling I was admitted into his realm of moral concern without passport credentials references of any sort. There I was a hobo boy lying on this cot in this weird place suppurating, for all he knew, in my dereliction, not a pot to pee in, and he was trying to recall me to my honor. He assumed I had it!

He saw me smiling and started to smile too. Then we were laughing.

"Of course it was wicked, a good wicked joke, God knows I can enjoy a joke at his expense. I wish there were more of them. Incidentally, he himself is not totally devoid of humor, you know."

"Who?"

"Bennett. I've studied him a long time. He's a very capable human being. Quite charming at times. The mistake most people make is to jump to conclusions before they even meet him."

"Well, I'll try not to," I said and we laughed again.

At that moment my mother-keeper came in, took my tray, gave Penfield a dirty look, and left.

"Dreadful woman," he said. "They all are. Except for Libby, of course. They despise me. I'm more than they are but I have no place as they have. They play all sorts of tricks on me, I have to beg for my meals. But when the Bennetts are here they'll invite me to dine and then I'm served like I'm the king of England."

I saw that he suffered from this, as from everything, in a state of expressive self-magnifying complaint.

"Well, I suppose I should go. How do you feel, by the way?"

"Lousy."

He pulled up his jacket sleeve and showed me on the inside of his left arm a pale scar from the wrist to the elbow. "You're not the only one, I want you to know. They treed me seven years ago when I came here one night—just like you."

One morning on his bed at the foot a folded suit of dark green. He dressed in it and looked for the first time into the hallway outside the room where he had been since he was carried there on some door was a mirror and there he was thin pale-faced boy pale as a sheet, with a sparse stubble on the rim of the jaw, a head of uncombed hair looking too big for the body, and a hunch as if he were still flinching from the teeth, from the snarling face of the mountainous night.

Something has leaked out through the stitches and some of the serious intention of the world has leaked in: like the sense of high stakes, the desolate chance of real destiny.

There was a distant railroad track with telephone poles regularly spaced down the side of my neck over the clavicle across the breastbone. There was another spur line on either arm and the right leg.

I had no feeling in the fourth finger of my right hand.

Thus I found myself on a brilliant morning raking leaves in the shadow of the great sprawling lodge house of the auto magnate F. W. Bennett. I was not to consider myself employed, however. My Loon Lake parents would as frankly have sent me on my way but they did nothing without the approval of their employer, who was still to return.

I felt weak in the knees, I couldn't have gone anywhere anyway. I was glad to hold on to the rake.

The lodge house was two stories on the land side, three on the lake side—the land dropped precipitously from the crest of the hill—and its walls were logs, uniformly brown, set with casement windows and crowned with a wood shingle roof of many angles and regularly spaced dormers. The trees oak maple elm, and though it was still September, a heavy leaf fall everywhere behind the meadow of my encounter, a burning wood of orange and gold and behind this on a distant mountain, ageless stands of evergreen against the bright blue sky.

As the morning advanced the sun was warm on my back. The air was sweet. I felt better. I was one of three or four workmen. A small truck with slat sides moved slowly among us to receive our leaves. We moved around to the back of the house and swept the leaves from two terraces, the upper with tables and chairs for dining, the lower with cushioned wooden wheeled lounge chairs for the view and the sun.

The lake out there a definite mountain lake, a water cupped high in the earth, its east and west shores hidden from view by intervening hills, its south shore across the water filled with pine and spruce that rose up straight on the mountainside in a kind of terror.

The lake glittered with fragments of sun, and flying over it were a couple of large black-and-white loons, big as swans. There was a boathouse down at the water in the same style as the main house. A dock going around the boathouse. A swimming float fifty yards out.

Between the terraces and the water line was a steep hillside garden of wild things, and through its paths we raked away the unwanted leaves from the bushes and plants.

I looked back up the hill to the house and felt the imposition of an enormous will on the natural planet. Stillness and peace, not the sound of a car or a horn or even a human voice, and I felt Loon Lake in its isolation, the bought wilderness, and speculated what I would do if I had the money. Would I purchase isolation, as this man had? Was that what money was for, to put a distance of fifty thousand acres of mountain terrain between you and the boondocks of the world?

The man made automobile bodies, and they were for connection, cars were democracy we had been told.

The wind rose in a sudden gust about my ears, and as I looked back to the lake, a loon was coming in like a roller coaster. He hit he water and skidded for thirty yards, sending up a great spray, and when the water settled he was gone. I couldn't see him, I thought the fucker had drowned. But up he popped, shaking and mauling a fat fish. And when the fish was polished off, I heard a weird maniac cry coming off the water, and echoing off the hills.

A while later I followed the workers going along the hillside with their rakes through the trees past the stables to the staff house for lunch. The people of the light and dark green ate in a sort of bunkhouse dining room with long tables and benches. The food was put out on compartmented metal trays as in a cafeteria.

Fifteen, twenty of them looking at me as I hesitated with my tray and then slid into a place next to Libby, who smiled and looked with some satisfaction to the rest of the table. I was inspected by a heavyset man with thick black eyebrows I took to be the uncle she had mentioned. I gave back a clear-eyed friendly face don't worry I'm no threat not me. After that I was ignored. I studied them all covertly: there were two, possibly three families of Bennett servants here. They did not make conversation. I had a palpable feeling of the politics of the place, the suspicious credential I had as a victim of the dogs. It wasn't enough to crack their guild. They seemed confident of that.

Well, screw them, they couldn't even understand that I wanted no part of it. When I was strong enough, a day or two, I'd be on my way down the railroad track and leave it to them to work out why. I still had the dollars I'd come with, stained brown with my blood but no less negotiable. Nobody here, not even Libby, knew my full name or had asked where I came from or where I'd been going.

The force of self-distinguishing which I found so foolish among stiffs and hobos was what I ran on. When you are nobody and have nothing, you depend on your troubles for self-respect. I had paid heavily for the bed and board. I wasn't one of them, I was a paying guest.

I finished and walked out while they were still drinking their coffee. I'd be damned if I'd lift a rake or anything else. What could they do, fire me? I stood on the porch and thought about leaving right away, immediately.

And it was at this moment that I saw over the rise to the meadow two people on the tennis court—one of them a girl with blond hair.

I fixed my eyes on her and walked forward already confirmed in expectation by the agonized heave of my heart.

Mr. Penfield the resident poet, an absurd roundish figure in white shorts and a shirt stretched dangerously by an enormous belly, was showing from his side of the net the proper form of the forehand. Once twice three times he stroked the air. His lithe student, trim in a tennis dress, watched him while holding her racquet on her shoulder.

Penfield now hit a ball to her. Careless of all his advice, she swung at it with a great wild lunge and poled it far over the fence across the meadow. I saw tennis balls lying like white flowers everywhere.

He reached into a round basket for another ball and hit it gently, and again she took a furious swing and the ball flew over the fence. Once more he hit to her and she spun herself around missing the ball entirely. He said something to her. She glared at him, dropped the racquet and left the court.

She strode across the grass toward the main house. She tossed her visor away unpinned her hair fluffing it to the breeze ignoring him as he stood on the court and called after her in a voice half reproach half apology, "Clara! Clara!"

But she went over the crest of a slope and descended by degrees until only her head could be seen moving toward the house. Mr. Penfield hurriedly collected the tennis balls lying about the court. I did the same thing in the grass. We met at the court gate. His large bleary face gazed upon mine.

"She can't bear to be taught," he said, admitting me with a stunning lack of ceremony to his thoughts. "All I said was 'Take a level swing, don't worry about hitting hard.' " He looked again in the direction she had gone. He smiled. "But what game can it be, after all, in which one doesn't hit one's hardest!"

He thrust into my hands the racquet and pail of balls and hurried off after her, moving lightly on the balls of his feet with that ability of some fat people to be quick and graceful. I stepped onto the court and picked up her racquet. I took everything to the shack not even thinking of it as the site of my grisly misfortune. I had forgotten misfortune. I headed back to the staff house, from one moment to the next, a worried probationary in my dark green shirt and pants no thought further from my mind than leaving. I wanted a job! Their job! Just as they knew I did. I would take up the rake or any other tool they had in mind oh God it was Clara, that was her name, Clara the girl on the train, no question about it, twice now the sight of her had stopped my heart.

I didn't know what would happen in my life but I knew whatever it was it would have to do with her, with Clara. I thought even having her name was an enormous inroad of intelligence. Was she a Bennett? But wouldn't they know their games, weren't they trained to their tennis and their riding? This one, so blazingly beautiful and pissed-off, knew nothing, this one standing pigeon-toed and swinging stiff-armed at balls so incredibly breath-takingly awkward and untrained—no, she was not a relation. Was she a guest? If so, where were the others, she had come with a train, maids in waiting! an entourage! but they were nowhere about, only the resident poet Penfield ambled after her like her pet bear. Was she related to Penfield?

I would do anything be anything to know her and know about her. Dressed in dark green, a spy! I worked to show them how worthy I was, how useful, to show them how I admired what *they* were and how I wanted to be like them and one of them. How much time did I have? Only until the big man arrived, I had only that time to prove I shouldn't be thrown out on my ass.

Of course I couldn't express to Libby even the most idly curious question about this princess living on the grounds. But she had loved showing me the guest book and I thought from her same peasant identification with Bennett wealth she would enjoy the wonder on my face as she secretly showed me the main house, where they lived and had their lives and Charlie Chaplin and the one-named kings sat down to dinner.

The Bennetts not at home there was a bending of the rules: on Saturday night two Loon Lake station wagons pulled out leaving a skeleton staff.

On Sunday afternoon with the sun coming through the trees at low angles to light the rooms, through rectangles of sun along dark corridors, Libby and I tiptoed about the vast upstairs with its hall alcoves of casement windows and window seats and bookshelves and its suites of rooms, each with its generous shade porch, and Adirondacks chairs and sofas.

Whatever empty room I saw led my mind to the next room, the next turn in the corridor, everywhere the light off the lake cast its silvery shimmer on the walls or in my eyes as we passed open doorways.

One wing was closed off. "We can't go there," Libby said.

"Why not?" I asked, casual as I could be.

"It's the Bennetts' wing, where they stay."

"Is someone there?"

"No. But I wouldn't feel right about it. Rose and Mary take care of it," she said.

She led me down a back stair through a kitchen with two black steel ranges and pantries of provisions and several iceboxes each crowned with its humming cylindrical motor.

Through a room of glass cabinets filled with sets of china and drawers of silver service.

Through the hexagonal dining room, three walls of glass and a table hexagonal in shape to seat thirty people.

To the huge living room, the grandest room of all, with tan leather couches built into the walls, the walls hung with the heads of trophy. There were two different levels of game tables and racks of magazines and clusters of stuffed chairs all looking out enormous windows to the lake.

I found myself tiptoeing, with a sense of intrusion, my chest constricted—and something else—the thinnest possibility of destructive intent, some very fine denial on my part to submit to awe. "Of course this is just one of their places," Libby said. "Can you imagine?"

One or two steps up and we were in the entrance hall. The walls were of dark rough wood. We stood under a chandelier made from antlers. I gazed up a wide curved staircase of halved logs polished to a high shine, with balusters of saplings. I gazed at this as at the gnarled and swirling access to a kingdom of trolls.

"Don't you love roughing it?" I said to Libby, running her up the staircase. "What!" she cried, but laughing too, entirely subject to my mood. In the long upstairs corridor I placed her hand on my arm and strolled with her as if we were master and mistress. I led her into one of the suites and flinging open the glass doors of the porch, I extended my arm and said, "Let us enjoy the view that God in his wisdom has arranged for us, my deah." She swept past me giggling in the game and we stood in the sun side by side looking over the kingdom.

"Do you mind if I smoke, old girl?" I said in my best imitation of wealthy speech. "No? Why, thank you, I think I'll light up one of these monogrammed cigs with my initials on them."

She was animated with pleasure, how easily she could be made to live! I kissed her to show her how the wealthy kissed, their noses so high in the air that their lips never met, only their chins. Then of course I kissed her properly. She was confused, she drew back blushing, she had thought it her secret that she was sweet on me.

Whatever I wanted from poor Libby I couldn't explain what I was doing solely to gain it. We had the run of the house and pretended to be masters. For those few minutes the upstairs maid and the hobo boy were the Bennetts of Loon Lake.

Libby took my hand and showed me a storage room where F. W. Bennett kept his stock of outfits that he provided his guests as gifts: riding habits and boots, tennis flannels, bathing suits, a goddamn haberdashery.

I stood in front of a full-length mirror and took off my greens and put on a pair of tan tweed knickers with pleats, ribbed socks, brown-and-white saddle shoes, my size, a soft white shirt, and a white sweater with an argyle design of large gold and brown diamonds across my chest.

I was stunned by the magnificent youth that looked back at me from the mirror. All the scars and deeper marks of hard life were covered in fine fashion. The face, a bit gaunt but unlined, the hair I combed back hastily with my fingers. He made a passing aristocrat! Well, I thought, so a lot of the effect comes from the outside, doesn't it? I might be a Bennett son!

And then I felt again my child's pretense that those two gray sticks in Paterson were not really my parents but my kidnappers! Who knew whose child I was!

I dreamed of recognition from her from Clara. It was her nearness that made me so crazy, and bold with Libby. So feverish so happy.

And as for Bennett I thought, He is no more aware of me than of some unfortunate prowler mauled by the wild dogs. But here I am, wearing his clothes, wandering freely through his house. Here I am, Mr. Muck-a-muck, and you don't even know it!

Then Libby came back from the female supply store and she was wearing jodhpurs and a silk blouse and a riding helmet perched none too securely on her thick hair and she wobbled in a pair of shiny boots too wide in the shank for her thin legs.

"You look swell, Libby," I said. She turned around with little shaky steps and gave me all the dimensions. Her gray eyes shone, her mouth stretched in her tremulous overbitten smile. I danced her out of there down the corridor doing a fast fox trot full of swirls while I hummed the tune I had heard the night I came, "Exactly Like You," Libby laughing and worrying at the same time, telling me to hush, looking back over her shoulder, giggling, falling against me every other step, brushing my cheek with her lips. And the light lay like a track along the carpet and shone in golden stations of the open doors.

There being no sign of her in the main house I knew she was staying in the smaller lodge perhaps a hundred yards west, into the woods and halfway down the hill to the lake.

I think I must have spent some while calculating how to get there, figuring out a pretext and then a script for the conversation we would have. But one evening, during the staff meal, one of the woodfolk, a grandmotherly one, said to me, "That Penfield called. You're to go over to the cottage."

"Who, me? What for?"

"How should I know?" she said. "I'll be glad when you're gone and them with you."

I finished my meal as slowly as I could, feigning the attitude of the workingmen of dark green. I washed my tray and lit a cigarette and sauntered back to my room.

I latched the door and changed from my work clothes to the knickers and shirt and sweater and ribbed socks and saddle shoes. Poor Libby, all happiness drained like the color in her face when I told her I was keeping these things. Shouldn't she have known that the fellow who'd write in the guest book would do that? Anyway, she understood the firm basis of our relationship, that whatever trust she placed in me I would betray.

And as for Mr. Penfield I knew in my bones I didn't have anything to fear from him. He had a way of canceling himself out if you let him talk long enough.

I washed my face and combed my hair and got out of the staff house without being seen.

Already dark on the path, the first stars coming out. Joe drew a sharp breath and tried to calm himself. He was trembling. He had followed her, navigating by her star, and by that means had been sleeping in a bed and eating well and indulging his self-regard for several weeks. An edited view but fervently held.

In his mind, his feelings were enough. He didn't need intentions, plans, the specificity of hope. Presenting his heart was enough.

"Here he is—and look at him!" Penfield said at the door. He held a bottle of red wine in one hand and a glass in the other. "Come in, come in!"

It was a low-ceilinged cottage with a living room and kitchen and stone hearth all in one. I tried not to look at her she was sitting on the sofa Indian style wearing a robe of white satiny material and it had fallen open across her thighs. I tried not to look she was not looking at me but taking a mighty pull from her wineglass head up neck beautiful pulsing neck.

"Here he is, Clara—Joe of Paterson, the man I wanted you to meet." A glass was put in my hand.

"Miss Clara Lukaćs," he said.

Pointing me at a chair, he crossed his ankles and sank his bulk down on the floor at her feet.

They were both facing me and to my right and their left a fire was going in the fireplace. The light flared and dimmed on their faces as some kind of wavering attention, I thought, especially from her she had not asked to meet me how absurd to have thought that. I sensed some purpose not entirely complimentary in the summons. Yet Penfield was smiling amiably indicating to me to drink and so I did, with the odd conviction that I had never tasted wine before. I had ridden the cars with the bums of three states worked with freaks and was wicked and shameless but in this moment it was my inexperience that shone.

What was the conversation? Mostly his, of course, the brilliant singsong of the failed poet, but how could I have been listening with the attention such beautiful words demanded, people from my world didn't talk with such embellishment such scrollwork. I had never before met someone who admitted to the profession of poet but believed it by the way he spoke. I kept my eyes on his face but it was her I looked at, this restless cat of inattention sitting quite still and staring into her wine careless of exposed limbs the inner thigh the rounded knee small cream cracked hummock of the underknees she sat quite still but her mind pacing from one wall to another, an expression on her small fair face of grief or petulance I couldn't tell. But how she felt was of overriding importance to me, how she felt!—then and every moment after—was my foremost concern, what I lived by. This was her quality and I think she was unconscious of it, that her presence occupied great moral space around her though she was surprisingly small, a small-boned slight thing with narrow shoulders. There was nothing stately about her except the alarming size of her moods. I studied her face with a fervent rush of recognition, a fair skin with a rouge of chapped cheeks, quick green eyes prominent upper lip everything framed in marcelled bleached blond hair I had friends playing as a child with such faces in Paterson I heard the fluent yowl of injustice from this face.

Mr. Penfield speaking of injustice explained how much more modest were his own rooms over the stables than this full cottage in the rustic log style. On the other hand he wrote well there he said in his way of negating his every point of view by obliging himself to express its opposite.

Then he recites some lines about the place, about Loon Lake. The glass in one hand, the bottle in the other, he sits with legs outstretched he is in his dirty sneakers with no socks his tweed jacket with the elbow patches his tennis shirt with the soft collar turned under on one side, he produces a deep melodious voice for his lines not his normal voice I was embarrassed by this sudden access to performance but she was not. She paid attention to his poetry as she had not to his conversation. But no audience was as responsive to Mr. Penfield's words as he was. His red eyes grew large with a film of tears.

I augment my memory with the lines actually printed in a private edition, the last of his three privately published volumes all recording different times of his life in the different places the same person. "The loons they heard were the loons we hear today"—in his deep reader's chant—"cries to distract the dying loons diving into the cold black lake and diving back out again in a whorl of clinging water   clinging like importuning spirits   fingers shattering in spray   feeling up the wing along the rounded body of the   thrillingly exerting loon   beaking a fish   rising to the moon streamlined   its loon eyes round and red."

And I, resonantly attuned to her, alive to the firelit moment—somewhere I had gotten at great cost, with the scars to show it, from such profound effort, the kind of unceasing insistence on my life's rights that was only now so exhausting in my release from it. As this absurd fat drunkard sang his words they seemed the most beautiful I had ever heard. But perhaps any words would have done. I heard them and I didn't hear them, I had no idea he had just written them I thought they were from some book already done, I heard the feeling they inspired in me, that I was living at last! That it was the way it should be, I was feeling Penfield's immense careless generosity, the boon of himself which granted me without argument everything I was struggling for, all of it assumed in the simple giving of words, so moving to this scruffy boy.

It was the moment of dangerous specification of everything I thought worth wanting. After the loon flew off whose red eyes were much like his own he cleared his throat and he poured wine all around although I'd barely sipped mine. He emptied the bottle on his turn and struggled to his feet for another bottle which he uncorked while continuing to speak and again he sat down with the new bottle as attached to his hand as the old.

I tried not to look at her. I saw the glance from under her brows toward the ceiling, the impatience, and then I began to feel the force of the occasion which was that somehow I was enlisted to help divert, distract or pacify Clara Lukács. That was the meaning of the self-dramatization of the man, that we were in some overburdened instant, with our backs to it, grounding our heels, digging in.

And then he was telling us about the war, of all things, a veteran, migod, would he bring out the poppies? But soon we were inside his images, listening like children, the mule-drawn caissons sinking in the mud, the troops in greatcoats and tin helmets riding the mules' backs, kicking their boots sharply against the mules' flanks, the bracing of backs on six-foot wheels, spokes like baseball bats tires of steel, each soldier alone and miserable inside his coat, charred trees beside the road the sky showing through city hall, gusts of acrid air blowing from the front, and here is Corporal Penfield riding the signal wagon, flag tubes strapped to his back like quivers, a helmet tilting over his eyes because the strap is too loose, and on his lap the crate covered with a khaki blanket shifts perceptibly, the pigeons whirring with each dull boom lighting the sky like lightning miles ahead.

He was dangling a medal. He had taken it from his pocket. He handed it to me. The colors of the ribbon had bled, there was thread and lint attached to it, but it was a Silver Star and it was his.

I leaned forward put it in her hand leaning forward over the bear rug between us, our hands grazed I felt the heat of her hand.

And there in our minds as we looked at the palpable proof was Signal Corporal Penfield during the battle of the Somme dispatched urgently to semaphore the artillery to drop some heavy stuff on the encircling Huns.

"The field telephone didn't work, there wasn't even a damn pigeon left." He paused to wet his throat. "So I took the old semaphore flags and went up to the top of a hill where I could be seen, because even though it was night the star shells were like the Fourth of July and it was brighter than day. I could see out over no man's land. I sent my message"—here he lifted his arms, attached to the glass and bottle and did a half-hearted pantomime—"and a while later the artillery came in on target, and that's what I got the medal for."

"You're a hero," she said, smiling. She dropped the medal in his lap and then raised her glass to her lips.

"No, but, love, you haven't heard the end." He dropped his chin to his chest. "I was so terrified I didn't send the message I was supposed to. What I semaphored was the first verse of a poem."

"What?" I said.

" 'There was a time when meadow, grove, and stream,   The earth, and every common sight,   To me did seem   Apparelled in celestial light,   The glory and the freshness of a dream,' and so on," he said. "And a while later the shells came in on target. It was very strange."

She was laughing. "In the war—in the battle?"

"Surely you know it," he said. "The Intimations Ode? Didn't you have it in school?"

"But why?"

"I don't know why. Maybe I thought I was going to die. Maybe it seemed to me the only appropriate thing *to* say. Anyway, after I got the medal I wrote a letter to the Secretary of the Army returning it and telling him it was more properly William Wordsworth's.''

''But it wasn't a medal for poetry,'' I said, and immediately felt like a fool.

''Apparently not, Joe of Paterson. Apparently not. I had to go for psychiatric tests. They pinned the medal on my bathrobe. They kept me under observation for ninety days in Nutley, New Jersey.''

''Where?'' she said, happily laughing. He looked up at her, victorious in her amusement. ''Oh, Warren, you old fuck, where?'' She threw back her head and laughed and laughed, I gazed at her throat, her neck, it was a moment in which I could look at all of her as she sat in her white satin robe, she bending forward now in her laughter, the robe unfolding like unfolding wings so that I could see her breasts.

Then I realized Penfield was looking at me, with his head lowered, with raised eyebrows, a characteristic expression, I knew at once, full of sadness, full of self-acknowledgment, and as she reached out and touched his head he too began to giggle, he was in love with her, and soon they were both laughing and I was laughing, but trying not to for some reason, feeling badly that I laughed, feeling ashamed.

I hadn't realized how drunk they were. A few moments later, in silence, she put her glass down and reached out, holding his head in her arms. He looked up at her, and behind her shingle of hair he kissed her, his hand with the bottle going up involuntarily, another semaphore, and I heard her sob, and then both of them were crying.

I tried to leave, but they wouldn't allow it. All at once they were very physical with me, placing themselves on either side of me and leading me back to the middle of the room. Penfield went to stoke up the fire. She led me to my chair and pressed my shoulders firmly with her small hands and then sat across from me and studied me solemnly. Until this moment her primary awareness had been of Penfield, she had not quite acknowledged me, as if one person at a time, and only one, could occupy her mind. She was always to be this way, intense and direct with whatever she fixed upon, and whatever the affront to those on the periphery. It was not snobbishness or anything like that—she was in fact reckless of her self-interest in a situation, and that I think was the center of her force and effect. She knew nothing about courtesy in the sense of not being subject to it. She blazed through her feelings and suffered the consequences.

I began to realize as we talked that she was no older than I was. I was stunned—I was not yet twenty—I equated power and position in the world with age.

''You live here?'' she said. ''How do you stand it?'' I rubbed my palms on my knickers. I looked with alarm at Warren Penfield, who said, ''Clara, he's my surprise for you,'' and came back to his place on the floor.

She had a throaty voice with a scratched quality. Her diction was of the street. "Whats 'at mean!" She gazed at me, her eyes widening, and I was certain, as if a chasm were opening around me, that she was as fraudulent in this place as I was. I drank off my wine.

"You remember the night you heard the dogs?" the poet said to her, and leaned forward to refill my glass. "Joe here is taking each day as it comes—like you, Clara."

I saw realization light her eyes. She went to the fire and sat down before it with her back to us. I don't remember much of what happened after that. I drank more than I should have. The fire looming her shadow across the low-ceilinged room. Later we heard the rain falling, a heavy rain that seemed to do something to the draught. Wood smoke came into the room on gusts. At this point we were all standing, I had removed my shirt, and she was tracing the scars on my chest and arms and neck with her fingertips.

I could smell her, the soap she used, the gel of her hair. The firelight flared on our faces as if we were standing with the poet in his war.

"He told me it was a deer, that they took a deer," she said. "That was a lie."

"Yes," Penfield said, watching her fingers.

"What class," Clara said. Tears were suddenly coming down her cheeks.

"I could help you leave," Penfield said. His eyes closed and he began moving his head from side to side like someone in mourning. "I can get you out of here. We can leave together." His sentences became a hum, a soft keening, as if he were listening to some private elegy and had no hope of an answer from her.

"That son of a bitch," she said with the tears streaming. "I wouldn't give him the satisfaction."

Certain contracts having quietly been made in mountains
certified convicts having mislaid their companions
I direct you eight hundred Mercator miles west
to the autobody works on the flat landscape
dawn whitening the frost on the corrugated shed roofs
the smokeless stacks the endless chain-link fence
the first trolley of the morning down Division Street
discharges workers in caps and open jackets but not workers.
The pickets roused from their sleep huddled by steel-drum fires
the cops awakened in their cars rubbing their misted windshields
the second trolley of the morning tolls down Division Street
discharges workers or workers at first glance
but somehow not resembling the strikers grouping uneasily
in front of the main gates of the autobody works.
The cops make calls from phoneboxes on the corners
the third trolley of the morning grinding its flanged wheels
on Division Street stopping the arrivals stepping down now
seen in the light their expressions of newly purchased loyalty
appearing as an unaccustomed cause in their shrewd appraising eyes
the insignia of their dereliction, jackets with pockets of pints
shoes tied around with rope, medals of filth,
mercenaries with callused fingers discovering
the cobblestones pried so easily
by ones and twos and hefted as many as until the tracks
of the trolleys of Division Street stand up from unpaved beds.
Open trucks arrive filled with the faces not of workers.
This army can take the city apart and put it back together
if it so wishes or perhaps wrap the electrified lines
stringing the utility poles overhead around each individual striker
until he may go self-powered into eternity.

Cops start patrol-car engines drive quietly away
certain black sedans now arrive between arrivals
of the crowded streetcars and trucks some men in overcoats appearing
among the seeming workers resembling only slightly now the pickets
with the eyes of lepers staring at them
no saints present on this wet gray morning to kiss them,
so numerous now they do not even have to look at whom they will
        face
when they walk over them into the plant and throw the switches.
And primly planning the action deploying forces
is a slim and swarthy man in overcoat and pearl-gray fedora
a dark-eyed man short but very well put together
friend of industrialists, businessman who keeps his word
and capable of a gracious gesture under the right conditions.
Only now, as with a gloved hand he beckons one of the strikers
an aged man with white hair and rounded shoulders
who has called out brothers don't do this to your brothers
to meet him between the lines alone in no man's land
does a small snapshot of rage light his brain.
He impassively demonstrates the function of the cobblestone
a sudden event on the workingman's skull who has met him
surprised now at the red routes of death mapped on his forehead
turning to share this intelligence with his brothers
hand lifted too late as the signal for the engagement to begin.

And then the life quickened, suddenly the people in green were scurrying about purposefully, there even seemed to be more of them, and I knew without being told that the master of Loon Lake, Mr. F. W. Bennett, was in place.

One morning I was mucking out the stables. Two horses were made ready for riding. The wide doors swung open admitting a great flood of light, the horses were led out, and I caught a glimpse of her in jodhpurs, velvet riding jacket, she was fixing the strap of her riding helmet. The doors closed. I climbed over the stall gate and ran to a window. A bay flank and a shiny brown boot moved through my field of vision. I heard a man's voice, a quiet word of encouragement, and then she, on her lighter mount, passed my eyes, the boot not quite secure in the stirrup.

I ran to the doors and put my eyes to the crack: the back and head of white hair were all I could see of Bennett before Clara's figure loomed up on her fat-assed horse, she didn't roll with its footfalls but took each one bumping, her black riding helmet slightly askew.

And then horses and riders passed behind some trees and were gone. I raked shit.

In the evening I went to Mr. Penfield's rooms and we listened to the scraps of dance music carried from the main house on the wind.

"I suppose I'll be out of here tomorrow," I said.

"What?" He had been staring into his wineglass.

"When it comes to his attention."

"You can't be sure, Joe of Paterson. I have made a great study of the very rich. The one way they are accessible is through their whim." He swallowed some wine. "Yes. I have not told you this, but six or seven years ago when I came up here at night along the track, as you did, I knew where I was going. I had traced Frank Bennett to Loon Lake and I intended to kill him."

"I have the idea myself," I said. He didn't seem to hear me.

"Mr. Bennett was amused. I was invited to remain on the grounds and write my poetry. Yes. And now you see me."

"I do," I said. "I see you."

"I know what you think. You think living this way year after year and not going anywhere, not doing anything, I have lost my perspective. It's true! It's true. So that everything that happens, every, oh God"—his eyes go heavenward, he swallows some wine—"small thing, is monumentally significant. I know! I lie in wait like a bullfrog lying in wait for whatever comes along for his tongue to stick to. Yes. That's the only part of me that moves, my tongue."

He dropped his chin on his chest and stared at me with his bleary red eyes. "You want to hear me croak?"

"What?"

He emitted the sound of a bullfrog, never had I heard such a blat of self-disgust I didn't want to. It was not one night like this but several I remember, sitting in his living room over the stables, piles of books on the floor, a desk covered with papers, composition notebooks the kind I used in school, clumps of dust on the floors, ashtrays filled to overflowing, ashes on the carpet, on the window seat, he drifts back and forth back and forth between the wine bottles and the window, and all the while Miss Clara Lukaćs dances rides swims dines in the provinces of Loon Lake, mysteriously advanced now to the rank of its mistress.

"I don't think it's a small thing," I said. "I think it is monumentally significant."

"Yes," he says, and he pulls his chair closer to mine, "this is not the first acquaintance. And it has nothing to do with who I am or the way I look, it's always the same—the immediate recognition I have for her when she appears, and the ease with which she comes to me whatever circumstances I'm in, whatever I've become. Because I have no particular appeal to women and I never have, except to this woman, and so the recognition must be mutual and it pushes us toward each other even though we don't talk the same language. And so, you see, now again, even though I'm indisputably fatter and more ridiculous as a figure of love than I ever was. And even though" his eyes brimmed—"she is faithful to nothing but her own life."

I didn't know what he was talking about.

He struggled out of his chair and ran to his bookshelves, and not finding what he wanted, he disappeared into a closet from which came the sounds of crashing and falling things.

He stumbled out with a book in his hand. He blew the dust off. "I want you to have this," he said, "my first published work, my first thin volume of verse"—he smiled unsmiled—"*The Flowers of the Sangre de Cristo.*" He did not hand me the book but examined it closely. "I printed it on a hand press and bound it myself in Nutley. It was my project for recovery, you see. The signatures in this one are out of order. But no matter, no matter."

He pressed the volume on me now and looked in my eyes as if hoping to see the wisdom that would flow into them from the book.

"Just a minute," he said. He ran back into the closet there was a terrible crash I jumped up but he came out coughing in a cloud of chalky dust waving his second published work. "This one too," he said, slamming the closet door. He swallowed a great draught of wine and slumped back in his chair wheezing from the exertion.

I held the two slim volumes, the second included a Japanese woodprint as frontispiece. "Don't read them now, don't ask me to watch you as you read them," he said.

I held the books, I could not help granting him the authority he craved as profound commentator on his own life—he was an author! Never mind that he published his books himself, I was impressed, nobody I ever knew had written a book. I held them in my hand.

Apart from everything else and despite the shadows of the wishes in my mind the vaguest shadows of the implementation of the wishes, I am moved to be so set up in the world with such a distinguished friend. I know he is a posturing drunk, how could I not recognize the type, but he has made me his friend, this poet, and I have a presence in the world.

He tells me his one remaining belief.

"Who are you to doubt it," he says angrily, "a follower of trains in the night!"

I don't doubt it I don't. I have listened to his life, heard it accounted indulged improved incanted and I believe it all. It is a life that goes past grief and sorrow into a realm, like the life of a famous gangster or an explorer, where sudden death is the ordinary condition. And somehow I'm invited to engage my instinct not to share his suffering but to marvel at it, a life farcically set in the path of historical and natural disaster it comes to me as entertainment—

The war before the war before the war
Before the rise of the Meiji emperor
Before the black ships—

his great accomplishment was his own private being the grandness and the depth of his failed affections each of his representations of himself at the critical moments of his past contributed to the finished man before me

Child Bride in a Zen Garden by Warren Penfield
In a poem of plum blossoms and boats poled down a river
Behind a garden wall the sun lighting its pediment of red tile

A fourteen-year-old girl aches for her husband.
One bird whistles in the foliage of a tree that stands on crutches.
Small things are cherished, a comb a hand mirror a golden carp
in a pool no more than eight inches deep. Curved wooden foot-
bridges of great age connect the banks of ponds. But everywhere
we know on the map are mountains with vertical faces
and thunderous waterfalls, escutcheons of burning houses
and suicidal armies, history clattering in contradistinction to
the sunlight melting itself in the bamboo grove.

Oh the fifty-three stations of the Tokaido. On the embankment
above the rice paddy travelers crouch under slants of rain.
Messengers run with their breechcloths flapping. Merchants
beat their donkeys. Boats with squared sails make
directly for shore. Paper lanterns slide down the waves.
Rain like the hammers of sculptors works the curved slopes
of water. When the sky clears at sunset fifty-three prefecture
officials arrive in the stations of the Tokaido. Fifty-three
women are prepared for them. Sunlit legends will be made tonight.
Beans are picked from the gardens, plump fowl slaughtered, and
in castles above the road unemployed warriors duel the firelight.
They weep they curse they raise wine cups to honor. Saints
of the wrong religion go unrecognized in the darkness beyond the
lighted windows of the inns. And at the end of the Tokaido
at the top of an inaccessible mountain sits the emperor himself,
a self-imperator, a self impersonating a self in splendor
in his empty room its walls painted with long-legged waterbirds,
its floor covered with ministers lying face down attending him.
The emperor is lacquered, his sword is set with suns, while
in another room doctors dispute the meaning of his stool.

Oh compact foreign devils flesh of rice
Everywhere we are smaller than the landscape.
I sit on the wood promenade overlooking my garden and I
am the real emperor. The small twisted tree is very old and has a
name. The rocks like islands in the sea of raked
gravel have names. The gravel waves break upon the rocks.
A girl with suncast eyes cries on the other side of the ancient
wall. I run across the gravel sea
and spy on her through the gate. Her blue-black hair is
undressed, like a child's. She sits on a bed of moss, her
bowed neck as long as a lady's of the court. The words rise
and fall in my throat growling and humming and making tunes.
I am breaking the laws of my religion. She is alert now to
the aviary of our language and stares at me with her wet mournful

eyes, the track of one tear surmounting the pout of her lip
and disappearing in the corner of her mouth. I speak and she
shifts to her knees, deferentially places her hands flat·upon
her thighs. The soles of her feet are pale. She listens.
She is as still as the fieldmouse in the talons of the hawk.

Oh the fifty-three stages of the Tokaido. The old monk and the girl
clamber up on the rock path. Along the path falls a stream
so vertically on rocks that the water, broken into millions of
drops, bounces pachinko pachinko like pellets of steel.
We find a ledge overlooking the ocean. I aspire to goodness.
I aspire to the endless serenity of the realized Buddha.
In the sun on the rock ledge I remove her clothing. I
remove my clothing she averts her eyes. We hunker in the
hairless sallow integument of our kind. Her haunches are
small and muscular. Her thighs are slender. Her backbone
is as ordered as the stones of a Zen garden. I see reflected
in the polished gray rock under her the entrance to her life.
It is like the etching of a fig.
Raising my hand in the gesture of tenderness, I see her chin
lift in trust and at that moment I fling myself at her
and she falls into the sea.
She falls in a slow spiral, wobbling like a spent arrow.
I feel her heart beating in my chest.
I feel all she is, her flesh and bone, her terror in the sky.

THE FIELD OF HIS ACCOMPLISHMENT WAS HIS OWN PRIVATE BEING, THE GRANDNESS
and depth of his failed affections. Each of his representations of himself
at the critical moments of this past contributed to the finished man before
me. He proved everything by his self-deprecation, his sighs, his lachry-
mose pauses, his prodigious thirst for wine, and he proved it in the scene
or two with Clara, when, at an hour he somehow always knew, he would
get me to help him over to her cottage not five minutes since she had come
in herself, her make-up and hair and dress all showing the use of the
evening, and she in some sort of sodden rage. What excited Mr. Penfield
was the idea of rescue. He wanted to save her, take her away, carry her off.
It was the pulsating center of his passion. And she seemed now not to
understand, as if they spoke different languages, hers being Realism.

"War-rin," she would say, "do I have to spell it out?"

"Oh God," he'd cry, lifting his eyes, "oh God who made this girl, give
her to me this time to hold, let me sink into the complacencies of fulfilled

love, let us lose our memories together and let me die from the ordinary insubstantial results of having lived!''

"Goddamnit," Clara shouted, and then, appealing to me, the audience, a role I embraced as I would any she chose, "what does he want from me? Oh Jesus! Joe," she'd say when, invariably, he broke down, "why did you bring him? Take him home. Get this fucking drunk out of here."

Another night or the one after, I went over to her cottage alone. I supposed it was midnight. No light on. It didn't matter. I sat in the shadow of her porch and I folded my arms and waited. A strong wind blowing over the mountains and sounding in the trees around the cottage. The trunks of the pine trees swayed and creaked. I sat with my back to the door and drew up my knees. I might be hearing her in her rut, singing somewhere with the wind going past an open window. That was all right. That was all right. If the poet could have her on her terms and the rich man on his, I could have her on mine. My revelation. Maybe she traveled like a princess on a private train, maybe poets thought they recognized her, but I knew her accent, she was an Eastern industrial child, she had come off streets like my streets she was born of the infinite class of nameless workers my very own exclusive class. Jesus, I had pressed against girls like her in the hallways, I had bent them backward on the banister, I had pulled their hair I had lifted their skirts I had rubbed them till they creamed through their underpants.

I reached over my head and tried the doorknob. Open. I decided to wait for her in comfort. I turned on a light. The wood smoke lay under the low ceiling. The hearth was cold. I put in some paper and kindling and got a fire going and stood with my back to the fire.

The green livery had as little regard for her as they did for Penfield. The place was a mess. I saw traces of our first party. Dirty dishes in the little alcove kitchen. Not that she'd care. I looked in her bedroom. Her clothes everywhere, stockings twisted and curled like strips of bacon, step-ins in two perfect circles on the floor as if disengaged in a meditative moment, or flung across a lampshade as if drop-kicked.

Poor Mr. Penfield. I knew what he couldn't possibly know. I knew what made his sympathies obsolete. Clara and Bennett had had breakfast together on the morning after he arrived. I managed to be raking leaves at the foot of the terrace wall under their line of sight. It was a bright windy morning and the clouds actually were below us over the lake and drifting through the trees on the mountains. "I think clouds should stay in the sky where they belong," Clara said, "don't you?" And Bennett had laughed.

Clara held a relentless view of the world. There were no visible principles. Every one of her moods and feelings was intense and true to itself—if not to the one before or the one after. She lightened and darkened like the times of the day.

I smoked a cigarette from the monogrammed cigarette box. Clearly, in my aspiration it was FWB I would have to contend with. FWB, the man who was paying for everything. Conceivably this gave him an advantage.

I mashed out the cigarette, stretched out on my back before the fire, put my hands under my head and closed my eyes.

I slept in that position for several hours. I remember coming awake with the fire out and sunlight glowing on the windows. The silhouettes of branches and leaves wavered on the log wall and a reddish gold light filled the room. I heard the sound of an airplane. It grew louder and then with a rise in pitch it receded and grew faint. I lay there and it got louder again and finally so close and thunderous that the cups rattled in the sink. Then the sound receded once more, the pitch of the engine rising. I went to the window: a single-engine plane with pontoons was banking over the mountain on the other side of the lake. I watched it, a seaplane with a cowled engine and an overhead wing. As it banked, its dimensions flared and I saw a smartly painted green-and-white craft zooming over the water and then lifting its nose and banking off again, the sun flashing on its wings. It was very beautiful to see. Again it was coming around. I ran outside. I watched several runs, each one was different in speed or angle of descent, it looked as if the pilot was practicing or doing tests. You didn't often see airplanes this close.

And then as the show continued here was Clara Lukács coming through the woods from the main house. She wore a white evening gown. She carried her shoes in her hand. She peered up through the trees, she turned, she walked backward, she stopped, she stood on her toes. She moved through patches of light and shade, and reaching the little clearing in front of the cabin, she took me in with a glance and turned to see the plane in its run.

It was very low this time. It drifted down the length of the lake and then dropped below the tree line.

"Are *you* here?" Clara said. She passed into the house and I followed. She stood in the middle of the room with her hands on her hips, and realizing she still held her shoes, she flung them away. At this moment the phone rang. It was in the bedroom and she ran in as if she was going to attack it.

"What!" I heard her shout by way of greeting. A pause. "Yeah, well, I wouldn't count on it!" she said and slammed the phone down.

I waited a minute. When she didn't come out, I moved to the doorway. She was sitting on the edge of her bed in some distraction slipping off one shoulder strap, then the other, shrugging her gown to her waist. Losing all volition, she dropped her hands in her lap and sat hunched over without glamour or grace. Her hair was matted and tears streamed down her cheeks.

She had no degrees of response, she lived hard, and the effect of her crying on my heart was calamitous. Her eyes were swollen almost immediately, her breasts were wet with her tears. Her looks collapsed as if they were a pretense.

"Hey," I said. "Come on. Come on."

After a while she stood up and let the gown fall to her ankles. She had nothing on underneath. She was big-breasted for such a thin narrow-shouldered girl. She stepped out of the gown and went into the bathroom and a moment later I heard the shower running. Her behind was small and firm, if a bit on the flat side. The prominence of her backbone made me smile. It made me think of the scrawny backs on sunburned little girls who came to the carnival in their bathing suits and convened at the cotton candy.

While she showered I found a percolator and put up some coffee. She came out wrapped in a white bath towel with a big maroon *FWB* monogrammed on the front. She accepted a mug of coffee and sat on the couch with her legs folded under her and held the mug with both hands as if for warmth. She had washed her hair, which lay about her head in wet curls, she was no longer crying but the exercise had left her eyes glistening and as she looked at me I wondered how I could have found anything to criticize. I had never in my life seen a woman more beautiful.

"This place is getting on my nerves," she said. "How do I get out of here?"

"I'll take care of it, leave it to me," I said without a moment's hesitation. Without a moment's hesitation. She glanced at me as she sipped her coffee. I waited for my justice. I wondered if I had taken her too literally if she would laugh now crack my heart with her laughter. But she said nothing and seemed satisfied enough by my assurance. Sun filled the room. She put her cup on the floor and curled up on the sofa with her back to me.

Drops of water glittered in her hair. After a while I realized she had gone to sleep.

I ran out of there determined not to be amazed. I should concentrate on what I was going to do next. Amazement would set me back. I wanted to sing, I was exhilarated to madness. But the way to bring this off was to think of my brazen hopes as reasonable and myself as a calm practical person matter-of-factly making a life for himself that was no more than he deserved.

Then Bennett himself was suddenly in full force in my life like a storm that had arrived.

I found myself that same morning with three or four of the ground-keepers, each of us with a pick or shovel on our shoulders, we were hurrying to a site in the woods off the main bridle path. Bennett was waiting. He was standing on a hill of some sort. His horse was tethered to a tree along the trail. "Come up here," he called.

We climbed up the face of an enormous boulder imbedded in the ground. "I've always wondered about this," he said. "I want it exposed."

The foreman of us, an older man long in the Bennett service, took off his cap and scratched his head. "You want us to dig this rock up?" he asked.

"Dig around it," Bennett said. "You see here? This is the top of it, we're standing on top of it. That's what this rise is. I want the whole thing uncovered, I don't know why it's here."

The workmen had trouble believing what he wanted. Bennett didn't get mad. Instead, he took one of the picks and started going at it himself. "You see?" he called out, breathing hard between swings of the pick. "Work it away, like this. You see that, how it extends? Goes all the way over here."

"Here, Mr. Bennett," the foreman said. "Don't you be doing that. You, you," he said to us. "Get to work."

So we started digging out a boulder that might be the size of a dirigible. Bennett watched each of us to see that we understood.

"That's the way," he said. "That's what I want."

He was sturdy and vigorous. Moved around a lot. A short wide-shouldered man with a large head. His hair was white but very full and combed as I combed mine, to a pompadour. He was well tanned. Blue eyes. A handsome blunt-faced old bastard in a riding outfit.

I had expected someone older, more restrained.

He climbed down off the rise and for several minutes crashed around in the woods nearby to see if he could find another rock like it. "You see," he shouted, "it's the only one. "Damnedest thing!" he called out as if we were all colleagues on some archaeological expedition.

Then he mounted his horse and rode off in the direction of the stables. As soon as he was out of sight the foreman leaned on his shovel, took off his cap and wiped his forehead with the back of his hand. "Jesus Mary and Joseph," he said.

We all sat down on the boulder.

But a while later two more diggers came along flushed from their dens, and soon there were a half-dozen of us standing shirtless in the woods swinging our picks and shovels at this mountainous stone.

It was interesting to me how the impulse of the man transformed into the hard work of the rest of us. By our digging we suggested something really important was going on, someone passing by would look at us and think it was serious—we ourselves were proof of the seriousness of the thing.

I had expected not to like F. W. Bennett. But he was insane. How could I resist that? There was this manic energy of his, a mad light in his eye. He was free! That was what free men were like, they shone their freedom over everyone.

I didn't want to think what he did with Clara. I could not dream that she could matter to him in any way at all that I would recognize. I swung my pick. All the intelligence I had of him, from his house and his lands and his train and his resident poets, had not prepared me for the impersonal force of him, the frightening freedom of him.

In the late afternoon we knocked off work, having unearthed the boulder to its southern polar slope. It sat now in an enormous trench at the bottom of which were packed several other stones. It looked as if it weighed several tons. On the way back we stopped in front of the main house to report these findings. Bennett stood on his front porch. He was very pleased. "We'll take it as far down as it goes, boys," he said. "And tomorrow we'll look for markings. I want to see if it has markings."

Apparently as he gazed at these dirty and sweat-stained workmen he saw in the face of one something that might have been disbelief.

"You, Joe," he said to me, "you think it's just a rock, don't you?"

I was so stunned that he knew my name I didn't know what to say.

"Come inside. I want you to see something." He turned and went in the house.

Someone reached over and took the pick from my shoulder. I heard a snicker. I followed F. W. Bennett into his front hall and went past the stairway of halved logs to the sunken living room.

There was a shimmering light on the ceiling, a reflection of the lake. But the floor was in shadow. In one corner, on a table, was a book with line drawings of primitive stone monuments: in all cases one large boulder rested on three or four smaller ones.

"You see?" he said. "I'm not as crazy as you think. They put down these megaliths, or dolmens, for their fallen chiefs."

He strode around the room lecturing me on the burial practices of ancient Indian tribes of New England. He compared them to the ancient burial practices of the Western desert tribes. Indoors he seemed older. He was vigorous and moved constantly but his voice was somewhat hoarse, it suggested age.

I stood in my filthy dark greens wondering how I was going to get out of there.

A maid came in holding a phone on a long cord. She brought it to his side and held it for him on her palm while he picked up the receiver. "Yes?" He continued to move about, and the maid in her light green uniform followed him dutifully where he went, dealing with the cord so that it wouldn't snag on the furniture. He was getting information. He asked short questions—How many? What time?—and listened to lengthy answers. I looked out the bay wall of windows. The late afternoon shadows made the lake a brilliant dark blue water.

On the terrace a woman was arranging flowers in a vase. I realized I was looking at Lucinda Bailey Bennett, the aviatrix. The small shock of seeing someone famous.

"You don't know how to work cameras, by any chance?"

The phone was gone. Bennett was talking to me.

"I've got all this equipment here but I can't get the hang of it myself," he said. "I want to take proper pictures of the excavation and send them out to see if I'm right."

"I don't know anything about cameras," I said.

"I thought you were smart . . . Well," he said, "I wanted to take a look at you, anyway, to see if you belong with me on a permanent basis. What's *your* opinion?"

"You mean a job?" I said.

"That's what I mean. You think you ought to be hired?"

I swallowed. "No," I said.

"No?" He seemed amused.

"I couldn't live here," I said. "It's not for me."

He laughed out loud. "You seemed to have adapted well enough. From what I understand you've made the place your own."

Something outside had caught his eye. He stepped onto the terrace, closing the glass doors behind him, and stood calling down the hill to somebody at the boathouse.

My muscles were tight and my hands clenched. I tried to loosen up.

Mrs. Bennett glanced through the window to where I was and said something to her husband. He turned to her smiling and said something back and she looked again in at me briefly, a half smile on her face. She was a very elegant, honest-looking lady, very well composed, with brown hair cut short, no make-up or anything like that, she wore a loose sweater and a longish skirt and low-heeled shoes. I thought you would not be able to tell, if you didn't know, that this slim handsome woman with her flowers knew how to fly the hell out of airplanes.

And then it came to me he was telling her who the boy inside was. The one and only Joe of Paterson. She was so elegant I realized that what I had written in anger and pride was from another point of view pathetic. I felt betrayed, like a child who gives out his most precious secret and hears it laughed about.

I turned to leave. I thought how powerful this Bennett was if I could be made to feel so bad from just a moment or two of his attention.

"Just a minute, Joe," he called. "I'm not finished with you."

He went past me into the front hall and then down the corridor of the other wing of the house. He opened a door and beckoned to me.

A large room filled with books, cabinets with silver cups, photographs of Mrs. Bennett standing in front of airplanes, Mr. Bennett in a railroad engineer's cap waving from the controls of a steam locomotive, photographs of cars and horses and presidents and governors and film stars. There were globes on stands and big dictionaries on lecterns, a ticker-tape machine under glass—a whole life of glory was in this room.

Bennett sat down behind his desk and took a manila folder out of a drawer and studied the papers in it for several minutes while I stood before him.

Without looking up, he said, "Are your injuries healed?"

"I suppose."

"Have you been in touch with your parents?"

"My parents?"

"They signed a waiver," he said, removing a document from the folder. "You mean you haven't talked to them? I am not at fault for the injuries you incurred on my property. They received two hundred and fifty dollars."

"How do you know my parents?"

"We looked through your billfold. You might have been on your way out."

I was too stunned to speak.

"They haven't called or written to see how you're getting along?" He shoved a paper along the desk and I saw at the bottom the shaky signature of my father. "I'm not lying to you," Bennett said. "By rights that's your money."

I shook my head.

"You don't want to work for me. Fine. You can go home and if you're smart you can use that money to make money. Buy something and sell it for profit. Anything, it doesn't matter. Some of the great fortunes in this country were built from less."

I pictured my father in the kitchen, coming to terms with this legal paper that had to be signed. Finding my school pen somewhere in a drawer and the bottle with Waterman's ink. Testing the penpoint on the oilcloth that covered the table and then rubbing the ink off with his thumb before it dried. My mother standing at the sink, washing the dishes, disguising the moment of the waiver in their lives as one more ordinary moment.

"No," I said. "It's theirs."

"I'll tell you," Bennett said. "I always respect a man's decision. Never try to argue him out of it. You're not staying here and you're not going home. That leaves you back on the road, doesn't it? Back on the bum. Well, I say why not, if that's what you want. But be sure you can handle it. Just be sure you've got the guts. So that if you have to steal or take a sap to someone's head for a meal, you'll be able to. Every kind of life has its demands, its tests. Can I do this? Can I live with the consequences of what I'm doing? If you can't answer yes, you're in a life that's too much for you. Then you drop down a notch. If you can't steal and you can't sap someone on the head when you have to, you join the line at the flophouse. You get on the bread line. If you can't muscle your way into the bread line, you sit at the curb and hold out your hand. You're a beggar. If you can't whine and wheedle and beg your cup of coffee, if you can't take the billy on the bottoms of your feet—why, I say be a poet. Yes"—he laughed at the thought—"like old Penfield, find your level. Get in, get into the place that's your nature, whether it's running a corporation or picking daisies in a field, get in there and live to it, live to the fullness of it, become what you are, and I'll say to you, you've done more than most men. Most men— and let me tell you, I know men—most of them don't ever do that. They'll work at a job and not know why. They'll marry a woman and not know why. They'll go to their graves and not know why."

He was standing at the window gazing out with his hands behind his back, gently slapping the back of one hand into the palm of the other. "I've never understood it, but there it is. I've never understood how a man could give up his life, give it up, moment by moment, even as he lives it, give it up from the second he's born. But there it is. Bow his head. Agree. Go along. Do what everyone's doing. Let it leach away. Sign it away. Drink it away. Sleep it away."

He was standing at the window meditating, eclipsing the window light so that the dark bulk of him was apparent. He was stocky and short-legged with a large head, like a mountain troll. "Well," he said, "you're brash enough. Where are you going?"

"I don't know. As far as I can get."

He came back to his desk and wrote something on a piece of paper. "You happen to need something—this is a private number, not to be given out, you understand?"

He folded the paper and handed it to me. He gave me a quick glance, one eyebrow arching over the lighted eye of shrewdness. "But don't leave until I've got my dolmen," he said, turning and picking up his telephone.

The first chance I had I hurried to Penfield's. He was the only one who could help me with Clara's escape. That was his word, escape. Clara would leave because she was dislodged by the returning wife, Clara would leave because with unforgivable haste she'd been removed from the cozy confidences of Loon Lake's master bedroom. But it wouldn't do to tell him that. He thought he was in torment for her sake. He brooded about rescuing her. That's the way poets are, I said to myself. They see what no one else can see, and what is clear to everyone else they don't see.

I found him in bed. His breath rasped. His skin was a strange pink-gray color and it shone in a glaze of perspiration. He stared at me mournfully from his pillows, his blue and bloodshot eyes swimming in helplessness.

Oh God. That was all I needed.

I went out and found Libby in the staff house.

"I'll have nothing to do with you," she said.

"It's not me, Libby. It's Mr. Penfield. Something's wrong with him. I think he needs a doctor."

She looked at me with suspicion. She went ahead of me to the stables and ran up the stairs to keep as much distance between us as she could.

She took one look at the poet and without troubling to remove herself from his hearing said, "There's nothing wrong with him, he just likes to carry on."

"What do you know, Libby?" he cried out, stung.

"I know what a hollow leg is," she said. "Look at this place, it's enough to make anyone sick."

"Get out, get out!" Penfield shouted. "Will everyone torture me? Am I to die with the scorn of servants in my ears?"

She ignored him and with a great flurry went into action, picking up papers books dirty socks.

"Go away," he shouted. "Don't touch a thing, damnit, you're disrupting everything!"

She straightened his bedcovers and plumped up his pillows while he shouted at her to leave him alone.

544

Furious with both of us, she marched out.

"Joe, there's a bottle of wine under the window seat," Mr. Penfield said.

I wondered what was wrong with me to be so gullible to the claims of this man. He lived here at Loon Lake sloshing in self-pity, the best aspect of him, his gift for poetry, put to the use of unsound notions. Obviously this was the solution of his life. I couldn't change that if I tried. Nobody could.

I handed him the bottle and a glass. He sat up.

"Mr. Penfield, I've got to tell you something," I said, pulling a chair to his bedside. "But I need some information first. Who is Clara? Who were those people who came with her on the train?"

"Tommy Crapo," he said.

"Who?"

"Tommy Crapo. The industrial consultant." He drank off a half-glass of wine. "Don't you read the newspapers? Don't you look at the tabloids? Tommy Crapo who has his picture taken on night-club banquettes with beautiful women."

Color was coming back to his face. He emptied the glass and lay back on his pillows.

"Is he in the rackets?"

"Mr. Crapo is a specialist in labor relations. Yes. I think that's a fair description."

"Does he work for Bennett? Does he knock heads for Bennett?"

He stared at the ceiling. A moment passed. "Why do you ask? You think I should get Miss Lukács away from here, don't you?"

"Well, she's ready."

"What?" He was not used to being taken at his word. He was not equipped for action.

"Miss Lukács is ready to get out of here," I said.

"What?"

"She's ready to make her escape."

I have committed many sins in my life. This precise sin—the sin against poets—is without absolution.

He was out of bed and struggling into a worn maroon robe that had a few tassels left on the belt. I could hear each breath he took. He got on his knees to look under the bed for his slippers. He found them, stood, stepped into them, and then went slapping across the floor, back and forth from one corner of his apartment to another without purpose or intent but busy with agitation.

I sat him down in his reading chair and brought him a cigarette and lit it for him, he held it between thumb and forefinger, his hand shaking.

"What did she say?" he asked.

"She wants me to get her away."

"You?"

"She thinks if you leave together, you'll be too easy to follow. Like a hot car."

"What?"

"Crapo doesn't know me from Adam."

"Crapo is back?"

"He's on his way, Mr. Penfield."

"I see. I see."

"Miss Lukács says once she's safe she can get in touch with you."

"She said that?"

"I've worked out a plan but I need money and I need a car."

"Yes, yes, so that's the way it happens. I see. I see." He was not fooled, he was not a fool, the large protuberant eyes stared through me. "Yes, yes. To be absolutely realistic I'm not in the picture. That's all right, it's just, I'm reconciled. The two young ones. Yes."

He kept talking this way.

I had the uncanny feeling that he was translating what I told him into another language. Yet I could hear everything he said. He rose, he seemed to gain strength, he strode back and forth from the window to the door. "Yes, of course, there is more than I knew. Yes. I want this for her. It's just. I put my faith in you, Joe. Yes, take her away from here. Two young people! It's right. Yes, it's the only way."

"I'll need money and a car," I said.

"Of course. Leave it to me. I'll help you. I'll get you both out. You'll see, you'll see. I have resources. Yes. You'll find Warren Penfield comes through. I have resources. I have allies."

He seemed joyful. He clapped his hands together and glanced heavenward to express his joy. In this moment he would rather have died than reveal his anguish.

As I was leaving he stood at the door and pulled back the sleeve of his robe. "Look here, Joe." he said. He held up his right arm. "The sign of the wild dog! Right?" He gave me a wan but demonstrably brave smile. I had to smile back. I rolled up my sleeve and showed my arm.

"That's right," he said. "You know what two men do who share the sign of the wild dog?" He touched his forearm to mine so that they crossed. "That's right," he said in a husky voice. "My pain is your pain. My life is your life."

Data linkage escape this is not an emergency
Come with me compound with me
A tulip cups the sun quietly in its color
Dixie cups hold chocolate and vanilla
Before the war after the war or

After the war before the war
A man sells me a Dixie cup for a nickel in a dark candy store.
The boy stands on the sidewalk in the sun
Licking the face of Joan Crawford free of ice cream.
A boy enjoys ice cream from a wooden spoon in the sun
before the war in front of the candy store on the corner
while he waits for the light to change. At this moment several
things happen. A horse pulling the wagon of a peddler
of vegetables trots by smartly golden balls of dung dropping
from the base of its arched tail. Then there was a whirring
in my ears and over the top of Paterson Grade School Three
a monumental dirigible nosed into view looming so low
I could see the seams of its paneled silver skin
and human shadows on the windows of its gondola. It was not
sailing straight through its bow but shouldering the wind shuddering
dipping and rising in its sea of air. It soared over the roof
of a tenement and disappeared. At the same time
the traffic light turned green and I crossed from sun to shade
noting that the not unpleasant odor of fresh horse manure
abruptly ceased with the change of temperature. In front of
the shoe repair on Mechanic Street at the sidewalk's edge
between a Nash and a Hudson parked at the curb a baby girl
was suspended from her mother's hands her pants pulled down.
It was desired of this child that she relieve herself there and then
schoolchildren going past in bunches peddlers at their cars
mothers pushing strollers and an older boy with ice cream
stopping shamelessly to watch. And this beautiful little girl
turned a face of such outrage upon me that I immediately
recognized you Clara and with then saintly inability to withstand
life you closed your eyes and allowed the thin stream of
golden water to cascade to the tar which was instantly black and
shone clearer than a night sky.

IN THE MORNING HACKING AWAY AT THE INDIAN-CHIEF MONUMENT, I SAW HIM
going down the bridle path, going right by without so much as a glance at
the strange work on the rock, walking a few steps, running, walking again
hurriedly, on the trail through the woods.

I waited five minutes and then I dropped my shovel and sauntered off.
"Where you going!" someone called behind me. I raised my hand to show
I knew what I was doing and that I'd be right back.

This was the trail the riders took to get to another shore of the lake, a
mile down from the main house. It was hoed regularly to keep it soft—

I had done some of that myself. It went through stands of towering pine and over small clearings where the grass was turning tan and gold in the autumn, and then it dropped down into an area where the leaves were falling like snowflakes. I felt the same turning season in me.

Where the trail cornered, along the shore of the wide lake, was an airplane hangar with a concrete ramp. Mr. Penfield sat on the ramp with his arms around his knees. He was looking at the water. The wind had whipped up a small white chop. Wavelets slapped at the concrete. He didn't seem to notice Lucinda Bailey Bennett coming out of the hangar and walking toward him. She pulled a big red trainman's handkerchief from the pocket of her overalls and wiped her hands.

I ducked around through the underbrush and came within a few feet of them. I could see inside: an engine was suspended from pulleys. A man was guiding it to a workbench.

"What do you do, Lucinda," said Mr. Penfield in a petulant tone. "Paint the innards like a new toy?"

"No, old bear. When I'm through, its innards will be dark and oiled, and refitted to tolerances that will take me to the top of the sky." She stuffed her handkerchief into the pouch of her overalls. "Why are you sulking? I thought you loved me."

"Since I gave up manhood to live here, I make no claims of that sort on anyone."

She smiled. "That's not the report I have."

"Oh, Lucinda," he said with a groan, and he turned to look up at her.

"So much suffering." She touched the back of her hand to his temple. "Poor Warren."

"How much better for me if when I came here my throat had been ripped out."

She sighed. "Yes," she said, "I suppose so."

After a moment she turned back and he lifted himself grunting to his feet. He lumbered after her. "Forgive me," he called.

"Oh, Warren, it's such a bore when you whine." She went into the hangar.

"Yes," he cried out bitterly. "Indeed. My agony does not divert." And he followed her.

I couldn't hear them now. The hangar was lit by electric lights that glimmered very faintly through the brightness of the morning. But I saw them moving around, she working and he talking with grand gestures. Every once in a while I heard the sound of his voice, and I knew Mr. Penfield well enough to know he was in good form, eloquent in his self-dramatization. I hoped so, because he was talking for me.

The man who'd been helping came out, lit a cigarette and went off along the trail. I moved to the hangar itself, staying out of sight of the doorway. I leaned my back to the wall.

"You have a good nature," I heard Mrs. Bennett say.

"Oh my dear!"

"Would you like to go on a flight? Probably not. But a really long flight. Just the two of us. Would you consider it?"

"What? Where?"

"I don't know. The Far East. Shall we do that? Fly across the Pacific."

"The Far East?"

"Yes, pooh bear. A long flight. You and I. Oh, that's a *good* idea! Who knows what might happen." She burst out laughing. "Warren, if you could see the expression on your face! The dismay!"

"Lucinda, what— How is it possible? Am I misunderstood?"

"Oh, foolish thing—I don't mean that! Good God!" She was merry now. "It's a practice made too thoroughly disreputable by its devotees, don't you think?"

That evening the four of them met for dinner. I stood on the terrace just out of the light cast through the windows and I watched them at their drinks. A fire blazed in the huge fireplace. Mounted prey gazed down at them. Clara was wearing a gown of sequined silver. She looked cheap. She sat staring at the floor, cowed, maybe even stunned into silence, by the nuances of civilization in that room. The gentlemen wore black tie, in which Mr. Penfield managed to look as rumpled and ill-prepared for life as ever. With his characteristic expression of appeal for love and understanding he glanced habitually at the others, but especially Clara. Lucinda Bennett smiled faintly and kept up her end of the conversation. Only F. W. Bennett seemed to be enjoying himself. He became so animated he stood up to deliver his sentences. He went to a table behind the leather sofa and held up a large flat book opened, and resting on his arm, and he read from it and laughed and looked at the others for their reaction.

I went through the woods to Clara's cabin and found her luggage standing just inside the front door. There were three bags and a hatbox. I got all of them under my arms or hanging from my hands, and struggled up the hill to the garage on the far side of the tennis court. This was the old Loon Lake stable. It housed five cars. In the last stall was Mrs. Bennett's car, a rarely used gray two-door Mercedes-Benz with a canvas top and spare tires in the front fender wells. I looked for the ignition key where Mr. Penfield had told me to—in the bud vase on the right-hand side in the back. Yes. I packed the bags in the trunk, which was not large, and put the hatbox in the back seat. I turned on the map light and by its glow learned the European-style shifting. There were four gears, and a diagram of their positions was imprinted on the mother-of-pearl knob of the floor shift. The dust on the seat cracked under me. I flicked at it with a chamois cloth. The odometer showed less than ten thousand miles. Then I saw it was not even miles, it was kilometers. Lucinda Bennett had told Mr. Penfield it was a 1933 model. Clearly, her interest in machines did not include cars. The license plate was up to date, however.

I swung open the doors as quietly as I could and got in and started the engine. I backed out. It was a noisy car—I later found it was only forty horsepower—and I drove it the few yards to the gas pump shushing it as if it were a baby. I filled it with Mr. Bennett's personal ethyl and then I gave each tire a shot of his air. I was wearing his knickers and argyle sweater and brown-and-white saddle shoes. I tried not to get them dirty.

I was ready to go. I waited behind the wheel. It was a snug little car. The seats were gray leather. The doors opened front to back. I went over some road maps. I sat there and got the feeling of the car and worried about driving it well, and wondered where to go and what I would say to Clara Lukács and what she would say to me. I worried that people seeing me behind the wheel would think I was rich. I didn't once reflect on the lately peculiar conforming of life to my desires. I didn't think of Lucinda Bennett's generosity or despair, or Mr. Penfield's, nor even reach the most obvious conclusion; that I was leaving Loon Lake in somewhat better condition than I had come. Calculating, heedless, and without gratitude, I accepted every circumstance that had put me there, only gunning my mind to the future, wanting more, expecting more, too intent on what was ahead to sit back and give thanks or to laugh or to feel bad.

I peered through the windshield. I watched the trees shaking in the night wind. I unlatched the canvas top and pushed it back a bit and looked at the stars, which seemed to shimmer and blur as if the wind were blowing through them.

Eventually she got there, hurrying along with Mr. Penfield holding her arm, while she held her gown off the ground to keep from tripping. She wore a fur jacket over the gown. He opened the door, but before she could slide in, he grabbed her and hugged her and started to gabble something. I saw all this with their heads cut off. I saw her push him away. "War-rin, please!" she said.

Then she was in the car beside me, in an atmosphere of fur and cold air, and she slammed the door. Penfield peered in, then ran around the front of the car to the driver's side. I started the engine and threw the toggle switch for the headlights. I adjusted the throttle. I rolled down my window and he thrust something in my hand, a wad of bills. "I wish it was more," he said. He gave us advice of many kinds, cheerful assurances, warnings about the road, the weather, appeals to keep in touch, phone numbers on bits of paper, promises, vows, thrown kisses—and to this fitful love song I put the car into first, and off we lurched down the road.

We were taking what was called the back road, away from the main house; there was a sudden bend, and Mr. Penfield, waving in the night in his black tie, veered out of my rear view.

I leaned forward, attentive to the clutching, and gradually, as we made our way bumping and sliding over this gravelly unpaved circuit through the Bennett preserve, I got the hang of it. We drove for quite a while. I glanced at her. In the glow of the dashboard I saw her young face.

I think now of that long drive down through the forest to the state road, dogs appearing from nowhere to gallop yelping alongside, their breath sounding metallic, like the engine; and disappearing just as suddenly, then again one or two of them, then for a mile a beating pack; and she saying nothing, only holding the leather strap by her window, looking out to the side, to the front, her eyes following them tracking them, the youth of her illuminated in the low light. Finally we outdistanced them all.

She sat back in her seat. She took a cigarette out of her purse and lit it.

"What do you think he'll do when he finds you gone?" I said.

"An interesting question," she said.

And so we descended from Loon Lake, Clara's clear eyes fixed on the farthest probe of the headlights, and I looking at her every other moment, in her composure of total attention, going with the ride.

Every morning she swept the dirt path outside the monastery wall. She always wore the same thing, a simple kimono and those wooden slippers, you know? She was fifteen or sixteen years old but her hair was cut in the bowl cut of young children. Hair as black as night. She never smiled, but when she glanced at me there was such a flash of recognition from my soul that I went weak with joy.

Oh, Warren.

I used to wake up before dawn and do my chores and manage always to be at the gate when the sun rose and she came to do hers. She was the daughter of some working family down the street. They sweep the streets there with straw brooms. The unpaved streets. They sweep the dirt, compose it. They compose everything, they pick the fallen leaves one at a time.

How did you get to her?

I wish you wouldn't phrase it that way, Lucinda. We knew each other on sight. We had to. My Japanese was less than rudimentary. Her English nonexistent. Only the upper classes studied English. It was a great social distinction to know English. A workman's daughter couldn't aspire to that.

Light me a cigarette, will you?

I have in my life just three times seen a face in dark light, at dusk or dawn or against a white pillow, in which there is a recognizably perfect perception of the world, some matched reflection of the world in her eye's light as terrifying and beautiful in equal measure. Am I coherent?

A moral light? Is that what you mean?

She lives through her fear to her curiosity, there is a stillness of apprehension, like an animal's stillness of perfect apprehension of its predator, and it is gallantry to break the heart.

I wish we had known each other when we were young.

Her father and several uncles made up a delegation to complain about my conduct to the monastery officials, who of course did not have to be told. I had broken every rule in the book. At the moment both sides gathered to come down on us we slipped away together and took the train to Tokyo. We found a room.

Is this when you became lovers?

I suppose so. I thought I could support us by teaching American customs and manners to Japanese businessmen. They wanted that. They were studying us intently. They listened to jazz and danced the Charleston. You're not crying, are you?

It makes me sad. I know what happened.

I left the house one morning. I had an appointment to see someone at the U.S. embassy. It was a Saturday, the first day in September, 1923. As I walked down the street, I lost my balance but suddenly people everywhere were screaming. The streets were cracking open. I ran back, the city was falling down everywhere, I climbed over rubble, I saw her coming after me with her arms raised, the cobblestones heaved, the street broke open, it filled with water, I reached her and grabbed her hand just as the earth sank away and she fell in, she fell from my hands and where the earth had been there was a steaming lake. What is that up ahead, Lucinda? It looks very dark.

It's nothing. A line squall.

The nights seemed to race by. The weather got colder. The freaks got nastier. We came one day to a town less promising than any I'd seen. It was shut down and boarded. One tavern and one store were open. I don't remember the name of this town, it was like a tree with just a branch or two still alive.

In a lot beside the boarded-up railroad depot Sim Hearn gave the signal and the carney put up for business. In the evening we turned on the lights and a few mountain people straggled in but most of the time the freaks talked to each other because nothing else was doing. The rides went around empty. I thought Sim Hearn had lost his marbles.

The next night the same thing, the wind blew through the booths and rattled the tent flaps, they sounded like over the mountains somewhere there was some gang war of Tommy guns going on.

I thought Sim Hearn was telling us the season was over by enacting the news. The cook built a fire on the ground and heated an ash can of water. He scrubbed his pots and pans with brown soap. Other people were packing. Mrs. Hearn grabbed my arm and we stepped behind a wagon.

"Hearn goes no farther," she said. "Look, a sweater I have for you so you wouldn't be cold."

She was a pain in the ass with her presents. She brought me cigarettes, oranges, she washed my clothes, all in secret of course. Nobody knew about it except the whole carney.

It chilled me to think Sim Hearn might know it. But his distance from me was unchanged and his peculiar authority maintained itself in my mind. It was as if no matter what I did to his wife I could never break through that supreme indifference. I decided no man was that godlike. I decided he didn't know. I wished he did know. Then I wouldn't be some nameless creature so low as to be beneath his line of vision.

The next morning we struck everything but the show tent. We raised the wood shutters on the wagons and nailed them shut. We pushed the wagons into an old car barn across the tracks from the depot. After lunch a few people left with their bags or bundles. Nobody said so long or even looked at anyone else. I think I was shocked. Despite all my other feelings about the carney, I could believe it was a privilege to be attached to it. It angered me that people would walk away as if Hearn Bros. had no more distinction than a mission flop.

On the other hand, why should it be different? Sim Hearn couldn't care less if any one of them lived or died and they knew that. He was going to take the trucks down to Florida for the winter and let them get down there on their own. If they showed up, he'd hire them; if they didn't, that was all right too.

Fanny the Fat Lady's wagon was in place and hadn't been moved. I saw Mrs. Hearn coming out of her trailer. "Fanny wheezes like calliope," she said.

"Well, why doesn't someone get a doctor?"

She put her hand on my cheek and looked in my eyes. "I worry to think someday if we are not together what will happen to you."

Several of the freaks were leaving in a group. I was told to take a truck and drive them about fifteen miles to a town called Chester, where there was a spur line to Albany. It was the afternoon, already getting dark. In the cab with me sat the woman who took care of Fanny. The whole ride she wept and blew her nose. She spoke to herself in Spanish as if her running stream of thoughts and sorrows came up over the banks every now and then. She thought I wasn't looking when she lifted her skirt and fingered the metal clip of her garter to make sure it was fastened properly. I saw tucked in the top of her stocking a wad of bills that looked like a lot of money.

I let off the truckload of freaks and their keepers in Chester, New York, and they hopped, climbed or were lowered from the tailgate. They went limping and scuttling into the waiting room carrying their bags like anyone. Why not? They were mostly immigrants, after all—the same people but with a twist who worked for pennies in the sawmills or stood on the bread lines. But I imagined the stationmaster seeing through his grill this company of freaks in ordinary streetclothes approaching him with questions of schedule and tickets.

Why didn't I get on the train with them? Did I really want to drive a truck to Florida? Did I want to bang Mrs. Magda Hearn in more states of the Union?

I thought of the freaks as pilgrims or revolutionaries of some angry religion nobody knew anything about yet.

When I got back it was already dark. I could tell something was wrong, there were lots of cars there and wagon teams. I cut the engine and stood on the running board. Beyond the lot was a hill that rose steeply, blacker than the sky, I could see its outline against the blue-black space of sky behind it. I thought I heard a scream. I listened—it was something else, a drumming of the earth or the sound of a rug being beaten. I walked toward the show tent, there was the dimmest light in there. A man stepped out of the shadow and put his hand on my arm. A flashlight shone in my eyes.

"Who's this?" a voice said.

And then I heard Magda Hearn. "It's all right. He's with the show."

My arm was still held and I could feel the consideration of this intelligence in the mind behind the light. The flashlight went off. I made out the figure of a state trooper, blocked hat and gun and Sam Browne belt. Then my arm was released, the marks of the fingers still on me, like the afterimage on the eye.

Magda Hearn was walking me toward the show tent. "Joe," she said, "I want you to see, to understand. And I wait for you in the car. Do you hear me?"

"What's going on?" I said. "What are the police doing here?"

"Joe, please to listen." She was whispering in my ear and in each cycle of her crippled gait, the sibilance rose and fell in waves of urgency.

Then I passed through the flaps.

The show tent had a few rows of wooden bleachers and a small ring where the ponies could run around and the bareback sisters, if they were so inclined, could do their turns. A cat act had been featured here for a while.

The bleachers were empty. One bulb burned from the tent pole. Eighty, maybe a hundred men stood in a circle in the dirt of the ring. I couldn't see over their backs but I heard the not unfamiliar night music, the grunts and gurgling moans and squeals of Fanny the Fat Lady. As the rhythm got faster the crowd shouted encouragement. Then I heard that peculiar basso thumping as if the earth itself was being drummed. Then an abrupt silence and the hoarse male roar of expiration. Whistles and cheers came from the crowd, men turned outward, I saw them drinking from bottles, exchanging money. Staggering through the ring, buttoning his pants, was a grifter I recognized. He sank down on his knees beside me, removed a flask from his back pocket and took a long pull.

Some sort of hot shame rose from the roots of my sex into my stomach and chest: it felt like illness. I pushed forward and saw Fanny on her back, arms and legs flung outward. She was naked. She lay twitching, each spasm jerking her flesh into ripples. She wheezed and fought for breath. The sweated slathered flesh was caked in dirt, but with white crevasses in the folds of her and a red blotch in the middle. I was pushed aside and spun around. A moment later another lover had fallen on her. The crowd yelled and jammed up around me. She was quickly brought to pitch, her great back rising and thumping into the earth, but this one didn't last long, and to great merry raucous hoots and jeers he stumbled out of the ring.

Almost immediately another rube was moving forward for his turn. I jumped him just as he unbuckled his belt. I knocked him down and kicked him in the groin. He yowled, doubling up and clutching himself and I took his place crouching beside Fanny, facing them all, my fists clenched. I was screaming something, I don't remember what, it stunned them for a second, and then they were laughing and taunting me and shouting at me to wait my turn.

Fanny lay there trembling in her agony and her eyes were rolled into her head. Her mouth was open and giving off gasping animal wheezes. Maniacally, I felt betrayed by her, as by life itself, the human pretense. I became enraged with her! In my nostrils, mixed with the sharp fume of booze, was an organic stench, a bitter foul smell of burning nerves, and shit and scum.

Then something flew out at me, a pint bottle, or a rock, and caught me low on the forehead. I went down, dazed, clutching my eyes, bright lights in my brain. I had fallen on Fanny, she was like some soft rotten animal carcass. Her arms helplessly went around me. I was panicked and tried to get free. My struggles were mistaken—I was pulled out of her grasp by my feet and dragged through the dirt and kicked and rolled and yanked to my feet and given a clout on the side of the head.

I found myself on my knees, behind the crowd. I was wet. Blood streamed in my eye. But the ceremony continued. There were men drooling there. There were onanists. There were gamblers betting on the moment of death. Later there were men leaping on her, on each other, squatting on her head, crawling over her, falling on her, shoving bottles in her. There were gallants calling for order, for some law of decency if all pleasure was not to be lost. And Fanny giving up a human appearance by degrees, trumpeting her ecstasies to the killing passion of the rubes.

From one only was there absolute quiet in this mayhem. I looked at him. His face was hidden in the shadow of his hat brim. You wouldn't know his connection with these spermy rites except for the indolence of his stance as he leaned against the bleacher supports with his bony arms folded and his ankles crossed. And I could swear I heard, through the hoarse cries and shouts and shrieking and orgiastic death, the thoughtful and preoccupied sucking of Sim Hearn's tongue on his teeth.

Riding over the mountain in the Model A, Joe became aware of where he was. She accelerated, the headlights brightened; she braked, the headlights dimmed. The bones of his legs sounded the ground pitch of the engine. Mrs. Hearn's face luminous in the night, she urged the car forward with her chin, her furrowed brow, her shoulders putting english on the turns. At the bottom of a hill she gunned it, halfway up plunged with her left leg, shifted to second, she came over the tops of the hills with her horn blowing, headlights making a quick stab at the night sky.

"Of course they never live long, such creatures—the heart won't beat for them . . . All summer Sim Hearn watches—he watches and then he sees the signs—she doesn't take breath as she should—from the bed she cannot lift herself . . . The people know Hearn—he gives something special at end of summer, a grand finale . . . The word goes through the mountains . . . Look where we are—we make time better than I hoped.''

In the early hours of the morning she judged us safely away and turned into a motor court and paid for a cabin in the pines farthest from the road. Wedged into the rumble seat was my broken-down valise with everything I possessed in the world. She had packed it for me. I carried it and her frayed black Gladstone into the room. She locked the car and locked the cabin door behind us and pulled the shades and then pulled the light cord.

The bed had a khaki blanket but no sheets. Two lumpy gray pillows. Magda Hearn rummaged in her bag for a white cotton face towel. She spread the towel on top of the bureau. The room had the shit smell of old untreated wood. She removed from her purse a manila envelope and from the envelope removed a stack of greenbacks which she placed on the cotton towel.

''Sim knows to get the money out before the fun starts,'' she said. ''To Albany to the bank he thinks I am going.''

She wet her thumb on her lower lip and stood at the bureau counting the money. I sat down on the bed and took off my shoes and socks. She wet her thumb on the inside of her lower lip, pulling it down so that for a moment her teeth showed her expression went slack. She was a while counting.

''Fifteen hundred and eighty-four dollars!''

She dug in her purse and extracted a wallet and from this withdrew another wad of bills.

''And plus salary which he never paid!'' she said in a tone of vengeful triumph. The thumb applied to the red inside of her lip. She counted aloud this time. ''Two hundred I squeeze from you, you bastard!''

She opened her Gladstone, interrupting herself to press her lips strongly on my mouth.

She pulled the string tie of a small canvas coin sack and spilled a stream of coins on the bed.

She lay on the bed making separate piles of nickels and dimes and quarters and halves, the little piles collapsed and came together because she was shaking the bed with her guttural glee. She started over, she was keen on pennies, too—if there had been coins of smaller denominations, she would have counted them, too. She was ready to count coins forever and to bitterly calculate the suffering she had done for each one.

''Joe Joe Joe! Tomorrow we trade his car and its license and buy new. We drive to California you and me. We are in our new car on way to California before even he thinks is something wrong!''

She gave up the count and lay on her back in the coins. She lifted her arms. ''Come to me, come to Magda. You know what?'' Kissing me, running hands on me, opening one by one the buttons on my fly. ''To Hollywood we are going. I have read the magazines, I understand the movie business. I sell my life story. A film of my life! Everyone will know who Magda is." She unbuckled my belt, she opened the buttons of my shirt. She kissed my chest and pulled the shirt down off my shoulders. "And who knows who knows, with your looks, my Joseph, with your body, why you cannot be movie star? And we will love each other and have great sooccess. Shall we?" Laughing, going down on me. "Shall we?"

She had no idea I had actually caught evil as one catches a fever, she didn't understand this, she thought my passion matched hers. I wanted to do to her what had been done to the Fat Lady, I wanted the force of a hundred men in unholy fellowship, I went at her like a murderous drunkard.

I fucked past her joy into her first alarm, I saw on her face under the weak glare of the hanging bulb the dilated eye. I was enraged by the flaws of her, the unnatural cleft of her left hip, one buttock was actually atrophied, the raised veins behind the knees, the hanging breasts like deflated balloons, the yellowed face with loosened folds of skin at the neck rising in parallel rows as she turned her head from me this stinking Hungarian hag this thieving crone bitch with the gall to think she had me for her toy boy her lover chuffing now like a fucking steam engine I brought the tears to her eyes she would acknowledge nothing she resisted and then the voice did come, and then the voice louder and more insistent, and finally she seemed to be urging me along as if we were together, the lying cunt in the Pine Grove Motor Court, our music mingling with the night wind in the pines the tree trunks creaking the million crickets. I ended and began again. We wrestled. She begged me to stop. Tears of mourning came from my eyes. I let her fall asleep. I woke her, made her moan. At one point the coins sticking to the wet ass, the wet belly, I invented a use of Magda Hearn so unendurable to her that with the same cry that must have come from her the day she fell twisting from the trapeze, she flung herself off the bed—a moment's silence, then the sickening shaming sound of bone and flesh slamming into the floor, a grunt. I lay on my back on the bed not daring to look, I heard a small soprano cry, a deeper moan, a whispered curse. I lay still. After a while I realized I was listening to the snores of an exhausted human being.

I thought I saw the first crack of light under the window shade. I got off the bed and rolled my clothes and shoes into a bundle. I grabbed the stack of bills from the bureau. I unlatched the door quietly and closed it behind me. There were no other guests at the Pine Grove Motor Court. A thin frost lay on the windshield of the Model A. The wind blew.

With all my might I reared back and threw the bills into the wind. I thought of them as the Fat Lady's ashes.

I found a privy up the hill behind the cabins and next to it an outdoor shower. I stood in the shower of cold springwater and looked up at the swaying tops of the pine trees and watched the sky lighten and heard through the water and the toneless wind the sounds of the first birds waking.

I dried myself as best I could and put on my clothes in a tremble of stippled skin and turned my back on the cabins and struck off through the woods. I had no idea where I was going. It didn't particularly matter. I ran to get warm. I ran into the woods as to another world.

At Kamakura he climbed the spiral stairs inside the largest Buddha in the world. In the head of the largest Buddha, on the ledge of its chin, sat a tiny Buddha facing in the opposite direction. Simple idolatry held no interest for him, but a religion that joked held genuine interest. He felt all at once the immense power of a communication that used no words. I acknowledge Warren's lifelong commitment—cancel lifelong commitment—fatal attraction for any kind of communication whether from words, flags, pigeons or the touch of fingertips in hope of a common language, but we must remember how we are vulnerable to the repetition of our insights so that they tend to come to us not as confirmation of something we already know but as genuine discoveries each and every time. And so he descended, and by degrees over a period of several days, drifted south along the route of the old Tokaido. He saw thousands of Buddhas lined up in trays in the tourist shops or ranked in legions at the shrines, some in lead, some in wood, some carved in stone and dressed in little knitted caps and capes. He came to see in this ubiquitous phenomenon the Buddha's godlike propensity for self-division, the endless fractioning of himself into every perceivable aspect, an allegory made by the people of Japan from the cellular process of life. Thus enlightened, he turned his eyes on the people in the streets and the narrow shopping arcades, old women in black slapping along on their sandals, black-haired children of incredible beauty staring at him with their thumbs stuck in their plump cheeks, giggling pairs of young women in brightly colored kimonos, old shopkeepers with wispy goatees bowing as he passed, thoughtful peddlers, and young men who stopped in their tracks to glare at him and bear themselves with brazen umbrage—they were all the Buddha too in his infinite aspect. Traveling down this avenue of thought lit only by stone lanterns filled with small stones in lieu of flames, he saw the true dereliction of the planet and realized anew that convictions of friendship, love, the assumption of culture, the certainty of calendars were fragile constructs of the imagination, and there was no place to live that was truly home, neither for him nor for the multitudinous islanders of Japan.

In this he-took-for-appropriate state of mind, Warren arrived one day at road's end, Kyoto, the strange city whose chief industry was meditation. He wandered from one monastery to the next, there were whole neighbor-hoods of them, but where, where was the sign that one was for him? He was afflicted with a fluttering humility, not daring even to make inquiries, hovering at this gate or in that garden or touching down for just a moment of indecision before the small window with the visitor admission in yen painted in black calligraphy on white cardboard stuck into the grate as if he were looking for a movie to see. Late in the afternoon, weary and full of self-condemnation, he happened to stumble up the step of a wooden verandah overlooking one of these beautiful monastery gardens of raked gravel and moss and stone. Thus launched, his large Caucasian person hurtled through a rice-paper door, splintering its laths, and like an infant being born, he found himself with the back half of him still on the porch side of the door and the front half in a room, looking with wide, even horrified eyes at the benign polished wood Buddha sitting facing him with a little altar of flowers on either side and the sinuous smoke of incense appearing to squinch up its eyes. He had made a terrible thunderous racket but nobody came running, nobody came shouting, and after he crawled the rest of the way into the room he set about calmly picking up the pieces and preparing in his mind the self-demeaning speech by which he would beg the chance to make the most extended and profound restitution. As it happened, the monastery was empty; he was to learn it was the rare annual holiday of this particular establishment in which everyone was set free for twenty-four hours. Only after searching the grounds did Warren find an old caretaker willing to come look and see the awful thing he had done. This old caretaker was smoking a cigarette, which he held in his teeth. He took in smoke with each inhalation and with each exhalation smoke streamed out of his nostrils. He gazed at the carnage, the plumes of smoke from his nostrils indicating the depth and strength of each drawn breath, and it seemed to fascinate him that such a perfect and modest structure as a sliding paper door should have been turned into this. He was a very short, extremely bald old man, and he wore a torn ribbed undershirt and a pair of dirty white muslin knickers with flapping ties at the waist but the peculiar thing was that he was not unpleasant to look upon, it did not create feelings of pity or fear or other degrees of patronization to look upon him. He picked up a broken length of lath and looked at it and asked a question in unintelligible Japanese. I'll pay for it, Warren said and removed from his pocket a wad of yen. He unfolded the bills and looked at the old man squinting at the money through the cigarette smoke. War-ren peeled off one bill and put it in the man's hand. Then another. Then another. He kept waiting for a sign that he'd met the cost. He hesitated. The old man looked at him and peremptorily slapped his arm with the lath. Warren was so astonished he dropped the whole wad of bills in the old man's hand. The caretaker put the bills into the pockets of his voluminous knickers, looked up at the Caucasian and swatted him again with the flat of the stick, this time across the side of his face. Then he laughed, and in so doing released his cigarette, which fell from his teeth and lay on the wooden floor glowing. Immediately Warren, thinking the whole place would go up, stepped on the tobacco ember with his large shoe, only realizing in that moment the defacement he had committed by stepping with street shoes on the monastery floors.

But the caretaker had turned and headed back to his garden shed with its straw brooms and clay pots and small pyramids of gravel. Warren experienced the uncanny sense of a sharply learned lesson. He slept that night at a Western hotel in the downtown section of Kyoto and found in the nightstand drawer a volume in English that seemed to be the Buddhist equivalent of the Bible. Gautama was an Indian prince kept at home by his father so as not to see life in any aspect but its most luxurious. But one day he went out and saw a beggar, an old crippled man, a monk and a corpse. He was thus able to conclude despite his own royal existence that life was suffering. Why couldn't he have figured that out without leaving the palace? Warren wondered. If death exists, life has to be suffering. Did his father hide death from Gautama? How was that done? The book said the cause of all suffering was desire, the desire to have the desire to be. Perhaps a prince would never experience the desire to have, but how could he avoid the desire to be? If desire by its nature is not gratified before it realizes itself, does it not exist in palaces too? Does it not exist especially in palaces? Nevertheless, he liked the story. He trusted Gautama Siddhartha and the simplicity of his reasoning. Not many people could get away with that sort of reasoning. He trusted the eightfold path for defeating desire and transcending suffering.

Early the next morning Warren went back to the monastery. The place was a shambles. Doors and shoji walls were splintered and torn everywhere. There were recumbent bodies on the verandah, and in the garden a monk lay in a pool of vomit. All the walls were torn and hanging, bodies lay about as if dead. There was even a body lying across the crest of the tile roof. The monastery looked as if it had been bombed. But even as he gazed at this dismal scene he heard the sound of small tinkling bells coming from somewhere in the main monastery building, and though the bells were soft and delicate they had the astonishing effect of rousing the Zen Buddhists from their drunken stupor. One by one they groaned, rose to their feet and staggered off.

And then around the corner came a man in white holding a staff of temple bells. His head was shaved, he was stout, the folds of his neck were like ruffles of a collar. He walked right up to Warren and inquired in heavily accented English if he could be of help. I want to discuss with someone the possibility of enrolling here for Zen training, Warren said. Of course, the monk said. If you don't mind waiting more than two moments but less than six, I will approach the Master for you.

More than two but less than six, Warren thought as he waited in an anteroom beside the front gate. That's a few. Shortly thereafter he was escorted by the monk to a small room with a beautiful Bodhisattva *pratima* and a vase of flowers and straw mats and cushions, and without having to be told, even by himself, he dropped to his knees and bowed to the resident Master, who was seated and facing him with a face of genial amusement. It was the old caretaker. On the one day off of the year for all his followers and monks, he, in perfect realization, had stayed where he was. The Master was smoking a cigarette. Another monk came by and listened. He was laughing and telling the monk, in Japanese, about his first meeting with Warren. Gusts of smoke came out of him. As the story was elaborated, the Master rose and began to act it out, and there to Warren's astonishment was a perfect imitation of himself, the way he carried himself, his walk, the tone of his voice, the shock on his face as the lath slapped his cheek. The Japanese laughed till there were tears in their eyes. Soon Warren began to smile and then he too exploded into laughter. He would come to understand in the months to follow that the Master so perfectly realized whatever he chose to do, that a kind of magnetic field was formed in which whoever was in his presence drew on its power. That is why interviews with the Master were so highly prized. His perfection was an impersonal force that you could feel and hope someday to manifest from yourself on a continuous basis. If he laughed, it was perfect laughter, and you had to laugh too. If he chose to cry, everyone around him would have to weep. But where did it come from, how did it happen? All Warren could work out was that the Master lived totally to the fullness of his being each and every moment of his existence. He was completely of the moment, then and there, in which you found him. Nothing of him was deadened by the suffering of his past life and there was no striving or fear in him for his future.

Would the Master feel a need to write poems?

No, because poems are the expression of longing and despair. Yes, because if the Master is one in every instant with what he sees and hears and feels, the poem is not the Master's written need but the world singing in the Master.

No, because the poem is a cry of the unborn heart. Yes, because the poem perfectly embodies the world, there is no world without poem.

Your register apologizes for rendering nonlinear thinking in linear language, the apperceptions of oneness in dualistic terminology. However, there is no difficulty representing the absolute physical torture of Warren Penfield's commitment to Zen meditation. He could not physically accomplish even the half lotus, his spine threatened to snap, his legs seemed to be in a vise; even the mudra—the bowl-shaped position of the hands, the thumbs lightly touching, a simple relaxed representation in the hand of the flow from right to left, from left to right, the rocking crescent continuity of the universe intimations of stars and ancient Eastern recognitions—became under the torment of his distracted physically weeping thought a spastic hand clench, a hardened manifestation of frozen fear and anguish, the exact opposite of the right practice, the body imprisoned, the mind entirely personal and self-involved and then God help you if you nod off every now and then as who could not, sitting like a damn beer pretzel twelve, sixteen hours a day he comes along and hits you with the damn slapstick the goddamn yellow-skinned bastard the next time he hits me with that stick I'm going to get up and wrap it around his goddamn yellow neck and break a goddamn Buddha doll over his goddamn shaven head this is not right thinking but tell me Gautama enlighten me if what you say is true why is it so difficult to attain wouldn't it all make a lot more sense if everyone could do it if everyone could be it without even thinking without being anything less before, without the death of my darling, and men drowning in the cold black coalwater of collapsed mines miles of coalstone sinking slowly upon their chests, or bullets perforating them like cutout coupons supposing I do attain it, supposing I find the right understanding what then what happens outside me how do I help Local 10110 of the Western Federation of Miners, Smelters, Sheepdippers and Zenpissers, and then there's the food, look what we wait for when at last the cute little tinkly bell rings and we may unpretzel ourself and try to regain the circulation in our swollen limbs, little bits of pickled leather, or some absolute excresence of the lowest sea life lightly salted or a congealed ball of rice dipped in some rank fermented fluid that smells to me like the stuff we dipped the pigeons in to kill the lice.

No, there is no problem expressing the inner record of Warren Penfield's quest for enlightenment: the whining despair, the uncharacteristic epithet, the rage, the backsliding giving up and consequent self-nauseation, the stubborn goings on, all of this silent, in a temple hall of inscrutable meditators, all of whom reminded him of the immigrant kids in the Ludlow Grade School around him totally serene and insulated in their lack of language the feeling what do they all know that I don't know why don't the storms of self taste fire and thunder across their brainbrow, why aren't they as sick and unsure of their dangerous selves as I am of mine, leading then to the false Zen-like casuistry as, for example, if we are to press ourselves on the world sticking to it like a decal, if I am one with the rocks the trees the stars why is my memory invalid and why then are the images of Clara on our beds of slag in the cool mountain dusk of Colorado forbidden me, I am my memory and the images of my past are me, and if I am the rocks and stones and trees, Wordsworth, rocked round in earth's diurnal course with rocks and stones and trees, why are my phantoms less real why are the ghostvoices of my mama and papa less real why is the mud of the Marne less real why must I exclude exclude, if everything is now and mind is matter is not everything valid is not meditation the substance of the mind as well as its practice?

Nor is it difficult to render the casually developed outer circumstances of this monastic life, the old Master becoming at some times demonic in his teaching, a destroyer of ego, of humble ordinary lines of thought, an army of right practice, right understanding overwhelming the frail redoubts and trenches of Warren's Western mind. One day they were in the temple and he came in screaming, naked, climbed the Buddha like a bee alighting on a flower and bending it with its own honeygravid weight and they watched shocked and stunned as a beautiful polished wood Buddha toppled to the floor under the Master, an act of profound desecration with sexual impact, and the Buddha lay split like a log, a piece of wood the aperture of an earthquake and nothing was ever said of it again. He was a violent old man, one day Warren was admitted for his counseling and the Master threw a cup of cold green tea in his face and that was the lesson of the day. One day he lectured them all, a particular holy day and he shouted at them saying you were all Masters when you first came through the gate and now look at you, I have more respect for the horse that pulls the shitwagon than I have for you—screaming and growling and trilling in the Japanese way of singsong, Warren prostrate with all the rest. But everyone took it as material to be pondered and worked out, it was only a style of pedagogy and only someone stupid enough to take emotions seriously would be shocked threatened or angered by the serene antics of the realized Buddha spirit of such a great Master. Warren finally reached the preliminary kindergarten stage of getting his own koan, a paradoxical question to form the empty mind of meditation. Each devotee received his own koan like a rabbit's foot to stroke and treasure, an unanswerable question to torment him month after month, perhaps year after year, until enlightenment burst over and he was able to answer it when the Master gently asked it of him the hundred millionth time. Warren walked in bowed, kneeled on the straw mat. The Master was smoking and making each breath visible as a plume of cigarette smoke and Warren knew the standard koans, the famous ones, there were actually collections of them like college course outlines but the one given to him he had never heard before or read anywhere and it was delivered by the Master with a shake of his head, a sigh and a glance of helpless supplication at the ceiling: Penfield-san, said the Master, if this is a religion for warriors, what are *you* doing here? Warren thanked him, bowed and backed out of the room even though the Master looked as if he was going to say something more. Later in his first pondering of this infinitely resounding question he squatted by his favorite place, near the garden gate beyond the gravel garden, and saw through the slats as for the first time the beautiful little girl who swept the street.

I drove out of the mountains through the night and found the way to Utica, New York, coming into city streets in the rain at three o'clock, passing freight yards, warehouses. She was asleep, I didn't want to wake her, I bumped the car gently across the railroad tracks and headed south and west toward Pittsburgh.

I wanted to log as many miles as I could before Bennett got up in the morning.

By dawn I was clear-eyed exhausted, feeling my nerves finely strung, the weariness in the hinges of my jaws, you are never more alert. Red lights in the dawn at intersections between fields, I saw the light of dawn shoot clear down the telegraph wires like a surge of power, I passed milk trucks and heard train whistles the sun came up and flooded my left eye suddenly it was day commerce was on the roads we had survived Loon Lake and were cruising through the United States of America.

I woke her for breakfast, we walked into a diner—some town in Pennsylvania. Clara in her fur jacket and long dress and Junior in his knickers and sweater. Someone dropped a plate. Clara is not awake yet— a hard sleeper, a hard everything—she sits warming her hands on her coffee cup, studies the tabletop.

"This won't do," I said, steering her by the arm to the car.

"What?"

"It's asking for trouble."

I found an Army-Navy Surplus Store. I bought myself a regular pair of pants, work shirt, socks, a wool seaman's cap and khaki greatcoat. I bought Clara a black merchant marine pullover and a pea jacket. I made her change her clothes in the back of the store. Then I did.

Mr. Penfield had pressed upon me about eighty dollars in clean soft ones and fives, bills that looked as if they had spent years in a shoe box. I added to this the forty dollars or so of my own fortune. The clothes had come to twenty-eight, and another dollar and change for breakfast.

"What kind of money do you have?"

"Money?"

"I want to see what our cash assets are."

"I don't have any money."

"That's really swell."

"Look in my bag if you don't believe me."

"Well, how far did you think you could go without money?"

"I don't know. You tell me."

It was the best of conversations, all I could have wished for. I scowled. I drove hard.

We took the bumps in unison, we leaned at the same angle on the curves. I didn't know where we were going and she didn't ask. I drove to speed. I stopped wondering what she was feeling, what she was thinking. She was happy on the move, alert and at peace, all the inflamed spirit was lifted from her. She had various ways of arranging herself in the seat, legs tucked up or one under the other, or arms folded, head down, but in any position definitive, beautiful.

Come with me

Late that afternoon we were going up a steep hill along the Monongahela, Pittsburgh spreading out below us, stacks of smoke, black sky, crucible fire. By nightfall I was numb, I couldn't drive another mile. We were in some town in eastern Ohio, maybe it was Steubenville, I'm not sure. On a narrow street I found the Rutherford Hayes, a four-story hotel with fire escapes and a barber's pole at the entrance. I took a deep breath and pulled up to the curb.

In the empty lobby were the worn upholstered chairs and half-dead rubber plants that would have been elegance had I not been educated at Loon Lake. I had never stayed at a hotel but I knew what to do from the movies.

I got us upstairs without incident and tipped the bellboy fifty cents. "Yes, suh!" he said. I chain-locked the door behind him.

We had a corner room with large windows, each covered with a dark green pull shade and flimsy white curtains. Everything had a worn-out look, a great circle of wear in the middle of the rug. I liked that. I liked the idea of public accommodation, people passing through. Bennett could keep his Loon Lake. I looked out the window. We were on the top floor, we had a view of greater Steubenville. In the bathroom was a faucet for ice water.

Clara, who had been in hotels before, found the experience unexceptional. She opened her overnight bag and took over the bathroom. I smoked a cigarette and listened to the sounds of her bathing. I kept looking around the room as if I expected to see someone else. Who? We were alone, she was alone with me and nobody knew where we were. I was smiling. I was thinking of myself crouched in the weeds in the cold night while a train goes by and a naked girl holds a white dress before a mirror.

This was a double bed I had booked and she hadn't even blinked. That would seem reason to hope. But for Clara Lukaćs there was no necessary significance in sleeping beside somebody in the same bed. She came out of the bathroom without a stitch. I undressed and turned out the light as cool in my assumptions as I could be. A high whine of impatience, a kind of child's growl, and a poke of her elbow was what I got when I happened to move against her in the dark. Just testing.

She curled up with her back toward me, and those vertebrae which I had noticed and loved were all at once deployed like the Maginot Line.

In the morning she woke out of sorts, mean.

"What in hell am I doing here?" she muttered. "Jesus," she said, looking at me. "I must be out of my mind."

I was stunned. My first impulse was to appeal.

"Look at him, hunky king of the road there. Oh, this is great—this really is great." She snapped up the window shade and looked out. "God damn him," she said. "And his wives and his boats and choo-choo trains."

She began to dress. She held up blouses, skirts, looked at them, flung them down. She sat abruptly on the bed with her arms full of clothes and she stared at the floor.

"Hey," I said. "I told you I'd get you out of there and I did. Didn't I?" She didn't answer.

"Hey, girlie," I said, "didn't I? You have a complaint? You think you're some hot-ass bargain?"

"You bet I am, hunky, I can promise you."

"Well then, go on," I said. "Go back to your fancy friends and see what they do for you. Look what they already done."

I got out of bed, pulled on my pants and socks, and stuck my feet in my shoes.

"Where are you going?" she said.

"Here," I said, taking out my wallet. I crumpled a couple of singles and threw them on the floor. "That and a twitch of your ass will get you back to the loons."

"You're not leaving," she said. "You're not leaving me here!"

"You can go back to your career fucking for old men," I said. I put on my shirt and combed my hair in the mirror over the dresser. "It's probably as good as you can do anyhow."

The mirror shattered. I didn't know what she had thrown. When I went for her she was reaching for the Gideon Bible to throw that. I grabbed her arm and we knocked the bedside lamp to the floor. I pinned her to the bed. She tried to bite me. I held her by the wrists and put my knees on each point of the pelvis.

"You're hurting me!" I moved back and let go of her. She lay still. A queer bitter smell came from her. It was anger that aroused her, confrontation was the secret.

But when I found her she was loving and soft and she shrank away softer and more innocent of her feelings than I had dreamed.

I held her, I loved the narrow shoulders, the small-boned frailness of her, the softness of her breasts against me. I was kissing her eyes, her cheeks, but she cried in the panic of the sensation, her legs couldn't find their place, she was like a swimmer kicking out or like someone trying to shinny up a pole.

I wanted her to know the sudden certainty declaring in me like God. I was where I belonged! I remembered this!

But she didn't seem to be aware of how I felt, there was this distracted spirit of her, her head shook from side to side with bursts of voice, like sobs, as if someone was mourned.

Our lovemaking was like song or like speech. "Don't you see," I asked again and again, "don't you understand?" And she shook her head from side to side in her distraction. I couldn't overcome this. I became insistent, I felt my time running out, I felt I had to break into her recognition. It's you, I wanted her to say, and she wouldn't she wouldn't say the words.

And then the tenderness was gone and I was pounding the breath from her, beating ugly grunts of sound from her, wanting her to form words but hearing savage stupid gusts of voiceless air coming from her.

In my moment of stunned paralytic grief I groan I go off bucking I think I hear her laugh.

For several days we made our life sleeping till mid-morning and getting on the road and driving again till the sun went down and we could find a bed. We drove through boarded-up towns, we ate blue-plate specials and we slept in rooming houses with linoleum on the floor and outhouses in back or in small motor-court cabins with the sound all night of the trucks rolling past. Night and morning we made love it was what we did our occupation our exercise. But always with great suspense in my mind. I never knew if it would happen again. I didn't have the feeling anything was established in her. She fucked in a kind of lonely self-intensification. She slept without touching me, she slept with no need to touch or hold me, she went off to sleep and it was as if I weren't there.

I would think about this lying in the dark while she slept. I was there for her, I was what she assumed, and I was willing to be that, to be the assumption she didn't even know she was making. And then one day she'd discover that she loved me.

Once in a while, usually in the numb exhaustion of daybreak, I'd look into her face and see an aspect there of the acknowledgment I wanted in the gold-washed green eyes. There would be humor in them. The lips slightly swollen and open, the small warm puff of breath. She'd giggle to see neither of us was dead and she'd give me a cracklipped kiss a soft dry kiss with the hot pulp of her lip against mine.

She liked to be inside her appetites and her feelings. Whatever they were. One day in a rainstorm I skidded off the road. I was frantically spinning the wheel, I couldn't see through the rain, it had turned white, opaque, but Clara was laughing and shrieking like a kid on a carnival ride. We thudded into a ditch. Water softened the canvas top and began to leak through and we sat at a tilt as if in a diving plane, in clouds. I thought we might drown. Then we felt the car rise, somehow the water floated us free, and when the storm passed over, we gently drifted a half mile or so in the flood like some stately barge down a stream. She loved it, she loved every second of it, her fingers gripping my arm, the nails digging into my skin.

Sometimes we went out at night walking some main street to a local movie. She liked to stop in a tavern and drink ten-cent beers, she liked the looks she got, the sexual alert that went off every time she walked into a bar or a diner. One time someone came over to the booth and started to talk to her as if I weren't even there. It seemed to me unavoidable what I had to do. He was an amiable fellow with a foolish grin, but with the strength in him of belonging in this bar, of being known in this bar, this town, he looked down and saw my knife, the tip making an indentation in the blue shirt and the sprung gut. He was genuinely astonished, they don't use knives in boondocks of the Midwest, he backed off with his palms up.

She had turned pale. "What's the idea, do you know what you're doing?" She spoke in a soft urgent whisper leaning toward me over the table.

"I do," I said, "and if you don't stand up and get your ass moving I'll do the same to you."

Outside I grabbed her arm. She was in a cold rage but I had the feeling, too, that I had done right, that I had shown her something she wanted to see.

"You know something?" she said as I hurried her along to our room. "You're crazy, you know that?"

I thought they were the first words of love I'd heard from her.

In Dayton, Ohio, I saw in the rear-view mirror the unmistakable professional interest of a traffic cop as we drove away from his intersection.

"I have not been smart," I said. "I suppose my mind has been on other things."

I made a sharp turn into a side street and started looking for the poor part of town.

"What's the matter?"

"A German convertible with bud vases and New York plates. You don't often see that in these here parts."

She thought awhile. "Is this a hot car?"

"In a manner of speaking."

Soon enough we were going through the dingy sections where the bums were standing on the sidewalks and the garbage spilled into the streets. The Buckeye State Used Cars enterprise looked grim and satisfactorily seedy, I turned in there and commenced a negotiation. The man with his fat dirty fingernails showed me there was not even a book on such a car. I said that was because it was so expensive they didn't figure anyone could afford it. He said maybe so, but how could he sell a car where you could not get the parts if they broke? I said nothing ever broke on a car like this. He said how could he take ownership on a car that had no papers? I said it was my family's car and since when did you walk around with papers of your own family's car? He said why did I want to sell my family's car? I said I was running away to get married and needed cash. "How are you going to run if you don't have no car anymore?" he said. "I'm going to buy a modest well-tuned vehicle from you," I said, looking with bright honest earnestness into his face.

He walked around the car several times. He glanced at Clara in the front seat, I had told her to put on her fur jacket. "That is my fiancée," I said to him softly, "of whom they don't approve." I could see him thinking: They wouldn't go after their own kid.

Come with me

Combust with me

"Someday," Clara said over the noise, "maybe you'll be able to buy it back, or one like it."

"What?"

"I said someday you could hope to get it back."

"I've got my car," I said, pounding the dashboard. "I've got papers for it. I've got a hundred fifty simoleons in my pocket. Is that bad? We can get to California if we're careful."

"California?"

"That's where we're going. Didn't you know?"

"I wasn't informed," she said, holding on to the leather strap over the door. She peered ahead, frowning. I had taken in partial trade a 1930 Chevrolet station wagon with wood-panel sides that shook and rattled, and floorboards that jumped in the air every time we hit a bump. It had a high polish on its tan-and-brown body and admitted to fifty thousand miles.

didn't know dead people were that unusual. I saw them all the time. I wandered around holding my bottle and seeing these dead hunkies lying on tables. I dragged my blanket around behind me. I wasn't frightened. My father would smile at me.

"When I was older I began to understand things a little more. I thought, for instance, that anyone who was dead had to have a hole in them. I didn't know people died without holes in them. Then I figured it out one day. Some old guy was being dressed who died of natural causes. He'd made it all the way. So I knew then about natural death.

"But it was just the business, you know, it was nothing special, we lived in an apartment right over the business I played after school outside in front of the stoop and there was my father driving up with his hearse, they'd back up into the garage and he and my brother took the body into the back. And that was the way things were on West Twenty-ninth Street.

"And then my mother died but my father didn't handle it, someone else from another funeral parlor came and took her away. Just like doctors don't treat their own families. But maybe it was because she was religious. None of our church got buried with us. We were Greek Orthodox but the business was nondenominational. My father was not highly regarded in church. I saw more Romans and Jewish rabbis at Lukaćs' than I did priests. Anyway, my father moped around a long time. He didn't know what to do with me. He hired this black lady to take care of me. She was okay but she drank. She stood at the window whenever there was a funeral downstairs. She'd count the numbers of cars to see how important the dead guy was. She'd count the number of flower cars. Sometimes she called me to come look and I began to look too. You'd see all these flowers in the flower cars, sometimes in three, four cars of flowers, it was too much, like huge mounds of popcorn, I didn't like it. I hate cut flowers. All my life they made a stink coming up through the floor below, there was always somebody downstairs you could smell flowers through the dumb-waiter.

"But then if it was really a big affair it would be worth watching. My father and brother all dressed up in their shiny black suits. He'd hire on men on these days. People coming to pay their respects, filling the parlor, crowds standing out on the street. And then outside all the cars in a line, double-parked with their headlights on, all these black mourners' cars twice around the block. And the cops would be there checking on who showed up, standing across the street and watching. And the photographers with their big flash cameras taking pictures, and the next morning in the *News* or the *Mirror* there was a picture of somebody and in the background the canopy said Lukaćs' Funeral Parlor.

"But he didn't need the publicity and he didn't care. He was just some dumb hunky, he didn't care about anything, he didn't talk much, he just did this work. And he got this clientele over the years, he wasn't in the rackets himself, but he kept his mouth shut and didn't make judgments and he just got to be the one they used. He didn't care who he buried, why should he, the kind of work he did why get excited. After a while he had to expand. He bought the brownstone next door, and put a new streamlined face across both houses. And then there was a showroom and a reception desk.

"And I was pretty grown-up now. I wouldn't stay in school. I'd worked for a while at the five-and-ten just to have something to do. But he was getting fancy now and he needed someone for the reception desk and to answer the phone who could talk right. So he asked me. So I thought, Why not? I mean when I was a kid I used to get it at school. That's why I had no friends at St. Clare's. They came around at Halloween with sheets on and rang the front bell. Clara Cadaver, Clara Cadaver. Well, shit, I only had boyfriends, anyway. I mean as a kid my friends were boys. I played street hockey.

"But anyway, I didn't mind. I wore a black dress. I wore stockings and high-heeled shoes. I had an allowance for the beauty parlor. And that was my job. I got to meet some real people. It was an entrée, as they say. What's that sound? The engine doesn't sound right."

"No," I said, "it's okay. Maybe I need a little oil."

"It's getting dark, anyway—where do you suppose we are?"

"Are you hungry?"

"A little."

I had a terrible feeling, a chilled feeling because of her lineage, her criminal lineage, I thought of it as a caste, some kind of contamination she had been born into through no fault of her own and I thought it was mine now too; if I wanted her, what she was was mine too, what she brought with her we both had now.

But I was also happy that she had told me, that in the dreamlife of the road the hours sitting next to each other and facing in the same direction brought things out we might not have otherwise said. We told each other about our lives, we gave each other our lives while we looked at the road backward into ourselves. Even though afterward we didn't remember what we said, or were too proud to admit we remembered.

"We lived across the river from each other, you realize that? We could have shouted at each other across the Hudson, two snot-nosed kids. Little did we know we were destined to meet! We saw the same Tom Mix movies. We ran along the sidewalks pointed to the sky at the same airships!"

"What?"

"No, really, playing hockey"—I wanted to make her smile—"don't you remember? Maybe our teams played each other. We made the puck from the end of the wooden cream-cheese box, right? We wrapped it in black tape, am I right?"

It seemed very important in this moment to make her smile.

"Don't you remember? Don't you remember the 'I cash clothes' man? On Twenty-ninth Street? The water wagon, running alongside it for the spray? Don't you remember how we went to the candy store for ice cream?"

"What are you talking about?"

"No, really, Clara. One hot afternoon we bought Dixie cups and stood on the sidewalk in the sun with our wooden spoons. You remember. Licking the ice cream off Joan Crawford's face?"

When Clara fell asleep I put on my coat, closed the door quietly and went out to look around. In addition to everything else snow had hit this burg, a heavy wet fall that stuck to your eyelashes and got into your shoes.

The rooming house was highway robbery—twelve dollars a week, paid in advance. Restaurants came to another two, three dollars a day. If I took her to the movies, another forty, fifty cents.

I had even bought her a gold wedding band—for her protection, I said.

I hadn't told her there was no money to get the valves reground. She thought we were in Jacksontown another day or two at the most. I could manage two day-coach fares to Chicago. But what would we do in Chicago—freeze our ass there?

And so, hunched in his khaki coat from the Great War, the big spender wandered through downtown Jacksontown, Indiana—Heart of the Hoosier Nation, as the sign said. Everything built of red brick, the bank, the library, the city hall, the armory. Stores occupied, the black cars parked at angles against the curbs, he notices the traffic, a heavy traffic rolling quietly through the snow, the sky gray, heavy flakes like soundproofing tamping down the horns, muffling the engines, even the streetcars grinding along hushed in the flanges, sparks flaring in the dark afternoon, the dark turrets of the armory the dark green cannon on the lawn with the mantle of white snow.

I saw everywhere on every street jalopies of every description, valises and boxes strapped to their fenders, children and grandparents high in the rear seats, scarfs wrapped around their heads. I saw furniture covered with blankets tied with rope on the beds of broken-down trucks. I saw out-of-state license plates: Kentucky Tennessee Georgia Arkansas Michigan Missouri.

I boarded the Railroad Street trolley to see what would happen. It banged its way sharply around corners and picked up speed. Soon it was out of the downtown area barreling between two endless rows of semiattached bungalows, block after block. Eventually it veered into a dark street, a canyon of the sides of buildings, moving slowly now, many men walking in the street, the bell clanged, an unbroken chain-link fence blurred my eyes, if I opened the window I could touch it.

Last stop the doors hissed open at the main gate. Here a crowd of men stood waiting to get in, a quiet intense crowd not orderly but silent. The snow came down. Even as I watched, the crowd grew pulsing like something underwater.

Behind the locked gates uniformed men stood chatting as if nothing was going on.

I looked up at the block-long sign across the tops of two buildings. BENNETT AUTOBODY NUMBER SIX was what it said.

That evening I took Clara to dinner at the Jacksontown Inn, the best restaurant in town. It had tablecloths, candles, black busboys, and the roast beef au jus went for two dollars and a half.

"I see in the paper where every state is covered with snow from here to the Rockies," I said.

She eyed me warily. The true color of her hair beginning to come through, her hair was fluffier too, she had given up the beauty parlor she believed they would ruin her if she had her hair done in the Midwest.

"Anyway," I said, "I did a little exploring while you were having a nap. We could be in worse places. There are jobs here, people have money in their pockets, they're shopping in the stores and going to the movies. They have three movie houses downtown."

She cut her roast beef.

"And you want to hear something funny? The big employer and why everything is humming is your friend and mine Frankie W. Bennett. His Number Six plant."

She put down her knife and fork, dabbed at her mouth with her napkin and sat there.

"Oh, Clara," I said. "I'd be happy if I could just look at you across this table for the rest of my life."

"That would be a lot of roast beef," she said.

"You didn't wear your gold ring!"

"I forgot."

I ate and drank energetically. "Anyway," I said, "as long as we're stuck here—so long—as we're here awhile—I thought I'd tap into old Frank—build up our cash reserve for the run to California."

"What does that mean?"

"Well, they're hiring at the Number Six plant."

"So?"

A sip of water from my cut-glass goblet. "I caught on there this afternoon. Nothing to it. I just gave them my shining innocent face. I mean there were these guys standing around with their toolboxes and employment records all wanting the same dumb unskilled jobs I put in for. No contest."

"Why?"

"Because it was obvious I didn't have a union background. They don't want someone who's a wiseass. They want the ones who don't know any better."

"Why did you do it?" she said.

"I thought I explained," I said. "I thought I explained that."

She didn't say anything, we resumed dining. Occasionally she'd look up and smile sweetly at me, in the silence there at the Jacksontown Inn the unarguable terror of things was driven home to me.

"I don't see why you should get on your high horse," I said. "Is it any worse than sleeping in his bed? Is it any worse than stealing his car?"

"I think I've got to leave now." She stood.

"Do you mind if I pay the damn check?"

We walked through the snow back to the room. I grabbed her elbow, she shrugged me off. "Clara, for God's sake, what is it I've done, after all? I got a job! A job! Is it a fucking crime to get a job? There's no money! We're here in the real world now, don't you understand? There's no money!"

In the room she started to pack. I willed myself to be calm, there were other roomers on the same floor, I didn't need landlady trouble on top of everything else. "Clara, please don't be like this. Please listen. All right, this is the worst shithole town in the frozenest fucking country there is. It's so fucking cold I can't believe how cold it is. And there's no reason to stay here. Except that it's Bennett's! That's why, Clara. That is the true reason why. Because I'm gonna work his line without his knowing and walk away from his machine with my wages in my pocket and he's going to get us to California! That's why."

She was still.

"You hear me, Clara? Because it's living right under his nose. That's why. Because it's the riskiest thing! It's the toughest and most dangerous and the classiest thing. That's why."

She sat on the side of the bed. "And what am I supposed to do here all day while you work his line and make your classy wages? Huh, big boy? What am I supposed to do?"

My God, it was laughable, it was heartbreaking but at least she asked the question. Neither of us was twenty! We were children—who were we, what chance did we have? In her question was one half of an instant's perceiving, dimly appreciated, of only the most obvious possibility of life comprising the history of mankind.

I sat on the side of the bed next to her, whispering in her ear, "You don't realize what you've done to me. Me, the carney kid! You're making an honest man of him, it's horrible. I have all these godawful longings to work to support you, to make a life with you, I want us to live together in one place, I don't care where, I don't care if it's the North Pole, I'll do any fucking thing to keep you in bonbons and French novels, Clara, and it's all your fault.''

''Oh Jesus, he's crazy, this boy is crazy.''

But I felt this weird tickle-behind-the-spine unprecedented truth of what I was saying. Before I said it I hadn't known I felt it: we could change, we could make our lives however we wanted! And the steps Clara had taken to molldom and to the high forest of Loon Lake were dainty steps, steps avoiding the muck of her reality and mine. And this was where we truly belonged, not on the road but stationary, in one place, working it all out in the hard life.

''You got anything better to do?'' I said.

She sighed. ''That's the crying shame of it.''

Data comprising life F. W. Bennett undergoing review.
Shown in two instances twenty-five years apart of labor
relations lacking compassion or flexible policy understanding
workers' needs. His dramatization suggests life devoted almost
entirely to selfish accumulation of wealth and ritual use thereof
according to established patterns of utmost class. It is
alleged he patronizes unsavory elements of society for his
business gain. It is alleged that he is sexually exploitative.
It is suggested he is at least unmoved by the violent death
of another human attributable to his calculated negligence.

Countervailing data re his apparent generosity to
worthless poet scrounge and likely drunkard Warren Penfield.
A hint too of his pride in Lucinda Bailey Bennett's aviation
achievements. A heart too for spunky
derelict kids.
Your register respectfully advises the need for additional
countervailing data. History suggests of the class of which Mr.
F. W. Bennett is a member no unalloyed spirit of evil the dimes
which John D. Rockefeller senior gave away compulsively to
people in the street became the multimillions of his sons'
philanthropies. Andrew Carnegie's beneficence well attested,
as well as William Randolph Hearst's Milk Fund for Babies.
And examination of the general practice of families of
immeasurable wealth in US suggests their generosity cannot
be explained entirely as self-serving public relations but
may be seen as manifesting anthropologically identified
principle of potlatch observed operating in primitive social
systems throughout the world from northern forest aboriginals
to unclad natives of tropical paradises. The principle
regardless of currency of benefaction breadfruit pigs palm

fronds or dollars is that wealth is accumulated so that
it can be given away thus bringing honor to the giver.
I refer to an American landscape from every region of which
rise hospitals universities libraries museums planetaria
parks think-tanks and other institutions for the public weal
all of which are the benefactions of the utmost class.
I cite achievements F. W. Bennett in his lifetime the original
endowments of the Western miners' Black Lung Research Facility,
Denver, Colorado. The Gymnasium of Miss Morris' School,
Briarcliff Manor NY, the Mexican Silver Workers' Church of the
Holy St. Clare, Popxacetl Mexico, The Bennett Library on the
grounds of Jordan College, Rhinebeck NY, the Bennett
Engineering Institute, Albany NY, plus numerous ongoing
benefactions of worthy charities and researches plus innumerable
acts of charity to individuals never publicized.

I attribute to F. W. Bennett in his death a last will and
testament of such public generosity as to receive acknowledgment
on the front page of the New York *Times* data available
upon request.

Generally speaking a view of the available economic systems
that have been tested historically must acknowledge the immense
power of capitalism to generate living standards food housing
education the amenities to a degree unprecedented in human
civilization. The benefits of such a system while occasionally
random and unpredictable with periods of undeniable stress
and misery depression starvation and degradation are
inevitably distributed to a greater and greater percentage
of the population. The periods of economic stability also
ensure a greater degree of popular political freedom
and among the industrial Western democracies today despite
occasional suppression of free speech quashing of dissent
corruption of public officials and despite the tendency of
legislation to serve the interests of the ruling business
oligarchy the poisoning of the air water the chemical adulteration
of food the obscene development of hideous weaponry the
increased costs of simple survival the waste of human resources
the ruin of cities the servitude of backward foreign populations
the standards of life under capitalism by any criterion are
far greater than under state socialism in whatever forms
it is found British Swedish Cuban Soviet or Chinese. Thus
the good that fierce advocacy of personal wealth accomplishes
in the historical run of things outweighs the bad. And while
we may not admire always the personal motives of our business

leaders we can appreciate the inevitable percolation of the
good life as it comes down through our native American soil.
You cannot observe the bounteous beauty of our country nor take
pleasure in its most ordinary institutions in peace and safety
without acknowledging the extraordinary achievement of
American civilization. There are no Japanese bandits lying
in wait on the Tokaidoways after all. Drive down the
turnpike past the pretty painted pipes of the oil refineries
and no one will hurt you.

No claim for the perfection of F. W. Bennett, only that like
all men he was of his generation and reflected his times in
his person. We know that by the nineteen-fifties at an advanced
age he had come finally to see unions as partners in
enterprise and to cooperate fully on a first-name basis with
major labor leaders playing golf of course at that age he
only drove a ball twenty or thirty yards but they called him
Mr. Frank and with humor admired his sportif outfits the
beige-yellow slacks the brown-and-white shoes with the tassels
the Hawaiian shirt with his breasts showing. Note is made here
too that this man had a boyhood, after all, woke
in the astonishment of a bedsheet of sap suffered acne
had feelings which frightened him and he tried to suppress
was cruelly motivated by unthinking adults perhaps rebuffed
or humiliated by a teacher these experiences are not the
sole prerogative of the poor poverty is not a moral
endowment and a man who has the strength to help himself
can help others. I cite too the ordinary fears of
mortality the inspection of a fast-growing mole on the side
of the nose blood in the stool a painful injury or the
mournful witness of the slow death of a parent all this is
given to all men as well as the starting awake in the
nether hours of the night from such glutinous nightmare
that one's self name relationships nationality place in life
all data of specificity wipe out amnesiatically asiatically you
don't even know the idea human it is such a low hour of the
night and he shares that with all of us. I therefore declare
F. W. Bennett to embody the fullness of the perplexity of
living, as they say.

I cite here his voice which people who knew him only in his
later years believed to be ridden and cracked with his age
but in fact his voice had always been rather high reedy
with a gravelly consistency around its edges and some people
found this menacing but others thought it avuncular

especially after his operation for cataracts when they wear
those goggle glasses. But it was one of those voices of such
individual character that people who never heard it can
imagine it just by the mention of his name and those standing
in the great crush of honors at his funeral could believe
themselves likely to hear it for many years afterward as if a
man of this strong presence could not release his hold on
life except very very slowly and, buried or not, manifest
a half life, probably, of twenty-five thousand years.

was on headlights. First I attached with four screws two metal frames the screws lay in a bin the frames met at the convergence of two small belts the left frame from the left belt the right down the line. Sometimes the pieces didn't match, sometimes the wrong piece came down the wrong side and sometimes, the thread not being true, I had to hammer the screws in, everybody did.

Next I affixed the crossed pieces to the inside of a curl of tin shaped like a flowerpot. I then inserted through a hole in the pot about four feet of insulated wire that came to hand dangling from a big spool overhead. I snipped the wire with a pair of shears, knotted the wire so it wouldn't slip and put the whole thing back on the line for the next man, who did the electrical connections, slapped on the chrome and sent it on to the main line for mounting on a fender.

That was the operation it's what I did.

High above my head the windows of the great shed hung open like bins and the sun came through the meshed glass already broken down, each element of light attached to its own atom of dust and there was no light except on the dust and between was black space, like the night around stars. Mr. Autobody Bennett was a big man who could do that to light, make the universe punch in like the rest of us.

And all around me the noise of running machines, conveyor belts, the creaking of pulleys, screeching of worked metal, shouts, the great gongs of autobodies on the line, the blast of acetylene riveting, the rattling of moving treads, the cries of mistakes and mysterious intentions.

And then continuously multiplied the same sounds repeated compounded by echoes. An interesting philosophical problem: I didn't know at any moment what I heard was what was happening or what had already happened.

It was enough to make me think of my father. The man was a fucking hero.

Then they speed things up and I'm going too slow I drop one of the tin pots on the wrong side of the belt the guy there is throwing tires on wheel rims and giving the tubes a pump or two of air he ignores my shouts he can't take the time. And then the foreman is coming down the line to pay me a call I can't hear him but I don't have to—a red bulging neck of rage.

And then they stop coddling us and throw the throttle to full and this is how I handle it: I am Fred Astaire in top hat and tails tossing up the screws into the holes, bouncing the frames on the floor and catching them in my top hat of tin. I twirl the headlight kick it on the belt with a backward flip of my heel. I never stop moving and when the belt is too slow for me I jump up and stomp it along faster, my arms outstretched. Soon everyone in the plant has picked up on my routine—everyone is dancing! The foreman comes pirouetting along, putting stars next to each name on his clipboard. And descending from the steel rafter by insulated wire to dance backward on the moving parade of car bodies, Mr. Bennett himself in white tie and tails. He's singing with a smile, he's flinging money from his hands like stardust.

Shit, how many more hours of this . . . I thought of Clara I thought of us driving to California in the spring. And then I thought, What if she just left, what if she met someone and said to him, *How do I get out of here?*

And then I resolved not to think at all, if I couldn't think well of Clara, I'd turn my mind from her knowing I was racked, knowing I couldn't physically feel hope in this hammering noise. But I didn't have to try not to think, by the middle of the afternoon my bones were vibrating like tuning forks. And so it had me, Bennett Autobody, just where it wanted me and I was screwed to the machines taking their form a mile away in the big shed, those black cars composed bit by bit from our life and the gift of opposition of thumb and forefinger, those precious vehicles, each one a hearse.

On the other hand everyone had the same problem I heard stories of people hauling off on a foreman, or pissing on the cars, or taking a sledge hammer to them, good stories, wonderful stories, probably not true. But the telling of them was important. I was the youngest on my line, jokes were made about that—what a woman could still hope for from someone my age. Jokes were important.

The line was a complex society with standards of conduct honor serious moral judgment. You did your work but didn't kiss ass, you stood up for yourself when you had to but didn't whine or complain, you kept your eyes open and your mouth shut, you didn't make outlandish claims brag threaten.

Yet none of this was visible when we pressed through the gates in the evening, a nameless faceless surge of men in soft caps in full flight.

Clara and I lived on Railroad, the street of the endless two-family bungalows. I had my choice—to take the streetcar, which was faster, or walk and save the carfare.

I ran.

I stopped only long enough to pick up a movie magazine or *True Confessions,* I liked to bring her small surprises keep her busy keep her occupied.

Sometimes I'd find her waiting at the window looking out the window—the dark industrial sky, the great bobbing crowd of men flowing down Railroad Street making a whispering sound on the cobblestones like some dry Midwestern sea—and she'd be holding her arms, the bleak mass life scared her as some elemental force she hadn't known, not even realized by the way she stood and watched that she gave it her deference.

We ate things heated from cans. We had two plates two cups two spoons two knives two forks. Our mansion was furnished army-camp fashion by the company. Behind the back porch was the outhouse.

We stayed in the kitchen till bedtime, I tossed pieces of coal in the stove, it never seemed to be enough. Clara sat reading, she wore her fur jacket she wore it all the time. She was fair and couldn't take the cold, the winter had done something to her face, coarsened it, rubbed the glamour from it. Five minutes out of doors her eyes watered, her cheeks flamed up. She didn't use make-up anymore.

All of it was all right with me. I still couldn't take my eyes off her. I tried to remember the insolent girl with the wineglass in her hand and the firelight in her eyes.

"I'm glad you're laughing," she said.

I had a scheme for getting us from kitchen to bed. I heated water in the black coffee pot and then ran the pot like a hot iron over the mattress. I undressed her under the covers.

I loved it cold, I loved the way she came to me when it was cold, as if she couldn't get close enough. But this particular evening I remember she stopped me in my lovemaking, she put her arm on my shoulder and said *Shhh.*

"You hear that?" she said.

"What?"

"Next door. They've got a radio."

I lay on my back and listened. I heard the wind blowing the snow in gusts along Railroad Street. Sometimes the snow came in through the cracks and in the morning you'd find it lying like dust inside the front door.

"I don't hear anything," I said.

"Listen."

And then I heard it, very softly through the wall, it was dance music, the swing band of a warmer world, it made me think of men and women on a terrace under a full moon.

Their place—the mirror of our three rooms—astounds me. No trace of company domicile, it's all been washed from the walls and strained from the light coming in off the street. We sit on stuffed horsehair chairs, there is a matching sofa, behind the sofa a lamp with a square translucent shade of the deco design. A braided rug covers the parlor floor and glass curtains adorn the windows. Amazing. On the desk in the corner a private phone. Who would have thought people on Railroad Street had their own phones?

The subtle giving to the newcomers of their protection. Lyle James smiles sitting on the sofa with his hands on his overalled knees, he's one of those crackers, hair like steel wool, reddish going to gray, a face of freckles so that he appears to be behind them looking from his pink-lidded eyes through them as from some prison of his own innocence, buckteeth smiling.

What does he see? In Jacksontown, crossroads of the world, he thinks he'll see everything given enough time. These two are just getting their legs, the boy looking at her as if she's sick about to die, or have a fit, but it's his fit more likely, that's what's important to this boy, not how he feels but how she feels. And she, one spooked little old girl, she smokes her cigarettes, crosses her legs, stares at the floor, that's the way it is with folks from the East.

Mrs. James comes in from the kitchen holding a platter with chocolate cake and cups and saucers and napkins. Another freckled-face redhead, but a pretty one with light eyes, a plump mouth sullen in a child, provocative in a woman. Which is she? She is very shy, blushing when her husband boasts that she baked the cake herself. She wears an unbuttoned sweater over her dress, school shoes, ankle socks.

We're all Bennett people, neighbors, fellow workers, this is Clara, hello, this is Sandy, hi, Clara, this is Lyle, this is Joe.

They are Southerners, like so many of them here, but with my tenacity, I recognize it, they talk slower but feel the same. He must be thirty-five, a lot older than his wife, crow's-feet under the freckles, they act dumb but I don't believe it.

I detected the sly rube who liked to take city slickers.

Clara talks to the wife. Clara in this conversation is the older woman from New York, Mrs. James maybe sixteen years old stands in awe of that sophistication. And then a baby is brought out, the child wife has a baby!

The establishment of them sitting modestly for our admiration: people are strong, they prove themselves. You see, Clara? You can wrest life from a machine and walk away.

" 'A course," he was saying, "all this work ain't just the season. You wouldn't know but they was a wildcat strike last summer. Quite a to-do at the main gate. The company brought in strikebreakers. A feller was killed. They closed the plant down, fired everone. Everone!"

I nod, this is man talk.

The baby began to cry, the young mother unbuttoned and gave her breast right in the parlor, neither of them made anything of it. I glanced at Clara. She was intent. She watched the infant suck, she watched the mother and child. Expressed in Sandy James' face just that absorption in the task as the doll mother's in her solemn game.

"I started out in trim," Lyle says. "Now I hang doors. You get a few more cents a hour. Hands don't cut up so bad. Lemme see your hands," he said. I held them out, swollen paws, a thousand cuts. "Yeah," he says, "that's it."

After a while he went over to the radio we had heard, obviously his pride and joy, a Philco console of burled wood big as a jukebox. A circular dial lit up green when he turned it on, it had regular and shortwave broadcasts, and a magic tuning eye like a cat's green eye with a white pupil that grew narrow when he brought in a station.

He had turned it on as casual as he could be and while it warmed up consulted a newspaper. "How 'bout *Mr. First Nighter,*" he said, "seein as you folks're from New York," he said to Clara.

Yes, they had culture!

We sat in dutiful appreciation and listened. Mrs. James had put her baby back to bed and sat now, a child herself, cross-legged on the floor right in front of the speaker, she wanted to get in there behind the cloth with those people.

In the casual grant of their warmth and circumstances we are so installed in the life as to have neighbors, we have started to live in their assumptions. I look at Clara she is way ahead of me, she is wearing her gold band.

As the drama crackled through the night the husband displayed enlightenment as to how the sound effects were made.

Someone kicked down a door. "They don't really wreck a door," he said. "'At's just a ordinary vegetable crate they stomp on. Splinters real good."

A horse-drawn carriage. ''Shucks, them's coconut shells rapped on the table.''

''Hush, Loll,'' his wife said. ''I cain't hear!''

After the program was over he lectured on how they made houses burn, typhoons blow, trees come down. He had us close our eyes and did these things up against our ears to get the effect of amplification. He was good, too, insane, I began to realize, once people got through their courtesy it was their madness they shared.

He had heard some *Arabian Nights* drama about a desert chieftain who skinned his victims alive.

''Ah don't wanna hear this, Loll,'' his wife said.

''Hold on, honey—see, Joe, I couldn't figger it out, Ah thought and thought, it was the damnedest thing! But I got it now, close your eyes a minute, this'll turn your hair white.''

I hear a piteous wail, screams, sinister laughter and the unmistakable stripping off of human skin inch by inch. I have to look. Off my left ear he was tearing a piece of adhesive tape down the middle.

No, not exactly my type, I would not under ordinary circumstances choose to associate with Lyle Red James, but I knew when we walked off to work together in the morning Clara would have coffee with his wife, maybe during the day they'd go to the grocery store together I saw the child given from one pair of arms to the other—I would listen to a hundred nights of radio for that.

And at the front gates of the plant every morning a car or two of cops parked there, just happening to be there. Not that I thought they were looking for me but if they were I imagined Red James as my disguise. If the cops were looking at all, it was for a man walking by himself—that was my reasoning. And anyway, what they would have to accomplish to get to this point wasn't very likely. They would have first of all to locate Mrs. Lucinda Bennett's car in Dayton, the guy wasn't that stupid that he wouldn't paint it. But even if they did, they would know only that they were looking for a wooden station wagon registered to clever Joseph Bennett Jr. But even then, how did that get them to Jacksontown, Indiana? But supposing they were here, they wouldn't find it anyway, it was parked off the street behind a garage and under a ton of snow. I probably couldn't find it myself. But supposing they found it, they'd be on the lookout for a hobo boy, a loner walking by himself to work in the morning and not Mr. Joe Paterson loping along step for step with the world's biggest fucking hayseed.

It always proved out to my satisfaction if I thought about it but that didn't stop me from thinking about it again each morning going to the punch clocks under the thousand fists like rifle fire we are going into the trenches and over the top in the barrage of time clocks, I always checked my position before I went down there.

I sought disguise, every change in Clara and me a disguise, nobody who knew Clara Lukaćs and was in his right mind would look for her on Railroad Street. I liked us having neighbors, yes, and living to the life the same as everyone else, living married, looking like an automobile worker's family for life, appearing to these people next door as mirrors of themselves, shining in their eyes so they couldn't even describe us after we'd gone.

I remember the way Red James walked. He wasn't especially tall but he took long stiff-kneed strides, loping along there in the freezing morning while everyone else was hunched up, head bent in the wind, it was something you had to tear to get through, but here was Red, shoulders back, head up out of his collar, the long neck bobbing, and he chattered constantly, made jokes, told stories.

"A smart man'll put beans in his mule's feedbag. You know why?"

"Why?"

"Doubles the rate of progress."

"Come on."

" 'Strue! The fartin moves 'em along. Clocked a mule once sixty miles a hour on a handful of dry beans. Fastern' 'ese here cars."

That was the kind of thing. He held out his arms; the snow driving thick like white sheets flapping in your eyes, yelling "Toughen me up, God, usen me up to it!"

And he sang, too, always some damn hillbilly song in that adenoidal tenor of his kind as we went down toward the plant one point of raw color bobbing crowing.

Hear the mighty eng-ine
Hear the lonesome hobos squall
. . . A-goin through the jungle
On the Warbash Cannonball!

And at work I found myself hearing his voice in the machines, in the rhythm of the racket, without even knowing it, doing headlight after headlight, I would sing to myself in Red James' tenor: keeping time to the pounding racket, I would hear the mighty eng-ine, hear the lonesome hobos squall, a-goin through the jungle, on the Warbash Cannonball.

One evening I came out of the gate and somebody tapped me on the shoulder. I turned around, no one was there. When I turned back, Red James was grinning at me.

"You comin to the meetin, ain't ya?"

"What meeting?"

"Union meetin."

"Well, I'm not a member, Red."

"I know you ain't. This is a recruitin meetin, anyone's got the balls."

"Well, I don't know," I said. "I never told Clara I wouldn't be home."

"Boy, the little woman sure has a holt a you. She's with Sandy anyways, you come on with me, they'll figger it out."

So I went along with him to this meeting in some decrepit fraternal lodge a few blocks from the plant. It was up a couple of flights, fifty or so men sitting on camp chairs in a badly lighted room. I recognized a few faces from the line, we smiled, catching each other out. I thought, Look, if you're doing the life, do it. I took a seat in the last row. Red had disappeared. The people running the meeting sat at a table in front of the room. I couldn't see all of them but they looked like Paterson toughs, they wore buttons or had their union cards stuck in the bands of their hats. I thought as Mr. Bennett was spread out and made into a corporation he may have enlarged, but so did the response, I couldn't see anyone in his personal service wearing his green putting a union button on their collar.

The meeting began with the pledge of allegiance and then the president rapped the gavel and called on the secretary to read the minutes.

Lyle Red James stood up and cleared his throat. "Herewith the o-fishul minutes a the last meetin," he said in a most formal manner. "As taken by yo Sec'tary Loll Jimes, Bennett Local Seventeen, union card number three six six oh eight?"

This called up a cheer and a burst of applause from the audience.

"Just read the damn minutes, James," the president said.

I hadn't known he was a union official, he had sprung it on me, it was queer, the faintest misgiving, I had thought the deception in our friendship was mine. I tried to think that whole meeting why I was bothered, I knew he was a damn clown I hadn't understood I was his audience.

I wanted to talk to Clara about it when I got home. Anyway, she'd be interested to know why I was late—but something else was on her mind entirely.

"Did you know," she said to me, "Sandy James is all of fifteen years old? Did you know that? She got married at thirteen. Can you beat that? And she does everything, she goes to the store she knows what's good and what isn't, she takes care of that kid like royalty, feeds that stupid hick better than he deserves, washes, shops, cleans, Jesus! The only thing I haven't seen her do is sew the American flag!"

What kind of time was this, a matter of a few weeks, a couple of days, minutes, and this other couple was in us, through us, I couldn't remember when we hadn't known them and lived next door.

In the second war we used to jam each other's radio signals, occupy the frequency, fill it with power.

Clara didn't think much of Red James but she never said no to one of their invitations, she had fixed on young Sandy, in that way she attached to people who interested her, locking on her with all her senses. I sometimes became jealous, actually jealous, I felt ashamed, stupid it was the diversion I had hoped for, it was just what I had counted on, I jammed myself when I saw the way Clara looked at Sandy, watched every move she made. Worrying about survival was something new to her and she was engaged by it, as by the little baby, the smell of milk and throwup, a bath in a galvanized-tin tub with water made hot on a coal stove, and all the ordinary outcomes of domestic life which presented themselves to her as adventure—how could I feel anything except gratitude! I thought every minute with Sandy James put Clara's old life further behind us, I felt each day working for my benefit I was a banker compounding his interest.

In the James kitchen Clara watches Sandy James dry the baby after her bath, the baby in towels on the kitchen table, two lovely heads together and laughing at the small outstretched arms, the gurgling infant, the women laughing with pleasure. I am noticed in the doorway, the heads conspire, the flushed faces, some not quite legible comment between them as they turn and look at me, smiling and giggling in what they know and what I don't.

I liked Sandy myself, I thought of her as my ally, the chaperone of my love, this child! I found her attractive especially in the occasional surprised look she gave me, as if she were an aspect of Clara and the current of attraction was stepped up by that.

"She was made to have babies," Clara said to me. "You can't see how strong she is because she doesn't know anything about clothes, all her things are too big for her, I don't know where she got them, but when she doesn't have anything on you can see how well built she is in the thighs and hips."

Clara's attentiveness to his wife did not go unnoticed by Red James, when we were all together he did what he could to affirm the universal order of things. One night he brought out his infant girl from their bedroom. Baby Sandy had no diaper or shirt. He held her up in his hand and said, "Looky here, Joe, you see this little darlin between her legs? You ever see them pitchers of gourami fish in the *National Geographical*? You know, them kissin fish? Ain't I right? Now I got two of em, two lovin women with poontangs just like that!"

This made Sandy James stare at the floor, her face reddening to the roots of her hair. "Lookit!" he said, laughing. "Colors up like the evenin sun!"

Clara sighed, stubbed out her cigarette and took Sandy and the baby into the other room.

He one night pours two shot glasses of Old Turkey I don't know what we're celebrating does he see Clara's hand touch Sandy's hair?

He says, "Hey, y'll see this here little girl, I kin make her do what I want, laugh, cry, anythang, watch." He begins to laugh, a silly high-pitched little laugh. Sandy ignores him, he jumps around to get in front of her puts his hand over his mouth, tries to keep from laughing, after a minute of his pyrotechnics she can't help herself, begins to laugh, protesting too of course, "*Shh, shh,* your gonna wake her Loll, *shhh,* you're wakin her up!," but he's really funny and she is laughing now, a child laughing, and in fact I'm laughing too at the mindlessness of the thing and suddenly he stops, face blank, staring at her puzzled his mouth turns down at the corners a sob comes out of him, he puts his arm up to his eyes, cries pitifully, we know what he is doing so does Sandy but she goes very quiet and asks him quietly to stop, he ignores her, keeps it up, crying to break your heart. "Oh Loll darlin'," she says, "you know I cain't tol'rate that," and then her eyes screw up, her lower lip protrudes, she is reduced, begins bawling, arm up, fist rubbing her eyes, she has a hole in the underarm of her dress, her red hair.

"What I tell you!" Red James says, laughing. "This li'l ole thang, look there she's a-just cryin her heart out!" and she is, she can't stop, he goes to her to comfort her maybe a bit sorry now that he's done this but she's furious. He tries to put his arms around her, she brings her leg up sharply, knees him in the groin, stalks off. Red James has to sit down, he takes a deep whistling breath.

And that's when Clara began to laugh.

n a great dramatic scrawl, full of flourishes:

To Joe—
    Herein all my papers, copies of chapbooks, letters, *pensées,* journals, night thoughts—all that is left of me. Dear Libby is to keep them for your return. And you will return, I have no doubt about it. I have thought a good deal about you. You are what I would want my son to be. More's the pity. But who can tell, perhaps we all reappear, perhaps all our lives are impositions one on another.

W.P.
Loon Lake
Oct 24 1937

hree little words. *Suree rittu waruz.* The girls had voices like cheap violins and they kept their wavery pitch as the car careened around abrupt corners, horns blasting, peddlers and old monks falling out of the way. It was three o'clock in the morning and the shopkeepers were already unrolling their mats heaving the flimsy boxes of fresh wet seagreens from the beds of trucks pitch-black the Tokyo sky above, Warren looked up as if to pray like a seasick sailor keeping his eye on a fixed point a light in the Oriental heavens channeled by tile roofs the heavens flowing in an orderly manner unlike the progress of the Cord, its headlights flashing the startled faces of the poor Japanese street class taking their morning fish soup hunkering beside small fires in metal drums. White-gowned attendants at the Shinto shrines sprinkled the cobblestoned courts with handfuls of water. *Suree rittu waruz.*

The car braked to a halt and Warren and the ladies pitched forward over each other hysteric laughter they all climbed down where are we he said and they led him triumphantly to the next bistro of the infinite night this one a *mirikubawa.* A what? Warren kept saying as they were led in through the smoke up on the platform three black musicians were playing *jazzu* and a waitress got to the little table almost before they sat down and they all watched the expression on Warren's face as the drinks were ordered and then the rollicking hysterico laughter as he tasted the white substance in the sake cup *mirik* it was milk this was a milk bar and their civilization had triumphed again in producing for the American their friend the one substance they never drank and were astonished that anyone could, cow's milk, the very sort of thing that made the Westerners smell that characteristic way from their consumption from birth of the squirted churned curded and boiled issue *issyouee* of the ridiculous cow. They did not like the smell of course and only one *garu* from whom he learned the *Chiara-stun* and what merriment that was that they had to teach him his dance, a bold brown-eyed bow-legged thing with her bobbed hair and low-waisted dress pleated to flare out above the knees had the nerve in the intimacy of his room one dawn to hold her fingers squeezing her own nostrils while he fucked her looking down over the upraised knees upon which he rested his bulk she was lying there holding her nose and squeezing her eyes shut but making the sounds of pleasure too how odd and later he said do I smell so bad do I need to bathe no no she said with *moga* merriment you can never washu away you it is *ura smerr,* you *smerra butta* Penfield-san a *whore tubba butta*

They were his friends his introduction to the world of flappers I had to come seven thousand miles from home to meet a flapper he thought and all the things he had read in the papers at home about the new people their jazz their late nights their haircuts and merry step up from provincialism he found there in Japan how odd they were relentless and because he was American he was an authority they came to him for authenticity and all the protests he made were regarded with approval as ritual modesty the kind of social grace they thought only they had so he was an ideal teacher they thought he understood the Japanese way so humble he fit right in and he learned to make decisions simply because he was their authority. I'm from the working class he had announced when he first arrived with his introductions from his Seattle labor movement friends but something was misinterpreted here or there the upper class liberals the modern boys and girls rebels of the loins of the Meiji the *mobo* and the *moga* they took him up and he was forced to have cards printed in the Japanese way everywhere you went you presented your card or received someone's card on a salver a lacquered salver Mr. Warren Penfield Teacher of Western Customs ordinarily this consisted in not much more than appearing somewhere and allowing yourself to be observed your dark suit and rolled umbrella, one man to his embarrassment asked him to disrobe in front of the whole family to his boxer shorts so the women could see the undergarments and sock garters and make them on their own for the father the brother. Mr. Warren Penfield slowly learning the contact language by which he could communicate The Handshake lesson one The Tip of the Hat lesson two The Stroll with the Umbrella lesson three Helping Ladies Across the Street very *difficurr resson* four the deference shown to women the most genuinely unpleasant of the customs but they did it he looked at the *jazzu* pianist and the *jazzu* pianist looked at him and smiled and shook his head here they were together in service the smile said the frank and somewhat contemptuous self-awareness mirrored in the other doing the same thing what are we doing here man I mean I got an excuse what's yours that look of economically dependent expatriate we really down the ladder man to be stuck on this island making nigger faces for these little yellow men.

But one day Warren's reputation was made when a low-level official of the American embassy called and asked him to come by for a chat and it was to see if he would consent to offer his services to certain Japanese diplomats preparing themselves to sail to Washington, D.C., for an international naval conference cutaway striped coats gray trousers top hats I don't know anything Warren said my father mined coal I was a corporal in the Signal Corps what do I know but the embassy man said we have no choice you're up on the latest fashions everybody else has been here too long our faces are turning yellow yours is still pink and white like a cherry blossom he laughed and so Warren gave a lecture in recent cultural history in America about which he thought he knew nothing but which from having observed the Japanese he knew by refraction. There is a great liberalizing trend he said because of the Great War and internationalization of taste a sense the old ways must be overthrown and the old beliefs and restrictions are absurd. Young men and women marry because they fall in love and sometimes when they fall in love they don't even marry they live together in defiance of propriety half the point to the way they live is to insult propriety. People generally expect more, I think that is what you can say about us at this modern age of the 1920s, more love more money more freedom more dancing *Chiara-stun jazzu* men and women hold each other to dance in public and there is a music industry that produces their dance music for them and wickedness is a form of grace, transgression is seen as the liberation of the individual spirit but, he said, looking with alarm on the impassive frowns of his distinguished audience, you won't find any of that in Washington, D.C. Washington under Mr. Harding is the soul of propriety, he spoke slowly so the translators could keep up one word was equivalent to three or four sentences before the word, the word, after the word, the three little words blossomed like a bowl of chrysanthemums Mr. Harding himself is devoted to Bach and Boccherini especially the andantes, and the distinguished audience leaned back in its chairs and the look of impassive disapproval was replaced by the look of impassive approval. Afterward there was a reception and he found himself bowing it was easy quite easy and the embassy man said you missed your calling you should have come into State and he bowed to him too. A junior Japanese diplomat said he had studied at Harvard University. A blond young woman glanced at him. A Japanese publisher asked him if he did any writing. The same young woman glanced at him. She had a ring on her finger eventually they spoke she spoke of the entire Japanese nation as if they were all servants, making remarks about their character and reliability, she was married to one of the embassy staff. They became friends, Warren had now established within himself those women he was prone to love and those with whom he was most intimate in conversation two separate classes and always he recognized them when they appeared, this young woman was of the second class. Her husband was always busy but they were totally married in spirit in purpose in confidence so that all possibly naughty emanations from her were totally muffled in marriagehood, that was more than all right with Warren they became devoted friends she was a Midwesterner not that smart but in some blind instinctive way constantly putting him in touch with just the experiences that provoked his deepest response which then expressed what she might have felt had she been that articulate or generally sensitive to the meanings of things. She knew he was a poet. She was a prim neat young woman with a slender figure and the most appalling provincial drawbacks she had even found herself a Methodist congregation for Sunday mornings but she methodically introduced him to Japanese civilization. She knew the secret restaurants where you could get the best raw sea bream or salted baby eggplant or bean paste flavored with thrush liver or chrysanthemum petals dipped in lemon vinegar, they went to the shrines he sat in rooms perfectly furnished with no furniture slowly very slowly the authority on Western manners customs and English speech began to see things with a Japanese eye to cherish small things a lovely comb a lacquered bowl a shallow pond with fat orange carp the way some trees looked in their foliage as if tormented by wind or a madwoman having just extended her hair with the pads of her fingers. The young Midwestern wife became the audience for the drama of his life if she had not been there watching and finding it important he might never have changed but found his period with the irreverent flappers or lapsed into the paternal delusions of the foreign diplomatic community enjoying with a smirk the Japanese discovery of *besbol* the humor of Adolph Menjou Lillian Gish speaking in ideograms. Instead he began his withdrawal first from the Americans then from the Japanese trying to be like the Americans then from the wide streets of the city in which he shuddered to see men in derbies and rolled umbrellas riding in bicycle cabs, he grew thin and ate no meat he turned sallow and began to look actively for a style of expiation he could manage without self-consciousness but he couldn't have been that brave unless someone like the young wife from Minneapolis was there to pay attention.

The afternoon before he left on his pilgrimage she took him to the Bunraku puppet theater. Each large puppet was manipulated by three figures in black hoods one for the right arm and spine and face including the lifting of the eyebrows one for the left arm one for the feet, the puppets moved dipped bowed gesticulated raised arms to heaven walked ran, each movement was accompanied by the three black shadows behind to the side and underneath and to further disintegrate the human idea the voices of the puppets their growling thrilling anguish was delivered from the side of the stage by a reader whose chants were punctuated by the plunks of the samisen like drops of water falling on a rock and Warren Penfield after several hours of this thought yes it's exactly true, when I speak I hear someone else saying the words when I decide to do something someone else is propelling me when I look up at the sky or down at the ground I feel the talons on my neck how true what genius to make a public theater out of this why don't we all stand up and tear the place apart what brazen art to tell us this about ourselves knowing we'll sit here and not do a thing.

The puppet play told the story of two lovers who, faced with adversity, decided to commit suicide together and so at the intimate crucial moment there were eight presences onstage.

Acold bright sun glittering on the snow, dazzling the eyes, you couldn't tell where you were, in what desolate tundra of the world. But men got to work. The stamping of thousands of feet muffled by the deep snow.

Inside the Autobody the great clamoring noise seemed distant, a distant hum, as if the peculiar light reflecting the snow outside were a medium of shushing constraint.

It was an ominous day, I felt something was wrong, from down the line it came like a conveyed thing, going through my station like a hunk of shapeless metal with no definable function.

But I knew secrets, I was in on secrets.

At lunchtime the whistle blew, belts slowed down and stopped. I listened to one generator in particular, pitch whine dropping deeper and deeper to nothing. I went to my locker, men rubbed their hands on rags and looked at each other. Then someone came in who thought he knew where the trouble was, and holding our sandwiches and thermoses, we drifted toward it, we climbed over the car bodies and trod the motionless belts as if walking on tracks, and we came finally to an area flooded with bright daylight.

Two great corrugated sliding doors were open, I could see outside to a flatbed railroad car. Granulated snow gusting in. Sticking to spots of oil and grease. The cold sting of the day blowing in.

"Here, you men, you don't belong here!" A uniformed guard coming toward us with a scowl.

They were dismantling a whole section of machines, unbolting them from the floor and preparing to hoist them on pulleys. Someone said they were tool-and-die machines for the radiator grilles.

At quitting time I waited in front of the tavern across the street from the main gate. Red didn't show up. I walked quickly in the dark down Railroad Street.

"The train I ride on is a hundred coaches long, you can hear the whistle blow nine hundred miles. You see, Joe, when the New Year comes soon as

everone's past the Xmas bonus, soon as everone begins to think a the spring layoffs as you cain't help but doin when the year swings round, that's when we're a-settin down. You understand the beauty o' that? The union's allotin considerable monies. You see what you don't know is that Number Six makes all the trim for the Bennett plants in three states. Do you take my meanin? Ever bumper. Ever hubcap. Ever runnin board. Ever light. When we set down come January, ever Bennett plant in Michigan, Ohio and Indiana is gonna feel it. 'Course I'm trustin you with this, you cain't tell no one, it's a powerful secret compris'n the fate of many. *Ohh-oh me, ohh-oh my, you can hear the whistle blow nine hundred miles.*''

When I got home Clara wasn't there. I went next door. She was standing in the bedroom doorway holding Sandy's baby.

Two men were sitting in the parlor. They were dressed in work clothes. Sandy introduced me, they were members of the board of the local and I thought I recognized one of them from the meeting. He was a skinny little man and he didn't look at me as he talked. ''Yeah, Paterson,'' he said, ''I seen you around.'' His eyes darted to the phone on the desk.

The other man was younger, bulkier, he had a fixed smile on his face as if he had trained himself to it. ''We're waitin fer Red,'' he said.

They sat back down. Sandy James didn't know what to do with them, she stood there rubbing her palms on her hips. The parlor was awfully crowded, I thought, with all of us and a Christmas tree too with the tip touching the ceiling the star awry.

''You and James buddies, Paterson?'' the little man said.

''Yes.''

He nodded, kept nodding as if unaware of the brevity of my answer.

And then the phone rang and he jumped up as if he had been waiting, and grabbed the receiver. ''Yeah,'' he said, ''yeah, that's it.'' He hung up.

''Well,'' he said looking at the other one, ''I guess we'll be on our way,'' indicating the door with his chin. ''Sorry to trouble you, Mrs. James.''

''Red should be home right soon.''

''No, no, that's okay,'' the little man said. ''Just tell him we were in the neighborhood. Nothin important.''

They left, she locked the door after them.

''Oh, it gives me the jitters,'' she said, ''strangers comin round and askin questions.''

''Like what?''

''Where we got our lovely furnishins? How long we had the radio?''

I went over to the desk, for the first time I noticed the phone had no number written on it the little white circle was blank.

''Where is Red?''

Sandy looked at me and down at the floor.

''Come on, Sandy, for God's sake,'' I said.

''To a meetin,'' she said. ''A secret union meetin.''

"A board meeting?"

"I guess."

I didn't argue with her. I motioned to Clara and we went back to our side. The house, banked with snow, was without draught, sealed, like a tomb. I didn't know why but I felt bad, I felt desolate, I didn't care about anything.

"Hey, big boy," Clara said. "Let me see you smile."

Later in our bed I was so huge with love for her it was a kind of mourning sound I made, plunged into my companion. The ceiling light was on. Her head was turned from me, her eyes were closed, her knuckles were in her teeth, high color spread up from her throat suffusing her face, her ears, this was not my alley cat of gasping contempt raking her nails down my back this was my wife connected to me by the bones of being, oh this clear ecstasy ravage on the skin, reluctance it was happening, lady's grief of coming.

said to Red James, "Will you tell me what's going on?," my voice feeble
and complaining. I already knew in this town of thirty thousand the
crucial action was at my eyes, I was centered in it, it could not be less clear
than something I would read in the newspaper. I was at the fulcrum where
the smallest movement signified distant matters of great weight.

And he answered wonderfully not as if he had until this moment
deceived me but as if I'd always known and admired him for what he was.

"See, Joe, I coulda stayed on, you know? Hell, I had it so finely made
I mighta run for somethin someday in the national. But the client don't
give a hoot fer that. He gets the intelligence and he spooks like a horse in
a hurricane. I mean I'd laugh if I didn't feel like cryin."

We were walking home men everywhere talking in groups LAYOFFS!
in the headlines flyers announcing a mass meeting trampled in the snow.
Red suggested we stop in for a drink. We stood in front of a tavern I'd not
been in before, the light in the window was gold and orange, it looked
warm in there, I felt I'd better have something.

We sat in a booth in the back under a dip in the patterned ceiling.
Behind us was the door to the toilet. We sat in this plywood booth drinking
twenty-cent shots with water chasers I smelled the whiskey in my head
odor of piss cigarette smoke the sweat of every man in the room.

"'Course I ain't without choice, they's a little job at the Republic Steel
in Chicago. Ain't no auto worker in Jacksontown gonna follow me to pull
steel in Chicago. An' ifn there is, just in case, looky here."

He pulled a paper bag from his lunch pail, shook a small bottle uncapped it put a drop of liquid on his right index finger rubbed the liquid
into the red hairs on the knuckles of his left hand. He spread the hand on
the table: the red hairs were black.

"You like that?" he grinned, my stunned silence, he signaled the
bartender for two more. "But hell, I'm thinkin to drop industrial work.
You been to the city of Los Angeleez?"

I shook my head.

"Well, they's a need for operators there. They's so much messin around what with them movie stars and all, you see, ever good wife needs to make her case sooner or later, if you get my meanin. As does ever good husband. Yessir, they's opportunity in Los Angeleez."

He was nervous, talking with much careless confidence his glance kept flying up to the room behind me and coming back to me and flying off. It happened in the crowded bar that the lower register of his voice was lost in the babble of the room, so half of what he said I couldn't hear, I only saw the trouble he was in enacted on his face, in the animated appearance of him spiky unshaven red hair around the Adam's apple, the suddenly large teeth threatening to engulf his chin, pale white eyelashes pink-lidded eyes staring through their mask.

Joe was suspended, blasted. Gone was the wiseass street kid, gone in love, gone in aspiration, gone in the dazzlement of the whole man, the polished being.

"See, if the union was smart they wouldn't never let on they knowed. Take their losses this hand, play for the next, string me along without me knowin and use me against the company and tell me one thing and do another and trick Bennett right out of their shoes. An' shit, everyone woulda made out all around, the union 'cause they knowed 'bout me, the company still thinkin they had their inside op, and me still drawin my pay in good faith and doin my work."

He slumped against the back of the booth. "Hell, it's all the same anyways, the boys'll get their wages and grievance committees and such and it won't matter, the company'll just hike their prices, everthin'll be the same. But you see, they let me know they know and the company knows they know and I'm not good to anyone anymore leastwise to myself and now I gotta take that poor chile and move her out of her home."

"Red, it is so weird! You recruited me!"

"I surely did. I brought in numbers a good men an' true."

"Let me ask you, does Sandy know?"

"What, about me bein a detective? Aw, Joe," he said with a grin, "the poor chile has so much of a man in me already did I tell her the whole truth she'd go out of her natural mind with love!"

It now occurred to me to ask why I had been told. I was at the point of perceiving his peculiar genius, which was to make a lie even of the truth. He was waving his hand, calling someone, I turned just as two men arrived at the table.

"Set yourself down!" Red greeted them.

One slid in beside me, the other beside Red. I had never seen them before. They were heavy middle-aged men, one wore a suit and tie and coat with the collar turned up, the other had on a lumber jacket and a blue knit cap.

"See," Red said to them without any preamble, "I ain't sayin I didn't make a mistake. I don't want you to think that, whatever happens."

"That's all right, Mr. James," the one in the overcoat said. He was sitting next to me. He pointed at me with his thumb. "And this is him?"

"My good friend and neighbor Mr. Paterson," Lyle Red James said.

"I see," the man in the overcoat said. He twisted in his seat and leaned back to look at me.

The fellow across from him pulled off his cap. He sat hunched over the table holding the cap in his fists. He was a white-haired man and his florid face was covered with gray stubble. He now spoke, his eyes lowered. "James," he said, "there is a particular place in hell, in fact its innermost heart, where reside for eternity the tormented souls of men of your sort. They freeze and burn at the same time, their skin is excoriated in sulfurous pools of their accumulated shit, the tentacles of foul slimy creatures drag them under to drink of it. This region is presided over by Judas Iscariot. You know the name, I trust."

Red began to laugh. "Aw, come on," he said, incredulous, "that ain't no kind of talk."

Then this man with the cap in his hands turned to Red and looked at him. I saw tears in his eyes. "On behalf of every workingman who has gone down under the club or been shot in the back, I consign you to that place. And may God have mercy on my soul, I will go to hell too, but it'll be a joyful thing if I can hear your screams and moans of useless contrition from now till the end of time."

"Hey, brother," Red James said, "come on now, you ain't even tried to see if I'm tellin the truth. That ain't exactly fair!"

Both men had risen. The man with the blue knit cap leaned over and spit in Red's face. The two of them made their way into the crowd and went out the door.

Red was impassive. He splashed some water from his glass onto his handkerchief and washed himself. He glanced at me. "Catholic fellers," he said.

A few minutes later we left the bar. My blood was lit with two whiskeys, and with the imagery of sin and death in my brain I wanted to ask him more questions—questions!—as if I didn't already know, like some fucking rube I beg your pardon would you spell it out for me please! Clara, I still had time, there was still time for me to get her and throw our things in a bag and get us the hell out of there. Instead I walked with Red James down Railroad Street in this peculiar identification I made with him, as if only he could guard me from what I had to fear from him, and on Railroad Street where it made a sharp turn there was a shortcut across an empty lot the moon was out and going across this terrain Red glanced at me as I tried to phrase my questions he looked at me with genuine curiosity, as if, with all his figuring he had not figured me to be, in this outcome, that stupid. And we went across the snow moon of the frigid night making our way to our joined homes and fates as if nothing had happened and two ordinary workers had only stopped for a drink in the time-honored way. He

was singing now in his nasal tenor the ritual that comes on the excommu-
nicated

> The train I ride on is a hundred coaches long
> You can hear the whistle blow nine hundred miles
> Ohh-oh me, ohh-oh my
> You can hear the whistle blow nine hundred miles.

At one point the police asked me if I knew who it was. I shook my head. "I never even saw them," I said. This technically was true. But I thought I knew them anyway. I recognized the sentiment. I heard in the furious contention the curses of my own kind. Swaying and tumbling all together, we were one being in the snow, one self-reproaching self-punishing being.

The police wore their blue tunics over sweaters. Their hips were made ponderous by all the belts and holsters and cuffs and sticks hanging from them. They were tough and stupid, there were four of them in the hospital emergency room, four cops writing their reports on pads wound with rubber bands. Then the reporter arrived from the local paper, a thin small man in a Mackinaw and fedora, and he asked them if they had found anything in the lot. I could tell it had not occurred to them to look.

When Clara got there with Sandy I was lying on a table in one of the treatment rooms and on the table next to me was the body. I think I'd been given something before they set my arm because I saw Sandy's stunned very white face but I didn't hear the sound she made. The attendant pulled away the sheet the lips were curled back from the teeth like he was grinning and Sandy passed out. Clara, who was holding the baby, grabbed Sandy's arm and kept her from falling while the attendant ran for the smelling salts. I thought it was still Red making her do whatever he wanted.

Sometime later I had a chance to talk to Clara for a minute.

"He was a company op," I said.

She shook her head. "The poor dumb galoot."

"None of this had anything to do with us," I said, "and I danced us right into it." I didn't want to talk this way. I looked in her eyes for the judgment and not finding it tried to put it there by talking this way.

She touched her fingers to my lips.

"He couldn't have been placed better," I said. "It was a secret strike plan, nobody knew except the officers. And then the company took out half the machines."

"Some men came to their house this afternoon," she said.

"What?"

"Just when it was getting dark. We happened to be on our side. At first Sandy thought it was the radio, that she left it on."

"Did you get a look at them?"

"I didn't want to. I heard what they were doing. They tore the place apart."

"Jesus."

"It's lousy that she got hit with all this," she said.

"Well, now I know why they didn't believe him."

"What? I don't think you should try to talk."

"No, it's all right, I'm doped up. I'm saying he was trying to pin it on me. I guess he couldn't think of anything better."

"What?"

"But they weren't buying it because they must have got into his files." I found myself panting in the effort to speak. I was having trouble catching my breath.

At this moment I saw in Clara's calm regard the disinterested understanding of a beat-up face—as if nothing I had to say was as expressive as the condition I was in.

"He tried to make me the fink," I said. I realized I was crying. "The son of a bitch. The goddamn hillbilly son of a bitch!"

She turned away.

I stayed that night in the hospital and once or twice I realized the moans on the ward were my own.

In the morning I caught a glimpse of myself in the metal mirror of the bathroom—arm in a sling, a swollen one-sided face, a beauty of a shiner. I found myself pissing blood.

I was released—I supposed on the grounds that I was still breathing. I walked a couple of blocks to the car line. A clear cold morning. I sat in the streetcar as it gradually was engulfed in the tide of men walking to work. I thought of trying to work the line with a broken arm. I was out of a job.

Men stepped aside to let the streetcar through. Faces looked up at me. I had pretended to be one of them. That was the detective's sin.

When I got home I found Clara and Sandy James and the baby asleep in my bed. The house was cold and there was a fetid smell, faintly redolent of throw-up or death, it was a very personal smell of mourning or despair. I got the fire going in the coal stove—I was learning with each passing moment the surprises of a one-armed life.

I went next door. The place was a shambles. Red's desk had been jimmied open, the sofa cushions and chair cushions were piled up, the braided rug was thrown back, his collection of pulp magazines was tossed everywhere. His secretarial ledgers were on the floor, one with the names and addresses of the membership, another with his meeting minutes. I found boxes of mimeographed form letters, a loose-leaf folder with directives of the National Labor Relations Board, a scattered pack of blank union cards.

Inside the splintered front door, stuck in a crack, was the carbon copy of a handwritten memo dated some months before. It had been stepped on. It was addressed to someone with the initials C.I.S. It was signed not with a name but with a number. But I could tell who the writer was, Red wrote a very chatty espionage report, very folksy. He spelled grievance *greevins.*

The bedroom was no less worked over. I straightened the mattress and lay down and pulled a blanket over me. I knew that I should be thinking but I couldn't seem to make the effort. Eventually I fell asleep. A wind came along and worked at the broken front door, banging it open, banging it closed, and I kept waking or coming to with the intention of seeing who it was, who it was at the door who wanted to come into this pain and taste of blood.

In the parlor a man was picking up papers and tapping them into alignment on the floor. It was the tapping that woke me.

"Hey, pal," he said.

He wore a topcoat that was open and followed him like a train as he duckwalked from one item to another. His hat was pushed back on his head.

He stood up with an effort. "Oh boy," he said, "these old bones ain't what they used to be."

A lean face, pitted and scarred, very thick black eyebrows, and carbon-black eyes with deep grainy circles of black under them. A heavy five o'clock shadow. But the skin under all was pale and unhealthy-looking. He had collected Red's union records and was stuffing them now in a briefcase. He righted the armchairs and looked under the cushions. He felt around the desk drawers. He stacked Red's pulps, flipping through each one to see if there was anything in it. He was very thorough. And all the while he talked.

"Whatsamatter, the lady's husband come home early? Well, you tell me: was it worth it? I'll tell you: no. I know about ginch. It is seldom worth it. It is seldom worth what you have to go through to get it. I been married twice myself. I was happy in love for maybe five minutes each of those women."

It was speech intending to divert, patronizing speech, his eyes and hands busy all the while.

"Put that stuff back," I said. "It doesn't belong to you."

He smiled and shook his head. He came toward me. "Where's the widow?" he said.

"What?"

"His bereaved."

"I don't know."

He came over to me. "Hey, kid, look at you. Look at how they worked you over. How much can you take? What's the matter with you?"

I immediately recognized the professionalism of the threat.

"Listen," he said, "don't be a wiseass. I'm here with the money, her death benefit." He waved an envelope in front of my eyes. I could feel the breeze on my hot face.

"She's at my place. I'll get her."

"I would be grateful," he said.

The women were up, they were in the kitchen, Clara was drinking coffee, she was wearing the clothes she had slept in, she looked gaunt, grim.

Sandy James' eyes were large and glistening with the unassuageable hurt of someone betrayed. The corners of her mouth were turned down. She was trying to feed her baby and the baby was enraged, it was twisting and turning, and making dry smacking sounds. It pulled on her breast and waved its tiny arms.

I explained, but even as I did he appeared in the doorway behind me. Sandy stood and thrust the baby at me and pulled her dress closed and buttoned the buttons while I held the crying baby, wriggling and twisting against my cast.

Now we all stood there frozen in that way of those overtaken by ceremony. Even the baby quieted down.

"I'm sorry for your trouble, Mrs. James," the man said. He held a legal-looking paper in one hand, an uncapped fountain pen in the other. "Your husband, Mr. James, was a brave man. The company knows it has a responsibility to his family. It ain't something we have to do, you understand, but in these cases we like to. If you will sign this receipt and waiver, both copies, I have a death-benefit sum of two hundred and fifty dollars cash on the barrelhead."

Sandy James looked at Clara. Clara sat with her head lowered, the fall of her hair hiding her face.

Sandy James looked at me. I knew what the waiver meant. Two hundred and fifty dollars seemed to be the going rate. Sandy James age fifteen was in no position to sue anybody. I nodded and she signed the waiver.

The fellow tucked one copy in his pocket and put the other on the table. He glanced at Clara. He took out his wallet and counted the money and put it in Sandy's hand. He came over to me and stuck his finger in the baby's cheek. "Hey, beauty," he said. He looked at me and laughed. "Beauty and the beast," he said.

When he was gone Clara found a cigarette and lit it.

"Two one-hundred-dollar beels," Sandy James said. "And a fifty-dollar beel."

I sat on the kitchen table and read the waiver. The party of the first part was Mrs. Lyle James and all her heirs and assignees.

The party of the second part was Bennett Autobody Corporation and its agents, C.I.S., Inc.

I said to Sandy, "You know what C.I.S. stands for?"

She shook her head.

Clara cleared her throat. "It means Crapo Industrial Services," she said. She took the baby from me. She hugged her and began to pace the room, hugging the baby and saying soft things to her.

"Mah milk's dried up," Sandy said. "She'll have to get on that Carnation?"

"Red worked for Crapo Industrial Services," I said to Sandy. "Did you know that?"

"Nossir."

"Neither did I. Why should it surprise me?" I said. "Clara? Does it surprise you?"

Clara didn't answer.

"No? Then why should it surprise me?" I said. "After all, a corporation like Bennett Autobody needs its industrial services. Spying is an industrial service, isn't it? I suppose strikebreaking is an industrial service. Paying off cops, bringing in scabs. Let's see, have I left anything out?"

"Why don't you take it easy," Clara said.

"I'm trying to," I said. "I'm just one poor hobo boy. What else can I do?" I went out to the privy. The sky was clear but a wind was blowing dry snow in gusts along the ground. I was still pissing blood. When I spit, I spit blood. Someone who had business connections with F. W. Bennett was big-time. Tommy Crapo was big-time. Surely he did not even know the name Lyle Red James. It was a coincidence that the fucking hillbilly who lived next door to me was an operative of Crapo Industrial Services. That was all it was. It was not a plot against me. It was not the whole world ganging up on one poor hobo boy.

But in my mind I saw the death-benefit man stepping into a phone booth and placing a call.

I went back inside.

"Can you eat anything?" Clara said. She spoke in a hushed voice that irritated me. "Do you want some coffee?"

"Sit down," I said. I faced her across the kitchen table. "You knew that joker."

She folded her hands in her lap. She sighed.

"Well, who is he?"

"Just some guy. I used to see him around."

"A friend of yours?"

"Oh Christ, no. I don't think I ever spoke five words to him."

"What's his name?"

She shrugged.

"What's his name, Clara?"

"I don't remember. Buster. Yeah, I think they called him that."

"Buster. Well, did Buster say anything? Did he recognize you?"

She didn't answer.

"Clara, for Christ's sake—do you think he recognized you!"

Clara bowed her head. "He may have."

"Okay," I said. I stood up. "Fine. That's what I wanted to know. See, if we know what we're dealing with we know what to do. Am I right? We need to know what the situation is in order to know what to do. Now. Is Tommy Crapo in Jacksontown? You tell me."

"How should I know? I don't think so."

"Well, where would he be?"

She shrugged. "He could be anywhere. Chicago. He lives in Chicago."

"Good, fine. When Buster calls Mr. Tommy Crapo in Chicago to tell him he's found Miss Clara Lukaćs, what is Mr. Tommy Crapo likely to do?"

"I don't like this. I don't want to talk about this anymore."

I leaned over the table. "Hey, Clara? You want to talk about us? You want to tell me how you love me? What is Mr. Tommy Crapo likely to do?"

"I don't know."

"Is he going to hang up the phone and laugh and call in his manicurist? Or is he going to come get you?"

She wouldn't answer.

"I mean what happened at Loon Lake? Why did he leave you there? Did you do something to make him mad? Or was it just a business thing?"

She slumped against the back of the chair. Her mouth opened. But she didn't say anything.

"Well?"

"You fuckin' bastard," she said.

"Oh, swell," I said. "Let's hear it. Step a little closer folks. Sandy!" I shouted. "Come in here and listen to this. Hear the lady Clara speak!"

We heard the front door close.

"You're terrific, you know?" Clara said, her eyes brimming. "That kid has just lost her husband."

"Don't I know it. And what a terrific guy he was. They're coming at me right and left, all these terrific guys. They run in packs, all your terrific friends and colleagues."

I ran next door.

Sandy James had put the baby in her carriage and was standing in the middle of the room pushing the carriage to and fro very fast.

"Sandy," I said, "I'm very sorry for all this and when we have the time we'll talk about it if you want to. I'll tell you everything I can. Did Red ever give you instructions who to call or what to do in case something happened to him?"

"Nossir."

"Does he have family in Tennessee, anyone who should be notified? Anyone who could come help you?"

She shook her head.

"How about your family?"

Her lower lip was protruding. "They cain't do nothin."

"Well, did Red carry life insurance?"

She shook her head.

"Do you know what that is?"

She shook her head.

"Well, where does he keep the family papers? I mean like the kid's birth certificate. He must keep that somewhere."

That's when Sandy James began to cry. She tried not to. She kept rubbing her eyes with the heels of her hands as if she could press the tears back in.

I looked around the room. With Buster's tidying, the parlor was not too badly messed now. I began to go through it myself, opening the desk drawers, tossing things around. What was in my mind? I thought if Red James had not told his wife of an insurance policy, he would be likely to have one. I was looking with absolute conviction in the clarity of my thought for an insurance policy but why it seemed to me the first order of business I couldn't have said. I supposed it would lead to something. Different pieces of Lyle Red James had been lifted—his espionage self by the union avengers, his union self by the industrial-service hoods, surely there must be something left for me, something of value to me, something he owed me. Maybe there was a strongbox and maybe along with a birth certificate and an insurance policy there would be cash. He owed me something. He owed me a broken arm and a battered face and a considerable portion of my pride. He owed me my abused girl, he owed me the care and protection of his own wife and child. He owed me a lot. I ran into the bedroom and began to go through the closet. Every move I made was painful, but the more I searched—for what? where was it?—the more frenzied I became. My body had thought it out: I needed to get us all off Railroad Street. I needed to save Clara. I needed to get Sandy James and her baby home to Tennessee. I needed the money for all of this. I think I must have whimpered or moaned as I searched. I was in a cold sweat. At one point from the corner of my eyes I saw the two women standing in the door watching me. I took the sling off my arm so that I could move around more easily. Without the sling I felt the true weight of my cast. I thought of the weight as everything that had to be done before I could get out of Jacksontown. I wanted to shake this cement cast from my bones as I wanted to shake free of this weight of local life and disaster. None of it was mine, I thought, none of it was justly mine. I had stopped over. That was all. I wanted to be going again. I wanted to be back at my best, out of everyone's reach, in flight. But I had all this weight and I felt there was no time for condolence or ceremony or grief or shock or tears, there was hardly time for what I had to do in order to lift it from me so that we could get free.

Eventually it dawned on him, the fucking radio of course, he pushed it away from the wall.

It was a small radio in a big cabinet. Under the tubes and behind the black paper speaker was a cigar box. In the box a .32-caliber pistol. He had never handled a gun before. It was heavy, felt loaded smelled oiled and sufficient. He put it back closed the box.

Wedged in the space between the tube chassis and the cabinet one of those cardboard accordion files with a string tie. This he lifted out. He pushed the radio back against the wall.

"Sandy!"

He sat on the floor. She knelt next to him. He watched her hands, she withdrew a marriage license a white paper scroll, she unrolled it holding it with both hands to her face as if she were near-sighted. She withdrew newspaper cutout coupons, a pack of them, the kind people saved for premiums, she withdrew the baby's birth certificate, she withdrew a wedding photo of Mr. and Mrs. Lyle James all dressed up smiling on the steps of a clapboard church. He had to let her cry over that one in her silent way palming the tears as they flowed. She withdrew a leather drawstring purse, he thought the deliberation of her movements would drive him out of his mind, she untied the string widened the mouth of the purse and shook out several shiny bright medals with ribbons.

"Was Red in the war?"

"Nossir."

"Stupid of me to ask."

She withdrew a printed policy of the Tennessee Mutual Life Insurance Policy. Its face value was a thousand dollars. That would have to do.

"Aren't there people who cash these things right away? Wills, IOUs, stuff like that?"

"Factors," Clara said.

"Yeah, factors. I bet I could get sixty, seventy cents on the dollar. This is as good as cash."

"It's not yours," Clara said.

"I didn't say it was. Would you mind coming into the other room a minute?"

Clara followed him into the Jameses' bedroom. He closed the door.

"I don't know," he said, "maybe you want to see your old sweetheart again. Have a few laughs."

"Is that what you think?"

"I don't know what I think. But if we don't move our ass out of here we're finished."

"Maybe so, but that's our problem, not hers."

"If we are all tending to our own problems," he said, "we can walk out this minute. We'll let the fifteen-year-old widow shift for herself. Is that what you want?"

"You're hurting my arm!"

"Why do I have to explain these things!"

"Let go of me. It was your idea, big boy. I didn't tell you to move to this shithole."

He went back to the parlor.

"Sandy, I'm prepared to take you back to Tennessee. I mean we're all finished in Jacksontown, I assume you understand that. You will spend Christmas with your family at your ancestral home. I am proposing we join forces, you and Clara and me, pool what we have and help each other. And I give you my word I will make good on every penny of the whole thousand."

The kid was silent. He waited. He realized this meant yes. "Okay," he said, "it's settled. We have a lot to do. He has to be buried. What are we going to do about that?" He looked at Clara. "Hey, Sandy, I bet you didn't know we had an expert among us."

The briefest bewilderment on Clara's face, what had she done wrong, did he blame his broken arm on her, his stitches? His mind was functioning now, he had calmed down, he was the old Joe of Paterson working things out. But one nick of this gem of a mind flashed the spectral light of treachery.

She smiled appreciatively almost shyly, with a dip of her head, a curl at the corner of her lips, her eyes sparkled, she had it, she knew it before he did, the secret wish, the resolution.

"Ah want the best," Sandy James said.

"Why not?" said Clara. She knelt down next to Sandy and put her arm around her. She tilted her head till their heads touched. "You'll have the best," Clara murmured. She looked up at him. "In Jacksontown it won't cost that much."

* * *

WHILE CLARA WAS ON THE PHONE I ASKED SANDY JAMES HOW SHE FELT ABOUT HER furniture.

"It's all paid," she said.

"So much the better. I could get it appraised and you'd make a clear profit."

She clutched her baby and looked around the parlor. Her eyes were large. "Wherever I live I'm gonna need a chair and table. I'm gonna need a bed to sleep in."

"Okay, okay, I'm just asking, is all. I'll figure something out."

An hour and a half later I had everyone packed. I called a Yellow Cab and by the time it pulled up I had both women and the baby and the bags out on the sidewalk.

Nobody was watching. No car followed us. I took us back to the rooming house Clara and I had stayed in when we first hit town. I rented two rooms adjoining. I got everyone settled.

"Do you mind telling me what you're doing?" Clara said.

"Not at all. I'm going to the factor. Then I'm going to pick up my back pay. Then I'm going to see what I can do about a truck for all that shit of theirs."

"You better slow down. You don't look so good."

"I can imagine."

"You can't leave town before the funeral."

"I understand that. But we'll get a good night's sleep. You don't object to a good night's sleep, do you?"

"She doesn't know what hit her yet. You're not giving her the chance."

"I'll leave that to you."

We stand on either side of Sandy James, who holds her baby. I hunch into my khaki greatcoat. It is buttoned over my cast and I have pinned the sleeve. The grave has been dug through the snow and through the ice and, with scalloped shovel marks, into the frozen earth. I study the crystal formations of the grave walls. I imagine lying there forever, as he is about to do.

The stones around us lean at all angles as if bent to the weight of the snow banked against them. The graveyard is in a desolate outlying section of town. It is on a rise that commands a view of the adjoining streets, one filled with the blank wall of a warehouse, the other fronting a lumberyard. A traffic light at the intersection. Over the racks and open sheds of the lumberyard I can see to the tracks and signals and swing gates of the Indiana Central.

The Baptist preacher is garrulous, Southern, like the fellow in the coffin. He speaks of God's peppers. An image comes into my mind of a green field of pepper plants and I wonder at the eccentricity of all the glories of God's fecund earth to speak of peppers.

I look from the corner of my eye at Sandy James. She stares into the grave. I see the tracks of her tears on her cheeks. I see the corneal profile of her green eyes. The baby comes into view, leaning forward in curiosity, her arms wave over the grave, cheeks puffing their steam of baby breath.

I cannot see Clara, the mother and baby block my view of Clara.

I shift my weight from one leg to the other. A dozen or so union men are standing behind us. They hold their caps. There are others too. The reporter who questioned me in the hospital, his ferret face under a brim hat, his plaid Mackinaw.

Two green-and-white police sedans and a police motorcycle and sidecar are parked in front of the warehouse across the street from the entrance to the graveyard. The cops sit on their fenders and smoke cigarettes.

A cream-colored La Salle with whitewall tires turns the corner and slowly cruises past the cops and out of my line of vision. I hear a motor cut off, the wrench of a handbrake.

"Do not question God's peppers," says the preacher.

I'm trying to think. What are all these people doing here? All night I sat in a chair by the door with a heavy pistol in my lap and I tried to think. I tried to lift my head and open my eyes, shake off the exhaustion of my bones to think.

Now I do have a thought. It is really very foolish. It is that these people—the union men, the cops, the reporter—they're all staying. I mean this is where they live, Jacksontown, Hoosier Heart of the Nation, it's their home, it's where they make their lives. The reason this preacher twangs on and on is because he too lives here. He's in no hurry, why should he be?

All of them, it's a big thing this funeral, an event. I look at the landscape, nothing is moving, even the sky looks fixed, residential.

I shiver, a chill ripples through me. I feel their entirety of interest and attention as some kind of muscling force. Some large proprietary claim in the presence of these people displaces me.

I am dispossessed.

I square my shoulders and stare straight ahead. It seems important not to reveal from my expression or my posture that I understand this. I know what it is now. It is the whispering return to my body of my derelict soul. Oh, my derelict soul of the great depression! What's happening to me— I feel guilty! Guilty of what? I don't know, I can't even imagine!

Finally the twanging ends and with great satisfaction in the holiness of his calling, he closes his Bible, turns his face upon me and I nod and shake his hand. The ten-dollar bill folded in my palm passes to his. He murmurs something to the widow and for no additional charge grazes the baby's cheek with the tips of his theistic fingers. Then he's gone. Clara moves around in front of Sandy and hugs her and turns her away from the gravedigger, who with his shovel propped against his hip is spitting on his hands getting ready to go to work.

We walk slowly to the gate, a hand taps me on the shoulder. "Paterson?"

I turn. The heavyset man with the blue knit cap the expert on hell. Behind him three or four others.

"We don't want to disturb Mrs. James at this time. We have made up a pot." He puts a folded wad of bills into my hand. "The boys from the local."

I must have looked shocked. He moves close to me.

"Do you think, Paterson," he says in my ear, "that we would be so stupid as to permit ourselves to be overheard threatening a man in public not ten minutes before we meant to jump him in a dark alley?"

"What?"

"Use your brains, lad. I'm sorry for the beating you took, but if it was us you'd be in the grave beside him."

He moves off, I find Sandy and Clara, I hold Sandy's arm, I feel her bewilderment of sorrow. Faces appear, condolences drift in the cold air flutter for a moment fall.

They knew my name.

They thought it matters to me who killed him.

Clara catches sight of the cream-colored La Salle. She frowns and turns away with an involuntary glance back uphill to the grave. The color in her cheeks, the thin skin she has for the cold, the blue translucence of the eyelids, the tears in the corners of her eyes.

We are through the gate, walking on pavement. I'm between the two women. I hold their arms. It is becoming more difficult to move forward. Several bulky policemen, awkward, they don't seem to know what to do with themselves.

"Pardon me." A man tips his hat to Sandy. "Mr. Paterson, I wonder if you'd mind." I can't hear him.

"What?" There seems to be some problem. It is some misunderstanding, it's becoming difficult to move forward, we're in a crowd, it banks higher and higher against our progress.

"What?" I hear my own voice. "What questions? I already answered questions."

"We just want to talk to you a few minutes, clear up some things."

I look behind me—we're completely hemmed in now, cops in front, the working stiffs behind us, the reporter at the edge of things his chin upraised. Everyone is terribly interested.

"I'm sorry," I say truthfully, "there's no time."

I hear laughter.

"I'm responsible for these ladies, I can't leave them alone here."

It is explained that they will come down to the station house with me. They can wait for me where it's warm. I am reasoned with. Just a few minutes. Sorry for the inconvenience. Clara and Sandy are being led to one police car, I to another. Just as the door opens for me I balk. "Clara!" I try to turn around, call her. I have changed my mind. I want to put her and Sandy in a cab. I want them to wait at the rooming house.

"Don't make it hard," a cop says.

My good arm is twisted behind my back I am bent forward at the waist the muffling of blue bulk a stick is brought up smartly between my legs I'm pushed into the car. I have the terrible sickness. I'm aware of people scattering as the police car makes a careening U-turn and picks up speed. A siren. I'm thrown against the back seat against the door we veer around the corner the cop next to me pushes me away with the tips of his fingers. "Relax, sonny," he says. "Enjoy the ride."

At a certain point Railroad Street made a ninety-degree curve and you could leave it, cut across an empty lot, and reach it again a block closer to home. The lot was filled with rubble, bricks, rusted sled runners, pieces of baby carriage, garbage a feast for Saint Garbage remnants of chimneys and basement foundations and all of it covered with snow. I was thinking it was the place to be, the place to be, I stumbled along drunk, to tell the truth, drunk on two glasses of rye through this moonscape of white shit. I heard the distant bell of the trolley and saw over a tenement roof the flash of its power line like the explosion of a star. I fell and fell again, cutting my knee on something sharp, getting a sockful of snow, but Red James jaunted along smoothly he even sang one of his songs the funeral dirge of the Southern mountains, hearing the whistle blow nine hundred miles, the condemned man in prison the betrayed lover the orphaned child everyone across the night suffering loss and failed love and time run out raising his head to hear the whistle blow through the valleys of the cold mountains. And then I was down again, hard this time and I shook my head to find myself on all fours I hadn't fallen. I heard something terrible, a grunt of punched-out breath, snapped bone, a man retching. I tried to stand I was flattened by a great weight, a violent steam-rolling weight pressing my face in the snow my forehead slashes on something sharp at my eye the snow turning wet and black the weight is gone, I scramble to my knees, breathing that is tearful, a desperate exertion, a mass of bodies tumbled past me I heard Red scream and hurtled myself against this mass of black movement butting it with my head taking purchase like a wrestler grabbing a leg a sleeve a back. Everything fell on me and I felt going down my arm twisted the wrong way I heard it break. This seemed to me worth a moment's contemplation. I lay still and even found a small space in the snow to spit out blood. I lay there under the murder. The intimacy of the shifting weights, the texture of their coats on my face, sobbing rages, one vehement crunch and I heard, we all heard, the unmistakable wail of a dead man. Then a hissing gurgling sound. Then no sound. After which, silence from us all and the night coming back in this silence, the weight lifted from me by degrees I look up portions of the night sky reappear suffused in the milk light of the moon I hear something sibilant, hoarse, it is my own breath, the wind brushing past my ears, I hear hitting hitting but it is the heart pounding in my chest.

He was heavier than he looked, I dragged him one-handed by the collar he kept snagging on things at the edge of the lot I found the right terrain, pulled him to the top of a flat rock and then sitting on the incline below it and easing him over my shoulder and sliding down in a sitting position to the sidewalk and standing up with the full heft of him in a fireman's carry on my good side, I took us to the curb under the streetlight to wait for someone passing by.

The police chief nods. It's cold in this room. I sit shivering in my coat. There's a clock on the wall, like the clocks in grade school. The minute hand leaps forward from one line to the next.

The chief is not cold. He sits at his desk in a short-sleeved shirt. Arms like trees. His wrist watch appears to be imbedded in the flesh. His badge, pinned to his shirt pocket, pulls the material to a point. He's enormous but with an oddly handsome unlined face prominent jawline straight nose. He is a freak who has managed to make himself a full life out of being born and raised in Jacksontown. I try to look as if this is not my opinion. He goes back to reading his file.

I have been very cooperative. Even though they did that to me I have told my story as completely and accurately as I can.

I hear the minute hand move on the clock.

We're in some room on the ground floor that looks into the courtyard. A couple of cops are standing around out there. The window has bars.

I don't even ask to smoke. I show no impatience. I don't want to give them anything to work on, if I don't seem to be in a hurry they'll be quicker to let me go.

A cream-white La Salle with whitewall tires pulls up in the courtyard just outside the window. The driver holds open the rear door and the man who gets out immediately has the attention of the cops. He wears a dark overcoat with a fur collar. A pearl-gray fedora. They seem to know him, they come over, they seem eager to shake his hand. He says something and one of the cops moves out of my view.

"Are you deaf, son?"

"What?"

"I said where are you from?"

"I'm from Paterson. Paterson, New Jersey."

"Like your name."

"Yeah."

He nods. "I see. What was your last job?"

"What? I rousted for a carnival."

"Whereabouts."

"Uh, upstate New York. New England."

"What carnival?"

"What?"

"What was the name of it?"

"I don't remember."

"You don't remember the name?"

"No."

"Well, how long did you work for them?"

"I don't know. Listen, is this going to take much longer?"

"It's up to you. You worked at this carnival?"

"Yeah. A couple of months. It was a summer job. Some lousy carnival."

"And before that?"

The man in the courtyard sees something. He removes one gray kidskin glove, takes off his hat. He's a short man, dark-complected, his black hair shines, shows the tracks of the comb. He is shaking his head, he seems genuinely relieved, he raises his arm, lets it fall. His eyes are large, dark, glistening, with long black lashes, they are shockingly feminine eyes.

There is Clara.

They look at each other, a wave of emotion overcomes them both and they hug. He holds her at arm's length and he laughs. He is charmed by her. He shakes his head as if to say, Oh what am I going to do with you!

"Sit down, son."

Side by side they lean against the cream-colored car and they talk. Clara's wearing her fur jacket. He says something to her, he smiles and holds her arm, whispers in her ear, it is as if he is in some night club somewhere at a dark table, and the intimate things he has to say are covered by the music of the swing band.

I am at the window.

"Son of a bitch, what does he see out there?"

"Clara!"

She has pulled her arm away, I hear something, I hear the high wordless whine of impatience with which she sometimes fends off the male approach.

"Clara!" I pound the window. He seems undismayed by her response, as if he knows too well it is a ritual, that it is in fact a form of encouragement.

"CLARA!" My arm, I am jerked back, a cop is pulling down the dark shade, is this my last sight of her head half turned as if she's heard something hair blowing back from her face eyes shining the winter courtyard as if she's heard something in her past, someone, just losing hold in her consciousness?

"Boy, don't you know you're being interrogated? Don't you understand that?"

I am slammed back in the chair.

"I gotta talk to Clara Lukács. She's out there."

"All in good time."

"It's important! Look, I'll answer anything any goddamn questions you can think of just let me talk to her a minute."

The cop is still behind me I have risen from my chair he presses me back down.

Another cop has come in and places Red James' gun on the desk. He takes up position with his back to the door, his arms folded.

The chief examines the gun. "A very serious piece of equipment. This is what the department should be carrying," he says to the cop. "Not the shit we got."

"Never been fired," the cop says.

Do I hear a car door slam? If I am to remain sane I must believe she is not leaving. I must believe she is handling things in her own way. I must believe that she is capable of dealing with Tommy Crapo as she knows he must be dealt with to get him off our backs. I will believe these things, and take heart and deal for my part with the situation in this room. An hour from now we'll be on our way. We'll make a slight detour down to Tennessee and then head for California. We'll be laughing about all of this. We'll be talking about the adventure we had.

"Where'd you get this, son?"

"It's his. Red James'."

He shakes his head and smiles. "Didn't do him much good, did it? You take it off him?"

"No, it was in his house. It was hidden behind the radio."

"Yesterday you went down to Mallory the pawnbroker's. You collected six hundred dollars on the deceased's insurance policy."

"That's right. The money belongs to Mrs. James. I'm holding it for her. She's fifteen years old and we're taking her home to her folks."

He nods, not to indicate he believes me, but as if to maintain the rhythm of the questioning. I look at the clear-eyed, steadfast face of the police chief, the lean face carved from his mountainous self. I've underestimated him.

"You expect them to give you trouble?" he says.

"Who?"

"Her folks you're taking her home to. That you were packing this thing."

"It wasn't for that."

"What was it for, then?"

"I was glad to find it. I sat up all night guarding the door with it."

"Why?"

"Until we got out of town, in case someone came after me."

He gives me his full attention. "Who?"

"I don't know who. Whoever killed Red."

"Why would they do that?"

"I don't know. If they thought I saw them? If they thought I could pin it on them?"

"Could you?"

"I told you. I didn't see anything. I got hit from behind and went down and it all fell on top of me. Could I see my girl, please?"

"Well, if you were afraid, why didn't you call the police? You think this is the Wild West?"

The policemen guffaw.

"Why would anyone want to kill him, anyway?" the chief says.

"I don't know."

"You're in the union, ain't you?"

"You have my billfold!"

"Maybe you killed him," he says.

"What? Jesus H. Christ!"

"Sit down, son. And watch your language."

"Oh, this is swell. This is really swell. No, I didn't kill him, he was my friend, we lived next door to each other!"

"Did you fool with his wife?"

I hear the ticking of the school clock. From far away comes the metallic screech and thunder of the car couplings as they make up the trains at the freight yards.

"Answer, please. Did you fool with his wife?"

The way is open for my full perception of official state-empowered rectitude. I am suddenly so terrified I cannot talk.

"Did you?"

I shake my head. A weakness, a palpable sense of my insufficiency drifts through my blood and bones.

"Okay," he says, "we could hold you for possession. But I think we have enough to hold you as material witness. You know what that is?"

I shake my head.

"You're all we have to go on. You were there when it happened. It means we hold you while we work up the case. I make it you diddled the wife and decided you liked it too much. The insurance didn't hurt neither."

And now I find my voice. I'm swallowing on tears, I'm producing tears and swallowing them so that they don't appear in my eyes. "Hey, mister," I say, "look at me, I don't look like much, do I? My arm's been broke, one side of my face is stitched up, I've been pissing blood . . . Jesus, since I came to this town I've been short-paid, tricked, threatened, double-crossed, and your Jacktown finest felt they had to work me over to get me here. I probably don't smell so good either. But I tell you something. You wouldn't hear from my mouth the filth that has just come from yours. I mean that is so rotten and filthy, I'd get down on my knees and beg that little girl's forgiveness if I was you."

"You oughtn't to tell me to do anything, son."

"Or else you're being funny. Is that it, are you being funny? I mean what's the idea—that I killed him before he broke my arm or did I kill him after he broke my arm? After? Oh yes. It makes great sense, it really does: with my one arm I was able to get him to hold still so as I could bash his head in. And then just to make sure everyone would know it I lifted him on my back and took him out to the street to get a ride to the hospital. Smart!"

"He's pretty stupid," the police chief says to the cop, "if he thinks we have to be smart."

The policeman laughs. The chief looks at me with the barest hint of a smile on his face. "You don't like my story, maybe you have a better one."

You don't like my story, maybe you have a better one.

Do you think, Paterson, we'd threaten a man in public a few minutes before we meant to jump him in a dark alley use your brains lad.

My brains.

Clara asked me about my work one day I told her she was furious. What's the matter? Don't move, look at how you're standing: it was so, my hands were in the air as if I were tying the cable, my feet were spread as if I were standing on the vibrating cement floor, I had not only told her, I had acted it out and I hadn't known I was doing that. I understood then the abhorrence of men on the line for bravado. The failure of perception is what did you in.

A murder is valuable property it gives dividends how much and to whom depends on how it's adjudicated.

I thought this was about Clara it is not it is about my life.

Tommy Crapo didn't think this up, he didn't do this to me, he didn't have to. You don't have to buy the police chief in a company town—he's in place! This dolmen stone skull has been here since the beginning of time.

I held up my hands. "Look," I say softly, new tone of voice, "you're making it wrong, it wasn't like that. We were family friends, Red and me. My fiancée Clara and his wife Sandy. We took care of their baby for them when they went to the movies."

"Your fiancée!"

"Yes, sir," I say, "that's what I'm trying to tell you. Clara and I are engaged to be married. You don't know my Clara or you wouldn't think I had an eye for another woman."

"She's something, eh?"

"Well"—I sit back in my chair and smile in reflection—"only the best, most beautiful girl in the world!"

The chief folds his arms. One of the cops leans over, whispers something to him. He listens while he stares at me. "Maybe we ought to see the little lady," he says.

The cop leaves, closing the door behind him. We all sit there waiting. It might be night the dark shade a globe light hangs from the middle of the ceiling the wood floor the oak furniture my chair creaks. The walls are painted dark green from the floor to halfway up, light green to the ceiling. I hear footsteps. I stand. The door opens the cop holds it open for Sandy James with her baby. From the empty hall behind her a cold wind sweeps into the room.

"Sandy, where's Clara?"

She stares at me unable to speak. But from her eyes gleams a sorrow not her own and a small light of courage or hope of possession. I see the decisive functioning matriarchy I have not before seen in her. It comes to them regardless of their age or intelligence when they have settled their claims.

In the winter of 1919 Penfield is in Seattle, walking the streets down by the docks, the rain green-gray, the escalloped seascape etched by rain. Life is a mist shining on his young face soothing his eyes, what his eyes have seen. He is wet and cold but not uncomfortable, there seems in this section of the world at this moment of his life a letting up of insistent death, no one he loves had died lately, he is all out, no mother father lover or signalman the bombs are still, the machine guns silent, the awful murderous insolence of mankind for the moment distracted. But the peace is killing him. Why is he here? He knows no one in Seattle, he knows no one in the whole country, he is one hundred percent bereft, he has come across the continent because it made the longest journey, there had been in his mind some expectation, the importance given to the being from the presumption of travel, but he has a room in a boarding house in West Seattle like the room they gave him in Nutley, New Jersey, in return for his medal and he walks down the hills to the docks. Why? He stands on pilings and looks at the water sloshing into itself infinitely accommodating to all blows objects hammers rainpocks taking it all, pour beaches in drop mountains in break off continental shelves the water gulps the water caresses it is the nature of the water to leave nothing untouched unloved even me thinks Warren Penfield. It is not that he has the urge to jump in but only that he lacks arguments why he should not. It is a rather thoughtful unemotional contemplation. This dark drizzly afternoon he throws his book in, one of the precious copies of his volume of verse, *Sangre de Cristo*, it blots, spreads, wafts, and solemnly raising its binding like wings dives into the great Sound. He leaves the pier and goes down a cobblestone alley and finds a bar a space for his own broad back collar up between the other broad-backed collars up a whiskey the bar dark wood honorably scarred a whiskey the damp air hung with smoke making the smoke of cigarettes a cloudmist he notices how crowded the bar is on a working afternoon he leaves the mist now inside the brain drifting over the lobes of the brain like clouds over the stone mountains the city is still. A block or two from the

waterfront it looks better to him at the end of streets the bows of steam-
ships loom over the clapboard buildings, he finds the conjunction of the
sea and the street exciting, bowsprits and lines of the old coal-fired riggers
gently bobbing over the cobblestones, the creak in the green-gray rain the
gulls in glistening drift through the rain there is another country, of
course! the sea is to connect waterfront streets at the far ends of the earth.
Such moments of elation keep him gliding over his despair he goes now
for the solace that never fails up the hill toward the center of town to the
public library. What goes on here the library is packed with men reading
the newspapers riffling the card boxes roaming the stacks making the
shapes of the words with their lips the librarians flustered by the sudden
accession to learning of the working world flush-faced, glasses slipping
down their noses they are reduced to whispering among themselves and
feeling hurt. But Warren likes this! He unbuttons his jacket pulls off his
cap sits at an oak table and feels the strength of these men reading the
papers on sticks quiet respectful as can be of this repository of words he
starts to ask a question quailed by the frown of the man next to him who
knows you're not supposed to talk in a library Warren goes to the granite
front steps the men clustered here smoking hunched in their collars in the
sweet rain he is too shy as usual but something is happening that is very
strange his landlady said nothing he will get a newspaper but block after
block no newsboys on the corners alarmed now it is February getting dark
in the afternoon the green is leaving the sky the street lamps beginning to
glow weakly the rained emptiness of the city he hears something missing,
no streetcars! the overhead wires gather the last light in silver lines an
inadequately populated city in the bakery window there is no bread in the
grocery no milk everyone knows something he does not know he waves
at a passing car black ignoring him he begins to run stores closed where
has he been follows men walking following other men walking stays close
stays in step hears now a human sound of population turns a corner a
suddenly illuminated warehouse great golden light pouring through the
doors they are all going here and suddenly he is inside the clatter of plates
and flatware, the steam of soup and the skyline of sliced bread he knows
what to do it is twenty-five cents, a bowl of soup two slices of bread gobs
of tub butter stew mashed potatoes an apple coffee in a tin cup twenty-five
cents rows of sawhorse tables in endless lines refectory benches under the
warehouse lights animation conversation all men thousands of men eating dinner and down at the end of one table at the far end in front of his
tray in wonder Warren Penfield poet coat open the sound is of raucous life
chopped fine in silver flutes and strings and drumfeet and shimmering
lifesong the men eat hot food drink strong coffee it is not Ludlow it is not
billets it is not distant thunder it is not the whingwhir of machine guns it
is the General Strike of Seattle February 6, 1919, the first of its kind in the
whole history of the United States of America.
    Everyone is out the printers and milk-wagon drivers butchers and

laundry workers hotel porters store clerks and seamstresses newsboys and
electricians and bakers and cooks steam fitters and barbers all under the
management of the central labor council and it is a very well organized
show Warren stands in the streets some trucks are running with signs
under the authority of the strike committee and the milk gets to the babies
and the lights stay on in the hospitals and the linen is picked up the food
cold storage continues to hum and the water from the waterworks and the
garbage trucks exempt by the strike committee continue to pick up the wet
garbage but not the ashes and the watchmen continue to guard the fences
and the mayor confers with the strike committee and not a shot is fired not
a fist flies not a harsh word they even have their own cops war veterans
big men standing with armbands the Labor War Veteran Guard to keep the
strike out of the streets, to break up crowds, keep the soldiers and cops
from finding excuses to make trouble they can't machine-gun air they tell
Warren move on brother keep your temper enjoy your vacation and by the
third day the provision trades are feeding thirty thousand men in their
neighborhood kitchen and the nonprofit stores are springing up everywhere not even the union newspaper is allowed to print for fear of unfair
competition to the struck big papers Warren is thrilled the city is being run
by workingpeople it is that simple they are learning the management
techniques it started with the shipyard strike and now it is Revolution pure
and simple says Warren's landlady big woman large jaw blue eyes taller
than he wiping red hands on her apron the Bolsheviks are in Seattle
they're here just like in Russia, they are a plague like the flu it spreads like
the flu they ought to be taken out and shot I've worked hard all my life and
never asked favors nor expected them and that's why I'm free and beholden to no one Warren tries to explain that's the same thing he's seen
the feeling beholden to no one independent men of their own fate and also
the incredible tangible emotion of solidarity key word no abstract idealiza-
tion but an actual feeling I had it too in the signal battalion the way we
looked after each other and were in it together an outfit many men one
outfit and I swear Mrs. Farmer that has got to be a good thing when you
feel it not necessarily the woman said the Huns felt the same feelings I'll
bet and took care of each other in their trenches and that don't make me
love them anymore they sank ships with babies in them she is in her way
a well-entrenched opponent and as always Warren thinks about this point
of view to which he is opposed to find the merit in it and test it against his
deepest suppositions they are having a good time at the kitchen table she
likes him he talks well and is a gentleman and a veteran and pays in
advance every two weeks look Mr. Penfield supposing they came in here
and told me how to run my house and when to clean the stairs and when
to change the sheets and what church to go to and how to teach my
children at this moment one of them runs in a remarkable five-year-old
little girl broad smooth brow wideset huge light eyes thick hair natural

grace dirty knees little socks drooping wild little thing stands between the
great-legged mother stares at the boarder with head tilted light in eye clear
recognition of his total flawed being what's that Mr. Penfield the great
granite mother how could she produce this wisp this unmistakable deity
she is scratching the inside of her thigh now with the heel of her shoe a
ballet dirty white underdrawers he says inspired well Mrs. Farmer I'll tell
you now not hesitant confident fearless of opposing opinion nobody
knows what human nature is in the raw it's never been seen on this earth
even Robinson Crusoe came from something even Friday and so it seems
to me the Huns like us shoot if you give them guns and enemies but love
if you will give them friendship and a common goal come down with me
and walk among these men and see their spirits change because they're
not under someone's heel you take away men's fear and be surprised how
decent they can be you don't make them climb over each other for their
sustenance give them their dignity and the right to run their lives you
release the genius of the race in the forms of art and love and Christian
brotherhood. Oh Mr. Penfield you're a good gentle man I'm afraid you
don't know the ways of the world very well I have some leftover pie here
let me make a pot of tea go along and play honey the child doesn't move
she is cleaning her lips with her tongue like a cat arms resting indolently
on her mother's skirted thighs outside the kitchen curtain the green rain
makes its soft hiss it is Warren who runs along in a flurry of stumbling
knocking over the kitchen chair proving his lack of ease in the ways of the
world she looks after him shaking her great jawed head sweet dupe he
goes to his room grabs books passport razor the child runs upstairs to the
hall-landing window looks out at Warren Penfield hurrying downhill he
sees turns his head back sees her the power of her eyes like a jolt to his
heart his face is wet the rain like her tonguelicks it is this more than
anything which sends him back to the docks in torment in scorn the
woman is right I am a fool if this strike goes on the committee who runs
things will be as bad as dictators everything'll be the same only with
different names do these men on strike absolve themselves of personal
private insensitivity in bed in kitchen do they know how to deal with their
own children or parents refrain from gossip and all the heavy baggage of
personal private evils vanity lust self-abuse the things in Latin the dreams
it was she God what are you doing she is come back in impossible form
God what are you doing I am haunted hounded you torment me with the
little I have to live for God what are you doing a basso horn from the sound
another from the harbor white smoke like Morse code from the stacks of
the ships berthed along the streets what is going on pardon me a small
Japanese turns what is all the horn-blowing he scintillating merry-un-
smiling we go now he says *stoorock ober*   What? Impatient Japanese
shouts to clarify to this white fool *stoorock ober! stoorock ober!* runs off from
the hills of the city church bells car toots the distant shouts of men who

have been men sounding like the gentle rain the Japanese runs up a
gangplank one bulb hung from the prow throwing a dazzling green halo
of rain over Warren's eyes the *stoorock* is *ober* Warren goes aboard the
Yokahama Trader books passage God what are you doing

You've got the wrong man," I said. The chief smiled. He wore his hexagonal blue cap now with the raised gold embroidery on the peak. He wore his tunic. He was sitting here for revelation, he had brought in a stenographer, more cops, and an older man in plain clothes.

I said, "The F. W. Bennett Company employs an industrial espionage agency to find out what's going on in their plants. The name of the agency is Crapo Industrial Services. Maybe you don't know this but I think you do. They put spies on the line and if possible in the unions themselves."

"Let's not waste time," the chief said.

"Red James was one of these spies. He came here two, three years ago just as the union began to organize the men. He got to be an officer of the local. He was secretary, he took minutes, he kept records, he made reports to his employer Crapo Industrial Services."

The chief turned to the stenographer, a gray-haired woman with a mole on her chin. She closed her book. I might be setting up to finger the union but I was talking funny. True! I had found a voice to give authority to the claim I was making—without knowing what that claim would be, I had found the voice for it, I listened myself to the performance as it went on. These fucking rubes!

"The union scheduled a strike just after the new year," I said. "The idea, see, was that if the trim line was shut down, eventually every other Bennett plant would have to shut down too because Number Six makes all the trim. So it was a big strategy of theirs and Red reported this. Right away there are layoffs, half the machines are dismantled and shipped to another plant, and the strike is up the creek."

"And that's why the union goons killed him," the chief said, looking at the plain-clothes man.

"But it wasn't them," I said. "It *looked* like it should be, I myself thought for a moment it was, let me tell you, Chief, you don't look for complications when your head's getting beat in. Does anyone have a Lucky?"

Where was this coming from? I had learned the basics from my dead friend Lyle James. But the art of it from Mr. Penfield, yes, the hero of his own narration with life and sun and stars and universe concentrically disposed on the locus of his tongue—pure Penfield.

"I'll try to make this as clear as I can," I said, taking a deep drag on my cigarette and nodding thanks to the cop with a match. "I know by sight every officeholder in the local, and every national big shot who's been in town since October. I know by sight most of the members—and this will surprise you but there aren't that many, considering the size of the work force at Number Six. But there are people who wear the same clothes and talk the same talk who don't work on the line and never will. And they are the ones who jumped us."

The police chief had risen. "You better know what you're doing, son."

"I made them for a traveling band, one of Crapo's industrial services," I said. "And that's who they were. If you really want Red James's killers, it's very simple. Speak to Mr. Thomas Crapo, president. You can reach him in the phone book—unless he's on his honeymoon."

The man in plain clothes stepped forward. It was clear to me now he was not in the department at all. He was dressed in a pin-stripe suit with a vest and a high collar and a stickpin in his tie. He had thin graying hair, and had the prim mouth of a town elder or business executive. To this day I don't know who he was—a manager of Number Six, a town councilman, but anyway, not a cop. I knew I could work him.

"What is it you're trying to say, young man?"

"I'll spell it out for you, sir. The agency murdered its own operative."

"That's a most serious charge."

"Yes, sir," I said. "It certainly is. But we're in a war, we're talking about a war here, and anything's possible. Once the company moved the machines, Red's days were numbered. The union found him out. That made him no longer of any use to Crapo, in fact he was worse than no use, he was a real danger."

"What?"

"He was an angry man. They'd left him to the dogs. He knew probably as much about Crapo as he knew about the local. He wasn't just your average fink who's been hooked for a few dollars and doesn't even know what he's doing. Red was a professional, an industrial detective, and he worked for Crapo in steel, he worked in coal, he'd done a lot of jobs and this particular assignment was very crucial and only the most experienced man could be trusted with it."

The police chief shook his head. He motioned to the stenographer to leave the room. He stood quite still and watched her close the door behind her. He turned to me he understood the reckless suicidal thing I was doing.

"But as I say, if you read your history of the trenches, the front lines at Belleau Wood, the Argonne, and so on, you find more than once the practice of sending out the patrol either to rescue or to kill their own man who has been captured—so that he doesn't give them away. War is war, other lives are at stake and war is war."

"I was with the Marines at Belleau Wood," the man in the business suit said. "I know of no such story."

"It was the British who did it," I said quickly. "I disremember the place and time, but it wasn't the Americans, it was the British and the French, and of course the Huns they did that all the time. But you don't have to believe it. Look at the chief here. First thing he thinks, a Crapo man is killed, it's the union who killed him. Why not, who would think different! And if he can make that case, if Crapo can trick him into making it, look what he's accomplished. He's set the union back twenty years. They're no union anymore, they're hoods and killers, nobody wants them, no working stiff wants comrades like that, not even Roosevelt wants that. Why, that in itself is enough to make it worthwhile—just to get the union defending itself from charges, just putting suspicion in people's minds—that's worth one op's life, I can tell you."

"All right, son," the chief said, coming around to the front of the desk.

"I know my rights," I said. "You are all witnesses. I'm telling you the truth as I know it, it's out now, it's out in this room and will be on every wire service in the country if you got any ideas of changing my testimony."

"I don't understand what's going on here," said the man in the business suit.

"This boy lies," the chief said. "He lied before and he's lying now. He's a punk from New Jersey who we found with a gun and the widow's insurance money in his kick. He's making this all up."

"That's right," I said. "I made up Tommy Crapo and I made up Crapo Industrial Services, didn't I? Or did I get it from the newspaper? That must be it, they must advertise in the newspaper. I can give you Red James' op number, the one he put on his reports, but that'll be made up too. I can give you the Illinois plate number of a cream-colored La Salle coupe with white sidewalls, but that's made up too. It's all made up. Buster is made up too, he doesn't exist."

"Who is Buster?"

"Buster who got Mrs. James to waive her rights for two hundred and fifty Industrial Services' dollars. Oh listen, mister, why doesn't anyone ask the right questions around here? Look at this, a roomful of ace detectives and not one of them thinks to ask how I know so much, how I knew Lyle James, how I got to be his friend, what I'm doing in this lousy town. Is it an accident? Do you think I like going around getting my arm broken and stitches taken in my face? Do you think I do this for laughs?"

An amazing current, a manic surge, I couldn't stop talking, listen Clara, listen! "I wonder at the human IQ when professionals cannot see through disguises. But if I was wearing a regular suit like this gentleman, if I was wearing my own suit and tie and my face was washed and my hair

E. L. DOCTOROW

combed, then you would listen, oh yes. And if I told you Lyle Red James was not just an operative for Crapo but a double operative, that he really worked for the union, that they made him not two weeks after he came to this town, because you know, don't you, he was not much good, he was a fool, a hillbilly, a rube, I mean they saw him coming! And they made him, and showed him how if he kept working and nobody the wiser, he'd get not only his pay envelope from Bennett and not only his salary from Crapo but his payoff from the union's cash box! Why, this strike at Number Six was a decoy! They never intended to strike Jacksontown, that was to send the company on a wild-goose chase shipping its damn machines every which way. Oh yes, gentlemen, when that strike comes, and it is coming, the birds will be singing in Jacksontown, it will be a peaceful day at Number Six and you won't know a thing till you hear it on the radio."

"What's this?" the businessman said. "What strike? Where?"

"Or maybe that isn't a good enough reason for taking care of Lyle Red James, that he was a dirty double-crossing Benedict Arnold."

It was an amazing discovery, the uses of my ignorance, a kind of industrial manufacture of my own. And the more it went on, the more I believed it, taking this fact and that possibility and assembling them, then sending the results down the line a bit and adding another fact and dropping an idea on the whole thing and sending it on a bit for another operation, another bolt to the construction, my own factory of lies, driven by rage, Paterson Autobody doing its day's work. I was going to make it! This was survival at its secret source, and no amount of time on the road or sentimental education could have brought me to it if the suicidal boom of my stunned heart didn't threaten my extinction.

"What strike, how do you know these things!" The businessman was beside himself. "Who is this fellow?" he said. "Damn it all, I want the truth. I want it now."

The police chief went back behind his desk and sat down. He looked at me, fingered the corners of his mouth. He lifted his hat and ran his fingers through his hair and put his hat back on.

"You don't like Crapo very much, do you?"

"We fancy the same girl," I said.

"And that's why you're fingering him—or trying to?"

"No more than he's done to me, Chief," I said. "But I got a better reason: I don't condone killing and neither does Mr. Bennett."

"Mr. who Bennett?" he said, frowning terribly.

"Mr. F. W. Bennett of Bennett Autobody. Is there any other?"

Here the man in the suit found a chair near the wall and sat down and glared at me.

"I'm a special confidential operative," I said. "I was sent here by Mr. F. W. Bennett personally to check on the Crapo organization. Their work has been falling off lately. Mr. Bennett takes nothing for granted, especially not the loyalty of gangsters. I worked into the confidence of Crapo's chief man in Number Six, Lyle James. Mr. Bennett himself arranged for the next door to be available. He thought I had a better disguise to be married and so I brought with me a lady''—here I faltered—''I happened to be serious about. This is the unofficial part, Chief, and I expect every man in this room to keep quiet about this part. I met this lady when she was with Mr. Crapo and we took to each other. We couldn't help it. And, well, he is not a man to forgive, as you can see by my condition and the circumstance of my being here before you.''

And now there was silence in the room.

''You are awful young to be what you say,'' said the police chief. He turned to the others. ''It's too crazy. Jacksontown don't need stuff like this. There are so many holes in this story it's like a punchboard. Why should Mr. Bennett need to do these things, you tell me? And if he did them, why would he find some kid like this not old enough to wipe the snot from his nose? No, I'm sorry, Mr. Paterson,'' he said, ''you're smart enough to throw the names around, but you were a punk when we pulled you in and as far as I'm concerned you're still a punk.''

''My name isn't Paterson,'' I said. I smiled and looked at the man in the suit and vest. ''It's easy enough to check,'' I said. ''In my billfold on a piece of paper is the phone number of Mr. Bennett's residence at Loon Lake in the Adirondack Mountains of New York. You may not know about that place, it's his hideaway. Call him for me. I get a phone call of my choosing anyway, isn't that the law? That's who I choose to call. Tell him also I'm sorry about the Mercedes. It may be on the lot of Buckeye State Used Cars in Dayton, Ohio. But it may not. Tell him I'm very sorry.''

I thought in the silence that ensued they could hear my heart beating its way back to survival.

''Yes, sir,'' the chief said, ''and who should we say is calling?''

One of the men laughed. I was livid with rage. Oh Penfield. Oh my soul. I could barely get the words out. ''You stupid son of a bitch,'' I said to the chief. ''Tell Mr. Bennett it's his son calling. Tell him it's his son, Joe.''

I don't remember the names of towns I remember the route, southwest through Kentucky and Arkansas, across northern Oklahoma and the top of the Texas Panhandle and then into New Mexico, a spooncurve that I thought would drop us gently into the great honeypot of lower California.

We drove through small boarded-up towns, we drove down dirt rut roads and through hollows where shacks were terraced on the hill beside the coal tipple. We drove through canyons of slag and stopped to pick up chunks of coal to burn in the stoves of our rented cabins. The road went along railroad tracks, alongside endlessly linked coalcars loaded and still.

We drove over wood-paved iron bridges I remember rivers frozen with swirls of yellow scum I remember whole forests of evergreen glazed in clear ice, shattered sunlight, I had to strap a slitted piece of cardboard over my eyes to see the road.

In January the thaw and false spring in the Southwestern air and when we were stopped at a roadside picnic grove for our lunch we could hear the thunderous cracks and groans of rivers we couldn't see. But then it froze again, cold and snowless and I remember stretches of brown land treeless swells of hardscrabble imbedded with rotted-out car frames and broken farm tools.

We had problems with the truck blown tires batteries fan belts oil-smoking flipping up the vented hood hot to the touch it was a journey fraught with peril. But you didn't have to think. It was simple, life was staying warm keeping on the move finding food beds being thrifty. We met people in trucks loaded like ours with furniture and we talked with them and gave the appraising looks of peers, the few chilled humans in motion. But most of the time we had the road to ourselves.

I bought the newspaper wherever we were. In Arkansas and Oklahoma lots of people were robbing banks, it seemed to me important to come into a town looking respectable. People on the go did not have social standing. The eyes of the waitresses in the cafés or the grudging grim men and women who rented rooms. I held the baby like a badge. Cleanliness, propriety, the cheerful honest face, mediation in a cold suspicious land. I made a point of tipping well and flashing my roll, I didn't like that moment of hesitation before the man cranked up the gas tank or the landlady took the key off the board.

In every state Sandy noticed the Justice of the Peace signs in front of clapboard houses. I told her they were legalized highway robbers who lifted travelers of five- and ten-dollar bills I said they handed out jail sentences to hobos but she knew them from the movies as kindly old men who would open their doors late at night to marry people they had wives in hair curlers and ratty bathrobes who smiled and clasped their hands Sandy and I were not mental intimates.

I don't mean she was stupid she was not, only that she asked no questions, she was already persuaded, like Libby at Loon Lake. She took instruction from the newspapers and radio she marveled at the Dionne quintuplets. But I was very kind to her and patient. We had shared sorrows, we knew something together, and this made me tender toward her. I liked the smell of her after a night in bed, the heat of her under the covers. I took a sweet pleasure in our lovemaking even though she was shockingly ignorant of what she could get from it. The first time as I sat on the edge of the bed she hiked up her flannel nightgown lay herself across my lap. "Not too hard?" she said over her shoulder and buried her face in a pillow. I caressed her ample buttocks and backs of the thighs I felt a film of clammy sweat in the small of her back I thought I had learned more of her late husband's tastes than I needed to know. She seemed relieved that I wanted no preliminaries and arranged herself on all fours on the bed presenting herself to me dog fashion here I did not demur. One had limits. She braced her arms and set her haunches and even gave them a little twirl now and then. I came quickly for which she afterward rewarded me with a quick kiss on the mouth before she went off to the bathroom.

She thought of it like cooking or changing the baby, a responsibility of domestic life. I wanted to awaken her surprise her but I was in no hurry. I enjoyed her the way she was. One morning with the light showing the streaks in the window shade I studied her face as she lay in my arms and suddenly her eyes flew open and she stared at me fearfully but not moving in that second or two before she remembered where she was who she was who I was. She drew a sharp breath and her green eyes swam with life. I hugged her and decided I loved her. I put her on her back and made love to her and took my time about it and detected a degree of thought or contemplation in her before the thing was done and she jumped out of bed to see to her baby.

Ahead of us on the road each morning a lowering sky, I felt under it as under a billowing tent as far as the eye could see. The roads became straighter, the land flattened out. No snow now, what blew across the land was a gritty red dust that shimmered on the road in the sun in rainbows of iridescence. Also accreting spindly balls of desert rubbish bouncing over the rocks and blowing up against the fences like creatures watching us go by. We went through one-street towns with red brick feed stores and tractors parked in the unpaved streets. We passed foreclosed farms with notices slapped on the fenceposts like circus bills. The towns were less frequent. There were no rivers creeks mountains trees, just this rocky flatland. But one day Sandy yelled to stop the truck. I pulled over. She thrust the baby in my hands and jumped down from the cab and ran back along the ditch. I watched her in the mirror. She came back with a sprig of tiny blue flowers, she was so happy, she tied them with a string and hung them from the sun visor.

The desert didn't alarm her. She had grown up in the mountains but country was country and she knew its rules and regulations. She knew the names of snakes and birds and pointed out the dry beds of creeks. One day the truck broke down in the middle of nowhere and she turned all around with her hand shading her eyes wise Indian maid and figured where to get help by the way the land was fenced. I remember that. We found a ranch about three miles down a dirt road intersecting the road we were on, just as she predicted.

But it was slow going, I began to think we were strung between outposts of civilization, the shadow range of mountains that cheered me when I first saw it one late afternoon seemed each new day as far away on the windshield. I didn't know what we would do in California but I knew it would take as much money as we could save to do it with. I came awake at night and wondered what I had in mind. The truth was I had no ambition, no ideas, no true desire or hope for anything. I was aware in the darkness of the forced character of my affections. I'd find myself angry at Sandy. I liked to surprise her in her sleep and be in her before her body could respond to make it easier. She would come awake gasping but throw her arms around me and hold on for dear life.

One evening, trying to do something about the way I felt, I found a reasonably good roadside café and we had steaks and beans and red wine. There were candles in little red glasses on the table.

"Clara told me about you," Sandy said.

"What?"

"Oh, long before I dreamed anything like this."

"What did she say?"

"Just that she was sweet on you. You know. The way girls talk."

"Yeah, well, I was sweet on her too."

"I thought you was married. I thought she was your wife!"

"Yeah, well, she'd be anything you wanted if you wanted it badly enough."

A particularly cold day, with the enormous blue sky turned almost white, we saw a man and a woman and a boy at the side of the road beside their old Packard touring car. I pulled up. Their gears were locked. A decision was made that the man would remain with the car and its heavy freight of steamer trunks and crates. He wrapped a scarf around his head and folded his arms and sat down on his running board and his family got up in the truck with us to ride to the next town. The woman must have been in her forties. She wore a dusty black coat with a fur collar half rubbed away and a tired felt hat that was nevertheless set off at a smart angle. She said her husband was a pharmacist. He had had his own store back in Wilmington, Delaware. Now they were on their way to San Diego, where they hoped to make a new start. "A new start!" Sandy said. "Why, that's what *we're* doing!"

When we had dropped them I said, "What do you mean we're making a new start?"

"What?"

"All they want is to open another drugstore. They want to do what they've always done. That's what a new start means."

"Well, I was just chattin with that lady."

"You think I want a job in an automobile factory? Or is it *your* new start you're talking about? I mean this furniture of yours we're dragging three thousand miles: Is *that* your new start? So you can find some rooms and put the furniture in them just the way you had it in Jacksontown? That kind of new start?"

"I don't know why you're so put out with me."

"Because if that's what you mean, say so. Let's settle it here and now. I'm not your husband and even if I was I wouldn't make my living as a stoolpigeon."

She looked at me now in bewilderment, and holding her baby to her, sat as far from me as she could get. She stared out the windshield with her chin on the baby's head. God knows her remark was innocent enough. But the confidence behind it I found irritating—as if living and traveling with her I must fit her preconceptions. I suppose what really bothered me was the strength of character behind this. I felt if she didn't even know what she was doing as she did it, I couldn't hope to change her.

Then of course in a few miles Joe was sorry, he apologized, which encouraged her to sulk and afterward to regain her good cheer.

Sandy could have said he was traveling on her money. But it never occurred to her. It occurred to him, however—he was not unaware of his talent for using other people's money, he was not unaware of his attraction to other men's wives, he was not unmindful that his life since leaving Paterson had been a picaresque of other men's money and other men's women, who in hell was he to get righteously independent with anyone? This kid was giving him her life everything she owned and all he could do was kick her in the ass for it.

He wondered seriously if love wasn't a feeling at all but a simple characterless state of shared isolation. If you were alone with a woman your feelings might change from moment to moment but the circumstance

of your shared fate did not change. Maybe that's where the love was, in
the combined circumstance. This was not the Penfield view but it could be
argued. Joe looked at other couples old and young and wondered what
they saw in each other, working their little businesses, or pushing their
jalopies west, or eating their meals together or holding the hands of a child
between them. Maybe all the world's pairs, dreary and toothless and
stumbling drunk, or picking at garbage pails or waiting on the street for
a flop knew about love as, say, he and Clara Lukács never had. They knew
it could incorporate passion or prim distaste, it might be joyous or full of
rage, it might carry extreme concern of any kind, or unconcern, but it was
presumed to survive challenge. All it was, was a kind of neutral constancy. Sandy knew it! You just made the decision, all you needed to do
was decide to have it and love was yours. Nothing grand, nothing monumental, and not a prison either, but a sort of sturdy structure of outlook,
one that wouldn't break under the weight of ideas and longing feelings
terrors visions and the world's awful mordant surprises.

"Sandy," he said, "let's get married."

She hugged him until he thought the truck would go off the road.

"We don't want a new start, Sandy, we want a new life. A whole new
life. When we get to California. Okay? That's the place."

She was more than amenable. "Oh my, oh my," she said, hugging the
baby. "You hear that, darlin? We're gonna have a proper daddy. Yes we
are! Oh my!"

There followed a period of solemn discussion. I explained that to make
a true marriage we both had to shuck the ways of our old lives, its
attitudes, its assumptions. "I know I won't be able to live a road life
anymore," I said. "I know I have to plan to make something of myself.
And I have ideas, Sandy, a man can do a lot starting from a small investment. More than one fortune has been made that way, I can tell you."

She nodded.

"So I know I've got to give up my past life and I want you to think
about giving up yours. Do you ask in what way?"

"Yes sir."

"In the way of style, Sandy honey. In the way of more ambition of
style. Now, take this truck for instance. They stop trucks like this by the
hundreds at the California state line. They don't want people coming in
looking like Okies, you know? In fact I've read if you can't prove you have
a job waiting they won't even let you in."

"This truck is bad?"

"Very bad."

"But how else we gonna move the furniture and all?"

"Ah, well, the furniture, that's the next thing I want to talk to you
about."

An hour later we were in a fair-sized town east of Albuquerque, New
Mexico. There was a big junk store at the edge of town. Sandy and I stood

with our luggage in the dusty street while the furniture was unloaded. A man scrawled a big number in chalk on each piece or tied a tag to its leg. Sandy watched her chair and sofa, her big Philco radio disappear into the darkness of the store. I patted her shoulder.

It was cold and very sunny. The man counted out sixty dollars into my hand.

"Where's there a used-car lot?" I said to him. He walked around the truck, looking it up and down. He leaned his weight on the lowered tailgate. "I'll take it off your hands," he said. "Not worth much, though."

I got seventy-five dollars for the truck, for which I had paid a hundred in Jacksontown. Twenty-five dollars to transport us across six states didn't seem at all bad.

I tied two of Sandy's bags with rope and slung them over my good shoulder. I held another valise under my good arm and a fourth in my good hand. Sandy carried the baby and the remaining bag and, slowly, and with many halts, we shuffled several blocks to the railroad depot. It was a small station on the Santa Fe line and in a couple of hours a train was coming through to Los Angeles.

I checked the bags and took my wife-and-baby-to-be across the street to a diner and left them there. I found a barbershop a few blocks away. The barber removed my bandages and pulled out the stitches. He shaved me and gave me a haircut. He gave me a hot towel.

Then I had an idea. I stopped in a drugstore. My cast was supposed to be on for six weeks, but it was a torment. The druggist did the job as several customers looked on.

I was shocked my my pale thin arm. The break had been down toward the wrist. My fingers ached when I tried to move them. But it was good to be rid of the weight of all that plaster and to sport instead a couple of splints and adhesive tape.

To celebrate I stopped in a haberdasher's and bought a dark suit with a vest and two pairs of pants. Eighteen dollars. The tailor did up the cuffs for me on the spot. I bought a white shirt and a blue tie for three-fifty. Even my old khaki greatcoat looked good after the man brushed it and put the collar down. "Wear it open," he said, "so the suit shows."

Sandy didn't recognize me when I walked back into the diner.

"Is that you?"

"It's either me or George Raft," I said.

The idea was coming clear to her. We still had an hour before the train arrived. She took one of her bags from the check-in and repaired to the ladies' room.

I remember that depot: it had wooden strip wainscoting and a stove and arched windows caked with chalk dust. I sat on the bench with Baby Sandy and held her on my lap. I felt her life as she squirmed to look at this or that. She wore a wool cap from which hair of the lightest color peeked through. I untied the string under her chin and pushed back the hat and it seemed to me now the hair was more red than I remembered. It seemed to me too as we regarded each other that her facial structure was changing and the father was beginning to show. "Oh, that would be a shame," I said aloud. She grabbed my tie in her fist.

And then I looked up and standing there Sandy James in a dress of Clara's and hose and Clara's high-heeled shoes. She was looking at the floor and holding her arms out as if she were on a high wire. Her face was flushed, she dropped her bag and grabbed hold of the bench.

"I'm fallin!" she said with a shriek.

"You're not falling," I said.

She had combed her hair back and put on lipstick a little bit crooked. She wore a coat open over the dress I hadn't seen it before it was creased but it was fine a dark creased coat not originally hers any more than the dress or the shoes, but it looked fine, it all looked fine.

She was awaiting judgment with mouth slightly open eyes wide.

"Aw, Sandy," I said, "you look swell. Oh honey, oh my, yes." And she broke into smiles, glowing through her freckles, her pale eyes crescented behind her cheekbones in a great face of pleasure, and there was our life to come in the sun of California—all in the beaming presence she made.

And so we sat waiting for our train, this young family, who would know what we had come from and through what struggle? We were an establishment with not a little pride in ourselves and the effect we made in the world. I thought of a bungalow under palm trees, something made of stucco with a red tile roof. I thought of the warm sun. I imagined myself driving up to my bungalow in the palm trees, driving up in an open roadster and tooting the horn as I pulled up to the curb.

A while later an interesting thing happened. The stationmaster told us through the gate that the famous Super Chief was coming through from Los Angeles. We went out on the platform to watch it go by on the far track. And after a minute it thundered by, two streamlined diesel engines back to back, and cars of ridged shiny silver with big windows. It shook the station windows with its basso horn, and a great swirl of dirt flew into our eyes. It was going fast but we could see flashes of people in their compartments.

Sandy grabbed my arm: "You see her! It's her, omigod, oh, she looked right at me!"

A moment later the train was gone and I stood watching it get smaller and smaller down the track. "Didn't you see her?" Sandy asked. "Oh, what's her name! Oh, you know that movie star, you know who I mean! Oh, she's so beautiful?"

It was true, the stationmaster said a few minutes later, you could get a glimpse of Hollywood stars every day, east and west, as the Super Chief and the Chief went by. But he wouldn't know in particular which one we had seen. "Oh, you know," Sandy kept saying to me. "You know who it is!" She stamped her foot trying to remember.

I had thought it was Clara. I laughed at myself and lit a cigarette, but long afterward something remained of the moment and located itself in my chest, some widening sense of loss, some heartsunk awareness of the value I once placed on myself.

The cars were crowded, valises and trunks piled near the doors at each end, bags and bundles stuffed in the overhead racks. We found a place toward the rear of one overheated car and we settled ourselves. We sat stiffly in recognition of the established residence of the other passengers. The car gave off the smell of orange peel and egg salad. People wore slippers instead of shoes, they slept covered with their own blankets and they chatted with each other like neighbors. Children ran up and down the aisle.

Passers-by stopped to admire the baby. We could not resist the social demands of the situation. Sandy was soon talking away, introducing us in our prematurely married state. Everyone else in the car, and in the car ahead of it and the car behind, was from the same town in Illinois. They were members of a Pentecostal church. A man told us they were moving to California to set up a new community on donated land south of Los Angeles. "Yes, thank Jesus Christ our Lord," he said. "We shall take ourselves into the Pacific and be baptized in the waters of His ocean." The idea so overwhelmed him that he broke into song. Soon everyone in the car was singing and clapping hands. Sandy smiled at me in the excitement of the moment, she was thrilled.

By evening I believed I had heard every number in the repertoire. They were good generous people if you didn't mind their conviction. After Sandy fell asleep across our seat they covered her with their blankets. An older woman happily shushed Baby Sandy to sleep in her arms.

I stood between the cars and smoked my cigarettes. This train was no Chief, it made frequent stops, and each time I got off to look around. As the night wore on, the train lingered at each stop although no one got on or off and only a sack or two was flung aboard the mail car. At one station, a small town in the desert, I thought I smelled something different in the air, like a warmer breeze or another land. It was very late. All the pilgrims on the train were asleep. Steam drifted back from the engine. I felt strange, as if coming out of shock. I felt as if I knew no one on earth.

I wondered if this wasn't really the last stop, if California was like heaven, unproven. In this flatland of grit and rubble, you might sense the barest whiff of it in the air or intimation in the light of the sky—but this was as far as you got.

I wandered to the rear to the end of the platform. I picked up a folded newspaper from a Railway Express baggage cart—the rotogravure section of a Sunday paper a week or two old. I looked at the pictures. I was looking at Lucinda Bailey Bennett the famous aviatrix, two whole pages of her at various times of her life. She stood beside different airplanes or sat in their cockpits. A separate ruled column listed her speed and endurance records by date. At the bottom right-hand page of the story she was shown under the wing of a big two-engine seaplane. She was waving at the camera. The caption said: HER LAST FLIGHT. Behind her, climbing into the cabin, was a large man, broad of beam, unidentified.

I turned back and found the beginning of the feature: Lucinda Bennett's plane *The Loon* had been given up for lost over the Pacific somewhere between Hawaii and Japan. F. W. Bennett was quoted as saying that if his wife had to die, surely this was the way she would prefer, at the controls of her machine, flying toward some great personal ideal.

Images of falling through space through sky through dreams
through floor downstairs down well down hole downpour.
Birds that fall into the sea as a matter of lifestyle include
kingfishers canvasbacks gulls heron osprey pipers tweaks.
Birds that fall most prominently into fresh water are loons
a type of grebe. Sixteen lakes in the Adirondack Mountains
named Loon Lake. The cry of loons once heard is not forgotten.

Clara has time to think, the space to realize her thinking mind. Never
in her life has her life been so uncrowded, something she never before
realized consciously how crowded her life was how people from her infancy had always been in her eyes, how the sounds of them had always
been in her ears, how their presence moved in her their wills directed her
even insofar as she created opposition she had been crowded by them their
wills their voices their appearance directing her their cars and trucks the
rumble of the elated horns horses pulling wagons splatting dung in the
street, peddlers pushing their carts the stone blasting out of the rock of
Manhattan tying in the girders with rivets, slapping in the stone, every
manner of machine whining growling rumbling roaring in its own pitch,
and all the gangsters of menace all the pain, others and her own, and the
sound of fear in her, her own fear which she hated most of all because it
was the loudest noise in the universe, the nuns at their prayers, kids
shouting down the street, the muttering of murderous intention, and every
square inch of space in her eyes blocked out by stone and tar and moving
metal, by dark stairs and painted apartment walls, by overstuffed furniture
by cots and pots and sinks and roaches and tin plates and later by phony
butlers and the pretensions of the earth's scum, there was nothing left in
her eyes for a bee gravid with being bending a flower to the earth, or for
simple blue skycolor unpenetrated by the spires of skyscrapers, or for
something small and lovely to be contemplated for its own seriousness,
like a comb or a hand mirror or a goldfish in a bowl, there was no chance,
nothing reflected, nothing gave back from the contemplation of it, even

her dreams were pure shit they did nothing for her, they were her days all over again, filled with the same people the same things in different arrangements or proportions but the same the same. So she stands quietly after some days molecularly reassembled widely spaced in her own density and watches through some branches and some leaves which have interest in themselves and pay her for the most marginal attention as she watches between them the lake water flung like a cast of silver grain in the gray day, two wakes widening behind the pontoons of the airplane finally losing the chase like porpoises turning back underwater as the green-and-white plane exchanges one environment for another and rising slowly turns, twists in the air rising turning its wings concentrating to a point then flaring out the plane falling swiftly away into the sky losing its color finally its shape and becoming possibly a speck of dust in her eye and when she blinks it is gone altogether, made of cloud made of sky gone even the sound of it gone, and she stares at the silver-scattered lake, the green leaves at her eyes, the branches and the big important journey of the ant along the twig.

So she's alone with him at Loon Lake and finds that still there is no intimacy and the mysteriousness of this fact begins to interest her. This is the way the rich do things. Getting herself dressed, she marches downstairs defiantly accepting it all and sits down for breakfast on the terrace overlooking the lake and waiting till they came out to see what she wants and eating a half grapefruit sitting in its silver shell in ice and daring anyone Bennett included to look at her the wrong way.

But nothing has happened, the schedule is unaltered, the drinks at certain hours, the meals at certain hours, the morning a certain time in a certain place, the afternoon and evenings all timed, the past between them unacknowledged, the past ignored, personal reactions forsworn, younaughty-girl forborne, every breath in its good time and Bennett keeps his distance with the utmost courtesy and only sees her at the times planned for seeing, at table, or on the tennis court her lesson or riding on the trail and she is left alone at her wish and settled into the timed ordered planned encounters of the rich in their family life who dole out time in carefully measured amounts to each other, they even sleep in separate rooms so as not to wear out their lives on each other, so as to avoid anything like the fluid mess of most people's lives, and those who are closest to each other are as timed to be apart as anyone else. So at last she understands what wealth is, the desire for isolation, its greatest achievement is isolation, its godliness is in its isolation and that's why never in her life before, her days and nights of time, has she enlarged this way, has her mind enlarged to the space this way, and has this voice been heard this way in reflection of herself. And the point is that she is growing to the environment, beginning to match it, and it is all beginning to make proportional sense, the timed encounters, the ceremony of courteous meetings, the space between people sharing space, the great distance to be traveled even in an obvious situation like this, so crudely obvious as to outcome, the aloneness of the two of them now, not the ironic wife not the fat poet sharing the fifty thousand acres, even now the isolated distance will have to be traveled before he can allow himself to put his hands on her. And that makes her smile. Because now she will know when that time is too, it will match her awareness and nothing will shock her or surprise her because the distance he must travel is the function of his wealth, as separative as it is powerful, and she waits in grim amusement knowing that by the time something happens he will have become recognizable to her, her familiar, and their intimacy will be all that's possible for her, so natural she will wonder what it ever was that enraged her when her gangster left her sleeping and took the private train.

But it was all in my mind, it was the furthest thing from everyone's mind except mine. She had not come back, he had not thought of bringing her back, the world had gone on and only I, like Warren Penfield, mourned its going. The ant on the twig was at my eye and I saw no plane and in fact knew I wouldn't, in fact felt the wolfish smile of secret satisfaction on my face, a simple mindless excitement just being back at this place, redballed home in comprehensive correction of my life, more comprehensive than the wild hope of seeing Clara again or the desire to take revenge. No simple motive could fill the totality of my return.

Following job description fall into sea: fighter pilot naval
bomber pilot naval, navigator bombardier gunner naval
carrier-based Pacific Fleet World War Two
with or without parachute drowned strafed dead of exposure
or rescued one thousand and eight six.
This is apart from individuals going down in their aircraft
shot down or deprived of carrier landing
from attack of Divine Wind or heavy seas
collapsing their landing gear or snapping constraint cable
or sailing into lower deck amidships or
otherwise stippling the sea like rain like the hammers of sculptors.

I thought oddly of eviction, a city street miniaturized in one cell of the remembering brain, a cityscape of old cheap furniture piled on the sidewalk and an old woman sitting on one of the chairs looking at old photographs of Paterson in an album. The chair arm had a doily. She showed me the picture she was looking at, herself as a girl, and she smiled. She smelled of urine, her hands were frighteningly swollen and twisted, she was totally unashamedly in residence on the sidewalk with her furniture, in some state of dreamy peace, careless of the cold, the first snowflakes came down toward evening and there was no derision from the tough kids on the street because she didn't weep or bow her head or display grief or fear in her misfortune and so not misfortune itself, but sat and thought her chin in her hand, her elbow propped on the armchair doily, while the snow turned her hair white. What frightened them off was the triumph of her senescence, only a stickler for custom would demand that such a lady of property be required to have four walls around her a ceiling above her a light in the lamp and tea in her cup.

I had this same mind, unhoused but triumphant coming off the streets through the dogs up the mountain to Loon Lake. And I greeted him like a complicitor while he stared at me quite astonished and then turned nodding as if he understood and continued to make his lunch in the spring sun. I was given Penfield's old room. That night I heard the sound of surging power, some transformed connection, an electric pungency and pop, and everywhere around all the houses of the compound great flood-lights came on, over every bit of space, the courts, the boathouse, the staff house, the stables. And a while later I heard the dogs but they came this time on leashes pulling three men with shotguns broken in one hand and leash straps in the other woven like reins, a dozen yelping matched hounds and uniformed guards with Sam Browne belts and boots.

I read the Penfield papers at his window from this outside light a peculiar bright amber night, and I heard the Poet's voice and saw his large debauched pleading eyes and tried to understand his death, what it was, what was terminated, if the voice and the face remained, if the presence lay in the rooms, and the faint winy redolence of his being was sniffed on my every breath. A wineglass still sat on the mantel, the dregs evaporated to a glazed scab in the bottom of the petal.

I mourn all change even for the better and in the days of my return I measured what I had known as the injured intruder against what I saw now as the sole guest. I mourned the absence of terror, the absence of hopeless desire, the absence of betrayals still to come.

I thought of Sandy James asleep in the train coach, curled on the seat and from the wrist under her cheek the trembling droop of her five-and-ten charm bracelet, a tiny tarnished lady's shoe, a tiny tarnished bottle, a tiny tarnished steam engine.

Bennett had changed too, he was in an interesting derelict state of mourning. A gray stubble grew on his face and he wore the same plaid flannel shirt day after day. The white hair of the careful shining pompa-dour was uncombed, shocked forward over his forehead and suggesting from a flash of boyishness what he might have been had he not been a Bennett—a farmer perhaps, a logger, or heavy-chested stevedore of some honest life. We took our meals together, the two of us alone, with a manservant serving heated canned food. All the women of the light green were gone, as if having lost Lucinda Bailey Bennett he wanted the race expunged. A couple of the outside men were now doing the household work and the cooking. In the kitchen the dishes were piled unwashed. I saw roaches going along the floor. It was as if the establishment was in some accelerating state of decrepitude, beginning with Bennett's heart and working outward. The grounds were immaculate as ever, Loon Lake was groomed for its spring. The stables were clean and horses shining and fit.

But if he went on like this, the men of dark green too would be sent away and the boats would sink in their berths, the earth around the dolmen would grow back and the fence around the tennis court would fall and the clay court would crack like the surface of a blasted planet. Mourning had illuminated the natural drift of his life to isolation, and if it was not corrected it would go on, outward in all directions, spreading out over the universe in some infinite looming reclusiveness.

But his eyes were curious when they lit on me for a moment or two at each measured meal. And the days were, after all, timed just as they had been, the hours appointed for drinking and eating, and naps, and exercise. He looked at me as if he were waiting. I met him each day in a renewed wonder of my own. I had seen his kingdom and I appreciated him almost more for the distracted humanity he displayed, broken as easily as anyone by simple events. For men all over the country he was, finally, a condition of their life. Yet he wandered about here in his grief, caring for nothing, barely raising his head when the phone rang. He moved slowly, almost listlessly, which brought out the natural lurch of the short-legged top-heaviness of him.

In the mornings I heard the horses stomping in the stable, and looking out the window, saw Bennett come out galloping, having spurred his horse from the very portal.

At noon we took lunch on the terrace if the day was fair and he'd glance at the sky over the lake as if expecting a plane to appear.

At night while the guards in their belted uniforms walked the floodlit grounds with their dogs I heard him playing his phonograph records, his favorites, I heard the song of the night of my arrival.

> I know why I've waited
> Know why I've been blue
> Prayed each night for someone
> Exactly like you.

He began to talk of Lucinda Bennett, imparting confidences that at first excited me inasmuch as I was there on the terrace in the sun at Loon Lake, in all the world the only one privileged to receive them. His voice lacked regret, his delivery was thoughtful, he chose his words as someone does who wants in as orderly a way as possible to impart information. So I hoped he was giving these thoughts to *me,* as instruction, and I trusted that his reasons would be forthcoming, that he had some plan, and that by being patient and attentive I would eventually learn what it was. Then I wondered if the confession itself was the gracious means by which I would pass through some subtle imperceptible moment of assumption from being something to being something else. But he went on, and the obsession of the subject became so apparent to me, and the confidences so intimate, I couldn't believe he was aware that I listened or that he would seriously divulge them if I did not lack all importance to him. Day after day I listened. I watched the white clouds disembowel themselves in the high pines across the lake. His man served canned soup, canned spaghetti, canned peaches. Bennett grew shaggier and smellier, looking more like a troll every day. I watched his beard grow. While I waited for a place in his mind I tested my status with the staff. I rode a horse one day with the stableman beside me showing me the elementals. I went upstairs to the storerooms that the maid Libby had shown me so long ago and took several outfits for myself, white ducks already cuffed, argyle sweaters, saddle shoes, shirts, ties, a pair of boots. I had the man in the boathouse bring out the mahogany speedboat and hold the line while I boarded her. I got the hang of it soon enough. I cruised around looking at the beaver lodges, the islands where the loons made their nests, and saw from the water the concrete ramp and hangar where Mr. Penfield and Mrs. Bennett began their round-the-world flight.

"She was a student when I met her. She was then, and remained, the most handsome woman I had ever seen. I secured a divorce to marry Lucinda. And in the years as they went by, no matter what passed between us, whenever she saw fit to spend time with me I was pleased to see her, I mean that no matter what the state of our affections I was always pleased when she came into a room. If she came into a room I had to look at her. I could not not look at her.

"I respect character in a man but I revere it in a woman. I am done in when I find it in a woman. That little doxie had it in a cheap sort of way. But in Lucinda it tested like the best ore, through and through, in the bones and in the beam of the eye.

"Long ago she lost the pleasure of—what?—the engagement. And I was able to appreciate her character in the depth of her withdrawal from me. And then how I wished she had less of it! Less pride, less distaste for—surprises. Less neatness of soul. I told her she liked the sky because it was clean. She liked to go up in rain. I never flew with her because I sensed that it was her realm. But everyone told me what a wonderful pilot she was. How cool. How capable. And then she began to pull down the prizes and I knew it was so.

"I was very proud of her. I bought her whatever she needed. She may have fallen in love with a fellow, some mail-service pilot, one of those adventurer types, and I was going to have it looked into. But when I thought about it I knew Lucinda would never permit herself an affair. It was not something to which she would give rein. And gradually she ceased to mention him. If it were possible for Lucinda to exist without a body she would have chosen to. Her body was of no interest to her. She did not like it . . . handled. She was a very orderly woman, Lucinda. If you look upstairs in her apartment you will see the order of her mind. She did everything with precision, and so was she affectionate with precision.

"She flew planes but her tastes were very delicate and refined. She

knew art, she knew music. She had small bones as befitting a fine mug-
wump family. They none of them liked me. I took great relish in that. It
was one of those things. I have no taste of my own but I could recognize
the quality of hers. She could look at something for a long time, a painting,
a piece of porcelain. Then I knew it was fine. I envied her vulnerability—
that she could be transfixed by something that was beautiful. She became
pregnant just once and immediately took measures to have it rescinded.
We had no children. I have one child by my first marriage but he is an
incompetent, I mean legally, a macrocephalic, he has water in the head,
and he lives in a home in Sweden. They take too good care of him. By all
rights he should have been dead years ago.

"Lucinda went once to see him. Thereafter she sent him thoughtfully
chosen gifts, toys, tins of cookies, picture books appropriate to his mental
age. She always sent him things. She liked helpless beings. I don't mean
that the way it sounds. I mean she had a heart for people. It was she who
saved Penfield a jail sentence. Penfield was from the working class and he
decided to come here in the late twenties to assassinate me. You knew that
of course. Well, the fellow was pathetic but she kept him on as a sort of
a cause in personal rehabilitation. A sort of one-woman Salvation Army,
except without the prayer. Lucinda was not religious except perhaps in
some vague pantheistic way. She decided the poor man was a poet. I got
to like him myself. He read aloud very well, he probably should have been
an actor. He read Wordsworth and Keats, all that kind of thing. He was a
sort of house pet she kept on and I indulged her. But then of course I did
something I shouldn't have. I took Penfield's own verses to the president
of the New York Public Library and asked him his opinion. In turn he
called on a professor who was an expert in the field of literature. Oh my.
And I showed Lucinda this fellow's letter. She perceived, accurately, that
the opinion didn't matter so much as my malice in having asked for it. She
threw the letter in the fire. She was a wonderful woman. She was not a
prey to fashion, didn't give a damn for it. She always looked smart by
looking herself. She always wore her hair the same way, cut short and
brushed back from her temples. I thought it was most seemly. She had a
thin, fit body. Thin waist. Ribs showed. She had good hands, small and
squarish, nails trim, cut close. She would not paint her nails or wear
make-up. I liked her mouth, a generous mouth. Sweet smile. A light came
into her eyes when she smiled. She had almost no bosom. Just a slight rise
there with good thick nipples. She told me once if I liked her body I must
really like boys."

He paused. "You've come here to kill me too, I suppose."
"What?"
"But you don't have the guts for it—anymore than he."
"What?"
"See? I'm not even carrying my gun."
He pushed his chair back from the table and held out his arms.

The room empties. They have gone to make the call. I walk back and forth shaking a fist in the air. The fuckers! By my wits I have done this thing and the stupid sons of bitches have gone for it. But why not? They will hear him laugh, they'll hear him say, *Yes, let him go*. My heart fills with a passionate conviction. He and I are complicitors. We're both against them. As if, having made this up, I cannot make it work unless I believe it myself.

And I am released. And I strut out of that room bone-cracked, skin-stitched and betrayed and I glare at them all as I lead her by the arm out the door. I take my time. I think the illusion will endure only if I do not break and run. I sleep in Sandy James' parlor. I sleep eighteen hours. I take her money, buy a truck. I hire two men to load it. In the rear-view mirror I see only a black industrial cloud where Jacksontown was. I press the accelerator. Cars turn on their lights, the red lights of moving cars ahead of me. The furniture shifts and bangs against the tailgate. The heavy furniture rises in the air on the bumps. I am in transit on the road, the child bride beside me, bracing herself with her knee against the dashboard and holding her baby tightly. I open the window for the cold air. I want the wind to blow these feelings out of my eyes, blow them away, leave me without memory or love, leave me to myself.

"If you thought I would want to kill you," I said, "why did you tell them to let me go?"

"What?"

"When the police called from Jacksontown," I said to him. "With that message." I was smiling like a fatuous idiot.

"What message? I don't know what you're talking about. From whom?"

I choked on the answer. Bennett got up and stood at the parapet. He stood looking over the lake with his hands in his pockets.

That night we steal upon a station of the Tokaido and purchase disguises. We are a country lord and his serving boy. She wears bloused trousers. We travel in this humble manner because my mission is clandestine. Soldiers of the daimyo eye us warily. We book rooms in a modest inn where, to avoid suspicion, I call for a woman. She is a tired fat *artiste* who responds to the humor of the situation. The two of us climb all over her, I with ordinary lasciviousness, my young ward with the affection of a child for her mother. Of course the old whore is terribly moved. She reaches into the child's pantaloons, and my hand, like a band of steel, clamps around her wrist. If she discovers my serving boy is a girl, all is lost. Even so the situation is difficult. I use all the sexual arts of which I am capable to divert the old bag. But in the midst of passion I intuit that the more undone she becomes, the more shrewd. It is actually interesting. At the moment of her release she is totally withdrawn and quietly aware that we are not what we appear to be. But her tongue is extended. I grab the tongue and impale it to the polished floor with an awl. I shout and stamp about and raise an uproar. The innkeeper comes to the door. Other travelers come running. I berate the innkeeper for the poor quality of his house. He is abject. The woman moans, rump up, head on the floor, eyes glazed like a pig to be served. I put my foot on her back and behead her. The innkeeper begs my pardon.

At dawn we continue our journey. The sky is pink. We climb the trail alongside an amazing stream, so rock-strewn that the water, broken into millions of drops, falls like the sound of hail and bounces like steel pellets. I scrape the bark from a small pine tree tortured by the wind to grow like sunrays toward the earth. This lime-green powdery moss I allow to dry for four minutes in the palm of my hand. I then lick this powder from my palm and immediately my young love becomes a giantess looking down at me with amazement. I trip her and she falls backward, quaking the earth, I run into her vulva and by that means continue my lifelong search for the godhead. It is some sort of gland somewhere. The way becomes slippery. In this viscous darkness I use my knees and my hands like a water spider. The way becomes narrower. Soon I am flattened, drawn like a mote toward some powerful brilliantly lit eye. I feel myself enlarging. The light is blinding. I become my own size and break her open like an egg.

You are thinking it is a dream. It is no dream. It is the account in helpless linear translation of the unending love of our simultaneous but disynchrous lives.

    Data linkage escape this is not emergency
    Come with me compute with me
    Coupling with me she becomes a couplet
    Lovers leap in the sea
    A drop of sunlit pee between two lips
    Substitute a priapic navigator
    I see inappropriate behavior
    I recall Father Damien seeing his own pale blue eyes
    Regarding him from a face resembling his own enlarged redblue
        heart
    It is a woman, a leperess, expressing his sentiments.
    I refer to the paired animals going up the ramp of the ark
    Leopard leopard aardvark aardvark porpoise porpoise inchworm
        inchworm
    The story of Noah is the religious vision of cloning.
    Scientists tweeze pollen eyedrop spermatozoa
    Dispatch flights of sexy sterile white moths to eliminate specie
    They notice human lovers commonly resemble each other
    Test it at home looking at their wives friends friends wives
    Or if not each other then each other's brother or sister
    But in any event that love conducts a shock of recognition

Question haven't I seen you somewhere before answer yes in the
    mirror
Given wars before wars after wars genocides
and competition for markets cloning will eliminate all chance
and love will be one hundred percent efficient
No *Sturm und Drang* German phrase no disynchronicity
but everyone having seen everyone else somewhere before
we will have realized serenity of perfect universal love
univerself love uniself love unilove
until the race withers and blows away like the dried husks
of moths but who's complaining

They had either believed me or not believed me. If they had believed
me I had been so effective, so frighteningly effective that they did not want
to confirm what I told them, they were afraid to. If they called, he would
want their names. So they had let me go.

If they had not believed me, then my desperation was so patent or my
cravenness so truly loathsome that they didn't have the heart to go on with
it. Perhaps there were moral operations in this world that transcended the
individual responsible for them and threatened to ruin everyone. Was that
it? Was I perceived as a leper who threatened to contaminate them?

In either case the result was the same, wasn't that so? I had been
released thinking I'd made contact with Bennett and I had not.

That night I lay in Penfield's bed and stared at the amber windowpanes
and listened to the watchdogs baying. I tried to compose my terrible
shame into something I could deal with, I tried to comprehend the weird
sick brokenness I felt, the sense of irreparable damage I had done to
myself the catastrophic discomposure of everything but the small light in
my mind. It was most difficult.

Sandy James asleep forever on the coach seat amid the pilgrims: I take
a few dollars out of my wallet and tuck the fat wallet with her death
benefits under her chin she does not wake the train begins to move the
small flaked tarnished charms of her charm bracelet swing in their arc the
train picks up speed I jump hit the embankment the cinders imbedding
themselves in my knees.

Compare the private railroad car of the Meiji emperor the imperial
beloved, as it makes its way through the sunlit valley of the Bunraku
province. It moves slowly and from the populated fields no closer than a
mile thousands of little children wave paper flags in time to the small
white puffs of smoke rising from the engine. The children are well
behaved. Their parents kneel beside them and hold their shoulders. Their
grandparents lie prostrate on the ground not even daring to glance toward
the distant train where the line of mounted imperial guardsmen cantering
at the base of the embankment alongside the dark green imperial car give
it the look of a lampshade with a rippling fringe.

The man resisted all approaches he was stone he was steel I hated his grief his luxurious dereliction I hated his thoughts the quality of his voice his walk the way he spent his life proving his importance ritualizing his superiority his exercises of freedom his arrogant knowledge of the human heart I hated the back of his neck he was a killer of poets and explorers, a killer of boys and girls and he killed with as little thought as he gave to breathing, he killed by breathing he killed by existing he was an emperor, a maniac force in pantaloons and silk slippers and lacquered headdress dispensing like treasure pieces of his stool, making us throw ourselves on our faces to be beheaded one by one with gratitude, the outrageous absurdity of him was his power, his clucking crowing mewing shouting whistling ridiculousness is what stunned us into submission but not this boy, I know what to do about this pompous little self-idolator, I'm going to put the fucker where he belongs I swear oh my Clara I swear Mr. Penfield I swear by the memory of the Fat Lady I know how to do it, I know how to do it and I have the courage to do it and it will be a beautiful monumental thing I do I will testify to God that he is a human being, that is how, I will save him from wasting away, I will save him from crumbling into a piece of dried shit, into a foul eccentric, you see, I will give him hope, I will extend his reign, I will raise him and do it all so well with such style that he will thank me, thank me for growing in his heart his heart bursting his son.

And in the morning the whole spring of the earth has come forth and Loon Lake is a bowl of light. A sweet blue haze hangs in the trees. The sun is shining, a filigree of pale green leaf laces through the evergreens across the water. I run down the hill to the lake side pulling off my clothes as I go. I stop to remove my shoes. My feet thump along the boathouse deck. I stand poised on the edge and dive into the water. With powerful strokes learned in the filth of industrial rivers Joe swims a great circle crawl in the sweet clear cold mountain lake. He pulls himself up on the float and stands panting in the sun, his glistening white young body inhaling the light, the sun healing my scars my cracked bones my lacerated soul, the sun powering my loins warming them to a stir. I toss my hair back, smooth it back, shake the water from my arms, open my eyes. Up on the hill Bennett stands on his terrace, a tiny man totally attentive. He has seen the whole thing, as I knew he would. He waves at me. I smile my white teeth. I wave back.

Herewith bio Joseph Korzeniowski.
Born to a working-class family Paterson New Jersey August 2 1918.
Graduated Paterson Latin Grade School 1930.
Graduated Paterson Latin High School 1936. Voted by classmates
Best Shape of the Head. Hobbies: Street hockey, petit larceny.
Roustabout Hearn Bros. Carnival, summer 1936.
Aka Joe of Paterson, Loon Lake NY autumn 1936.

Employed Bennett Autobody Number Six, headlight man, winter
    1936.
Enrolled Williams College September 1937. Letters in Lacrosse,
Swimming. Graduated *cum laude,* honors in Political Science, 1941.
Voted by classmates Captain ROTC and Most Likely to Succeed.
Commissioned Second Lieutenant U.S. Air Corps.
Legal name change Joseph Paterson Bennett, June 1941.
Assigned newly formed Office of Strategic Services 1942
parachuting into France in black sweater flight jacket trousers
black boots false passport black wool cap black parachute
pockets of francs four thousand feet into windy void
face blackened teeth blackened, heart blackened dropping into
    blackness.
Awarded Bronze Star with oak leaf cluster 1943.
Awarded Silver Star with oak leaf cluster 1944.
Decommissioned 1945 rank of Major, Office of Strategic Services.
Appointed organization staff Central Intelligence Agency 1947.
Married Dru Channing Smith 1947, divorced 1950; no issue.
Married Kimberly Andrea Kennedy 1951, divorced 1954; no issue.
Continuous service Central Intelligence Agency to resignation
1974. Retiring rank Deputy Assistant Director.
Retired US State Department rank of Ambassador 1975.
Chairman and Chief Operating Officer Bennett Foundation.
Board of Directors James-Pennsylvania Steel Corporation.
Board of Directors Chilean-American Copper Corporation.
Trustee Jordan and Naismith colleges, Rhinebeck NY.
Trustee Miss Morris' School for Young Women, Briarcliff Manor
    NY.
Member Knickerbocker, Acropolis, New York; Silks, Saratoga
    Springs;
Rhode Island Keel, Newport.
Master of Loon Lake.

ABOUT THE AUTHOR

E.L. DOCTOROW has written a number of other critically acclaimed bestsellers, including *The Book of Daniel, Ragtime,* and *Lives of the Poets.* Both of his novels, *Ragtime* and *Billy Bathgate,* have been made into major motion pictures. Mr. Doctorow is a two-time winner of the National Book Critics Circle Award and a recipient of the National Book Award, the Pen/Faulkner Award, the Simon Guggenheim Fellowship, and the William Dean Howells Medal of the American Academy of Arts and Letters. His newest novel, *The Waterworks,* will be published in June 1994.

This edition contains the complete and unabridged texts of the original editions. They have been completely reset for this volume.

This 1994 edition is published by Wings Books,
distributed by Random House Value Publishing, Inc.
40 Engelhard Avenue, Avenel, New Jersey 07001,
by arrangement with Random House, Inc.

Random House
New York • Toronto • London • Sydney • Auckland

Printed and bound in the United States of America

Library of Congress Cataloging-in-Publication Data
Doctorow, E. L., 1931–
   [Novels. Selections]
     E.L. Doctorow : three complete novels.
       p. cm.
     Contents: Billy Bathgate — World's fair — Loon Lake.
     ISBN 0-517-10078-9
     1. New York (State)—History—Fiction.   2. Historical fiction.
American.   I. Title.   II. Title: Three complete novels.
PS3554.O3A6   1994
813'.54—dc20   93-40651
                          CIP

8   7   6   5   4   3   2   1